BOOKS BY HARRY TURTLEDOVE
The Guns of the South

THE WORLDWAR SAGA
Worldwar: In the Balance
Worldwar: Tilting the Balance
Worldwar: Upsetting the Balance
Worldwar: Striking the Balance

COLONIZATION
Colonization: Second Contact
Colonization: Down to Earth
Colonization: Aftershocks

THE VIDESSOS CYCLE
The Misplaced Legion
An Emperor for the Legion
The Legion of Videssos
Swords of the Legion

THE TALE OF KRISPOS
Krispos Rising
Krispos of Videssos
Krispos the Emperor

THE TIME OF TROUBLES SERIES
The Stolen Throne
Hammer and Anvil
The Thousand Cities
Videssos Besieged

Noninterference
Kaleidoscope
A World of Difference
Earthgrip
Departures

How Few Remain

THE GREAT WAR
The Great War: American Front
The Great War: Walk in Hell
The Great War: Breakthroughs

American Empire: Blood and Iron
American Empire: The Center Cannot Hold
American Empire: The Victorious Opposition

Settling Accounts: Return Engagement

Settling Accounts:
Return Engagement

HARRY TURTLEDOVE

SETTLING ACCOUNTS: RETURN ENGAGEMENT

BALLANTINE BOOKS

NEW YORK

A Del Rey® Book
Published by The Random House Publishing Group

Copyright © 2004 by Harry Turtledove

All rights reserved under International and Pan-American Copyright Conventions. Published in the United States by Del Rey Books, an imprint of The Random House Publishing Group, a division of Random House, Inc., New York, and simultaneously in Canada by Random House of Canada Limited, Toronto.

Del Rey is a registered trademark and the Del Rey colophon is a trademark of Random House, Inc.

Library of Congress Cataloging-in-Publication Data is available from the publisher upon request.

ISBN 0-345-45723-4

Manufactured in the United States of America

This one is for Al and Craig

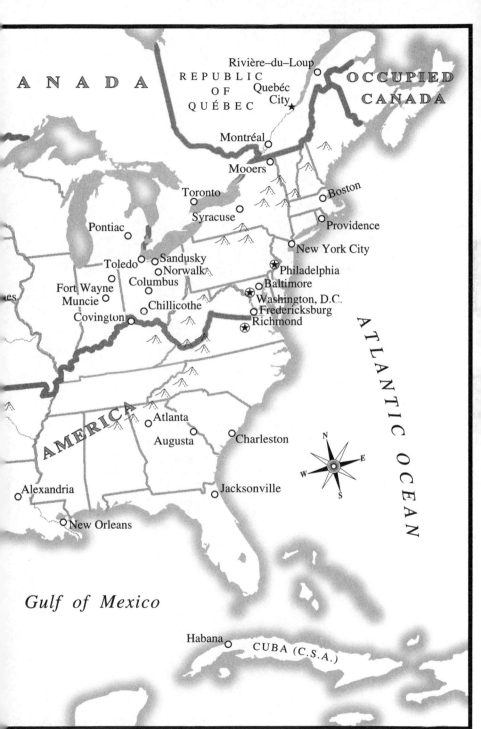

Settling Accounts:
Return Engagement

I

Flora Blackford woke from nightmare to nightmare. She'd dreamt she was trapped in a burning building, with fire alarms and sirens screaming all around her. When her eyes opened, she thought for a dreadful moment that she was still dreaming, for sirens *were* wailing outside. Then reason returned along with consciousness, and the Congresswoman from New York groaned. Those were air-raid sirens, which could only mean the war had started at last.

Or maybe it's a drill, Flora thought, snatching desperately at hope, though a drill at—she looked at the alarm clock on the nightstand—four in the morning struck her as madness. Of course, a new round of war between the United States and the Confederate States struck her as madness, too.

Antiaircraft guns in the defense ring around Philadelphia began to pound. That sound banished the last vestiges of doubt. Guns inside the de facto capital of the USA opened up a moment later. Through the gunfire and the sirens, she heard a deep, distant throbbing that rapidly grew louder. Those were Confederate bombers overhead.

She sprang out of bed and threw a housecoat on over the thin cotton nightgown she'd worn against the muggy heat of the first days of summer in Philadelphia. She had one arm in the quilted housecoat and one arm out when she suddenly stopped in outrage that seemed ridiculous only later. "That *bastard*!" she exclaimed. "He didn't even declare war!"

A new sound joined the cacophony outside: the thin whistle of falling bombs. As the first explosions made the windows of her flat rattle and shake, she realized President Jake Featherston of the CSA wouldn't have to send Al Smith, his U.S. counterpart, any formal messages now.

Fear joined outrage. She could die here. So could her son. She ran to his bedroom and threw open the door. "Joshua! Get up!" she shouted. "We've got to get down to the basement! The war is here!"

Only a snore answered her. At sixteen, Joshua could sleep through anything, and he'd proved it. Sirens? Antiaircraft guns? Droning bombers? Bombs? Probing searchlights? His mother yelling? They were all one to him, and likewise all nothing to him.

"Get up!" Flora shouted again. Still no response. She went over to the bed and shook him. *"Get up!"*

That did the job. Joshua Blackford sat up and muttered for a moment. He didn't doubt what was going on around him the way his mother had. "They really went and did it!" he said.

"Yes, they really did," Flora agreed grimly. Bombs were bursting closer now, underscoring her words. "Come on. Get moving. Put on a bathrobe or something and get downstairs with me. We don't have time to dawdle."

Later, she would discover that putting on a bathrobe when you were already wearing pajamas was dawdling, too. But that would be later. In the wee small hours of June 22, 1941, she was doing as well as she could.

Someone pounded on the door. "Get out! Get downstairs!" a hoarse male voice yelled.

"We're coming!" Flora shouted back. Joshua flew into a terry-cloth robe. Flora grabbed a key and locked the door behind her when she and her son left the apartment. Those niceties would also go by the board later on.

Down the stairs they scurried, along with the other members of Congress and bureaucrats and businessmen and their families who rented here. For the moment, everybody was equal: equal in fear and equal in fury. In the darkness of the stairwell, people said exactly what they thought of Jake Featherston, the Freedom Party, and the Confederate States of America. Flora heard some things she'd never heard before. No one cared if women were within earshot. Some of the most inflammatory things came from the mouths of women, as a matter of fact.

The basement was dark, too, dark and crowded and hot and stuffy. Someone lit a match to start a cigarette. The brief flare of light might have been a bomb itself. Flora wished she hadn't thought of that comparison. If a bomb did hit this building . . . *"Sh'ma yisroayl, adonai elohaynu, adonai ekhod,"* she murmured, just in case.

More bombs burst, some of them very close. The basement shook, as if at an earthquake. Plaster pattered down from the ceiling. A woman screamed. A man groaned. Beside Flora, Joshua whispered, "Wow!"

She wanted to hit him and kiss him at the same time. He was reacting to the spectacle, to what people were doing all around him. Fear? He knew nothing of fear because at his age he didn't really believe anything could happen to him. Flora was heading into her mid-fifties. She knew perfectly well that disaster could knock on the door.

A rending crash came from outside, different from the sharp, staccato roars of the exploding bombs. "We got one of the fuckers, anyway," a man said in tones of ferocious satisfaction.

A bomber. That was what that had to be. A Confederate bomber had smashed to earth somewhere not far away. How many young men had been aboard it? How many had managed to get clear and parachute away before it went into its last fatal dive? And how many Philadelphians had they killed before they were shot down? If you were going to ask the other questions, you had to ask that one, too.

The raid lasted a little more than an hour. Little by little, bombs came at longer intervals. The drone of engines overhead faded. The antiaircraft guns kept ravening away for several minutes after the bombers were gone. Some of them went on shooting even after the continuous all-clear note replaced the warbling rise and fall of the air-raid alarm.

"Well, that was fun," somebody behind Flora said. Along with half a dozen other people, she laughed—probably louder than the joke deserved. But it cut the tension, and there had been enough tension in the air to need a lot of cutting.

"What do we do now, Mom?" Joshua asked.

"We go back up to the flat and see what happened to it," Flora answered. "Then I have to go in to Congress. Featherston may not have bothered with a declaration of war, but President Smith will, and they'll need me to vote for it."

Back in 1914, as a Socialist agitator in New York City, she'd urged her party not to vote for the credits that financed the opening act of the Great War. She remained a Socialist. These days, though, the country had a Socialist President (which would have seemed unimaginable in 1914) and had been wantonly attacked by the Confederate States (which wouldn't have seemed surprising at all).

As they left the basement, morning twilight was brightening toward dawn. "That's why the Confederate bombers went home," Joshua said as they climbed stairs. "They didn't want to hang around when our gunners and fighter pilots could get a good look at them."

"I didn't know I had a son on the General Staff," Flora said. Joshua snorted but looked immensely proud of himself.

When they went back into the apartment, they found glass everywhere: on the floors, on the beds, some glittering shards driven deep into the plaster of the far wall. The windows were gone, every single one of them. Flora eyed the shards with a fresh horror. What would those flying fragments of glass have done to people whose soft flesh happened to get in the way? Butchered them. That was the only word Flora could think of.

Joshua was staring out at the city. His head slowly swung from left to right, taking it all in like a panning newsreel camera. Flora joined him. There were bomb craters half a block down the street. A little farther away, a black, greasy pillar of smoke rose into the sky. Was that the bomber's pyre? She thought so.

More columns of smoke rose all over Philadelphia. Most of them came from the center of town, where government buildings had gone up ever since the 1880s. Most, but not all. The Confederates had dropped bombs all over the city. Bad aim? Deliberate terror? Who could guess?

Fire engine sirens screeched as the sun came up over the horizon. When Flora tried to turn on the bathroom lamp, she discovered the power had gone out. "Don't leave the icebox open very long—it lets the cold out," she called to Joshua as she dressed. They had an electric refrigerator, but she was used to the older word. "I'm going to Congress." She hurried out the door and down the stairs.

Two Representatives and a Senator were already at the curb trying to flag a taxi. Flora got one by walking out in the street in front of it. The driver didn't—quite—run over her. All the elected officials piled in. "To Congress!" they bawled.

The neoclassical mountain of a building where the Senate and House met had escaped damage, though firemen were fighting flames in the office building across the street and dragging bodies out of it. "Joint session!" Flora didn't even know where she first heard it, but it was everywhere as soon as she got into the rotunda. "President Smith will address a joint session."

A joint session meant shoehorning the Senate into the far larger House chamber along with the Representatives. Today, there were still some empty seats after that: members of Congress who couldn't get to the session or who were injured or dead. A joint session also meant the risk of a lucky bomb taking out the whole legislative branch and the President. Flora wished she hadn't thought of that.

"Ladies and gentlemen, the President of the United States!" the Speaker of the House boomed out. The wave of applause that greeted Al Smith was fierce and savage.

Smith himself looked like hell. People had called him the Happy Warrior, but he seemed anything but happy as he mounted the podium. He had aged years in the months since his acceptance of a U.S.-C.S. plebiscite in Kentucky and Houston (now west Texas again) and Sequoyah proved such a spectacularly bad idea. His hands shook as he gathered the pages of his speech.

But his voice—even more strongly New York–flavored than Flora's—rang out strong and true. A thicket of microphones picked it up and carried it across the USA by wireless: "I have to tell you now that this country is at war with the Confederate States of America. At the close of my address, I shall ask the Congress to make the official declaration, a formality the Confederate States have forgotten." Another furious round of applause said he would get what he asked for.

He went on, "You can imagine what a bitter blow it is for me that all my long struggle to win peace has failed. Yet I cannot believe that there is anything more or anything different that I could have done and that would have been more successful. Up to the very last it would have been quite possible to have arranged a peaceful and honorable settlement between the CSA and the USA, but Featherston would not have it. He had evidently made up his mind to attack us whatever happened, and although he may claim he put forward reasonable proposals which we rejected, that is not a true statement.

"His action shows convincingly that there is no chance of expecting that this man will ever give up his practice of using force to gain his will. He can only be stopped by force. We have a clear conscience. We have done all that any country could do to establish peace. But now that it has come to war, I know every American will play his part with calmness and courage.

"Now may God bless you all. He *will* defend our cause. It is the evil things that we shall be fighting against—brute force, bad faith, injustice, oppression, and persecution—and against them I am certain that the right shall prevail."

Flora applauded till her palms hurt. It was a good speech. The only way it could have been better was if Al Smith hadn't had to give it at all.

When the air-raid sirens screeched in the middle of the night, Armstrong Grimes thought it was a drill. He figured some sadistic officer had found a new way to rob him of sleep, as if basic training didn't take enough anyhow. But listening to a sergeant screaming, "Get moving, assholes! This is the real thing!" sent him bouncing out of his cot in a hurry.

He could normally dress in three minutes. He had his green-gray uniform on in under two. "Do we line up for roll call?" somebody yelled.

"Jesus Christ, no!" the sergeant hollered back. "Get your asses into the shelter trenches! If you bastards live, we'll count you later."

They'd dug the shelter trenches near the Fort Custer barracks outside Columbus, Ohio, the week before. Wasted work, Armstrong had thought. And it had been then, in the dim dark disappearing days of peace. Now war was coming, riding closer every second on the screams of the sirens. War was coming, and what had been waste might save his life. A lesson lurked there somewhere, if only he could find it.

No time now, no time, no time. Along with the other raw recruits, he dove for the trenches. A mosquito whined through the din, the song of its wings somehow penetrating the greater madness all around. If it pierced him, he would itch. If fragments of steel from the greater madness pierced him, he would scream till he could no longer hear the sirens, till he choked on the song of death.

Antiaircraft guns pounding, pounding. Lights in the sky: bursting shells. And the buzz of engines overhead. Armstrong had never known anything like it before. He hoped he never did again. When the U.S. Army conscripted him, he'd looked forward to war. What point to putting on the uniform if you weren't going to see action? Well, here it was, and it wasn't what he'd thought it would be.

He'd pictured himself shooting at Confederate soldiers in butternut uniforms while they shot back at him. He'd pictured them missing, of course, while his bullets knocked them over one after another as if they were part of a funhouse shooting gallery. He'd pictured the enemy soldiers who managed to survive throwing up their hands and surrendering in droves. He'd pictured generals pinning medals on him, and pretty girls giving him a hero's reward.

What he hadn't pictured was lying in a muddy trench—it had rained two days before—while the Confederates dropped bombs on his head and while he didn't even have a Springfield in his hand so he could shoot back. Whether he'd pictured it or not, that was his introduction to war.

Somebody not far down the trench started screaming as soon as he heard the bombs falling. Armstrong had thought he would laugh about something like that. It seemed funny and cowardly, both at the same time. He wasn't laughing, not for real. It was all he could do not to scream himself.

And then the bombs weren't falling any more. They were bursting. The noise was like the end of the world. He'd got used to the bang of Springfields on the firing range. These, by contrast, were hammer blows against the ears. They picked him up and slammed him down. They tried to reach down his throat and tear his lungs out through his nose. The ground twisted and quivered and shook under him, as if in torment. By then, plenty of people were screaming. After a little while, he realized he was one of them.

Fragments of bomb casing hissed and whistled past overhead. Armstrong wondered again what would happen if they ran into flesh, then wished he hadn't. Mud and dirt thrown up by bomb bursts rained down into the trench. *I could be buried alive,* he thought. The notion didn't make him much more frightened than he was already.

A chunk of metal thumped into the soft ground about six inches from Armstrong's head. He reached out and touched it, then jerked his hand away—it was hot as hell. Maybe it was a chunk of casing, or maybe a shell fragment from a round out of an antiaircraft gun. If it had come down on his head instead of near it, he would have had himself a short and ignominious war.

A bomb hit the barracks he'd come out of a few minutes before. That rending crash was different from the ones he'd heard when bombs hit bare ground. "McCloskey!" Armstrong sang out, doing his best to imitate a pissed-off sergeant. "Pick up your fucking socks!"

Four or five scared recruits stopped screaming and laughed. Somewhere up the trench, Eddie McCloskey gave his detailed opinion about what Armstrong could do with and to his socks.

Then a bomb burst *in* the trench, less than a hundred feet away. The earthwork zigzagged, so the blast didn't travel far. What the bomb did do was bad enough anyway. Something thumped Armstrong in the shoulder. He automatically reached out to see what it was, and found himself holding a little less than half of somebody's hand.

Blood splashed and streaked his palm. With a cry of disgust, he threw away the ruined part of a man. But shrieks from close by where the bomb had hit sent him moving in that direction. (Only silence came from the very place where the bomb had landed. Nothing right there lived to shriek.)

He stumbled over a man's head. It moved when his foot hit it— moved like a kicked football, moved in a way that proved it was no longer attached to a body. He gasped out a couple of horrified curses. He'd made a joke about Eddie McCloskey's socks when he didn't know how bad things could be. Now he was finding out, and whatever jokes might have lived within him withered.

It was still nighttime. He couldn't see very well. But he knew the bloody smell of a butcher's shop. He knew it, and he'd never expected to find it here, especially not mingled with the darker outhouse reeks of offal.

Along with the young men who were dead were several who wished they were. They shouted loudly for someone to kill them. Armstrong would have done it, too, if only to make them shut up, had he had any kind of weapon. Since he didn't, he had to try to keep them alive instead.

That was hardly easier than putting them out of their misery. He had no bandages, no medicines, no nothing. He found one fellow clutching a gaping wound in his calf. He tore the laces out of the injured soldier's shoes and used them for a tourniquet. He never knew for sure if that did any good, for he went on to someone else right away, but he dared hope.

Somebody let out a whoop of savage glee, shouting, "We got one of the sons of bitches, anyhow!" And so they had. A C.S. bomber overhead trailed fire from one engine. The flames slid up the wing toward the fuselage.

"I hope all the cocksuckers in there roast," Armstrong snarled.

Several other men nodded or wished something even worse on the Confederate fliers. "Shitheads didn't even declare war on us," someone said.

"Well, what do you think?" another soldier asked. "You think we're at war with them now—or shall we invite 'em in for tea?"

Armstrong kept hoping this was a nightmare from which he'd wake up. The hope kept getting dashed, again and again and again. The bombers didn't linger overhead very long—they must have had other targets besides Fort Custer. It only seemed like forever, or ten minutes longer. As the bombs started falling somewhere else, Armstrong came out of the trench and looked around.

Nothing was left of the barracks except burning rubble. Several other buildings were also on fire. So were autos and trucks. Bomb craters made the paths and lawns resemble what people with high foreheads said the surface of the moon was like. Armstrong didn't know much about that. He did know it was the biggest, most godawful mess he'd ever seen in his life. His mother and his granny had gone on and on about what Washington, D.C.—his home town—was like during the Great War. He hadn't taken them too seriously. *He* didn't remember such things, after all. But now, with a convert's sudden zeal, he believed.

"Who the hell is that?" One of the other men pointed at somebody walking in out of the predawn darkness.

The newcomer wore coveralls of an unfamiliar cut. Even by the light of blazing buildings and vehicles, Armstrong could see the coveralls were the wrong color, too. The stranger had a pistol on his hip, but he didn't try to use it. Instead, he raised his hands above his head. "Reckon y'all got me," he drawled, sounding cheerful enough. "Isn't much point for a flyin' man to go on with the fight once his airplane goes down, now is there?"

Just hearing that Southern accent made Armstrong wish he had a gun handy. The bastard thought he could murder U.S. soldiers and then bail out of the war as easily as he'd bailed out of the bomber? Growling like an angry dog, Armstrong took a couple of steps toward him.

A rock sailed out of the darkness and caught the Confederate airman above the ear. In the firelight, he looked absurdly surprised. As he started to crumple, he tried to get the pistol out of the holster. He couldn't. His hands didn't seem to remember what they were supposed to do.

And it probably wouldn't have made any difference anyway. Armstrong and eight or ten others rushed him. He wouldn't have been able to hold on to the gun for more than a heartbeat. He might have shot one of the U.S. soldiers, or two, but after that. . . . After that, he would have been a dead man. Which he was anyway.

By the time the soldiers finished pounding and kicking and stomping, he didn't look anything like a man any more. He resembled nothing so much as a large broken doll lying there on the grass, all of its limbs bent in directions impossible in nature. His neck had an unnatural twist in it, too.

A corporal came up right after the recruits realized the flier had no more sport left in him. "Jesus Christ, you bastards, what the hell did you go and do?"

"Gave this asshole what he deserved," Armstrong answered. Morning twilight was beginning to paint the eastern sky with gray.

"Well, yeah." The noncom stared at the crumpled corpse. "But do you know how much of a stink there'll be if the Confederates find out what the hell you did? They're liable to start doing the same thing to our guys, too."

Armstrong hadn't thought of that. It was the only reason he could imagine for regretting what he'd just helped do. He would have rid the world of ten or a hundred Confederates as cheerfully, if only he'd got his hands on them.

One of the other men who'd mobbed the flier said, "Hell with it, Corporal. We'll throw the motherfucker in the trench where the bomb hit, toss his clothes on the fire, and bury the pistol somewhere. After that, who's gonna know?"

After a little thought, the soldier with two stripes on his sleeve nodded. "All right. That's about the best we can do now, I guess. Get the identity disk off from around his neck, too, and bury it with the piece. That way, people will think he was one of ours when they deal with the bodies." He came closer and took a long look at the dead Confederate. "Fuck! Nobody'll recognize him, that's for sure."

"It's a war, Corporal," Armstrong said. "You wanted us to give him a big kiss when he came in here with that shit-eating grin on his face? We kissed him, all right. We kissed him good-bye." The noncom waved for him and the others to take care of the body. They did. The corporal didn't do any of the work himself. That was what having those stripes on his sleeve meant.

Brigadier General Clarence Potter had spent three years up near the front in the Great War. He hadn't had to do a lot of actual fighting; he'd been in Intelligence with the Army of Northern Virginia. He was in Intelligence still—or rather, after close to twenty years out of the Confederate Army, in Intelligence again—but wished he could get up to the front once more instead of being stuck in Richmond.

A tall, well-made man in his mid-fifties, Potter had close-cropped hair now closer to white than to its original dark brown. His cold gray eyes surveyed the world from behind steel-rimmed spectacles. The spectacles, these days, were bifocals. That had annoyed him when he first got them. By now, he was used to them and took them for granted.

A telephone on his desk rang. "Potter speaking," he said briskly. His accent was clipped and Yankeelike. He'd gone to college at Yale, and the way of speaking up there had stuck. That made some of his fellow Confederates look at him suspiciously. It also made him and those like him valuable in intelligence work. The CSA and USA spoke the same language, with minor differences in accent and vocabulary. A man from the Confederate States who could sound as if he came from the United States made a valuable spy.

A man from the United States who could sound as if he came from the Confederate States . . . was somebody else's worry to hunt down, though Potter had been the one who first realized such a man might pose problems.

"Good morning, General. Saul Goldman," said the voice on the other end of the line.

Potter came alert at once. "What can I do for you, Mr. Goldman?" he asked. The little Jew held an innocuous-sounding title: Director of Communications. But he was a force to be reckoned with in the Featherston administration. He shaped the news that went out over the wireless, in newspapers, and in cinema newsreels. His wireless station here in Richmond had helped Jake Featherston rise, and Featherston, who never forgot an enemy, also never forgot a friend.

The only problem being, he hasn't got many friends. Considering what a charming fellow he is, it's no surprise, either, Potter thought. He didn't count himself among that small group. Five years earlier, he'd come to Richmond with a pistol in his pocket, intending to rid the CSA of Jake Featherston once for all. Instead, he'd ended up shooting a black frankfurter seller who had the same idea but who sprayed bullets around so wildly, he endangered everybody near him—including Potter.

Memory blew away like a dandelion puff on the breeze as Goldman answered, "I would like to know how I can give your outfit the attention it deserves. I want the people to understand we're doing everything we can to find out what the Yankees are up to and to stop it."

"You want to give us the attention we deserve, eh?" Potter said. "Well, I can tell you how to do that in one word."

"Tell me, then, General," Goldman said.

"Don't."

"But—" Saul Goldman wasn't a man who usually spluttered, but he did now. "We need to show the people—"

"Don't," Potter repeated, this time cutting him off. "D-O-N-apostrophe-T, don't. Anything you tell us, you tell the damnyankees, too. Now you may want Joe Dogberry from Plains, Georgia, to be sure we're a bunch of clever fellows. That's fine, when it's peacetime.

When it's war, though, I want the United States to be sure we're a pack of goddamn idiots."

"This is not the proper attitude," Goldman said stiffly.

"Maybe not from the propaganda point of view. From the military point of view, it sure as hell is." Potter didn't like defying the director of communications. But, Intelligence to his bones, he liked the idea of giving away secrets even less.

Unlike the swaggering braggarts who made up such a large part of the Freedom Party, Saul Goldman was always soft-spoken and courteous. When he said, "I guess I'll have to take it up with the President, then," a less alert man might not have recognized that as a threat.

"You do what you think you have to do, Mr. Goldman," Potter said. "If President Featherston gives me an order . . ." He decided not to say exactly what he'd do then. Better to keep his choices open.

"You'll hear from me—or from him. Good-bye." Saul Goldman hung up.

Potter went back to work. Since the war started, his biggest worry was how to hear from his agents in the United States. Postal service between the two countries had shut down. So had the telegraph lines. *Where there's a will, there's a lawyer,* Potter thought cynically. He'd managed so far. North America was a big place. Slipping over the border one way or another wasn't that hard, especially west of the Mississippi. Advertisements on wireless stations and in local newspapers along the border that sounded innocent weren't always. If they were phrased one way, they could mean this. If they were phrased another, they could mean that.

Some of his people had wireless transmitters, too. That was risky in any number of ways, but sometimes the rewards outweighed the risks. Potter knew he was going to be busy as a one-armed man with poison ivy all through the war. The front? He'd be lucky if he saw the sun once a week.

The telephone rang again. He picked it up. "Clarence Potter."

"Hello, Potter, you stubborn son of a bitch." That harsh rasp was infinitely familiar all the way across the Confederate States, from Norfolk to Guaymas.

"Hello, Mr. President. Saul Goldman talked to you, did he?"

"He sure as hell did," Jake Featherston answered. "I want you to cooperate with him just as far as you can. Have you got that?"

"Yes, sir. I do. Who decides how far I can cooperate?"

"You do and he does, together."

"In that case, sir, you'd better take me out of this job, give me a rifle, and send me to Ohio or Indiana," Potter said. "I wouldn't mind going. I was thinking about that a little while ago. By the nature of things, Saul and I aren't going to see eye to eye about this."

"What do you mean?" As always when somebody bucked him, suspicion clotted Featherston's voice.

"Goldman's a publicist. He's got a story he wants to tell, and he wants to shout it from the housetops," Potter replied. "Me, I'm a spy. That's why you put the uniform back on me."

"That's not why, and we both know it," Jake said. "I put the uniform back on you because shooting you five years ago would've raised a stink."

"I believe it," Clarence Potter said cheerfully. "If you give me a rifle, though, you've got a pretty good chance the damnyankees'll do it for you."

"Don't tempt me." The President of the Confederate States laughed. It was not a pleasant sort of laugh. "God damn you, why won't you ever be reasonable?"

"Mr. President, I *am* being reasonable—from my own point of view, anyway," Potter said. "I told you: I'm a spy. The best thing that can happen to me is that the bastards on the other side don't even remember I'm here. And Saul wants to shine a searchlight on me. No, thanks."

"Then you jew him down to shining a flashlight on you," Featherston said. "Whatever you don't want to show, you don't show, that's all."

"I don't want to show anything." Potter did his best to keep his temper. It wasn't easy, not when everyone around him seemed willfully blind. "Don't you understand, sir? For every one thing I show, the damnyankees are going to be sure I'm hiding half a dozen more. And the bastards will be right, too."

"But even if you don't show anything, the Yankees will know you're hiding something," Jake Featherston returned. "You reckon they don't know we've got spies? They're bastards, but they aren't stupid bastards—you know what I'm saying? They might not have your telephone number, but they know where you work. Now you tell me, Potter—is that the truth or ain't it?"

"Well . . . maybe," Potter said reluctantly.

"All right, then. In that case, quit your bellyaching," Jake said. "Let Saul take his photos and write his story. If you want to say this is your supersecret brand-new spy headquarters in Williamsburg or something, you can go ahead and do that. I don't mind one goddamn bit. Maybe it'll make the USA drop some bombs on that ratty old place. Nobody'd mind if they blew it to hell and gone, and they wouldn't hurt anything we want to hold on to. How does that sound?"

Potter thought it over. He didn't like Jake Featherston, and knew he never would. He'd had to develop considerable respect for Featherston's driving will, but he'd never thought the President was what anybody would call smart. Smart or not, though, no denying Jake could be shrewd.

"All right, sir. New supersecret spy headquarters in Williamsburg it is," he said. "But Goldman will have to be careful taking pictures with windows in them. Now that some of the people I boss actually work above the ground here, people who take a good look at what's in the windows will be able to see it's Richmond."

"You talk to Saul about that kind of crap," Featherston said. "He'll take care of it. You know your business. You'd best believe he knows his." He hung up.

So did Potter, slowly and thoughtfully. Featherston had just got him to do what he was told. *If I'd pushed it, I could have gone to the front,* the intelligence officer realized ruefully. But you didn't push things against Jake Featherston, not when he was pushing on you. Potter knew himself to be no weakling. Featherston had imposed *his* will even so.

A young lieutenant came in and dropped eight or ten envelopes on Potter's desk. "These just came in, sir," he said. "Not likely we'll be getting any more like 'em."

"No, not likely," Potter agreed. The envelopes were from his agents in the USA, and they'd gone to mail drops in the CSA—mail sent directly to the War Department in Richmond might have made U.S. postal clerks just a trifle curious. All of them were postmarked in the last few days before the war broke out. Potter opened one from Columbus, Ohio. "Well, let's see what we've got."

The agent in Columbus played the role of a businessman. He played it so well, he was getting rich up there in the United States.

He'd acquired a Packard and a mistress. While Potter knew about the latter, he didn't think the man's wife in Jacksonville did. Codes were crude. The agent wrote that his competition was alert, that the other fellows were sending salesmen down into towns close by the Ohio River, and that they'd ordered more heavy machinery. Potter didn't have to be a genius to figure out that salesmen were soldiers and heavy machinery meant barrels. Neither would any other reasonably suspicious fellow who happened to read the letter.

But if you weren't suspicious, it looked like an ordinary business letter. So did the others. They all told about the same story: the damnyankees knew something was coming, and they were getting ready to try to stop it.

Clarence Potter muttered to himself. Had he been running things, he wouldn't have been so belligerent ahead of time. That way, the attack might have been a strategic as well as a tactical surprise. But he didn't run things. For better and for worse, this was and would be Jake Featherston's show.

Jefferson Pinkard slept badly. In part, that was because the weather at Camp Dependable—not far outside Alexandria, Louisiana—was even hotter and muggier than it was in Birmingham, where he'd lived most of his life. And in part . . . He mostly didn't remember his dreams, even when they woke him up with his heart pounding and his eyes wide and staring. Considering the kind of dreams a camp commandant was likely to have, that made him more lucky than not.

Camp Dependable wasn't desperately crowded any more. The camp had a limited capacity. The number of black prisoners who came into it from all over the CSA seemed unlimited. Rebellion had smoldered and now and then burst into flame ever since the Freedom Party came to power—and Jake Featherston and his followers didn't believe in turning the other cheek. When they got hit, they hit back—hard.

When a new shipment of captured rebels came into the camp, guards led a matching number of prisoners out to the nearby woods and swamps. The guards always came back. The prisoners they escorted didn't.

The first time Jeff had to order something like that, he'd been appalled. He'd had to do it several times now, and it did grow easier. You could get used to damn near anything. He'd seen that in west Texas during the war, and again in the civil war down in Mexico. But, even though he didn't break out in palpitations whenever he had to do it again, it told on him when he went to bed at night.

It told on the guards, too, or on some of them, anyhow. The ones who went out on those disposal jobs often drank like fishes. Pinkard couldn't clamp down on them as hard as he would have liked. He knew what they were doing out there. They needed some way to blow off steam. One of them, the very first time, had stuck his pistol in his mouth and blown off the top of his head instead.

Others, though, didn't seem bothered at all. They came back to camp laughing and joking. Some took it as all in a day's work. And some took it as the best sport this side of coon hunting. When Jeff said as much after the latest operation, one of those fellows grinned at him and said, "Hell, it is coon hunting, ain't it?"

"Funny, Edwards. Funny like a goddamn crutch," Pinkard had answered. But a lot of the returning guards thought it was the funniest thing they'd heard in all their born days. Pinkard said, "All right, you bastards. Go ahead and laugh. But you better not be laughing and screwing around when you're watching the niggers. You'll be sorry if you are, by Jesus."

That got their attention. *By God, it had better,* Jeff thought. Camp Dependable didn't hold political prisoners any more (well, except for Willy Knight, and the ex–Vice President was a special case if ever there was one). These days, the prisoners were Negroes who'd fought against the Confederate States. If they saw a chance, they would rise up against the guards in a heartbeat.

Pinkard's gaze went to the machine-gun towers rising above the barbed-wire perimeter of the camp. If the spooks in here did try to get cute, they'd pay for it. Of course, they were going to pay for it anyway, so what did they have to lose? Guarding desperate men had its disadvantages.

Some of the guards in the towers were men who had the toughest time going out on population-reduction maneuvers. (Jeff wanted to think about what he did with the Negroes who left the camp and didn't come back in terms like those. That way, he didn't have to dwell on the details of what went on out there in the woods and swamps. He had his weaknesses, too.) Even so, he didn't worry about them where they were. If it came down to their necks or those of the prisoners, he knew they'd save themselves.

"Keep your eyes open," he urged for what had to be the millionth time. "Keep your ears open, too. Don't let those sneaky black bastards tell you what they want you to hear." He looked around. "Any questions?"

The guards shook their heads. Pinkard, who was an ordinary Joe himself, knew a lot of them weren't any too bright. It didn't matter, as long as they were tough and as long as they followed orders. They were more than tough enough. And they obeyed pretty well. If nothing else, the fear of disaster kept them in line.

He nodded. "All right, then. Dismissed."

Off they went. Mercer Scott, the guard chief, stayed behind to talk privately to Pinkard. Scott was plenty sharp, or sly anyway, and about as tough as they came. His jowly face looked as if it were made out of boot leather. Pausing to shift his chaw from one cheek to the other, he said, "Boss, we got to do a better job of what we're doin'."

"Yeah?" Jeff said noncommittally. He worried that Scott was after his job. He also worried that the guard chief told tales on him back to Richmond. Jake Featherston (or Attorney General Ferd Koenig, which amounted to the same thing) kept an eye on everybody. Pinkard had been in the Freedom Party since the first time he heard Featherston speak, and he'd stayed in it through good times and bad. *You'd think they'd cut me a little slack.* But that wasn't how things worked, and he knew it.

Mercer Scott nodded now. "Yeah, I reckon so. Taking a batch of niggers out and shooting 'em . . . That wears on the men when they got to do it over and over, you know what I mean?"

"Well, we wouldn't have to do it if Richmond didn't keep sending us more smokes than we got any chance of holding, let alone feeding," Jeff said. "If you've got any clout back there, make 'em stop."

There. Now he'd told Scott at least some of what he suspected. But the guard chief shook his bullet head. "Not me. Not the way you mean. I don't believe I've got as much as you."

Was he sandbagging? Pinkard wouldn't have been surprised. He said, "Well, what the hell are we supposed to do? We've got to get rid of the extra niggers, on account of the camp sure as shit won't hold as many as they send us. Got to keep the goddamn population down." No, he didn't like talking—or thinking—about shooting people. That Mercer Scott didn't seem to mind only made him ruder and cruder than ever in Pinkard's eye.

Now he said, "Yeah, boss, we got to get rid of 'em, but shooting 'em ain't the answer. That's what I'm trying to tell you."

Pinkard began to lose patience. "You're telling me you don't like it, so—"

"It ain't just me," Scott broke in. "It's the men, too. This here business is hard on 'em, way we're doing it now. Some can take it, yeah, but some can't. I got me a ton of transfer requests I'm sitting on. And folks around this place know what we're doing, too— whites and niggers. You hear all those guns goin' off every so often, nobody needs to draw you a picture after that."

"Fine," Jeff said. "Fuckin' wonderful. I told you, Mercer, I know what you've got your ass in an uproar about. You tell me what sort of notion you've got for fixing it, then I'll know whether we can try it or we need to keep on doin' what we're doin' undisirregardless of whether anybody likes it. So piss or get off the pot, is what I'm telling you."

That got him a sullen look from the guard chief. "It's your camp, dammit. You're the one who's supposed to keep it running smooth."

"You mean you don't know what to do," Jeff said scornfully. "Get the hell out of here."

"Oh, I'll go." But Scott turned back over his shoulder to add, "I'm telling you, boss, there's got to be a better way."

"Maybe there does," Pinkard said. "You figure out what it is, you let me know. Till then, you got to shut up and do your job just like the rest of us."

Black prisoners—Willy Knight a white crow among them—lined up to get their noon rations. Those rations, even now, were none too large. They'd never caught up with the capacity of Camp Dependable. If Pinkard hadn't carried out periodic population reductions, he wouldn't have been able to feed the population he had. That would have reduced it, too, but not neatly or efficiently.

The blacks sent Pinkard looks in which hate mingled with fear. They knew what he was doing to them. They couldn't help knowing. But they were warier about showing their hatred than they had been. Anything that put them on the wrong side of any guard was liable to get them included in one of the reductions. If that happened, they'd die quickly instead of slowly.

Pinkard went into the dining area and watched them gulp down their soup—cooked up from whatever might be edible that the camp got its hands on—and grits. The food disappeared amazingly fast. Even so, there was never enough. Day after day, prisoners got scrawnier. Less and less flesh held their skin away from their bones.

One of them nodded to Pinkard. "You give me a gun, suh," he said. "You give me a gun and I shoots me plenty o' damnyankees. Give me a gun and give me a uniform and give me some food. I be the best goddamn sojer anybody ever see."

Maybe he would. He'd fought against the Confederate States. Why not for them? Sometimes a fellow who'd learned what to do with a rifle in his hands didn't care in which direction he pointed it. Jeff had been that way himself when he went down to Mexico. The only reason he'd fought for Maximilian and not the republican rebels was that his buddies were on the Emperor's side. He'd cared nothing for the cause as a cause.

Of course, this Negro was hungry to the point where his ribs would do duty for a xylophone. If his number came up in a population reduction, hunger would be the least and last of his worries, too. He'd probably say and do anything to keep breathing and to put real rations in his belly. He was at least as likely to desert the first chance he saw, or to start aiming his rifle at Confederates again.

Any which way, that wasn't Jeff's call. He said, "You're eating at the table you set when you did whatever the hell you did to land yourself in here. You don't like it now, you shouldn't've done whatever the hell it was."

He waited to see if the colored man had some kind of smartmouth comeback ready. Some of these bastards never learned. But this fellow just poured down the soup and spooned up his grits and kept his mouth shut otherwise. That was smart. Of course, if he were really smart, he wouldn't have been here.

Some of the Negroes in here insisted they were guilty of nothing but being black. They could insist as much as they wanted. It wasn't going to change a goddamn thing. And if Jake Featherston wanted to run every Negro man, woman, and child through Camp Dependable . . . Pinkard laughed. If he wanted to do that, he'd have to build himself a hell of a lot bigger camp.

Jeff didn't see that happening. If anything, the start of the war would probably starve Dependable and the other camps in the CSA of guards and resources. Fighting the USA was a hell of a big job. Everything else, he figured, would have to wait on a siding while that train rolled by.

Which also meant he didn't have to flabble like a turtle jumping off a rock to figure out better ways to deal with population reductions. No matter what Mercer Scott thought, they wouldn't be too urgent. If some of the guards couldn't stand the strain, he'd get others. There'd be wounded veterans not fit for tougher duty who could take care of this just fine.

There's a relief, Pinkard thought. All the same, finding other ways to go about it kept gnawing at him, like the very beginnings of a toothache.

The wind came out of the west, off the Carolina coast. That made Lieutenant, j.g., Sam Carsten happy. It meant the USS *Remembrance* could steam toward the coast when she launched her bombers and torpedo aircraft at Charleston harbor. Had the wind blown in the other direction, she would have had to head straight away from land to send her aircraft towards it.

Not that Sam expected to watch much of the fight either way. His battle station was down in the bowels of the carrier. He was assistant damage-control officer, under Lieutenant Commander Hiram Pottinger. He would rather have had more to do with aviation, but the Navy wanted what it wanted, not what he wanted.

And, in late June off the Carolina coast, being where he was had its advantages. With fair, fair skin, pale blond hair, and blue eyes, he was *this* far from being an albino. Even the mild sun of northern latitudes was a torment to him. Down in Confederate waters, the sun came closer to torture than torment. He painted himself in zinc-oxide ointment till he was blotchy as a leper, and burned anyhow.

One more airplane roared off the deck. Silence came down. "Now we wait," Pottinger said. He was twenty years younger than Sam, but he'd graduated from Annapolis and was on his way through a normal officer's career. Carsten had started as an ordinary seaman. He was a mustang, up through the hawse hole. He'd spent a long time as an ensign, and even longer as a j.g. If he ever made lieutenant, he'd be proud. If he made lieutenant commander, he'd be ecstatic.

Of course, there was a war on. All the naval yards on both coasts would start cranking out ships as fast as they could. They'd need bodies to put into them. And some ships would go to the bottom, too, or suffer battle damage and casualties. They'd need replacements. Sam wasn't thrilled at the idea of getting a promotion on account of something like that, but he knew those things happened. He'd seen it in the last war.

An hour and a half later, the intercom buzzed and squawked. Sam's head swung towards it. One of the sailors in the damage-control party said, "Oh, God, what the hell's gone wrong now?" Carsten had the same thought. The intercom seldom brought good news.

"Men, this is the captain speaking," came from the squawkbox. Whatever the news was, then, it wasn't small. Captain Stein didn't waste his time on small stuff. He left that to Commodore Cressy, the exec. After a tiny pause, the skipper went on, "The government of Great Britain has announced that a state of war exists between their country and the United States."

"Aw, shit," somebody said, softly and almost reverently. Again, Sam was inclined to agree. The Royal Navy could play football on anybody's gridiron. It had written the book from which other navies around the world cribbed—and it had been building hard these past few years.

"Prime Minister Churchill said, 'We have not journeyed all this way across the centuries, across the oceans, across the mountains, because we are made of sugar candy. We know the United States are strong. But the destiny of mankind is not decided by material computation. Death and sorrow will be the companions of our journey; hardship our garment; constancy and valor our only shield. We must be united, we must be undaunted, we must be inflexible. Victory at all costs.' " Captain Stein paused again, then continued, "Well, he gives a nice speech, doesn't he? But we'll whip him and the limeys anyhow."

"Yeah," several sailors said together. The skipper had gauged their feelings well. No matter how good a speech Churchill gave, Sam wondered how smart he was. He could have stayed out of the American war and concentrated on helping France and Russia whip Germany and her European allies. He might have had a pretty good chance of bringing that off, too, and the USA would never have declared war on him.

But Churchill was rolling the dice. He'd always been a man for whom Britain without her empire was like eggs without ham. Beating Germany alone wouldn't get back what she'd lost at the end of the Great War. Beating Germany and the United States might.

"Where we are now, we don't have to worry about the Royal Navy right away," Lieutenant Commander Pottinger said. "We have plenty of other things to worry about instead."

The sailors laughed. Sam did, too, not that it was all that funny. Land-based bombers had damaged his battleship off the South American coast during the last war. The state of the art had improved a lot since then. By attacking Charleston harbor, the *Remembrance* was sticking her head in the lion's mouth.

To keep from thinking about that, he thought about something else: "If the one that started in 1914 was the Great War, what are we going to call this one? The Greater War?" He got a laugh. He almost always could. He had a knack for that, whenever he felt like using it.

Hiram Pottinger said, "Let's hope we call it the 'This Was Easy and We All Went Home in a Hurry War.' " He got a bigger laugh. Sam joined it and softly clapped his hands. He liked that kind of name just fine.

A few minutes afterwards, the intercom came to life again. "This is Commander Cressy." As usual, the executive officer sounded cool, calm, and collected. "Our wireless ranging gear shows aircraft not our own approaching the ship from the west. It is a wee bit unlikely that those aircraft will be friendly. I know you'll give them the warm reception they deserve."

"Happy days," Sam said. The lion was trying to bite.

"Better this news than a surprise," Pottinger said, and Sam could only nod. The wireless ranging gear had gone into the *Remembrance* just the year before. She'd made a special trip to the Boston Navy Yard for the installation. Without it, she would have been blind to the approaching menace, maybe till too late.

Sam wondered whether the Confederates also had wireless ranging gear—Y-range, people were calling it. They'd figured out where the *Remembrance* was pretty damn quick. Nobody'd said anything about their having it. But then, how much of war was finding out the hard way what the other fellow had that you didn't know about ahead of time? Put that way, it sounded quietly philosophical. Put another way, it meant Sam was likely to get killed because some dimbulb in Philadelphia was asleep at the switch.

"They're going to throw up a lot of antiaircraft all around us," said one of the sailors in the damage-control party. Maybe he'd had the same nasty thought Sam had, and was trying to reassure himself.

And maybe whoever'd given the order for this raid hadn't stopped to figure out the likely consequences of sending an airplane carrier within range of land-based aircraft. Hardly anybody had had to worry about land-based attacks on ships during the Great War. Sam was a rare exception. If an admiral hadn't had a new thought since 1917, he'd figure everything would go fine. And maybe he'd turn out to be right, and maybe he wouldn't. And the *Remembrance* was going to find out which.

If the Confederates happened to have a submarine in the neighborhood, too . . . Well, that was another reason destroyers and cruisers ringed the carrier. They were supposed to carry better antisubmersible gear than they'd had in the Great War, better even than they'd had in the Pacific War against Japan.

Would you be able to hear the ships around the *Remembrance* shooting at Confederate airplanes if you were way the hell down here? Carsten cocked his head to one side, listening intently. All he could make out were the carrier's usual mechanical noises.

And then, without warning, all hell broke loose. The *Remembrance*'s dual-purpose five-inch guns and all her smaller quick-firing antiaircraft weapons let go at once. Sam could sure as hell hear that. The engines started working harder. The ship heeled to the left, then to the right. Captain Stein was handling her as if she were a destroyer, dodging and twisting on the open sea like a halfback faking his way past lumbering defensive linemen.

Trouble was, airplanes didn't lumber. By comparison, the *Remembrance* was the one that was slow.

A bomb burst in the water close by the ship. That felt almost like being inside a bell when it was rung. Two more went off in quick succession, a little farther away. Fragments would cause casualties

up on deck. The blasts might spring seams, too. Nobody was screaming for damage control, though, so maybe not.

Then, up near the starboard bow, a bomb burst on the *Remembrance.*

The ship staggered, as if she'd taken one right on the chin—and
she had. Lights flickered, but they stayed on. The reassuring deep
throb of the engines went on. So did the antiaircraft fire. Not a mortal wound, then—not right away, anyhow. But it could be.

"Carsten, take a party and deal with that!" Pottinger rapped
out.

"Aye aye, sir!" Sam turned to the sailors. "Come on, boys.
We've got work to do. Sections one and two, with me."

The ship was buttoned up tight. They had to open and close a
slew of watertight doors to get where they were going. Carsten
wished there were something to be done about that. It slowed aid.
But it also helped keep the ship afloat, which counted for more.

He'd been out on deck under air attack during the Pacific War. It
was just as much fun as he remembered. A Confederate airplane
went into the sea almost without a splash. Another flew by nearly
low enough to land, spraying machine-gun bullets down the flight
deck. Men dove for cover, not that there was much. Screams rose
when bullets struck home.

Sam sprinted up the deck toward the bomb hit. He skidded to a
stop at the smoking edge of the damage. The explosion had torn off
a corner of the flight deck, exposing one of the five-inch gun positions just below. The gun seemed intact. Red smears and spatters
said the gunners were anything but. Sam turned to a petty officer—
one of the flight-deck crew—beside him. "Can you still take off and
land with the deck like this?"

"Hell, yes, sir," the man answered. "No problem. It was a
glancing hit—should have been a miss, I think, but we zigged instead
o' zagging." He didn't seem very worried.

"All right." Carsten gave orders to most of the men he commanded to help set things right. Then he said, "Doheny, Eisenberg,
Bengough—follow me. We can still fight that gun, God damn it." He
hadn't been in charge of a five-inch for years, but he knew how.

He scrambled down through the wreckage to the gun. He cut his
hands a couple of times, but he wouldn't notice till later. A fighter
from the carrier's combat air patrol, flame licking back from the en-

gine cowling toward the eagle with crossed swords on the tail, cartwheeled into the Atlantic. Another Confederate airplane shot up the *Remembrance.*

"Doheny, jerk shells. Bengough, you load and shoot. Eisenberg, handle azimuth! Can you do that?" Sam waited for a nod, then grabbed the elevation screw. "Come on, you bastards! Like the skipper said, we've got company!"

At his orders, the gun started banging away. Black puffs of smoke dotted the sky. A Confederate airplane, hit square in the fuselage, broke in two. Both burning chunks went into the drink. The pilot never had a chance to hit the silk. Carsten and his makeshift crew cheered like maniacs. Even as he yelled, though, he was looking for a new target. How many waves of attackers would the Confederates send at the *Remembrance?* And how long till her own bombers and torpedo airplanes came home and she could get the hell out of range? It already seemed like forever.

Anne Colleton looked across the warm blue water of Charleston harbor toward Fort Sumter. A plaque said General Beauregard had stood right here when the Confederacy opened fire on the island fortress the United States and that damned fool Abraham Lincoln refused to surrender. FIRST SHOTS IN THE BATTLE FOR OUR FREEDOM FROM YANKEE OPPRESSION, the plaque declared.

That little island remained fortified to this day. Big coast-defense guns could reach far out to sea. But they couldn't reach far enough to smash all the threats the United States might throw at Charleston. Antiaircraft guns bristled on the island and around the harbor. If the damnyankees flew airplanes off the deck of a ship at the ships and the shore installations here, they would catch as much hell as the gunners could give them.

A Freedom Party stalwart named Kirby Walker stood at Anne's right hand. "If they try anything, we'll be ready for 'em," he declared. Despite the heat and breathless humidity of early summer in Charleston, he looked cool and well pressed in crisp white shirt and butternut slacks. "We know—darn well they can't lick us."

He couldn't have been more than thirty years old. He would have been a little boy when the Great War ended. She wondered how long it would be till this new one put him in a real uniform instead of the imitation he wore. She also wondered if he had any brains at all. Some stalwarts didn't—they were all balls and fists, and they didn't need to be anything else. She said, "We don't know anything of the sort. If they hadn't licked us the last time, this war would look mighty different."

"Well, but we were stabbed in the back then." Walker sounded as positive as if he'd been there to watch the knife go home. "It'll be a fair fight this time, so of course we'll lick 'em."

He talked just the way Jake Featherston and Saul Goldman would have wanted him to. He talked just the way the President and his director of communications had been training Confederates to talk ever since Featherston took the oath of office. He thought the way they wanted him to think. He was the new Confederate man, and there were an awful lot just like him.

Anne, in fact, had come to Charleston to put on a rally for the new Confederate men and their female opposite numbers. When a lot of those men would be going into uniform, and when, in due course, they would start coming back maimed or not coming back at all, they needed to be reminded of what this was all about. Speeches on the wireless went only so far. Nothing like a real rally where you could see your friends and neighbors jumping up and yelling along with you, where you could *smell* the fellow next to you getting all hot and bothered, to keep the juices flowing.

A gray-mustached man who walked with a limp and carried a submachine gun led a gang of Negroes towards a merchant ship. The blacks wore dungarees and coarse, collarless cotton work shirts. Their clothes weren't quite uniforms. They weren't quite prison garb, either. But they came close on both counts.

Kirby Walker followed the blacks with his eyes. "Lousy niggers," he muttered. "We work 'em hard enough, they won't have a chance to get themselves in any trouble this time around."

"Here's hoping they won't," Anne said.

"If they do, we start shooting first," Walker said. "We'd've shot a few of 'em early on in the last war, we never would've had half the trouble with 'em we did. We were too soft, and we paid for it."

Again, he sounded as if he'd been there. This time, Anne completely agreed with him. She *had* been there. The Marshlands plantation, these days, was nothing but ruins. Before the war, she'd treated her Negroes better than anyone else nearby. And what had she got for it? Half—more than half—the leaders of the Red Congaree Socialist Republic came from her plantation.

She muttered to herself. Not very long before, she'd been sure she found Scipio, her old butler, waiting tables at a restaurant in Augusta, Georgia. He'd been in the Congaree Socialist Republic up to his eyebrows, and he'd managed to stay hidden for more than twenty years after its last vestiges collapsed. She wanted him dead. She'd been so sure she had him, too, till the restaurant showed her paperwork proving the black man she thought was Scipio really was the Xerxes he claimed to be, and that he'd worked there since before the Great War.

Anne muttered some more. She hated being wrong about anything. She especially hated being wrong about anything that meant so much to her. As far as she knew, that black man was *still* waiting tables at that restaurant. What would have happened to him if he really were Scipio . . . Her nails bit into the flesh of her palms. How she'd wanted that!

And she'd been so very certain! Half of her still was, though she couldn't imagine how that manager might have had faked paperwork that went back close to thirty years handy. Then she shrugged and laughed a singularly unpleasant laugh. Her gaze swung to the Negro work gang, which was hauling crates out of a freighter under the watchful eye of that half-disabled veteran with the submachine gun. Whether the Negro in Augusta really was Scipio or Xerxes, he might yet get his.

"What's funny, Miss Colleton?" Kirby Walker asked.

"What?" Anne blinked, recalled from dreams of vengeance to present reality. "Nothing, really. Just thinking of what might have been."

"Not a . . . heck of a lot of point to that, I don't reckon," the Freedom Party stalwart said. "You can't change things now."

"No?" Back at the start of the Great War, the glance Anne sent him would have melted him right out of his shoes. Now it only made him shrug stolidly. Her blond good looks hadn't altogether left her, but they slipped away day by day. She could still hope for vengeance against Scipio and against the United States. Nobody got even with time. She sighed. "I want to have another look at the hall, if that's all right."

"Sure enough, ma'am. I'm here to do what you need me to do,"

Walker said. He made himself a liar without even knowing he was doing it. What she needed him to do was acknowledge her as the beauty she had been. That wouldn't happen. She knew it wouldn't, couldn't. Knowing was an ulcer that ate at her and would not heal.

It was, perhaps, just as well that Clarence Potter would not know where this rally was being held. The hall had belonged to the Whigs for generations. Clarence had gone to God only knew how many meetings here himself. It wasn't far from the harbor, and it was right across the street from a bar: a good location. These days, nobody but the Freedom Party held meetings. The hall had stood vacant for quite a while. It wouldn't stay vacant long. And the Freedom Party, unlike the Whigs, did meetings *right*.

Stalwarts and Freedom Party guards and ordinary Party members started filling the place more than an hour before the scheduled meeting time. Everyone wore a Freedom Party pin: the Confederate battle flag with red and blue reversed. Most of the pins had a black border. That showed that the people who wore them had joined the Party after March 4, 1934, when Jake Featherston became President of the CSA. Members who'd belonged before that day looked down their noses at the johnny-come-latelies and opportunists, which didn't keep them from using the newcomers whenever they needed to.

A young Congressman named Storm or something like that was the first one up to address the meeting. Anne had heard him before. He was very good on the Negro question, weaker elsewhere. Here, he didn't get to show his paces. He'd barely started his speech when air-raid sirens outside began to wail.

"You see?" he shouted. "Do you see?" He shook a fist at the sky. "The damnyankees don't want you to hear the truth!"

People laughed and cheered. "Go on!" somebody shouted. "Who cares about a damned air raid?"

And the Congressman *did* go on, even when the antiaircraft guns around the harbor started pounding and bombs started falling. The Freedom Party men in the audience clapped their hands and stomped their feet to try to drown out the din of war. That made the Congressman shout to be heard over them and over the fireworks not far away.

Anne thought they were all insane. She'd been through a bombing raid in the last war. Sitting here in this exposed place was the last thing she wanted to do now. But she knew what would happen if she yelled, *Take cover, you damned idiots!* The Freedom Party stalwarts would think she was nothing but a cowardly, panicky woman. They wouldn't listen to her. And they wouldn't take her seriously any more afterwards, either. That was the biggest part of what kept her quiet.

Resentment burned in her all the same. *Because you're so stinking stubborn, I'm liable to get killed.*

More bombs burst. Windows rattled. Not all the Yankees' presents were falling right on the harbor. Maybe that meant the anti-aircraft fire was heavier than the enemy had expected. Maybe it meant his bombardiers didn't know their business. Either way, it meant more of Charleston was catching hell.

Finally, a man about her age whose Party pin showed he'd been a member before 1934 and who wore the ribbon for a Purple Heart just below it, stood up and bellowed, "Time to get the hell out of here, folks, while the getting's good!"

They listened to him. Anne saw that with a mixture of relief and resentment. The veteran had a deep, authoritative rasp in his voice. Would they have paid that kind of attention to her contralto? Not likely!

"Where's a shelter?" somebody called. "This goddamn building hasn't got a cellar."

"Across the street," someone else said. He sounded as if he knew what he was talking about. People got up and started leaving. Anne wasn't sorry to go—far from it. She had all she could do not to run for the door. Again, fear of being thought weak carried more weight than fear of death. She didn't know why that should be so, but it was.

Out in the street, the noise was ten times worse. Chunks of shrapnel from spent antiaircraft shells rained down out of the sky. A man cried out in pain when one hit him in the shoulder. He sat down, hard, right there in the middle of the road.

Anne looked around for the U.S. airplanes that were causing all the commotion. She didn't see any—and then she did. Here came one, over the tops of the buildings, straight toward her. It was on fire, and still had a bomb slung below the fuselage. Maybe the pilot was dead. If he wasn't, he couldn't do anything with or to his airplane.

"Run!" Half a dozen people yelled it. It was good advice, but much too late. The bomber screamed down. The world blew up. When Anne came back to consciousness, she wished she hadn't. She'd heard you often didn't feel pain when you were badly wounded. Whoever had said that was a goddamn liar. Someone very close by was screaming. She needed a little while to realize those noises were pouring out of her own mouth. She tried to stop, and couldn't.

Kirby Walker lay a few feet away, gutted like a hog. He was lucky. He was already dead. Anne looked down at herself, and wished she hadn't. Consciousness faded. Black rose up to swallow it.

Somewhere down below Major Jonathan Moss was Ohio, somewhere Kentucky. He saw the ribbon of the Ohio River, but could not for the life of him have said which side of it he was on, not just then. He'd just broken off a dogfight with a Confederate fighter pilot who'd run into a cloud to get away from him, and he didn't know north from his elbow.

Then he saw shells bursting on the ground, and he realized that had to be Ohio. The CSA had kicked the USA in the teeth, attacking without bothering to declare war first. The Confederates had the edge right now. They were across the river in Indiana and Ohio, across with infantry and artillery and barrels, and they were pushing forward with everything they had.

No Great War army had ever moved like this. Moss knew that from experience. Going from Niagara Falls to Toronto had taken three long, bloody years. The Canadians had defended every foot of ground as if they were holding Satan's demons out of heaven. And, with trenches and machine guns, they'd been able to make every foot of ground count, too. Moss had started out flying a Curtiss pusher biplane, observing the front from above. He'd imagined himself a knight of the air. He'd ended up an ace in a fighting scout, knowing full well that his hands were no cleaner than any ground-pounding foot slogger's.

Living conditions were better for fliers, though. He hadn't got muddy. He'd had his own cot in a barracks hall or tent out of artillery range of the front. He'd eaten regularly, and well. And people with unpleasant attitudes had tried to kill him only every once in a while, not all the time.

So here he was back again for another round, something he never would have imagined when the Great War ended. He'd spent a lot of years as a lawyer specializing in occupation law in Canada. He'd married a Canadian woman. They'd had a little girl. And a Canadian bomb-maker had blown them up, maybe under the delusion that that would somehow help Canada toward freedom. It wouldn't. It couldn't. It hadn't. All it had done was wreck his life and drive him back to flying fighters.

He pushed the stick forward. The Wright 27 dove. The ground swelled. So did the Confederate soldiers and barrels in front of Lebanon, Ohio—he thought it was Lebanon, anyway, and if he was wrong, he was wrong. He wasn't wrong about the advancing Confederates. Thanks to the barrels, they'd already smashed through trench lines that would have held up a Great War army for weeks, and the war was only a couple of days old.

Someone down there spotted him. A machine gun started winking. Tracers flashed past his wings. He jabbed his thumb down on the firing button on top of the stick. His own machine guns spat death through the spinning disk of his propeller. Soldiers on the ground ran or threw themselves flat. That damned machine gun suddenly stopped shooting. Moss whooped.

Here and there, Confederates with rifles took potshots at him. Those didn't worry him. If a rifle bullet knocked down a fighter, the pilot's number was surely up. He checked six as he climbed. No Confederate on his tail. In the first clash, the CSA's machines—they were calling them Hound Dogs—seemed more maneuverable, but U.S. fighters had the edge diving and climbing. Neither held any enormous advantage over the other.

The Confederates had some real antiaircraft guns down there. Puffs of black smoke appeared in midair not far from Moss' fighter. They weren't quite round; they were longer from top to bottom than side to side. "Nigger-baby flak," Moss muttered to himself. With extensions of gas out from the main burst that could have been arms and legs, the smoke patterns did bear a certain resemblance to naked black dolls.

A bang said a shell fragment had hit the fighter somewhere.

Moss' eyes flicked anxiously from one gauge to another. No loss of oil pressure. No loss of coolant. No fuel leak. No fire. The controls answered—no cut wires or bad hydraulics. He breathed a sigh of relief. No damage done.

Trouble was, he hadn't done the Confederates on the ground much harm, either. They would keep right on pushing forward. They weren't trying to break into Lebanon, which looked to be heavily fortified. They were doing their best to get past it and keep pushing north. If it still had some U.S. soldiers in it afterwards . . . well, so what?

Neither side had fought that way during the Great War. Neither side could have. That had mostly been a war of shoeleather, with railroads hauling soldiers up to the front and with trucks lugging supplies. But no army then had moved faster than at a walk.

Things looked different here. Barrels were a lot faster than they had been a generation earlier. Trucks didn't just haul beans and bullets. They brought soldiers forward to keep up with the barrels. The internal-combustion engine was supercharging this war.

His fighter's internal-combustion engine was running out of gas. He streaked north to find another airstrip where he could refuel. He'd started the war in southern Illinois, but they'd sent him farther east right away. For the time being, the action was hottest along the central part of the Ohio River.

The strip he found wasn't even paved. He jounced to a stop. When he pulled back the canopy and started to get out of the fighter, a lieutenant on the ground shouted, "Can you go up again right away?"

Moss wanted nothing more than sleep and food and a big glass of something strong. But they didn't pay him for ducking out of fights. He said, "Fill me up and I'll go."

"Thanks—uh, thank you, sir," the young officer said. "Everybody down south is screaming for air support."

"Why aren't they getting more of it?" Moss asked as ground-crew men in coveralls gave the fighter gasoline. Another man in coveralls, an armorer, wordlessly held up a belt of machine-gun ammunition. Moss nodded. The armorer climbed a ladder and went to work on the airplane's guns.

"Why? 'Cause we got sucker-punched, that's why," the lieutenant said, which fit too well with what Moss had seen and heard in the past couple of hectic days. The younger officer went on, "God only knows how many airplanes they got on the ground, either, the sons of bitches."

"No excuse for that," Moss said. "No goddamn excuse for that at all."

"Yeah, I know," the lieutenant answered. "That doesn't mean it didn't happen. Some heads ought to roll on account of it, too."

"You bet your—" Moss broke off. Antiaircraft guns south of the airstrip had started banging. Through them, he heard the rising note of fighters. They were Confederates, too. The engine roar was slightly deeper than that of U.S. aircraft. And he was standing in what was at the moment a bomb with wings. He got out of the cockpit and leaped to the ground as fast as he could, shouting, "Run!"

None of the groundcrew men had needed the advice. They were doing their best to imitate Olympic sprinters. When bullets started chewing up the airstrip, some of them hit the dirt. Others ran harder than ever.

Three bullets slammed into the armorer's back. He was only a few bounds ahead of Jonathan Moss, who saw dust puff out from the man's coveralls at each hit. When the bullets went out through his belly and chest, they took most of his insides with them. He crumpled as if all his bones had turned to jelly. He was surely dead before he stopped rolling.

Moss wanted to go flat. He also wanted to get as far away from his fighter as he could. When he heard a soft *whump!* behind him and felt a sudden blast of heat at his back, he knew he'd been smart.

The Confederates came back for another strafing run. By then, Moss was on the ground, in a wet, muddy ditch by the side of the hastily made airstrip. Cold water helped fear make his balls crawl up into his belly. The lieutenant lay a few feet away from him, staring foolishly at his right hand. He had a long, straight, bleeding gouge along the back of it, but his fingers all seemed to work when he wiggled them.

"You're lucky as hell, kid," Moss said, glad to have something to talk about besides the pounding of his heart. "That's only a scratch, and you'll get yourself a Purple Heart on account of it."

"If I'd been lucky, they would have missed me," the lieutenant said, which held more than a little truth. If he'd been unluckier, though, all the infinite cleverness and articulation of that hand would have been smashed to bloody, bony ruin in less than the blink of an eye.

Ever so cautiously, Moss stuck up his head. The Confederate fighters—there'd been three of them—were streaking away. Futile puffs of flak filled the sky. He'd hoped to see at least one go down in flames, but no such luck. His own machine burned on the strip. The ammunition the luckless armorer had been loading into it started cooking off. Bullets flew in all directions. He ducked again.

"You have transportation?" he asked. "I've got to get to my unit, or at least to an air base with working fighters."

"There's an old Ford around here somewhere, if the Confederates didn't blow it to hell and gone," the young officer said. "If you want to put it on the road, you can do that. We don't exactly have control of the air right here, though."

That was a polite way to put it—politer than Moss could have found. What the shavetail meant was, *If you start driving around, the Confederates are liable to shoot up your motorcar, and we can't do a whole hell of a lot to stop 'em.*

"I'm not worth much to the country laying here in this goddamn ditch." Moss crawled out of it, dripping. "Point me at that Ford."

It was old, all right—so old, it was a Model T. Moss had never driven one in his life. His family had had too much money to get one. After the war, he'd gone around in a lordly Bucephalus for years—a make now extinct as the dodo, but one with a conventional arrangement of gearshift, clutch, and brake. He tried the slab-sided Ford, stalled it repeatedly, and had a devil of a time making it go. Finally, a corporal with a hard, flat Midwestern accent said, "Sir, I'll take you where you want to go. My folks are still driving one of them buggies."

"Thanks." Moss meant it. "I think I'm more afraid of this thing than I am of Confederate airplanes."

"All what you're used to." The corporal proceeded to prove it, too. Under his hands, the Model T behaved for all the world as if it were a normal, sane automobile. Oh, it could have stopped quicker, but you could say that about any motorcar of its vintage. The only way it could have gone faster than forty-five was by falling off a cliff, but that also turned out not to be a problem.

Refugees clogged every road north. Some had autos, some had buggies, some had nothing but shank's mare and a bundle on their backs. All had a serious disinclination to staying in a war zone and getting shot up. Moss couldn't blame them, but he also couldn't move at anything faster than a crawl.

And the Confederates loved shooting up refugee columns, too, just to make the madness worse. Moss had done that himself up in Canada during the Great War. Now he got a groundside look at what he'd been up to. He saw what people looked like when they burned in their motorcars. He smelled them, too. It put him in mind of roast pork. He didn't think he'd ever eat pork again.

Colonel Irving Morrell had always wanted to show the world what fast, modern barrels could do when they were well handled. And so, in a way, he was doing just that. He'd never imagined he would be on the receiving end of the lesson, though, not till mere days before the war broke out.

He would be fifty at the end of the year, if he lived that long. He looked it. His close-cropped sandy hair was going gray. His long face, deeply tanned, bore the lines and wrinkles that showed he'd spent as much time as he could in the sun and the wind, the rain and the snow. But he was a fit, hard fifty. If he could no longer outrun the men he commanded, he could still do a pretty good job of keeping up with them. And coffee—and the occasional slug of hooch—let him get by without a whole lot of sleep.

He would have traded all that fitness for a fat slob's body and an extra armored corps. The Confederates were putting everything they had into this punch. He didn't know what they were up to on the other side of the Appalachians, but he would have been amazed if they could have come up with another effort anywhere close to this one. If this wasn't the *Schwerpunkt,* everything he thought he knew about what they had was wrong.

His own barrel, with several others, lurked at the edge of the woods east of Chillicothe, Ohio. The Confederates were trying to get around the town in the open space between it and the trees. Morrell spoke into the wireless set that connected him to the others: "Wait till their move develops more fully before you open up on them. That's the way we'll hurt them most, and hurting them is what we've got to do."

"Hurt them, hell, sir," said Sergeant Michael Pound, the gunner. "We've got to smash them."

"That would be nice." Pound was nothing if not confident. He wasn't always right, but he was always sure of himself. He was a stocky, broad-shouldered man with very fair skin and blue eyes. He came from the uppermost Midwest, and had an accent that might almost have been Canadian.

He should have commanded his own barrel. Morrell knew as much. But he didn't want to turn Pound loose. The man was, without a doubt, the best gunner in the Army, and they'd spent a lot of time together in those periods when the Army happened to be interested in barrels. Pound had also done a stretch as an ordinary artilleryman during that long, dreary dry spell when the Army stopped caring that cannon and armor and engine and tracks could go together into one deadly package. Trouble was, the package was also expensive. To the Army, that had come close to proving the kiss of death.

It was, in fact, still liable to prove the kiss of death for a lot of U.S. soldiers. Even though the factories up in Pontiac were going flat out now, they'd started disgracefully late. The CSA had factories, too, in Richmond and Atlanta and Birmingham. They weren't supposed to have been working so long and so hard. But the Confederates were using more barrels than anybody in what was alleged to be U.S. Army Intelligence had suspected they owned.

Here came three of them, a leader and two more behind him making a V. They didn't look much different from the machine he commanded. They were a little boxier, the armor not well sloped to deflect a shell. But they hit hard; they carried two-inch guns, not inch-and-a-halfers. All things considered, U.S. and C.S. machines were about even when they met on equal terms.

Morrell didn't intend to meet the Confederates on equal terms. Hitting them from ambush was a lot more economical. "Range to the lead barrel?" he asked Sergeant Pound.

He wasn't surprised to hear Pound answer, "It's 320 yards, sir," without the slightest hesitation. The gunner had been traversing the turret to keep that barrel in the gunsight. He wasn't just ready. He was eager. That eagerness was part of what made him such a good gunner. He thought along with his commander. Sometimes he thought ahead of him.

"Let him have it," Morrell said.

"Armor-piercing, Sweeney!" Pound said, and the loader slammed a black-tipped round into the breech. The gunner traversed the turret a little more, working the handwheel with microscopic care. Then he fired.

The noise was a palpable blow to the ears. It was worst for Morrell, who'd just stuck his head out the cupola so he could see the effect of the shot. Fire spurted from the muzzle of the cannon and, half a second later, from the side of the Confederate barrel. Side armor was always thinner than at the front or on the turret.

"Hit!" Morrell shouted. "That's a goddamn hit!" Easier to think of it as the sort of hit you might make in a shooting gallery, with little yellow ducks and gray-haired mothers-in-law and other targets going by on endless loops of chain. Then you didn't have to contemplate that hard-nosed round slamming through armor, rattling around inside the fighting compartment, and smashing crewmen just like you—except they wore the wrong uniforms and they weren't very lucky.

Smoke started pouring from the wounded barrel, which stopped dead—and *dead* was the right word. A hatch at the front opened. A soldier in butternut coveralls—probably the driver—started to scramble out. Two machine guns opened up on him from Morrell's barrel. He crumpled, half in and half out of his ruined machine.

As Morrell ducked down inside the turret, it started traversing again. Sergeant Pound had commendable initiative. "Another round of AP, Sweeney!" he bawled. "We'll make meat pies out of 'em!" The loader gave him what he wanted. The gun bellowed again—to Morrell, a little less deafeningly now that he was back inside. The sharp stink of cordite filled the air inside the turret. The shell casing came out of the breech and clanged on the floor of the fighting compartment. It could mash toes if you weren't careful. Peering through the gunsight, Pound yelled, "Hit!" again.

"Was that us, or one of the other barrels here with us?" Morrell asked.

"Sir, that was us." The gunner was magisterially convincing. "Some of those other fellows couldn't hit a dead cow with a fly swatter."

"Er—right." Morrell stuck his head out of the cupola. All three of the lead Confederate barrels were burning now. Somebody in one of the other U.S. machines must have known what to do with his fly swatter.

A rifle shot from a Confederate infantryman cut twigs from the oaks above Morrell's head. He didn't duck. His barrel was well back in the shade. Nobody out there in the open could get a good look and draw a bead on him. That didn't mean a round not so well aimed couldn't find him, but he refused to dwell on such mischances.

He hoped the Confederates would try to charge his barrels. He could stand them off where he was for quite a while, then fall back to another position he'd prepared deeper in the woods. Defense wasn't his first choice, but that didn't mean he couldn't handle it. And the enemy, charging hard, might well be inclined to run right on to a waiting spear.

But the Confederates had something else in mind. After about ten minutes of confusion, they started lobbing artillery shells toward the woods. At first, Morrell was scornful—only a direct hit would make a barrel say uncle, and hits from guns out of visual range of their targets were hard as hell to come by. But then he caught the gurgling howl of the shells as they flew through the air and the white bursts they threw up when they walked toward the barrels.

Swearing, he ducked down into the turret and slammed the cupola hatch behind him. "Button it up!" he snarled. "Gas!" He got on the wireless to all the barrels he commanded, giving them the same message. "Masks!" he added to the men in his own machine. "That's an order, God damn it!"

Only when he put on his own mask did Pound and Sweeney reach for theirs. He couldn't see the driver and the bow gunner up at the front of the hull. He hoped they listened to him. If the barrel stayed buttoned up, the men would start to cook before too long. It might have been tolerable in France or Germany. In Ohio? Right at the start of summertime? In gas masks to boot?

Sergeant Pound asked an eminently reasonable question: "Sir, how the hell are we supposed to fight a war like this?"

"How would you like to fight it without your lungs?" Morrell answered. His own voice sounded even more distant and other-worldly than Pound's had. He couldn't see the gunner's expression.

All he could see were Pound's eyes behind two round portholes of glass. The green-gray rubber of the mask hid the rest of the sergeant's features and made him look like something from Mars or Venus.

Looking out through the periscopes mounted in the cupola hatch was at best a poor substitute for sticking your head out and seeing what was going on. Shoving one of those glass portholes up close enough to a periscope to see anything was a trial. What Morrell saw were lots of gas shells bursting.

He did some more swearing. The barrel wasn't perfectly airtight, and it didn't have proper filters in the ventilation system. That was partly his own fault, too. He'd had a lot to say about the design of barrels. He'd thought about all sorts of things, from the layout of the turret to the shape of the armor and the placement of the engine compartment. Defending against poison gas hadn't once crossed his mind—or, evidently, anyone else's.

"What do we do, sir?" Sergeant Pound asked.

Morrell didn't want to fall back to that prepared position without making the Confederates pay a price. His lips skinned back from his teeth in a fierce grin the gas mask hid. "Forward!" he said, first to Pound, then on the intercom to the driver, and then on the wireless. "Let's see if those bastards want to drop gas on their own men."

The barrel rumbled ahead. Morrell hoped not too much gas was getting into the fighting compartment. He could tell the instant they came out into the sunlight from the shade of the trees. It had been hot in the barrel before. It got a hell of a lot hotter when the sun started beating down on the hull and the turret.

Bullets began hitting the barrel as soon as it came out into the open, too. Morrell didn't worry about ordinary rifle or machine-gun rounds very much, not while he wasn't standing up and looking out through the cupola. (He didn't worry about them while he was, either. Afterwards, sometimes, was a different story.) But the Confederates had the same sort of .50-caliber antibarrel rifles as U.S. troops. Even one of those big armor-piercing bullets wouldn't penetrate the front glacis plate or the turret, but it might punch through the thinner steel on the barrel's sides.

Sergeant Pound and the bow machine gunner, a redheaded mick

named Teddy Fitzgerald, opened up on the Confederate soldiers they'd caught in the open. Pound abandoned the turret machine gun after a little while. "H.E.!" he called to Sweeney, who fed a high-explosive round into the cannon. It roared. Through the periscopes, Morrell watched the round burst. A couple of enemy soldiers went flying.

The Confederates didn't put gas down on top of their own men. They didn't break through east of Chillicothe, either. Morrell's barrels gave them a good mauling there. But they did break the U.S. line west of town. Morrell had to fall back or risk being surrounded. Even pulling back wasn't easy. He fought a brisk skirmish at long range with several C.S. barrels. If the Confederates had moved a little faster, they might have trapped him. He hated retreat. But getting cut off would have been worse. So he told himself, over and over again.

As Mary Pomeroy walked to the post office in Rosenfeld, Manitoba, with her son Alexander in tow, she laughed at herself. She'd always thought she couldn't hate anyone worse than the green-gray-clad U.S. soldiers who'd occupied the town since 1914. Now the Yanks, or most of them, were gone, and she discovered she'd been wrong. The soldiers from the Republic of Quebec, whose uniforms were of a cut identical to their U.S. counterparts but sewn from blue-gray cloth, were even worse.

For one thing, the Yanks, however much Mary despised them, had won the war. They'd driven out and beaten the Canadian and British defenders of what had been the Dominion of Canada. If not for them, there wouldn't have been any such thing as the Republic of Quebec. Quebec had been part of Canada for more than 150 years before the Yanks came along. The USA had no business splitting up the country.

For another, hardly any of the Quebecois soldiers spoke more than little fragments of English. You couldn't even try to reason with them, the way you could with the Yanks. Some Yanks—Mary hated to admit it, but knew it was true—were pretty decent, even if they did come from the United States. Maybe some Quebecois were, too. But if you couldn't talk to them, how were you supposed to find out?

They jabbered away in their own language, and it wasn't as if Mary or anybody else in Rosenfeld had ever learned much French. And not only did the men in blue-gray speak French, they *acted* French. She'd long since got used to the way American soldiers eyed her. They'd done it in spite of her wedding ring, later in spite of little Alec. She was a tall, slim redhead in her early thirties. Men did notice her. She'd grown used to that, even if she didn't care for it.

But the two Quebecois soldiers who walked by her were much more blatant in the way they admired her than the Yanks had been. It wasn't as if they were undressing her with their eyes—more as if they were groping her with them. And when, laughing, the Frenchies talked about it afterwards, she couldn't understand a word they said. By their tone, though, it was all foul and all about her. She looked straight ahead, as if they didn't exist, and kept on walking. They laughed some more at that.

"Are we almost there yet?" Alec asked. He'd be starting kindergarten before long. Mary didn't want to send him to school. The Yanks would fill him full of their lies about the past. But she didn't see what choice she had. She could teach him what he really needed to know at home.

"You know where the post office is," Mary said. "*Are* we almost there yet?"

"I suppose so," Alec said in a sulky voice. He didn't take naps any more. Mary missed the time when he had, because that had let her get some rest, too. Now she had to be awake whenever he was. But even if he didn't actually take naps any more, there were still days when he needed them. This felt like one of those days.

Mary did her best to pretend it didn't. "Well, then," she said briskly, "you know we cross the street here—and there it is."

There it was, all right: the yellow-brown brick building that had done the job since before the last war. The postmaster was the same, too, though Wilfred Rokeby's hair was white now and had been black in those distant days. Only the flag out front was different. Mary could barely remember the mostly dark blue banner of the Dominion of Canada. Ever since 1914, the Stars and Stripes had fluttered in front of the post office.

Alec swarmed up the stairs. Mary followed, holding down her pleated wool skirt with one hand against a gust of wind. She was damned if she'd give those Frenchies—or anybody else—a free show. She opened the door, the bronze doorknob polished bright by God only knew how many hands. Her son rushed in ahead of her.

Stepping into the post office was like stepping back in time. It was always too warm in there; Wilf Rokeby kept the potbellied stove in one corner glowing red whether he needed to or not. Along with the heat, the spicy smell of the postmaster's hair oil was a link with Mary's childhood. Rokeby still plastered his hair down with the oil and parted it exactly in the middle. Not a single hair was out of place; none would have dared be disorderly.

Rokeby nodded from behind the counter. "Morning, Mrs. Pomeroy," he said. "New notices on the bulletin board. Directions are I should tell everybody who comes in to have a look at 'em, so I'm doing that."

Mary wanted to tell the occupying authorities where to head in. Getting angry at Wilf Rokeby wouldn't do her any good, though, or the Yanks and Frenchies any harm. "Thank you, Mr. Rokeby," she said, and turned toward the cork-surfaced board with its thumbtack holes uncountable.

The notices had headlines in big red letters. One said, NO HAR-BORING ENEMY AGENTS! It warned that anyone having anything to do with people representing Great Britain, the Confederate States, Japan, or France would be subject to military justice. Mary scowled. She knew what military justice was. In 1916, the Yanks had taken her brother Alexander, for whom Alec was named, and shot him because they claimed he was plotting against them.

NO INTERFERENCE WITH RAILWAY LINES! the other new flyer warned. It said anyone caught trying to sabotage the railroad would face not just military justice but summary military justice. As far as Mary could tell, that meant the Yanks would shoot right away and not bother with even a farce of a trial. The notice was relevant for Rosenfeld. The town would have been only another patch of Manitoban prairie if two train lines hadn't come together there.

She turned back to Wilf Rokeby. "All right. I've read them. Now you can sell me some stamps without getting in trouble in Philadelphia."

"It wouldn't be quite as bad as that," the postmaster answered with a thin smile. "But I did want you to see them. You have to remember, it's a war again, and those people are jumpier than they used to be. And these here fellows from Quebec . . . I've got the feeling it's shoot first and ask questions later with them."

"I wouldn't be surprised," Mary said. "They hardly seem like proper human beings at all."

"Well, I don't know there," Rokeby said. "What I do know is, I wouldn't do anything foolish and get myself in trouble with 'em."

"Why do you think I would want to get myself in trouble with them?" Mary asked.

Rokeby shrugged. "I don't suppose you'd want to, exactly, but. . . ."

"But what?" Mary's voice was sharp.

"But I recollect who your brother was, Mrs. Pomeroy, and who your father was, too."

Hardly anyone in Rosenfeld mentioned Arthur McGregor, her father, to her. He'd been blown up by a bomb he meant for General George Custer, who'd passed through the town on his way into retirement. All that was left of Arthur McGregor these days was his Christian name, which was Alec's middle name. And Mary couldn't remember the last time anyone had spoken of Alexander McGregor. A lot of people in town were too young even to remember him. Twenty-five years was a long time.

But she didn't quite like the way the postmaster had spoken of them. "What do you mean?"

"I mean I wouldn't like to see the same sort of thing happen to you as happened to them," Rokeby answered.

She stared at him. Except for Alec, they were the only two people in the post office, and Alec paid next to no attention to what grownups said to each other unless they started shouting or did something else interesting or exciting. "Why on earth would anything like that happen to me?" she asked, deliberately keeping her voice calm and her face straight.

"Well, I don't know," Wilf Rokeby said. "But I do recall a package you posted to a cousin of yours in Ontario not so long ago—a cousin named Laura Moss."

"Do you?" Mary said tonelessly.

The postmaster nodded. "I do. And I recall reading in the paper a little later on about what happened to a woman named Laura Moss."

What had happened to Laura Moss—who'd been born Laura

Secord, descended from the Canadian patriot of the same name, and who'd been a Canadian patriot herself till she ended up in a Yank's bed—was that a bomb had blown her and her little girl sky high. "What's that got to do with me?" Mary asked, again with as little expression in her voice or on her face as she could put there. "Do you think I'm a bomber because my father was?" There. The challenge direct. What would Rokeby make of it?

He looked at her over the tops of the old-fashioned half glasses he wore. "Well, I don't know anything about that for certain, Mrs. Pomeroy," he said. "But I also believe I recollect a bomb that went off at Karamanlides' general store after he went and bought it from Henry Gibbon. He's from down in the USA, even if he's been here a while now."

"I didn't have anything to do with that—or with this other thing, either," Mary said. After the challenge direct, the lie direct.

Wilf Rokeby didn't raise an eyebrow. He didn't call her a liar. He showed not the slightest trace of anything but small-town interest. "Did I say you did, Mrs. Pomeroy?" he asked easily. "But I thought, with those new notices up there, you maybe ought to remember how nervous the Yanks and Frenchies are liable to be. You wouldn't want to do anything, oh, careless while you're near a train track, or anything like that."

The only place where Mary had ever been careless was in letting Rokeby get a look at the name on the package she'd posted. She didn't see how she could have avoided that, but she hadn't imagined he would remember it. It only went to show you never could tell.

She studied the postmaster. If he'd wanted to, he could have told the Yanks instead of bringing this up with her. Searching her apartment wouldn't have told them anything. Searching the basement of her apartment building would have. Her father's bomb-making tools were hidden, but they could be found.

So what did he want? Money? She and Mort had some, but not a lot. The same probably applied to Wilfred Rokeby. Did he want something else from her, something more intimate? He was a lifelong bachelor. He'd never had any sort of reputation for skirt-chasing. She'd heard a couple of people over the years wonder if he was a fairy, but nobody had ever had any real reason to think so except that he didn't have much to do with women.

"I always try to be careful," she said, and waited to see what would happen next.

Rokeby nodded. "Good. That's good. Your family's seen too many bad things. Wouldn't think you could stand a whole lot more of 'em."

"Can I buy those stamps now?" Mary asked in a tight voice.

"You sure can," the postmaster answered. "Just tell me what you need." She did. He got out the stamps and said, "That'll be a dollar and a half all told." She paid him. He nodded as he would have to any other customer he'd been seeing for years. "Thank you kindly, Mrs. Pomeroy. Like I say, you want to be careful, especially now that there's a war on."

"I heard you," Mary said. "Oh, yes. I heard you."

Alec in tow, she left the post office and started back to their apartment. They hadn't gone far before her son asked, "Mommy, what was that man talking about?"

It was a good question. Did Wilf Rokeby really sympathize with her? He hadn't told the Yanks and he hadn't asked for anything from her. He'd just warned her. So maybe he did. Could she trust everything to the strength of a maybe? She had to think about that. She had to think hard. She also had to tell Alec something. "Nothing important, sweetie," she said. "Grownup stuff, that's all." He accepted that with a nod. His question was easily answered. Her own? No.

When the last war broke out, Chester Martin had been a corporal taking a squad of U.S. soldiers from West Virginia into Virginia. He'd been through the mill, sure as hell, and he'd been lucky, too, as luck ran in wartime: three years of hard fighting, and only one wound. Back in 1914, he'd been a Democrat. He'd lived in Toledo.

A lot of things had changed since. He wasn't a kid any more. He was closer to fifty than forty. His light brown hair had gone gray. His features had been sharp, almost foxy. Now he had jowls and a belly that stuck out farther than his chest, though not much. He had a wife and a young son. He was a Socialist, a construction workers' organizer in Los Angeles.

He was a Socialist these days, yes. But he'd voted for Robert Taft in the 1940 presidential election, not Al Smith. He'd been through the mill. He didn't want to see the Confederate States strong. As his wife set a plate of ham and eggs in front of him, he said, "Things don't look so good back East."

"No, they don't," Rita agreed. Chester was her second husband. Her first had gone to war a generation earlier, but he hadn't come back. That was as much luck of the draw as Chester's survival. If you happened to end up in the wrong place at the wrong instant, you could be the best soldier in the world and it wouldn't matter one goddamn bit. Your next of kin would get a wire from the War Department, and that would be that.

"I wish . . ." Chester began, and then let it trail away.

He might as well not have bothered. Rita knew what he hadn't said. "It wouldn't have made any difference if Taft beat Al Smith," she said. "We'd still have a war right now, and we wouldn't be any readier than we are."

She was a Socialist, too. She'd never been anything else. Her folks were Socialists, where Chester's were rock-ribbed Democrats. And she sometimes had a hard time forgiving him when he backslid—that was how she looked at it, anyhow.

Here, she was probably right. Al Smith had agreed to the plebiscites in Houston and Sequoyah and Kentucky before the election. Even if Taft had won, they were scheduled for early January, before he would have been inaugurated. And once Kentucky and Houston went Confederate in the vote, could he have thrown out the elections? That would have touched off a war all by itself.

Of course, it would have touched off a war with Kentucky and what was once more west Texas in U.S. hands, which might have made things better. Chester almost said so—almost, but not quite. He and Rita had been married a while now. He'd learned a wise man didn't antagonize his wife over something inherently unprovable, especially when she'd just given him breakfast. He finished the ham and eggs and some toast, gulped his coffee, put on a cap, and headed out the door. Rita gave him a kiss as he left, too, one more reason to make him glad he hadn't got her angry.

"Chillicothe falls!" a newsboy shouted. "Read all about it!"

He forked over a nickel for a copy of the *Los Angeles Times*. He hated giving the *Times* his money. It thought labor unions were nothing but a bunch of Reds; reactionary didn't begin to go far enough to describe it. But it was the only morning paper he could buy on the way to the trolley stop. Sometimes convenience counted for more than ideology.

Another nickel went into the trolley's fare box, and four pennies for two transfers. He was going all the way down to Torrance, in the South Bay; he'd have to change trolleys twice. He plopped his fanny into a seat and opened up the *Times*. He had some time to kill.

Long shadows of early morning stretched out toward the west. The day was still cool, but wouldn't stay that way for long. It would be better in Torrance, which got the sea breeze, than here in Boyle Heights on the east side of town; the breeze didn't usually come in this far. It got hotter here than it ever did in Toledo. Chester didn't mind. Hot weather in Toledo was steam-bath central. He'd known worse in Virginia during the war, but Toledo was plenty bad. Next to that kind of heat, what L.A. got was nothing. Your clothes didn't stick to you. You didn't feel you'd fall over dead—or at least start panting like a hound dog—if you walked more than a hundred yards. And he didn't miss snow in the wintertime one bit.

His smile when he thought of not getting snowed on slipped as he read the lead story. Chillicothe wasn't the only Ohio town that had fallen to the Confederates. They looked to be pushing north through Ohio and Indiana with everything they had: men and airplanes and barrels and poison gas.

"God damn Jake Featherston," Chester muttered under his breath. Neither side had moved like this during the Great War. Machine guns had made attacks almost suicidally expensive. Railroads behind the lines had stayed intact. That meant defenders could move men forward faster than attackers could push through devastated terrain. That was what it had meant in the last war, anyhow. This time, trucks and barrels seemed to mean the rules had changed.

Other news wasn't good, either. Confederate bombers had hit Washington and Philadelphia again, and even New York City. The Empire of Japan had recalled its ambassador to the USA. That probably meant a new war in the Pacific, and sooner, not later. And the war in the Atlantic already looked insane, with ships from the USA, Germany, the CSA, Britain, and France all hammering at one another.

From what Chester remembered, the naval war in the Atlantic had been crazy the last time around, too. He didn't remember much of that, though. He'd been too busy trying not to get shot to pay it a whole lot of attention.

And Governor Heber Young of Utah said his state would react with "disfavor and dismay" if the USA tried to declare martial law there. Chester didn't have much trouble translating that into the kind of English somebody who wasn't the governor of a state might speak. If the United States tried to put their foot down in Utah, the state would explode like a grenade. Of course, if the United States didn't put their foot down in Utah, the state was liable to explode like a grenade anyhow. Mormons thought the USA had been oppressing them since before the Second Mexican War sixty years ago, if not longer than that. If they had a chance to break away and get their own back, wouldn't they grab it with both hands?

The French were claiming victories in Alsace-Lorraine. The Germans were loudly denying everything. They were also loudly denying that the Ukraine's army had mutinied when the Tsar's forces crossed the border from Russia. Maybe they were telling the truth and maybe they weren't. Time would show, one way or the other.

Suddenly sick of everything that had to do with the war, Chester turned to the sports section, which was mostly full of news of football games canceled. The Los Angeles Dons, his favorite summer league team, had been up in Portland to play the Wolves. Now a quarter of the squad had got conscription notices, and the rest were arranging transportation back to Los Angeles. He sighed. He hadn't really thought about what the war would do to ordinary life. He hadn't been part of ordinary life the last time around.

He got so engrossed in the paper, he had to jump off the trolley at the last moment to make one of his transfers. He was still reading when he got off in Torrance. He walked three blocks to the construction site the union was picketing. The builders had done everything under the sun to drive away the pickets. They'd even sicced Pinkerton goons on them. That hadn't worked; the union men had beaten the crap out of the down-and-outers the detective agency hired.

Chester expected more trouble here. What he didn't expect was a man of about his own age in a double-breasted gray pinstripe suit and a straw hat with a bright plaid hatband who came up to him, stuck out his hand, and said, "You must be Martin."

"Yeah." Chester automatically took the proffered hand. The other fellow didn't have a worker's calluses, but his grip was strong. Martin said, "Afraid I don't know you."

"I'm Harry T. Casson," the other man said.

Son of a bitch, Chester thought. Harry T. Casson might not have been the biggest builder in Los Angeles, but he was sure as hell one of the top three. He was also, not coincidentally at all, the man trying to run up the houses here. "Well, what do you want with me?" Chester asked, hard suspicion in his voice.

"Cooperation," Casson said. "Things are different with a war on, don't you think?"

"If you're going to try to use the war for an excuse to exploit the people who work for you, you can go straight to hell, far as I'm concerned," Chester said.

He almost hoped that would make Casson spit in his eye. It didn't. Calmly, the builder said, "That's not what I meant. I know I have to give some to get some."

Give some to get some? Chester had never heard anything like that before from the men who hired construction workers here. He wondered why he was hearing it now. Smelling a rat, he said, "You know what we want. Recognize the union, dicker with us in good faith over wages and working conditions, and you won't have any trouble with us. No matter what the *L.A.* goddamn *Times* says, that's all we've ever wanted."

Harry T. Casson nodded. He was a cool customer. He said, "We can probably arrange something along those lines."

"Christ!" Chester didn't want to show his astonishment, but he couldn't help it. "I think you mean it."

"I do," Casson said.

Visions of glory danced in Martin's head. All these years of struggle, and a victory at the end of them? It seemed too good to be true. Of course, things that seemed too good to be true commonly were. "What's the catch?" he asked bluntly, and waited to hear what sort of smooth bushwah Harry T. Casson could spin.

"Look around," Casson said. "Plenty of people I'm hiring"—he meant scabs—"are going to go into the Army. Plenty of your people will, too. That's already started to happen. And a lot of the others will start working in munitions plants. Those will pay better than

I've been. If I'm going to have to pay high to keep things going, I don't want to stay in a scrap with you people, too. That just adds insult to injury. So—how about it?"

Chester considered. Try as he would, he couldn't see a whole lot of bushwah there. What Harry T. Casson said made good, hard sense from a business point of view. Martin said, "Make your offer. We'll vote on it. If it's something we can live with, we'll vote for it. I just wish to God you'd said something like this a long time ago."

The building magnate shrugged. "I had no reason to. I made more money without you people than I would have with you. Now it looks like things are different. I hope I'm not stupid. I can see which way the wind is blowing."

It all came down to dollars and cents for him—his dollars and cents. How his workers got by? If they got by? He didn't care about that. It wasn't his worry, or he didn't see it as such. *Capitalist,* Chester thought, but then, *Now the wind's blowing in our direction.*

"I think we can work together," he said. "You're right about one thing: it's high time we tried." He put out his hand now. Harry T. Casson took it.

For a long time, Cincinnatus Driver had thought of himself as a lucky man. He'd been in Covington, Kentucky, when it passed from the CSA to the USA at the start of the Great War. Escaping the Confederate States was a good start on luck all by itself for a black man.

Then he'd got out of Kentucky. Escaping what had been the Confederate States was good luck for a black man, too. Negroes didn't have it easy in Des Moines, but they had it a lot easier. His son had graduated from high school—and married a Chinese girl. Achilles and Grace seemed happy enough, so he supposed that was luck . . . and he loved his grandchildren. Amanda, his daughter, was going to graduate, too. When Cincinnatus was a boy in Covington, any schooling for Negroes had been against the law.

He'd built up a pretty fair trucking business in Des Moines. That wasn't luck. That was hard work, nothing else but. But his father and mother had stayed behind in Covington. His mother began to slip into her second childhood. When Al Smith agreed to the plebiscite in Kentucky, Cincinnatus knew he would have to get his folks up to Des Moines. The Confederates would win that vote, and he didn't want two people who were born as slaves to go back under the Stars and Bars, especially not with Jake Featherston running the CSA.

And so he'd come back to Covington to help his father bring his mother out of Kentucky and back to Iowa . . . and his luck had run out. His mother, senile, had wandered away from home, as she was doing more and more often. He and his father went after her. Cincinnatus found her. He ran across the street to get her—and never saw the motorcar that hit him.

Fractured leg. Fractured skull. Everybody said he was lucky to be alive. He wasn't sure he called it luck. He'd been laid up when the plebiscite went off. He'd been laid up during the grace period afterwards, when people who wanted to stay in the USA could cross the Ohio. By the time he could travel at all, the USA had sealed the border. Now he was trapped in the Confederate States with a war on. If this wasn't hell, you could see it from here.

He still limped. A stick helped, but only so much. He got blinding headaches every now and again, or a little more often than every now and again. Worse than any of that were the reflexes he had to learn all over again, the things he'd put aside in almost twenty years in Iowa. There, he was a man among men—oh, not a man at the top of the heap, but a man nonetheless.

Here, he was a nigger.

Whenever he left Covington's colored district near the Licking River for any reason, he had to expect a cop to bear down on him and growl, "Let me see your passbook, boy." It didn't matter if the cop was only half his age. Negro males in the CSA went straight from *boy* to *uncle*. They were never *misters*, never men.

The cop this particular day had a white mustache and a limp almost as bad as Cincinnatus'. He wouldn't be any good in the army chewing north through Ohio and Indiana. He also had a gray uniform, an enameled Freedom Party flag pinned next to his badge, and the sour look of a man who was feeling a couple too many from the night before. He could be mean just for the fun of being mean.

"Here you are, suh," Cincinnatus said. His passbook looked official. It wasn't. Before he left Covington, he'd had connections with both the Red Negro underground and the Confederate diehards who'd resisted Kentucky's incorporation into the USA. He hadn't much wanted those connections, but he'd had them. Some of the

Reds were still around—and still Red. False papers weren't too hard for them.

The policeman looked at the photo in the passbook and compared it to Cincinnatus' face. That was all right. The photo really was his. "Go on," the cop said grudgingly, handing back the passbook. "Don't you get in no trouble, now."

"Don't want no trouble, suh," Cincinnatus said, which was true. He put the passbook in his pocket, then gestured with his cane. "Couldn't get in no trouble even if I did want to."

"I never yet knew a nigger who couldn't get in trouble if he wanted to," the policeman said. But then he walked on by, adding, "You get your ass back into your own part of town pretty damn quick, you hear?"

"Oh, yes, suh," Cincinnatus said. "I hear you real good."

Newsboys hawked papers, shouting of Confederate victories all along the border with the USA. By what Cincinnatus gathered from U.S. wireless stations, the headlines in the Confederate papers weren't lying too much, however badly he wished they were. Since the war started, tuning in to the wireless had become an iffy business. It was suddenly against the law to listen to U.S. stations. The Confederates tried to back that up by jamming a lot of them. The USA fought back in kind against Confederate broadcasts. What you mostly heard these days was faint but urgent gabbling through roaring waterfalls of static.

With the cynicism black men learned early, Cincinnatus figured both sides would soon be lying just as hard as they could.

Antiaircraft guns poked their snouts up from parks and vacant lots. Some had camouflage netting draped over them in case U.S. airplanes came over in the daytime. Others didn't bother, but just stood there in their bare deadliness. So far, U.S. bombers had paid a couple of brief calls on Covington by night. They'd cost people some sleep, but they hadn't hit anything worth hitting.

Here was the grocery store he needed to visit. He had to wait a while to get noticed. The man behind the counter dealt with white customers till he didn't happen to have any in the store. Then he deigned to pay attention to Cincinnatus. "What do you want?" he asked. He didn't say, *What can I do for you?* the way he had for his white customers. Not many whites in the CSA thought about what they could do for Negroes.

"I need a gallon of ketchup for the barbecue place," Cincinnatus answered.

"Oh, you do, do you?" The white man paid some real attention to him for the first time. "Heinz or Del Monte?"

"Del Monte, suh. It's the best." Cincinnatus knew he sounded like a wireless advertisement, but he couldn't help it. The clerk eyed him for a long moment. Then he said, "Hang on. I have to get it from the back room." He disappeared, returning a moment later with a carton that prominently featured the gold-bordered red Del Monte emblem. He set it on the counter. "Jug's inside. Thirty-six cents." Cincinnatus gave him a half-dollar, got his change, and stuck it in his pocket. The white man asked, "You carry that all right with the cane? You don't want to drop it, now."

Cincinnatus believed him. "I'll be careful," he promised. He tucked the carton under his free arm, then left the grocery and made his slow way back toward the Negro district. The policeman who'd asked him for his passbook saw him again. Since he was walking east, the cop didn't trouble him any more. *As long as you know your place and stay there, you're all right.* The white man didn't say it, but he might as well have.

Don't trip. Don't fall down. Cincinnatus was listening to what he himself wasn't saying as well as to what the cop wasn't. *Got to pay for my passbook some kind o' way. I fall down, though, I pay too much.*

Even before he got back into the colored part of town, his nostrils twitched. The breeze was out of the east, and brought the sweet, spicy, mouth-watering smell of barbecue to his nostrils. First Apicius Wood and then his son, Lucullus, had presided over what locals had long insisted was the best barbecue place between the Carolinas and Kansas City. The Woods, over the years, had had just about as many white customers as black. Freedom Party stalwarts weren't ashamed to get Lucullus' barbecue sauce all over their faces as they gnawed on falling-off-the-bone tender pork or beef ribs. They might despise Lucullus Wood. Nobody but a maniacal vegetarian could despise those ribs.

And the smell just got stronger and more tempting as Cincinnatus came closer. Walking inside was another jolt, because the Woods cooked indoors. It was like walking into hell, though Cincinnatus didn't think the sinners on the fire there would smell anywhere near so tasty. Carcasses spun on spits over pits of prime hickory wood. Back after the USA took Kentucky away from the CSA, Apicius had chosen his surname from that wood.

Assistant cooks didn't just keep the spits and carcasses going round and round. They also used long-handled brushes to slather on the spicy sauce that made the barbecue something more than mere roast meat. Fat and juices and sauce dripped down onto the red-hot coals, where they hissed and popped and flamed.

Coming in here on a dubious errand took Cincinnatus back in time. How often had he done that during and just after the Great War? Back then, he'd been whole and strong and young, so goddamn young. Now the years lay on his shoulders like sacks of cement. His body was healing, but it was a long way from healed. That fellow in the auto had almost done for him. But it had been his own fault, no one else's. He'd run out in the street, though he still didn't remember doing it, or actually getting hit. The pain when he came back to himself afterwards? That he remembered all too well.

One of the cooks pointed with a basting brush. Cincinnatus nodded. He already knew the way back to the office that had been Apicius' and now belonged to Lucullus. He'd been going there longer than that pimply high-yellow kid had been alive. He set down the box and knocked on the door. There had been times when he barged in there without knocking. He'd got away with it, but he wondered how.

"Yeah?" came the deep, gruff voice from the other side of the door. Cincinnatus opened it. Lucullus' scowl disappeared when he came in. "Oh. Sorry, friend. Thought you might be somebody else. Set yourself down. Here. Have some of this." He reached into his battered desk, pulled out a bottle, and offered it to Cincinnatus.

"Thank you kindly." Before taking the bottle, Cincinnatus carefully lifted the Del Monte carton and set it on the desk. "This here's for you. Ofay who gave it to me said not to drop it."

Lucullus Wood rumbled laughter. His father had been unabashedly fat. He was big and solid and heavy, but too hard for the word *fat* quite to fit him. He said, "I didn't aim to do that anyways. I know what's in there."

"Suits me. Reckoned I better speak up, though, just in case." Now Cincinnatus picked up the bottle and tilted it back. The whiskey wasn't very good, but it was strong. It went down his throat hot and snarling. "Do Jesus!" he wheezed. "That hit the spot." "Good. Glad to hear it." Lucullus' Adam's apple worked as he took a formidable knock of hooch himself. He said, "Part of me's sorry you stuck here with your folks, Cincinnatus, but you got to answer me somethin', and answer it for true. Ain't it better to give them Confederate sons of bitches one right in the teeth than it is to sit up North somewheres and make like everything's fine?"

Cincinnatus owed Lucullus for his passbook, so he didn't laugh in his face. He said, "Mebbe," and let it go at that. But he would have given anything he had, including his soul for the Devil to roast in a barbecue pit, to be back in Des Moines with his family again.

Hot, humid summer weather was always a torment to Brigadier General Abner Dowling. An unkind soul had once said he was built like a rolltop desk. That held an unpleasant amount of truth. And now, after long years as General George Custer's adjutant, after an even longer stretch as occupation commander in Salt Lake City, after the infuriating humiliation of being kept in that position during the Pacific War against Japan, he finally had a combat command of his own.

He had it, and he could feel it going wrong, feel the ground shifting under his feet as if he were stumbling into quicksand. When the fighting broke out, he'd worried that his headquarters in Columbus was too far behind what would be the front. Now he worried that it was too far forward. He also worried about holding on to Columbus, and if that wasn't bad news, he couldn't imagine what would be.

Chillicothe was gone. Dowling hadn't expected to keep the former state capital forever. He hadn't expected to lose it in the first few days of fighting, either. He'd had several defense lines prepared between the Ohio and Chillicothe. He had only one between Chillicothe and Columbus. He was likely to lose the present state capital almost as fast as he'd lost the earlier one.

Of course, how much good his defense lines had done him was very much an open question. The Confederates had pierced them, one after another, with what seemed effortless ease. A few local counterattacks had bothered the men in butternut, but nothing seemed to slow them down for long. They kept coming: barrels and airplanes to punch holes in U.S. positions, foot soldiers and artillery to follow up and take out whatever the faster-moving stuff had left behind. It was a simple formula, but it had worked again and again.

The window in Dowling's office was open, to give a little relief from the heat. Masking tape crisscrossed the windowpane. If a bomb or a shell burst nearby, that would keep flying glass splinters from being quite so bad. The open window also let him hear a low rumble off to the south, a rumble like a distant thunderstorm. But it wasn't a thunderstorm, or not a natural one, anyhow. It was the noise of the approaching front.

It was also only background noise. What he heard in the foreground was a horrible cacophony of military transport and raw panic. Trucks full of soldiers and barrels were trying to push south, to get into position to hold back the Confederate flood. They needed to move quickly, and they were having a hard time moving at all. The whole population of southern Ohio seemed to be fleeing north as fast as it could go.

Dowling had trouble blaming the people running for their lives. If he were a farmer or a hardware-store owner and somebody started shooting off cannon and dropping bombs all around him, he would have got the hell out of there, too. But refugees were playing merry hell with troop movements. And Confederate fighters and light bombers had taken to tearing up refugee columns whenever they got the chance. That spread panic farther and wider than ever. It also coagulated road traffic even worse than simple flight could.

A knock on the door interrupted Dowling's gloomy reflections. A lieutenant stuck his head into the office and said, "Excuse me, sir, but Colonel Morrell is here to confer with you."

"Send him in," Dowling said. Morrell still wore a barrel man's coveralls. Grime and grease stains spotted them. Dowling heaved his bulk up out of the chair. "Good morning, Colonel. Good to see you."

"I wish I were back at the front," Irving Morrell said. "We've got to do something about those bastards, got to slow them down some kind of way. Can you get me more barrels? That's what we need most of all, dammit."

"I've been screaming into the telephone," Dowling answered.

"They say they need them back East. They can't leave Washington and Philadelphia uncovered."

Morrell's suggestion about what the U.S. War Department could do with Washington and Philadelphia was illegal, immoral, improbable, and incandescent. "Is the General Staff deaf, dumb, *and* blind?" he demanded. "We're liable to lose the war out here before those people wake up enough to take their heads out of their—"

"I know," Dowling broke in, as soothingly as he could. "I'm doing my best to get them to listen to me, but. . . ." He spread pink, pudgy hands.

"The Confederate attack is coming in on the line I predicted before the balloon went up," Morrell said bitterly. "Fat lot of good anticipation does if we haven't got the ways and means to meet it."

"I've heard good things about the action you fought east of Chillicothe," Dowling said. "You did everything you could."

"Yes? And so?" Morrell, Dowling rediscovered, had extraordinary eyes. A blue two shades lighter than the sky, they seemed to see farther than most men's. And, at the moment, they were remarkably cold. "They don't pay off for that, sir. They pay off for throwing the bastards back, and I didn't do it. I couldn't do it."

"You've done more than anybody else has," Dowling said.

"It's not enough." Nothing less than victory satisfied Irving Morrell. "If I'd had more to work with, I'd have done better. And if pigs had wings, we'd all carry umbrellas. If Featherston had held off a little longer, we'd have been in better shape. Every day would have helped us. Every—"

He broke off then, because the air-raid sirens started to howl. Some of the wireless-ranging stations along the border had had to be destroyed to keep them from falling into Confederate hands. That cut down the warning time Columbus got. Dowling rose from his chair. "Shall we go to the basement?" he said.

"I'd rather watch the show," Morrell said.

"Let me put it another way: go to the basement, Colonel. That's an order," Dowling said. "The country would probably muddle along without me well enough. It really needs you."

For a moment, he thought he would have a mutiny on his hands. Then Morrell nodded and flipped him as ironic a salute as he'd ever had. They went down to the basement together. Bombs were already falling by the time they got there. The noise was impressive.

Safety, here, was a relative thing. They weren't risking splinter and blast damage, the way they would have if they'd stayed in Dowling's office. But a direct hit could bring down the whole building and entomb them here. Buried alive . . . except they wouldn't stay alive very long.

Antiaircraft guns started hammering. Someone in the crowded cellar said, "I hope they knock a lot of those shitheads out of the sky."

Dowling hoped the same thing. But antiaircraft fire, no matter how ferocious, couldn't stop bombers. All it could do, at best, was make raids expensive. The Confederates had already proved they didn't mind paying the bill.

Bomb bursts walked closer to the building. After each one, the floor shook more under Dowling's feet. A captain a few feet away from him started screaming. Some men simply couldn't stand the strain. A scuffle followed. Finally, somebody clipped the captain, and he shut up.

"Thank God," Dowling said. "A little more of that, and I'd've started howling like a damn banshee, too."

Colonel Morrell nodded. "It really can be catching," he remarked, and rubbed the knuckles of his right hand against his trouser leg. Had he been the one who'd laid out the captain? He'd been in the brawl, but Dowling hadn't seen him land the punch.

The stick of bombs passed over the headquarters building. Dowling thought of the Angel of Death, and wondered if someone had slapped lamb's blood on the doorframe at the entrance. The bursts diminished in force as they got farther away.

"Whew," somebody said, which summed it up as well as anything else.

"Columbus is catching hell, though," someone else said. "Too goddamn bad. This is a nice town."

"Too goddamn bad is right," Morrell said. "This is a town we've got to hold." He plainly didn't care whether Columbus was nice, dreary, or actively vile. All he cared about was Columbus as a military position.

After about half an hour, the all-clear sounded. Confederate air bases weren't very far away. The bombers could loiter for a while if U.S. fighters didn't rise to drive them off. That didn't seem to have happened this time. Of course, the C.S. bombers would have had fighters of their own riding shotgun.

"Well," Dowling said in what he hoped wasn't black despair, "let's see what they've done to us this time."

He and Morrell and the rest of the officers and enlisted men climbed the stairs out of the basement. A corporal looked up and said, "Jesus God, but it's good to see the sky again!" He crossed himself.

Dowling was more than happy to see the sky again, too, even if clouds and streamers of smoke and the contrails left by airplanes now departed still marred its blue perfection like burn scars on what would have been a beautiful face. A staff officer pointed to a tall pillar of smoke off to the west and said, "They've gone and pasted Camp Custer again, the sons of bitches."

"No big surprise there," Dowling said. The Confederates had been hitting the training facility every chance they got ever since the war broke out. It was, without a doubt, a legitimate military target. But they were also punishing civilian sectors of Columbus and other U.S. cities. In retaliation—President Smith said it was in retaliation—the United States were visiting the same sort of destruction on C.S. towns.

Colonel Morrell was thinking along the same lines. "Going to be a swell old war, isn't it?" he said to nobody in particular.

The air-raid sirens started up again, not the usual shrill warble but one that got louder and softer, louder and softer, over and over again till back-teeth fillings started to ache. "What the hell?" Dowling said.

Everybody stared for five or ten seconds, trying to remember what that signal was supposed to mean. At last, a sergeant exclaimed, "It's a goddamn gas alert!"

There was a new wrinkle. The Confederates hadn't dropped that kind of death from the air before, at least not on Columbus. The soldiers dashed back into the building they'd so gratefully vacated moments before. Some of them found gas masks. Others had to take their chances without.

From behind his hot, heavy rubber monstrosity, Dowling said, "This is going to be hell on civilians. They don't have anywhere near enough masks." Even he could hear how muffled his voice was.

Morrell wore a mask, too. He did so self-consciously, as if he didn't want to but knew he had to. He said, "The Confederates only need to drop a few gas bombs, too, to make us flabble all over the place. You can't help taking gas seriously, and they get a big payback for a small investment."

"So they do," Dowling said morosely. "But I'll tell you this, Colonel: they won't be the only ones for long."

III

When it came to waiting tables at the Huntsman's Lodge, summer was the worst season of the year. Scipio had to put on his tuxedo in the Terry—Augusta, Georgia's, colored quarter—and then walk through the heat and humidity to the restaurant where he worked. The walk would also expose him to what passed for wit among the whites of Augusta. If he had a dime for every time he'd heard *penguin suit,* he could have retired tomorrow and been set for life.

He would have liked to retire. He was, these days, nearer seventy than sixty. But if he didn't work, he wouldn't eat. That made his choices simple. He would work till he dropped.

Bathsheba, his wife, had already left their small, cramped apartment to clean white folks' houses. Scipio kissed his daughter and son and went out the door. They'd had a better flat before the white riots of 1934 burned down half the Terry. Not much had been rebuilt since. The way things were, they were lucky to have a place at all.

A couple of blocks from the apartment building, a long line of Negroes, almost all men, stood waiting for a bus. It pulled up just as Scipio walked by. Some of the blacks stared at him. Somebody said something to his friend that had *penguin suit* in it. Scipio kept walking. He shook his head. Real wit was hard to come by, whether from whites or blacks.

The placard on the bus that pulled up said WAR PLANT WORK. Scipio shook his head again. Negroes weren't good enough to be

Confederate citizens, weren't good enough to be anything but the CSA's whipping boys. But when the guns started going off . . .

When the guns started going off, the whites went to shoot them. But the soldiers went right on needing more guns and ammunition and airplanes and barrels. If the CSA took whites out of the line to make them, it wouldn't have enough men in uniform left to face the USA's greater numbers. That meant getting labor out of black men and white women.

Scipio wouldn't have wanted to make the tools of war for a government that also used those tools to hold Negroes down. But none of the blacks getting on that WAR PLANT WORK bus seemed unhappy. They had jobs. They were making money. And if they were doing something Jake Featherston needed, Freedom Party stalwarts or guards were less likely to grab them and throw them in a camp. Those camps had a reputation that got more evil with each passing day.

Scipio didn't believe all the rumors he'd heard about the camps. Some of them had to be scare stories, of the sort that had frightened him when he was a pickaninny. Nobody in his right mind could do some of the things rumor claimed. Confederate whites wanted to keep blacks down, yes. But killing them off made no sense. Who would do what whites called nigger work if there were no blacks to take care of it?

He imagined white women cleaning house for their rich sisters. And he imagined white men out in the cotton fields, picking cotton dawn to dusk under the hot, hot sun. It was pretty funny.

And then, all of a sudden, it wasn't. One of the things the Freedom Party had done was put far more machinery in the fields than had ever been there before. A few men on those combines could do the work of dozens, maybe hundreds, with hand tools. *It's almost as if they were working out ahead of time how they would get along without us.* That precisely formed sentence made Scipio nervous for two reasons. First, it had the unpleasant feel of truth, of seeing below the surface to the underlying reality. And second, it reminded him of the education Anne Colleton had forced on him when he was her butler at the Marshlands plantation. Again, she hadn't given it to him for his benefit, but for her own. But that didn't mean it hadn't benefited him.

And now Anne Colleton was dead. He'd read that in the *Augusta Constitutionalist* with astonished disbelief. He hadn't thought anything could kill her, could stop her, could turn her aside from a path she'd chosen. She'd always seemed as much a force of nature as a mere human being.

But even a force of nature, evidently, could get caught in a damnyankee air raid. For years, Scipio had lived in dread of her showing up at the Huntsman's Lodge. And then one day she had, and sure as hell she'd recognized him. She wanted him dead. He knew that. But he'd managed to slither out from under her wrath, and now he didn't have to worry about it any more.

Without looking at the people around him, he could tell the minute he left the Terry and entered the white part of Augusta. Buildings stopped having that bombed-out look. They started having new coats of paint. The streets stopped being minefields of potholes. The stripes between lanes were fresh and white. Hell, there *were* stripes between lanes. On most of the streets in the Terry, nobody'd ever bothered painting them.

A cop pointed his nightstick at Scipio. "Passbook," he said importantly.

"Yes, suh." Scipio could talk like an educated white man. If he didn't—and most of the time he didn't dare—he used the thick dialect of the Congaree River swampland where he'd been born.

The gray-uniformed policeman peered at the passbook through bifocals. "How the hell you say your name?" he demanded, frowning.

"It's Xerxes, suh," Scipio answered. He'd had the alias for a third of his life now. He took it more for granted than the name his mama gave him. After escaping the ruin of the Red Congaree Socialist Republic, keeping that real name would have been suicidally dangerous.

"Xerxes," the cop repeated. He looked Scipio up and down. "Reckon you wait tables?"

"Yes, suh. Huntsman's Lodge. Mistuh Dover, he vouch fo' me."

"All right. Get going. You're too goddamn old to land in a whole lot of trouble anyways."

Scipio wanted to do something right there to prove the policeman wrong. He didn't, which went some way toward proving the man right. He did go on up the street to the Huntsman's Lodge. Sometimes no one bothered him on the way. Sometimes he got endless harassment. Today, in the middle, was about par for the course. He went into the kitchen and said hello to the cooks as soon as he got to the restaurant. If they were happy with you, your orders got done quickly. That meant you had a better chance for a good tip. If you got on their bad side, you took your chances.

Jerry Dover was going through the kitchens, too. The manager was making sure who was there and who wasn't, and that they had enough supplies to cover the day's likely orders. All the cooks except the head chef were black. Dover himself, of course, was white. A Negro manager would have been unimaginable anywhere in the CSA except a place that not only had exclusively colored workers but also an exclusively colored clientele.

"Afternoon, Xerxes," Dover said.

"Afternoon, Mistuh Dover," Scipio answered. "How you is?"

"Tolerable. I'm just about tolerable," the manager said. He didn't ask how Scipio was. He wouldn't, unless he saw some obvious sign of trouble. As white men in the Confederate States went, he wasn't bad in his dealings with blacks . . . but Confederate whites had a long way to go.

"People comin' in like they ought to?" Scipio asked.

"Yeah. Doesn't look like we'll be shorthanded tonight," Dover said. "But we may lose some fellas down the line, you know."

"War plant work, you mean?" Scipio asked, and the other man nodded. Jerry Dover was thin and wiry and burned with energy. From the owners' point of view, the Huntsman's Lodge couldn't have had a better manager. Scipio had to respect him, even if he didn't always like him. He said, "I seen dat de las' war."

"Where'd you see it?" Dover asked. Scipio didn't answer right away. After a moment, the white man waved the question aside. "Never mind. Forget I asked you that. It was a long time ago, and you weren't here. Whatever you did, I don't want to know about it."

Thanks to Anne Colleton, he already knew more than Scipio wished he did. No help for that, though, not unless Scipio wanted to get out of Augusta altogether. The way police and stalwarts checked passbooks these days, that was neither easy nor safe.

Then Dover said something that rocked Scipio back on his heels: "This place is liable to be losing me down the line, too."

"You, suh?" Scipio said. "Wouldn't hardly be no Huntsman's Lodge without you, suh." The people who ate there might not understand that, but it was certainly true for those who worked there. "How come you go, suh? You don't like it here no mo'?"

Dover smiled a crooked smile. "It ain't that," he said. "But if they conscript me, I got to wear the uniform." He chuckled. "You imagine me trying to feed a division's worth of soldiers all at once instead of worrying about whether the goddamn venison's marinated long enough?"

"You do good, I reckon," Scipio said, and he meant that, too. He didn't think there was anything Jerry Dover couldn't do when it came to handling food and the people who fixed it. But Dover was past forty. "They puts a uniform on *you?*"

The manager shrugged. "Never know. I wouldn't be surprised. I was a kid when the last war came along. Didn't see much action. But I saw how it sucked in more and more men the longer it went on. They were putting uniforms on fellows older than I am now. No reason they won't do it again, not unless we win pretty goddamn quick."

If he thought he would be conscripted, he didn't think the Confederate States would win in a hurry. Scipio didn't, either. He wouldn't say so. A black man dumb enough to doubt out loud wouldn't last long.

When he started waiting tables, he found, as he had before, that Augusta's big shots had far fewer doubts about how things were going than Jerry Dover did. When they weren't trying to impress the women with them with how magnificent they were, they blathered on about how degenerate the damnyankees had become and how they were surely riding for a fall. Anne Colleton had talked that way when the Great War broke out. She'd found she was wrong. These big-talking fools hadn't learned anything in a generation.

They hadn't even learned that black men had ears and brains. Had Scipio had a taste for blackmail, he could have indulged it to the fullest. He didn't; he'd always been a cautious man. But what were the odds for Confederate victory if such damn fools could rise high in the CSA? Did the same hold true in the United States? He dared hope not, anyhow.

* * *

Jake Featherston studied an immense map of Indiana and Ohio tacked to a wall of his office in the Gray House, the Confederate Presidential residence. Red pins showed his armies' progress, blue pins the positions U.S. defenders still held. The President of the CSA nodded to himself. Things weren't going exactly according to plan, but they were pretty close.

Someone knocked on the door. "Who is it?" Featherston rasped. His voice was harsh, his accent not well educated. He was an overseer's son who'd been an artillery sergeant all through the Great War before joining the Freedom Party and starting his rise in the world.

The door opened. His secretary came in. "Mr. Goldman is here to see you, Mr. President," she said.

"Thanks, Lulu. Send him right on in." Jake spoke as softly to her as was in him to do. She'd stuck with him through bad times and good, even when it seemed as if the Freedom Party would go down the drain. And it might have, if she hadn't helped hold things together.

Saul Goldman came into the office a moment later. The director of communications—a drab title for the Confederate master of propaganda—was short, and had lost his hair and grown pudgy in the nearly twenty years Featherston had known him. Jake himself remained lanky, rawboned, long-jawed, with cheekbones like knobs of granite. He'd lately had to start wearing reading glasses. Nobody ever photographed him with them on his nose, though.

"Good morning, Mr. President," Goldman said.

"Morning, Saul," Jake answered cordially. Goldman was another one who'd stayed loyal through thick and thin. There weren't that many. Featherston gave back loyalty for loyalty. He repaid disloyalty, too. Oh, yes. No one who crossed him or the country could expect to be forgotten. He put on a smile. "What can I do for you today?"

The round little Jew shook his head. "No, sir. It's what I can do for you." He held out a neat rectangular package wrapped in plain brown paper and string. "This is the very first one off the press."

"God*damn!*" Jake snatched the package with an eagerness he hadn't known since Christmastime long before the last war. He tugged at the string. When it didn't want to break, he reached into a trouser pocket on his butternut uniform and pulled out a little clasp knife. That made short work of the string, and he tore off the brown paper.

OVER OPEN SIGHTS was stamped in gold on the front cover and spine of the leather-bound book he held. So was his name. He almost burst with pride. He'd started working on the book in Gray Eagle scratch pads during the Great War, and he'd kept fiddling with it ever since. Now he was finally letting the whole world see what made him tick, what made the Freedom Party tick.

"You understand, of course, that the rest of the print run won't be so fancy," Saul Goldman said. "They made this one up special, just for you."

Featherston nodded. "Oh, hell, yes. But this here is mighty nice—*mighty* nice." He opened the book at random and began to read: " 'The Confederate state must make up for what everyone else has neglected in this field. It must set race at the center of all life. It must take care to keep itself pure. Instead of annoying Negroes with teachings they are too stupid to understand, we would do better to instruct our whites that it is a deed pleasing to God to take pity on a poor little healthy white orphan child and give him a father and mother.' " He nodded. "Well, we've gone a hell of a long way towards doing just that."

"Yes, Mr. President," the director of communications agreed.

Jake held the book in his hands. It was there. It was real. "Now folks will see why we're doing what we're doing. They'll see all the things that need doing from here on out. They'll see how much they need the Freedom Party to keep us going the way we ought to."

"That's the idea," Goldman said. "And the book will sell lots and lots of copies. That will make you money, Mr. President."

"Well, I don't mind," Jake Featherston said, which was not only true but an understatement. He'd lived pretty well since coming up in the world. But he added, "Money's not why I wrote it." And that was also true. He'd set things down on paper during the war and afterwards to try to exorcise his own demons. It hadn't worked, not altogether. They still haunted him. They still drove him. Now they were all out in the open, though. That was where they belonged.

"Everyone who joins the Freedom Party should have to buy a copy of this book," Goldman said.

Featherston nodded. "I like that. It's good. See to it." The Jew pulled a notebook from an inside pocket of his houndstooth jacket and scribbled in it. Jake went on, "Other thing you've got to do is arrange to get it translated into Spanish. The greasers in Texas and Sonora and Chihuahua may not be everything we wish they were, but they don't much fancy niggers and we can trust 'em with guns in their hands. An awful lot of 'em are good Party men even if their English isn't so hot. They need to know what we stand for, too."

Goldman smiled and said, "Sir, I've already thought of that. The Spanish version will only be a couple of weeks behind the English one."

"Good. That's damn good, Saul. You're one sharp bastard, you know that?" Jake was usually sparing of praise. Finding fault was easier. But without Saul Goldman, the Freedom Party probably wouldn't have got where it was. The wireless web he'd stitched together sent the Party's message all over the Confederate States. It got that message to places where Jake couldn't go himself. And now all the wireless stations and newspapers and magazines and newsreels in the CSA put out what Goldman told them to put out.

"I try, Mr. President," Goldman said now. "I owe you a lot, you know."

"Yeah, you've said." Jake waved that away. Inside, he wanted to laugh. Right at the start of things, Goldman had worried that the Freedom Party might come after Jews. It was a damn silly notion, though Featherston had never said so out loud. Why bother? There weren't enough Jews in the Confederate States to get hot and bothered about, and the ones who were here had always been loyal. Blacks, now, blacks were a whole different story.

"Well . . ." Goldman dipped his head. All these years, and he was still shy. "Thank you very much, Mr. President."

"Don't you worry about a thing." Jake shook his head. "No—you worry about one thing. You worry about how we're going to tell the world we've kicked the damnyankees' asses, on account of we're going to." He looked toward the door. Saul Goldman took a hint. He dipped his head again and stepped out.

Jake went back to the desk. He spent the next little while flipping through *Over Open Sights*. The more he read, the better he liked it. Everything—everything!—you wanted to know about what the Freedom Party stood for was all there in one place. Everybody all over the Confederate States, even those damn greasers, would be able to read it and understand.

He expected the telephone to ring and ruin the moment. As far as he could see, that was what the lousy thing was for. But it held off. He had twenty-five minutes to flip through twenty-five years' worth of hard work. Oh, he hadn't fiddled with the book every day through all that time, but it had never escaped his mind. And now the fruits of all that labor were in print. The more he thought about it, the better it felt.

In the end, the telephone didn't interrupt him. Lulu did. "Sir, the Attorney General is here to see you," she said.

"Well, you'd better send him in, then," Jake answered. His secretary nodded and withdrew. Ferdinand Koenig came into the President's office a moment later. Jake beamed and held up his fancy copy of *Over Open Sights.* "Hello, Ferd, you old son of a bitch! Ain't this something?"

"Not bad," Koenig answered. "Not bad at all, Sarge." He was one of the handful of men left alive who could call Featherston a name like that. A massive man, he'd been in the Freedom Party even longer than Jake. He'd backed the uprising that put Jake at the head of the Party, and he'd backed him ever since. If anybody in this miserable world was reliable, Ferdinand Koenig was the man.

"Sit down," Featherston said. "Make yourself comfortable, by God."

The chair on the other side of the desk creaked as Koenig settled his bulk into it. He reached for the book. "Let me have a look at that, why don't you? You've been talking about it long enough."

"Here you are," Jake said proudly.

Koenig paged through the book, pausing every now and then to take a look at some passage or another. He would smile and nod or raise an eyebrow. At last, he looked up. "You saw a lot of this before the last war even ended, didn't you?"

"Hell, yes. It was there, if you had your eyes open," Jake answered. "Tell me you didn't know we'd never be able to trust our niggers again. Everybody with an eye to see knew that."

"That's what I came over here to talk about, as a matter of fact," Koenig said. "Way things are going, I need to ask you a couple of questions."

"Go right ahead," Featherston said expansively. With *Over Open Sights* in print and in his hands at last, he felt happier, more mellow, than he had for a hell of a long time. Maybe this was what women felt when they had a baby. He didn't know about that; he'd never been a woman. But this was pretty fine in its own way.

Koenig said, "Well, the way things are, we're doing two different things, seems to me. Some of these niggers are going into camps like the one that Pinkard fellow runs out in Louisiana."

"Sure." Jake nodded. "Bastards are going in, all right, but they're not coming out again. Good riddance."

"That's right," the Attorney General said. "But then we've got all these other niggers we're roping into war production work, and they just live wherever they've been living when they aren't at the plant."

"So?" Featherston said with a shrug. "They'll get theirs sooner or later, too. The more work we can squeeze out of 'em beforehand, the better."

"I agree with you there," Ferdinand Koenig said. Hardly anyone dared disagree with the President of the CSA these days. Koenig went on, "I've been thinking, though—there might be a neater way to do this."

"Tell me what you've got in mind," Jake said. "I'm listening."

"Well, Sarge, the word that really occurs to me is consolidation," Koenig said. "If we can find some kind of way to put the war work and the camps together, the whole operation'll run a lot smoother. And then, when some of these bucks get too run down to be worth anything on the line . . ." He snapped his fingers.

Featherston stared. Slowly, a grin spread across his face. "I like it. I like it a hell of a lot, matter of fact. Get it set up so it doesn't disrupt everything else going on too much, and we'll do it, by God."

As Saul Goldman had a little while before, Koenig took a notebook from an inside jacket pocket and wrote in it. He said, "I'll have to see exactly what needs doing. Whatever it is, I'll take care of it. It does seem to be a way to kill two birds with one stone."

"You might say that," Jake answered. "Yeah, you just might. But we'll do a hell of a lot more killing than that." He threw back his head and laughed like a loon. He was not a man to whom laughter came often. When it did, the fit hit him hard.

"Damn right we will." Koenig got to his feet. "I won't bother you any more, Sarge. I know you've got the war with the USA to run. But I did want to keep you up to date on what we're doing."

"That's fine." Featherston laughed again. "Oh, hell, yes, Ferd. That's just fine. And the war with the USA and the war against the niggers go together. Don't you ever forget that."

Down in southern Sonora, Hipolito Rodriguez could have thought the new war against the USA nothing but noise in a distant room. No U.S. bombers appeared over the small town of Baroyeca, outside of which he had his farm. No U.S. soldiers were within a couple of hundred miles, and none seemed likely to come any closer. Peace might have continued uninterrupted . . . except that he had one son in the Army and two more who might be called to the colors at almost any time. For that matter, he was only in his mid-forties himself. He'd fought in the last war. It wasn't unimaginable that they might want to put butternut on his back again.

He didn't want to leave his farm. He even had electricity these days, something he couldn't have imagined when he left Sonora the first time. That went a long way toward making the place a paradise on earth. Electric lights, a refrigerator, even a wireless set . . . what more could one man need?

One evening when the war was still very new, he kissed his wife and said, "I'm going into town for the Freedom Party meeting."

Magdalena raised an eyebrow. "Do you think I didn't know you were going to?" she asked. "You've been going as many weeks as you can for more than fifteen years now. Why would you change tonight?"

They spoke Spanish between themselves, a Spanish leavened with English words absorbed in the sixty years Sonora and Chihuahua had belonged to the CSA. Their children used more English, an English leavened with many Spanish words from the 350 years Sonora and Chihuahua had belonged first to Spain and then to Mexico. Their grandchildren and great-grandchildren might one day speak an English more like that heard in the rest of the Confederacy. Thinking about that occasionally worried Rodriguez. Most of the time, though, it lay too far beyond the horizon of now to trouble him very much.

Out the door he went. He still hadn't had a letter from Pedro since the shooting started. There was a worry much more immediate than any over language. He also hadn't had a telegram from the War Department in Richmond. That made him think everything was all right, and that his youngest son was just too busy to write. He hoped so, anyway.

Baroyeca lay in a valley between two ridge lines of the Sierra Madre Occidental. The westering sun shone brightly on them, burnishing their peaks and gilding them. From lifelong familiarity, Rodriguez hardly noticed the mountains' stern beauty. The wonders of our own neighborhoods are seldom obvious to us. What he did notice were the men coming out of the reopened silver mine, the railroad that had closed in the business collapse but was running again, and the poles that carried electricity not only to Baroyeca but also to outlying farms like his. Those, to him, were the real marvels.

He lived about three miles outside of town. The power poles ran alongside the dirt road. Hawks sat on the wires, looking for rabbits or mice or ground squirrels. He had never understood why they didn't get electrocuted, but they didn't. Some of them let him walk by. Others flew away when he got too close.

The country was dry—not disastrously dry, not with water coming down out of the mountains, but dry enough. Somewhere off in a field, a mule brayed. In the richer parts of the Confederate States, tractors did most of the field work that horses and mules had done since time out of mind. Around Baroyeca, a man with a good mule counted for wealthy. Hipolito had one.

The town could have been matched by scores of others in Sonora and Chihuahua. The *alcalde*'s house and the church stood across the square from each other; both were built of adobe, with red tile roofs. Baroyeca had one street of business. The most important of those, as far as Rodriguez was concerned, were Diaz's general store and *La Culebra Verde,* the local cantina. Down near the end of the street stood Freedom Party headquarters.

It had both FREEDOM! and ¡LIBERTAD! painted on the big window out front. The Freedom Party had always been scrupulous about using both English and Spanish in Sonora and Chihuahua. That was one reason it had prospered. The Whigs used to look down their snooty noses at the citizens they'd acquired in the states they bought from the Empire of Mexico. Even the Radical Liberals had dealt with the rich men, the *patrones*, and expected them to deliver votes from their clients. Not the Freedom Party. From the start, it had appealed to the people.

Rodriguez went in. Robert Quinn, the Party representative in Baroyeca, nodded politely. "*Hola, Señor* Rodriguez," he said in English-accented Spanish. "*¿Como está Usted?*"

"*Estoy bien, gracias,*" Rodriguez answered. "And how are you, *Señor* Quinn?"

"I am also well, thanks," Quinn said, still in Spanish. Not only had he learned the language, he treated people who spoke it like anyone else. The Freedom Party didn't care if you were of Mexican blood. It didn't care if you were a Jew. As long as you weren't black, you fit right in.

Carlos Ruiz waved to Rodriguez. He patted the folding chair next to him. Rodriguez sat down by his friend. Ruiz was a veteran, too. He'd fought up in Kentucky and Tennessee, where things had been even grimmer than in west Texas. He too had a son in the Army now.

Quinn waited another fifteen minutes. Then he said, "Let's get started. For those of you without wireless sets, the war news is good. We are driving on Columbus, Ohio. The town will fall soon, unless something very surprising happens. In the East, our airplanes have bombed Washington and Baltimore and Philadelphia and New York. We have also bombed the oil fields in Sequoyah, so *los Estados Unidos* will not get any use from the state they stole from us. We are going to beat those people."

A pleased murmur ran through the Freedom Party men. A lot of them had fought in the Great War. Hearing about things happening on U.S. soil instead of a massive U.S. invasion of the Confederate States felt good.

"You will also have heard that the Empire of Mexico has declared war on the United States," Quinn said. Another murmur ran through the room. This one was half pleased, half scornful. Sonorans and Chihuahuans, these days, looked at Mexicans the way a lot of white Confederates looked at *them*: as lazy good-for-nothings living in the land of perpetual *mañana*. That might not have been fair, but it was real.

Somebody behind Rodriguez asked, "How much good can Mexico do us?"

"Against *los Estados Unidos, los Estados Confederados* need men," Quinn replied. "We have the factories to give them helmets and rifles and boots and everything else they require. But getting more *soldados* up to the front can only help."

"If they don't run away as soon as they get there," Rodriguez whispered to Carlos Ruiz. His friend nodded. Neither of them had much faith in the men who followed Francisco José II, the new Emperor of Mexico.

Quinn went on, "But that is not the only news I have for you tonight, *mis amigos.* I am delighted to be able to tell you that I have a copy of President Featherston's important new book, *Over Open Sights,* for each and every one of you." He picked up a crate and set it on the table behind which he sat. "You can get it in Spanish or English, whichever you would rather."

An excited murmur ran through the Freedom Party men. Rodriguez's voice was part of it. People had been talking about *Over Open Sights* for years. People had been talking about it for so long, in fact, that they'd begun to joke about whether Featherston's dangerous visions would ever appear. But here was the book at last.

Only a few men asked for *Over Open Sights* in English. Rodriguez wasn't one of them. He spoke it fairly well, and understood more than he spoke. But he still felt more comfortable reading Spanish. Had his sons been at the meeting, he suspected they would have chosen the English version. They'd had more schooling than he had, and more of it had been in English.

"Pay me later, as you have the money," Quinn said. "Some of the price from each copy will go to helping wounded soldiers and the families of those who die serving their country. *Señor* Featherston, *el presidente,* was a soldier himself. Of course you know that. But he has not forgotten what being a soldier means."

Hipolito Rodriguez wasn't the only one who nodded approvingly. Now that Jake Featherston was rich and famous, he could easily have forgotten the three dark years of the Great War. But Quinn was right; he hadn't.

The local Freedom Party leader went on, "At the end of the last war, our own government tried to pretend it didn't owe our soldiers anything. They'd fought and suffered and died—*por Dios,* my friends, *you'd* fought and suffered and died—but the government wanted to pretend the war had never happened. It had made the mistakes, and it blamed the men for them. That's one of the reasons I'm so glad we finally came to power. What the Whigs did then, the Freedom Party will never do. Never!"

More nods. Some people clapped their hands. But the applause wasn't as strong as it might have been. Rodriguez could see why. Instead of giving *Señor* Quinn all their attention, men kept opening their copies of *Over Open Sights* here and there and seeing just what Jake Featherston had to say. The President would never come to Baroyeca, especially not now, not with a war on. But here, in his book, Featherston was setting out all his thoughts, all his ideas, for his country to read and to judge.

Rodriguez held temptation at bay only long enough to be polite. Then he, too, opened *Over Open Sights*. What *did* Jake Featherston have to say? The book began, *I'm waiting, not far behind our line. We have niggers in the trenches in front of us. As soon as the damnyankees start shelling them, they'll run. They don't want anything to do with U.S. soldiers—they'd sooner shoot at us. I'd like to see the damnyankees dead. But I'd rather see those niggers dead. They aim to ruin this country of ours. And most of all, I want to pay back the stupid fat cats who put rifles in those niggers' hands. I want to, and by Jesus one of these days I will.*

And he had. And he was paying back the *mallates*, and he was paying back the damnyankees, too. Rodriguez had always thought Jake Featherston was a man of his word. Here once again he saw it proved.

Quinn laughed. He said, "I am going to ask for a motion to adjourn. You are paying more attention to the President than you are to me. That's all right. That's why Jake Featherston *is* the President. He makes people pay attention to him. He can do it even in a book. Do I hear that motion?" He did. It passed with no objections. He went on, "*Hasta la vista, señores.* Next week, if it pleases you, we will talk about some of what he has to say."

The Freedom Party men went out into the night. Some of them headed for home, others for *La Culebra Verde.* After a brief hesitation, Rodriguez walked to the cantina. He didn't think people would wait for next week's meeting to start talking about what was in *Over Open Sights.* He didn't want to wait that long himself. He could read and drink and talk—and then, he thought with a smile, drink a little more.

* * *

Dr. Leonard O'Doull was not a happy man. He found that all the more strange, all the more disheartening, because he'd been so happy for so long. He'd come up to Quebec during the Great War to work at the hospital the U.S. Army had built on a farmer's land near the town of Rivière-du-Loup. He'd ended up marrying the farmer's daughter, and he and Nicole Galtier had come as close to living happily ever after as is commonly given to two mortals to do. Their son, Lucien, named for his grandfather, was a good boy, and was now on the edge of turning into a good young man.

Oh, they'd had their troubles. O'Doull had lost his father, a physician like himself, and Nicole had lost both her mother and her father in the space of a few years. But those were the sorts of things that happened to people simply because they were human beings. As a doctor, Leonard O'Doull understood that better than most.

He'd made a good life, a comfortable life, for himself in the Republic of Quebec. He'd spoken some French before he ever got up here. These days, he used it almost all the time, and spoke it with a Quebecois accent, not the Parisian one he had of course learned in school. There had been times when he could almost forget he was born and raised in Massachusetts.

Almost.

He'd been reminded his American past still stayed a part of him when war clouds darkened the border between the United States and the Confederate States. To most people in Rivière-du-Loup—even to his relatives by marriage—the growing strife between the USA and the CSA was like a quarrel between strangers who lived down the street: interesting, but nothing to get very excited about.

Now that war had broken out, the locals still felt the same way. The Republic of Quebec was helping the USA with occupation duty in English-speaking Canada, but the Republic remained neutral, at peace with everyone even when most of the world split into warring camps.

As Leonard O'Doull walked from his home to his office a few blocks away, he did not feel at peace with the rest of the world. Far from it. He was a tall, lean man, pale as his Irish name suggested, with a long, lantern-jawed face, green eyes that usually laughed but not today, and close-cropped sandy hair now grayer than it had been. He didn't feel fifty, but he was.

People nodded to him as he walked by. Rivière-du-Loup wasn't such a big town that most folks didn't know most others. And O'Doull stood out on account of his inches and also on account of his looks. He didn't look French, and just about everybody else in town did. Most people were short and dark and Gallic, the way their ancestors who'd settled here in the seventeenth century had been.

Oh, there were exceptions. Nicole's brother, Georges Galtier, was as tall as O'Doull, and twice as broad through the shoulders. But Georges looked like a Frenchman, too; he just looked like an oversized Frenchman.

Here was the office. O'Doull used one key to open the lock, another to open the dead bolt. His was one of the few doors in Rivière-du-Loup to have a dead bolt. But he was a careful and reputable man. He kept morphine and other drugs in here, and felt an obligation to make them as hard to steal as he could.

He got a pot of coffee going on a hot plate and waited for his receptionist to come in. Stephanie was solidly reliable once she got here, but she did like to sleep in every so often. While he waited for the coffee to perk and for her to show up, O'Doull started skimming medical journals. With vitamins and new drugs and new tests appearing seemingly by the day, this was an exciting time to be a doctor. He had a chance of curing diseases that would have killed only a few years before. Every journal trumpeted some new advance.

The outer door opened. "That you, Stephanie?" O'Doull called.

"No, I'm afraid not." It was a man's voice, not a woman's, and used a clear Parisian French whose like Leonard O'Doull hadn't heard for years. Then the man switched to another language with which O'Doull was out of touch: English. He said, "How are you today, Doctor?"

"*Pas pire, merci,*" O'Doull replied in Quebecois French. He had no trouble understanding English, and thanks to his journals read it all the time, but he didn't speak it automatically the way he once had. He needed a conscious effort to shift to it to ask, "Who are you?"

"Jedediah Quigley, at your service," the stranger said. He paused in the doorway to the private office till O'Doull nodded for him to come in. He was trim and lean, still erect and probably still strong though he had to be past seventy, and he had the look of a man who'd spent a long time in the military. Sure enough, he went on, "Colonel, U.S. Army, retired. I've done a fair amount of liaison work between the U.S. and Quebecois governments in my time. I confess to taking it easier these days, though."

"Jedediah Quigley." O'Doull said the name in musing tones. He'd heard it before, and needed to remember where. He snapped his fingers. "You're the fellow who took my father-in-law's land for the military hospital, and then ended up buying it from him after the war."

"That's right." Quigley gave back a crisp nod. "He skinned me for every sou he could, too, and he enjoyed doing it. I was sad to hear he'd joined the majority."

"So was I," O'Doull said. "He was quite a man. . . . But you didn't come here to talk about him, did you?"

"No." The retired officer shook his head. "I came here to talk about you."

"Me? Why do you want to talk about me?" O'Doull pulled open a couple of desk drawers to see if he could find a spare cup. He thought he remembered one, and he was right. He stuck it on his desk, filled it with coffee, and shoved it across to Quigley. Then he poured the usual mugful for himself. After a sip, he went on, "I'm just a doctor, doing my job as best I can."

"That's why." Quigley sipped his own coffee. He chuckled as he set down the cup. "Some eye-opener, by God. Why you, Dr. O'Doull? Because you're not just a doctor. You're an American doctor. What I came to find out is, how much does that mean to you?"

"Isn't that interesting?" O'Doull murmured. "I've been wondering the same thing myself, as a matter of fact. What have you got in mind?" Even as he asked the question, a possible answer occurred to him.

When Jedediah Quigley said, "Your country needs doctors, especially doctors who've seen war wounds before," he knew he'd got it right. Quigley added, "Things aren't going as well as we wish they were. Casualties are high. If you still think of yourself as an American . . ."

"Good question," Dr. O'Doull said. "Till this mess blew up, I really didn't. I was as much a Quebecois as anybody whose umptygreat-grandfather fought alongside Montcalm on the Plains of Abraham. But there's nothing like seeing the country where you were born in trouble to make you wonder what you really are."

"If you think we're in trouble now, wait till you see what happens if those Confederate bastards make it all the way up to Lake Erie," Quigley said.

"You think that's what they're up to?" O'Doull asked.

"I do." Quigley spoke with a good officer's decisiveness. "If they can do that, they cut the country in half. All the rail lines that connect the raw materials in the West with the factories in the East run through Indiana and Ohio. If those go . . . Well, if those go, we have a serious problem on our hands."

Leonard O'Doull hadn't thought of it in those terms. He'd never been a soldier. At most, he'd been a doctor in uniform. But a picture of the USA formed in his mind—a picture of the factories in eastern Ohio and Pennsylvania and New York and New England cut off from Michigan iron and from Great Plains wheat and from oil out of Sequoyah and California. He didn't like that picture—didn't like it one bit.

"What do we do about it?" he asked.

"We do our damnedest to stop them, that's what," Quigley answered. "If you cut me in half at the belly button, I won't do too well afterwards. The same applies to the United States. I can tell you one thing stopping the Confederates means, too: it means casualties, probably by the carload lot."

"Well, I do understand why you're talking to me," O'Doull said.

The retired colonel nodded. "I would be surprised if you didn't, Doctor. You're good at what you do. I don't think anybody in town would say anything different. And you've got plenty of experience with military medicine, too, as I said before."

"More than I ever wanted," O'Doull said.

Jedediah Quigley waved that aside. "*And* you're an American." He cocked his head to one side and waited expectantly. "Aren't you?"

No matter how much O'Doull wanted to deny it, he couldn't, not when he'd been thinking the same thing on his way to the office. "Well, what if I am?" he asked, his voice rough with annoyance—at himself more than at Quigley.

"What if you are?" Quigley echoed, sensing he had a fish on

the hook. "If you are, and if you know you are, I'm going to offer you the chance of a lifetime." He sounded like a fast-talking used-motorcar salesman, or perhaps more like a sideshow barker at a carnival. Before going on, he made a small production of lighting up a stogie. The match hissed when struck, sending up a small gray cloud of sulfurous smoke. What came from the cheroot wasn't a whole lot more appetizing. Quigley didn't seem to care. After blowing a smoke ring, he said, "If you're an American, I'm going to offer you the chance to get close enough to the front to come under artillery fire, and probably machine-gun fire, too. You'll do emergency work, and you'll swear and cuss and fume on account of it isn't better. But you'll save lives just the same, and we need them saved. What do you say?"

"I say I'm a middle-aged man with a wife and a son," O'Doull answered. "I say that if you think I'm going to try to keep them going on a captain's pay, or even a major's, you're out of your mind."

Quigley blew another smoke ring, even more impressive—and even smellier—than the first. He steepled his fingers and looked sly. "They aren't Americans, of course," he said. "They're citizens of the Republic of Quebec."

"And so?" O'Doull asked.

"And so the Republic, out of the goodness of its heart—and, just between you and me, because we're twisting its arm—will pay them a stipend equal to your average income the last three years, based on your tax records. That's over and above what we'll pay you as a major in the Medical Corps."

You do want me, O'Doull thought. And the USA had set things up so the Republic of Quebec would pay most of the freight. That seemed very much like something the United States would do. O'Doull laughed. He said, "First time I ever wished I didn't have a good accountant."

That made Jedediah Quigley laugh, too. "Have we got a bargain?"

"If I can persuade Nicole," O'Doull answered. His wife was going to be furious. She was going to be appalled. He was more than a little appalled himself. But, for the first time since the war broke out, he also felt at peace with himself. At peace with Nicole was likely to be another matter.

* * *

George Enos, Jr., scanned the waters of the North Atlantic for more than other fishing boats, sea birds, and fish and dolphins. He'd heard how a Confederate commerce raider had captured his father's boat, and how a C.S. submersible had tried to sink her, only to be sunk by a U.S. sub lurking with the boat. He hardly remembered any of that himself. He'd been a little boy during the Great War. But his mother had talked about it plenty, then and afterwards.

He bit his lip. His mother was dead, murdered by the one man she'd fallen for since his father. That Ernie had blown out his own brains right afterwards was no consolation at all.

Inside of a day or two, the *Sweet Sue* would get to the Grand Bank off Newfoundland. Then George wouldn't have the luxury of leisure to stand around. He'd be baiting hooks with frozen squid, letting lines down into the cold, green waters of the Atlantic, or bringing tuna aboard—which always resembled a bout of all-in wrestling much more than anything ordinary people, landlubbers, thought of as fishing. He'd barely have time to eat or sleep then, let alone think. But the long run out gave him plenty of time to brood.

Under his feet, the deck throbbed with the pounding of the diesel. The fishing boat was making ten knots, which was plenty to blow most of the exhaust astern of her. Every so often, though, a twist of wind would make George notice the pungent stink. The morning was bright and clear. The swells out of the north were gentle. The Atlantic was a different beast in the wintertime, and a much meaner one.

George ducked into the galley for a cup of coffee. Davey Hatton, universally known as the Cookie, poured from the pot into a thick white china mug. "Thanks," George said, and added enough condensed milk and sugar to tame the snarling brew. He cradled the mug in his hands, savoring the warmth even now. Spin the calendar round half a year and it would be a lifesaver.

Hatton had the wireless on. They were beyond daytime reach of ordinary AM stations in the USA or occupied Canada and New-foundland, though they could still pull them in after the sun went down. Shortwave broadcasts were a different story. Those came in from the USA, the CSA, Britain, and Ireland, as well as from a host of countries where they didn't speak English.

"What's the latest?" George asked.

Before answering, the Cookie made a production of getting a pipe going. To George's way of thinking, it was wasted effort. The tobacco with which Hatton so carefully primed it smelled like burning long johns soaked in molasses. Old-timers groused that all the tobacco went to hell when the USA fought the CSA. George didn't see how anything could get much nastier than the blend the Cookie smoked now.

Once he'd filled the galley with poison gas, Hatton answered, "The Confederates are pounding hell out of Columbus."

"Screw 'em," George said, sipping the coffee. Even after he'd doctored it, it was strong enough to grow hair on a stripper's chest— a waste of a great natural resource, that would have been. "What are we doing?"

"Wireless says we're bombing Richmond and Louisville and Nashville and even Atlanta," Hatton answered. He emitted more smoke signals. If George read them straight, they meant he didn't believe everything he heard on the wireless.

"How about overseas?" George asked.

"BBC says Cork and Waterford'll fall in the next couple of days, and that'll be the end of Ireland," the Cookie replied. "That Churchill is an A-number-one son of a bitch, but the man makes a hell of a speech. Him and Featherston both, matter of fact. Al Smith is a goddamn bore, you know that?"

"I didn't vote for him," George said. "What about the rest of the war over there?"

"Well, the BBC says the French are kicking Kaiser Friedrich Wilhelm's ass. They say the Ukraine's falling apart and Poland's rebelling against Germany. But they tell a hell of a lot of lies, too, you know what I mean? If I could understand what's coming out of Berlin, you bet your butt the krauts would be singing a different tune. So who knows what's really going on?"

At that moment, the *Sweet Sue* gave a sudden, violent lurch to starboard, and then another one, just as sharp, to port. "What the hell?" George exclaimed as coffee slopped out of the mug and burned his fingers.

Then he heard a new noise through the chatter on the wireless and the diesel's deep, steady throb: a savage roar rising rapidly to a mechanical scream. It seemed to come from outside, but filled the galley, filled everything. George got a glimpse of an airplane zooming toward them—and of flames shooting from its wings as it opened up with machine guns.

Bullets stitched their way across the fishing boat. One caught the Cookie in the chest. He let out a grunt—more a sound of surprise than one of pain—and crumpled, crimson spreading over the gray wool of his sweater. His feet kicked a few times, but he was plainly a dead man. A sudden sharp stench among the good smells of the galley said his bowels had let go.

Screams on the deck told that the Cookie wasn't the only one who'd been hit. George saw right away that he couldn't do anything for Hatton. He hurried out of the galley. *Chow'll be rotten the rest of the run* went through his mind. Then he realized that was the least of his worries. Getting home alive and in one piece counted for a hell of a lot more.

Chris Agganis was down on the deck clutching his leg. Blood spilled from it. George was used to gore, as anybody who made his living gutting tuna that could outweigh him had to be. But this blood spilled out of a person. He was amazed how much difference that made.

"Hurts," Agganis moaned in accented English. "Hurts like hell." He said something else in syrupy Greek. This was his first time on the *Sweet Sue*. The skipper'd hired him at the last minute, when Johnny O'Shea didn't come aboard—was probably too drunk to remember to come aboard. Agganis knew what he was doing, he played a mean harmonica, and now he'd been rewarded for his hard work with a bullet in the calf.

George knelt beside him. "Lemme see it, Chris." Agganis kept moaning. George had to pull the Greek's hands away so he could yank up his dungarees. The bullet had gone through the meat of his calf. As far as George could see, it hadn't hit the bone. He said, "It's not good, but it could be a hell of a lot worse." He stuffed his handkerchief into one hole and pulled another one out of Chris Agganis' pocket for the second, larger, wound.

He was so desperately busy doing that—and fighting not to puke, for hot blood on his hands was ever so much worse than the cold stuff that came out of a fish—that he didn't notice how the shriek of the airplane engine overhead was swelling again till it was almost on top of the fishing boat.

Machine-gun bullets dug into the planking of the deck. They chewed up the galley once more, and clanged through the metal of the smokestack. Then the fighter zoomed away eastward. The roundels on its wings and flanks were red inside white inside blue: it came from a British ship.

"Fucking bastard," Chris Agganis choked out.

"Yeah," George agreed, hoping and praying the limey wouldn't come back. Once more and the fishing boat was liable to sink. For that matter, how many bullet holes did she have at the waterline? And how many rounds had gone through the engine? Was she going to catch fire and burn right here in the middle of the ocean?

The engine was still running. The *Sweet Sue* wasn't dead in the water. That would do for a miracle till a bigger one came along.

And she still steered. That meant the skipper hadn't taken a bullet. George got to his feet and went back into the galley. He knew where the first-aid kit was. Shattered crockery crunched under the soles of his shoes. The air was thick with the iron stink of blood, the smell of shit, and the nasty smoke from the cheap pipe tobacco the Cookie had lit a couple of minutes before he died.

George took a bandage and a bottle of rubbing alcohol and, after a moment's hesitation, a morphine syringe out to Chris Agganis. The fisherman let out a bloodcurdling shriek when George splashed alcohol over his wound. "You don't want it to rot, do you?" George asked.

Agganis' answer was spirited but incoherent. He hardly noticed when George stuck him with the syringe and injected the morphine. After a few minutes, though, he said, "Ahhh."

"Is that better?" George asked. Agganis didn't answer, but he stopped thrashing. By the look on his face, Jesus had just come down from heaven and was patting him on the back. George stared at him, and at the syringe. He'd heard what morphine could do, but he'd never seen it in action till now. He hadn't imagined anybody with a bullet wound could look that happy.

With Chris Agganis settled, George could look over the *Sweet Sue. Chewed to hell but still going* seemed to sum things up, as it had before. Captain Albert had swung her back toward the west. With one dead and at least one hurt man on board, with the boat probably taking on water, with the engine possibly damaged, what else could the skipper do? Nothing George could see.

But heading west produced a painful pang, too. They'd get into Boston harbor with nothing on ice except the Cookie, and they couldn't sell him. What the hell would they do without a paycheck to show for the trip? What the hell would Connie say when George walked into the apartment with nothing to show for his time at sea? *She'll say, "Thank God you're alive," that's what,* George thought. She'd hug him and squeeze him and take him to bed, and all that would be wonderful. But none of it would pay the rent or buy groceries. What the hell good was a man who didn't bring any money with him when he walked through the front door? No good. No good at all.

He went up to the wheelhouse. The fighter hadn't shot that up. The skipper was talking into the wireless set, giving the *Sweet Sue*'s position and telling a little about what had happened to her. He raised a questioning eyebrow at George.

"Chris got one in the leg," George said. "And the Cookie's dead." He touched his own chest to show the hit Hatton had taken.

"At least one dead and one wounded," the skipper said. "We are returning to port if we can. Out." He set the microphone back in its cradle, then looked at—looked through—George. "Jesus Christ!"

"Yeah," George said.

"See who else is still with us, and what kind of shape the boat's in," Albert told him. "I don't know what the hell the owners are going to say when we get back like this. I just don't know. But I'll be goddamn glad to get back at all, you know what I mean?"

"I sure do, Skipper," George answered. "You better believe I do."

Somewhere out in the western North Atlantic prowled a British airplane carrier with more nerve than sense. The USS *Remembrance* and another carrier, the *Sandwich Islands,* steamed north from Bermuda to do their damnedest to send her to the bottom.

Sam Carsten peered across the water at the *Sandwich Islands.* She was a newer ship, built as a carrier from the keel up. The *Remembrance* had started out as a battle cruiser and been converted while abuilding. The *Sandwich Islands'* displacement wasn't much greater, but she could carry almost twice as many airplanes. Carsten was glad to have her along.

Repairs still went on aboard the *Remembrance*. The yard at Bermuda had done most of the work. In peacetime, the carrier would have stayed there a lot longer. But this was war. You did what you had to do and sent her back into the scrap. It had been the same way aboard the *Dakota* during the Great War. Sam wondered whether the battleship's steering mechanism was everything it should be even now.

Destroyers and cruisers ringed the two carriers. That reassured Sam less than it had before the raid on Charleston. The screening ships hadn't been able to keep land-based aircraft away from the *Remembrance*. Would they and the combat air patrol be able to fend off whatever the limeys threw at this force? Carsten hoped so. He also knew that what he hoped and what he got were liable to have nothing to do with each other.

He rubbed more zinc-oxide ointment on a nose already carrying enough of the white goo to resemble one of the snow-capped peaks of the Rockies. He only wished the stuff did more good. With it or without it, he burned. Without it, he burned a little worse.

Up at the top of the *Remembrance*'s island, the antennas for the wireless rangefinder spun round and round, round and round. The gadget had done good work off the Confederate coast, warning of incoming enemy airplanes well before the screening ships or the combat air patrol spotted them. As the carriers got more familiar with their new toy, they said Y-range more and more often. The whole name was just too clumsy.

Some of the cruisers also sported revolving Y-range antennas. They used them not only to spot incoming enemy aircraft but also to improve their gunnery. Y-ranging gave results more precise than the stereoscopic and parallax visual rangefinders gunners had used in the Great War.

A signalman at the stern wigwagged a fighter onto the deck. Smoke stinking of burnt rubber spurted from the tires. The hook the airplane carried in place of a tailwheel snagged an arrester wire. The pilot jumped out. The flight crew cleared the machine from the deck. Another one roared aloft to take its place.

"You're in unfamiliar territory, Carsten," said someone behind Sam.

He turned and found himself face to face with Commander Dan Cressy. "Uh, yes, sir," he answered, saluting the executive officer.

"I'm like the groundhog—every once in a while, they let me poke my nose up above ground and see if I spot my own shadow."

The exec grinned. "I like that."

Sam suspected Cressy would have a ship of his own before long. He was young, brave, and smarter than smart; he'd make flag rank if he lived. *Unlike me,* Carsten thought without rancor. As a middle-aged mustang, he had much slimmer prospects of promotion. He'd dwelt on them before. He didn't feel like doing it now, especially since all of them but getting the *junior grade* removed from his lieutenant's rank would take an uncommon run of casualties among officers senior to him.

"Glad you do, sir," Sam said now. He sure as hell didn't want the exec to catch him brooding.

"Damage-control parties have done good work for us," Cressy said. "The skipper is pleased with Lieutenant Commander Pottinger—and with you. You showed nerve, fighting that five-inch gun when the Confederates hit us off Charleston."

"Thank you very much, sir," Sam said, and meant it. The exec usually did Captain Stein's dirty work for him. The skipper got the credit, the exec got the blame: an ancient Navy rule. Winning praise from Cressy—even praise he was relaying from someone else—didn't happen every day.

"You were on this ship when you were a rating, weren't you?" Cressy asked.

"Yes, sir, I sure was, just after she was built," Sam said. "I had to leave her when I made ensign. There wasn't any slot for me here. When I came back, they put me in damage control. If I'd had my druthers, I'd have stayed in gunnery, or better yet up here with the airplanes." He knew he was sticking his neck out. Grumbling about an assignment he'd had for years was liable to land him in dutch.

Commander Cressy eyed him for a moment. "When you're so good at what you do, how much do you suppose your druthers really matter?"

"Sir, I've been in the Navy more than thirty years. I know damn well they don't matter at all," Sam answered. "But that doesn't mean I haven't got 'em."

That got another grin from Cressy. Sam had a way of saying things that might have been annoying from somebody else seem a joke, or at least nothing to get upset about. The exec said, "Well, fair enough. If we ever get the chance to give them to you . . . we'll see what we can do, that's all."

"Thank you very much, sir!" Sam exclaimed. It wasn't a promise, but it came closer than anything he'd ever heard up till now.

"Nothing to thank me for," Cressy said, emphasizing that it was no promise. "There may not be anything to do, either. You have that straight?"

"Oh, yes, sir. I sure do," Sam said. "I can handle the job I've got just fine. It isn't the one I would have picked for myself, that's all."

Klaxons began to hoot. "Now we both get to do the jobs we've got," Commander Cressy said, and went off toward the *Remembrance*'s island at a dead run. Carsten was running, too, for the closest hatchway that would take him down to his battle station in the carrier's bowels.

Closing watertight doors slowed him, but he got where he was going in good time. Lieutenant Commander Pottinger came down at almost exactly the same moment. "No, I don't know what's going on," Pottinger said when Sam asked him. "I bet I can guess, though."

"Me, too," Sam said. "We must've spotted that British carrier."

"I can't think of anything else," Pottinger said. "Their pilot was probably stupid, shooting up that fishing boat."

"One of ours would've done the same thing to their boat off the coast of England," Sam said. "Flyboys are like that."

In the light of the bare bulb in its wire cage overhead, Pottinger's grin was haggard. "I didn't say you were wrong. I just said the limey was stupid. There's a difference."

The throb of the *Remembrance*'s engines deepened as the great ship picked up speed. One after another, airplanes roared off her flight deck. Some of those would be torpedo carriers and dive bombers to go after the British ship, others fighters to protect them and to fight off whatever the limeys threw at the *Remembrance* and the *Sandwich Islands*.

As usual once an action started, the damage-control party had nothing to do but stand around and wait and hope its talents weren't needed. Some of the sailors told dirty jokes. A petty officer methodically cracked his knuckles. He didn't seem to know he was doing it, though each pop sounded loud as a gunshot in that cramped, echoing space.

Time crawled by. Sam had learned not to look at his watch down here. He would always feel an hour had gone by, when in fact it was ten minutes. Better not to know than to be continually disappointed.

When the *Remembrance* suddenly heeled hard to port, everybody in the damage-control party—maybe everybody on the whole ship—said, "Uh-oh!" at the same time. If the antiaircraft guns had started banging away right then, Sam would have known some of the British carrier's bombers had got through. Since they didn't . . .

"Submersible!" he said.

Lieutenant Commander Pottinger nodded. "I'd say the son of a bitch missed us—with his first spread of fish, anyhow." He added the last phrase to make sure nobody could accuse him of optimism.

Not much later, explosions in the deep jarred the *Remembrance*. "They're throwing ashcans at the bastard," one of the sailors said.

"Hope they nail his hide to the wall, too," another one said. Nobody quarreled with that, least of all Sam. He'd seen more battle damage than anybody else down there. If he never saw any more, he wouldn't have been the least bit disappointed.

Another depth charge burst, this one so close to the surface that it rattled everybody's teeth. "Jesus H. Christ!" Pottinger said. "What the hell are they trying to do, blow our stern off?"

Nobody laughed. Such disasters had befallen at least one destroyer. Sam didn't think anybody'd ever screwed up so spectacularly aboard a carrier, but that didn't mean it couldn't happen.

Then the intercom crackled to life. "Scratch one sub!" Commander Cressy said exultantly.

Cheers filled the corridor. Carsten shouted as loud as anybody. A boat with somewhere around sixty British or Confederate or French sailors had just gone to the bottom. *Better them than me,* he thought, and let out another whoop. Lieutenant Commander Pottinger stuck out his hand. Grinning, Sam squeezed it.

Thuds on the deck above told of airplanes landing. One of the sailors said, "I wonder what the hell's going on up there." Sam wondered the same thing. Everybody down here did, no doubt. Until the intercom told them, they wouldn't know.

An hour later, the all-clear sounded—still with no news doled out past the sinking of the one submarine. Sam would have made a beeline for the deck anyway, just to escape the cramped, stuffy, paint- and oil-smelling corridor in which he'd been cooped up so long. The added attraction of news only made him move faster. He found disgusted fliers. "The limeys hightailed it out of town," one of them said. "We went to where they were supposed to be at—as best we could guess and as best we could navigate—and they weren't anywhere around there. We pushed out all the way to our maximum range and even a little farther, and we still didn't spot the bastards. They're long gone."

"Good riddance," Sam offered.

"Well, yeah," the pilot said, shedding his goggles and sticking a cigar in his mouth (he wasn't fool enough to light it, but gnawed at the end). "But that's a hell of a long way to come to shoot up a goddamn fishing boat and then go home."

"I think they were trying to lure us out to where the submarine could put a torpedo in our brisket," Sam said. "The Japs did that to the *Dakota* in the Sandwich Islands, and she spent a lot of time in dry dock after that."

"Maybe," the pilot said. "Makes more sense than anything I thought of."

"It didn't work, though," Sam said. "We traded one of our fishing boats for their sub—and I hear they didn't even sink the fishing boat. I'll make that deal any day."

IV

Clarence Potter's promotion to brigadier general meant inheriting his luckless predecessor's office. Not being buried under the War Department had a couple of advantages. Now he could look out a window. There wasn't much point to one when all it would show was dirt. And now a wireless set brought in a signal, not just static.

He knew, of course, that Confederate wireless stations said only what the government—that is, the Freedom Party—wanted people to hear. Broadcasters could not tell too many lies, though. If they did, U.S. stations would make them sorry. Unjammed, U.S. broadcasts could reach far into the CSA, just as C.S. programs could be heard well north of the border.

And so, when a Confederate newsman gleefully reported that the Confederate Navy and the Royal Navy had combined to take Bermuda away from the United States, he believed the man. "In a daring piece of deception, HMS *Ark Royal* lured two U.S. carriers away from the island, making the joint task force's job much easier," the newscaster said.

Slowly, Potter nodded to himself. That must have been a nervy piece of work. The Royal Navy must have believed that Bermuda was worth a carrier. It hadn't had to pay the price, but it might have.

Eyeing a map, the Intelligence officer decided the British were dead right. The game had been worth the candle. With Bermuda lost, U.S. ships would have to run the gauntlet down the Confederate coast to resupply the Bahamas. He didn't think the United States could or would do it. Taking them away from the USA would probably fall to the Confederacy rather than Britain, but it would eliminate a threat to the state of Cuba and make it much harder for U.S. ships to move south and threaten the supply line between Argentina and the United Kingdom. Cutting that supply line was what had finally made Britain throw in the sponge in the Great War.

And if we take the Bahamas, what will we do with all the Negroes there? he wondered. That was an interesting question, but not one he intended to ask Jake Featherston. If he was lucky, Featherston would tell him it was none of his goddamn business. If he was unlucky, something worse than that would happen.

He didn't waste a lot of time worrying about it. As Confederates went, he was fairly liberal. But Confederates—white Confederates—did not go far in that direction. What happened to Negroes—in the Confederate States or out of them—wasn't high on his list of worries. Blacks inside the CSA deserved whatever happened to them, as far as he was concerned.

There, Anne Colleton would have completely agreed with him. He shook his head. He made a fist. Instead of slamming it down on the desk, he let it fall gently. He still couldn't believe she was dead. She'd been one of those fiercely vital people you thought of as going on forever. But life didn't work like that, and war had an obscene power all its own. What it wanted, it took, and an individual's vitality mattered not at all to it.

His fist fell again, harder this time. He was damned if he knew whether to call what he and Anne had had between them love. There probably wasn't a better name for it, even if the two of them had disagreed so strongly about so many things that they'd broken up for years, and neither one of them ever really thought about settling down with the other. Anne had never been the sort to settle down with a man.

"And neither have I, with a woman," Potter said softly. He tried to imagine himself married to Anne Colleton. Even if what they'd known had been love, the picture refused to form. Domestic bliss hadn't been in the cards for either one of them.

Potter laughed at himself. Even if he'd had a wife who specialized in domestic bliss—assuming such a paragon could exist in the real world—he wouldn't have had time to enjoy it. When he wasn't here at his desk, he was unconscious on a cot not far away. The coffee he poured down till his stomach sizzled made sure he was unconscious as little as possible.

He lit a cigarette. Tobacco didn't help keep him awake. It did, or could every now and then, help him focus his thoughts. Since the war started, getting instructions to the spies the CSA had in the USA and getting reports back from them had grown a lot harder than it was during peacetime.

Where was that roster? He pawed through papers till he found it. One of the Confederates who spoke with a good U.S. accent worked at a Columbus wireless station. Potter scribbled a note: *"Satchmo's Blues" at 1630 on the afternoon of the 11th, station CSNT.*

The note would go to Saul Goldman. Goldman would make sure the right song went out at the right time from the Nashville wireless station. The Confederate in Columbus listened to CSNT every afternoon at half past four. If he heard "Satchmo's Blues," he made his coded report when he went on the air in the wee small hours. Someone on the Confederate side of the line would hear and decipher it. Potter didn't know all the details, any more than Goldman knew exactly who would be listening for that tune. Someone was listening. Someone would hear. That was all that mattered.

Sooner or later, some bright young damnyankee would be listening, too, and would put two and two together and come up with four. At that point, the Confederate in Columbus would start suffering from a sharply lower life expectancy, even if he didn't know it yet.

Or maybe, if the men from the USA were sneaky enough, they wouldn't shoot the Confederate spy. Maybe they would turn him instead, and make him send their false information into the CSA instead of the truth.

How would the people who listened and deciphered know the agent had been turned? How would they keep the Confederates from acting on damnyankee lies? Mirrors reflecting into other mirrors reflecting into other mirrors yet . . . Intelligence was that kind of game, a chess match with both players moving at the same time and both of them blindfolded more often than not.

Somewhere not far from Columbus, some other Confederate

spy would be waiting for a different signal. He would have a different way to respond. If what he said didn't match what the fellow at the wireless station reported, a red flag would—with luck—go up. Potter snorted. Without luck, nobody would notice the discrepancy till too late. In that case, some Confederate soldiers would catch hell. It wasn't as if soldiers didn't catch hell all the time.

Air-raid sirens began to warble. That was what the instruction posters said, anyhow. *When the siren begins to warble, that is your signal to take cover.* It didn't sound like a warble to Potter. It sounded like the noise a mechanical dog would make if a giant stepped on its tail. HOWLhowlHOWLhowlHOWLhowl endlessly, maddeningly repeated . . .

The damnyankees had nerve, coming over Richmond in broad daylight—either nerve or several screws loose. Potter locked up his important papers in a desk drawer, then headed for the stairway to the shelters in the War Department subbasement—not far from where he'd formerly worked, in fact. He'd just reached the stairwell when the antiaircraft guns started banging away. "I hope we shoot down all of those bastards," a young lieutenant said.

"That would be nice," Potter agreed. "Don't hold your breath till it happens, though." The lieutenant gave him an odd look. It was one he'd seen a great many times before. "Don't worry, sonny," he said. "I'm as Confederate as you are, no matter what I sound like."

"All right, sir," the lieutenant said. "I don't reckon they'd make you a general if you weren't." His voice was polite. His face declared he didn't altogether believe what he was saying. Potter had seen that before, too.

Bombs were already screaming down when Potter got into the shelter. It was hot and crowded and not very comfortable. The ground shook when bombs started bursting. The lights overhead flickered. The shelter would be a hell of a lot less pleasant if they went out. Crammed into the sweaty dark with Lord only knew how many other people . . . He shuddered.

More bombs rained down. A woman—a secretary? a cleaning lady?—screamed. Everybody in the shelter seemed to take a deep breath at the same time, almost enough to suck all the air out of the room. One scream had probably come close to touching off a swarm of others.

Crump! The lights flickered again. This time, they did go out, for about five seconds—long enough for that woman, or maybe a different one, to let out another scream. A couple of men made noises well on the way toward being screams, too. Then the lights came on again. Several people laughed. The mirth had the high, shrill sound of hysteria.

Behind Potter, somebody started saying, "Jesus loves me. Jesus loves me. Jesus loves me," again and again, as relentless as the air-raid siren. Potter almost shouted at him to make him shut up— almost but not quite. Telling the man that maybe Jesus loved him but no one else did might make the Intelligence officer feel better, but would only wound the poor fellow who was trying to stay brave.

The next explosions were farther away than the blast that had briefly knocked out the lights. Potter let out a sigh of relief. It wasn't the only one.

"How long have we been down here?" a man asked.

Potter looked at his watch. "Twenty-one—no, twenty-two— minutes now."

Several people loudly called him a liar. "It's got to be hours," a man said.

"Feels like years," someone else added. Potter couldn't very well quarrel with that, because it felt like years to him, too. But it hadn't been, and he was too habitually precise to mix up feelings and facts.

After what seemed like an eternity but was in truth another fifty-one minutes, the all-clear sounded. "Now," somebody said brightly, "let's see if anything's left upstairs."

Had the War Department taken a direct hit, they would have known about it. Even so, the crack spawned plenty of nervous laughter. People began filing out of the shelter. This was only the third or fourth time the USA had bombed Richmond. Everybody felt heroic at enduring the punishment. And someone said, "Philadelphia's bound to be catching it worse."

Half a dozen people on the stairs nodded. Potter started to himself. He wondered why. Yes, there was a certain consolation in the idea that the enemy was hurting more than your country. But if he blew you up, or your family, or your home, or even your office, what your side did to him wouldn't seem to matter so much . . . would it? Vengeance couldn't make personal anguish go away . . . could it?

That near miss hadn't blown up Potter's office. But it had blown the glass out of the windows, except for a few jagged, knife-edged shards. The soles of his shoes crunched on glittered pieces of glass in the carpet. More sparkled on his desk. He couldn't sit down on his swivel chair without doing a good, thorough job of cleaning it. Otherwise, he'd get his bottom punctured. He shrugged. A miss *was* about as good as a mile. An hour or two of cleanup, maybe not even that, and he'd be back on the job.

Lieutenant-Colonel Tom Colleton peered north toward Grove City, Ohio. It wasn't much of a city, despite the name; it couldn't have held more than fifteen hundred people—two thousand at the outside. What made it important was that it was the last town of any size at all southwest of Columbus. Once the Confederate Army drove the damnyankees out of Grove City, they wouldn't have any place to make a stand this side of the capital of Ohio.

Trouble was, they knew it. They didn't want to retreat those last eight miles. If the Confederates got into Grove City, they could bring up artillery here and add to the pounding Columbus and its defenses were taking. U.S. forces were doing their best to make sure that didn't happen.

Grove City lay in the middle of a fertile farming belt. Now, though, shells and bombs were tearing those fields, not tractors and plows. Barrel tracks carved the most noticeable furrows in the soil. The smell of freshly turned earth was sweet in Colleton's nostrils; he crouched in a foxhole he'd just dug for himself, though the craters pocking the ground would have served almost as well.

More shells churned up the dirt. The U.S. soldiers had an artillery position just behind Grove City, and they were shooting as hard and as fast as they could. Somewhere not far away, a Confederate soldier started screaming for his mother. His voice was high and shrill. Tom Colleton bit his lip. He'd heard screams like that in the last war as well as this one. They meant a man was badly hurt. Sure enough, these quickly faded.

Tom cursed. He was in his late forties, but his blond, boyish good looks and the smile he usually wore let him lie ten years off his age. Not right now, not after he'd just listened to a soldier from his regiment die.

And when bombs or shells murdered his men, he couldn't help wondering whether his sister had made those same noises just before she died. If Anne hadn't been in Charleston the day that goddamn carrier chose to raid the city . . . If she hadn't, the world would have been a different place. But it was what it was, and that was all it ever could be.

"Wireless!" Tom shouted. "God damn it to hell, where are you?"

"Here, sir." The soldier with the wireless set crawled across the riven ground toward the regimental commander. The heavy pack on his back made him a human dromedary. "What do you need, sir?"

"Get hold of division headquarters and tell 'em we'd better have something to knock down those Yankee guns," Colleton answered. "As best I can make out, they're in map square B-18."

"B-18. Yes, sir," the wireless operator repeated. He shouted into the microphone. At last, he nodded to Tom. "They've got the message, sir. Permission to get my ass back under cover?"

"You don't need to ask me that, Duffy," Tom said. The wireless man crawled away and dove into a shell hole. Soldiers said two shells never came down in the same place. They'd said that in the Great War, too, and often died proving it wasn't always true.

Within a few minutes, Confederate shells began falling on map square B-18. The bombardment coming down on the Confederate soldiers south of Grove City slowed but didn't stop. Tom Colleton shouted for Duffy again. The wireless man scrambled out of the shell hole and came over to him, his belly never getting any higher off the ground than a snake's. Duffy changed frequencies, bawled into the mike once more, and gave Tom a thumbs-up before wriggling back to what he hoped was safety.

Dive bombers screamed out of the sky a quarter of an hour later. *Screamed* was the operative word; the Mules (soldiers often called them Asskickers) had wind-powered sirens built into their nonretractable landing gear, to make them as demoralizing as possible. They swooped down on the U.S. artillery so fast and at so steep an angle, Tom thought they would surely keep going and crash, turning themselves into bombs, too.

He'd watched Mules in action before. They always made him worry that way. He'd seen a couple of them shot down—if Yankee fighters got anywhere near them, they were dead meat. But they didn't fly themselves into the ground, no matter how much it looked as if they would. One after another, they released the bombs they carried under their bellies, pulled out of their dives, and, engines roaring, raced away at not much above treetop height.

Mules aimed their bombs by aiming themselves at their target. They were far more accurate than high-altitude bombers—they were, in effect, long-range heavy artillery. Counterbattery fire hadn't put the U.S. guns out of action. A dozen 500-pound bombs silenced them.

"Let's go, boys!" Colleton yelled, emerging from his foxhole and dashing forward. His men came with him. If he'd called for them to go forward and hung back himself, they wouldn't have moved nearly so fast. He'd discovered that in the Great War. He was one of the lucky ones. He'd had only minor wounds, hardly even enough to rate a Purple Heart. An awful lot of brave Confederate officers—and damnyankees, too—had died leading from the front.

Even without their artillery, the U.S. soldiers in Grove City didn't intend to leave. Tracer rounds from several machine guns sketched orange lines of flame across the fields. Men went down, some taking cover, others because they'd been hit. The volume of fire here was less than it had been on the Roanoke front; this was a war of movement, and neither side got the chance to set up defenses in depth the way both had a generation earlier. But even a few machine guns could take the starch out of an attacking infantry regiment in a hurry.

"Goddammit, where the hell are the barrels?" somebody shouted.

Whoever that fellow was, noncom or more likely private, he thought like a general. Barrels—a few stubborn Confederates called them tanks, the way the British did—were the answer to machine-gun fire. And here they came, five—no, six—of them, as if the belly-aching soldier really had summoned them. The U.S. machine guns started blazing away at them. You needed a bigger door knocker than a machine-gun round to open them up, though. The bullets sparked off their butternut-painted armor.

The barrels also carried machine guns. They started shooting up the U.S. position at the southern edge of Grove City. And the barrels' cannon spoke, one by one. One by one, the Yankees' machine guns stopped shooting back. Rifle fire still crackled, but rifle fire couldn't wreck advancing foot soldiers the way machine guns could.

"Let's go!" Tom Colleton yelled again. He panted as he dashed forward. He'd been a kid during the Great War. He wasn't a kid any more. He flinched when a bullet whined past him. Back then, he'd been sure he would live forever. Now, when he had a wife and kids to live for, he knew all too well that he might not. He didn't hang back, but part of him sure as hell wanted to.

Young soldiers on both sides still thought they were immortal. A man in U.S. green-gray sprang up onto a Confederate barrel. He yanked a hatch open and dropped in two grenades. The barrel became a fireball. The U.S. soldier managed to leap clear before it blew, but Confederate gunfire cut him down.

Five trained men and a barrel, Tom thought glumly. The damnyankee had thrown his life away, but he'd made the Confederates pay high.

Another barrel hit a buried mine. Flames spurted up from it, too, but most of the crew got out before the ammunition inside started cooking off. The remaining barrels and the Confederate infantry pushed on into Grove City. Tom waited for barrels painted green-gray to rumble down from the north and stall the Confederate advance. He waited, but it didn't happen. The USA didn't seem to have any barrels around to use.

They're bigger than we are, Colleton thought as he peered around the corner of a house whose white clapboard sides were newly ventilated with bullet holes. *They're bigger than we are, but we're a lot readier than they are. If we'd waited much longer, we'd be in trouble.*

But the Confederate States hadn't waited, and their armies were going forward. In the last war, they'd thrust toward Philadelphia, but they'd fallen short and been beaten back one painful mile at a time. Other than that, they'd fought on the defensive all through the war. Tom had been part of it from first day till last, and he'd never once set foot on U.S. soil.

Here he was in Ohio now. Jake Featherston had always said he would do better than the Whigs had when it came to running a war against the United States. Tom had had his doubts. He'd never sold his soul to the Freedom Party, the way he often thought his sister had. You couldn't argue with results, though. A couple of weeks of fighting had taken the Confederacy halfway from the banks of the Ohio River to the shores of Lake Erie. If another two or three weeks could take the CSA the rest of the way . . .

If that happens, the United States get to find out what it's like when an axe comes down on a snake. Both halves wiggle for a while afterwards, but the damn thing dies just the same. Tom grinned fiercely, liking the comparison.

Freight-train roars in the sky reminded him that the damn-yankees weren't cut in half yet. Half a dozen soldiers yelled, "Incoming!" at the same time. The Mules might have knocked out the battery that had flayed the regiment as it advanced, but the USA had more guns where those came from.

And, along with the usual roaring and screaming noises shells made as they flew toward their targets, Tom also heard sinister gurgles. He knew what those gurgles meant. He'd known for more than a quarter of a century, though he'd hoped he might forget what he knew.

"Gas!" he shouted. "They're shooting gas at us!" He pulled his mask off his belt and thrust it over his face. He had to make sure the straps that held it on were good and tight and that it sealed well against his cheeks. No soldier who wanted to make sure he was safe against gas could afford to grow a beard.

Shells thudded home, one after another. Most were the robust black bursts with red fire at their heart that Tom had long known and loathed. A few of them, though, sounded more like sneezes. Those were the gas shells going off. Tom wondered what kind of gas the Yankees were using. A mask alone wasn't really enough protection against mustard gas. It would blister your hide as well as your lungs. A few gas specialists wore rubberized suits along with their masks. A rubberized suit in Ohio in July was torture of its own.

The gas would also torment the defenders in Grove City, who were falling back toward the racetrack at the north end of town. The Yankee high command didn't seem to care. The more they slowed down the Confederates, the longer they would have to fortify Columbus.

Tom wondered if his own side could be that ruthless. Part of him hoped so, if the need ever arose. But he prayed with every fiber of his being that such a day of need would never come.

Brigadier General Abner Dowling stood by the side of Highway 62, watching U.S. soldiers fall back from the south and into Columbus.

Dowling didn't think he had ever seen beaten troops before. In the Great War, he'd watched George Custer throw divisions into the meat grinder, sending them forward to take positions that couldn't possibly be taken. Where divisions went forward, regiments would come back. Before barrels changed the way the war was fought, machine guns and artillery made headlong attacks impossibly, insanely, expensive—which hadn't stopped Custer from making them, or even slowed him down.

Those who lived through his folly had been defeated, yes. By the nature of things, what else could have happened to them? But they hadn't been *beaten,* not the way these soldiers were. They'd been ready to go back into the fight as soon as the trains disgorged some more newly minted, shiny troops to go in with them.

Looking at the men trudging up the asphalt towards and then past him, Dowling knew they weren't going to be ready for battle again any time soon. They weren't running. Most of them hadn't thrown away their Springfields. Their eyes, though . . . Their eyes were the eyes of men who'd seen hell come down on earth, who'd seen it, been part of it, and had no intention of being part of it again for a long time, if ever.

Beside Dowling stood Captain Max Litvinoff, a short, skinny young man with a hairline mustache. The style was popular these days, but Dowling didn't think much of it. He was used to the bushier facial adornments men had worn in years gone by. He didn't think much of Captain Litvinoff, either. Not that the man wasn't competent—he was. He was, if anything, the USA's leading expert on gas warfare. That by itself was plenty to give Dowling the cold chills.

"If we are to hold this city, sir, we need a wider application of the special weapons." Litvinoff's voice was high and thin, as if it hadn't quite finished changing. He wouldn't call poison gas poison gas, from which Dowling concluded his conscience bothered him. If he used an innocuous-sounding name, he wouldn't have to think about what his toys actually did.

"We've already used enough gas to kill everything between the Ohio and here, haven't we, Captain?" Dowling growled.

Behind the lenses of his spectacles, Litvinoff's eyes registered hurt. "Obviously not, sir, or the opposing forces would not have succeeded in advancing this far," he replied.

"Right," Dowling said tightly. "Have we really accomplished anything by using gas? Except to make sure that Featherston's bastards are using it, too, I mean?"

"Sir, don't you think it likely that we would be in an even worse situation if we were not using gas?" Litvinoff replied. "The Confederates would be under any circumstances, would you not agree?"

Dowling muttered under his breath. However much he didn't want to, he did agree with that. Jake Featherston's main goal in life was to kill as many U.S. soldiers as he could, and he wasn't fussy about how he did it. As for Litvinoff's other comment, though . . . Dowling asked, "Captain, how in damnation *could* we be in a worse situation than we are now? If you can tell me that one, you take the prize."

You Take the Prize was the name of a popular quiz show on the wireless. Dowling listened to it every once in a while. Part of the attraction, for him, was finding out just how ignorant the American people really were. By the way Max Litvinoff blinked, he'd not only never listened to the show, he'd never heard of it.

"What do you recommend, sir?" he asked.

"How about going back in time about five years and building three times as many barrels as we really did?" Dowling said. Captain Litvinoff only shrugged. However good that sounded, they couldn't do it. What *could* they do? Dowling wished he knew.

Soldiers weren't the only people retreating into Columbus. Civilian refugees kept right on clogging the roads. Naturally, nobody in his right mind wanted to hang around where bullets and shells were flying. And a good many people didn't want to live where the Stars and Bars flew. Three generations of enmity between USA and CSA had drilled that into citizens of the United States. What nobody had told them before the war was that running for their lives wasn't the smartest thing they could have done.

Had they sat tight, the fighting would have passed them by. On the road, they kept blundering into it again and again. And Confederate pilots had quickly discovered that the only thing that blocked a highway better than a swarm of refugees was a shot-up, bombed-out swarm of refugees. U.S. propaganda claimed they attacked refugee columns for the fun of it. Maybe they had fun doing it, but it was definitely business, too.

Dowling wished he hadn't thought of air attacks just then.

Sirens began yowling, which meant the Y-range gear had picked up Confederate airplanes heading for Columbus. Those rising and falling electrified wails were enough to galvanize soldiers where nothing else had been able to. They scrambled off the road, looking for any cover they could find.

Civilians, by contrast, stood around staring stupidly. To them, the air-raid sirens were just one more part of the catastrophe that had overwhelmed their lives. Maybe this bunch had never been attacked from the air before. If not, they were about to lose their collective cherry.

Captain Litvinoff nudged Dowling. "Excuse me, sir," he said politely, "but shouldn't we think about finding shelter for ourselves?"

Dowling could already hear airplane engines. Overeager anti-aircraft gunners began shooting too soon. Black puffs of smoke started dotting the sky. "I think it's too late," Dowling said. "By the time we can run to a house, they'll be on top of us." He threw himself down on the ground, wishing he had an entrenching tool.

Litvinoff flattened out beside him. "What will the United States do if we are killed on account of this incaution?" he asked.

By the way he said it, the USA would have a tough time going on if the two of them got hit. Also by the way he said it, *he* was the one the country would particularly miss. Dowling didn't blame him for that. Any officer who didn't think he was indispensable was too modest for his own good.

On the other hand, reality needed to puncture egotism every once in a while. "What will the United States do?" Dowling echoed. "Promote a colonel and a first lieutenant and get on with the goddamn war."

Captain Litvinoff sent him a wounded look. That was the least of his worries. As he answered, his voice had risen to a shout to make itself heard above the rapidly rising roar of the Confederate bombers. *Mules,* Dowling thought as the airplanes screamed down. No other machines made that horrible screech or had those graceful gull wings.

They seemed to be diving straight down. Dowling knew they weren't, knew they couldn't be, but that was how it seemed just the same. "Crash, you bastards!" he shouted. "Fly it right into the ground!"

The Mules didn't, of course, but that bellowed defiance made him feel better. He pulled his .45 out of its holster and banged away at the Confederate dive bombers. That also did no good at all. He consoled himself by thinking that it might. He wasn't the only one shooting at the airplanes. Several other soldiers were doing the same. Every once in a while, he supposed they might bring one down by dumb luck. Most of the time, they didn't.

Then the bombs fell from the Mules' bellies. The airplanes leveled off and zoomed away. Blast picked Dowling up and slammed him down on the dirt as if it were a professional wrestler with the strength of a demon. "Oof!" he said. He tasted blood. It ran down his face, too. When he raised a hand, he discovered it came from a bloody nose. It could have been worse.

A few feet away, Max Litvinoff was trying to get his feet under him. By his dazed expression, he might have taken a right to the kisser. Missing glasses accounted for some of that. Without them, he looked even more confused than he was. He also had a bloody nose, and a cut on one ear that dripped more blood down onto the shoulder of his uniform tunic.

Dowling pointed. "Your spectacles are a couple of feet to the left of your left foot, Captain."

"Thank you, sir." Litvinoff plainly had to think about which foot was his left. He groped around on the grass till he found the eyeglasses, then set them on the bridge of his beaky nose. He peered over at Dowling with a worried frown. "I'm afraid I must have suffered some sort of head injury, sir. You look clear enough through one eye, but with the other one I might as well not have the glasses on at all."

"Captain, if you check them, I think you'll discover that you've lost one lens," Dowling said.

Litvinoff raised a shaky forefinger. When he almost poked himself in the left eye, he said, "Oh," in a small, wondering voice. After a moment, he nodded. "Thank you again, sir. That hadn't occurred to me." Another pause followed. "It should have, shouldn't it? I don't believe I'm at my best."

"I don't believe you are, either," Dowling said. "Unless I'm wrong, you got your bell rung there. If that bomb had hit a little closer, the blast might have done us in."

"Yes." Litvinoff looked down at himself. He seemed to realize for the first time that he was bleeding. The damage wasn't serious, but at the moment he was unequipped to do anything about it.

Dowling plucked a handkerchief from his own trouser pocket and dabbed at the younger man's nose and at his cut ear. "That's definitely a wound, Captain. I'll write you up for a Purple Heart."

"A Purple Heart? Me?" That needed a while to penetrate, too. Dowling suspected Litvinoff's likely concussion was only part of the reason. The gas specialist had done most of his work at the War Department offices back in Philadelphia. Thinking of himself as a front-line soldier wouldn't seem easy or natural. Slowly, a smile spread across his face as the idea sank in. "That will impress people, won't it?"

"Provided you live long enough to show off your pretty medal, yes," Dowling answered. "I'll be damned if I know how good your chances are, though."

As if to underscore his words, Confederate shells began landing a few hundred yards away. The bursts walked closer. "No special weapons in any of those," Captain Litvinoff said distinctly. Concussed or not, he still knew his main business.

"Happy day," Dowling said. "They can kill us anyway, you know." Litvinoff looked astonished again. That hadn't occurred to him, either. Abner Dowling wished it hadn't occurred to *him*.

Properly speaking, Armstrong Grimes hadn't had enough training to go into combat. After the Confederates bombed Camp Custer, nobody seemed to worry about anything like that. He had a uniform. They gave him a Springfield all his own. True, he was still missing some of the finer points of the soldier's art. The theory seemed to be that he could pick those up later. If he lived.

Getting bombed had gone a long way toward clearing notions of immortality from his head. The first bullet that cracked past his head missed him but slew several more illusions. Bombs fell out of the sky, the way rain or snow did. That bullet had been different. That bullet had been *personal*. He'd dug his foxhole deeper as soon as it flew by.

West Jefferson, the town he and his fellow frightened foot soldiers were supposed to defend, lay about fifteen miles west of Columbus. It was on the south bank of Little Darby Creek, and had probably been a nice place to live before the Confederates started shelling it. Brick houses from the nineteenth century stood side by side with modern frame homes. When shells hit the brick houses, they crumbled to rubble. When shells hit the frame homes, they started to burn. Six of one, half a dozen of the other, as far as Armstrong could see.

Up ahead, something that might have been a man in a butternut uniform moved. Armstrong Grimes still had a lot to learn about being a soldier, but he understood shooting first and asking questions later. He raised the Springfield to his shoulder, fired, worked the bolt, and fired again.

Maybe he'd hit the Confederate soldier. Maybe the fellow flattened out and took cover. Or maybe there hadn't been a Confederate soldier in those bushes to begin with. Any which way, Armstrong saw no more movement. That suited him fine.

His company commander was a pinch-faced, redheaded captain with acne scars named Gilbert Boyle. "Keep your peckers up, boys!" Boyle called. "We've got to make sure Featherston's fuckers don't ford the creek."

A corporal named Rex Stowe crouched in a foxhole about ten feet from Armstrong's. He was swarthy, unshaven, and cynical. A cigarette dangled from one corner of his mouth. It jerked up and down as he said, "Yeah, keep your pecker up. That way, Featherston's fuckers can shoot it off you easier."

The mere thought made Armstrong want to drop his rifle and clutch himself right there. He'd seen a lot of horrible things since the war started. He hadn't seen *that* yet, for which he thanked the God in Whom he believed maybe one morning in four.

A submachine gun stuttered, somewhere not far away. Bullets stitched up dirt and grass in front of Armstrong. Then, when the burst went high the way they always did, more rounds clipped twigs from the willow tree behind him. He tried to disappear into his foxhole. It wasn't big enough for that, but he did his damnedest.

Stowe fired a couple of times in the direction from which the burst had come. More submachine-gun fire answered him. He curled up in his hole, too. "I think everybody in the whole goddamn Confederate Army carries an automatic weapon," he growled, a mixture of disgust and fear in his voice.

"Seems that way," Armstrong agreed. "There's always more of us, but they put more lead in the air."

After another burst of fire, this from a new direction, a Southern voice called, "You Yankees! Y'all surrender now, get yourselves out o' the fight, make sure y'all live through the war!"

"No," Captain Boyle shouted back, and then, "Hell, no! You want us, you come get us. It won't be as easy as you think."

"You'll be sorry, Yank," the Confederate answered. "Sure you don't want to change your mind? . . . Going once . . . Going twice . . . Gone! All right, you asked for it, and now you'll get it."

Armstrong's father went on and on about Confederate attacks during the Great War, about artillery barrages and then thousands of men in butternut struggling through barbed wire toward waiting machine guns and riflemen. Merle Grimes had a Purple Heart and walked with a cane. Armstrong thought he was a blowhard, but he'd never figured his old man didn't know what he was talking about.

These Confederates, though, had a different set of rules—or maybe just a different set of tools. Instead of an infantry charge to clear the U.S. soldiers out of West Jefferson, four barrels rattled forward.

Foot soldiers ran along with the machines, but Armstrong hardly noticed them. He started shooting at the lead barrel. His bullets threw off sparks as they ricocheted from the frontal armor. For all the harm they did, he might as well have been throwing peaches.

"Where's our barrels?" he shouted. It was, he thought, a hell of a good question, but no one answered it.

Behind an oak tree, three artillerymen struggled to make a 1.5-inch antibarrel gun bear on the Confederate machines. "Fire!" yelled the sergeant in charge of the gun. The shell exploded between two of the barrels. The gun crew reloaded. The sergeant shouted, "Fire!" again. This time, they scored a hit. As flame and smoke spurted from a barrel, the artillerymen whooped in delight.

They didn't enjoy their triumph long. Two of the surviving barrels turned their machine guns and cannon fire on them. The splinter shield on their piece wasn't big enough to protect them. Down they went, one after another. Armstrong didn't know what artillerymen learned while they trained. Whatever it was, it didn't include much about taking cover. Shell fragments hissed and squealed through the air, right past his head. *He* sure as hell ducked.

On came the three remaining Confederate barrels. They looked as big as houses to Armstrong. The soldiers who advanced with them also shot and shot and shot, making the U.S. defenders keep their heads down. Some of the C.S. foot soldiers carried submachine guns. Others had automatic rifles, which were even nastier weapons. Submachine guns fired pistol cartridges of limited range and hitting power. But an automatic rifle with a round as powerful as a Springfield's . . . that was very nasty news indeed.

"Hang tough, men!" Captain Boyle shouted. "We can stop them!"

The Confederate barrels shelled the houses on the south side of town. They knocked down a couple of them and started several new fires. Coughing at the smoke, Armstrong didn't think they accomplished much else.

In spite of Captain Boyle's commands, U.S. soldiers started slipping back towards and over Little Darby Creek. West Jefferson didn't seem worth dying for. Facing barrels and infantrymen with automatic weapons when they had none of their own looked like a bad bargain to more and more men.

"How long you going to stick, Corporal?" Armstrong asked. He figured he could honorably leave when Rex Stowe pulled out.

Stowe didn't answer. Armstrong looked over to his foxhole, fearing the noncom had stopped a bullet while he wasn't looking. But the foxhole was empty. Stowe had already decided this was a fight the U.S. Army wouldn't and couldn't win.

"Shit," Armstrong muttered. "You might have told me you were bugging out."

Escaping was harder than it would have been five minutes earlier. With the barrels and the Confederate foot soldiers so close, getting out of his foxhole was asking to get killed. Of course, staying where he was was liable to be tough on living to get old and gray, too.

Captain Boyle kept on yelling for everybody to stand his ground. "Screw you, Captain," Armstrong muttered. He looked back over his shoulder. If he ran like hell, he could get around the corner of that garage before anybody shot him—as long as he was lucky.

He didn't feel especially lucky. But he did feel pretty damn sure he'd get his head blown off if he hung around. Up! Run! Pounding boots. Bullets kicking up dirt around his feet. One tugging at his trouser leg like the hand of a friend. Others punching holes in the clapboard ahead. But none punching holes in him.

Panting, trotting along all doubled over to make himself a small target, he headed for the creek. He knew where the ford was. That had to be why the Confederates wanted West Jefferson. Soldiers could cross Little Darby Creek damn near anywhere. It wasn't so easy for barrels. They couldn't swim. They couldn't even wade all that well. They had to have shallow water to cross.

Captain Boyle had stopped yelling about standing fast. Maybe he'd seen the light. Maybe he was too dead to grumble any more. Either way, Armstrong didn't have to worry about disobeying orders now. He was going to do it, but he didn't have to worry.

The creek was crowded with men in green-gray floundering across to the north bank. Some of them carried their Springfields above their heads. Others had thrown away the rifles to get across faster. The discarded Springfields lay here and there on the south bank, the sun now and then glinting from a bayonet. Armstrong thought about throwing away his piece. In the end, he hung on to it. The Confederates were going to cross the creek, too, sure as hell they were. He'd need the rifle on the other side.

He hurried down toward the ribbon of water. He was only about thirty feet from the creek when a Confederate fighter skimmed along it, machine guns chattering with monstrous good cheer. Armstrong threw himself flat, not that that would have done him a hell of a lot of good. But the fighter pilot was shooting up the men already floundering across Little Darby Creek. They couldn't run, they couldn't hide, and they couldn't fight back. All they could do was go down like stalks of wheat before a harvester's blades.

The Hound Dog fighter roared away. Armstrong lifted his head out of the dirt. Bodies floated in the water. Next to them, men who hadn't been hit—and who had and who hadn't was only a matter of luck—stood as if stunned. Little Darby Creek ran red with blood. Armstrong had heard of such things. He'd never imagined they could be true.

But he couldn't afford to hang around here staring, either, not with C.S. soldiers and barrels coming up behind him any minute now. He scrambled to his feet and ran for the water. He splashed into it. It was startlingly cold. The stream came up to his belly button at the deepest. If the Hound Dog came back while he was fording it, he was likely a dead man. If he didn't ford it, though, he was also a goner.

He got across and, dripping, dashed for the bushes on the far bank. He flopped down behind them. Not ten feet away lay Corporal Stowe, rifle pointed toward the south. Out of curiosity just this side of morbid, Armstrong asked, "What would you have done if I'd kept going?"

Stowe didn't waste time pretending to misunderstand him. "Shot you in the back," he answered laconically.

"Figures," Armstrong said. He peered through the undergrowth, then stiffened. "Here they come." Sure as hell, the men approaching Little Darby Creek wore butternut and had on helmets of slightly the wrong shape. He drew a bead on a Confederate and squeezed the trigger. Down went the soldier in a boneless sprawl. *Got that bastard,* Armstrong thought, and swung the rifle towards a new target.

Plain City, Ohio, was a neat little town north and west of Columbus. Big Darby Creek chuckled through it. Shade trees sheltered the houses, and also the stores in the two-block shopping district. A fair number of Amish lived nearby; in peaceful times, wagons had mingled with motorcars on the roads. Had Irving Morrell been a man who cared to settle down anywhere, he could have picked plenty of worse places. Agnes and Mildred would have liked Plain City just fine.

At the moment, though, Morrell wasn't worried about what his wife and daughter might think of the place. He wanted to keep the Confederates from getting over Big Darby Creek as easily as they'd crossed Little Darby Creek a few miles to the south. Every thrust of their barrels put them closer to outflanking Columbus and threatening to encircle it.

Morrell knew the kind of defensive campaign he would have run if he'd had the barrels. If he'd had enough machines, he could have made his Confederate opposite number's life very unhappy. He'd already slowed the C.S. forces down several times. He counterattacked whenever he saw the chance. Trouble was, he didn't see it often enough.

"Ten years," he growled to Sergeant Michael Pound. "Ten mortal years! We figured the Confederates would never get back on their feet again, and so we sat there with our thumb up our ass."

"And now we're paying for it," the gunner agreed. "You and I both thought this would happen. If we could see it, why couldn't the War Department?"

What the War Department had seen was that barrels cost money, airplanes cost money, submersibles and airplane carriers cost money. It had also seen that, under twelve years of Socialist administrations, money was damned hard to come by. And it had seen that the United States had won the war and the Confederate States were weak, and if they got a little less weak, well, who cared, really? The United States were still stronger. They always would be, wouldn't they?

Well, no. Not necessarily.

Morrell stuck his head out of the cupola for a look around. Unless the Confederates planned on throwing a pontoon bridge across Big Darby Creek somewhere west of Plain City, they would have to come through here. This was where the ford was, where their barrels could easily get over the stream and keep pushing north. And he knew without being told that that was what they wanted to do. It was what he would have wanted to do if he'd worn butternut instead of green-gray. Whoever was in charge on the other side thought very much the way he did. It was like fighting himself in a mirror.

But the fellow on the other side had more barrels. He had more airplanes. And he had one other thing going for him. It was the edge the United States had had in 1914. The Confederates here were convinced they owed the USA one, and they intended to pay the United States back. It made them come on where more sensible soldiers would have hung back. Sometimes it got them killed in carload lots. More often, though, it let them squeeze through holes in the U.S. line that less aggressive troops never would have found.

Morrell had about two dozen barrels. More were supposed to be coming down from the north, but he didn't know when they'd get here. As far as he was concerned, that meant they were out of the fight. During a war, nobody ever showed up on time, except possibly the enemy. He'd found few exceptions to that rule during the Great War. So far in this one, he hadn't found any.

He couldn't see more than a couple of his barrels. They waited behind garages and in hedgerows and hull-down behind little swells of ground. All of them had secondary and tertiary positions to which they could fall back in a hurry. Morrell didn't like standing on the defensive. He would much rather have attacked. He didn't have the muscle to do it. If he was going to defend, he'd do the best job he could. *Nothing comes cheap*—that was his motto.

A soldier in green-gray came pelting up a driveway toward him. "They're heading this way, sir!" he called.

"Give me today's recognition signal," Morrell said coldly.

"Uh, hamster-underground," this man said.

"All right. Tell me more." The Confederates had no trouble getting hold of U.S. uniforms. They didn't have much trouble finding men whose drawls weren't too thick. Add those two together and they'd made a couple of holes for themselves where none had been before, simply by telling the right lie at the right time. That made U.S. officers leery about trusting men they didn't know by sight.

With luck, U.S. soldiers in butternut were also confusing the enemy. Both sides had used such dirty tricks in the last war. They both seemed much more earnest about them this time around.

The man in green-gray pointed southwest. "Barrels kicking up dust, sir. You'll see 'em yourself pretty soon. And infantrymen moving up with 'em, some on foot, some in trucks."

"How many barrels?" Morrell asked. He worried about the Confederate soldiers in trucks, too. This war was being fought at a pace faster than men could march. The CSA seemed to understand that better than his own side did.

"Don't know for sure, sir," the man answered. *Was* he really a U.S. soldier? The Confederates could have wrung the signal out of a prisoner. He went on, "Looked like a good many, though."

Artillery started coming in out of the south. That argued the fellow was telling the truth. Morrell hoped all the civilians were out of Plain City. Artillery killed.

Up ahead, machine guns started rattling. They sealed the messenger's truth for Morrell. Up there, grizzled noncoms would be teaching their younger disciples the mysteries of the two-inch tap, mysteries into which they themselves had been initiated during the last war. Tap the side of the weapon so that it swung two inches to right or left, keep tapping back and forth through its whole arc of fire, and it would spit out a stream of bullets thick enough that advancing against it was death for foot soldiers.

Small-arms fire answered the machine guns. But it was not small-arms fire of the sort Morrell had heard in the Great War, not the steady *pop-pop-pop!* that came from bolt-action rifles. These stuttering bursts were like snippets of machine-gun fire themselves. Some of the Confederates had submachine guns, whose racket was relatively weak and thin. But others carried those damned automatic rifles that were young machine guns in their own right.

And here came the Confederate barrels. The lead machines did what they were supposed to do: they stopped and began taking out the U.S. machine-gun nests. Once those were silenced, the infantry could go forward without being bled white. But the Confederates didn't seem to suspect U.S. barrels were in the neighborhood. Stopping to fire gave irresistibly tempting targets.

"Pick your pleasure, Sergeant Pound," Morrell said with an odd, joyous formality.

"Yes, sir." Pound traversed the turret, peered through the range-finder, and turned a crank to elevate the gun ever so slightly. He barked a hyphenated word at the loader: "Armor-piercing!"

"Armor-piercing!" Sweeney set a black-tipped shell in the breech; high-explosive rounds had white tips.

Pound fired. The gun recoiled. The roar, Morrell knew, was softer inside the turret than it would have been if he had his head out the cupola. He coughed at the cordite fumes.

"Hit!" Pound shouted, and everyone in the crowded turret cheered and slapped everyone else on the back. Morrell popped up like a jack-in-the-box to get a better look at what was going on. Three Confederate barrels were burning. Men were bailing out of one, and U.S. machine-gun and rifle fire was cutting them down. The poor bastards in the other two barrels never had even that much chance to get away.

Now the C.S. barrel crews knew they weren't facing infantry alone. They did what Morrell would have done had he commanded them: they spread out and charged forward at top speed. A moving target was a tough target. And they had, however painfully, developed the U.S. position: now they knew where some of their assailants hid. A glancing blow from a shell made one of them throw a track. It slewed sideways and stopped, out of the fight. The rest came on.

Sergeant Pound fired twice in quick succession. The first round set a barrel on fire. The second missed. The Confederates started shooting back. A U.S. barrel brewed up. Ammunition exploded inside the turret. An enormous and horribly perfect smoke ring rose from what must have been the open cupola. Morrell hoped the men inside the barrel hadn't known what hit them.

He got on the wireless to his machines: "Fall back to your second prepared positions now!" He didn't want the Confederates outflanking his barrels, and he didn't want them concentrating their fire on the same places for very long, either.

His own barrel retreated with the rest. The second prepared position was under a willow tree that made the great steel behemoth next to invisible from any distance. He wished he could have offered more support to the foot soldiers, but his main task was to keep the Confederate barrels on this side of Big Darby Creek.

Sergeant Pound fired again. He swore instead of whooping: a miss. And then, as much out of the blue as a sucker punch in a bar fight, a shell slammed into Morrell's barrel.

The front glacis plate almost kept the round out—almost, but not quite. The driver and the bow machine gunner took the brunt of the hardened steel projectile. They screamed, but not for long. The loader likewise howled as the round smashed his leg before crashing through the ammunition rack—luckily, through a slot without a shell in it—and into the engine.

As smoke and flame began filling the turret, Morrell threw open the cupola. "Out!" he shouted to Pound. "I'll give you a hand with Sweeney."

"Right you are, sir," the gunner said, and then, to the loader, "Don't worry. It will be all right."

"My ass," Sweeney ground out.

They got him and themselves out of the barrel before ammunition started cooking off. One look at his leg told Morrell he'd lose it—below the knee, which was better than above, but a long way from good. A tourniquet, a dusting of sulfa powder, and a shot of morphine were all Morrell could do for him. He shouted for medical corpsmen. They took the wounded man away.

"Now we have to get out of this ourselves. That could be interesting." Michael Pound sounded more intrigued than alarmed.

U.S. barrels were falling back towards and then across the ford over Big Darby Creek. The Confederates pressed them hard. Morrell would have done the same thing. It might cost a few more casualties now, but the rewards were likely to be worth it.

The two barrel men splashed through the creek. A Confederate barrel whose machine gun was swinging their way took a round in the flank and caught fire. The crew lost interest in them and started bailing out. Morrell and Pound made it across and into the bushes on the far side. For the time being, the Confederates couldn't force a crossing here. But Morrell wondered how long that would last and whether they could get over the creek somewhere else.

Major Jonathan Moss was not the man he had been half a lifetime ago, not the bright young flying officer who'd gone into the Great War all bold and brave and chivalrous. The desperate campaign in the skies above Ohio and Indiana rubbed his nose in that.

Last time around, he'd been able to live practically without sleep for weeks at a time, and to make up for it when the weather was too bad to let him get his rickety machine off the ground. Now, more than a quarter of a century further on, he needed a rest every so often. Despite coffee and pep pills, he couldn't bounce from mission to mission as fast as the younger men in his squadron.

He went to a doctor at the airstrip just outside Winchester, Indiana, and asked what the fellow could do to help him. The doctor was a tall, skinny, middle-aged man with bags under his eyes and yellow hair heavily streaked with gray. His name was Clement Boardman; he went by Doc or Clem. After a brief pause to light a cigarette and take a deep drag, he said, "Goddammit, Major, if I had the fountain of youth, don't you think I'd use it on myself?"

"I don't want miracles," Moss said.

"Like hell you don't. I want 'em, too," Boardman said. "Difference between us is, I know I won't get 'em."

"What can I do?" Moss demanded.

"Shack up with an eighteen-year-old blonde," the doctor answered. "That'll have you walking on air for a few weeks, anyhow—if it doesn't remind you you're not a kid any more some other ways, either."

He didn't know how Moss' wife had died. The flier had to remind himself of that to keep from getting angry. He said, "I already know I can't screw like I did when I was in college. But that's just me. This is my country."

"All you can do is all you can do," Clem Boardman said. "If you fly into a tree or you get shot down because you're too goddamn sleepy to check six, what good does that do your country—or you?"

It was an eminently sensible question. Moss didn't want good sense, though. He wanted to be told what he wanted to hear. That he was thinking like a three-year-old was a telling measure of how tired he was, but he was too tired to realize it.

"Here. Take these." The doctor handed him two pills.

"What are they?" Moss asked suspiciously.

"They'll make a new man out of you." Boardman filled a glass from a metal pitcher of water. "Come on. Down the hatch. In my medical opinion, they're what you need."

"All right. All right." Moss swallowed both pills at once. He could take almost any number of pills at the same time. That had amazed, amused, and horrified his wife, who couldn't . . . and try as he would, he couldn't get Laura out of his mind. He wondered if she'd ever fade, even a little. He also still wondered about the pills. "I don't feel any different than I did before."

"Wait twenty minutes," Boardman said.

"Then what happens?"

"Your hair turns blue, your nose catches fire, you start spouting Shakespeare, you grow fins, and your balls swell up to the size of cantaloupes," Boardman answered, deadpan. "I told you, they'll make a new man out of you."

"I think maybe I like the old man better." Moss yawned. "Dammit, who knows what the Confederates are liable to do if I'm not up there to shoot 'em down?"

"You're not going to win the war singlehanded," Dr. Boardman said. "If you can't see that, you're in even worse shape than I thought."

Moss yawned again, enormously. The hinges of his jaws creaked. He'd been tired before, but he hadn't been sleepy. So he told himself, anyhow. But no matter what he told himself, he kept on yawning. Pointing an accusing finger at Boardman took real effort; his arm seemed to weigh half a ton. "God damn you, Doc, you slipped me a mickey," he said, his voice slurring more with every word.

"Guilty as charged," Boardman said cheerfully. "If you won't take care of yourself, somebody's got to do it for you."

Moss cussed him with sleepy sincerity. The pills took the edge off his inhibitions, and then more than the edge. They also left him swaying like a badly rooted tree in a high wind.

He never did remember blowing over. One minute, he was calling Doc Boardman every name in the book—or every name he could come up with in his ever more fuddled state. The next—so it seemed to him, anyhow—he was in a cot, still in uniform except for his hat and his shoes. He was also still sleepy as hell. He never would have awakened, except he had to piss fit to bust. He put on the shoes, staggered out to a slit trench, did what he needed to do, and then lurched back to the cot. He'd just realized he had a godawful hangover when he passed out again, still with the shoes on.

It hadn't gone away by the time he woke up again, some unknown while later. He'd done his share of drinking, and his share of waking up wishing he hadn't. This topped all of that. He had trouble remembering his name. His head didn't ache. It throbbed, as if bruised from the inside out. Cautiously, he looked down along the length of himself. No fins. He remembered that, all right. He looked again. Nothing wrong with his balls, either.

He needed to take another leak. The room spun around him when he stood up. He went out and did his business. When he came back, he found Dr. Boardman waiting for him. "How long have I been out?" he croaked.

"Two and a half days," Boardman answered. "You slept through an air raid. That's not easy. You slept through getting picked up and flung in a shelter trench. That's a hell of a lot harder. Of course, you had help."

"Two and a half days?" Moss shook his head, which made it want to fall off. "Jesus." His stomach growled fearsomely. He didn't think the doctor was lying. "Got to get something to eat. Got to get some coffee, too. Sure as hell can't fly like this. Feel like I'm in slow motion."

"You are," Dr. Boardman agreed. "But it'll wear off. And you're smart enough to realize you're stupid now, which you weren't before. This is progress. Food and coffee will do for you, yeah."

Moss plowed into scrambled eggs and a young mountain of fried potatoes. He washed them down with mug after tin mug of corrosive coffee partly tamed by lots of cream and sugar. Once he got all that inside him, he felt amazingly lifelike. But when he asked Boardman for clearance to fly, the doctor shook his head. "Why not?" Moss demanded irately.

"Because your reflexes are still shot," Boardman answered. "Tomorrow? Fine. Today? Nope. Let the pills wear all the way off. The Confederates haven't marched into Philadelphia while you were out, and I don't expect one more day with you on the sidelines will lose us the war."

He only laughed when Moss suggested what he could do to himself. But as it happened, Moss did fly out of Winchester late that afternoon. It wasn't a flight he much wanted to make, but he had less choice than he would have liked. The Confederates had come far enough north to let their heavy artillery start probing for the airstrip. That likely meant the town would fall before long. Sure as hell, Moss spotted barrels nosing up from the south when he took off.

The squadron came down at a field near Bluffton, a town about two-thirds of the way from Muncie to Fort Wayne. The town looked pleasant as Moss flew over it. It sat on the south bank of the Wabash River. The streets downtown were paved with red brick; those farther out were mostly just graveled. So many shade trees grew around the houses that some of those were hard to see from the air. Nobody'd bombed the place yet.

He wondered how long the landing field had been there. Not long, probably: it had been gouged out of the middle of a wheat field. Groundcrew men threw camouflage tarps over the fighters as they came in, but how much good would those do? How much good would anything do? Moss was gloomy as he headed for the tent where he'd flop that night. The field stuck out like a sore thumb. They hadn't mowed BOMB ME! in the wheat, but they might as well have.

As evening fell, trucks brought up three antiaircraft guns. More camouflage netting went over them. Camouflaged or not, they were still going to stick out, too. The younger pilots weren't worried about a thing. They laughed and joked and bragged about the havoc they'd wreak on the Confederates the next day.

Was I like that up in Canada in the last war? Moss wondered. He clicked his tongue between his teeth. He probably had been. Everybody'd been like that back then. Flying was brand new. It hadn't been around long enough to attract gray, middle-aged pilots who could see farther than the end of their noses.

Up in the sky, he still knew what he was doing. He'd proved it the only way you could: he'd gone into combat and come back alive. Down here? Down here, he wanted to talk with grownups. The only one anywhere close by who seemed to meet the description was Dr. Clement Boardman.

"Take a walk with me, will you, Doc?" Moss said.

Boardman glanced at him sidelong. By the evil gleam in his eye, he almost said something like, *You aren't my type.* But he didn't. Maybe the look on Moss' face convinced him it wasn't a good idea. They strode out into the night.

Crickets chirped. A whippoorwill sang mournfully. Off in the distance, a dog howled. Fireflies blinked on and off like landing lights. The muggy air smelled of growing things, and faintly of exhaust and hot metal. Moss' footfalls, and Boardman's, were almost silent on the soft ground.

When they'd gone a hundred yards or so from the tents, the doctor asked, "Well, what's on your mind now?"

"We're losing the war, aren't we?" Moss said bluntly.

Boardman stopped. He pulled out a pack of cigarettes, lit one, and offered them to Moss. The pilot shook his head. Boardman shrugged, dragged till the coal glowed red, and blew out a cloud of smoke. Only then did he answer, "Mm, I expect things could look a little better."

"What are we going to do?" Moss said. "We can't let Featherston take a bite out of us. He'll just want another one as soon as he can get it."

"Why are you asking me? I'm not the President. I didn't even vote for him." The doctor blew out more smoke. As always, what he exhaled smelled milder than the harsh stuff spiraling up off the cigarette.

Moss' Canadian law practice meant he hadn't voted for close to twenty years. He said, "It's either talk about it or start screaming, you know what I mean? It's not just *could look better.* Things don't look good. For God's sake, tell me I'm wrong. Make me believe it." Dr. Boardman walked along in silence. After a few steps, Moss realized that was all the answer he'd get. "Give me a smoke after all, would you?" he said, and Boardman did.

V

Jake Featherston had fought through the Great War in the First Richmond Howitzers. Even then, the name had been a misnomer; the artillery outfit had had quick-firing three-inch field guns—copies of the French 75—instead of the howitzers its gunners had served during the War of Secession and the Second Mexican War.

Nowadays, the First Richmond Howitzers used four-inch guns. They could fire a shell twice as heavy almost half again as far as the last war's models. But the principles hadn't changed one goddamn bit.

If the crew that was shelling damnyankee positions north of Fredericksburg, Virginia, was nervous about performing under the knowing eye of the President of the CSA, it didn't show. Bare to the waist and gleaming with sweat in the July sunshine, they loaded, aimed, and fired again and again. The gun pit in which they served their piece was bigger and deeper than the ones Jake remembered, but the gun was bigger, too. It needed more digging in.

A sergeant named Malcolm Clay commanded not only the gun but the battery of which it was a part. He was about thirty-five, blond with strawberry stubble on his cheeks and chin, and did a perfectly capable job. All the same, watching him, Jake smiled behind his hand.

He turned to Saul Goldman and asked quietly, "Did you put them up to this, or were they smart enough to come up with it on their own?"

Goldman looked silly in a helmet, the way a coal miner would have looked silly in a top hat: it wasn't his style at all. The director of communications conscientiously wore it just the same. Peering out from under the steel brim, he said, "I don't know what you're talking about, Mr. President."

"Hell you don't," Jake said genially. "I was a sergeant in charge of a battery, too. They let me run it on account of I could and I was good, but the bastards never would promote me." He raised his voice: "Clay! Come on over here!"

"Yes, sir?" Red dust kicked up from the noncom's boots as he obeyed. He smelled hot and sweaty, too, but it wasn't a nasty stink. He was working and sweating too hard for that.

"How'd you get command of this here battery?" Featherston asked.

"Sir, Captain Mouton got wounded four or five days ago, and I'm in charge till they drop another officer into his slot."

"No, goddammit." Jake shook his head. "It's your battery now, Lieutenant Clay. You can do the job, so you deserve the rank."

"Thank you very much, sir!" Sergeant—no, Lieutenant—Clay's eyes were a bloodshot blue. They shone now. His grin showed a missing front tooth.

"You're welcome," Featherston answered. "In this here war, people who deserve to be promoted are going to get promoted. Nobody's gonna get screwed over like I got screwed over twenty-five years ago."

"You won't be sorry, sir!" Clay exclaimed. "We'll give those damnyankees what-for—you wait and see. Freedom!" He shouted the Party greeting.

"Freedom!" Jake said. "On this front, what I want is for you to keep the Yankees from giving us what-for. That's what we need here: to stop those sons of bitches in their tracks. Can you do that?"

"Hell, yes," Clay said, and then, "Uh, yes, sir."

Jake Featherston laughed. "I understood you the first time. I used to do your job, remember?"

Newsreel cameras ground away. They would capture Jake daring to visit the front, brave Confederate soldiers blasting the hell out of the damnyankees, and as much other good news as they could find. Before long, the result would be in theaters all across the CSA, running in front of thrillers from before the war and, soon, melodramas that would help people see things the way the Freedom Party wanted them to.

U.S. artillery wasn't idle around here. Every so often, a few shells would come down on the Confederate positions behind the town of Fredericksburg. No doubt they did some harm, in the sense that they did wound or kill a few men in butternut. But Featherston, having fought here in the last war, knew Fredericksburg was a damn tough nut to crack. From where he was when the order came to cease firing, he could have slaughtered all the U.S. soldiers in the world if they'd kept coming at him, and they wouldn't have been able to do much to hurt him.

Things weren't quite the same this time around, of course. Bombers and barrels had both been babies in the Great War. They'd grown up now. If the USA got barrels across the Rappahannock, they might tear the defenses to pieces. They might—but it wouldn't be easy even so.

Saul Goldman plucked at his sleeve. "We've done everything we came here to do, Mr. President," he said, half good flunky, half mother herding would-be rebellious child on its way before it could get into trouble.

"All right, Saul," Featherston said indulgently. He could play the role of good little boy, too. He could play any role he wanted. If more than twenty years on the stump had taught him anything, it was how to do that.

He went back to Army of Northern Virginia headquarters, a few miles farther behind Fredericksburg—out of artillery range. There, Nathan Bedford Forrest III was hashing things out with Lieutenant General Hank Coomer, currently in charge of the army that had once belonged to Robert E. Lee. The two officers stood in front of a map table so big, they needed pointers to show what they wanted to do; their arms weren't long enough to reach.

"Dammit, they can't bring that off, Nate," Coomer was saying when Featherston walked into the middle of the argument. Like Forrest, he was a new man. He was just a few years past forty, and had been a lieutenant in the Great War. He came from no fancy-pants family; his father had pressed pants in Atlanta. He'd belonged to the Freedom Party since 1922.

Nathan Bedford Forrest III did some pointing of his own. "They can't bring it off *now*," he said. "But they're building up for it. Do you think some spoiling attacks on the flanks will disrupt them, make them spread out? Because we sure as hell don't want them pushing down toward Richmond with everything they've got."

Coomer scowled. When he did, a scar over his right eye pulled his eyebrow out of shape. The ribbon for the Purple Heart was among the fruit salad above the left breast pocket of his tunic. He said, "Even if they do get over the Rappahannock, we can stop 'em."

"Don't even let 'em try, not if you can help it," Jake said. "We've got to hang in here till what we're doin' farther west takes hold. They can hurt us bad right now if they get the chance. Later on, it'll be a hell of a lot harder for 'em. I don't believe they've quite figured that out yet."

"Some of them have," Forrest said. "That Morrell is squealing like a shoat caught in a fence. He knows what's going on."

"He's the bastard who took Nashville away from us last time," Coomer said. "He knows his business, all right."

"Damnyankees paying any attention to him?" Featherston asked.

"Not yet. Not by what they're putting into the Midwest," Forrest answered.

"Good. Outfuckingstanding, as a matter of fact," Jake said. "If we get where we're going, they are screwed."

"That's true, Mr. President," his chief of staff said. "But it's like any coin: it's got another side to it. What the damnyankees aren't sending to the *Schwerpunkt*, they *are* sending here."

"Damn right they are," Coomer agreed. "They want to make Virginia the *Schwerpunkt*, same as they did in the War of Secession. They reckon they can smash on through to Richmond and give us one in the nuts."

"I understand that. Your job is to make sure they don't do it," Jake said. "This isn't the best country for barrels—too many river barriers, not enough space between the mountains and the ocean—so we've got to keep blocking their punch till ours lands on their chin. If we can't do that, we've got a lot more trouble than we figured on."

He eyed Hank Coomer. *If you can't do that, you've got a lot more trouble than you ever figured on,* he thought. He'd pumped

Coomer up. He'd deflate him and pick somebody else just as fast if the fellow in charge of the Army of Northern Virginia let him down.

But Coomer said, "I understand what we need, sir." By the look in his eye, he probably understood what Featherston was thinking along with what he was saying. "All the bombing we're doing helps keep the Yankees from concentrating. And the sabotage problem on the roads and railways back of their lines is pretty bad."

"Damn well better be," Featherston said. He and Hank Coomer and Nathan Bedford Forrest III all had the identical gleam in their eye. At the end of the Great War, the United States had annexed as much of northern Virginia as they'd occupied, and they'd tacked it on to West Virginia. They could do that. They'd won the war, and the Confederate government was in no condition to tell them no. They could do it, but they couldn't make the people they'd done it to like it.

The annexed part of Virginia had given the USA trouble ever since they took it. Even the Whigs had had sense enough to encourage that. But the damnyankees wouldn't cough it up, because it protected Washington as long as they had it, and Washington had been threatened in the War of Secession, shelled in the Second Mexican War, and occupied during the Great War.

So what had been northern Virginia remained part of West Virginia. And it remained a place where roads were mined, where machine guns shot up trucks and troop trains and then disappeared, where switches got left half open, and where stretches of rail vanished into thin air so locomotives derailed. It also remained a place where the Yankees hanged anybody whose looks they didn't like, which only made survivors love them better still.

"We've got to hold 'em," Jake repeated. "If we can keep their attack here from coming off at all, that's best. If we can't, though, we've got to blunt it, contain it. We've *got* to, God damn it, on account of we can't afford to pull anything away from our own main attack."

"That's always been our problem," Forrest said. "The United States are bigger than we are. They've got more people than we do, and more factories, too. They can afford to make some mistakes. We can't. We've got to do it right the first time."

"We've done it before," Jake said. "We did it in the War of Secession and in the Second Mexican War. It was only in the Great War that the Whigs screwed the pooch."

They'd done the most obvious thing they could: they'd driven straight for Philadelphia. He'd known better than that this time, anyway. So far, everything was going fine. In the War of Secession, the damnyankees had tried to come down the Mississippi and cut the CSA in half. It hadn't worked. But turnabout was fair play. How would the USA do if it got split in two? Jake smiled hungrily. If things went well for just a little longer, he'd find out.

Gasoline rationing had come to Canada as soon as fighting broke out between the Confederate States and the United States. Mary Pomeroy resented that. The USA had made sure her country wasn't in the fight this time. Why did the Yanks have to steal gas from people who weren't at war? She knew the answer perfectly well: so they could use it against the Confederates. Knowing the answer didn't make her like it.

Not long after the war began, the wireless announced that gasoline rationing had also been imposed in the USA. That didn't make Mary any happier. The Yanks deserved it. Her own people didn't.

Rationing didn't keep her and Mort and Alec from going for a picnic one warm, bright Sunday afternoon. Such days didn't come to Rosenfeld all that often. Wasting this one would have felt sinful.

Mary did the cooking. They could have taken food from the Pomeroy diner, but it wouldn't have seemed like a real picnic to her then. She fried chicken and made potato salad and cole slaw and deviled eggs and baked two cherry pies. She filled an enormous pitcher with iced tea. And, though she didn't brew the beer herself, she didn't forget it, either.

By the time the picnic basket was full of food—and ice from the diner, to keep the cold things fresh—it weighed about a ton and a half. She happily let Mort show how strong he was by carrying it down the stairs to the Oldsmobile. "What did you put in here, an anvil?" he asked halfway down.

"That's right," she answered. "I roasted it special—it's one of Ma's old recipes." Alec giggled at that.

Mort just shook his head. "Ask a silly question, get a silly answer." But when he put the picnic basket in the back seat of the motor-

car, it made the springs visibly settle. Mary's husband shook his head
again. "Maybe there really is a roasted anvil in there."

"Is there, Mommy?" Alec asked eagerly. "Can I have a piece?"

"It'll make all your teeth fall out," Mary said. Her son didn't
seem to mind. He hadn't lost any teeth yet, but he had heard of the
tooth fairy. He liked the idea of getting money whenever a tooth
came out.

The road they took ran west, parallel to one of the railroad
tracks that came into Rosenfeld. Getting out of town wasn't hard;
inside of ten minutes, they'd put all memory of the place behind
them. To Mary, being out in the middle of that vast, gently rolling
farm country seemed the most natural thing in the world. Her husband and her son had grown up in town. They weren't used to a
horizon that stretched out forever.

After a while, Mort pulled off onto the shoulder and stopped the
auto. "As good a place as any," he said. "If I don't fall over lugging
the picnic basket away from the road . . ."

"It's not as heavy as all that," Mary said indignantly. She
grabbed blankets with one hand and Alec with the other.

Mort mimed staggering under the weight of the basket. Mary
mimed tripping him so he really would fall. They both laughed. She
spread out the blankets on the grass. Mort set down the basket with
a theatrical groan of relief. Even after he set it down, he kept listing
to the right, as if the weight had permanently bent him. Alec thought
that was funny, too.

Mort's condition improved remarkably once Mary opened a
Moosehead for him. He gulped about half the bottle and then sat
down. "Is that a hawk up there in the sky?" he asked, pointing towards a wheeling shape high overhead.

"No, that's a turkey vulture," Mary answered at once. "See how
the wings go slanting up a bit from the body? Hawks mostly carry
theirs flat."

"A vulture, is it?" Mort said. "It must know how worn out I am
from hauling that basket."

"Well, you can make it lighter so you won't have to carry so
much back to town," Mary said.

"I aim to do that very thing," he answered. "Let me have some
of the fried chicken, if you'd be so kind."

Before long, he'd turned a lot of chicken into bones. He liked light meat, Mary liked dark, and Alec was partial to giblets. They damaged the cole slaw and the potato salad, too, and the two grownups got rid of several bottles of beer. The bones, inevitably, drew ants. That vulture, or another one, soared past again. "We're not going to leave it much to eat," Mary said.

"Good," Mort said. "I'd rather gobble up all this good stuff myself than leave it for an ugly old bird with a bald pink head."

Every so often, a motorcar would rattle past. A couple of drivers honked their horns at the picnickers. When they did, Mary would wave and Mort solemnly lift the straw hat from his head. Alec paid no attention to salutations from the passersby. He was busy picking wildflowers and hunting bugs.

They'd been there a little more than an hour, and had reached the filling-in-the-corners stage of things, when an eastbound train roared past. That made Alec sit up and take notice, even if he'd ignored the passing autos. The great wheel-churning, smoke-belching locomotive was too grand and noisy to ignore. The engineer blew a long, mournful blast on his whistle, too. And once the steam engine had gone by, there were still all the boxcars and flatcars and tank cars to admire, and at last the caboose—this one painted yellow instead of the more usual red.

"Wow!" Alec's eyes shone. "I want to make one of those go when I get big."

"Maybe you will," Mort said. "It's a good job."

For all the sense he made to his son, he might as well have started speaking Eskimo. Alec couldn't imagine that being an engineer was work, and often hard work to boot. He would have paid, and paid anything he happened to have, for the privilege of riding in that thundering monster.

"Want another piece of pie, anyone?" Mary asked.

"Twist my arm," Mort said lazily. "Not too big a piece, or I'm liable to explode."

"Kaboom!" Alec yelled. "Can I have another piece, too, Mommy?" If he hadn't been eating cherry pie, the sticky red all around his mouth would have meant he'd got a split lip.

Mary was cutting him the new piece when a truck pulled off the road behind their Oldsmobile. It had a blue-gray body and a green-gray canvas top over the bed. Half a dozen soldiers who wore blue-gray uniforms and carried bayoneted rifles jumped out and advanced on the Pomeroys.

Their leader was a sergeant with a salt-and-pepper mustache. "What you do here?" he asked in bad English.

"We're having a picnic." Mort waved to the basket. "Want some fried chicken?"

The sergeant spoke to his men in French. They plundered the picnic hamper as if they'd heard food might be outlawed tomorrow. All the leftovers and all the beer—and even the iced tea—vanished inside of fifteen minutes. Mary knew she'd made more food than her family needed. She hadn't made enough for a squad of hungry Quebecois infantry.

"You too close to train tracks," the sergeant said, gnawing the last meat off a drumstick. "You no come here no more. It could be I have to run you in. But you not doing nothing bad, you just have food. You go home, you don't get in no trouble. You be happy, we be happy. *C'est bon?*"

"*Oui, monsieur. Merci.*" Mort had picked up a little French at the diner.

The Quebecois sergeant beamed at him. He ruffled Alec's reddish-brown hair. "*Mon fils,* he about this big," he said. He added something in French. His men got back in the truck. It rolled away.

"That was funny," Alec said.

"Ha," Mary said in a hollow voice. "Ha, ha. Ha, ha, ha."

Mort picked up the basket. It hardly weighed anything now. "So much for leftovers," he said, and then, "Damn Frenchy was right. We might as well go home now. There's sure no point to staying any more."

"If they do things like that, they only make people want to blow up trains," Mary said. "Can't they see?"

"Doesn't look like it," Mort said. "Me, I'd sooner blow up their barracks right now." He carried the basket to the auto and put it in.

Mary rolled up the picnic blankets. Alec tried to get rolled up in one of them. When he kept trying till he annoyed her, she swatted him on the bottom. After that, he behaved—for a little while. She tossed the blankets into the Olds. Mort, of course, had been joking about blowing up the garrison's headquarters in Rosenfeld. Mary had really contemplated it. She'd never done more than contemplate it, though. It wouldn't have been easy to pull off, and would have been risky.

Blowing up a train, on the other hand, or the tracks, or a train *and* the tracks . . . The Canadian prairie was enormously wide. Only bad luck the Frenchies' patrol had driven past while they were picnicking. To come out here by herself would be easy. In spite of the signs on the bulletin board inside the post office, it didn't seem dangerous.

For the first time, she looked forward to the day when Alec would go off to school. That would give her back several hours of free time during the day. She laughed. She hadn't even thought about free time in years.

"What's funny?" Mort asked.

"Nothing, really." She looked back toward where they'd been eating. "Have we got everything?"

"Everything the Frenchies didn't eat, yeah," her husband answered. "I'm surprised they didn't walk off with our plates and our spoons."

"They're the occupiers. They can do what they want," Mary answered.

Mort came back with something suggesting exactly what the Frenchies could do, and where. Alec's eyes got big and round. Mary was surprised, too, though she didn't show it. Mort had always been a Canadian patriot, but he'd always been a lukewarm Canadian patriot, one who grumbled about the occupation and disliked it, but who wasn't likely to do anything more than grumble. Now . . .

Experimentally, Mary said, "This is what the Yanks have done to us."

"I didn't mind the Yanks all that much," Mort said. "I guess maybe I'd got used to them—I don't know. But these Frenchies . . . I can't stand 'em. They think they're better than white people, and we just have to stand here and take it."

That was moderately promising, but only moderately. It wasn't anything that gave Mary a real handle to pull. But maybe she'd get one with him, sooner or later. Meanwhile . . . Meanwhile, she opened the passenger-side door. "Let's go home."

Mort started the auto. Making a U-turn back onto the road was easy—no traffic in either direction. Back toward Rosenfeld they went.

*   *   *

Like a lot of people in the Confederate States, Jefferson Pinkard had been waiting for *Over Open Sights* for a long time. The prison-camp boss liked having things spelled out for him. As long as they were, he didn't have to do a whole lot of thinking on his own. And he was an orderly man. If he had the rules, he'd follow them, the same way as the prisoners in Camp Dependable had to follow the rules he laid down.

Now, at last, he had a copy of *Over Open Sights* in his hand. So what if it had a cheap paper dust jacket over a cheap cloth binding? So what if it had cost him six dollars? Now he could get the straight dope, just the way Jake Featherston wanted him to have it.

And now he was one sadly confused stalwart. He'd skimmed through *Over Open Sights* the way a younger man might have gone through a sex book looking for the dirty parts. He'd found some of what he was after, too—stuff about revenge against blacks and against the USA that set his pulse pounding. But most of it was just . . . dull. Of all the things he'd expected from Jake Featherston, a dull book was among the last.

Jake was still settling accounts with people who'd wronged him back in the Great War. Many of them were dead now. He gloated over that. He was still refighting Freedom Party squabbles from the earliest days, still getting even with people the world had long forgotten. (For that matter, the world hadn't heard enough about most of them to forget them.)

And he was lecturing. He didn't just explain why he couldn't stand blacks. He went on and told why everybody had hated blacks since the beginning of time. That was more than Jeff wanted to know. He thought it was more than anybody wanted to know. He thought the same about the endless lectures on why the United States were dangerous to the Confederate States. Pinkard knew why. They were next door, they were too goddamn big, and they didn't like the CSA. How much more did you need to say?

Pinkard wasn't the only fellow in Camp Dependable to have shelled out for *Over Open Sights*. Damn near everybody had, as a matter of fact. Most of the guards were Freedom Party stalwarts. It would have looked funny if they hadn't bought the President's book.

Not getting a copy might not have landed them in trouble, but who wanted to take a chance on something like that?

But, now that people had it, they had to pretend they'd read it. They had to pretend that they'd kept track of everything, too, instead of dozing off partway through as if they were reading Shakespeare back in school.

Conversations were . . . interesting. "Hell of a book, ain't it?" Pinkard said to Mercer Scott one hot, sticky morning. Thunderheads were piling up in the sky to the south. Maybe it would rain and cut the humidity a little. Maybe, on the other hand, it would just tease, like a woman who wore tight dresses and shook her ass but wouldn't put out. Jeff would have been inclined to slap a woman like that around to get her to change her mind. He couldn't very well slap the weather around, though.

The guard chief's leathery face assumed a knowing expression. "Goddamn right it is," he said, and paused to light a cigarette. After a couple of drags, Scott added, "Tears the goddamn niggers a new asshole."

"Oh, you bet," Pinkard agreed. He lit a cigarette, too. After that welcome pause, he said, "And he really lays into the damnyankees, too."

"Fuckers deserve it," Mercer Scott said.

"That's right. That's just right," Jeff said. They beamed at each other and both blew smoke rings. They'd done their duty by *Over Open Sights*.

It didn't take long for the prisoners in Camp Dependable to find out Jake Featherston's book had finally seen print. Most of them didn't care once they did know; Pinkard would have bet more than half the Negroes waiting their turn for a population reduction couldn't read or write.

But all rules had their exceptions. Willy Knight was nothing but an exception. He had his letters. He was the only white prisoner in the camp. Had things gone a little differently, he would have been President of the CSA in Jake Featherston's place.

His Redemption League in Texas had done the same sorts of things as the Freedom Party had farther east. But the Freedom Party got bigger faster and swallowed the Redemption League instead of the other way round. Knight had been Featherston's running mate when the Freedom Party finally won. A few years later, tired of playing second fiddle, he'd tried to get Jake killed. If he'd pulled it off . . . But he hadn't, and here he was, getting what was coming to him.

At morning roll call, he asked, "Can I get me a copy of that there *Over Open Sights*, please?"

"You? What for?" Pinkard asked suspiciously.

Willy Knight smiled. His face was skinny and filthy. None of the Negroes in Camp Dependable had had the nerve to do anything to him, fearing punishment even though he was in disgrace. Jefferson Pinkard hadn't had the nerve to include him in a population reduction, either. If people back in Richmond changed their minds about Knight . . . It wasn't likely, but why take chances?

"How come?" Pinkard demanded.

"How come? On account of I've got the galloping shits, and where else around here am I gonna get me more asswipes all at once?"

Several Negroes snorted laughter. They probably wouldn't have had the nerve to come out with anything like that themselves. They'd seen that Knight wasn't expendable, and they knew damn well they were. But just because Willy Knight couldn't be casually killed didn't mean he could get away with whatever he wanted. He might think so, but he was wrong. "Teach that man some respect," Pinkard told the guards with him.

They did. They pulled him out of the roll-call formation and worked him over. None of what they did would cause him permanent damage. All the same, Jeff wouldn't have wanted any of it happening to him. After a last kick, one of the guards stared down at Knight in cold contempt. "Get up," he growled. "You think you can lie around the whole goddamn morning?"

A trickle of blood running from the side of his mouth, Knight staggered upright. "Punishment cell. Bread and water. Ten days," Pinkard said. "Take him away."

Two guards half led, half dragged Knight off to the row of punishment cells. They weren't big enough to stand up in, or to lie down at full length. All you could do in one of them was squat or sit and take whatever the weather did to you. In this season, you'd bake.

Jeff eyed the assembled Negroes. "Anybody else feel like cracking wise? Want to show off how clever y'all are?" Nobody said a word. The black men stood at stiff attention. Their faces stayed as impassive as they could make them. Pinkard nodded: not approval, but acceptance, anyhow. "Good. You're showing a little sense. 'Course, if y'all had had any real sense, you wouldn't be here, now would you?"

That was another dangerous question. A couple of Negroes stirred. Jeff waited. Would they be fools enough to grouse about the way the Confederacy treated its black residents? Again, no one said a word.

Again, Jefferson Pinkard nodded. He turned to the remaining guards. "All right. Let's get 'em counted. Remember to take one off for that little trip to the punishment cell."

"Right, boss," they chorused, and set to work. Until the count was right, nothing else happened: no breakfast, no work details, nothing. The Negroes knew that, and tried to make things as simple as they could. Things didn't always go smoothly even so. Some of the guards had trouble counting to eleven without taking off their shoes. Making the prisoner count come out the same way twice running sometimes seemed beyond them. This was one of those mornings.

The prisoners didn't say anything. Pointing out the obvious would only have landed them in trouble, the way so many things here did. But Jeff could see what they were thinking even so. He fumed quietly. If whites were the superior race and blacks inferior, ignorant, and stupid, why wasn't the count going better?

Had Pinkard been a different sort of man, that might have made him wonder about a lot of the ruling assumptions the Confederate States had held since they broke away from the United States. Being who and what he was, though, he only wondered why he'd got stuck with such a pack of lamebrains. Even that wasn't a question easy to answer.

At long last, everything tallied. The prisoners trooped off to the mess hall. Jeff prowled through one of the barracks halls, peering at everything, looking for contraband and for signs of escape tunnels.

He found none. That might have meant the Negroes didn't have the nerve to try to break the rules. Or it might have meant they were too sneaky to let him notice anything they did have going on. He hoped and thought it was the former, but didn't rule out the latter. People who underestimated the opposition had a way of paying for it.

After the inspection, he went on to the next hall, and then to the ncxt, till he'd been through the whole camp. Mercer Scott gave him a quizzical look as he finished his tour. Jeff stared back stonily. He'd learned down in Mexico to rely on his own eyes and ears, not just on what the guards told him. You could count on what you saw for yourself. Guards? If guards were so goddamn smart, why couldn't they keep the count straight?

And if other camp commandants didn't have the brains to keep an eye on things for themselves, that was their tough luck. Jeff knew he could screw up in spite of inspections. Better that than screwing up because he hadn't made them.

He went back to his office and started plowing through paperwork. He'd never imagined how much paperwork went with keeping people locked up where they couldn't get in trouble. You had to keep track of who you had, who'd died, who was coming in. . . . It never seemed to end.

A guard walked into the office with a yellow telegram. Pinkard's heart sank. He knew what it was going to be. And he was right. Ferdinand Koenig was pleased to inform him of a shipment of so many prisoners, to arrive at Camp Dependable on such and such a day— which happened to be four days away.

"You son of a bitch," Jeff muttered. That wouldn't have delighted the Attorney General, but Koenig wasn't there to hear it. Koenig wasn't there to deal with the mess he was causing, either. Oh, no. Hell, no. He left that to Jeff to clean up.

A population reduction inside of four days? *Mercer Scott'll scream bloody murder when I tell him,* Pinkard thought. Well, too bad. Just as Jeff was stuck with what Richmond did to him, so Scott was stuck with what Jeff needed from him. And bloody murder it would be, even if nobody called it that.

If they hadn't done it before, they wouldn't have been able to bring it off. It wouldn't be easy even now, because the prisoners would know what was going to happen to them when they went out into the bayou. They'd know they weren't coming back. They would have to be manacled and shackled. But the job would get done. That was all that counted.

Iron wheels squealing and sending up sparks as they scraped against the rails, the westbound train pulled into the station at Rivière-du-

Loup. Dr. Leonard O'Doull stood on the platform. He hugged and kissed his wife, and then his son.

"I wish you weren't doing this," Nicole said. Tears stood in her dark eyes, but she was too proud, too stubborn, to let them fall.

"I wish I weren't, too," he answered. "But it's something I need to do. We've been over it before." That was a bloodless way of putting it. They'd screamed and yelled and done everything but throw crockery at each other.

"Be careful," she said. He nodded. It was useless advice. They both knew it. He made a show of accepting it just the same.

"Take care, Papa," Lucien said. He was twenty-three now. He had his full height, but was still three or four inches shorter than his rangy father. He didn't need to worry about going to war. His country was still at peace. In the end, though, the Republic of Quebec wasn't Dr. O'Doull's homeland. He belonged to the USA.

"All aboard!" the conductor shouted.

Black bag in hand, O'Doull got on the train. Nicole and Lucien waved to him after he found a seat. He waved back, and blew kisses. He kept on waving and blowing kisses as the train began to roll, even after his wife and son disappeared.

"God damn Jedediah Quigley," he muttered in English. But it wasn't Quigley's fault. The retired officer couldn't have sold him on returning to the service if he hadn't wanted to be sold. Blaming the other man was easier than blaming himself, though.

The train ran along the southern bank of the St. Lawrence for a long time. The river, through which the Great Lakes drained into the Atlantic, hardly seemed to narrow as O'Doull went south and west. The ocean was bigger, but the Great Lakes might not have known it. They sent a lot of cold, clean, fresh water out into the sea. Even well beyond Rivière-du-Loup to the east, where the St. Lawrence river gradually became the Gulf of St. Lawrence, the water remained at most brackish.

Farm country much like that which O'Doull's father-in-law had worked for so many years met the doctor's eye through the rather smeary window. Fields of wheat and barley and potatoes alternated with pear and apple orchards. The farmhouses also reminded O'Doull of the one in which Lucien Galtier had lived. They were built of wood, not stone. Almost all of them were white, with red roofs whose eaves stuck out to form a sort of verandah above the front door. The barns were white, too. O'Doull had got used to that. Now he recalled that most barns in the USA were a dull red that got duller each year it wasn't touched up.

Towns came every few miles. They commonly centered on Catholic churches with tall spires made of pressed tin. Near the church would be a school, a post office, a few stores, and a tavern or two. Sometimes there would be a doctor's office, sometimes a dentist's, sometimes a lawyer's. Houses with shade trees in front of them surrounded the little business centers.

Even if he hadn't been familiar with such small Quebecois towns, he would have come to know them well on the journey back to the United States, for the train seemed to stop at every one. That cut its speed down to a crawl, but nobody except O'Doull seemed to mind, and even he didn't mind very much.

Now a man in overalls would get on and light up a pipe, now a woman with squealing children or squealing piglets in tow, now a priest, now a granny. They would get to where they were going, get off at a station just like the one at which they'd boarded, and be replaced by other similar types. Once a handful of soldiers in blue-gray, probably coming back from leave, livened up O'Doull's car for a while. A couple of them were still drunk. They sang songs that made the grannies blush and cover their ears—except for one old dame who sang along in a voice almost as deep as a man's.

From Rivière-du-Loup to Longeuil, across the river from Montréal, was about 250 miles. The train didn't get there till evening, though it had left Rivière-du-Loup early in the morning. An express could have done the run in less than half the time. Leonard O'Doull laughed at himself for even imagining an express that ran out as far as Rivière-du-Loup. Where were the people who might make such a run profitable? Nowhere, and he knew it.

No matter how much the U.S. Army Medical Corps wanted his services, they hadn't wanted them badly enough to spring for a Pullman berth. His seat reclined, a little. He dozed, a little. His route went south, away from the river at last and down toward the United States. Even so, the train kept right on stopping at every tiny town.

Here in what people called the Eastern Townships, Quebec changed. English-speakers replaced Francophones. The towns, from what he could see of them, lost their distinctively Quebecois look and began to resemble those of nearby New England. Most of the settlers in this part of Quebec were descended from Loyalists who'd had to flee the USA during and just after the Revolution.

O'Doull wondered how loyal those people were to the government in Quebec City even now. French-speaking Catholics dominated the Republic of Quebec—as well they might, when they made up close to seven-eighths of the population. The Republic's constitution guaranteed freedom of religion, and no one had yet tried to ram French down the throats of the people here, but where in the world did minorities ever have an easy time? Nowhere.

Not my worry, thank God, O'Doull thought, and dozed some more.

When he woke up again, the train was passing from the Republic of Quebec to the United States. Customs inspectors in dark green uniforms went up and down the aisles, asking people from the Republic for their travel documents. What O'Doull had was sketchy: a U.S. passport from just before the Great War and a letter from Jedediah Quigley certifying that he had been invited down to the USA to rejoin the Medical Corps.

The customs inspector who examined his papers looked as if he'd swallowed a lemon. "Hey, Charlie!" he called. "Come take a gander at this. What the hell we got here?"

In due course, Charlie appeared. He had slightly fancier gold emblems on his shoulder boards than the other customs man did. He frowned at the ancient passport, and frowned even harder at the letter. "Who the devil is Jedediah Quigley?" he demanded. "Sounds like somebody out of Dickens."

A literate official—who would have believed it? O'Doull answered, "Actually, I think he's from New Hampshire or Vermont. He's been the middleman for a lot of deals between the USA and Quebec. As far as he's concerned, I'm just small change."

Charlie might have been literate, but he wasn't soft. "As far as I'm concerned, you're just small change, too, buddy," he said coldly. "I think you better get off the train till we can figure out if you're legit. There's a war on, you know."

"If there weren't a war on, I wouldn't be back in the United States," O'Doull said. "You can count on that."

"I don't count on anything," Charlie said. "That's why I've got this job, and that's why you're getting off this train."

O'Doull wanted to punch him in the nose. If he had, he probably would have ended up in jail instead of in the train station at Mooers, New York. By the time the sun came up, the distinction seemed academic. Mooers lay in the middle of what had been forest and was now stubble, as if the earth hadn't shaved for several days. O'Doull had seen haphazard logging jobs in Quebec, but this one seemed worse than most.

Adding to the surreal feeling his weariness gave him, almost everybody in the train station except the customs inspectors seemed to be an immigrant from Quebec. When he spoke French to a girl who brought him coffee, her face lit up. But he just made the customs men more suspicious.

"How come you parlez-vous?" Charlie demanded. "You're supposed to be a Yankee, aren't you?"

"I *am* a Yankee, dammit," O'Doull answered wearily. "But I've lived in Quebec for twenty-five years. My wife speaks French. All my neighbors speak French. All my patients, too. I'd better, don't you think?"

"I think we'll get your cock-and-bull story checked out, that's what I think," Charlie said. "Then we'll figure out what's what."

The girl brought O'Doull a plate of scrambled eggs and fried potatoes and more coffee. The customs men sent her sour stares; maybe she wasn't supposed to. O'Doull doubted she would have if he'd just used English with her. The potatoes were greasy and needed salt. He wolfed them down anyhow.

When he went to the men's room to get rid of some of that coffee, one of the customs men tagged along. "Do you really think I'd try to run away?" O'Doull asked. "Where would I go?"

"Never can tell," said the man in the green uniform. O'Doull thought he was nuts, but didn't say so. Mooers might not have been in the middle of nowhere, but it wasn't right at the edges, either.

Instead of escaping, he went back and sat down on the padless metal folding chair he'd vacated to whizz. His backside was sick of sitting, and this chair was even less comfortable than the seat on the train. He twisted and turned. Whenever he stood up to stretch, the customs men got ready to jump him.

He bought a hamburger and more greasy fries for lunch. By then, he'd started to wonder if he could open a practice here, because he seemed unlikely to go any farther. The customs men did finally let him buy a newspaper, too: a copy of the *Plattsburg Patriot* from two days before. The headline insisted that Columbus wasn't cut off and surrounded, and denied that the U.S. Army had pulled its Ohio headquarters out of the city. O'Doull had seen headlines like that before. They were usually lies. He didn't say so. It would have made the customs men think him a defeatist.

Finally, at half past four, Charlie came up to him and said, "As far as we can tell, Dr. O'Doull, you are what you say you are. We're going to let you go on as soon as the next train gets in."

"That's nice," O'Doull answered. "It would have been a lot nicer if you'd decided that a while ago, but it's still nice. When does the next train get in?" If Mooers hadn't been on the border, no railway would have come anywhere near it.

"Tomorrow evening," Charlie said, a little uncomfortably.

A little—not nearly enough. *"Tomorrow evening!"* Leonard O'Doull exploded. "Jesus Christ! I'm stuck in this lousy place for two stinking days? No wonder we're losing the goddamn war!" In the face of two days in Mooers, New York, defeatism suddenly seemed a small thing.

"We are not," Charlie said, but he didn't sound as if he believed himself. "And if you'd had proper travel documents—"

"I did," O'Doull said. "It only took you about a year and a half to check them." Charlie looked sullen. O'Doull didn't care. "I don't suppose there's actually a hotel here?" The customs man's face told him there wasn't. He made more disgusted noises. If he wasn't going to enjoy himself in Mooers, he was damned if Charlie was going to enjoy having him here.

After the Second Mexican War, Philadelphia became the de facto capital of the USA for one simple reason: it was out of artillery range of the CSA. During the Great War, Philadelphia hadn't quite come within artillery range of the CSA, either. Confederate bombers had visited the city every now and then, but they hadn't done much damage.

That was then. This was now. Flora Blackford had already come to hate the rising and falling squeal of the air-raid siren. Confederate bombers came over Philadelphia every night, and they weren't just visiting. They seemed bound and determined to knock the town flat.

Hurrying down to the cellar of her apartment building after the latest alarm, Flora complained, "Why didn't they move the government to Seattle?"

"Because then the . . . lousy Japs would bomb us," said a man ahead of her.

She scowled. The stairwell was dark. No one noticed, not even Joshua beside her. She'd been in Los Angeles in 1932, campaigning with her husband in his doomed reelection bid, when Japanese carrier airplanes came over the city. It had been only a pinprick, but it had let the last of the air out of his hopes.

Someone else on the stairs said, "Japan hasn't declared war on us yet."

"Yeah? And so?" another man replied. "Confederates didn't declare war on us, either. Slant-eyed so-and-sos are probably just waiting till they've got a big enough rock in their fist."

That made more sense than Flora wished it did. But she couldn't brood about it, not right then. Bombs started coming down. She took them more seriously than she had when the war began. Every time she went out during the day, she saw what they could do.

Into the cellar. It filled up fast. Fewer people bothered about robes and slippers than they had that first night. As long as you weren't naked, none of your neighbors would give you a second look. They had on pajamas and nightgowns, too. They hadn't combed their hair or put on makeup, either. Quite a few of them hadn't had baths. If you hadn't, it didn't matter so much. Nobody was going to get offended.

The floor shook under Flora's feet. "They're after the War Department again," Joshua said. "That's where most of the bombs are coming down." He pointed like a bird dog.

And Flora could tell he was right. The knowledge brought horror, not joy. Learning how to tell where bombs were falling was nothing she'd ever wanted to do. "Damn Jake Featherston," she said quietly.

"Amen," said somebody behind her. Half a dozen other people rumbled agreement.

She guessed they were damning him for bombing Philadelphia and routing them out of bed again. She damned Featherston for that, too. But she had bigger reasons. She damned the President of the CSA for murdering hope. In the time the Socialists held the Presidency of the USA after the Great War, they'd been reluctant to spend money on weapons. They'd thought the world had learned its lesson, and that nobody would try to kill anybody any more any time soon. Better to set things to rights inside the United States than to flabble about the Confederate States. After all, the CSA had suffered even more than the USA in the Great War. The Confederates wouldn't want to risk that again, would they? Of course not! You'd have to be a madman to want to put your country through another round of torment.

As long as the Whigs ruled in Richmond, cool heads prevailed. The Whigs did what they could to rebuild. The Confederate States enjoyed a modest prosperity. The United States weren't sorry to see that prosperity—or its modesty. The Freedom Party howled outside the door, but who was mad enough to invite it in?

Then came the worldwide collapse. Where cool heads had failed, hotheads prevailed. No one in the USA had imagined Featherston could actually win an election. Flora knew she hadn't. The very idea had struck her as *meshuggeh*.

But, crazy or not, Featherston had gone about doing what he'd promised all along he would: getting even. If anyone in power in the USA had believed he would be giving orders one day, War Department budgets would have looked different through the 1920s.

A few Democrats had screamed bloody murder about the way the budgets looked. They'd proved right, even if some of their own party reckoned them reactionaries at the time. They had been reactionaries. Some of them, crowing on the floor of Congress now, were still reactionaries, and proud of it. But even reactionaries could be right once in a while. After all, a stopped clock was right twice a day.

Those Democrats, damn them, had picked something important to be right about. Flora hated admitting they had been right all the more because she thought them wrong about so many other things. She'd been wrong here. She hated admitting that, too. She'd done it, though. It hadn't won her much respect from the Democrats. She hadn't expected it to.

"I think the AA is hotter than it was when the war started," Joshua said, bringing her back to the here and now.

"Maybe you're right," she said. "I hope you are."

"I'm not sure *I* hope I am," her son answered. "If the Confederates get shot at more, they won't hit their targets so much."

"That's good, isn't it?" Flora said.

Joshua shrugged. "Well, maybe. But if they don't hit their targets, they'd want to hit *something* before they get out of here. That means they're liable to drop their bombs any old place."

"Oh, joy," Flora said.

Not far away, a man muttered, "Oh, shit," which amounted to the same thing.

Flora had already accused her son of belonging to the General Staff. He got proved right here with alarming speed. A stick of bombs came down right in the neighborhood. Flora didn't know all that much about earthquakes, but this felt the way she imagined an earthquake would. She cast a frightened eye at the ceiling, wondering if it would stay up.

It did. The lights went out for a couple of minutes, but then they came back on. Everybody in the cellar let out a sigh of relief when they returned. "Isn't this fun?" a woman said. Several people laughed. With a choice between laughing and shrieking, laughing was better.

After that, the bombs hit farther away. The Confederate bombers lingered over Philadelphia for more than an hour. Their bases weren't far away. Antiaircraft guns and searchlights and fighters hunting through the black skies of night were not enough to drive them off or even to slow them down very much. Every so often, one or two of them would crash in flames. What was that, though, but the cost of doing business?

The all-clear sounded. Yawning and sleepily cursing the Confederates, people went up to their flats. The air in the stairwell smelled of sweat and smoke.

Fire-engine sirens wailed, some nearer, some farther away. Flora had just opened the door to the flat she shared with Joshua when a big boom only a few blocks away made things shake all over again. "That was a bomb!" she said indignantly. "But the Confederates went away."

"Time fuse." Her son's voice was wise. "That way, people and stuff come close, and then it blows up." He did his teenaged best to sound reassuring: "Don't worry, Mom. We've got 'em, too."

"Oh, joy," Flora said again, in the same tone and with the same meaning as she'd used down in the cellar. Wasn't that a lovely piece of human ingenuity? It lay there quietly to lure more victims into the neighborhood, then slaughtered them. And the USA and CSA both used such things. Whoever had invented them had probably got a bonus for his talents.

She would have liked to give him what he really deserved. The Geneva Convention probably outlawed that, though.

Lying down, she looked at the alarm clock's luminous dial, the only light in the bedroom. Half past three. She said something more pungent than *Oh, joy* under her breath. It could have been worse. She knew that. It could have been better, too.

She yawned and stretched and tried to get comfortable and also tried to free her mind from the fear she'd known. That wasn't easy. She looked at the alarm clock again—3:35 now. Why did the dots by the numbers and the lines on the hour and minute hands glow? Radium—she knew that. But why did radium glow? Because it did; that was all she knew. Somewhere, there were probably scientists who could give a better explanation. She hoped so, anyhow.

She yawned again. Somewhat to her surprise, she did fall back to sleep. More often than not, she couldn't. She wasn't the only one doing without, either. Half the people in Philadelphia seemed to be stumbling around with bags under their eyes these days. If the Confederates cut off coffee imports, the city would be in a bad way.

When the alarm went off not quite three hours later, she felt as if another bomb had exploded beside her head. The first time she tried to make it shut up, she missed. The second time, she succeeded. Yawning blearily, she got out of bed.

Coffee, for the time being, she had. She made herself a pot. Joshua's snores punctuated the wet *blup-blup* of the percolator. He didn't have school and he didn't have a job. He could sleep as long as he wanted. Flora marveled at that as she fried eggs to go with the coffee. Sleep as long as you wanted? Till Joshua, no one in her family had ever been able to do that. What else could more clearly mark an escape from the proletariat?

She dressed, went downstairs, and hailed a cab. The driver was a man with a gray mustache and only two fingers on his left hand. "Congress," she told him.

"Yes, ma'am," he answered, and put the elderly Buick in gear. "You a Congressman's wife, ma'am?"

"No," Flora said. "I'm a Congresswoman."

"Oh." The cabby drove on for a little while. Then he said, "Guess I just killed my tip." Flora said neither yes nor no, though the same thought had crossed her mind. The driver went on, "Any way you can make 'em pass a law to get me back into the Army? I can still shoot in spite of this." He held up his mutilated hand. "Stinking recruiting sergeants just laugh at me, though."

"I'm sorry," Flora told him. "I can't do much about that. The Army knows what it needs." There was something strange for a Socialist to say. It was true all the same, though. They rode the rest of the way into downtown Philadelphia in glum silence.

Every day, Flora saw more damage to the city where she'd lived the second half of her life. A woman sat on the sidewalk with three little children and a dog. The children clung to odds and ends of property—shoes, framed pictures, and, ridiculously, a fancy china teapot. Flora knew what that meant: they'd lost everything else. They weren't the only ones, or anything close to it.

"Here you are, lady," the cab driver said, pulling to a stop in front of the Congressional building. "Fare's forty cents."

Flora gave him a half dollar. She hurried up the stairs. Even as she did, though, she wondered why. Congress wouldn't change things much now. It was up to the men in green-gray and butternut.

Chester Martin and Harry T. Casson approached the table from opposite sides. Chester wore his usual workingman's clothes. Casson was natty in a white summer-weight linen suit. The builder could have bought and sold the labor organizer a dozen times without worrying about anything but petty cash.

Despite their differences, they sat down side by side. Martin stuck out his hand. Casson shook it. Flashbulbs popped, even though nothing much had happened yet. Casson reached into an inside pocket and took out a sheet of paper and some glasses. Setting those on his nose, he looked at the waiting reporters and said, "I'd like to read a brief statement, if I might."

"Why are you making this deal with the construction workers' union?" a reporter called.

"Well, that's what the statement's about," the builder said. He glanced down at the typewritten sheet. "In this time of national emergency, the only enemy we have is our foreign foe. There is no place now for strife between labor and capital. Since that is obviously true even to those who have disagreed about other issues before, I have decided to sign a contract with the union at this time. Peace at home, war with the Confederate States and their allies." He folded the paper and looked at Chester. "Mr. Martin?"

"We've been working toward this moment for a long time." Chester had no notes. He felt like a hick next to the smooth Casson, but they sat here as equals. "A fair wage for a day's work and decent working conditions are all we ever wanted. With this contract, I think we're going to get 'em."

Harry T. Casson pulled a gold-nibbed fountain pen from his breast pocket. He signed all four copies of the contract, then ceremoniously offered Chester the pen.

"No, thanks. I've got my own." Martin had a plain steel nib, but it was plenty good enough for signatures. After he signed, he stuck out his hand again. Casson shook it. The flash photographers took more pictures.

"This is a great day for Los Angeles!" one of the reporters said.

He worked for the *Times*. "It'd be a better day, and it would have come sooner, if your paper hadn't spent the last I don't know how many years calling us a pack of lousy Reds," Chester said. "I bet you don't print that—I bet you pretend I never said it—but it's true just the same."

"I'm writing it down," the reporter said. Men from the other, smaller, papers in town were writing it down, too. It would show up in their rags. Whether or not the guy from the *Times* put it in his piece, Chester's bet was his editor would kill it before it saw print.

"How much will this help the war effort?" asked a man from the *Torrance Daily Breeze*, a paper that had given labor's side of the class struggle a much fairer shake.

Chester nodded to Harry T. Casson, as if to say, *You know more about that than I do.* Chester wasn't shy about admitting it, not when it was true. The builder said, "We hope it will help quite a bit. We think everything will go better now that we're all pulling in the same direction."

"Will the other builders settle with the union?" asked the reporter from the *Breeze*.

"I can't speak for them," Casson said, which was half true at most. "I hope they will, though. We've had too much trouble here for too long."

"Amen to that," Chester said. "I think we could have settled earlier—the union hasn't made any secret about the terms it was after—but I'm awfully glad we've got an agreement at last."

A man from the *Pasadena Star-News* asked, "With so many workers going into defense plants, how much will this deal really mean? Can the union keep its members? Except for war work, how much building will be going on?"

"You want to take that one?" Martin and Casson both said at the same time. They laughed. So did everybody else at the press conference. With a shrug, Chester went on, "Steve, to tell you the truth, I just don't know. We'll have to play it by ear and see what happens. The war's turned everything topsy-turvy."

"That about sums it up," Harry T. Casson agreed. "We're doing the best we can. That's all anybody can do, especially in times like these." He held up a well-manicured hand. "Thank you very much, gentlemen."

Some of them still scribbling, the reporters got up from their folding chairs and headed off toward typewriters in their offices or towards other stories. "Well, Mr. Casson, we've gone and done it," Chester said. "Now we see how it works."

"Yes." The building magnate nodded. "That's what we have to do." He took out a monogrammed gold cigarette case that probably cost at least as much as Martin had made in the best three months of his life put together. "Smoke?"

"Thanks." Martin got out a book of matches that advertised a garage near his place. He lit Casson's cigarette, then his own. The tobacco was pretty good, but no better than pretty good. He'd wondered if capitalists could get their hands on superfancy cigarettes, the way they could with superfancy motorcars. That they couldn't— or at least that Casson hadn't—came as something of a relief.

Casson eyed him. "And where do you go from here, Mr. Martin?"

"Me? Back to work," Chester answered. "Where else? It's been way too long since I picked up a hammer and started working with my hands again."

"I wonder if you'll get the satisfaction from it that you expect," Casson said.

"What do you mean?"

"You said it yourself: you haven't worked with your hands for a long time," Casson answered. "You've worked with your head instead. You've got used to doing that, I'd say, and you've done it well. You're not just a worker any more. For better or worse, you're a leader of men."

"I was a sergeant in the last war. I commanded a company for a while, till they found an officer who could cover it," Chester said.

Harry T. Casson nodded. "Oh, yes. Those things happened. I was a captain, and I had a regiment for a couple of weeks. If you lived, you rose."

"Yeah." Chester nodded, too. He wasn't surprised at what Casson said; the other man had the air of one who'd been through the mill. "Point is, though, I didn't miss it when the shooting stopped. I don't much like people telling me what to do, either."

Casson tapped his ash into a cheap glass ashtray on the table. "Maybe not, but you've done it, and done it well. You're in command of more than a regiment these days. Will the people you're in charge of let you walk away? Will the lady who's in charge of you let you do it?"

"Rita's my worry," Chester said, and Casson nodded politely. Rita hadn't wanted him to start a union here. He remembered that. Why would she care if he went back to what he'd done before? If *local president* sounded grander than *carpenter*, so what? As for the other members of the union . . . "There's bound to be somebody who can do a better job than I can."

"You may be surprised," Harry T. Casson said. "You may be very surprised indeed. You've been stubborn, you haven't been vicious, and you've been honest. The combination is rarer than you'd think. I made a bargain with you in half an hour, once I decided I needed to. I wouldn't even have dickered with some of your, ah, colleagues."

"That's flattering, but I don't believe it for a minute," Martin said.

"Believe it," the magnate told him. "I don't waste time on flattery, especially not after we've made our deal. What's the point? We've already settled things."

"I'm glad we have, too," Chester said.

"Yes, well, this poor miserable old country of ours is going to take plenty more knocks from the damned Confederates. I don't see much point in hurting it ourselves," Casson said.

"Makes sense," Chester said, and then, "Is Columbus really surrounded?"

"All I know is what I read in the newspapers and hear on the wireless," Casson answered. "The Confederates say it is, we say it isn't. But both sides say there's fighting north of there. Draw your own conclusions."

Martin already had. He liked none of them. He said, "I'm from Toledo. I know what holding on to Ohio means to the country."

"I hope people back East do," Casson said. "If they don't, I think the Confederates'd be happy to teach them." He grimaced, then tried a smile on for size. "Not much either one of us can do about that."

"No, not unless we want to put on the uniform again," Chester said. Harry T. Casson grimaced again, in a different way. Chester laughed, but not for long. "If Ohio goes down the drain, it could come to that. If Ohio goes down the drain, we'll need everything and everybody we can get our hands on."

He hoped Casson would tell him he was wrong, tell him that he was flabbling over nothing. He wouldn't have agreed with the building magnate, but he hoped so anyhow. Casson didn't even try. He just said, "You're right. We're a little long in the tooth, but only a little, and we've been through it. They'd put green-gray on us pretty damn quick if we gave 'em the chance."

"I've thought about it," Martin said.

"Have you?" Casson pointed a finger at him. "You're mine now. I can blackmail you forever. If you don't do what I say, I'll tell *that* to your wife."

"Rita already knows," Chester said. That was true. He didn't say anything about how horrified she'd been when she found out. He didn't suppose he could blame her. Her dismay was probably the biggest single thing that had kept him from visiting a recruiting station. He didn't say anything about that, either; it was none of Harry T. Casson's business. He just took his copies of the agreement they'd signed. "I'd better get home."

"You don't have an auto, do you?" Casson asked.

"Nope." Chester shook his head.

"That's hard here," the magnate said. "Los Angeles is too spread out to make getting around by trolley very easy." Chester only shrugged. Casson went on, "I'd be happy to give you a lift, if you like."

"No, thanks," Chester said. "I took the trolley here. I can take it back. If you give me a ride, half the people in the union will think I've sold 'em down the river. And that's liable to be what you've got in mind."

The other man looked pained. "Times are pretty grim when a friendly gesture can get misunderstood like that."

"You're right. Time *are* pretty grim when something like that can happen," Chester said. "But these are the times we've got. We've made a deal. I'm glad we've made a deal—don't get me wrong. We're class enemies just the same, and pretending we're not isn't going to change things even a dime's worth."

"I'm surprised you'd rather fight Featherston than me," Casson said.

"Up yours, Mr. Casson," Chester said evenly. "He's a class enemy, too, and he's a national enemy." Before the Great War, Socialists hadn't realized how nationalism could trump the international solidarity of the proletariat. They had no excuse for not seeing that now.

Harry T. Casson snorted. "Have it your way. I still think the whole notion of class warfare is a bunch of crap."

"Of course you do. You can afford to." Chester walked out with the agreement and the last word.

VI

Early one stiflingly hot and sticky July morning, Cincinnatus Driver watched colored men lining up at the edge of Covington, Kentucky's, Negro district. A sign said, WAR WORK HERE. Three or four policemen—whites, of course—hung around just to make sure nobody got out of line literally or metaphorically.

Half a dozen buses rolled up. They were old and rickety. The nasty black diesel fumes that belched from their tailpipes made Cincinnatus cough. It wasn't the poison gas the Confederates and Yankees were shooting at each other on the far side of the Ohio, but it was bad enough.

Doors wheezed open on the buses. The blacks filed aboard. They filled each bus to overflowing, taking all the seats and packing the aisles. More fumes poured from tailpipes as the buses rolled away. Disappointed blacks who hadn't managed to get aboard milled around on the sidewalk.

"Form a new line!" one of the cops bawled. "Form a new line, goddammit! Next buses come along in fifteen minutes!"

The Negroes obeyed. They might have been so many sheep. *Lambs to the slaughter,* Cincinnatus thought. He got moving again, putting weight on his cane so he didn't have to put it on his bad leg. He couldn't go fast enough to get out of his own way. By now, the policemen were used to seeing him around. They hardly ever asked for his passbook any more, at least as long as he stayed in the colored district.

He couldn't have worked in a war plant even if he'd wanted to, not unless they found him a job that involved sitting down all the time. Such jobs undoubtedly existed. Did blacks have any of them? Cincinnatus doubted that. It would have been unlikely in the USA. In the CSA, it was inconceivable, or as close as made no difference. But these Negroes, swarms of them, lined up for the chance to work at whatever kind of jobs their white rulers deigned to give them. Kentucky hadn't been back in the Confederate States for very long. Blacks here had already learned the difference between bad and worse, though. This was bad: long hours, lousy pay, hard work, no choice, no possible complaint.

Worse? Worse was drawing the notice of Confederate authorities—in practice, of any suspicious white. If that happened, you didn't go on a ride to a war plant. You went for a ride, all right, but you didn't come back. People talked about camps. People talked about worse things than camps. A strange phrase had crept into the language since Cincinnatus found himself stuck in Covington. *You gonna git your population reduced,* one Negro would say to another when he meant the other man would end up in trouble. Cincinnatus hadn't heard that one before. He knew endless variations on *git your tit in a wringer* and *git your ass in a sling,* but *git your population reduced* was new—and more than a little ominous. The next person he heard of who'd come out of a camp would be the first.

He shuffled on. His father was sprier than he was these days. He hated that. With his mother slipping deeper into her second childhood every day, his father needed someone who could help keep an eye on her and take care of her. Cincinnatus had come down from Des Moines so he could take them both back to the USA before Kentucky returned to the Confederate fold. Thanks to the man who'd run him down, Seneca now had two to take care of.

Somebody'd pasted a crudely printed flyer to a brick wall. SABOTAGE! it said in bold black letters, and underneath, *Don't make things the Freedom Party can use against the USA! If the Confederacy wins, Negroes lose!* Below that was a set of broken chains.

Cincinnatus read the flyer out of the corner of his eye. He didn't turn his head towards it. Someone could have been watching him. Besides, he'd seen that particular flyer before. During the Great War, he'd become something of a connoisseur of propaganda posters. This one, he judged, was . . . fair.

Nothing wrong with the message. If the CSA and the Freedom Party beat the USA, things would only get worse for blacks here. But calling for sabotage was calling for a worker to take his life in his hands. Those who got caught paid. Oh, how they paid.

He also saw lots of places where a flyer—probably the same one—had been torn down. Not many people would want that message on their wall or fence or tree. It would land them in trouble with the Confederate authorities, and trouble with the Confederate authorities was the last thing any black man in Covington needed.

Not entirely by coincidence, Cincinnatus' amble took him past Lucullus Wood's barbecue place. He started to go inside, but he was still reaching for the knob when the door opened—and out strode a gray-uniformed policeman gnawing on a beef rib as long as a billy club.

"You comin' in, uncle?" the cop said around a mouthful of beef. Grease shone on his lips and chin. He held the door open for Cincinnatus.

"Thank you kindly, suh," Cincinnatus said, looking down at the ground so the policeman wouldn't see his face. The man had done something perfectly decent: not the sort of thing one necessarily expected from a cop in Covington at all. But then he'd gone and spoiled it with one word. *Uncle.* Like *boy*, it denied a black male his fundamental equality, his fundamental humanity. And, worse, the policeman seemed to have no idea that it did.

Lucullus' place did a brisk breakfast business, mostly on scraps and shreds of barbecued beef and pork cooked with eggs and with fried potatoes or grits. Cincinnatus sat down at a bench and ordered eggs and pork and grits and a cup of coffee. Everything came fast as lightning; Lucullus ran a tight ship. Cincinnatus' eyes widened when he took his first sip of the coffee. He sent the waitress an accusing stare. "You reckon I don't know chicory when I taste it? There any real coffee in this here cup at all?"

"There's some," she answered. "But we havin' trouble gettin' the real bean. Everybody havin' trouble gettin' the real bean, even white folks. We got to stretch best way we know how."

Cincinnatus took another sip. Some people in the CSA—especially blacks—had a taste for coffee laced with chicory. Some even liked it better than the real bean. He hadn't even tasted it since he moved up to Iowa. It did help pry his eyes open. He couldn't deny that. "You go on, girl," he told the waitress. "It'll do. But you let Lucullus know he got somebody out front who wants a word with him."

"I do that," she said, and hurried off.

Lucullus didn't come out right away. Cincinnatus would have been astonished if he had. When he did, he planted his massive form across the table from Cincinnatus and said, "So you ain't much for chicory, eh?"

"It's all right. It's tolerable, anyways," Cincinnatus answered. "What it says that you can't get no coffee . . . that's another story."

"There's some. There's always some, you wanna pay the price for it," Lucullus said. "But it ain't cheap no more, like it was before the war. I charge my customers a quarter a cup, pretty damn quick I ain't got no customers no more."

With his barbecue, he would always have customers. Cincinnatus took his point just the same. After another forkful of grits, he spoke in a low voice: "I seen six buses first pickup this mornin'. More comin' in fifteen minutes, police say."

"Six, with more comin'," Lucullus echoed quietly. Cincinnatus nodded. Lucullus clicked his tongue between his teeth. "They got a lot o' niggers workin' for 'em."

"You don't work for 'em, somethin' worse happen," Cincinnatus said. "You don't work *hard* for 'em, somethin' worse happen. You seen that sabotage flyer?"

"Yeah, I seen it," Lucullus answered. His smile was broad and genuinely amused. Cincinnatus hadn't asked him if he'd had anything to do with putting it up. Seeing it was safe enough. The other wasn't.

"Lots o' colored folks try that, they end up dead," Cincinnatus said.

"Colored folks don't try somethin' like that, we all liable to end up dead," Lucullus said. Cincinnatus made a face. That was going too far . . . wasn't it? But Lucullus nodded. "You reckon Jake Featherston don't want us dead?"

"Well, no," Cincinnatus said; nobody in his right mind could believe that. But he went on, "There's a difference between wantin' us dead an' makin' us dead."

"You go on thinkin' that way, you gonna git your population reduced." Lucullus pointed at Cincinnatus with a thick, stubby fore-finger. "You hear that before?"

"I heard it," Cincinnatus said unwillingly.

"You suppose the folks who say it, they jokin'?" Lucullus persisted.

"How the hell do I know?" Cincinnatus spoke with more than a little irritation. "I ain't been in the goddamn Confederate States for a hell of a long time. Never wanted to be in the Confederate States again, neither. How do I know how you crazy niggers talk down here?"

That made Lucullus laugh, but not for long. He said, "We talks that way on account o' what goes on at them camps in Alabama and Mississippi and Louisiana. You don't believe they reduces their population there? You don't believe they kills people so they don't got to worry 'bout feedin' 'em no more? You don't believe that?"

Cincinnatus didn't know what he believed. "Don't want to believe it," he said at last. "Even Featherston ain't that much of a son of a bitch."

"Hell he ain't." Lucullus had no doubts. "Mebbe they kills us whether we fights back or no. We sits quiet, though, they kills us for sure."

"He's fightin' the damnyankees," Cincinnatus said. "How's he gonna do that if he's doin' all this other shit, too? USA's bigger'n the CSA. Featherston's a bastard, but he ain't no fool. He got to see he can't waste his men and waste his trains and waste all his other stuff goin' after niggers who ain't doin' him no harm."

"You been up in Ioway. You ain't been payin' enough attention to the CSA. Even when Kentucky was in the USA, I had to," Lucullus said. "Why you reckon Confederate factories make about nine million tractors and harvesters and combines a few years back?"

"I seen that when it happened. Don't tell me I don't pay no attention," Cincinnatus said angrily. "Any damn fool can tell you why they done it: on account of any factory that can make tractors can make barrels, too, that's why."

Lucullus looked surprised, and not just at his vehemence. "That's part o' why, I reckon," he admitted. "But they's more to it than that. They put all them machines in the fields. Just one of 'em do the work of a hell of a lot o' nigger farmhands. Niggers want to work, they got to go to town. Mister Jake Featherston got hisself a whole new proletariat to exploit . . . an' the niggers who fights back, or the niggers who can't find no work no way, nohow, he goes an' he reduces their population."

Cincinnatus stared at him. That had to be the most cynical assessment he'd ever heard in his life, and he'd heard a lot of them. But, along with the cynicism, it made a lot more sense than he wished it did. Then Lucullus went back to his office. He returned a minute or so later. Cincinnatus wouldn't have minded if the barbecue king had brought back a bottle. Even though it was early, he could have used a drink after the talk they were having. But Lucullus wasn't carrying a bottle. Instead, he set a book on the table between them.

"*Over Open Sights*," Cincinnatus read aloud.

"It's all in here," Lucullus said. "Featherston ain't just a bastard, like you say. He's a bastard who knows what he wants to do. An' he wrote some of this shit back during the Great War. He *say* so, for Chrissake. He's knowed what he wants to do for *years*."

Scipio watched a plump, prosperous white businessman eat his venison at the Huntsman's Lodge. The man's supper companion was a very pretty blonde half his age—not his wife, as Scipio knew. He was saying, "Have you had a look at *Over Open Sights*, sweetcakes?"

That wasn't, to put it mildly, the approach Scipio would have taken. The girl said, "I've seen it, but I haven't read it—yet." She added the last word in a hurry.

"Oh, baby, you have to." The man paused to take a big gulp from a glass of burgundy whose rich bouquet Scipio savored from ten feet away. He'd ordered it because it was expensive. Treating a vintage like that was a disgrace, to say nothing of a waste. Scipio couldn't do a thing about it, though. Nor could he do anything but stare impassively as the man went on, "He's sound on the nigger question. He's very, very sound. He knows just what he wants to do about coons."

Did he even remember Scipio was standing close by? Remember or not, he didn't care. What was a black waiter but part of the furniture? The man's companion said, "Good. That's good. They're a pack of troublemakers." She had no trouble forgetting about Scipio's existence, either.

They remembered him when they ordered peach cobbler for dessert, but gave no sign of knowing he'd been around while they were eating. Scipio was tempted to spit in the desserts. With something gooey like peach cobbler, they'd never know. He finally didn't, though he had trouble saying why. *Life is too short,* was all that really occurred to him.

The white man tipped well. He left the money where the girl could see it. He aimed to impress her, not to make Scipio happy. Scipio didn't care. Money was money.

Jerry Dover saw him pocket the brown banknotes. The manager missed next to nothing. He would have said—he did say—his job was to miss next to nothing. "Got yourself a high roller, did you?" he said as Scipio came back toward the kitchen.

"Not too bad," Scipio allowed.

"How come you don't look happy, then?" Dover asked.

"I's happy enough," Scipio said. His face became the expressionless mask he used to shield his feelings from the outside world, the white man's world. Even Jerry Dover had trouble penetrating that reserve.

He had trouble most of the time. Not tonight. "Sidney goin' on about niggers again?" he asked.

"Well . . . yeah, he do dat some," Scipio said unwillingly.

"Can't be a whole lot of fun for you to listen to," Dover said. Scipio only shrugged. His boss asked, "You want to go home early? All right by me."

"An' leave you shorthanded? Nah. I be fine," Scipio said, angry at himself for letting the white man see he was upset.

"Buy something nice for your missus with the money," Jerry Dover said. "Sidney figures if his new girl thinks he's one tough guy, she's more likely to suck him off. Haven't you seen that before?"

Damnfool buckra, Scipio thought. But he couldn't say that. A white could make cracks about another white. He could even do that in a black's hearing. But for a black to make cracks about a white, even with another white who'd just made a crack about the same man, broke the rules. Scipio didn't consciously understand that. For him, it was water to a fish. But a fish without water would die. A black who broke the rules of the CSA would die, too.

He got through the rest of the night. When he left the restaurant, he went into a world of darkness. Blackout regulations had reached

Augusta, though the next U.S. airplane the city saw would be its first. Scipio went south toward the Terry with reasonable confidence. The colored part of town had never had street lights to black out. That made Scipio more used to getting along without them than most whites were.

Every so often, an auto would chug by, its headlights reduced to slits by tape or by hastily manufactured blinkers that fit over them. The muted lamps gave just enough light to keep a driver from going up on the sidewalk—as long as he didn't go too fast. The *Constitutionalist* seemed to report more nighttime smash-ups every day.

Lights or no lights, Scipio knew when he got to the Terry. No more motorcars. The pavement under his feet turned bumpy and hole-pocked. The stink of privies filled his nostrils. There even seemed to be more mosquitoes. He wouldn't have been surprised. Public-health men were likely to spray oil on puddles in the white part of town first and worry about the Terry later, if at all. If some Negroes came down sick, well, so what? They were only Negroes.

He tried to walk quietly in the Terry. Lately, lots of hungry black sharecroppers had come into Augusta from the nearby cotton farms and cornfields. Tractors and harvesters and combines had stolen their livelihood. Here in the Terry, they weren't fussy about what they did to eat, or to whom they did it.

Some of them would sneak out and prey on whites. But that was risky, and deadly dangerous if they got caught. Most preyed on their own kind instead. The police were much less likely to go after blacks who robbed other blacks. Blacks who stole from other blacks got easier treatment even when the police did catch them.

Scipio scowled, there in the midnight gloom. *The white folks reckon we're worthless,* he thought bitterly. *Is it any wonder a lot of us reckon we're worthless, too?* That was perhaps the most bitter pill blacks in the CSA had to swallow. Too often, they judged themselves the way their social superiors and former masters judged them.

But how can we help it? Scipio wondered. Whites in the CSA had always dominated the printed word. Now they had charge of the wireless and the cinema, too. They made Negroes see themselves as they saw them. Was it any wonder skin-lightening creams and hair-straightening pomades made money for druggists all over the Confederacy?

Some of the pomades worked, after a fashion. A lot of them, Scipio had heard, were mostly lye, and lye would shift damn near anything. What it did to your scalp while it straightened your hair was liable to be something else again. But then, some people judged a pomade's quality by how much it hurt. As far as Scipio knew, all the skin-lightening creams were nothing but grease and perfume. None of them was good for more than separating a sucker from his—or more likely her—hard-earned dollars.

His own hair, though cut short, remained nappy. His skin—he looked down at the backs of his hands—was dark, dark brown. But would he have found Bathsheba so attractive if she'd been his own color and not a rather light-skinned mulatto? He was damned if he knew.

After a few paces, he shook his head in a mixture of guilt and self-disgust. He *did* know. He just didn't want to admit it to himself. Whites had shaped his tastes, too, so that he judged Negro women's attractiveness by how closely they approached their white sisters' looks.

There were black men who'd been warped more than he had, who craved the genuine article, not the approximation. Things seldom ended well for the few who tried to satisfy their cravings. In the right circumstances, white male Confederates might put up with some surprising things from blacks. They never put up with that, not when they found out about it.

When he heard footsteps coming up an alley, he shrank back into the deeper shadow of a fence and did his best to stop breathing. One . . . two . . . three young black men crossed the street in front of him. They had no idea he was there. Starlight glittered off the foot-long knife the biggest one carried.

"Slim pickin's tonight," the trailing man grumbled.

"We gits somebody," the one with the knife said. "We gits somebody, all right. Oh, hell, yes." On down the alley they padded, beasts of prey on the prowl.

Scipio waited till he couldn't hear their footfalls any more. Then he waited a little longer. Their ears were younger than his, and likely to be keener. The three didn't come running back toward him when he crossed the alley, so he'd waited long enough.

He hated them. He despised them. But next to the Freedom Party stalwarts—and especially next to the better disciplined Freedom Party guards—what were they? Stray dogs next to a pride of lions. And the Freedom Party men were always hungry for blood. He got to his apartment building without incident. The front door was locked. Up till a little while before, it hadn't been. Then a woman got robbed and stabbed in the lobby. That changed the manager's mind about what was needed to make the building stay livable. Scipio went in quickly, and locked the door behind him again.

Climbing the stairs to his flat was always the hardest part of the day. There seemed to be a thousand of them. He'd been on his feet forever at the Huntsman's Lodge—it felt that way, anyhow. His bones creaked. He carried the weight of all his years on his shoulders.

I was born a slave, he thought; he'd been a boy when the Confederate States manumitted their Negroes in the 1880s. *Am I anything but a slave nowadays?* Most of the time, he had no use for the Red rhetoric that had powered the Negro uprisings during the Great War. He'd thought them doomed to fail, and he'd been bloodily proved right. But when he ached, when he panted, when the world was too much with him, Marx and revolution held a wild temptation. *Like cheap booze for a drunk,* he thought wearily, *except revolutions make people do even stupider things.*

The apartment was dark. It still smelled of the ham hocks and greens his family had eaten for supper. His children's snores, and Bathsheba's, floated through the night. He sighed with pleasure as he undid his cravat and freed his neck from the high, tight, hot wing collar that had imprisoned him for so long.

Bathsheba stirred when he walked into their bedroom to finish undressing. "How'd it go?" she asked sleepily.

"Tolerable," he answered. "Sorry I bother you."

"Ain't no bother," his wife said. "Don't hardly see each other when we's both awake."

She wasn't wrong. He hung his clothes on the chair by the bed. He could wear the trousers and jacket another day. The shirt had to go to the laundry. He'd put on his older one tomorrow. If Jerry Dover grumbled, he wouldn't do any more than grumble.

Scipio asked, "How *you* is?" He let his cotton nightshirt fall down over his head.

Around a yawn, Bathsheba answered, "Tolerable, like you say." She yawned again. "Miz Finley, she tip me half a dollar—more'n I usually gits. But she make me listen to her go on and on about the war while I work. Ain't hardly worth it."

"No, I reckons not," Scipio said. "Could be worse, though. Buckra at the restaurant, he go on about de niggers to his lady friend—only she ain't no lady. He talk like I's nothin' but a brick in de wall."

"You mean you ain't?" Bathsheba said. Scipio laughed, not that it was really funny. If you didn't laugh, you'd scream, and that was—he supposed—worse. His wife went on, "Why don't you come to bed now, you ol' brick, you?" Laughing again, Scipio did.

Connie Enos clung to George. "I don't want you to go down to T Wharf," she said, tears in her voice.

For how many years had Boston fishermen's wives been saying that to the men they loved? It took on special urgency when George was going out again after coming home aboard the shot-up *Sweet Sue.* He had no really good answer for Connie, and gave the only one he could: "We got to eat, sweetie. Going to sea is the only thing I know how to do. We were lucky when the company paid us off for the last run. I don't suppose they would have if the *Globe* hadn't raised a stink."

He hadn't expected the company to pay off even with the stink. But next to the cost of repairing the boat, giving the surviving crewmen what they would have got after an average trip was small change. There were times when George understood why so many people voted Socialist, though he was a Democrat himself.

"Do you think the company will pay me blood money after the goddamn limeys sink your boat? Do you think I'd want it if they did?" Connie, born McGillicuddy, hardly ever swore, but made an exception for the British.

George shrugged helplessly. "Lightning doesn't strike twice in the same place," he said, knowing he was lying. Lightning hit wherever something tall stuck up, and hit again and again. But the *Sweet Sue* wasn't an especially remarkable boat. She'd been unlucky once. Why would she be again? *Because there's a war on,* he told himself, and wished he hadn't.

"Why don't you get a job in a war plant?" Connie demanded. "They're hiring every warm body they can get their hands on."

"I know they are." George tried to leave it at that.

Connie wouldn't let him. "Well, then, why don't you? War work pays better than going to sea, and you'd be home with your family. You'd be able to watch your kids grow up. They wouldn't be strangers to you. What's so bad about that?"

Nothing was bad about any of it. George's father would have been a stranger to him even if his destroyer hadn't been torpedoed at—after—the end of the Great War. Fishermen *were* strangers to their families, those who had families. That was part of what went into their being fishermen.

George knew that, felt that, but had no idea how to say it. The best he could manage was, "That isn't what I want to do."

His wife exhaled angrily. She put her hands on her hips, something she did only when truly provoked. She played her trump card: "And what about me? Do you want to end up being a stranger to your own wife?"

Wearily, George shook his head. He said, "Connie, I'm a fisherman. This is what I do. It's all I ever wanted to do. You knew that when you married me. Your old man's been going to sea longer than I've been alive. You know what it's like."

"Yeah, I know what it's like. Wondering when you're coming home. Wondering *if* you're coming home, especially now with the war. Wondering if you'll bring back any money. Wondering why I married you when all I've got is a shack job every two weeks or a month. You call that a marriage? You call that a *life*?" She burst into tears.

"Oh, for God's sake." George didn't know what to do with explosions like that. Connie had them every so often. If he'd accused her of acting Irish, she would have hit the ceiling and him, not necessarily in that order. He said, "Look, I've got to go. The boat's not gonna wait forever. This is what I do. This is what I *am*." That came as close to what he really meant as anything he could put into words.

It wasn't close enough. He could see that in Connie's blazing eyes. Shaking his head, he turned away, slung his duffel over his shoulder, and started down the hall to the stairs. Connie slammed the door behind him. Three people stuck their heads out of their apartments to see if a bomb had hit the building. George gave them a sickly smile and kept walking.

T Wharf was a relief. T Wharf was home, in many ways much more than the apartment was. This was where he wanted to be. This was where his friends were. This was where his world was, with the smells of fish and the sea and tobacco smoke and diesel fuel and exhaust, with the gulls skrawking overhead and the first officers cursing the company buyers in half a dozen languages when the prices were low, with the rumble of carts full of fish and ice, with the waving, sinuous tails of optimistic cats, with the scaly tails of the rats that weren't supposed to be there but hadn't got the news, with . . . with *everything*. He started smiling. He couldn't help it.

The *Sweet Sue* had a fresh coat of paint. She had new glass. You could hardly see the holes the bullets had made in her—but George knew. Oh, yes. He knew. He'd never be able to go into the galley again without thinking of the Cookie dead on the floor, his pipe beside him. They'd have a new Cookie now, and it wouldn't be the same.

On the other hand . . . There was Johnny O'Shea, leaning over the rail heaving his guts out. He drank like a fish whenever he was ashore, and caught fish when he went to sea. He wasn't seasick now, just getting rid of his last bender. He did that whenever he came aboard. Once he dried out, he'd be fine. Till he did, he'd go through hell.

I don't do that, George thought. *I never will—well, only once in a while. So what does Connie want from me, anyway?*

"Welcome back, George," Captain Albert called from his station at the bow.

"Thanks, Skipper," George said.

"Wasn't sure the little woman'd let you come out again."

"Well, she did." George didn't want anybody thinking he was henpecked. He went below, tossed the duffel bag in one of the tiny, dark cabins below the skipper's station, and stretched out on the bunk. When he got out of it, he almost banged his head on the planks not nearly far enough above it. He'd get used to this cramped womb again before long. He always did.

After stowing the duffel, George went back up on deck. But for the skipper and Johnny O'Shea, it was going to be a crew full of strangers. The old Cookie was dead, Chris Agganis was still getting over his wound, and the rest of the fishermen who'd been aboard on the last run didn't aim to come back.

A round man in dungarees, a ratty wool sweater, and an even rattier cloth cap approached the *Sweet Sue*. He'd slung a patched blue-denim duffel over his left shoulder. Waving to George, he called, "Can I come aboard?"

"You the new cook?" George asked.

"Sure as hell am," the newcomer answered. "How'd you know?" The gangplank rattled and boomed as his clodhoppers thumped on it.

Shrugging, George said, "You've got the look—know what I mean?" The other man nodded. George stuck out his hand and gave his name.

"Pleased t'meetcha." The new cook shook hands with him, then jabbed a thumb at his own broad chest. "I'm Horton Everett. Folks mostly call me Ev." He pointed to Johnny O'Shea. "Who's that sorry son of a bitch?"

"I heard that," O'Shea said. "Fuck you." He leaned over the rail to retch again, then spat and added, "Nothing personal."

"Johnny'll be fine when he sobers up and dries out," George said. "He's always like this when we're setting out."

Horton Everett nodded. He took a little cardboard box of cheap cigars from a trouser pocket, stuck one in his mouth, and offered George the box. George took one. Everett scraped a match alight on the sole of one big shoe, then lit both cigars. He liked a honey-flavored blend, George discovered. That made the smoke smooth and sweet, and helped disguise how lousy the tobacco was. And, with the Confederates shooting instead of trading, it would only get worse.

Other new hires came aboard. One of them, a skinny oldster who talked as if he wore ill-fitting dentures, joined Johnny O'Shea in misery by the rail. *Terrific,* George thought. *We've got two lushes aboard, not just one. The skipper better keep an eye on the medicinal brandy.*

After they pulled away from the wharf, the *Sweet Sue* had to join a gaggle of other fishing boats going out to sea. Actually, the skipper could have taken her out alone. But the fast little patrol boat shepherding his charges along had a crew who knew the route through the minefields intended to keep Confederate raiders away from Boston harbor. George suspected that was snapping fingers to keep the elephants away. Nobody much worried about his suspicions.

The *Sweet Sue's* diesel sounded just the way it was supposed to. George remained amazed that the British fighter could have shot up the boat so thoroughly without doing the engine much harm, but that was how things had turned out. Luck. All luck. Nothing but luck. If the fighter pilot had aimed his nose a little differently, he would have shot George and not the Cookie. George shivered, though summer heat clogged the air.

He shivered again when, after the *Sweet Sue* had threaded her way through the minefields, he went into the galley. Horton Everett had a pot of coffee going. "You want a cup?" he asked.

"Sure, Ev," George said. "Thanks." The new Cookie's cigar smoke gave the place a smell different from the one Davey Hatton's pipe tobacco had imparted. The coffee was hot and strong. George sipped thoughtfully. "Not bad."

"Glad you like it." Everett puffed on a new cigar. "You and the skipper and what's-his-name—the sot—are gonna measure every goddamn thing I do against what the other Cookie did, ain't you?"

"Well . . ." George felt a dull embarrassment at being so transparent. "I guess maybe we are. I don't see how we can help it. Do you?"

The new Cookie took off his cap and scratched tousled gray hair. "Mm, maybe not. All right. Fair enough. I'll do the best I can. Don't cuss me out too hard if it ain't quite the same."

For lunch, he fried up a big mess of roast-beef hash, with eggs over easy on top and hash browns on the side. Neither Johnny O'Shea nor the other drunk was in any shape to eat, which only meant there was more for everybody else. It wasn't a meal Davey Hatton would have made, but it was a long way from bad.

The skipper ate slowly, with a thoughtful air. He caught George's eye and raised an eyebrow ever so slightly: a silent question. George gave back a tiny nod: an answer. Captain Albert nodded in turn: agreement. Then he spoke up: "Pretty damn good chow, Cookie."

"Thanks, Skipper," Everett answered. "Glad you like it. Of course, you'd be just as much stuck with it if you didn't."

"Don't remind me," the skipper said. "Don't make me wish another British fighter'd come calling, either."

Horton Everett mimed getting shot. He was a pretty good actor. He got the skipper and the new fishermen laughing. George managed to plaster a smile on his face, too, but it wasn't easy. He'd been right here when the old Cookie really did take a bullet in the chest. The one good thing was, he'd died so fast, he'd hardly known what hit him.

Everett said, "You guys better like the hash and eggs now, on account of it's gonna be tuna all the goddamn way home."

They cursed him good-naturedly. They knew he was right. Maybe he could even keep tuna interesting. That would make him a fine Cookie indeed. And, with any luck, they'd never see a British airplane. *Lightning doesn't strike twice.* George tried to make himself believe the lie.

Sometimes the simplest things could bring pleasure. Hipolito Rodriguez had never imagined how much enjoyment he could get just by opening the refrigerator door. An electric light inside the cold box came on as if by magic, so he could see what was inside even in the middle of the night. Vegetables and meat stayed fresh a very long time in there.

And he could have a cold bottle of beer whenever he wanted to. He didn't need to go to *La Culebra Verde.* He could buy his *cerveza* at the general store, bring it home, and drink it as cold as if it were at the cantina—and save money doing it. Not only that, he could drink a cold beer with Magdalena, and his *esposa* would not have been caught dead in *La Culebra Verde.*

Such thoughts all flowed from opening a refrigerator door. If that wasn't a miracle of this modern age, what would be? As soon as the question formed in his mind, so did an answer. What about the new wireless set? He'd left the valley in which Baroyeca sat only twice in his life: once to go to war and once to go to Hermosillo, the capital of Sonora, to agitate for a second term for Jake Featherston. But the wireless set brought the wider world here.

Magdalena came into the kitchen. She wasn't thinking about miracles. She said, "Why are you standing there in front of the refrigerator letting all the cold air out?"

"I don't know," he answered, feeling foolish. "Probably because I'm an idiot. I can't think of any other reason." Watching the light come on didn't seem reason enough, that was for sure.

By the way his wife smiled, she had her suspicions. She said,

"Well, whatever the reason is, come into the front room. It's just about time for the news."

The wireless set wasn't a big, fancy one, a piece of furniture in its own right. It sat on a small table. But the room centered on it. Chairs and the old, tired sofa all faced it, as if you could actually see the pictures the announcer painted with his words.

Magdalena turned the knob. The dial began to glow—another little electric light in there. After half a minute or so of warming up, music started to play: it wasn't quite time for the news. Some people had had wind-up phonographs before electricity came to Baroyeca. Those were fine, but this was even better. Any sort of sound could come out of a wireless set, any sound at all.

"This is radio station CSON, telling you the truth from Hermosillo," the announcer said in a mixture of Spanish and English almost anyone from Sonora and Chihuahua—and a lot of people in Texas, U.S. New Mexico and California, and several of the Empire of Mexico's northern provinces—could understand. The announcer went on, "One more song to bring us up to the top of the hour, and then the news."

Like most of what CSON played, the song was *norteño* music, full of thumping drums and accordion. The singer used the same blend of Sonora's two languages as the announcer. That made Rodriguez frown a little. When he was a young man, *norteño* music had been in Spanish alone—even though its instruments were borrowed from German settlers along the old border between Texas and Mexico. Because that was what he'd grown up with, he thought it right and natural. As the years went by, though, English advanced and Spanish retreated in his home state.

When the syrupy love song ended, a blaring march—a Confederate imitation of John Philip Sousa—announced the hour and introduced the news. "Here is the truth," the newscaster said: the Freedom Party's claim to it, these days, was far from limited to Jake Featherston alone. Another march, a triumphant one, rang out. That meant the newscaster was going to claim a victory. Sure enough, he spoke in proud tones: "Your brave Confederate soldiers have closed an iron ring around Columbus, Ohio. Several divisions of Yankee troops are trapped inside the city. If they cannot break out, they will be forced to surrender."

"That's amazing," Rodriguez said to Magdalena. "To have

come so far so fast . . . Neither side did anything like this in the last war."

"Shh," she told him. "If we're going to listen, let's listen." He nodded. A wise husband didn't quarrel even when he was right. Quarreling when you knew you were wrong was a recipe for disaster.

The newscaster said, "Here is Brigadier General Patton, commander of the Army of Kentucky's armored striking force."

In pure English, a man with a raspy, tough-sounding voice said, "We've got the damnyankees by the neck. Now we're going to shake them till they're dead." For those who couldn't follow that, the announcer translated it into the mixed language commonly used in the Confederacy's Southwest. The officer—General Patton—went on, "They thought they were going to have things all their own way again this time. I'm here to tell them they've missed the bus."

Hipolito Rodriguez followed that well enough. He glanced over to Magdalena. She was waiting for the translation. He hadn't had much English, either, before he went to war. These days, he dealt with it without thinking twice.

The announcer went on to talk about what he called a terror-bombing raid by U.S. airplanes over Little Rock. "Forty-seven people were killed, including nineteen children sheltering at a school," he said indignantly. "Confederate bombers, by contrast, strike only military targets except when taking reprisals for U.S. air piracy. And President Featherston vows that, for every ton of bombs that falls on the Confederate States, three tons will fall on the United States. They will pay for their aggression against us."

"This is how it ought to be," Rodriguez said, and his wife nodded.

"In other news, the reckless policies of *los Estados Unidos* have earned the reward they deserve," the newscaster said. "The Empire of Japan has declared war on the United States, citing their provocative policy in the Central Pacific. The United States claim to have inflicted heavy losses on carrier-based aircraft attacking the Sandwich Islands, but the Japanese dismiss this report as just another U.S. lie."

"They are supposed to be very pretty—the Sandwich Islands," Magdalena said wistfully.

"Nothing is pretty once bombs start falling on it," Rodriguez replied with great conviction. "That was true in the last war, and it is bound to be even more true in this one, because the bombs are bigger."

"Prime Minister Churchill calls the entry of Japan into the war a strong blow against the United States," the announcer went on. "He says it will restore the proper balance of power in the Pacific. Once the United States are driven from the Sandwich Islands, Japanese-Confederate cooperation against the West Coast of the USA will follow as day follows night, in his opinion."

That was a very large thought. Rodriguez remembered that the Japanese had bombed Los Angeles during the Pacific War. But that had been only a raid. This could prove much more important. Of course, the Japanese hadn't pushed *los Estados Unidos* out of the Sandwich Islands. If they did, that would be wonderful. If they didn't, they would still tie up a big U.S. fleet. Too bad they wouldn't be able to pull off a surprise attack, the way the USA had against Britain at the start of the Great War.

In portentous tones, the newscaster continued, "Prime Minister Churchill also spoke of the pounding Berlin, Munich, Frankfurt, and other German cities have taken from the French and British air fleets. Smoke climbs thousands of feet into the sky. German efforts to retaliate are feeble indeed. The Prime Minister also declares that the collapse of the Ukraine at Russia's first blows and the clear weakness of Austria-Hungary argue the war in Europe will go differently this time."

Hipolito Rodriguez tried to imagine another war across the sea, a war as big as the one here in North America and even more complicated. He had trouble doing it. He would have had trouble imagining the war here if he hadn't fought in the last one. That was what came of peacefully living most of his life on a farm outside a small town in Sonora.

"In a display of barbarism yesterday, the United States executed four Canadians accused of railroad sabotage," the newsman said. "Confederate security forces in Mississippi, meanwhile, smashed a squadron of colored bandits intent on murdering white men and women and destroying valuable property. The *mallates* and their mischief *will* be suppressed."

He sounded full of stern enthusiasm. Rodriguez found himself nodding. He'd suppressed *mallates* himself—niggers, they called them in English. That had been his first taste of war, even before he faced the Yankees. As far as he was concerned, black men caused nothing but trouble. He had another reason for despising them, too. They were below folk of Mexican descent in the Confederate social scale. If not for blacks, the white majority would have turned all its scorn on greasers. Rodriguez was as sure of that as he was of his own name.

A string of commercials followed. The messages were fascinating. They made Rodriguez want to run right out and buy beer or shampoo or razor blades. If he hadn't lived three miles from the nearest general store, he might have done it. Next time he was in Baroyeca, he might do it yet.

More music followed the commercials. The news was done. Rodriguez said, "The war seems to be going well."

"No war that has our son in it is going well." Now Magdalena was the one whose voice held conviction.

"Well, yes," Rodriguez admitted. "*Tienes razón.* But even if you are right, wouldn't you rather see him in a winning fight than a losing one? Winning is the only point to fighting a war."

His wife shook her head. "There is no point to fighting a war," she said, still with that terrible certainty. "Win or lose, you only fight another one ten years later, or twenty, or thirty. Can you tell me I am wrong?"

Rodriguez wished he could. The evidence, though, seemed to lie on his wife's side. He shrugged. "If we win a great victory, maybe *los Estados Unidos* won't be able to fight us any more."

"They must have thought the same thing about *los Estados Confederados,*" Magdalena said pointedly.

"They did not count on Jake Featherston." Rodriguez missed that point.

His wife let out an exasperated sniff. "Maybe they will have that kind of President themselves. Or maybe they will not need a man like that. They are bigger than we are, and stronger, too. Can we really beat them?"

"If *Señor* Featherston says we can, then we can," Rodriguez answered. "And he does, so I think we can."

"He is not God Almighty," Magdalena warned. "He can make mistakes."

"I know he can. But he hasn't made very many," Rodriguez said. "Until he shows me he *is* making mistakes, I will go on trusting him. He is doing very well so far, and you cannot tell me anything different."

"So far," his wife echoed.

Sometimes Rodriguez let her have the last word—most of the time, in fact. He was indeed a sensible, well-trained husband. But not this time, not when it was political rather than something really important. They argued far into the night.

Brigadier General Abner Dowling had never expected to command the defense of Ohio from the great metropolis of Bucyrus. The town—it couldn't have held ten thousand people—was pleasant enough. The Sandusky River, which was barely wide enough there to deserve the name, meandered through it. The small central business district was full of two- and three-story buildings of dull red and buff bricks. A factory that had made seamless copper kettles now turned out copper tubing; one that had built steamrollers was making parts for barrels.

How long any of that would last, Dowling couldn't say. With Columbus lost, he had no idea whether or how long Bucyrus could hold out. He counted himself lucky to have got out of Columbus before the Confederate ring closed around it. A lot of good U.S. soldiers hadn't. The Columbus pocket was putting up a heroic resistance, but he knew too well it was a losing fight. The Confederates weren't trying very hard to break into the city. Cut off from resupply and escape, sooner or later the U.S. soldiers would wither on the vine. The Confederates, meanwhile, kept storming forward as if they had the hosts of hell behind them.

Dowling's makeshift headquarters were in what had been a grain and feed store. The proprietor, an upright Buckeye named Milton Kellner, had moved in with his brother and sister-in-law. Sentries kept out farmers who wanted to buy chicken feed and hay. Dowling wished they would have kept out all the soldiers who wanted to see him, too. No such luck.

Confederate artillery could already reach Bucyrus. Dowling wondered if he should have retreated farther north. He didn't like making his fight from a distance, though. He wanted to get right up there and slug it out with the enemy toe to toe.

The only problem was, the enemy didn't care to fight that kind of war against him. Confederate barrels kept finding weak spots in his positions, pounding through, and forcing his men to fall back or be surrounded. Fighters shot up his soldiers from the sky. Dive bombers wrecked strongpoints that defied C.S. artillery. He didn't have enough barrels or airplanes to do unto the enemy as the enemy was doing unto him.

Boards covered the front window to Kellner's store. That wasn't so much to protect the window as to protect the people inside the building from what would happen if the glass shattered. Bucyrus still had electricity; it drew its power from the north, not from Columbus. The environment inside the store wasn't gloomy. The atmosphere, on the other hand . . .

A young lieutenant stuck pins with red heads ever farther up a big map of Ohio tacked to the wall over a chart that luridly illustrated the diseases of hens. Dowling was just as glad not to have to look at that. Hens' insides laid open for autopsy reminded him too much of men's insides laid open by artillery.

"By God, it's a wonder every soldier in the world isn't a vegetarian," he said.

"Because we do butchers' work, sir?" the young officer asked.

"It isn't because we parade so prettily," Dowling growled. The lieutenant, whose name was Jack Tompkins, blushed like a schoolgirl.

"What are we going to do, sir?" Tompkins asked.

Dowling eyed him sourly. He couldn't possibly have been born when the Great War ended. Everything he knew about fighting, he'd picked up in the past few weeks. And, by all appearances, Dowling knew just as little about this new, fast-moving style of warfare. The idea was humiliating, which made it no less true. "What are we going to do?" he repeated. "We're going to go straight at those butternut sons of bitches, and we're going to knock the snot out of them."

Custer would be proud of you, a small mocking voice said in the back of his mind. Custer had always believed in going straight at the enemy, regardless of whether that was the right thing to do. Dowling wouldn't have thought his longtime superior's style had rubbed off on him so much, but it seemed to have.

And no sooner were the words out of his mouth than a messenger came into the feed store with what, by his glum expression, had to be bad news. "Well?" Dowling demanded. Since the war started, he'd already heard about as much bad news as he could stand.

No matter what he'd heard, he was going to get more. "Sir," the messenger said, "the Confederates have bombed a troop train just the other side of Canton. Those reinforcements we hoped for are going to be late, and a lot of them won't come in at all. There were heavy casualties."

Custer would have screamed and cursed—probably something on the order of, *Why do these things happen to me?* He would have blamed the messenger, or the War Department, or anyone else who happened to be handy. That way, no blame was likely to light on him.

With a grimace, Dowling accepted the burden. "Damnation," he said. "So the antiaircraft guns on the flatcars didn't work?"

"Not this time, sir," the messenger answered.

"Damnation," Dowling said again. "I was counting on those troops to go into the counterattack against the Confederates' eastern prong. If I hold it up till they do come in . . . well, what the devil will the enemy do to me in the meantime?"

The messenger only shrugged. Dowling dismissed him with an unhappy wave of the hand. Lieutenant Tompkins said, "Sir, we haven't got the men to make that counterattack work without reinforcements."

"Now tell me something I didn't know," Dowling said savagely. Tompkins turned red again. Dowling felt ashamed of himself. He had to lash out at someone, but poor Tompkins was hardly a fair target. "Sorry," he mumbled.

"It's all right, sir," the young lieutenant answered. "I know we've got to do something." His eyes drifted to the ominous map. He spread his hands in an apology of his own. "I just don't know what."

The U.S. Army wasn't paying him to know what to do. It was, unfortunately, paying Abner Dowling for exactly that. And Dowling had no more inkling than Tompkins did. He sighed heavily. "I think the counterattack will have to go in anyway."

"Yes, sir." Lieutenant Tompkins looked at the map again. "Uh, sir . . . What do you think the chances are?"

"Slim," Dowling said with brutal honesty. "We won't drive the enemy very far. But we may rock him back on his heels just the same. And if he's responding to us, he won't be able to make us dance to his tune. I hope he won't." He wished, too late, that he hadn't tacked on those last four words.

With no great hope in his heart, he started drafting the orders. In the last war, Custer had fed men into the meat grinder with a fine indifference to their fate. Dowling couldn't be so dispassionate—or was it simply callous? He knew this attack had no real hope past spoiling whatever the Confederates might be up to. That that was reason enough to make it was a measure of his own growing desperation.

Artillery shells began falling on Bucyrus again not long after he got to work on the orders. He didn't think the Confederates knew he was here. They would have hit harder if they did.

And then, off in the distance, an automobile horn started honking, and another, and another. Dowling swore under his breath. Soldiers by the thousands—by the tens of thousands—were trapped in and around Columbus, but the Confederates were letting out women, children, and old men: anyone who didn't seem to be of military age. Why not? It made them seem humane, and it made the USA take care of the refugees—whose columns Confederate pilots still gleefully shot up when they got out beyond the C.S. lines.

"What do we do with them, sir?" Lieutenant Tompkins asked.

"We get them off the roads so they don't tie up our movements," Dowling answered. That had been standard operating procedure ever since the shooting started. It had also proved easier said than done. The refugees wanted to get away. They didn't give a damn about moving over to let soldiers by. After some more low-voiced swearing, Dowling went on, "Once we do that, we see to their food and medical needs. But we've got to keep the roads clear. How are we supposed to stop the Confederates if we can't even get from here to there?"

"Beats me, sir," Tompkins said. He didn't say the U.S. Army hadn't been able to stop the Confederates even when it had moved freely. Of course, he didn't need to say that, either. Headquarters for U.S. forces in Ohio wouldn't have been in a feed shop in Bucyrus if it weren't true.

The horns went on and on. The refugees had probably bumped up against the U.S. lines on the south side of town. Abstractly, Dowling could know a certain detached sympathy for them. They hadn't asked to have their lives turned upside down. Concretely, though, he just wanted to shunt them out of the way so he could get on with the business of fighting the enemy.

He wasn't thrilled about letting them through his lines, either. Sure as hell, the Confederates would have planted spies among the fugitives. They seemed to be taking espionage and sabotage a lot more seriously in this war than they had in the last one. The USA had trouble gauging how seriously they were taking it, because not all their operatives were getting caught.

He knew his own side was doing the same in the CSA. He'd commanded in Kentucky before the state fell back into Confederate hands. After U.S. forces had to pull out, he'd arranged to keep the new occupiers occupied. He only wished he would have seen more results from U.S. efforts and fewer from the Confederates'.

An auto screeched to a stop in front of the feed store. A harried-looking sergeant came in. "Sir, what are we going to do with those bastards?" he said. "They've got a lawyer out in front of 'em. He says they've got a Constitutional right to come through."

Abner Dowling did not like lawyers. He said, "Tell the guy to go to hell. Tell him Ohio's under martial law, so all his Constitutional rights are straight down the toilet. If he gives you any lip after that, tell him we'll goddamn well conscript him into a ditch-digging detail unless he shuts up. If he doesn't shut up, you do it—and if he doesn't have bloody blisters on his hands inside of two hours after that, you're in big trouble. Got it?"

"Yes, sir!" The sergeant saluted. He did a smart about-face and got out of there in a hurry. The motorcar roared away.

A few minutes later, the auto horns stopped very suddenly. Dowling grunted in an odd kind of embarrassed satisfaction. He'd done what he needed to do. That didn't make him very proud of himself. It didn't do a thing to help the poor refugees. But it did mean he could get on with the war without having those people get in his way.

He finished drafting the order for the counterattack that would now have to start without the men from the westbound troop train. That didn't make him very proud of himself, either. He knew what was likely to happen to the soldiers who did go in. What he didn't know was what the Confederates would do to him if he failed to make that attack. He was afraid to find out. He handed the orders to Lieutenant Tompkins, who hurried off to get them encoded and transmitted. "Poor bastards," Dowling muttered, feeling very much a poor bastard himself.

During the Great War, Dr. Leonard O'Doull had never actually seen action. He'd served in a hospital well back of the lines, a hospital artillery couldn't reach. He'd met his wife in that hospital. When the retired Colonel Quigley talked him into putting on a U.S. uniform again, he'd assumed he'd be doing the same kind of thing again.

So much for assumptions. War had changed in the past generation. Treating the wounded had changed, too. The sooner they got help, the better they did. Taking them back to hospitals far behind the lines often let them bleed to death, or quietly die of shock, or come down with a wound infection that would do them in. People had known about that during the Great War. This time around, they were actually trying to do something about it.

O'Doull worked in an aid station about half a mile behind the line. The tents had red crosses prominently displayed. He didn't think the Confederates would shell them or bomb them on purpose. That didn't make him feel any better when machine-gun bullets or rifle rounds cracked past, or when artillery shells came down close by. Even before he got there, all the tents had bullet holes as well as the red crosses.

When U.S. lines moved back, the tents moved with them. And when U.S. soldiers counterattacked and regained ground, the aid station went along. The latest counterattack in eastern Ohio was aimed at Zanesville, which had fallen to the Confederates two weeks before.

Just because it was aimed at Zanesville didn't mean it would get there. Confederate dive bombers had stalled it outside of Cooper-dale, twenty miles north of the target. The aid station was operating in an oak wood a few miles north of the hamlet, which the Confederates were defending as if it were Columbus.

O'Doull himself was operating on a man with a wounded leg. An X ray would have shown just where the shell fragment lay. The X-ray machine was at a field hospital five miles farther back. O'Doull was finding the sharp metal the old-fashioned way, with a probe.

He'd given the soldier a local, but it hadn't really taken hold. The man wiggled and cussed every time the probe moved. O'Doull couldn't blame him. He thought he would have done the same thing had he been on the other end of the probe. It did make his job harder, though.

"Try to hold still, Corporal," he said for about the dozenth time. "I think I'm very close to— Ah!" The probe grated on something hard.

"Shit!" the corporal said, and wiggled again. O'Doull felt like saying *shit,* too; the writhe had made him lose the fragment.

But he knew it couldn't be far. He found it again a minute later. He slid the probe out of the wound and slipped a long-handled forceps in instead. The noncom gave his detailed opinion of that, too. O'Doull didn't care. He felt like cheering when the jaws of the forceps closed on the fragment. "Now you have to hold still," he warned the corporal. "This *will* hurt, but it'll be the end of it."

"Awright, Doc." The man visibly braced himself. "Go ahead."

When O'Doull did, a torrent of horrible curses broke from the corporal's lips. He did hold still, though. O'Doull eased the shell fragment out through the man's torn flesh. When he drew it out, he found it about the size of his thumbnail. He opened the forceps. The fragment dropped with a clank into a metal basin.

"That it?" the corporal asked, staring with interest at what had laid him up. "That goddamn little thing?"

"I think so. I hope so." O'Doull dusted the wound with sulfa powder and sewed it up. After a moment's hesitation, he put a drain in it. Maybe it would heal clean—the new drugs did some wonderful things. But you never could tell.

He'd just straightened up when a yell came from outside: "Doc! Hey, Doc! We got a sucking chest!"

Now O'Doull did say, "Shit," but under his breath. "Bring him in," he called. "I'll do what I can."

He cut the soldier's tunic off him—that being the fastest way to get rid of it—to work on the wound on the right side of his chest. One of the corpsmen who'd come in with the casualty said, "Pulse is fast and weak and thready, Doc. He's losing blood in there like a son of a bitch."

One look at the wounded man's pale face would have told O'Doull that. The man was having trouble breathing, too. That blood was drowning him. O'Doull clapped an ether cone over his face. "Plasma!" he shouted. "Run it into him like it's going out of style." He might not have spoken English much over the past quarter of a century, but it came back.

All he could do was hope the wounded man was under when he started using the scalpel. If he waited, the soldier would die on him. He didn't need to be a medical genius to know that. The bullet, he saw when he got in there, had chewed up the lower lobe of the right lung. No chance to save it; he cut it out. A man could live on a lung and a half, or even on a lung. He cleared the blood from the chest cavity, stuck a big drain in the wound—no hesitation this time—and closed.

"That's a nice piece of work, Doc," the corpsman said. The war was less than a month old, but he'd already seen plenty to have some professional expertise. "He may make it, and I wouldn't have given a wooden nickel for his chances when he got here."

"I dealt with the worst of the damage," O'Doull said. "He's young. He's strong. He's healthy—or he was before he got hit. He does have a shot." He stretched, and let out a sigh of relief. Only his right arm had been moving while he worked on the patient.

"Morphine?" the corpsman asked. "He ain't gonna be what you call happy when he comes out from under the ether."

"Half a dose, maybe," O'Doull answered after considering. He nodded to himself. "Yes, half a dose. He'll have a devil of a time breathing anyway, what with the wound and the collapsed lung I gave him opening up his chest."

"He'd be dead if you hadn't," the other man observed.

"Yes, I know," O'Doull said. "But morphine weakens the breathing reflex, and that's the last thing he needs right now."

"I suppose." The corpsman took out a syringe and injected the unconscious soldier. "Half a dose, like you say. If it was me laying there, though, I bet like anything I'd want more."

"He can have more when he shows it won't kill him," O'Doull answered. "He wouldn't want that, would he?"

The corpsman took a somber look at the long, quickly sutured wound across the injured man's chest. "Damned if I know. He'll wish he was dead for a while, I'll tell you."

He was bound to be right on that score. O'Doull didn't feel like arguing with him, and ducked out of the tent for a while. He couldn't light a cigarette in there, not with the ether. If he lit one out here, he was taking his chances with snipers. But it would steady his hands. He needed about fifteen seconds to rationalize it and talk himself into doing what he already wanted to do anyhow.

Now that, for a moment, he wasn't frantically busy, he listened to the way things were going up at the front. He didn't have much experience there, but he didn't like what he heard. All the artillery and machine guns in the world seemed to be pointing back at him. The front was alive with the catamount screech soldiers on both sides still called the rebel yell. The Confederates had their peckers up, and the U.S. soldiers facing them didn't.

A couple of men in green-gray came back through the trees. They both carried their rifles. Neither one looked panic-stricken. But they didn't look like men who intended to do any more fighting any time soon, either.

They eyed Dr. Leonard O'Doull. "Got some butts you can spare, buddy?" one of them asked. Wordlessly, he held out the pack. They each took a cigarette and leaned close to him for lights. Then, nodding their thanks, they kept on heading north.

He started to call after them, but checked himself. It wasn't fear they would turn their rifles on him, though that crossed his mind, too. What really stopped him was just the conviction that they wouldn't pay any attention to him. He saw no point in wasting his breath.

He ground out his cigarette under his heel. Army boots were a discomfort he'd forgotten in the years since taking off his uniform. He felt as if he had a rock tied to each foot. He understood why infantrymen had to wear such formidable footgear. He was much less sure why he did.

Back into the tent. Back to work. He checked the man with the chest wound. The fellow wasn't in great shape, but he was still breathing. If sulfa drugs let him dodge a wound infection, he might pull through.

O'Doull looked around in sudden confusion. He'd been maniacally busy for he'd forgotten how many hours, running on nerves and nicotine and coffee. Now, all at once, he had nothing to do. His tremble was like the last lingering note from an orchestra after a piece had ended.

"Jesus, I'm bushed!" he said to nobody in particular.

"Why don't you flop, then, Doc?" said a corpsman named Granville McDougald: a man who had no degree in medicine but who would have made a good general practitioner and a pretty fair jackleg surgeon.

"I don't know, Granny. Why don't I?" O'Doull answered, and yawned.

"Go sleep," McDougald told him. "We'll kick your ass out of bed if we need you. Don't you worry about that."

"I'm not." O'Doull yawned again. "What I'm worried about is, will I have any brains if you wake me after I've been sleeping for a little bit? Or will I be too far underwater to do anybody any good for a while?"

"If you *don't* go to sleep, will you be able to do anybody good?" McDougald asked reasonably. "Sleepy docs kill patients."

He was right about that. O'Doull knew it. It got proved all too often. He found his cot and lay down on it. He couldn't sleep on his belly the way he liked to, not without taking off his boots. That demanded too much energy. He curled up on his right side and fell asleep as if someone had pulled his plug.

He had no idea when Granny McDougald shook him awake. All he knew was, he hadn't been asleep nearly long enough. "Wha' happened?" he asked muzzily. "Who's hurt? What do I have to do?"

"Nobody's hurt," the corpsman replied. "Nobody's hurt that you gotta deal with, anyway. But we're pulling back, and we figured you better come along. It's that or you do your doctoring in a Confederate POW camp."

"What the hell?" O'Doull said. "Something go wrong while I was out?"

"Either you've got a clean conscience or you really were whupped," McDougald told him. "Didn't you hear all the shooting and bombing off to our right? The Confederates have smashed our line. If we don't get out, we get caught."

"Oh." O'Doull left it at that, which McDougald thought was pretty funny. They took down the tents, loaded them and their patients into trucks, and headed north. They didn't stop for quite a while. Nobody thought that was funny, nobody at all.

VII

Jefferson Pinkard prowled Camp Dependable like a hound hunting a buried bone. The black prisoners got out of his way. Even his own guards were leery of him. When the boss wanted something he couldn't figure out how to get, everybody was liable to suffer.

What Pinkard wanted was a bigger camp, or fewer shipments of Negroes coming in from all over the CSA. He wasn't likely to get either one of those. He would have settled for a way to reduce population quickly, efficiently, and above all neatly. He hadn't been able to manage that, either.

The morning's news was what had set him prowling. Mercer Scott had come to him with a scowl on his face. Scott always scowled, but this was something special. "Chick Blades is dead," he'd told Pinkard. "Killed himself."

"Aw, shit," was what Pinkard had said. Some of that was dismay. More was a sort of resigned disgust. Blades was a man who'd gone out on a lot of population-reduction details. After a while—how long depended on the man—some people cracked. They couldn't keep doing it, not and stay sane. Blades was the second or third suicide Camp Dependable had seen. One or two men were wearing straitjackets these days. And others got drunk all the time or ruined themselves other ways.

Mercer Scott had nodded. "That's what I said when I found out." He took a somber satisfaction in passing on bad news.

"How'd he do it? Wasn't a gun—somebody would've reported the shot." Pinkard liked to have things straight. "He hang himself?"

"Nope. Went out to his auto, ran a hose from the exhaust to the inside, closed all the windows, and started up the motor."

"Christ!" That had damn near made Pinkard lose his breakfast. The idea of sitting there waiting to go under, knowing what you'd done to yourself . . . If you were going to do it, better to get it over with all at once, as far as he was concerned.

"Yeah, well . . ." Scott had only shrugged. "Healthiest-looking goddamn corpse you ever seen."

"What do you mean?"

That question had surprised the head guard. Then he looked sly. "Oh, that's right—you never were a real cop or anything like that, were you?" He knew damn well Pinkard hadn't been. He went on, "When they kill themselves with exhaust, they're always pink instead of pale the way dead bodies usually are when you find 'em. Something in the gas does it. It's got a fancy name—I misremember what."

"Oh, that." Pinkard had nodded. "Now I know what you're talkin' about. Burn a charcoal fire in a room that's closed up tight and you're liable not to get out of bed the next morning, or ever. And if you don't, you look like that—all pink, like you say."

"Didn't figure Chick'd be the one to do it," Mercer Scott had said. "He never fretted over getting rid of niggers, not that I ever knew."

Jeff Pinkard hadn't noticed that Blades carried any special burden, either. That bothered him. If he'd pulled the guard off of population reductions, would Blades still be alive today? How could you know something like that? You couldn't. You could only wonder. And so Pinkard prowled and prowled and prowled.

He kept chewing on what had happened. The worst thing about a guard's suicide was what it did to the morale of those who survived. He'd have to watch three or four people extra close for a while, to make sure they didn't get any bright ideas. And they were free citizens, like everybody else—everybody white, anyhow—in the CSA. You couldn't watch them every damn minute of every damn day. If they decided to kill themselves, you probably couldn't do much about it.

Chick Blades, if he remembered straight, had a wife and kids. Pinkard supposed it was a good thing the man hadn't hauled them into the motorcar with him. Exhaust from an engine could have done in four or five for the price of one.

A hurrying Negro almost ran into him. "Where the hell you think you're going, God damn you?" Jeff roared.

"Latrine, suh," the black man answered. "I got me the gallopin' shits, an' I don't want to get it on nothin'." He shifted anxiously from foot to foot.

"Go on, then." Pinkard watched him with narrowed eyes till he squatted over the slit trench. The chief of Camp Dependable could see flies rising in a buzzing cloud. The guards put down chloride of lime every day. But a lot of prisoners came down with dysentery. The chemical didn't do much good, and didn't do good for long. For the moment, the breeze blew from him toward the latrine trenches. That cut down on the stink, but didn't kill it. Nothing could kill it. When the wind blew in the other direction, it really got fierce.

The black man rose and set his tattered trousers to rights. He went on about his business. Had he waved to Pinkard or done anything cute, the camp commandant would have hauled him in for questioning. Here, no. Not worth the bother.

"Labor gang!" a guard bawled. "Get your lazy nigger asses over here, you stinking labor-gang men!"

The Negroes came running. A man who showed himself useful building roads or crushing rock wasn't likely to be added to the next population reduction. So the blacks thought. They fought to get included in labor gangs, and worked like maniacs once they were. Lazy? Not likely!

Chick Blades' funeral came two days later, at a church in Alexandria. Behind her black veil, his widow looked stunned, uncomprehending. Pinkard got the idea the dead guard hadn't told her everything he did at Camp Dependable. Nobody would tell her now, either. She wouldn't understand. Neither would his little boys. His wife would wonder if she'd done something that pushed him over the edge or failed to notice something that might have saved him. Jeff didn't believe it for a minute, but he couldn't explain why, not without talking more than he should.

After the preacher read the graveside service and the body went into a hole in the ground, Mrs. Blades—her name, he thought, was

Edith—walked up to him and said, "Thank you for coming." Her face was puffy and swollen and pale. Had she slept at all since she found out about her husband? Jeff would have bet against it. "Least I could do," he mumbled. "He was a good man." Edith Blades nodded with frantic eagerness. "He was. He really was. He was a kind man, a gentle man. He wouldn't have hurt a fly, Chick wouldn't."

Jeff bit back a sardonic reply. He also bit back a burst of laughter that would have turned the funeral into a scandal. No, the widow didn't know what her husband had been up to. How many Negroes had Chick Blades shot in the head from behind? Hundreds? Thousands? Pinkard shrugged. He'd shot one too many to keep doing it and go on breathing, and that was the only thing that mattered.

"Everybody liked him real good," Jeff managed at last. "He could play the mouth organ like you wouldn't believe."

"He courted me with it," she said, and broke down in tears again. She wouldn't have been a bad-looking woman, not at all, if she were herself. She was somewhere in her thirties, dishwater blond, with a ripe figure the mourning dress couldn't hide. "He was such a funny fellow."

"Yes, ma'am," Pinkard said uncomfortably. "I'll do what I can to make sure you get his pension."

She blinked in surprise. "Thank you!"

"You're welcome," Pinkard said. "I can't promise you anything, on account of this has to go through Richmond. But I sure think you ought to have it. If any man ever died for his country, Chick Blades did."

"That's true," Blades' widow breathed. It was a lot more true than she knew. With any luck, she wouldn't find out how true it was. Chick had got rid of more enemies of the Confederacy than any general except maybe that Patton fellow up in Ohio, but would anybody ever give him any credit for it? Not likely. The only credit he'd ever get was a pine box. Dirt thudded down on it as the gravediggers started filling in the hole.

"You take care of yourself, ma'am," Jeff said, and then startled himself by adding, "You ever need anything, you let me know. Like I say, I dunno if I can manage everything, but I'll do my best."

"I may take you up on that, sir, after things settle a bit," she answered. "I don't know, but I may." She shook her head in confusion. "Right now, I don't know anything—not anything at all. It's like somebody picked up my world and shook it to pieces and turned it upside down."

"I understand," Jeff said. She shook her head again, and then looked sorry she had. She didn't want to make him angry or anything. But he wasn't. It was no wonder she didn't believe him. But he knew more than she thought he did—he knew more than she did, come to that.

What would happen when she found out? Sooner or later, she would, sure as hell. Pinkard shrugged. He couldn't do anything about that.

He went back to Camp Dependable in a somber mood. What he saw in Alexandria did nothing to cheer him up. People who spoke English gestured and flabbled like Cajuns. People who spoke French—fewer than the English-speakers—peppered it with fiery Anglo-Saxon obscenities. Rusty decorative ironwork from before the War of Secession ornamented downtown businesses and houses. The whole town seemed rusty and rustic. He wondered if Pineville, on the other side of the Red River, was any better. The town's name was ugly enough to make him doubt it.

Mercer Scott had the same feeling. "Ass end of nowhere, ain't it?" he said as their motorcar carried them out of town.

"Maybe not quite, but you can see it from there," Jeff answered.

Scott's chuckle, like a lot of his mirth, had a nasty edge. "Some of the white trash back there'd count themselves lucky to be living in the camp. I'm from Atlanta, by God. I know what a real city's supposed to be like, and that one don't measure up."

Jeff hit the brakes to keep from eradicating an armadillo scuttling across the road. "Atlanta, is it?" That explained a lot. Atlanta was too big for its britches, and had been since before the turn of the century. People who came from there always acted as if their shit didn't stink just because they were Atlantans. Pinkard said, "Me, I come out of Birmingham. I could give you an argument about what makes a good city."

"If you want to be a horseshoe or a nail or anything else made out of iron, Birmingham's a fine enough town, I reckon. You want anything else, Atlanta's the place to be."

That struck home, after all the time Jeff had spent at the Sloss Foundry working with molten steel. He was damned if he'd admit it. "Atlanta says it's a big city, but all you've got is fizzy water. And the fellow who invented the number one brand outa that place sucked up cocaine like it was going out of style."

Mercer Scott only laughed. "You had that kind of scratch back at your house, wouldn't you do the same?"

Since Jeff probably would have, he changed the argument in a hurry: "Besides, next to Richmond you ain't so much of a much."

"You don't want to push me too far," Scott said in suitably menacing tones. "You really don't . . . boss."

That could have provoked a fight between the two men as soon as they got out of the auto. It could also have made Pinkard pull off the road and settle things then and there. But he judged the other man's menace was put on, not genuine, and so he laughed instead. Mercer Scott laughed, too, and the moment passed.

"Hell of a thing about Chick," Pinkard said a minute or so later.

"Well, yeah." But Scott didn't seem unduly upset, not any more. "We're here to get rid of niggers. If you can't do the job, you don't belong."

"I wish he'd've asked for a transfer out or something, though," Jeff said. "I'd've given him a good notice. He did the best he could, dammit." His hands tightened on the wheel. If that didn't sound like an epitaph, he didn't know what did.

"Whole country did the best it could in the last war," Scott replied. "That's not good enough. Only thing that's good enough is doing what you got to do."

He had no give in him, not anywhere. That made him good at what he had to do. A camp guard who showed mercy was the last thing anybody needed. But it made Scott uncomfortable to be around. He was always looking for signs of weakness in other people, including Jefferson Pinkard. And if he found one, he'd take advantage of it without the least pity or hesitation. He made no bones about that at all.

"There's the camp," he said when Jeff swung the rattling Birmingham—iron, sure enough—around a last corner.

"Yeah," Jeff said. "Wonder when they're gonna send us some more population."

"Whenever they do, we'll reduce it," Mercer Scott declared. "Only thing that can stop us is running out of ammo." He laughed again. So did Pinkard, not quite comfortably.

Flora Blackford's secretary stuck her head into the Congresswoman's office. She said, "Mr. Jordan is here to see you."

"He's right on time," Flora said. "Show him in."

Orson Jordan was a tall blond man in his mid-thirties. He was so pink, he looked as if he'd just been scrubbed with a wire brush. "Very pleased to meet you, ma'am," he said. By the way he shook Flora's hand, he was afraid it would break if he squeezed it very hard.

"Please sit down," Flora told him, and he did. She went on, "Shall I have Bertha bring us some coffee—or tea, if you'd rather?"

"Oh, no, thank you, ma'am." Orson Jordan shook his head. He turned pinker than ever. Flora hadn't thought he could. He said, "Go right ahead yourself, if you care to. Not for me, though. I don't indulge in hot drinks."

He sounded like an observant Jew politely declining the shrimp cocktail. There were parallels between Jews and Mormons; Mormons had a way of making more of them than Jews did. Flora shrugged. That wasn't her worry, or she didn't think it was. "It's all right," she said. "Tell me, Mr. Jordan, what do you think I can do for you that your own Congressman from Utah can't?"

"It's not what I think you can do, ma'am," Jordan said earnestly. "It's what Governor Young hopes you can do." Heber Young, grandson of Brigham, had headed the Mormon church in Utah during the occupation after the Great War, when legally it did not exist. He was elected Governor the minute President Smith finally lifted military rule in the state. By all appearances, he could go on getting elected Governor till he died of old age, even if that didn't happen for the next fifty years.

Patiently, Flora asked, "Well, what does Governor Young think I can do for him, then? He's not my constituent, you know."

Orson Jordan smiled at the joke, even though Flora had been kidding on the square. He said, "In a way, ma'am, he thinks he is one of your constituents. He says anyone who respects liberty is."

"That's . . . very kind of him, and of you," Flora said. "Flattery will get you nowhere, though, or I hope it won't. What does he want?"

"Well, ma'am, you're bound to know Utah is a bit touchy about soldiers going through it or soldiers being stationed there. We've earned the right to be touchy, I'd say. I was only a boy when the last troubles happened, and I wouldn't want my own children to have to worry about anything like that."

"I believe you," Flora said. When the Mormons rose during the Great War, they'd fought till they couldn't fight any more. Plenty of boys no older than Orson Jordan would have been had died with guns in hand. The United States had triumphed in a purely Tacitean way: they'd made a desert and called it peace.

"All right, then," Jordan said. He wore a somber, discreetly striped suit and a very plain maroon tie. A faint smell of soap wafted from him. So did a much stronger aura of sincerity. He meant everything he said. He was a citizen the United States would have been proud to have as their own—if he hadn't continued, "Governor Young wants to make it real plain he can't answer for what will happen if the United States keep on doing things like that. A lot of people there hate Philadelphia and everything it stands for. He's been holding them back, but he isn't King Canute. He can't go on doing it forever. Frankly, he doesn't want to go on doing it forever. We want what ought to be ours."

"Should what you want be any different from what other Americans want?" Flora asked. "When you got military rule lifted, part of the reason you did was that you convinced people back here you were ordinary citizens."

"We're citizens, but we're not ordinary citizens," Jordan said. "We got hounded out of the USA. That's why we went to Utah in the first place. It belonged to Mexico then. But the First Mexican War put us under the Stars and Stripes again—and the government started persecuting us again. Look at 1881. The oppression after that was what made us rise in 1915. Do you think we can trust the United States when they start going back on their solemn word?"

He still sounded earnest and sincere. Flora still had no doubt he meant every word he said, meant it from the bottom of his heart. She also had no doubt he didn't have any idea how irritating he was to her. She said, "Another way you're special is that you're not conscripted. Shouldn't you count your blessings?"

Orson Jordan shook his head. "No, ma'am. We want to be trusted to do our duty, like anybody else."

She pointed a finger at him. "I'm afraid you can't have that both ways, Mr. Jordan. You want to be trusted, but you don't want to trust. If you don't trust, you won't be trusted. It's as simple as that."

The Mormon emissary looked troubled. "You may have a point there. I will discuss it with the Governor when I get back to Salt Lake—you can count on that. But we have been through so much, trust will not come easy. I wish I could say something different, but I can't."

"Learning to trust Mormons won't come easy for the rest of the country, either," Flora said. "As I told you, the knife cuts both ways."

"Yes, you did say that." Jordan gave no hint about what he thought of her comment. After a moment, he went on, "You will take my words to President Smith?"

"You can certainly trust me on that," Flora said, and her guest gave her a surprisingly boyish smile. She continued, "He needs to hear what you just told me. I can't promise what he'll do about it. I can't promise he'll do anything about it. There is a war on, in case you hadn't noticed."

"I rather thought there might be." So Jordan was capable of irony. That surprised Flora, too. She wouldn't have guessed he had such depths. She wondered what else might be lurking down there below that bland exterior. Orson Jordan politely took his leave before she had the chance to find out.

When Flora phoned Powel House—the President's Philadelphia residence—she thought at first that his aides were going to refuse to give her an appointment. That infuriated her. They both went back a lot of years in Socialist affairs in New York. But when she mentioned Heber Young's name, hesitation vanished. If she had news about Mormons, Al Smith wasn't unavailable any more.

She took a cab to Powel House. The driver had to detour several times to avoid bomb craters in the road. "Lousy Confederates," he said. "I hope we blow them all to kingdom come."

"Yes," agreed Flora, who also hoped Confederate bombers wouldn't come over Philadelphia by daylight, as they had a couple of times. They hadn't been back in the daytime for almost two weeks, though; heavy antiaircraft fire and improved fighter coverage were making that too expensive. But air-raid sirens howled most nights, and people scrambled for shelters.

Presidents had spent more time in Powel House than in the White House since the Second Mexican War. Flora had spent much of four years there herself, when Hosea Blackford ran the country. Her mouth tightened. The country remembered her husband's Presidency only for the economic collapse that had followed hard on the heels of his inauguration. He'd done everything he knew how to do to pull the USA out of it, but hadn't had any luck. Calvin Coolidge had trounced him in 1932, and then died before taking office—whereupon Herbert Hoover had proved the Democrats didn't know how to fix the economy, either.

Such gloomy reflections vanished from Flora's mind when an aide led her up a splendid wooden staircase and into the office that had been her husband's and now belonged to Al Smith. What replaced those reflections was something not far from shock. She hadn't seen the President since he came to Congress to ask it to declare war on the CSA. If Smith hadn't aged fifteen years in the month since then . . . he'd aged twenty.

He'd lost flesh. His face was shrunken and bloodless. By the bags under his eyes, he might not have slept since the war began. A situation map hung on the wall to one side of his battleship of a desk. The red pins stuck in the map showed Confederate forces farther north in Ohio than press or wireless admitted. Maybe that was why Smith hadn't slept.

"How are you, Flora?" Even his voice, as full of New York City as Flora's own, had lost strength. It didn't show up on the wireless, where he had a microphone to help, but was all too obvious in person. "So what are these miserable Mormons trying to gouge out of us now?"

Had he been in other company, he might have asked what the Mormons were trying to jew out of the government. But Flora had met plenty of real anti-Semites, and knew Al Smith wasn't one. And she had more urgent things to worry about anyhow. As dispassionately as she could, she summed up what Orson Jordan had told her.

"Nice of them," the President said when she was through. "As long as we don't try to get them to do what other Americans do or try to govern them at all, they'll kindly consent to staying in the USA. But if we do try to do anything useful with them or with Utah, they'll go up in smoke. Some bargain." His wheezy laugh was bitter as wormwood.

"They . . . don't like us any better than we like them," Flora said carefully. "They . . . think they have good reason not to like us, or to trust us."

"You know what? I don't give a damn what they like or what they trust," Al Smith said. "I let Jake Featherston take me for a ride, and the country's paying for it now. I'll take that shame to my grave. But if you think—if anybody thinks—I'll let Heber Young take me for a ride, too, you've got another think coming."

Was he reacting too strongly against the Governor of Utah because he hadn't reacted strongly enough against the President of the Confederate States? Flora wouldn't have been surprised. But that wasn't something she could say. She did ask, "Are you all right, Mr. President?"

"I'll do," Al Smith answered. "I'll last as long as I last. If I break down in harness, Charlie LaFollette can do the job. It seems pretty plain, wouldn't you say?" Except for a nod, Flora didn't have any answer to that, either.

Every time Mary Pomeroy turned on the wireless, it was with fresh hope in her heart. She lived for the hourly news bulletins. Whenever the Yanks admitted losses, she felt like cheering. Whenever they didn't, she assumed they were lying, covering up. The Confederates were bombing them in the East and pounding on them in the Midwest. *Now you know how it feels, you murdering sons of bitches!* she exulted.

The news on other fronts was good, too—good as far as she was concerned, that is. The Japanese were making menacing moves against the Sandwich Islands. The U.S.-held Bahamas were being bombed from Florida. In Europe, the German and Austro-Hungarian positions in the Ukraine seemed to be unraveling. Bulgaria wavered as a German ally—although she couldn't waver too much, not with the Ottoman Turks on her southern border.

And the wireless kept saying things like, "All residents of

Canada are urged to remain calm during the present state of emergency. Prompt and complete compliance with all official requests is required. Sabotage or subversive activity will be detected, rooted out, and punished with the utmost severity."

Mary laughed whenever she listened to bulletins like those. If they weren't cries of pain from the occupying authorities, she'd never heard any. And the more the Americans admitted they were in distress, the bigger the incentive the Canadians had to make that distress worse. Didn't they?

If the bulletins didn't do it, the way the Quebecois troops in Rosenfeld acted was liable to. The Americans, whatever else you could say about them, had behaved correctly most of the time. They'd known how to keep their hands to themselves, even if their eyes were known to wander. The Frenchies didn't just look. They touched.

Not only that, the soldiers in blue-gray spoke French. Most of them had grown up since the Republic of Quebec broke away from Canada. They'd never had much reason to learn English. Nor had the local Manitobans had any more reason to pick up French. Hearing the Quebecois troopers jabber away in a language the locals couldn't understand made them seem much more foreign than the Americans ever had.

They came in to eat at the Pomeroys' diner fairly often. Even if they had to pay for it, the food there was better than what their own cooks dished out. Mort and his father took their money without learning to love them.

"It's humiliating, that's what it is," he said when he got home one summer's evening. "At least the lousy Yanks licked us. The Frenchies never did."

"The Yanks shouldn't have, either," Mary said.

Mort only shrugged at that. "Maybe you're right and maybe you're wrong. I don't know. I've never been much good at might-have-beens. All I know is, they did. I used to think they were pretty bad. Now I know better. The Frenchies showed me the difference between bad and worse."

"Well, the Frenchies wouldn't be here if they weren't doing the Yanks' dirty work for them," Mary pointed out.

"That's true," her husband admitted. "I hadn't thought of it like that."

"May I be excused?" asked Alec, who'd finished the drumstick and fried potatoes in front of him.

"Yes, go ahead," Mary answered. He hurried off to play. Mary looked after him with a smile half fond, half exasperated. "Little pitchers have big ears."

"He is getting old enough to repeat anything he hears, isn't he?" Mort said.

"Yes, but he's not old enough to know there are times when he shouldn't," Mary answered. "Whenever we start talking about the Yanks, we start coming close to those times, too."

"I don't want to talk sedition. I'm too tired to talk sedition," Mort said.

Mary was never too tired to talk sedition. She didn't talk it very much with Mort. For one thing, she knew he was more resigned to the occupation than she was. For another, since she'd done more than talk, she didn't want him to know that. The more people who knew something, the more who could give you away.

She did say, "The Yanks are flabbling about sedition on the wireless more than they used to."

Mort smiled and cocked his head to one side. "That's not a word I expected to hear from you."

"What?" Mary didn't even know what she'd said. She had to think back. "Oh. Flabbling?" Her husband nodded. She shrugged. "People say it. You hear it on the wireless. They'll probably stop saying it in a little while."

"I even heard a Frenchy use it today," Mort said. "This little kid started to cry and have a fit in the diner, and this soldier, he goes, 'Ey, boy! Vat you flabble for?'" He put on a French accent.

"Did the kid stop?" Mary asked, intrigued in spite of herself.

"Not till his mother warmed his fanny for him," Mort answered. "Then he really had something to cry about."

"Good for her." Mary didn't approve of children who made scenes in public. She didn't know anyone who did, either. The sooner you taught them they couldn't get away with that kind of nonsense, the better off everybody was. She said, "The Yanks must be worried about sedition and sabotage, or they wouldn't talk about them on the wireless so much."

"Does sound like they're hurting down south, doesn't it?" Mort allowed. "Couldn't happen to a nicer bunch of folks." He didn't love the Yanks. He never had. But he'd hardly ever been so vocal about showing how little he liked them, either.

Mary was tempted to let him know she still carried on the fight against the occupiers. She was tempted to, but she didn't. Three could keep a secret, if two of them were dead. That was Benjamin Franklin: a Yank, but a Yank who'd known what was what. The Americans routinely broke up conspiracies against them. Traitors to Canada and blabbermouths gave the game away time after time. But her father had carried on the fight against the USA undetected for years, simply because he'd been able to keep his mouth shut. Collaborators hadn't betrayed him; only luck had let him down. Mary intended to follow the same course.

Her husband went on, "The worst of it is, probably none of what happens down there matters to us. Even if the Confederates lick the Yanks, how can they make them turn Canada loose? They can't. If you think straight, you've got to see that. We're stuck. England can't get us back, either, not if she's fighting Germany. Even if she isn't, she's an ocean away and the Yanks are right next door. I don't know what we're supposed to do about that."

Fight them ourselves! Mary thought. She didn't say it out loud, though. She knew what she needed to do. She waited only on opportunity. But dragging Mort in, when he plainly didn't want to be dragged in, wouldn't have been fair to him and might have proved dangerous to her. One man—or one woman—going it alone: that was the safe way to do it.

Every now and again, she wished she could be part of a larger movement. Many people working together could harry the Yanks in a way a loner couldn't. But a large operation could also go wrong in ways a small one couldn't. She was willing to give her life for her country. She wasn't willing to throw it away.

Mort said, "I may be wrong, but I do believe there's fewer Frenchies in town lately. Maybe they've decided we aren't going to start turning handsprings right here."

Mary shook her head. "That's not it. A lot of them are out guarding the railroad lines."

Her husband gave her an odd look. "How do you know?"

Careful! She couldn't tell him the truth, which was that she'd driven around and looked. She'd taken care not to examine any one stretch more than once; she hadn't done anything to rouse the least suspicion in any Quebecois corporal's heart. She didn't want to make Mort wonder, either, so she answered, "I heard somebody talking about it in Karamanlides' general store."

"Oh." Mort relaxed, so she must have sounded as casual as she hoped she had. He went on, "Good luck to them if somebody does decide to sabotage the railroad. Too many miles of train tracks and not enough Frenchies."

"Wouldn't break my heart," Mary said. Mort only smiled. He already knew how she felt about the Yanks. Saying she hoped somebody else did them a bad turn was safe enough. The only thing she couldn't tell him—couldn't tell anybody—was that she intended to do them a bad turn herself.

"Talk about hearing things," Mort said. "Reminds me of what else I heard in the diner today. Wilf Rokeby's retiring."

"You're kidding!" Mary exclaimed. "He's been postmaster as long as I can remember."

"He's been postmaster as long as anybody can remember," Mort agreed. "He's been here since dirt. But he's going to give it all up at the end of the year. Says he's getting too old for all the standing and lifting he's got to do." He chuckled. "Says he's had it with being polite to people all the time, too."

"But him going! I can't believe it," Mary said. "And what will the post office be like without the smell of that hair oil he uses? It won't be the same place."

"I know," Mort said. "We've got to do something nice for him when he does quit. The whole town, I mean. You said it: it'll hardly be Rosenfeld without Wilf."

"Good luck to him. I wonder what he'll do when he's not being polite to people all day long," Mary said. Mort snorted at that.

Mary certainly did wonder what Wilf Rokeby would be doing. Rokeby knew things he shouldn't. He hadn't done anything with the knowledge. The proof was that Mary was still sitting at the supper table talking things over with Mort. If Rokeby had gone to the Yanks, she'd be in jail or shot like her brother.

But just because Wilf hadn't talked didn't mean he wouldn't talk. When you were worried about your life, you couldn't be too careful, could you? Mary suddenly understood why robbers often shot witnesses. Dead men told no tales. It sounded like something straight out of a bad film—which didn't mean it wasn't true.

I have to think about this. Mary had been thinking about it for a while. Wilf Rokeby had been doing what the Yanks told him ever since they occupied Rosenfeld in 1914. That was a long time by now. He'd never shown any signs he was unhappy about cooperating with U.S. authorities. All he'd cared about was running the post office, and he hadn't worried about for whom.

That didn't mean he would go to the occupying authorities. But it didn't mean he wouldn't, either. *Can I take the chance? Do I dare take the chance?* The sky hadn't fallen. It hadn't, but it could.

Just then, the cat yowled and hissed. Alec yelled and started to cry. Mary stopped worrying about Wilf Rokeby. She ran into the front room to see what had happened. The cat crouched under the coffee table, eyes blazing. Alec clutched a scratched arm. He also clutched a small tuft of what looked like cat fur. Cause and effect weren't hard to figure out.

"Don't pull the kitty's tail," Mary said. "If you do, you can't blame him for scratching."

"I didn't," Alec said, but his heart wasn't in it.

Mary whacked him on the backside, not too hard. "Don't tell fibs, either."

He looked amazed. She could read his thoughts. *How can she tell I'm lying?* She almost laughed out loud. Alec hadn't had much practice yet.

There was a saloon not far from Cincinnatus Driver's parents' house in Covington. There were a lot of saloons in the colored district in Covington. Blacks had troubles aplenty there, and needed places to drown them. Had Cincinnatus been all in one piece, he wouldn't have given the Brass Monkey the time of day. Since he was what he was, he spent a good deal of time there.

The inside of the Brass Monkey was dim, but not cool. A couple of ceiling fans spun lazily, as if to show they were doing their best. Next to one of them hung a strip of flypaper black with flies in every stage of desiccation. Sawdust lay in drifts on the floor. The place smelled of beer and cigars and stale piss.

"What can I get for you?" the barkeep asked when Cincinnatus gingerly perched on a bar stool.

"Bottle of beer," Cincinnatus answered. He pulled a dime from his pocket and set it on the bar. It was a U.S. coin. The bartender took it without hesitation. Not only had Kentucky been part of the USA till a few months before, but the U.S. and C.S. dollars had officially been at par except during the Confederacy's disastrous inflation after the Great War. A dime held the same amount of silver in both countries, though you could buy a little more with one in the United States.

"Here you go." The barkeep took the beer out of the icebox behind him.

"Thank you kindly." Cincinnatus didn't bother with a glass. He took a sip from the bottle, then pressed it against his cheek. "Ah! That feels mighty good."

"Oh, yeah. I know." The barkeep fiddled with the white shirt and black bow tie that marked him for what he was. "Wish this here was looser. Feels like I'm cookin' in my own juice."

"I believe it." Cincinnatus sipped again. Two old black men, one bald, the other white-haired, sat in a corner playing checkers. He nodded to them; he'd seen them around in Covington since he was a kid. One had a beer, the other a whiskey. They nodded back. He was as familiar to them, and his being away for close to twenty years meant very little.

A man about his own age sat on a stool at the far end of the bar. He had a whiskey in front of him. He knocked it back, his face working, and signaled to the bartender for another. "You sure, Menander?" the barkeep asked. "Somebody gonna have to carry you home?"

"Don't you worry about me none," Menander answered. "Just give me the damn whiskey, an' I'll give you the money. That's how it goes, ain't it?"

"Yeah. That's how it goes." The bartender sighed and gave him what he wanted. He gulped down the whiskey and set another quarter on the bar. The barkeep took it, but he sighed again. "Ain't like you to get shit-faced like this. You should oughta leave it to them what does."

"Ain't I earned the right?" Menander came back. "Do Jesus, ain't I earned the goddamn right?"

"Damfino." The bartender ran his rag along the countertop before setting another whiskey there. "What happen, make you wanna git wide?"

"Didn't they go an' haul my brother off to one o' them goddamn camps?" Menander said. "Ain't I never gonna see him no more? Ain't the world one fucked-up place? You bet your ass it is."

That made Cincinnatus prick up his ears. He'd hated and feared the Freedom Party for those camps long before he got stuck in the CSA. He looked down the bar toward Menander. "What did your brother do, you don't mind me asking?"

"Do?" The other man stared blearily back at him. "He didn't do nothin'. What you need to do? Don't you just got to be in the wrong place at the wrong time? Don't the ofays jus' got to reckon, *We needs us another nigger*? Ain't that how it goes?" Now he waved to the barkeep for support.

The bartender said, "I done heard all kinds o' things."

"I believe that," Cincinnatus said.

He got a thin smile for a reward. "Yeah, a barkeep, he hear *all* kinds o' things," the bartender said. "But none o' what I hear tell about them camp places is good. You go in, you don't come out no more—not breathin', anyways. Menander, he ain't wrong about that there."

Slowly, Cincinnatus nodded. "I heard the same," he said, and also heard the trouble in his own voice. "I heard, they want to take you down to Louisiana, you're just as well off lettin' 'em kill you, on account of you ain't gonna stay 'mong the living real long."

Menander put his head down on the bar and started to weep. Did that mean his brother had gone to Louisiana? Or did it only mean he'd drunk himself maudlin? Cincinnatus didn't have the heart to ask.

"We ought to do somethin' about that," he said instead.

He wasn't even sure Menander heard him. The barkeep did. He asked, "What you got in mind?"

Cincinnatus started to tell him what he had in mind. He started to say that no black man should quietly let himself be arrested. He started to say that if every black man answered the door with a gun in his hand when police or Freedom Party stalwarts or guards came calling—not impossible, not with as many guns as there were floating around the CSA—the powers that be might start thinking twice before they arrested people quite so freely. If Negroes didn't just submit, how many dead white men would the Freedom Party need before it got the message? Not many, not unless Cincinnatus missed his guess.

He started to tell the bartender all those things. He started to, but the words never passed his lips. Instead, after a thoughtful pull at his beer, he answered, "Well, now, I don't rightly know. We *can't* do a whole hell of a lot, don't look like to me."

The bartender polished the bar some more with his rag. It wasn't especially clean. If there was any dirt on the bar, he was just spreading it around, not getting rid of it. His face was expressionless, but barkeeps weren't supposed to show much of what they were thinking. Cincinnatus didn't want to show much of what he was thinking, either. He didn't like his own thoughts, which didn't keep him from having them.

He'd never set eyes on the man behind the bar before coming back to Covington. Oh, maybe he had, but the man would have been a boy when the Drivers moved to Iowa. He didn't *know* him. That was what counted. That . . . and he could see how useful Confederate authorities would find it to have a black bartender letting them know which Negroes were getting uppity, and how.

No, he didn't know this fellow. Because he didn't know him, he couldn't trust him. Back when Kentucky belonged to the USA, Luther Bliss, the head of the Kentucky State Police (which might as well have been the Kentucky Secret Police), hadn't worked him over too badly when he had him in his clutches. Whoever Bliss' counterpart was now that Kentucky had gone back to the CSA, Cincinnatus didn't think he would show such restraint.

At the far end of the bar, Menander raised his head. Tears streaked his cheeks. His face might have been one of those masks of tragedy you sometimes saw on theater curtains. "I tell you what we ought to do," he said in a terrible voice. "We ought to kill us some o' them white cocksuckers. We should ought to *kill* 'em, I say. Reckon they leave us alone then, by Jesus."

"Reckon they kills us, too," the bartender said quietly.

"They killin' us *now*," Menander cried. "We gots to make 'em stop."

The bartender got busy with the rag. It swished over the top of the bar. He watched it intently as he worked, but it didn't seem to be enough to distract him from his thoughts. He tossed it into that secret space under the bar that could hold almost anything: a cleaning rag, a bottle of maraschino cherries, a smaller bottle of knockout drops, a blackjack, a sawed-off shotgun. The rag disappeared with a damp splat. He lit a cigarette and took a long, meditative drag. Cincinnatus wondered if all the smoke would stay in the man's lungs, but he blew out a blue cloud of it. Only after that did he say, "Menander, I know you is hurtin', but you got to watch what you say and where you say it."

He might have been a father warning his little boy to look both ways before he crossed the street. Like the little boy if he happened to be in a crabby mood, Menander wasn't having any of it. "For Chrissake!" he burst out. "You tellin' me some nigger here—some lousy nigger here—give me away to the motherfuckin' Freedom Party?"

"I didn't say that," the bartender answered. "You done said that."

"Some ofays sell their souls for a quarter," Cincinnatus answered. Menander nodded eagerly at that. But then Cincinnatus went on, "How come you reckon niggers is any different?"

Back in Iowa, *nigger* was a term of abuse. Here in Kentucky, blacks used it casually among themselves to describe themselves. Some whites here used it as a casual descriptive term, too—some, but not all. In the mouth of a Freedom Party stalwart, it was ugly as could be. Despite the hot, muggy day, Cincinnatus shivered. In a stalwart's mouth, the word had an evil rasp he'd never heard with any other.

Menander stared at him. "I don't reckon any nigger'd be a dog low enough to sell out his own kind."

Both Cincinnatus and the bartender laughed at him. So did both old men playing checkers in the corner. Menander's eyes heated with drunken rage. "Calm yourself," Cincinnatus told him. "I didn't say niggers was worse'n white folks. That ain't so. But if you reckon they's better, you got a ways to go to prove it."

"Don't see no niggers goin' 'round yellin, 'Freedom!' " Menander spat.

"Well, no," Cincinnatus admitted, "but I figure you would if we was on top and the ofays was on the bottom. When the Reds rose up in the last war, what was they but Freedom Party men with different flags shoutin' different slogans?"

By the time the black Marxists rose in the CSA, Covington and most of Kentucky were under U.S. occupation. The rebellion had been muted here. Lucullus Wood, a Marxist still, would have been irked to hear Cincinnatus compare the Reds to the Freedom Party. Word of what was said in the Brass Monkey was likelier to get back to him than it was to reach the Freedom Party, too. Cincinnatus sighed. It wasn't as if he hadn't said what he believed.

"There's a difference, though," Menander insisted.

"What's that?" Cincinnatus asked.

"The ofays, they *deserves* it," Menander said savagely. "Got my brother, got . . ." His voice trailed away into a slur of curses. How much whiskey *had* he downed?

That was the obvious question. From cursing, Menander started crying again. He'd put down a lot of whiskey, which answered the obvious question. But wasn't there another related question, maybe not so obvious? Wasn't Jake Featherston saying, *The niggers, they* deserve *it* over in Richmond? Too right he was.

And what could anybody do about that? In the short run, fight back and hope Featherston couldn't lick the USA. In the long run . . . In the long run, was there any answer at all to whites and blacks hating each other?

Cincinnatus hadn't seen all that much hate in Des Moines. But there weren't that many Negroes in Des Moines, either: not enough to trigger some of the raw reactions only too common in the Confederate States. The United States were happy they didn't have very many Negroes, too. Immigrants—white immigrants—took care of what was nigger work in the CSA.

Yeah, the USA can do without us, Cincinnatus thought glumly. *Can the CSA?* Over in Richmond, Jake Featherston sure thought so.

"**K**eep them moving forward, goddammit!" Lieutenant-Colonel Tom Colleton yelled into the mike on his portable wireless set. The company commanders in his regiment, or at least their wireless men, were supposed to be listening to him. If they weren't, he'd hop in a motorcar and shout sense right into their stupid faces.

In many ways, Ohio was an ideal place for a mechanized army to fight. The country was mostly flat. It had a thick road and railroad net, which was the whole point of pushing up through it in the first place. And if the Confederate Army ever ran short of transport, which happened now and again, motorcars commandeered from the damnyankees often took up the slack. There were even gas stations where autos and trucks and barrels could tank up.

Right now, his regiment stood just outside of Findlay, Ohio. The town lay in the middle of rich farming country punctuated by oil wells. Back in the 1890s, the oil had set off a spectacular boom in these parts. The boom had subsided. Some of the oil still flowed. The Yankees were fighting like the devil to keep the Confederates from seizing the wells that did survive.

Tom didn't give a particular damn about the oil wells. He would have, but he'd been ordered not to. As far as he was concerned, the only thing that was supposed to matter was getting to Lake Erie. He'd promised the men he would strip naked and jump in the lake when they did.

That had produced a mild protest from the regimental medical officer, Dr. David Dillon. "Why don't you promise them you'll jump in an open sewer instead?" Dillon asked. "It would probably be healthier—a little more shit, maybe, but not nearly so many nasty chemicals."

"Seeing how many nasty chemicals the Yankees have been shooting at us, to hell with me if I'm going to flabble about what they pour in the lake," Colleton had answered. The medical officer found nothing to say to that.

Now Tom could see Findlay through his field glasses. It had been a nice little city, with a lot of ornate Victorian homes and shops and office buildings left over from the boom-town years. Now bombardment and bombing had leveled some of the buildings and bitten chunks out of others. Smoke from fires in the town and from destroyed wells nearby made it harder to get a good look at the place.

Somewhere in all that smoke, U.S. artillery still lurked. Shells fell a few hundred yards short of where Tom Colleton was standing. If he and his men stayed where they were, they'd get badly hurt when the Yankees found the range.

He wouldn't have wanted to stay there anyhow. The Confederates hadn't invaded Ohio to hold in place. "Advance!" he shouted again. "We aren't going to shift those sons of bitches if we stand around with our thumbs up our asses!"

Behind him, somebody laughed. He whirled. There stood a rawboned man about his own age with the coldest pale eyes he'd ever seen. He wore three stars in a wreath on each side of his collar: a general officer's rank markings. Among the fruit salad on his chest were ribbons for the Purple Heart and the Order of Albert Sidney Johnston, the highest Army decoration after the Confederate Cross. Also on his chest was the badge of a barrel man, a bronze rhomboid shape like the Confederate machines from the last war.

"That's telling 'em!" he said, his voice all soft Virginia.

"Thank you, sir," Tom answered. "General Patton, isn't it?"

"That's right." The Confederate officer's smile didn't quite reach his eyes. "George Patton, at your service. I'm afraid you have the advantage of me." Tom gave his own name. "Colleton," Patton repeated musingly. His gaze sharpened, as if he were peering down the barrel of one of the fancy revolvers he carried in place of the usual officer's .45. "Are you by any chance related to Anne Colleton?"

"She was my sister, sir." If Tom had a dime for every time he'd answered that question, he could have bought the Army instead of serving in it.

"A fine woman." But then Patton's gaze sharpened further. " 'Was,' you say? She's suffered a misfortune?"

"Yes, sir. I'm afraid so. She was in Charleston when the Yankee carrier raided it. One of the bombs hit nearby, and—" Colleton spread his hands.

"I'm very sorry to hear that. You have my sincere sympathies." General Patton reached up to touch the brim of his helmet, as if doffing a hat. The helmet was of the new style, like Tom's: rounder and more like what the Yankees wore than the tin hats the C.S. Army had used in the Great War. Patton went on, "It's a loss not only to you personally but also to the Confederate States of America."

"Very kind of you to say so, sir."

"I commonly say what I mean, and I commonly mean what I say." Patton paused to light a cigar. "She helped put the Freedom Party over the top, and we all owe her a debt of gratitude for that. We can't be too careful about the dusky race, can we?"

Tom Colleton considered that. His politics were and always had been less radical than Anne's. But when he thought about Marshlands as it had been before 1914 and the ruin it was now . . . "Hard to argue with you there."

"It usually is." Patton looked smug. Considering how far north the armor under his command had driven, that wasn't surprising. He pointed toward Findlay. "Are you having difficulties there?"

"Some, sir," Tom replied. "The damnyankees want to hold on to the oil in the neighborhood as long as they can. They've got machine guns and artillery, and they've slowed down our push. If you've got a few barrels you could spare, either to go right at them or for a flanking attack, it would help a hell of a lot."

"I have a few. That's about what I do have," Patton said. "I wish I could say I had more than a few, but I don't. Colonel Morrell, who's in charge of the U.S. barrels, knows what he's doing. He wrote the book, by God! If not for him, we'd be swimming in the lake by now."

Tom decided not to mention his promise to his men, much less the medical officer's opinion of it. He also marveled that Patton, who'd come so far so fast, was disappointed not to have come farther faster. He said, "Whatever you can do, sir, would be greatly appreciated."

"Give me an hour to organize and consolidate," Patton said. "Then I'll bring them in along that axis"—he pointed west, where a swell in the ground would offer the barrels some cover—"unless the situation changes in the meantime and requires a different approach."

"Yes, sir." *This I have to see,* Tom thought. He'd expected Patton would talk about tomorrow, if not the day after. An hour? Could anybody really put together an attack so fast? Tom held up his own troops till he found out.

Patton proved as good as his word. About five minutes before the appointed time, three three-barrel platoons showed up and started shelling the U.S. positions in front of Findlay. Whooping gleefully, Tom Colleton sent his men forward with them. He went forward, too. He fired his .45 a couple of times, but didn't know if he hit anything.

He did know he wanted Patton to see him at the front. The man plainly had no use for laggards. He wouldn't have done what he had if he'd tolerated failure, or even incompetence.

The U.S. soldiers blew up the oil wells as they retreated from them. That sent more clouds of black, noxious smoke into the hot, blue summer sky. One of Tom's men asked, "Should we put on our masks, sir? This here stuff's got to be as poisonous as mustard gas."

He was exaggerating, but by how much? When Tom spat, he spat black. The inside of his mouth tasted oily. What *was* that horrible smoke doing inside his lungs? He said, "Do whatever you think best. If you can stand to wear the mask in this heat, go ahead."

One of Patton's barrels hit a mine and blew up. Colleton didn't think any of the crew got out. The rest of the barrels pounded Findlay from the edge of town. They didn't actually go in. Tom couldn't blame them for that. Barrels weren't made for street fighting.

For that matter, he didn't send his own men into Findlay, either. Now that the way around it was open, he gladly took that. The U.S. soldiers inside would have to fall back to keep from being cut off or wither on the vine, holding a little island in a rising Confederate sea. There were still islands like that all the way back to the Ohio River, though they went under one by one, subdued by second-line troops.

A few of them, the larger ones, still caused trouble. Tom knew that, but refused to worry about it. Someone else had the job of worrying about it. His job was to push toward the Great Lakes with everything he had. If he did that, if everybody at the front did that, the islands would take care of themselves.

The U.S. soldiers in Findlay seemed to think so. They pulled out of the town instead of letting themselves be surrounded. Their rear guard kept the Confederates from taking too big a bite out of them. Tom Colleton regretted that and gave it the professional respect it deserved at the same time.

He was glad to flop down by a fire when the sun went down. One drawback to a war of movement for a middle-aged man was that you had to *keep* moving. He could keep up with the young soldiers he commanded, but he couldn't get by on three hours' sleep a night the way they could. He felt like an old car that still ran fine—as long as you changed the oil and the spark plugs every two thousand miles.

His men had liberated some chickens from a nearby farm. Chicken roasted over an open fire—even done as it usually was, black on the outside and half raw on the inside—went a long way towards improving the rations they carried with them. Tom gnawed on a leg. Grease ran down his chin.

In the darkness beyond flames' reach, a sentry called a challenge. Tom didn't hear the answer, but he did hear the sentry's startled,

"Pass on, sir!" A few seconds later, George Patton stepped into the firelight.

"Good thing there aren't wolves in this country, or the smell would draw them," he said. "You boys think you can spare a chunk of one of those birds for a damn useless officer?"

"You bet we can, General," Tom said before any of his men decided to take Patton literally. "If it weren't for those barrels you loaned us, likely we'd still be stuck in front of Findlay."

Patton sprawled in the dirt beside him and attacked a leg of his own with wolfish gusto. As he had been earlier in the day, he was perfectly dressed, right down to his cravat and to knife-sharp trouser creases. Off in the distance were spatters of small-arms fire. Telling the two sides apart was easy. The Yankees still used bolt-action Springfields, as they had in the last war. With submachine guns and automatic rifles, Confederate soldiers filled the air with lead whenever they bumped into the enemy.

"Your boys did handsomely yourselves," Patton said, throwing bare bones into the bushes. "You understand the uses of outflanking." His eyes glittered in the firelight. "Were you in the Army all through the dark times?"

"No, sir," Tom answered. "They took the uniform off my back in 1917, and I didn't put it back on till things heated up again."

"That's what I thought," Patton said. "I would have heard of you if you'd stayed in. Hell, you'd probably outrank me if you'd stayed in. You may not be a professional in name, but by God you are in performance." Maybe he meant it. Maybe he was just making Tom Colleton look good to his men. Either way, Tom felt about ten feet tall.

About the only thing Armstrong Grimes knew these days was that the United States were in trouble. He shook his head. He knew one other thing: he was still alive. He hadn't the faintest idea why, though.

"I figured we were going to keep that fucking Findlay place," he said as he lay down by a campfire somewhere north of the fallen town.

"We would have, if those stinking barrels hadn't shown up," said a new man in the squad, a New York Jew named Yossel Reisen.

He was a few years older than Armstrong. He'd been conscripted in the peaceful 1930s, done his time, and been hauled into the Army again after the shooting started.

They'd fallen back to the northeast through the hamlet of Astoria toward the larger town of Fostoria. Five rail lines fanned through Fostoria. It also boasted a carbon electrode factory and a stockyard. It was not the sort of place the USA wanted to see in Confederate hands.

"Where the hell were *our* barrels?" Armstrong demanded of everyone within earshot. "What were they doing? I'm sick of getting run out of places because the other guys have barrels and we can't stop 'em."

Off not far enough in the distance, artillery rumbled. The noise came from the north, which meant the guns belonged to the USA. Armstrong hoped that was what it meant, anyhow. The other possibility was that the Confederates had badly outflanked U.S. forces, and that Armstrong and his comrades were cut off and in the process of being surrounded. There were times when sitting out the rest of the war in a Confederate prison camp didn't seem so bad.

That was one thing Armstrong didn't say. Everybody who outranked him was awfully touchy about defeatism. You could grouse about why the Army wasn't fighting back as hard as it might have; that was in the rules. But if you said you'd just as soon not be fighting at all, you'd gone too far. He didn't know exactly what happened to soldiers who said such things. He didn't want to find out, either.

Overhead, shells made freight-train noises. They flew south, south past the U.S. lines, and came down somewhere not far from Astoria. That was Confederate-held territory now, which meant those were U.S. guns firing, and that the soldiers in butternut and their swarms of barrels hadn't broken through.

Counterbattery fire came back very promptly. It might be dark, but the Confederates weren't asleep. Those shells flew over Armstrong's head, too, roaring north. As long as the guns traded fire with one another, he didn't mind too much. When the Confederates started pounding the front line, that was something else again.

That was trouble, was what it was.

Armstrong rolled himself in his blanket and went to sleep. He'd discovered he could sleep anywhere when he got the chance. All he needed was something to lean against. He didn't have to lie down;

sitting would do fine. Sleep, in the field, was more precious than gold, almost—but not quite—more precious than a good foxhole. Whenever he could, he restocked.

Corporal Stowe shook him awake in the middle of the night. Armstrong's automatic reaction was to try to murder the noncom. "Easy, tiger," Stowe said, laughing, and jerked back out of the way of an elbow that would have broken his nose. "I'm not a goddamn infiltrator. Get your ass up there for sentry duty."

"Oh." Now that Armstrong knew it wasn't kill or be killed in the next moment, he allowed himself the luxury of a yawn. "All right." He pulled on his shoes, which he'd been using for a pillow. "Anything going on? Those bastards poking around?"

"That's why we have sentries," the squad commander answered, and Armstrong really wished that elbow had connected. Stowe went on, "Seems pretty quiet. You run into trouble, shoot first."

"Bet your ass," Armstrong said. "Any son of a bitch tries to get by me, he pays full price."

When the war first broke out, Stowe would have laughed at him for talking like that. But he'd lived through more than a month of it. Not only that, he'd shown he was one of the minority of soldiers who did the majority of damage when fighting started. The corporal thumped him on the shoulder and gave him a little shove.

He got challenged by the man he was replacing. Gabby Priest hardly ever said anything that wasn't line of duty. He and Armstrong spoke challenge and countersign softly, to keep lurking Confederates from picking them off—another drawback to a war where both sides used the same language.

Gabby went back the way Armstrong had come. Armstrong settled himself as motionlessly as he could. He listened to chirping crickets. They didn't know anything about war, or how lucky they were to be ignorant. An owl hooted. A whippoorwill called mournfully.

Armstrong listened for noises that didn't belong: a footfall, a twig breaking under a boot heel, a cough. He also listened for sudden silences that didn't belong. Animals could sense people moving even where other people couldn't. If they stopped in alarm, that was a good sign there was something to be alarmed about.

He heard nothing out of the ordinary. Somebody fired off a burst of machine-gun fire over to the west, but it had to be at least half a mile away. As long as nothing happened any closer than that, he didn't need to worry about it.

He yawned. He wished he were back under the blanket. After another yawn, he swore at himself in a low whisper. One of the things they'd made very plain in basic training, even before the war started, was that they could shoot you if you fell asleep on sentry duty. That didn't necessarily mean they would, but he didn't care to take the chance. If the Confederates broke through because he was snoring, his own side wouldn't be very happy with him even if he survived—which wasn't particularly likely.

Some guys carried a pin with them when they came on sentry duty, to stick themselves if they started feeling sleepy. Armstrong never had. From now on, though, he thought he would.

Was that . . . ? He tensed, sleep forgotten as ice walked up his back. Was that the clatter of barrel tracks, the rumble of engines? Or was it only his imagination playing tricks on him? Whatever it was, it was either just above or just below his threshold of hearing, so he couldn't decide how scared he ought to be.

If those were barrels coming forward, the Springfield he clutched convulsively wouldn't do him a damn bit of good. He could shoot it at a barrel till doomsday, and he wouldn't hurt a thing. He listened as he'd never listened before—and still couldn't make up his mind whether he'd heard anything. He didn't hear any more. That meant the barrels weren't coming any closer, anyhow, which suited him fine.

The artillery duel between U.S. and C.S. guns started up again, each side feeling for the other in the night. Listening to death fly back and forth overhead was almost like watching a tennis match, except both sides could serve at once and there could be more than one ball in the air at the same time.

One other difference belatedly occurred to Armstrong. Tennis balls weren't in the habit of exploding and scattering deadly shell fragments, or perhaps poison gas, all over the court. Artillery shells, unfortunately, were.

Armstrong longed for a cigarette. It would make him more alert and help the time pass. Of course, a sniper who aimed at the coal could blow his face off. Even someone who didn't spot the coal could smell smoke and know he was around. He didn't light up, but let out a soft snort of laughter. Somebody might smell *him* and know he was around. He couldn't remember the last time he'd bathed. Of course, any Confederate sneaking up was liable to be just as gamy as he was.

He crouched in the foxhole, peering into the night, hunter and hunted at the same time. With trees overhead, he couldn't even watch the stars go by and gauge the time from them. Little by little, though, black gave way to indigo gave way to gray gave way to gold gave way to pink in the east.

Soft motion *behind* him. He whirled, swinging his rifle toward the noise. "Halt!" he called. "Who goes there?"

"Nagurski," came the response: not a name but a recognition signal.

"Barrel," Armstrong answered. Any U.S. football fanatic knew the hard-pounding Barrel Nagurski. The Confederates had their own football heroes. With luck, they didn't pay attention to muscular Yankee running backs.

Yossel Reisen came out into the open just as the sun crawled over the horizon. "Anything going on?" he asked.

"I'm not sure," Armstrong answered, and told him of what he thought he'd heard. He finished, "They've been quiet since then. I *am* sure of that. Whether they were there at all"—he shrugged—"who the hell knows?"

Reisen started to say something. Before he could, he and Armstrong both looked to the sky. Airplanes were coming up out of the south, motors roaring. At the same time, the Confederate bombardment not only picked up, it started falling on the front line and not on the U.S. artillery. The foxhole Armstrong stood in wasn't really big enough for two. Yossel Reisen jumped in anyhow. Armstrong said not a word. He would have done the same thing.

Screaming sirens added to the engine roars: dive bombers stooping like hawks. "Mules!" Reisen yelled, at the same time as Armstrong was shouting, "Asskickers!" He hoped the Confederate artillery shells would shoot down their own airplanes. *Wish for the moon while you're at it,* went through his mind. It was a one-in-a-million chance at best.

Bombs began bursting, back a few hundred yards where the other men in the squad rested. Some of the shells came down much closer to the foxhole. Fragments snarled past, some of them bare inches above Armstrong's head. He yelled—no, he screamed, and was unashamed of screaming. Yossel Reisen probably couldn't hear him through the din. And Yossel's mouth was open, too, so he might have been screaming himself.

Armstrong's father went on and on about the day-long bombardments he'd gone through during the Great War. He had a limp and the Purple Heart to prove he wasn't kidding, too. Armstrong had got sick of hearing about it all the same. Now he understood what his old man was talking about. Experience was a great leveler.

This bombardment didn't go on all day. After half an hour, it let up. "We're in for it now," Armstrong said. Reisen nodded gloomily.

Confederate soldiers loped forward, bent at the waist to make themselves small targets. Armstrong and Yossel both started shooting at them. They went down—hitting the dirt, probably, rather than dead or wounded. Sure as hell, some of them began shooting to make the U.S. soldiers keep their heads down while others advanced.

"We better get out of here before they flank us out," Armstrong said. Yossel Reisen nodded. The two of them scrambled back through the trees, bullets snapping all around them.

Nothing was left of the encampment except shell holes and what looked like a butcher's waste. As the two U.S. soldiers fell back farther, they fell in with other survivors. Nobody seemed interested in anything but getting away. They didn't find anything like a line till just in front of Fostoria. No one there asked them any questions. The position farther south had plainly been smashed. Now, would this one hold? With no great optimism, Armstrong hoped so.

VIII

With the bulk of the Americas in the way, getting from the Atlantic to the Pacific was a long haul for a U.S. warship. For many years, people in the USA and the CSA had talked about cutting a canal through Colombia's Central American province or through Nicaragua. No one had been able to agree on who would do the work or who would guard it once done. The United States had threatened war if the Confederate States tried, and vice versa. And so, in spite of all the talk, there was no canal.

The *Remembrance* and her accompanying cruisers and destroyers and supply ships steamed south toward Cape Horn and Tierra del Fuego. She kept her combat air patrol constantly airborne. The Empire of Brazil was neutral. When they got as far south as Argentina, on the other hand, she was on the same side as England and France, which meant the same side as the CSA.

Sam Carsten had seen in the last war that land-based airplanes could be hard on ships. He knew from the raid on Charleston that they could be a lot harder now. The CAP also kept an eye out for British, Confederate, and French submersibles—maybe even Argentine ones, for all Sam knew.

Even in wartime, though, some rituals went on. Carsten had crossed the Equator several times. That made him a shellback, immune from the hazing men doing it for the first time—polliwogs—had to go through. Officers suffered along with ratings. They got their backsides paddled. They had their hair cut off in patches. They got drenched with the hoses. They had to kiss King Neptune's belly. The grizzled CPO who played King Neptune had a vast expanse of belly to kiss. To make the job more delightful, he smeared it with grease from the galley.

Everybody watched to see how the polliwogs took it. A man who got angry at the indignities often paid for it later on. If you went through things with a smile—or, better, with a laugh and a dirty joke for King Neptune—you won points. And the suffering polliwogs needed to remember that they were turning into shell-backs. One of these days, they would have the chance to get even with some new men.

Commander Dan Cressy came up to Carsten as he watched the hijinks. "Well, Lieutenant, what do you think?" the exec asked.

"Damn good show, sir," Sam answered. "Szymanski makes about the best King Neptune I've ever seen."

"Can't argue with you there," Cressy said. "But I didn't mean that. A lot of officers just do their jobs and don't worry about anything outside them. You look at the bigger picture. What do you think of our move to the Pacific?"

"Thank you, sir," Sam said. That the exec should ask his opinion was a compliment indeed. After a moment, he went on, "If we have to go, it's probably a good thing we're going now. That's how it looks to me: we're grabbing the chance while it's still there."

"I agree," Cressy said crisply. "With Bermuda lost and the Bahamas going, we'll have a much tougher time getting a task force into these waters once the Confederates and the British consolidate their positions." He looked unhappy. "They snookered us very nicely to draw us out of Bermuda so they could hit it. We shouldn't have fallen for the lure of the British carrier—but we did, and now we have to live with it."

"Yes, sir," Sam said. "Other thing that occurs to me is, will this task force be enough help for the Sandwich Islands?"

"Damn good question," Cressy said. "We have to try, though, or else we'll lose them, and that would be a disaster. You see the difficulty we face, I presume?" He cocked his head to one side like a teacher waiting to see how smart a student was. The impression held even though Sam was the older man.

"I think so, sir," Sam said, and then spluttered as water splashed off a luckless polliwog and onto him. He wiped his face on his sleeve and tried to remember what he'd been about to say. "We have to be strong in the Atlantic and the Pacific, because we've got enemies to east and west. The Japs can concentrate on us."

Commander Cressy brought his hands together, once, twice, three times. They made hardly any sound at all. Even so, Sam felt as if he'd just got a standing ovation from a capacity crowd at Custer Stadium in Philadelphia. "That is the essence of it, all right," the exec said. "And the Japs have a running start on us, too. Since they gobbled up what was the Dutch East Indies, they've got the oil and the rubber and a lot of the other raw materials they need for a long war. Going after them starting from the Sandwich Islands will be hard. Going after them from the West Coast would be impossible, I think."

"Yes, sir," Sam said, "Especially if—" He broke off.

He hadn't stopped soon enough. "Especially if what?" Cressy asked—and when he asked you something, he expected an answer.

Unhappily, Sam gave him one: "Especially if the Confederates cut us in half, sir, is what I was going to say. That would leave the West on its own, and it just doesn't make as much or have as many people as they do back East."

Commander Cressy rubbed his chin. Slowly, he nodded. "This isn't the first time I've thought it was a shame you're a mustang, Carsten. If you'd come up through the Naval Academy, you'd outrank me now."

"You do what you can with the cards they deal you, sir," Sam said. "I joined the Navy when I was a kid. It's been my home. It's been my family. Least I can do to pay it back is to work hard. I've done that. I'm happy I've got as far as I have. When I signed up, being an officer was the last thing on my mind. I figured I'd end up where Szymanski is, except maybe without the grease on my stomach. And I could've done a lot worse'n that, too."

The exec glanced over toward Szymanski, who was bawling obscenities at a lieutenant, j.g., less than half Carsten's age. "He's a good man, a solid man," Cressy said. "The big difference between the two of you is that he's got no imagination. He just accepts what he finds, while you've got that itch to figure out how things work."

"Do I?" Sam thought about it. "Well, maybe I do. But I could have thrown it into, say, being a machinist's mate just as easy."

"So what? *Could have* doesn't count for anything, not in this man's navy," Commander Cressy said crisply. "You are what you are, and I'm damn glad to have you on my ship." He clapped Carsten on the back and went on his way, dodging the stream from another hose as smoothly as a halfback sidestepping a tackler. Whatever he did, he did well.

And he likes me, Sam thought. *I'm only a mustang, a sunburned sea rat up through the hawse hole, but he likes me.* That made him feel better about himself than he had since . . . since . . . He laughed. He was damned if he remembered when anything had made him feel better.

A sunburned sea rat he certainly was. Orders had gone out for all hands to wear long sleeves and not to roll them up regardless of the weather. Action had shown that protected against flash burns when shells and bombs burst. Sam had been wearing long sleeves for more than thirty years. That way, he burned only from the wrists down and from the neck up: a dubious improvement, but an improvement nonetheless.

After the festivities that went with crossing the Equator, routine returned to the *Remembrance.* Drills picked up as the ship and the accompanying task force neared Argentine waters. General quarters sounded at all hours of the day and night. It bounced men out of their bunks and hammocks. It pulled them out of the showers. Sailors laughed when their comrades ran to battle stations naked and dripping, clothes clutched under one arm. But they didn't laugh too much. Most of them had been caught the same way at one time or another. And besides, with the task force where it was, nobody could be sure when a drill might turn into the real thing.

The summer sun receded in the north. Sam still suffered, but not so severely. He might have been the only man aboard who looked forward to rounding Cape Horn in the Southern Hemisphere's winter. There, if nowhere else south of the Yukon, the weather suited his skin.

One of the destroyers in the task force detected, or thought she detected, a submersible. She dropped depth charges. Down deep in the bowels of the *Remembrance,* Sam listened to the ashcans bursting one by one. They were too far away to shake the ship as they would have at closer range.

"Hope they sink the son of a bitch," one of the soldiers in the damage-control party said savagely.

"Not me," Sam said. Everybody looked at him as if he'd lost his mind. He explained: "I hope there's no sub there at all. I hope they're plastering the hell out of a whale, or else that the hydrophone operator's got a case of the galloping fantods."

"Why?" Lieutenant Commander Hiram Pottinger asked, real curiosity in his voice. "Don't you want to see the enemy on the bottom?"

"Oh, hell, yes, sir, if that's the only boat out there," Sam told his superior. "But they're liable to hunt in packs. If we get one, there may be more. I'd just as soon there weren't any."

Pottinger pursed his lips, then slowly nodded. "You've got kind of a lefthanded way of looking at things, don't you? Can't say you're wrong, though."

They never found out whether the destroyer sank the submersible, or whether a sub had been there at all. The only evidence was negative: no torpedoes streaked toward any ship in the task force. If the sub had been there, and if it had been sunk, it was a lone wolf, not part of a pack.

No Argentine airplanes came out to harry the *Remembrance* and her satellites. Argentina and the USA were formally at war, but that was because Argentina did so much to feed England and France, and the United States threatened her commerce. The task force was bound for the Pacific. If provoked, though, it might pause. Maybe the Americans had quietly warned they *would* pause if provoked. Sam didn't know anything about that. As far as he could tell, nobody on the *Remembrance* did. He did know he was glad not to have to fight his way past Argentina.

The Argentines hadn't unbent enough to let the task force through the Straits of Magellan. The U.S. ships had to go around Tierra del Fuego and through the thunderous seas of Cape Horn. It felt like the devil's sleigh ride: up one mountainous wave after another, then down the far side. Some of those waves broke over the carrier's bow, sending sea surging across the flight deck and carrying away anything that wasn't lashed down and quite a bit that was. A sailor on one of the accompanying destroyers got washed overboard. He was gone before his mates had any chance to rescue him.

Vomit's sharp stink filled the corridors of the *Remembrance*. The stoves in the galleys were put out; the pitching was too much for them. Chow was sandwiches and cold drinks, not that many men had much appetite. Sam was a good sailor, but even he was off his feed.

What really amazed him was the knowledge that things could have been worse. A hundred years earlier, clippers had rounded the Horn on sail power, going into the teeth of the howling westerly gale. He admired the men aboard those ships without wanting to imitate them. The passage was hard enough with 180,000 horsepower on his side.

And then, at last, they were through. The Pacific began to live up to its name. The stoves were lit again. Hot meals returned. The crew felt good enough to eat them, and to clamor for more. And all the task force had to deal with were the Chileans, who were irked the U.S. ships hadn't punished their Argentine enemies. After what the *Remembrance* had just been through, mere diplomacy felt like child's play.

Jonathan Moss spotted a flight of Mules buzzing along above northern Ohio. His lips skinned back from his teeth in a predatory grin. The gull-winged Confederate dive bombers raised hell with U.S. infantry. But they were sitting ducks for fighters. He spoke into the wireless for the men of his squadron: "You see 'em, boys? Two o'clock low, just lollygagging along and waiting for us. Let's go get 'em."

He pushed the stick forward. The Wright fighter dove. The squadron followed him down. They'd been trying to do too much with too little for too long. Now they had a chance to take a real bite out of the Confederates. Those damned Asskickers were like flying artillery, pounding U.S. positions ordinary shellfire couldn't hurt. Take them out and the Confederate ground attack would suffer.

Nobody could say the men who flew the Mules were asleep at the switch. They scattered when they spotted the U.S. fighters stooping on them. Some dove for the deck. Others hightailed it back toward the Confederate lines.

Moss picked his target: a Mule scooting along just above the treetops. The rear gunner saw him, and started shooting. A stream of tracers flew from the back of the Mule's long cockpit toward him.

His grin got wider and more savage. The Mule had one machine gun. He had half a dozen, and a much steadier gun platform than a jinking bomber. His finger jabbed the firing button on top of the stick. The leading edges of the Wright's wings spouted flame as the guns hammered away. He held the dive, careless of the enemy's fire. The best way to knock an airplane down was to do your shooting from as close as you could.

He fired another burst into the Mule. The rear gunner stopped shooting. Moss was close enough to see him slumped over his gun. Flame ran back from the wing root along the dive bomber's fuselage. The Mule suddenly heeled over and slammed into the ground. Flame and smoke volcanoed upward. The pilot had never had a chance.

"Scratch one bandit!" Moss shouted exultantly, and then clawed for altitude. He wanted more of those Asskickers burning, and he thought he knew how to get what he wanted, too.

But then one of his pilots yelled, "Bandits! Bandits at three o'clock high!" Moss' exultation turned to cold sweat on the instant.

As his fighters had had the advantage of altitude against the Mules, so the Confederate Hound Dogs had the edge on the Wrights. The C.S. fighters tore into them, guns blazing. Frantic shouts came from Moss' wireless set. A couple of them cut off abruptly as fighters or pilots were hit.

He'd been late pulling up. Too late. Here came a Hound Dog, diving on him. He twisted to try to meet it. Too late again. Machine-gun bullets and a couple of shells from the cannon that fired through the Confederate fighter's propeller hub stitched across his machine's left wing and fuselage. The engine made a horrible grinding noise. Smoke poured from it. Suddenly Moss was flying a glider that didn't want to glide.

He had to get out—if he could. The controls still answered, after a fashion. He got the crippled fighter over onto its back, opened the canopy, undid the harness that held him in his armored seat, and fell free.

The slipstream tore at him. He just missed killing himself by smashing into the Wright's tail. Then he was clear of the airplane, clear and falling toward the ground far below—far below now, but drawing closer with inexorable speed.

He yanked the ripcord. Folded silk spilled out from the pack on his back. He'd put the parachute in there himself. If it didn't open the way it was supposed to, he'd curse himself all the way down.

Whump! The shock when the canopy opened was enough to

make him bite his tongue. He tasted blood in his mouth. Considering what might have happened, he wasn't complaining. He hung in midair. All at once, he went from brick to dandelion puff. Even so, he would sooner have done this for fun than to save his own neck.

His fighter hit the ground and burst into flames, just like the Mule he'd shot down. And he hadn't finished saving his own neck, either—here came the Hound Dog that had knocked him out of the sky. Or maybe it was another one—he couldn't tell. But he'd never felt more helpless than he did now, hanging in the air.

During the Great War, hardly any fliers had worn a parachute. The ones who did were reckoned fair game till they got to the ground. If that Confederate pilot wanted to fire a machine-gun burst into him, he couldn't do one goddamn thing about it. He had a .45 on his hip, but he didn't bother to reach for it.

Instead of shooting, the Confederate waggled his wings and zoomed away. Moss thought he saw the other man wave inside the cockpit, but the Hound Dog was gone too fast for him to be sure. He waved his thanks, but he didn't know if the Confederate could see that, either.

"They aren't all bastards," he said, as if someone had claimed they were. He felt weak and giddy with relief. To his disgust, he also realized he felt wet. Somewhere back there, he'd pissed himself. He shrugged inside the parachute harness. He wasn't the first flier who'd done that, and he wouldn't be the last. When he got down on the ground, he'd clean himself off. That was all he could do. Only dumb luck he hadn't filled his pants, too.

He swung his weight to the left, trying to steer the chute away from the trees below and towards a stretch of grass. Was he over Confederate-held territory, or did the USA still have a grip here? He didn't know. Pretty damn soon, he'd find out.

He passed over a pine almost close enough to kick it on the way down. There was the meadow, coming up. He bent his knees, braced for the impact—and twisted his ankle anyhow. "Son of a bitch!" he said loudly. The chute tried to drag him across the field. He pulled out his knife and sawed at the shrouds. After what seemed a very long time, he cut himself free. He tried to get to his feet. The ankle didn't want to bear his weight. He could hobble, but that was about it.

From behind him, somebody said, "Hold it right there, ass-hole!" Moss froze. Was that a U.S. or a C.S. accent? He hadn't been able to tell. The soldier said, "Turn around real slow, and make sure I can see both hands are empty."

Moss couldn't turn any way but slowly. He whooped when he saw the man pointing a rifle at him wore green-gray. "I'm Jonathan Moss, major, U.S. Army Air Force," he said.

"Yeah, sure, buddy, and I'm Queen of the May," the U.S. soldier said. For a dreadful moment, Moss thought his career would end right there, finished by someone on his own side. But then the soldier said, "I see you're heeled. Drop your piece, and don't do anything stupid or you'll never find out who wins the Champions' Cup this year."

"Whatever you say." Moss fished his pistol out of the holster with the thumb and forefinger of his right hand. He dropped it on the ground, then took a couple of limping steps away from it. "Get me back to your CO. I'll show him I'm legit."

The soldier came forward and scooped up the .45. Never for an instant did his Springfield stop pointing at Moss' brisket. "Maybe you will and maybe you won't," he said. "But all right—I've pulled your teeth. Come along. You better not try anything funny, or that's all she wrote."

"I'm coming," Moss said. "I can't run, not on this leg." The soldier in green-gray only shrugged. Maybe he thought Moss was fak-ing. Moss wished he were. He asked, "Where the hell are we, anyway? I flew out of Indiana, and I got all turned around in the last dogfight."

"If my lieutenant wants you to know, he'll tell you," the soldier answered. "Can't you move any faster than that?"

"Now that you mention it," Moss said, "no." Behind him, the soldier scattered unprintables the way Johnny Appleseed had scat-tered seeds. The sputter of bad language eased but didn't stop when they got in under the trees. Moss was glad to get out of the meadow, too; one of those Hound Dogs might have paid a return visit, and shooting up soldiers caught in the open was any pilot's sport.

"Halt!" an unseen voice called. "Who goes there?"

"No worries, Jonesy—it's me," Moss' captor (rescuer?) replied. "I got me a flyboy—says he's one of ours. He don't talk like a Confederate, but he don't quite talk like one of us, neither." *That's what I get for living in Canada for most of twenty years—I started sounding like a Canuck,* Moss thought unhappily.

"Well, bring him on," Jonesy said. "Lieutenant Garzetti will figure out what the hell to do with him."

Lieutenant Giovanni Garzetti was a little dark man in his late twenties who looked as if he'd never smiled in his whole life. He made his headquarters in a barn that had had one corner blown off by a shell. He looked Moss and his gear over, asked him a few questions, and said, "Yeah, you're the goods, all right." He turned to the soldier who'd brought in the fighter pilot. "Give him back his sidearm, Pratt."

"Yes, sir," the soldier said. This was the first time Moss had heard his name. Pratt took the .45 off his belt and handed it back. "Here you go. I didn't want to take any chances with you, you know what I mean?"

Moss could tell he wouldn't get any more of an apology than that. He nodded as he slid the pistol into the holster again. "Don't worry about it."

"So what can we do for you, Major?" Lieutenant Garzetti asked.

"A bandage for my ankle and a lift to the closest airstrip would be good," Moss answered. "I can't walk for beans, but I expect I can still fly."

"Pratt, go chase down a medic," Garzetti said. The soldier sketched a salute and departed. Garzetti nodded to Moss. "We'll get you wrapped up good. Meanwhile . . ." He pulled a little silver flask out of his pocket. "Have a knock of this."

This was some of the best—certainly the most welcome—bourbon Moss had ever drunk. "Anesthetic," he said solemnly, and Garzetti nodded. The lieutenant took a drink from the flask when Moss returned it. Then he put it in his pocket once more. Was he a quiet lush? He didn't act like one. If he fancied a drink every now and then . . . well, Moss fancied a drink every now and then, too. "Boy, that hit the spot. You sure you aren't part St. Bernard?"

Lieutenant Garzetti still didn't smile. His eyes twinkled, though. "If you said on my mother's side, you'd've called me a son of a bitch."

"That's not what I meant!" Moss exclaimed.

"I know it's not, and I'm not flabbling about it," Garzetti said. A man with a Red Cross armband came in through the missing corner of the barn. "Here's the medic. Let's see what he can do." After poking and prodding at Moss' ankle, the medic said, "I don't *think* it's busted, Major, but you sure as hell ought to get it X-rayed first chance you find."

Moss only laughed. "And when's that likely to be?"

"Beats me, sir, but you ought to. You can mess yourself up bad, trying to do too much on a busted ankle. In the meantime . . ." In the meantime, the medic used what seemed a mummy's worth of gauze to wrap the injured part. "There you go. Try that. Tell me how it is. If you're not happy, I'll put some more on."

How? Moss wondered. He got to his feet. The ankle still complained when he put weight on it, but it didn't scream so loud. He could walk, after a fashion. "Thanks," he said. "It's not perfect, but it's an awful lot better. And as long as I can get into a fighter, what else do I need?" Neither the medic nor Lieutenant Garzetti had anything to say to that.

Scipio watched bored cops herd colored factory workers onto their buses near the edge of the Terry. He'd got used to that. It bothered him less than it had when he first saw it. The buses brought the workers back every evening. They really did take the men and women to do war work. They didn't haul them off to those camps from which nobody ever came back. "Come on. Keep moving," a cop said. "You got to—"

The world blew up.

That was how it seemed to Scipio, anyhow. One minute, he was walking along the streets, watching the workers board the buses and thinking about what he'd be doing once he got to the Huntsman's Lodge. The next, he was rolling on the ground, tearing out both knees of his tuxedo pants and clapping his hands to his ears in a useless, belated effort to hold out that horrible sound.

Afterwards, he realized that the buses had shielded him from the worst of the blast. The motorcar bomb went off across the street from them. If they hadn't been in the way, the twisted metal junk screeching through the air in all directions probably would have cut him down, too. As things were, he got a couple of little cuts from flying glass, but nothing worse than that.

Head ringing from the force of the explosion, he staggered upright again. He heard everything as if from very far away. He knew his hearing could come back to normal in a couple of days. *A hell of a country,* he thought, *when you know how things are after a bombing on account of you've been through them before.*

When he looked at what the bomb had done to the buses and to the people waiting for them, his stomach did a slow lurch. All four buses were burning furiously. That would have been even worse if they'd had gasoline engines rather than using diesel fuel, but it was plenty bad enough as things were. One of them lay on its side; another had been twisted almost into a right angle. And the people . . .

"Do Jesus!" Scipio whispered, realizing just how lucky he'd been. The bomb might have been a harvester for people; the blast had cut them down in windrows. Men and women and bleeding chunks that had belonged to men and women lay everywhere. A policeman's head stared sightlessly at a black woman's arm. A disemboweled worker—still somehow wearing his cloth cap—tried to rearrange his guts till he slumped over, unconscious or dead. A man whose face was nothing but raw meat lay on his back and screamed agony to the uncaring sky.

The worst of all this was, Scipio knew what to do. He *had* been through the nightmare before. This wasn't the first motorcar bomb to hit Augusta—Negroes who hated the Freedom Party had struck before. Scipio began looking for people who'd been badly hurt but might live if someone stanched their bleeding in a hurry. He used whatever he could to do the job: socks, hankies, shirts, shoelace tourniquets.

He wasn't the only one, either. Passersby and the lucky few the bomb hadn't hurt badly did what they could to help the wounded. Scipio found himself bandaging a white policeman with a gaping hole in his calf. "Thank you kindly, uncle," the cop said through clenched teeth.

He meant well. That made the appellation sting more, not less. Even in his pain, all he saw was . . . a nigger. Scipio wanted to find some way to change his mind. If doing his best to save the white man's life couldn't turn the trick, he was damned if he knew what could.

Clanging bells announced ambulances and fire engines—a building across the street, by the scattered smoking fragments of the auto that had held the bomb, was burning. Scipio hadn't even noticed. He was intent on more urgent things close by him. He did hear the ambulance crews' exclamations of dismay. The men pitched in and helped. To give them their due, they didn't seem to care whether they aided whites or the far more numerous blacks.

"Here, Pop, scoot over—I'll take care of that," one of them said, elbowing Scipio aside. And he did, too, digging a jagged chunk of metal out of a man's back and bandaging the wound with practiced dispatch. Scipio minded *pop* much less than he'd minded *uncle*. The fellow from the ambulance could have called anyone no longer young *pop* regardless of his color, and Scipio's hair was gray heading toward white.

One of the ambulances had a radio. A blood-spattered driver was bawling into the microphone: "Y'all got to send more people here, Freddy. This is a hell of a mess—worst damn thing I've seen since the end of the war . . . Yeah, whatever you can spare. I hope they catch the goddamn son of a bitch who done it. Hang the bastard by his balls, and it'd still be too good for him."

Scipio was inclined to agree with the driver. He would have bet his last dime that the man who planted the bomb was black. That didn't change his opinion. What did the bomber hope to accomplish? He'd killed at least twenty of his own kind, and wounded dozens more. He'd wrecked buses that were taking the Negroes to work that kept them out of camps. And the Freedom Party would probably land on the Terry with both feet after this. Would Jake Featherston's men squeeze another indemnity out of people who had very little to begin with? Or would stalwarts and guards simply fire up Augusta's whites and start a new pogrom? Oh, they had plenty of choices—all of them bad for Negroes.

More ambulances clattered up to the disaster. The fellow who'd pushed Scipio aside nudged him now. "Thanks for your help, Pop. You can go on about your business, I reckon. Looks like we're getting enough people to do the job."

"Yes, suh," Scipio said. "I stays if you wants me to."

The ambulance man shook his head. "That's all right." He

looked Scipio up and down. "If you don't have a job you need to get to and a boss who's wondering where you're at, I'm a damnyankee. Go on, get going."

Till the man mentioned them, Scipio had forgotten about the Huntsman's Lodge and Jerry Dover. He surveyed himself. Except for the ruined trousers, he'd do. He didn't have much blood on his boiled shirt, and his jacket was black, so whatever he had on that didn't show.

He thought about going back to the flat to change trousers— thought about it and shook his head. He was already badly late. He supposed he could get another pair at the restaurant. Even if he couldn't, those ruined knees would silently show the rich white customers a little about what being a black in the Confederate States of America was like.

"You sure it's all right?" he asked the ambulance man. The fellow nodded impatiently. He made shooing motions. Scipio left. He discovered his own knees had got scraped when he hit the pavement. Walking hurt. But he was damned if he'd ask anybody to paint him with Merthiolate, not when there were so many people who were really injured.

Whites often stared at him when he walked to the Huntsman's Lodge. A black man in a tuxedo in a Confederate town had to get used to jokes about penguins. Today, the stares were different. Scipio knew why: he was a singularly disheveled penguin. People asked him if he'd got caught in the bombing. He nodded over and over, unsurprised; they must have heard the blast for miles around.

He'd just put his hand out to open the side door to the restaurant when another blast shook Augusta. The sound came from back in the Terry—from the very direction in which he'd just come. "Do Jesus!" he said again. In his mind's eye, he could imagine bombers setting timers in two motorcars parked not too far apart, not too close together. The first one would wreak havoc. Ambulances and fire engines would come rushing to repair the damage— and then the second bomb would go off and take out their crews. Scipio shivered. If he'd guessed right, someone had a really evil turn of mind.

Still shaking his head, he opened the door and went in. He almost ran into Jerry Dover, who'd come hurrying up to find out what the second blast was about. The restaurant manager gaped at him, then said, "Xerxes! You all right? When you didn't show up for so long, I was afraid the bomb—the first bomb, I mean—got you."

"I's all right, yes, suh," Scipio said. "Bomb damn near do get me." He explained how being behind the buses had shielded him from the worst of the blast, finishing, "I he'ps de wounded till de ambulances gits dere. Now—" He spread his hands. His palms were scraped and bloody, too.

"Huh? What do you mean?" Jerry Dover hadn't put the two explosions together. Scipio did some more explaining. Dover's mouth tightened. Now that Scipio had pointed it out to him, he saw it, too. He made a fist and banged it against the side of his leg. "Son of a bitch. *Son* of a bitch! That's . . . devilish, is what it is."

"Yes, suh," said Scipio, who would have had trouble coming up with a better word. "I don't know it's so, mind you, but I reckon dat what happen."

"I reckon you're right," Dover said. "You're damn lucky that ambulance man sent you away. If he'd asked you to stay instead . . ."

"Lawd!" That hadn't occurred to Scipio. But his boss was right. If the man had asked him to stay, he would have, without hesitation. And then that bomb would have caught him, too.

Jerry Dover clapped him on the shoulder. "You sure you're all right to work? You want to go home, I won't say boo. Hell, I'll pay you for the day. You went through a lot of shit there."

"Dat right kind of you, Mistuh Dover." Scipio meant it. His boss was actually treating him like a human being. The restaurant manager didn't have to do that. Few bosses with black workers bothered these days. Why should they, when the Freedom Party and the war gave them a license to be as nasty as they pleased? After a moment, Scipio went on, "All de same to you, though, I sooner stay here. I hopes they keeps me real busy, too. Busier I is, less I gots to think about what done happen."

"However you want. I ain't gonna argue with you," Dover said. "But you better rustle up another pair of pants from somewhere. The ones you got on don't cut it."

"Somebody let me borrow a pair, I reckon," Scipio said.

The cook's trousers he got didn't really go with his jacket and shirt. But they were black. Anybody who saw the rest of the outfit would probably fill in what he expected to see. The pants didn't fit all that well, either. They would do for a shift. He had that other pair back home. Now he'd have to go out and buy one more. Jerry Dover didn't offer to cover that expense.

Customers talked about the bombing. A lot of them thought, as Scipio did, that it was foolish for Negroes to bomb their own kind. "I bet they're in the damnyankees' pay," one man said. "They're trying to disrupt our production."

"Wait till we catch them," said another white man, this one in a major's uniform. "We'll send them to—" But he broke off, noticing Scipio within earshot.

What was he going to say? Did he know about the camps? Did he think Scipio didn't? Whatever it was, Scipio never found out, because the major did know how to keep his mouth shut.

None of the prosperous whites eating at the Huntsman's Lodge thought to ask Scipio if he'd been anywhere near the bomb when it went off. He looked all right now, so it didn't occur to them. No one here cared what he thought about it. He wasn't a person to these people, as he was to Jerry Dover. He was only a waiter, and a colored waiter at that. His opinions about the day's specials and the wine list might be worth hearing. Anything else? No.

That didn't surprise Scipio. Normally, he hardly even noticed it. Today, he did. After what he'd been through, didn't he deserve better? As far as the Confederate States were concerned, the answer was no.

All Irving Morrell wanted to do was put together enough barrels to let him counterattack the Confederates in Ohio instead of defending all the time. If he could act instead of reacting . . . But he couldn't. He didn't know where all the barrels were going, but he had his dark suspicions: infantry commanders were probably snagging them as fast as they appeared, using them to bolster sagging regiments instead of going after the enemy. Why couldn't they see barrels were better used as a sword than as a shield?

Fed up, Morrell finally took a ride in a command car to see Brigadier General Dowling. The ride proved more exciting than he wanted it to be. A low-flying Confederate fighter strafed the motorcar. Morrell shot back with the pintle-mounted machine gun. The stream of tracers he sent at the fighter made the pilot pull up and zoom away. The fellow hadn't done much damage to the command car, but the flat tire from one of his bullets cost Morrell almost half an hour as he and the driver changed it.

"Good thing he didn't take out both front tires, sir," the driver said, tightening lug nuts. "We've only got the one spare, and a patch kit's kind of fighting out of its weight against a slug."

"Try not to attract any more Hound Dogs between here and General Dowling's headquarters, then," Morrell said.

"I'll do my best, sir," the driver promised.

Morrell got into Norwalk, Ohio, just as the sun was setting. Norwalk was the last town of any size south of Sandusky and Lake Erie. It had probably been pretty before the fighting started. Some of the houses still standing looked as if they dated back to before the War of Secession. With their porticoes and column-supported porches, they had an air of classical elegance.

Classical elegance had a tough time against bombs, though. A lot of houses probably as fine as any of the survivors were nothing but charred rubble. Here and there, people went through the wreckage, trying to salvage what they could. The sickly-sweet smell of decay warned that other people were part of the wreckage.

Dowling had his headquarters in one of those Classic Revival houses. He was shouting some thoroughly unclassical phrases into a field telephone when Morrell came to see him: "What the hell do you mean you can't hold, Colonel? You have to hold, hold to the last man! And if you *are* the last man, grab a goddamn rifle and do something useful with it." He hung up and glared at Morrell. "What the devil do *you* want?"

"Barrels," Morrell answered. "As many as you can get your hands on. The Confederates are smashing us to pieces because they can always mass armor at the *Schwerpunkt*. I don't have enough to stop them when they concentrate."

"I'm giving you everything that's coming into Ohio," Dowling said.

"If that's true, we're in worse trouble than I thought," Morrell said. "My guess was that infantry commanders were siphoning some of them off before I got my hands on them. If we're not making enough new ones . . ."

"Production isn't what it ought to be," Dowling said. "Confederate bombers don't have any trouble reaching Pontiac, Michigan, from Ohio, and they've hit the factories hard a couple of times. They're also plastering the railroad lines. And"—his jowly features twisted into a frown—"there are reports of sabotage on the lines, too: switches left open when they should be closed, bombs planted under the tracks, charming things like that."

Morrell used several variations on the theme Dowling had set on the telephone. The Confederates were doing everything they could with saboteurs this time around. That looked to be paying off, too. Anything that added to the disarray of U.S. forces in Ohio paid off for the CSA.

"I'm sorry, Colonel," Dowling said. "Believe me, I'm sorry. We're doing everything we can. Right now, it isn't enough."

"I've got an idea." Morrell snapped his fingers. He pointed at the fat general. "Once the barrels come off the line in Michigan, let 'em *drive* here. It'll cost us fuel, but fuel we've got. I'd like to see one of those Confederate bastards try to sabotage all the roads between Pontiac and here, by Jesus."

Dowling scribbled a note to himself. He grunted when he finished. "There. I've written it down. I'd forget my own head these days if I didn't write down where I kept it. That's not a bad idea, actually. It'll tear up the roads—they aren't made for that kind of traffic—but—"

"Yes. But," Morrell said. "The damned Confederates can already plaster Sandusky. But what they plaster, we can repair. If they break through again, if they reach the lake, they cut us in half. I saw this coming. That doesn't make me any happier now that it's here."

If the Confederates broke through to Lake Erie, the War Department would probably put General Dowling out to pasture. Someone, after all, had to take the blame for failure. Morrell realized the War Department might put *him* out to pasture, too. That was the chance he took. They were asking him to make bricks without out straw. They'd deliberately withheld the straw from him, withheld it for years. And now they could blame him for not having enough of it. Some people back in Philadelphia would leap at the chance.

"Sorry I haven't got better news for you, Colonel," Dowling said.

"So am I," Morrell told him. "I think I've wasted my trip here. The way things are, we can't afford to waste anything."

Before Dowling could answer, the field telephone jangled again. Looking apprehensive, the general picked it up. "Dowling speaking— what now?" He listened for a few seconds. His face turned purple. "*What?* You idiot, how did you let them get through? . . . What do you mean, they fooled you? . . . Oh, for Christ's sake! Well, you'd better try and stop them." He hung up, then glowered at Morrell. "Goddamn Confederates got a couple of our damaged barrels running again and put them at the head of their column. Our men didn't challenge till too late, and now they're making us sorry."

"Damn!" Morrell said. At the same time, he filed away the ploy in the back of his mind. Whoever'd thought it up was one sneaky son of a bitch. Morrell would have loved to return the favor. But the Confederates were advancing. His side wasn't. The enemy had more access to knocked-out U.S. barrels then he did to C.S. machines. He saluted. "If you'll excuse me, sir, I'm going to get back to the front." As he left, General Dowling's field telephone rang once more.

Out in front of the house, Morrell's driver was smoking a cigarette, his hands cupped around it to hide the coal in the darkness. "Get what you wanted, sir?" he asked.

"No." Morrell shook his head. "The commanding general tells me it's unavailable. So we'll just have to do the best we can without it." He climbed into the command car. "Take me back to our encampment. Try not to run over anything on the way."

"Do my best, sir," the driver answered. Only the narrowest of slits let light escape from his headlamps. He might as well have done without for all the good it did. But if he showed enough to light the road, he invited attack from the air. Blackout was a serious business on both sides of the border.

Off they went. They'd just left Norwalk when Morrell heard bombers droning far overhead. The airplanes were coming up from the south and heading northwest. Morrell swore under his breath. If that didn't mean Pontiac was about to get another pounding . . .

The driver almost took him straight into a Confederate position. They'd gone past there without any trouble on the way to Norwalk. Whatever Abner Dowling was yelling about on the field telephone must have happened in these parts. Morrell fired a few bursts from the machine gun at the Confederate pickets, who were at least as surprised to see him as he was to encounter them. They shot back wildly. Tracers lit the night. Bouncing along little country roads, the driver made his getaway.

"You know where you're going?" Morrell asked after a while.

"Sure as hell hope so, sir," the driver answered, which could have inspired more confidence. He added, "If those bastards have come farther than I thought, though, getting back to where we were at is liable to take some doing."

"If they've come that far, the barrels won't be where they were, either," Morrell pointed out. The driver thought that over, then nodded. He was going much too fast for the meager light the headlamps threw. Morrell said not a word. Had he been behind the wheel, he would have driven the same way.

The next time they got challenged, Morrell couldn't tell what sort of accent the sentry had. The driver zoomed past before he could exchange recognition signals. A couple of shots followed. Neither hit. Then the driver rounded a corner he noticed barely in time.

"That was one of ours," Morrell said mildly.

"How do you know?" The driver paused. His brain started to work. "Oh—single shots. A Springfield. Yeah, I guess you're right." He paused again. "Wish to God I had one of those automatic rifles Featherston's fuckers carry. That's a hell of a nice piece."

"Wouldn't do you as much good as you think," Morrell said. "Caliber's different from ours, so we can't use our own ammo in it. That was smart." He scowled in the darkness. Too much of what the Confederates had done in this fast-moving war was smart.

If I were trying to whip a country twice the size of mine, what would I do? Morrell scowled again. Jake Featherston's blueprint looked alarmingly good. That remained true, even though in effective manpower the USA's lead was closer to three to one than two to one. If you got the Negroes doing production work, if you mechanized your farming so it used the fewest possible people, if you went straight for the throat . . . If you did all that stuff, why then, goddammit, you had a chance.

"Hold it right there, or you're fucking dead." That challenge came from a sandbagged machine-gun nest blocking the narrow road. Morrell set a hand on the driver's shoulder to make sure they did stop. He thought those were U.S. forces behind the sandbags. He also doubted the command car could get away.

Cautiously, he exchanged password and countersign with the soldiers. They were as wary about him as he was about them. As usual, nobody wanted to say anything very loud. "Never can tell if those butternut bastards are listening," a sentry said. And he was right, too. But Morrell worried all the same. If U.S. soldiers spent more time thinking about the enemy than about what *they* were going to do next, didn't that give the Confederates an edge?

He got past the machine-gun nest. What should have been a half-hour ride to his own position outside the hamlet of Steuben ended up taking close to three hours. To his relief, he found the barrels still there. The Confederate penetration farther east hadn't made them pull back—yet.

Sergeant Michael Pound handed him the roasted leg of what was probably an unofficial chicken. "Here you are, sir," the gunner said. "We figured you'd be back sooner or later. Any good news from the general?"

He assumed he had the right to know—a very American thing to do. And Morrell, after gnawing the meat off the drumstick and thigh, told him: "Not a bit of it. We get to go right on meeting what Patton's got with whatever we can scrape together."

"Happy day," Sergeant Pound said. "Hasn't it occurred to anybody back in Philadelphia that that's a recipe for getting whipped?"

"It probably has, Sergeant," Morrell answered. "What they haven't figured out is what to do about it. The Confederates have been serious about this business longer than we have, and we're paying the price."

Sergeant Pound nodded gloomily. "So we are, sir. Have they realized it's liable to be bigger than we can afford to pay?" Morrell only shrugged. The noncom could see that. Morrell could see it himself. He too wondered if the War Department had figured it out.

Clarence Potter was, if not a happy man, then at least a professionally satisfied one. Seeing that his profession kept him busy eighteen to twenty hours a day, seven days a week, satisfaction there went a long way toward simulating happiness.

Sabotage along U.S. railroad lines wasn't easy to arrange. The lines were guarded, and the guards were getting thicker on the ground every day. Even so, he'd had his successes. And every railroad guard toting a Springfield two hundred miles from the front was a man who wasn't aiming a Springfield at Confederate soldiers in the field.

He wondered if he ought to sacrifice a saboteur, arrange for the Yankees to capture somebody and shoot or hang him. That might make the United States flabble about spies and hurt their war effort.

"Have to do it so the poor son of a bitch doesn't know we turned him in," Potter said musingly. The idea of getting rid of a man who'd worked for him didn't horrify him. He was coldblooded about such things. But it would have to be done so that nobody suspected the tip had come from Confederate Intelligence. He'd have a hell of a time getting anyone to work for him if people knew he might sell them out when that looked like a profitable thing to do.

If you had scruples about such things, you didn't belong in Intelligence in the first place. Potter snorted and lit a cigarette. If he had any scruples left about anything, he wouldn't be here in the Confederate War Department working for Jake Featherston. But love of country came before anything else for him, even before his loathing of the Freedom Party. And so . . . here he was.

The young lieutenant who sat in the outer office and handled paperwork—the fellow's name was Terry Pendleton—had a security clearance almost as fancy as Potter's. He stuck his head into Potter's sanctum and said, "Sir, that gentleman is here to see you." Along with the clearance, he had an even more useful attribute: a working sense of discretion. Very often, in the business he and Potter were in, that was a fine faculty to exercise. This looked to be one of those times.

"Send him in." Potter took a last drag at the cigarette, then stubbed it out. The smoke would linger in his office, but he couldn't do anything about that. At least he wouldn't be open in his vice.

"That gentleman" came in. He was in his fifties: somewhere not too far from Potter's age. He was tall and skinny, and carried himself like a man who'd fought in the Great War. Potter was rarely wrong about that; he knew the signs too well. The gentleman wore a travel-wrinkled black suit, a white shirt, a dark fedora, and a somber blue tie. "Pleased to meet you, General Potter," he said, and held out his hand.

Potter took it. The newcomer's grip was callused and firm. "Pleased to meet you, too, ah. . . ." Potter's voice trailed away.

"Orson will do," the other man said. "It was enough of a name to get me across the border. It will be enough of a name to get me back. And if I need another one, I can be someone else—several someones, in fact. I have the papers to prove it, too."

"Good," Potter said, thinking it was good if the Yankees didn't search Orson too thoroughly, anyhow. "You didn't have any trouble crossing into Texas?"

Orson smiled. "Oh, no. None at all. For one thing, the war's hardly going on in those parts. And, for another, you Easterners don't understand how many square miles and how few people there are in that part of the continent. There aren't enough border guards to keep an eye on everything—not even close."

"I see that. You're here, after all," Potter said.

"Yes. I'm here. Shall we find out how we can best use each other?" Orson, plainly, had had fine lessons in cynicism somewhere. He went on, "You people have no more use for us than the United States do. But the enemy of one's enemy is, or can be, a friend. And so . . ."

"Indeed. And so," Clarence Potter said. "If Utah—excuse me, if Deseret—does gain its independence from the United States, you can rest assured that the Confederate States will never trouble it."

The Mormon smiled thinly. "A promise worth its weight in gold, I have no doubt. But, as it happens, I believe you, because no matter how the war goes the Confederate States and Deseret are unlikely to share a border."

Not only a cynic but a realist. Potter's smile showed genuine good nature. "I do believe I'm going to enjoy doing business with you, Mr. . . . uh, Orson."

"That's nice," Orson said. "Now, what kind of business can we do? How much help can you give a rising?"

"Not a lot, not directly. You have to know that. You can read a map—and you've traveled over the ground, too. But when it comes to railroads and highways—well, we may be able to do more than you think."

"Maybe's a word that makes a lot of people sorry later," Orson observed.

"Well, sir, if you'd rather, I'll promise you the moon," Potter said. "I won't be able to deliver, but I'll promise if you want."

"Thanks, but no thanks," Orson said. "Maybe isn't much, but it's better than a lie."

"We're going in the same direction—or rather, we both want to push the USA in the same direction," Potter said. "It's in the Confederacy's interest to give you a hand—and it's in your interest to work with us, too, because where else are you going to find yourselves any friends?"

"General, we've been over that. We aren't going to find any friends anywhere, and that includes you," Orson answered calmly. "Do you think I don't know that the Confederacy persecutes us, too? We've also been over *that*. But it's all right. We're not particularly looking for friends. All we want is to be left alone."

"Well, Jeff Davis said the same thing when the Confederate States seceded," Potter answered. "We have a few things in common, I'd say. And you haven't got any more use for niggers than we do, have you?"

"Depends on what you mean," Orson said. "We don't really want to have anything to do with them. But I don't think we'd ever do some of the things you people are doing, either. I don't know how much of what I hear is true, but. . . ."

Clarence Potter had a pretty good idea of how much of rumor was true. Here, he didn't altogether disapprove of what the Freedom Party was up to. He hadn't trusted the Negroes in the CSA since 1915. He said, "You can afford to take that line, sir, because you can count the niggers in Utah on your thumbs, near enough. Here in the CSA, they're about one in three. We have to think about them more than you do."

"I don't believe, if our positions were reversed, that we would do what you are doing, or what I hear you're doing," Orson replied.

Easy enough for you to say. But the words didn't cross Potter's lips. That wasn't for fear of insulting Orson. He could afford to insult him if he wanted to. The Mormon was a beggar, and couldn't be a chooser. On reflection, though, Potter decided he believed Orson. His people had always shown a peculiar, stiff-necked pride.

Instead, the Confederate Intelligence officer said, "And how are the Indians who used to live in Utah? Will you invite them to join your brave new land?"

Orson turned red. Potter wasn't surprised. The Mormons had got on with the local Indians no better than anyone else in the United States did. The USA might have a better record dealing with Negroes. The CSA did when it came to Indians.

"What do you want from us?" Potter asked again, letting the Mormon down easy. "Whatever it is, if we've got it, you'll have it."

"Grenades, machine guns—and artillery, if you can find a way to get it to us," Orson answered. "But the first two especially. Rifles we've got. We've had rifles for a long time."

"We can get the weapons over the border for you. If you got in, we can get them out," Potter promised. "It's just a matter of setting up exactly where and when. How you get them to where you use them after that is your business."

"I understand." Orson snapped his fingers. "Oh—one other thing. Land mines. Heavy land mines. They're going to throw barrels at us. They didn't have those the last time around. We'll need something to make them say uncle."

"Heavy land mines." Potter scribbled a note to himself. "Yes, that makes sense. How are you fixed for gas masks?"

"Pretty well, but we could probably use more," Orson answered. "We didn't have to worry much about gas the last time around, either."

"All right." Potter nodded. "One more question, then. This one isn't about weapons. What will Governor Young do when Utah rises? What will you do about him if he tries to clamp down on the rising?" That was two questions, actually, but they went together like two adjoining pieces of a jigsaw puzzle.

Orson said, "There are some people who still think we can get along with the USA. We'll take care of them when the time comes. We have a list." He spoke without anger but with grim certainty. He didn't name Heber Young—one of Brigham's numerous grandsons. On the other hand, he didn't say the governor wasn't on the list, either.

"That's good," Clarence Potter said. "I was hoping you might."

The Mormon—nationalist? patriot? zealot? what was the right word?—eyed him with no great liking. "Occurs to me, General, that it's just as well we won't share a border no matter how things turn out. You'd be just as much trouble as the United States are."

"You may be right," Potter said, thinking Orson certainly was. "But what does that have to do with the price of beer?"

Beer. Orson's lips silently shaped the word. Potter wondered how badly he'd just blundered. The man in the somber suit undoubtedly didn't drink. But Orson could be practical. After a small pause, he nodded. "Point taken, sir. Right now, it doesn't have anything to do with anything."

"We agree on that. If we don't agree on other things—well, so what?" Potter said. "I'm going to take you to my colleagues in Logistics. They'll arrange to get you what you need when you need it." He got to his feet.

So did Orson. He held out his hand. "Thank you for your help. I realize you have your own selfish reasons for giving it, but thank you. Regardless of what you're doing here in the CSA, you really are helping freedom in Deseret."

I love you, too, Potter thought. Whatever his opinion of Orson's candor, it didn't show on his face. But as they walked to the door, he couldn't help asking, "Would the, um, gentiles in your state agree with you?"

Orson stopped. His face didn't show much, either. But his pale eyes blazed. "If they'd cared what happened to us for the past sixty years, maybe I would worry more about what happens to them. As things are, General . . . As things are, what do they have to do with the price of beer right now?"

"*Touché,*" Potter murmured. He took the Mormon down the hall to Logistics. People gave the obvious civilian curious looks. He didn't seem to belong there. But he was keeping company with a brigadier general, so no one said anything. And, even if he didn't belong in the War Department, he had the look of a man of war.

Logistics didn't receive Orson with glad cries. Potter hadn't expected them to. They parted with ordnance as if they made it themselves right there in the War Department offices. But they'd known the Mormon was coming. And they knew one other thing: they knew Jake Featherston wanted them to do what they could for Orson. In the Confederate States these days, nothing counted for more than that.

*   *   *

George Enos, Jr., found himself facing the same dilemma as his father had a generation earlier. He didn't want to join the U.S. Navy. He would much rather have stayed a fisherman. If he tried, though, his chances of being conscripted into the Army ranged from excellent to as near certain as made no difference. He relished the infantry even less than the Navy.

"I'd better do it," he told his wife on a morning when the war news was particularly bad—not that it had ever been good, not since the very start of things.

Connie began to cry. "You're liable to get killed!" she said.

"I know," he replied. "But what's liable to happen to me if they stick a rifle in my hands and send me off to Ohio? Where are my chances better? And it's not safe just putting to sea these days." He remembered too well the gruesome strafing the British fighter had given the *Sweet Sue*.

"Why don't you just get a job in a war plant here in Boston and come home to me every night?" Connie demanded.

They'd been over that one before—over it and over it and over it again. George gave the best answer he could: "Because I'd start going nuts, that's why. The ocean's in me, same as it is with your old man."

She winced. Her father had been a fisherman forever. As long as he could keep going out, he would. She and George both knew it. She said, "That's not fair. It's not fair to me, it's not fair to the boys. . . ." But she didn't say it wasn't true. She couldn't, and she knew it.

"I'm sorry, hon. I wish I was different," George said. "But I'm not. And so . . ."

And so the first thing he did the next morning was visit the Navy recruiting station not far from T Wharf. It was in one of the toughest parts of Boston, surrounded by cheap saloons, pawnshops, and houses where the girls stripped at second-story windows and leaned out hollering invitations to the men passing by below and abuse when they got ignored. George wouldn't have minded stripping himself; the day was breathlessly hot and muggy. Even walking made sweat stream off him.

A fat, gray-haired petty officer sat behind a sheet-steel desk filling out forms. He finished what he was doing before deigning to look at—look through—George. "Why shouldn't I just be shipping your ass on over to the Army where you belong?" he asked in a musical brogue cold enough to counteract the weather.

"I've been going to sea for more than ten years," George answered, "and my father was killed aboard the USS *Ericsson* at—after—the end of the last war."

The petty officer's bushy, tangled eyebrows leaped toward his hairline. He pointed a nicotine-stained forefinger at George. "We can check that, you know," he rumbled. "And if you're after lying to me for sympathy's sake, you'll go to the Army, all right, and you'll go with a full set of lumps."

"Check all you please," George said. "Half the people in Boston know my story." He gave his name, adding, "My mother's the one who shot Roger Kimball."

"*Son* of a bitch," the petty officer said. "They should have pinned a medal on her. All right, Enos. That's the best one I've heard since the goddamn war started, so help me Hannah." He pulled open a desk drawer. It squeaked; it needed oiling, or maybe grinding down to bright metal. "I've got about five thousand pounds of forms for you to be filling out, but you'll get what you want if you pass the physical." One of those eyebrows rose again. "Maybe even if you don't, by Jesus. If you come from *that* family, the whole country owes you one."

"I can do the job," George said. "That's the only thing that ought to matter. I never would have said a word about the other stuff if you hadn't asked me the way you did."

"You've got pull," the petty officer said. "You'd be a damn fool if you didn't use it." He pointed again, this time towards a rickety table against the far wall. "Go on over there and fill these out. To hell with me if we won't have the doctors look you over this afternoon. You can say your good-byes tonight and head off for training first thing tomorrow mornin'."

He sent three men away while George worked on the forms. Two went quietly. The third presumed to object. "I'll go to another station—you see if I don't," he spluttered. "I was born to be a sailor."

"You were born to go to jail," the petty officer retorted. "Think I don't know an ex-con when I see one?" The man turned white—

that shot struck home like a fourteen-inch shell from a battleship. The petty officer went on, "Go on, be off with you. Maybe you can fool some damn dumb Army recruiting sergeant, but the Navy's got men with eyes in their heads. You'd be just right for the Army—looks like all you're good for is running away."

"What's he got that I haven't?" The man pointed at George.

"A clean record, for one, like I say," the petty officer answered. "And a mother with more balls than you and your old man put together, for another." He jerked a thumb toward the door. "Get out, or I'll pitch you through the window."

The man left. Maybe he would have made a good Navy sailor and maybe he wouldn't. George wouldn't have wanted to put to sea with him in a fishing boat. A quarrelsome man in cramped quarters was nothing but a nuisance. And if this, that, and the other thing started walking with Jesus . . . George shook his head. No, that was no kind of shipmate to have.

He finished the paperwork and thumped the forms down on the petty officer's desk. The man didn't even look at them. He picked up his telephone, spoke into it, and hung up after a minute or two. "Go on over to Doc Freedman's. He'll give you the physical. Here's the address." He wrote it on a scrap of paper. "You bring his report back to me. Unless you've got a glass eye and a peg leg you haven't told me about, we'll go on from there."

"Yes, sir. Thank you, sir," George said.

The petty officer laughed. "You've still got some learning to do, and that's the God's truth. You don't call me *sir*. You call me *Chief*. Save *sir* for officers."

"Yes—" George caught himself. "Uh, right, Chief."

"That's the way you do it." The older man nodded. "Go on. Get the hell out of here."

George left. The doctor's office wasn't far. The receptionist, a sour old biddy, sent the new arrival a disapproving look. "You are unscheduled, Mr. Enos," she said, as if he had a social disease. But she sent him on in to see the sawbones.

Dr. Freedman was a short, swarthy Jew with a pinkie ring. He looked as if he made his money doing abortions for whores, and maybe selling drugs on the side. His hands were as cold and almost as moist as a cod just out of the Atlantic. But he seemed to know what he was doing. He checked George's ears, looked in his mouth and ears and nose, listened to his chest, took his blood pressure, and stuck a needle in his arm for a blood sample. Then he put on a rubber glove and said, "Bend over." Apprehensively, George obeyed. That was even less fun than he thought it would be. So was getting grabbed in intimate places—much less gently than Connie would have done—and being told to cough.

After half an hour's work, the doctor scrawled notes on an official Navy form. "Well?" George asked as he got back into his clothes. "How am I?"

"Except for being a damn fool for wanting to do this in the first place, you're healthy as a horse," Freedman answered. "But if they disqualified every damn fool in the Navy, they'd have twenty-seven men left, and how would they win the war then?"

George blinked. He didn't think he'd ever run into such breathtaking cynicism before. He asked, "You think going into the Army is better?"

The doctor laughed, a singularly unpleasant sound. "Not me. Do I look that stupid? I'd get a job where they weren't going to conscript me and sit this one out. Wasn't the last one bad enough?"

Connie had said much the same thing. George hadn't wanted to hear it from her. He really didn't want to hear it from a big-nosed Hebe with all the charm of a hagfish. "Don't you care about your country?" he asked.

"Just as much as it cares for me," Freedman said. "It takes my money and throws it down ratholes. It tells me all the things I can't do, and none of the things I can. So why should I get all hot and bothered?"

"Because the Confederates are worse?" George suggested.

Freedman only shrugged. "What if they are? This is *Boston,* for God's sake. We could lose the next three wars to those bastards, and you'd still never see one within a hundred miles of here."

"What if everybody felt the way you do?" George said in something approaching real horror.

"Then nobody would fight with anybody, and we'd all be better off," Freedman replied. "But don't worry about that, because it isn't going to happen. Most people are just as patriotic"—by the way he said it, he plainly meant *just as stupid*—"as you are." He scratched his name at the bottom of the form. "Take this back to the recruiting station. It'll get you what you want. As for me, I just made three dollars and fifty cents—before taxes."

Slightly dazed, George carried the form back to the petty officer. He had to wait; the man was dealing with another would-be recruit. At last, he set the form on the petty officer's desk, remarking, "The doc's a piece of work, isn't he?"

"Freedman? He is that." The petty officer laughed. "He thinks everybody but him is the world's biggest jerk. Don't take him serious. If he was half as smart as he thinks he is, he'd be twice as smart as he really is, you know what I mean?"

George needed a couple of seconds to figure that out. When he did, he nodded in relief. "Yeah."

"All right, then. It won't be tomorrow after all—I was forgetting they'd need a few days to run your Wasserman. Report back here in a week. If the test is good, you're in. If it's not, you're likely in any way. In the meantime, get lost. Don't put to sea, though. If you're not back here in a week now, we have to notice, and you won't like it if we do."

"A week." It felt like an anticlimax to George. "My wife'll want me out of her hair by the time I have to come back here. And she'll be nagging me all the time while I'm there. Why'd I go and do this? I can hear it already in my head."

The petty officer only shrugged. "You just volunteered, Enos. Nobody was after holding a gun to your head or anything like that. This is part of what you volunteered for. You don't like it, you should have joined the Army. The way things are these days, they sure as hell wouldn't give a damn about your Wasserman. You're breathing, they'll take you."

"No, thanks," George said hastily. The petty officer's laugh was loud and raucous.

When George went back to his apartment, he found Connie red-eyed, her face streaked with tears. She shouted at him. He gave back soft answers. It didn't do him any good. Now that he had volunteered and couldn't take it back, she was going to get everything she could out of her system. She didn't quite throw a flowerpot at him, but she came close.

Despite that, they spent more of the following week in bed than they had since their brief Niagara Falls honeymoon. George was used to going without on fishing runs. But how long would it be this time before he saw Connie again? He tried to make up in advance for time to be lost in the future. It wouldn't work. He could sense that even as he tried. But he did it anyway—why not?

He reported back to the Navy recruiting station on the appointed day. The petty officer greeted him with, "You live clean." From then on, he belonged to the Navy.

IX

Chester Martin sat with Rita and Carl in the dark of a Los Angeles movie theater, waiting for the night's feature to come on. The war hadn't laid a glove on California. No Confederate bombers had flown this far from Texas or Sonora. No Confederate or Japanese ships had appeared off the West Coast. If you wanted to, you could just go on about your business and pretend things weren't going to hell in a handbasket back East.

People all around crunched popcorn and slurped sodas. The Martins were crunching and slurping, too. That was what you did when you came to one of these places. Somebody behind them bit down on a jawbreaker. It sounded as if he were chewing a bunch of rocks.

The newsreel came on after the cartoon. Carl enjoyed it. He liked watching things blow up, and wasn't fussy about whose things they were. But Chester and Rita got very quiet. Watching Ohio torn to pieces hurt them all the more because they'd lived most of their lives there. Rita reached out and squeezed Chester's hand when the newsreel showed bomb damage in Toledo.

They didn't cheer up much at seeing the wreckage of Confederate bombers, either. "We are fighting back," the announcer declared. "Every day, the vicious enemy has a harder time going forward. We will stop him, and we will beat him back."

Was he whistling in the dark? It sure seemed that way to Chester. So far, U.S. forces had done nothing but retreat. *Could* they do anything else? If they could, when? When would it be too late? What would happen if the Confederates cut the United States in half? The resolutely cheerful announcer not only didn't answer any of those questions, he didn't acknowledge that they existed.

Then the newsreel camera cut away to SOMEWHERE BEHIND THE LINES, as the card at the head of the feature declared. Soldiers sat on the ground watching four men with long beards cavort on a makeshift stage with a pathetically dignified woman. "The Engels Brothers entertain the troops," the announcer said. "Their mad hijinks help our brave men forget the dangers of battle."

Sure enough, the soldiers were laughing. Chester remained dubious. He'd laughed, too, when he escaped from the trenches for a little while. But he'd never forgotten the dangers. How could he? He still woke up screaming every so often, though now it was once every two or three years, not once every two or three weeks.

After the Engels Brothers left the stage, bathing beauties paraded across it. The soldiers liked them even better, even if they could only look and not touch. The girls were wearing much less than they would have in a Great War entertainment. Chester approved of that. He was sure the young soldiers enjoyed it even more.

Al Smith appeared on the screen. Some people in the theater cheered the President. Others booed. By Smith's ravaged face, he was hearing those boos—and the roar of the guns—even in his sleep. He looked out at the audience he would never see in the flesh. "Our cause is just," he insisted, as if someone had denied it. "We will prevail. No matter how fierce and vicious our enemy may be, he will only destroy himself with his wickedness. Stand together, stand shoulder to shoulder, and nothing can hold you back."

That sounded good. Chester wondered if it was true. So far, the evidence looked to be against it. But then the newsreel cut from President Smith to the Stars and Stripes flying in front of a summer sky. "The Star-Spangled Banner" swelled on the soundtrack. People sang along in the theater. For a couple of minutes, Socialists, Democrats, and the handful of remaining Republicans *did* stand shoulder to shoulder.

The film started. It was a story of intrigue set in Kentucky between the wars. All the villains had Confederate drawls. The hero and heroine sounded as if they came from New York and Boston, respectively. They foiled the villains' plot to touch off a rebellion and fell in love, both at the same time.

"Kentucky will be ours forever," he said, gazing into her eyes. "Kentucky will be free forever," she replied, gazing into his. They kissed. The music went up. The credits rolled. The film had to have been made in a tearing hurry—certainly since the plebiscite early in the year. Did it help? Or did it only make people feel worse by reminding them that Kentucky was lost?

"Is there another picture after this one?" Carl asked.

"The cartoons and the newsreel and the movie weren't enough for you?" Chester asked.

Carl shook his head. "Nope." But he betrayed himself by yawning.

"Well, it doesn't matter, because there isn't another picture," Rita said. "And you're up way past your bedtime."

"Am not," Carl said around another yawn.

Since there wasn't another picture, though, arguments for staying out later had no visible means of support. They walked back to the apartment where they'd lived since moving from Toledo. It was only a few blocks, but they had to go slowly and carefully through the blacked-out streets. Cars honked to warn other cars they were there as they came to intersections. That no doubt cut down on accidents, but it didn't do much for people who were trying to get to sleep.

To Chester's relief, Carl went to bed without much fuss. Chester knew he wouldn't sleep well himself, and the honks out in the street had nothing to do with anything. "Things are lousy back East," he said heavily.

"Looks that way," Rita agreed. "Doesn't sound like they're telling everything that's going on, either."

"Oh, good," Chester said, and his wife looked at him in surprise. He explained: "I didn't want to think I was the only one who was thinking something like that."

"Well, you're not," his wife said. "We've both been through this before. If we can't see past most of the pap, we're not very smart, are we?"

"I guess not," Chester said unhappily. He lit a cigarette. The tobacco was already going downhill. The Confederate States grew more and better than the United States. He hoped losing foreign exchange would hurt them. Blowing a moody cloud of smoke toward the ceiling, he went on, "Got to do something about it."

"Who's got to do something about what?" Rita's voice was sharp with fear. She'd been married once before. Her first husband hadn't come home from the Great War. Had he talked like this before joining the Army? Chester wouldn't have been surprised. Everybody'd been openly patriotic in 1914. Machine guns hadn't yet proved heroism more expensive than it was often worth.

Chester sucked in more smoke. It didn't calm him as much as he wished it would. He said, "Doesn't hardly feel right, being out here all this way away from the fighting."

"Why not? Isn't one Purple Heart enough for you?"

He remembered the wound, of course. How not, when he would take its mark to the grave with him? He remembered hitting a man in butternut in the face with an entrenching tool, and feeling bone give beneath the iron blade. He remembered cowering in trenches as shells came down all around him. He remembered his balls crawling up into his belly in terror as he went forward in the face of machine-gun fire. He remembered poison gas. He remembered lice and flies and the endless stench of death.

But, toward the end, he also remembered the feeling that everything he'd gone through was somehow worthwhile. That wasn't just his looking back from almost a quarter of a century's distance; he'd felt it in 1917. Only one thing explained it—victory. He and so many like him had suffered so much, but they'd suffered for a reason: so the USA could get out from under the CSA's thumb.

That was why the plebiscites in Kentucky and Houston had disturbed him so much. They returned to the Confederates for nothing what the United States had spent so much blood to win. What was the point of everything he and so many millions like him had gone through if it was thrown away now?

Slowly, he said, "If they lick us in Ohio, they'll turn the clock back to the way it was before 1914."

"So what?" Rita said. "So *what*, Chester? What difference will that make to you? You'll still be right here where you've been for years. You'll be doing the same things you've done. Your hair is going gray now. You're not a kid any more. You've given the country everything it could want from you. Enough is enough."

Every word of that made good, solid sense. But how much sense did good, solid sense make when the United States were in trouble? "I don't feel right standing on the sidelines and watching things go down the drain," he said.

"And how much difference do you think you're going to make if you do put the uniform back on?" his wife demanded. "You're not General Custer, you know. The most they'd do is give you your sergeant's stripes back. How many thousands of sergeants are there? Why would you be better than any of the others?"

"I wouldn't," Chester admitted. "But the Army needs sergeants as much as it needs generals. It needs more of them, but it can't get along without them." He thought the Army could get along without lieutenants much more easily than it could without sergeants. Lieutenants, no doubt, would disagree with him—but what the hell did lieutenants know? If they knew anything, they wouldn't have been lieutenants.

Rita glared at him. "You're going to do this, aren't you? Sooner or later, you are. I can see it in your face. You're going to put the uniform back on, and you'll be all proud of yourself, and you won't care two cents' worth what happens to Carl and me after you . . . after you get shot." She burst into tears.

Chester couldn't even say he wouldn't get shot. He'd been a young man during the Great War, young enough to be confident nothing could kill him. Where had that confidence gone? He didn't own it any more. He knew he could die. He'd known it even in brawls with union-busting Pinkertons. If he went back to where they were throwing lead around with reckless abandon . . . Well, anything could happen. He understood that.

He started to tell Rita something reassuring, but gave it up with the words unspoken. He couldn't be reassuring, not knowing what he knew, understanding what he understood. All he could do was change the subject. He got up and turned on the wireless. A little music might help calm Rita down—and it would make him feel better, too.

He had to wait for the tubes to warm up. Once they did, it wasn't music that came out of the speaker, but an announcer's excited voice: "—tial law has been declared in Utah," the man said. "At present, it is not clear how much support the insurrection commands. There are reports of fighting from Ogden down to Provo.

Governor Young has appealed for calm and restraint on all sides. Whether anyone will listen to him may be a different question. Further bulletins as they break."

"Oh, Jesus Christ!" Chester exclaimed, and turned off the wireless with a vicious click. The Mormons had caused the USA endless grief by rising in the last war. If they were trying it again, they might do even more harm this time.

"I wish you hadn't heard that," Rita said in a low voice.

"Why? Are you afraid I'll run right out to the nearest recruiting station?"

Chester had intended that for sarcasm, but his wife nodded. "Yes! That's exactly what I'm afraid of," she said. "Every time you go out the door, I'm afraid I'll never see you again. You've got that look in your eye. Ed had it, too, before he joined the Army." She didn't mention her first husband very often, and hardly ever by name. More than anything else, that told Chester how worried she was.

He said, "I'm not going anywhere right now." He'd hoped to make her feel better. The fright on her face told him that *right now* had only made things worse. He started to say everything would be fine and he'd stay where he was. He kept quiet instead, though, for he realized he might be lying.

Summer lay heavy on Baroyeca. The sun was a white-hot blaze in the blue dome of the sky. Vultures circled overhead, riding the invisible streams of hot air that shot up from the ground. Every so often, when a deer or a mule fell over dead, the big black birds would spiral down, down, down and feast. And if a man fell over dead under that savage sun, the vultures wouldn't complain about turning his carcass into bones, either.

Hipolito Rodriguez worked in his fields regardless of the weather. Who would do it for him if he didn't? No one, and he knew it. But he always wore a sombrero to shield his head from the worst of the sun. And he worked at a pace a man who forgot the weather might have called lazy. If he cocked his head skyward, he could see the vultures. He didn't want them picking *his* bones.

When the weather was less brutal, he worried about meeting snakes in the middle of the day. Not now. They might come out in the early morning or late afternoon, but they stayed in their holes in the ground the rest of the time. They knew they would die if they crawled very far along the baking ground. Even the scorpions and centipedes were less trouble than usual.

Rodriguez had one advantage the animals didn't. It was an edge he hadn't had for very long. He sometimes had to remind himself to use it. When he felt worst, he could go back to the house, open the refrigerator, and pour himself a big glass of cold, cold water. The luxury of that seemed more precious than rubies to him. He wouldn't drink the water right away. Instead, he would press the chilly, sweating glass against his cheek, savoring its icy feel. And when he did drink, it was as if the water exorcised the demons of heat and thirst at the very first swallow.

He made sure he filled the pitcher up again, too. He could go out to the fields again, come back in a couple of hours, and find more deliciously chilly water waiting for him. It wasn't heaven—if it were heaven, he wouldn't have had to go out to the fields in the first place. But the refrigerator made life on earth much more bearable.

Magdalena enjoyed the cold water no less than he did. Once they both paused for a drink at the same time. "Is it true," she asked him, "that in parts of *los Estados Confederados* they have machines that can make the air cold the same way as the refrigerator makes water cold?"

"I think it is," Rodriguez answered cautiously. "I think that's what they call air conditioning. Even in the rich parts of the country, they don't have it everywhere, or even very many places."

"I wish we had it here," his wife said.

He tried to imagine it: going from the back oven of a summer to winter just by opening and closing a door. It was supposed to be true, but he had trouble believing it. He said, "Electricity is one thing. This air conditioning is something else. It's very fancy and very expensive, or so they say."

"I can still wish," Magdalena said. "I wished for electricity for years before we got it. I wished and I wished, and here it is. Maybe if I do enough wishing, we will have this air conditioning, too, one of these years. Or if we don't, maybe our children will. With all the changes we've seen, you never can tell."

"You never can tell," Rodriguez agreed gravely. "As for me, what I wish for is an automobile."

"An automobile," his wife breathed. She might have been speaking of something as distant and unlikely as air conditioning. But then her eyes narrowed. "Do you know, Hipolito, we could almost buy one if we wanted to badly enough."

"Yes, that occurred to me, too," he answered. The motorcar they could get for what they could afford to spend wouldn't be anything fancy: a beat-up old Ford or some Confederate make of similar vintage. But even a beat-up old auto offered freedom of a sort nothing else could match. Rodriguez went on, "The only times I was ever out of the valley were to fight in the last war and to go to Hermosillo to help get President Featherston a second term. It's not enough."

In a small voice, Magdalena Rodriguez said, "I've never been outside this valley at all. I never really thought about what was going on anywhere else till we got the wireless set. But now . . . If I can hear about the world outside, why can't I see it?"

For years, even trains had stopped coming to Baroyeca. They were back again, now that the silver (and, perhaps not so incidentally, lead) mines in the hills above the little town had reopened. But traveling by train was different from hopping into an auto and just going. Trains stuck to schedules, and they stuck to the rails. In a motorcar, you could go where and when you wanted to go, do whatever you wanted to do. . . .

You could—if they let you. Rodriguez said, "I think this would be something for after the war. We might buy a motorcar now, *sí*. But whether we could buy any gasoline for it is a different question."

Rationing hadn't meant much to him. It still didn't, not really. He'd even stopped worrying about kerosene. With electricity in the house, the old lamps were all packed up and stored in the barn. But gasoline, these days, was for machines that killed people, not for those that made life easier and more pleasant.

"If we had an automobile to go with electricity . . . Ten years ago, only the *patrones* had such things, and not all of them," Magdalena said.

"That was before the Freedom Party took over," Rodriguez answered. "Now ordinary people can have the good things, too. But even if I had a motorcar, I wouldn't be a *patrón*. I would never want to do that. To be a *patrón*, you have to like telling others what to do. That has never been for me."

"No, of course not." Magdalena's voice had a certain edge to it. She might have been warning that if he thought he could tell *her* what to do, he had better think again.

Since he didn't have an automobile, he walked into Baroyeca for the next Freedom Party meeting. He would have grumbled if he'd had to walk because his motorcar was in the garage. Because he'd never done anything but walk, he didn't grumble at all. He took the journey for granted.

A drunken miner staggered out of *La Culebra Verde* as Rodriguez came up the street toward Freedom Party headquarters. The man gave him a vacant grin, then sat down hard in the middle of the dirt road. Rodriguez wondered how many drunks had come out of the cantina and done the exact same thing. He'd done it himself, but no more than once or twice. Miners drank harder than farmers did. They might have worked harder than farmers did, too. Rodriguez couldn't think of anyone else for whom that might be true. But to go down underground all day, never to see the sun or feel the breeze from one end of your shift to the other . . . That was no way for a man to live.

He walked past Diaz's general store. A storekeeper, now, had it easy. If Diaz wasn't sitting in the lap of luxury, who in Baroyeca was? Nobody, not that Rodriguez could see. And yet Jaime Diaz complained about the way things went almost as if he tilled the soil. He wasn't too proud to act like anybody else.

"Good evening, *Señor* Rodriguez," Robert Quinn said in Spanish when the farmer came into the headquarters. "Good to see you."

"*Gracias, señor.* The same to you," Rodriguez answered gravely. He nodded to Carlos Ruiz and some of his other friends as he sat down on a second-row folding chair. The first row of chairs, as usual, was almost empty. Not many men were bold enough to call attention to themselves by sitting up front.

Freedom Party headquarters filled up with men from Baroyeca and peasants from the surrounding countryside. Some of them had walked much farther to come to town than Rodriguez had. "Freedom!" they would say as they came in and sat down—or, more often, "*¡Libertad!*"

Quinn waited till almost everyone he expected was there. Then, still in Spanish, he said, "Well, my friends, let's get on with it." When no one objected, he continued, "This meeting of the Freedom Party, Baroyeca chapter, is now in session."

He went through the minutes and old business in a hurry. Hipolito Rodriguez yawned a little anyhow. He hadn't joined the Freedom Party for the sake of its parliamentary procedure. He'd become a member because Jake Featherston promised to do things—and kept his promises.

As quickly as Quinn could, he turned to new business. "I know we'll all pray for Eduardo Molina," he said. "He can't be here tonight—he just got word his son, Ricardo, has been wounded in Ohio. I am very sorry, but I hear it may be a serious wound. I am going to pass the hat for the Molinas. Please be generous."

When the hat came to him, Rodriguez put in half a dollar. He crossed himself as he passed it along. He could have got bad news about Pedro as easily as Eduardo Molina had about Ricardo. What happened in war was largely a matter of luck. So many bullets flew. Every so often, one of them was bound to find soft, young flesh.

A man at the back of the room brought the hat up to Robert Quinn. It jingled as the Freedom Party organizer set it down beside him. "*Gracias,*" he said. "Thank you all. I know this is something you would rather not have to do. I know it is something some of you have trouble affording. Times are not as hard as they were ten years ago, before we came to power, but they are still not easy. But all of you understand—but for the grace of God, we could have been taking up a collection for *your* family."

Rodriguez started. Then he nodded. It really wasn't that surprising to have *Señor* Quinn understand what was in his mind. Quinn knew how many men here had sons or brothers in the Army, and what could happen to those men.

"On to happier news," the Freedom Party man said. "Our guns are now pounding Sandusky, Ohio. Let me show you on the map where Sandusky is." He walked over to a campaign map pinned to the wall of Freedom Party headquarters. When he pointed to the city on the shore of Lake Erie, a low murmur ran through the men who crowded the room. Quinn nodded. "*Sí, señores, es verdad*—we have cut all the way through Ohio and reached the water. Soon our men and machines will be on the lake. The United States cannot send anything through the middle of their country. It is cut in half. And do you know what this means?"

"It means victory!" Carlos Ruiz exclaimed.

Quinn nodded. "That is just what it means. If *los Estados Unidos* cannot send the raw materials from the West to the factories in the East, how are they going to make what they need to go on fighting?" He beamed. "The answer is simple—they cannot. And if they cannot make what they need, they cannot go on with the fight."

Could it be as simple as that? It certainly seemed to make good sense. Rodriguez hoped it did. A short, victorious war . . . The North American continent hadn't seen one like that for sixty years. Maybe this wouldn't be a fight to the finish, the way the Great War had been. He could hope not, anyhow.

"War news elsewhere is mostly good," Quinn said. "There is no more U.S. resistance in the Bahamas. Some raiding does go on, but it is by black guerrillas. The *mallates* may be a nuisance, but they will not keep *los Estados Confederados* from occupying these important islands."

As far as Rodriguez was concerned, *mallates* were always a nuisance—a deadly nuisance. He'd got his baptism of fire against black rebels in Georgia. That fight had been worse than any against U.S. troops. The blacks had known they couldn't surrender, and fought to the end.

Well, the Freedom Party was putting them in their place in the CSA. And if it was doing the same thing in the Bahamas, too . . . good.

"**S**andusky." Jake Featherston spoke the ugly name as if it belonged to the woman he loved. When the thrust up into Ohio began, he hadn't known where the Confederates would reach Lake Erie— whether at Toledo or Sandusky or even Cleveland. From the beginning, that had depended as much on what the damnyankees did and how they fought back as on his own forces.

"Sandusky." He said it again, eyeing the map on the wall of his office as avidly as if it were the woman he loved slipping out of a negligee. Where Confederate troops reached Lake Erie didn't matter so much. *That* they reached it . . . That they reached it mattered immensely. He'd seen as much before the fighting started. The United States were only starting to realize it now.

"Sandusky." Featherston said it one more time. Getting to Sandusky—or anywhere else along the shores of Lake Erie—didn't mean victory. He had a hell of a lot of work to do yet. But if his barrels had been stopped in front of Columbus, that would have meant defeat. He'd done what he had to do in the opening weeks of his war: he'd made victory possible, perhaps even likely.

Lulu knocked on the door. Without waiting for his reply, she stuck her head in the office and said, "Professor FitzBelmont is here to see you, Mr. President."

"Send him in," Jake said resignedly, wondering why he'd given the man an appointment in the first place. "I promised him, what—ten minutes?"

"Fifteen, Mr. President." Lulu spoke in mild reproof, as if Featherston should have remembered. And so he should have, and so he had—but he'd done his best to get out of what he'd already agreed to. Lulu was better at holding him to the straight and narrow path than Al Smith dreamt of being. She ducked out, then returned with a formal announcement: "Mr. President, here is Professor Henderson V. FitzBelmont of Washington University."

Henderson V. FitzBelmont looked like a professor. He wore rumpled tweeds and gold-framed eyeglasses. He had a long, horsey face and a shock of gray hair that resisted both oil and combing. When he said, "Very pleased to meet you, Mr. President," he didn't tack on a ringing, "Freedom!" the way anybody with an ounce of political sense would have done.

"Pleased to meet you, too." Jake stuck out his hand. FitzBelmont took it. To the President's surprise, the other man had a respectable grip. His hand didn't jellyfish under Featherston's squeeze. Obscurely pleased, Featherston waved him to the chair in front of his desk. "Why don't you take a seat? Now, then—you're a professor of physics, isn't that right?"

"Yes, sir. That is correct." FitzBelmont talked like a professor, too. His voice had the almost-damnyankee intonation so many educated men seemed proud of, and a fussy precision to go with it, too.

"Well, then . . ." Jake also sat, and leaned back in his chair. "Suppose you tell me what a professor of physics reckons I ought to know." He didn't quite come out and say that a professor of physics couldn't tell him anything he needed to know, but that was in his own voice and manner.

Henderson V. FitzBelmont didn't seem to notice. That didn't surprise Featherston, and did amuse him. The professor said, "I was wondering, Mr. President, if you were familiar with some of the recent work in atomic physics coming out of the German Empire."

Jake didn't laugh in his face, though for the life of him he couldn't have told why not. All he said was, "Sorry, Professor, but I can't say that I am." *Or that I ever wanted to be, either.* He looked at his watch. Damned if he would give this fellow a minute more than his allotted time.

"The Germans have produced some quite extraordinary energy releases through the bombardment of uranium nuclei with neutrons. *Quite* extraordinary," Professor FitzBelmont said.

"That's nice," Jake said blandly. "What does it mean? What does it mean to somebody who's not a professor of physics, I ought to say?"

He didn't know how he expected FitzBelmont to answer. The tweedy academic made an unimpressive fist. "It means you could take this much uranium—the right kind of uranium, I should say—and make a blast big enough to blow a city off the map."

"Wait a minute," Jake said sharply. "You could do that with one bomb?"

"One bomb," Professor FitzBelmont agreed. "If the theoretical calculations are anywhere close to accurate."

Featherston scratched his head. He'd heard things like that before. Theory promised the moon, and usually didn't even deliver moonshine. "What do you mean, the right kind of uranium? Up till now, I never heard of uranium at all, and I sure as hell never heard of two kinds of it."

"As you say, sir, there are two main kinds—isotopes, we call them," the professor answered. "One has a weight of 238. That kind is not explosive. The other isotope only weighs 235. That kind is, or seems to be. The trick is separating the uranium-235 from the uranium-238."

"All right." Featherston nodded. "I'm with you so far—I think. The 235 is the good stuff, and the 238 isn't. How much 235 is there? Is it a fifty-fifty split? One part in three? One part in four? What?"

Henderson V. FitzBelmont coughed. "In fact, Mr. President, it's about one part in a hundred and forty."

"Oh." Now Jake frowned. "That doesn't sound so real good. How do you go about separating it out, then?"

The professor also frowned, unhappily. "There is, as yet, no proven method. We cannot do it chemically; we know that. Chemically, the two isotopes are identical, as any isotopes are. We need to find some physical way to capitalize on their difference in weight. A centrifuge might do part of the job. Gaseous diffusion might, too, if we can find the right kind of gas. The only candidate that seems to be available at present is uranium hexafluoride. It is, ah, difficult to work with."

"How do you mean?" Featherston inquired.

"It is highly corrosive and highly toxic."

"Oh," Jake said again. "So you'd need to do a lot of experimenting before you even have a prayer of making this work?" Professor FitzBelmont nodded. Jake went on, "How much would it cost? How much manpower would it take? There's a war on, in case you hadn't noticed."

"I had, Mr. President. I had indeed," FitzBelmont said. "I confess, it would not be cheap. It would not be easy. It would not be quick. It would require a very considerable industrial effort. I do not minimize the difficulties. They are formidable. But if they can be overcome, you have a weapon that will win the war."

Jake Featherston had heard that song before. Crackpot inventors sang it every day. Professor FitzBelmont didn't seem like the worst kind of crackpot, the kind with an obviously unworkable scheme for which he wanted millions of dollars—all of them in his own personal bank account. *That* kind of crackpot always said things would be easy as pie. Sometimes he knew he was lying, sometimes he didn't.

Because FitzBelmont seemed basically honest, Jake let him down as easy as he could. "If you'd come to me with this here idea six years ago, Professor, I might have been able to do something for you."

"Six years ago, sir, no one in the world had the slightest idea this was possible," FitzBelmont said. "Word of the essential experiment was published in a German journal about eighteen months ago."

"Fine. Have it your way. But you don't see the point," Featherston said. "The point is, right now we *are* in the middle of a war. We're stretched thin. We're stretched thin as can be, matter of fact. I can't take away God knows how much manpower and God knows how much money and throw all that down a rathole that won't pay off for years and may not pay off at all. You see what I'm saying?" Professor FitzBelmont nodded stiffly. "Yes, sir, I do understand that. But I remain convinced the benefits of success would outweigh all these costs."

Of course you do. You wouldn't be here bending my ear if you didn't, Jake thought. *But that doesn't mean you're right.* He stayed polite. One of the drawbacks of being President, he'd discovered, was that you couldn't always call a damn fool a damn fool to his face. Sometimes, no matter how big a damn fool he was, you knew you might need him again one of these days.

After he'd shown Professor FitzBelmont the door, Jake let out a sigh. For a moment, the man had had him going. If you could take out a whole city with just one bomb, that would really be something. It sure would—if you could. But odds were you couldn't, and never would be able to. Odds were the professor wanted the Confederate government to pay for a research project he couldn't afford any other way. Odds were nothing but a few papers with Fitz-Belmont's name on them would ever come out of the research project. Since becoming President, Jake had become wise in the ways of professors. He'd had to.

He lit a cigarette, sucked in smoke, and blew a wistful cloud at the ceiling. It was too goddamn bad, though.

Distant thunder muttered, off to the north. Jake's lips tightened on the cigarette. The day was fine and clear. Oh, it was hot and muggy, but it was always going to be hot and muggy in Richmond this time of year. It wasn't thunder. It was the artillery duel that went on between Yankee and Confederate forces. If the United States had wanted to drive for Richmond the way the Confederates had driven for Lake Erie, the Confederate defenders would have had a bastard of a time holding them back.

It hadn't happened, though, and defenses at the river lines grew stronger every day. A thrust the damnyankees could have easily made a month before would cost them dear now. In another few weeks, it would—Jake hoped—be impossible.

He walked over to his desk and stubbed out the cigarette. Somewhere in the pile of papers was one Clarence Potter had sent him. Where the devil had that disappeared to? He reached into the stack and, like Little Jack Horner pulling out a plum, came up with the document he needed. The desk always looked like hell. It was Lulu's despair. But he could find things when he needed to.

From what Potter said—and, Featherston remembered, General Patton agreed—the USA's most aggressive officer who was worth anything was a barrel commander named Morrell. Jake grinned. He thought he'd remembered the name, and he was right. If the fellow had been in charge in northern Virginia, he could have raised all kinds of Cain. But he was busy over in Ohio, playing defense instead of getting the chance to attack. That suited Featherston—to say nothing of the Confederate cause—down to the ground.

The United States made most of their barrels in Michigan. It made sense that they should. That was where their motorcar industry had grown up. But with a corridor from the Ohio River to Lake Erie in Confederate hands, how were they going to get those barrels to the East? And if they couldn't, what would happen when the Confederate States hit them again?

"Yeah," Jake said softly. "What will happen then?" His grin got wider. He had his own ideas about that. Al Smith probably wouldn't like them very much, but Jake didn't give a damn about what Al Smith liked or didn't like. He'd pried the plebiscite out of the President of the USA. He would have fought without it, but the odds wouldn't have been so good. Getting what the Yankees called Houston back was nice. Getting Kentucky back was essential. Kentucky was the key to everything.

And he had it, and the key was turning in the lock.

Like anyone else who got a halfway decent education in the Confederate States before the Great War, Tom Colleton had fought his way through several years of ancient Greek. He didn't remember a hell of a lot of it any more, but one passage had stuck in his head forever. In Xenophon's *Anabasis,* the Greek mercenaries who'd backed the wrong candidate in a Persian civil war had had to fight their way out of the Persian Empire. They'd come up over a rise, looked north, and started yelling, *"Thalatta! Thalatta!"*—"The sea! The sea!" Once they reached the sea, they knew they could get home again.

Looking north toward the gray-blue waters of Lake Erie, Tom felt like shouting, *"Thalatta! Thalatta!"* himself. As Xenophon's Greeks had more than 2,300 years earlier, he'd come in sight of his goal. He still intended to jump in the lake when he got the chance. Now he had to get there, and to get there without throwing away too many of his men. Sandusky sprawled along the southern shore of Lake Erie. It was about five miles wide and two miles deep. Not far from the water was Roosevelt Park—it had been Washington Park till the United States decided they would rather not remember a man from Virginia. The factories and foundries lay south of town. The business district—brick buildings that had gone up between the War of Secession and the turn of the century—lay to the north. The whole damn town crawled with U.S. soldiers. Trains were still trying to get through, even though Confederate gunners had the tracks in their sights.

As Tom watched, a steam engine hauled a long train toward the town from the west. What was it carrying? Men? Barrels? Ammunition? All three? Artillery opened up on it right away. The engineer had nerve—either that or an officer was standing behind him with a gun to his head. He kept coming.

He kept coming, in fact, after two or three shells hit the passenger cars and flatcars he was hauling. Not till an antibarrel round of armor-piercing shot went right through his boiler did he stop, and that halt wasn't voluntary on his part.

Sure as hell, soldiers in green-gray started spilling out of the passenger cars. Artillery bursts and machine-gun fire took their toll among them, but the Yankees mostly got away. By how the survivors dove for whatever cover they could find, they'd been under fire before. Tom Colleton felt a certain abstract sympathy for them. It wasn't as if he hadn't been under fire himself.

Then the damnyankees did something he thought was downright brilliant. He would have admired it even more if it hadn't almost cost him his neck. Despite bullets striking home close by, the U.S. soldiers managed to get a handful of barrels off the train and send them rattling and clanking against the advancing Confederates.

All by themselves, those barrels almost turned advance into retreat for the CSA. One driver plainly knew what he was doing; either he was a real barrel man or he'd driven a bulldozer or a big harvester in civilian life. The others were far more erratic, learning as they went along. The Yankees at the machine guns and cannon had more enthusiasm than precision. As long as they kept shooting, they made it almost impossible for Confederate infantry to get anywhere near them. And they shot up the crews of some of the guns that had been punishing the U.S. soldiers from the train.

An antibarrel round set one of the snorting horrors on fire. A brave Confederate flung a grenade into an open hatch on another— the U.S. soldiers manning the barrel hadn't known enough to slam it shut. That machine blew up; Tom didn't think anybody got out of it. A third barrel bogged down in an enormous bomb crater. The amateur driver couldn't figure out how to escape. That limited the damage that machine could do.

But the last one, the one with the driver who wasn't an amateur, kept on coming. The antibarrel cannon that had put paid to the first U.S. machine scored a hit, but a hit at a bad angle—the round glanced off instead of penetrating. Then machine-gun fire from the mechanical monster drove off the cannon's crew. And then, in an act of bravado that made Tom Colleton clap his hands in startled admiration, the barrel drove right over the gun. Nobody would use that weapon again soon.

Without infantry support, though, a lone barrel was vulnerable. Confederate soldiers sneaked around behind it and flung grenades at the engine decking till—after what seemed like forever—the barrel finally caught fire. They showed their respect for the men who'd formed the makeshift crew by taking them prisoner instead of shooting them down when they bailed out of the burning barrel.

Tom Colleton looked at his wristwatch. To his amazement, that hour's worth of action had been crammed into fifteen minutes of real life. He turned to a man standing close by him. "Well," he said brightly, "*that* was fun."

"Uh, yes, sir," the young lieutenant answered.

"Now we have to make up for lost time." Tom pointed toward downtown Sandusky. "Any bright ideas?"

The lieutenant considered, then asked what had become the inevitable question in the Ohio campaign: "Where are *our* barrels?"

"I think I'd better find out," Tom said. He didn't want to send infantry forward without armor—he was sure of that. If U.S. soldiers felt like fighting house-to-house, his regiment would melt like snow in springtime. He looked for outflanking routes, and didn't see any the damnyankees hadn't covered. With a sigh, he shouted for the man with a wireless set on his back.

Ten minutes of shouting into the mouthpiece at a colonel of barrels named Lee Castle showed him the armor wasn't that eager to get involved in house-to-house fighting, either. "That's not what we do," Castle said. "Place like that, they could tear us a new asshole, and for what? Sorry, pal, but it's not worth the price."

"What are you good for, then?" Tom knew that wasn't fair, but his frustration had to come out somewhere.

"I'm doing this the way I'm doing it on orders from General Patton," Colonel Castle said, and he might have been quoting Holy Writ. "You don't like it, take it up with him—either that, or bend the flyboys' ears."

Tom doubted Patton would bend. He could see why the commander of armor would want to keep his machines from being devoured while clearing a few blocks of houses and factories. He didn't like it, but he could see it. Calling in the bombers to soften up Sandusky was a happier thought. It wasn't as if the town hadn't been hit before. But now it would get hit with a purpose.

A couple of hours later, bombs rained down on Sandusky from a flight of Razorback bombers that droned along a couple of miles up in the sky. Their bombsights were supposed to be so fancy, they were military secrets. That didn't particularly impress Tom, not when some of the bombs came down on his men instead of inside enemy lines. He lost two dead and five wounded, and shook his fist at the sky as the bombers flew south toward the field from which they'd taken off.

But then the Mules started hammering Sandusky. The dive bombers screamed down to what seemed just above rooftop height before releasing their bombs and pulling up again. Their machine guns blazed; their sirens made them sound even more demoralizing than they would have otherwise. What they hit stayed hit. No wonder the soldiers on the ground called them Asskickers.

No matter how hard they hit, though, they couldn't work miracles. When Confederate troops poked forward after the Mules flew away, machine guns and mortars and rifles greeted them. Bombers could change a town from houses to ruins, but that didn't mean stubborn soldiers wouldn't keep fighting in those ruins. And ruins, as Tom had discovered, sometimes offered better cover than houses did.

Try as they would, his men couldn't clear the U.S. soldiers from one factory. By the sign painted on the side of its dingy brick walls, it had manufactured crayons. Now it turned out trouble, and in carload lots, too. It was too big and too well sited to bypass; it had to fall before the rest of Sandusky could.

Tom almost got shot reconnoitering the place. A bullet tugged at his shirtsleeve without hitting his arm. He drew back, figuring he'd tempted fate far enough for the moment. Then he got on the wireless and summoned the Mules again. They wouldn't get rid of all the enemy soldiers in the place, but they were the best doorknockers the Confederate Army had.

Back came the dive bombers. They blew the factory to hell and gone. The walls fell in. A great cloud of dust and smoke thickened the pall that had already turned a blue sky brownish gray. This time, though, the Mules didn't get away scot-free. U.S. fighters knocked two of them out of the sky. The Asskickers seemed impressively fast diving on ground targets, but they couldn't measure up against fighters. And the airplanes with eagles on their sides shot up Confederate soldiers on the ground, too, before streaking off towards Indiana.

Gunfire still blazed from the crayon factory when the Confederates attacked again. Colleton swore. The Yankees weren't making things easy or simple. Tom decided to try a trick that had worked for Nathan Bedford Forrest in the War of Secession. He showed a flag of truce till firing on both sides died away, then sent in a man calling on the Yankees to surrender. "Tell 'em we can't answer for what happens if they keep fighting," he told the young officer.

The man came back through the eerie silence a few minutes later. "Sir, a captain in there says, 'And the horse you rode in on,' " he reported.

"Does he?" Tom said. The officer nodded. Tom sighed. Forrest must have been facing a different breed of Yankee. With another sigh, Tom pointed toward the factory. "All right, then. We'll just have to do it the hard way." He shouted for a wireless man, then shouted into the set.

Artillery fire rained down on the crayon factory. A lot of shells gurgled through the air as they flew: gas rounds. By the time the Confederate gunners were done pounding the place, nothing without a mask could have survived for more than a breath. Even though the wind was with them, Tom's men had to don gas gear, too.

He gave the order to attack again. Submachine guns and automatic rifles blazing, his men obeyed. By then, the crayon factory was nothing but a poison-filled pile of rubble. Not all the U.S. soldiers inside were dead, though. Machine guns and rifles in the ruins greeted the Confederates. This time, though, the men in butternut gained a toehold inside the factory.

It was still an ugly business. Here and there, the fighting came down to bayonets and entrenching tools, as it had in trench raids during the Great War. The damnyankees had to be cleared from what was left of the building one stubborn knot at a time. The Confederates took very few prisoners. That wasn't deliberate brutality. Their foes were in no mood to give up while they could still hit back.

At last, not long before sunset, the fight for the factory ebbed. A handful of damnyankees fell back to the north. Tom's men let them go. They couldn't do much else. They'd been chewed to red rags themselves. He looked at the prize they'd won. By itself, the crayon factory wasn't worth having. How many more stands like that did U.S. soldiers have in them?

Tom recalled his classical education. It wasn't Xenophon this time; it was Plutarch. King Pyrrhus of Epirus had won his first battle against the Romans. Then he looked at his battered army and exclaimed, "One more such victory and we're ruined!" If he'd seen the fight for the crayon factory, he would have understood.

Jonathan Moss enjoyed hunting Mules. U.S. foot soldiers hated and feared the Confederate dive bombers—he knew that. Asskickers could pound ground positions to a fare-thee-well . . . if they got the chance. When U.S. fighters caught them in the air, they often didn't. Their pilots and rear gunners were more than brave enough. But the machines weren't fast enough to run away or maneuverable enough to fight back. They got hacked out of the sky in large numbers.

The Confederates didn't take long to figure out they had a problem. In the fight for Sandusky, they quickly took to sending in swarms of Hound Dogs along with the Mules. The fighter escorts tried to keep U.S. fighters away from the dive bombers till they'd done their dirty work and headed back for where they came from. Unlike the Asskickers, Hound Dogs *were* a match for the Wrights U.S. pilots flew. Moss had discovered that the hard way not long before. He found out again in a heated encounter above the embattled lakeside city. The Confederate pilot couldn't bring him down, but he couldn't get rid of the enemy, either. The flak bursting all around could have knocked down either one of them. He didn't think the gunners on the ground could tell them apart—or much cared who was who.

After ten or fifteen nerve-wracking minutes, he and the Confederate pilot broke off by what felt like mutual consent. Moss hoped he never saw that particular Confederate again. The fellow was altogether too likely to win their next encounter. He hoped the Confederate felt the same way about him.

His fuel gauge showed he was getting low. He wasn't sorry to have an excuse to leave. His flight suit was drenched in sweat despite the chill of altitude. He knew nothing but relief when the enemy pilot seemed willing to break off the duel, too. Maybe they'd managed to put the fear of God in each other.

The latest airstrip from which he was flying lay near Defiance, Ohio, in the northwestern corner of the state. Once upon a time, it had been all but impenetrable forest. These days, it was corn country, and the airstrip had been carved out of a luckless farmer's field. When Mad Anthony Wayne first ran up a fort at the junction of the Maumee and Auglaize Rivers, he'd said, "I defy the English, the Indians, and all the devils in hell to take it." The English and Indians were no longer worries in Ohio. From what Moss had seen, the devils in hell were busy in Sandusky.

He bumped to a landing. The strip had been cleared in a tearing hurry, and was a long way from smooth. As soon as he got out of his fighter, groundcrew men pushed it off towards a camouflaged revetment. If a bomb hit it, fire wouldn't spread to any other aircraft.

Camouflage netting also concealed the tents where pilots slept and ate and drank, not necessarily in that order. The heavy leather clothes that had kept him warm three miles up in the sky were stifling in August on the ground. He unfastened toggles and unzipped zippers as fast as he could. (He remembered from the Great War that he would be glad to have such gear when winter rolled around, assuming he was still alive by then.)

Twilight seemed to close in around him when he ducked under the netting. He trudged wearily to the headquarters tent. It was even gloomier inside there, which perfectly suited his mood. Another major, a knobby-cheeked Irishman named Joe Kennedy, Jr.—he insisted on the *Junior*—was doing paperwork by the light of a kerosene lamp. He was a boy wonder, half Moss' age, the son of a Boston politico. That went a long way towards accounting for his rank, but he could fly. He'd already shot down three Confederate airplanes—and, as the bandages on his left arm showed, been shot down himself. Till the burns healed, he was grounded.

He looked up and nodded to Moss. "How'd it go?" he asked, a New England accent broadening his vowels.

"Got myself a Mule," Moss answered. "Our own antiaircraft was doing its goddamnedest to shoot me down. So was a Hound Dog. We were a match—neither one of us could get the drop on the other. Finally we both gave up and went home. How about you, Joe? How's the arm?"

"Hurts a little," Kennedy admitted. He dry-swallowed a couple of small white pills. They were codeine, not aspirin; he hadn't graduated to aspirin yet. Moss suspected his arm hurt more than a little, but he didn't bitch about it. No matter how he'd got his rank, he seemed to be doing his best to deserve it. After the pills went down, he asked, "How's Sandusky look?"

"Kicked flat and then stomped on," Moss said. "It's not going to hold, and life gets a hell of a lot more complicated when it falls."

"Yeah." Joe Kennedy, Jr., nodded. "You should hear my old man go on about Al Smith. Two Irishmen, two Catholics—but it doesn't matter a hill of beans, not as far as Dad's concerned. He's a Democrat and Smith's a Socialist, and that's what really counts."

Moss only grunted. "Far as I can see, how we got into this mess stopped mattering as soon as the shooting started. Now we've got to get out of it the best way we can."

"Makes sense to me," Kennedy said mildly; even though his father was at least a medium-sized wheel back in Boston, he didn't try to ram his own politics down anybody else's throat.

Come to that, Moss wasn't precisely sure what the younger Kennedy's politics were. He didn't ask now, either. Instead, he said, "What's new out of Utah?"

Kennedy's face twisted with a pain that had nothing to do with his injury. "It's as bad as it was in the last war," he said, swallowing that final consonant. "The Mormons are up in arms, all right. Governor Young's run for Colorado." More r's vanished, while one appeared at the end of the state's name.

"What are we going to do about those bastards?" Moss aimed the question at least as much at himself, or perhaps God, as at Joe Kennedy, Jr.

But Kennedy had an answer. His face went hard and ruthless as he said, "Bomb them, shoot them, blow them up, and hang the ones that are left. Smith was nice to them, same as he was nice to Featherston. He thought that was all it took. Just be nice, and everybody'd love you and do what you wanted. It's really worked out great, hasn't it?"

"I think it's a little more complicated than that, at least with the Mormons," Moss said. "Utah's been a mess longer than I've been alive. It didn't start with the Great War."

"They got one bite then." Kennedy waved complications away with his good arm; he didn't want to hear about them. "That's what you give a mean dog—one bite. If it bites you again, you get rid of it."

"Shall we do the same for the Confederates?" Moss' voice was dryly ironic. He had no more use for simplicity than Kennedy did for complexity.

The younger man refused to acknowledge the sarcasm. "We'd better, don't you think? They'd get rid of us if they had the chance. The way things are going, they think they do. I happen to think they're full of shit. I don't suppose you'd be wearing the uniform if you didn't feel the same way. But if we can beat them, they'd better not get another chance to do this to us. If they do, we deserve whatever happens to us afterwards, wouldn't you say?"

"If you think occupying Canada's been expensive, occupying the CSA'd be ten times worse," Moss said.

"Maybe." Kennedy shrugged, then bit his lip; the pain pills must not have kicked in. "Maybe you're right. But if occupying the Confederate States will be expensive, how expensive will *not* occupying them be?"

He had no give in him. He wanted the United States to have no give in them, either. Moss said, " 'They make a desert and call it peace,' eh?"

Kennedy recognized the quotation. Moss had figured his education included Latin. Kennedy said, "Tacitus was a stiff-necked prig who didn't like anything the Roman government did. The Romans might have made a desert out of Britain, but they hung on to it for the next four hundred years after that."

"Have it your way." Moss was too weary to argue with him. "What I could use right now is a drink"—*or three,* he added to himself—"and then some sack time."

"Go ahead." Kennedy jerked his thumb toward the tent that held what passed for the officers' club. "I've got to finish this crap first." He attacked the paperwork.

In the Great War, pilots had drunk as if there were no tomorrow. For a lot of them, there hadn't been. This time around, men seemed a little more sober. Maybe they were thinking more about what they were doing. Moss' chuckle came sour. If people really thought about what they were doing, would they have started wars in the first place?

Instead of bar stools, the officers' club had metal folding chairs that looked as if they'd been liberated from an Odd Fellows' hall in Defiance. Moss wasn't inclined to be unduly critical. He sat down in one of them and called for a whiskey sour.

"Coming right up, sir," answered the soldier behind the bar, which was as much a makeshift as the seating arrangements. He brought the drink, then took fresh beers to a couple of fliers who already had a lot of dead soldiers in front of them.

Moss poured down half his drink. He hardly knew anybody else who flew out of this airstrip. He'd got acquainted with Joe Kennedy, Jr., in a hurry, because Kennedy liked to hear himself talk. Most of the others remained ciphers, strangers. Squadron organization hadn't held up well under the relentless pressure of the Confederate onslaught. Moss hoped victory had disrupted the enemy as much as defeat had disorganized the USA, but he wouldn't have bet on it.

He finished the whiskey sour and held up the glass to show he wanted another one. Two stiff drinks started to counter the adrenaline still coursing through him after his inconclusive duel with the Confederate fighter pilot. He got up and headed for his cot. Sleep seemed the most wonderful thing in the world.

He was deep underwater when C.S. bombers paid a call on Defiance. The roar of the antiaircraft guns around the field didn't wake him. When bombs started falling, though, he sat up and blearily looked around. He thought about going back to sleep again, but didn't. He got up and ran for a trench carrying his shoes; he was still wearing the rest of his clothes.

The airplanes overhead were Razorbacks, not Mules. They dropped their bombs from three miles up in the sky. That meant they mostly couldn't hit the broad side of a barn. Bombs fell on and around the airstrip almost at random. "We ought to scramble some of our fighters and shoot those bastards down," Moss called to Joe Kennedy, Jr., who sprawled in the trench about ten feet away.

"Can't," Kennedy answered.

"Why the hell not?"

"On account of they put a couple of 250-pounders right in the middle of the strip," Kennedy said. "We aren't going anywhere till the 'dozers fill in the holes."

"Oh, for the love of Mike!" Moss said, too disgusted even to swear.

Major Kennedy only shrugged. "Sometimes you'd rather be lucky than good. Maybe some of the guys from other fields'll get after their asses."

"Hope somebody's home," Moss said. Most U.S. fighters spent as much time as they could over the corridor the Confederates had carved up through Ohio and Indiana. They'd done all they could to keep the CSA from reaching Lake Erie. They'd done all they could— and it hadn't been enough.

What were they going to do now? Huddled in the trench, Moss had no idea.

Flora Blackford's secretary looked into the office. "Mr. Caesar is here to see you, ma'am," she said, and let out a distinct sniff.

"Send him in, Bertha," Flora answered.

Bertha sniffed again. Flora understood why. It saddened her, but she couldn't do much about it. In came the man who'd waited in the outer office. He was tall and scrawny, and wore a cheap suit that didn't fit him very well. He was also black as the ace of spades, which accounted for Bertha's unhappiness.

"Please to meet you, Mr. Caesar," Flora said. She waved the Negro to a chair. "Sit down. Make yourself comfortable. I gather you had quite a time getting to Philadelphia."

"Caesar's not my last name, ma'am, so I don't hardly go by *Mister*," he said. "It's not my first name, neither. It's just . . . my name. That's how things is for black folks down in the CSA." He folded himself into the chair. "Gettin' here . . . ? Yes, ma'am. Quite a time is right. Confederate soldiers almost shot me, and then Yankee soldiers almost shot me. But I got captured instead, like I wanted to, and they sent me up here. When they did, I knew you was the one I wanted to see."

"Why?" Flora asked.

"On account of I heard tell of you down in Virginia. You're the one they call 'the conscience of the Congress,' ain't that right?"

A flush warmed Flora's cheeks. "I don't know that I deserve the name—" she began.

Caesar waved that aside. "You got it. It's yours." He was plainly intelligent, even if his accent tried to obscure that. "Figured if anybody would take me serious, you're the one."

"Take you seriously about what?" Flora asked.

"Ma'am, they are massacrin' us," Caesar answered solemnly. "They got camps in the pinewoods and in the swamps, and black folks goes into 'em by the trainload, and nobody never comes out."

"People have been telling stories like that about the Freedom Party since before it came to power," Flora said. "What proof have you got? Without proof, those stories are worse than useless, because the Confederates can just call us a pack of liars."

"I know that, ma'am. That's how come I had to git myself up here—so I could give you the proof." Caesar set a manila envelope on her desk. "Here."

She opened the envelope. It held fifteen or twenty photographs of varying size and quality. Some showed blacks in rags and in manacles lined up before pits. Others showed piles of corpses in the pits. One or two showed smiling uniformed white men holding guns as they stood on top of the piles of dead bodies. She knew she would remember those small, grainy, cheerful smiles the rest of her life.

She both did and didn't want to look all the way through the photos. They were the most dreadful things she'd ever seen, but they also exerted a horrid, almost magnetic, fascination. Before she saw them, she hadn't dreamt humanity was still capable of such things. This was a sort of education she would rather not have had.

At last, after she didn't know how long, she looked up into Caesar's dark, somber features. "Where did you get these?" she asked, and she could hear how shaken her voice was. "Who took them?"

"I got 'em on account of some folks—colored folks—knew I wanted to prove what people was sayin'," Caesar answered. "We had to do it on the sly. If we didn't, if the Freedom Party found out what we was up to, I reckon somebody else'd take a photo with me in one o' them piles."

"Who *did* take these?" Flora asked again.

"Some of 'em was took by niggers who snuck out after the shootin' was done," Caesar said. "Some of 'em, though, the guards took their ownselves. Reckon you can cipher out which. Some of the guards down at them places ain't always happy about what they're doin'. Some of 'em, though, they reckon it's the best sport in the world. They bring their cameras along so they can show their wives an' kiddies what big men they are."

He wasn't joking. No one who'd had a look at those photographs could possibly be in any mood to joke. Flora made herself examine them once more. Those white faces kept smiling out of the prints at her. Yes, those men had had a good time doing what they did. How much blood was on their boots? How much was on their hands?

"How did your friends get hold of pictures like this?" she asked.

"Stole 'em," he answered matter-of-factly. "One o' them ofays goes out with a box Brownie every time there's a population reduction, folks notice. Plenty o' niggers cook and clean for the guards. They wouldn't do nigger work their ownselves, after all. They got to be ready to take care o'—that." He pointed to the photos on the desk.

Ofays. Population reduction. Neither was hard to figure out, but neither was part of the English language as it was spoken in the United States. The one, Flora guessed, was part of Confederate Negro slang. The other . . . The other was more frightening. Even though she heard it in Caesar's mouth, it had to have sprung from some bureaucrat's brain. If you call a thing by a name that doesn't seem so repellent, then the thing itself also becomes less repellent.

Sympathetic magic—except it wasn't sympathetic to those who fell victim to it.

Flora shook herself, as if coming out of cold, cold water. "May I keep these?" she asked. "I'm not the only one who'll need to see them, you know."

"Yes, ma'am. I understand that," Caesar said. "You can have 'em, all right. They ain't the only ones there is."

"Thank you," Flora said, though she wished with all her heart that such photographs did not, could not, exist. "Thank you for your courage. I'll do what I can with them."

"That's what I brung 'em for." Caesar got to his feet. "Much obliged. Good luck to you." He dipped his head in an awkward half bow and hurried out of her office with no more farewell than that.

If Flora put the photos back in the manila envelope, her eyes wouldn't keep returning to them. She told her secretary, "Cancel the rest of my appointments for this morning. I have to get over to Powel House right away."

Bertha nodded, but she also let out another sniff. "I don't know why you're getting yourself in an uproar over whatever that . . . that person told you."

"That's my worry," Flora said crisply. She went outside to flag a cab. Fifteen minutes later, she was at the President's Philadelphia residence. Antiaircraft guns poked their long snouts skyward on the crowded front lawn. They were new. She walked between them on the way to the door.

She was a Congresswoman. She was a former First Lady. She'd known Al Smith for more than twenty-five years, since before she was either. Put that all together, and it got her fifteen minutes with the President after half an hour's wait. When a flunky escorted her into his office, she had to work hard to keep her face from showing shock. Smith hadn't looked well the last time she came here. He looked worse now, much worse. He looked like hell.

He'll never live through this term, Flora thought. She bit her tongue, even though she hadn't said anything at all. "Are you . . . getting enough sleep, Mr. President?" she asked carefully.

"I get a little every night, whether I need it or not." His grin came from the other side of the grave, but his voice, though weaker than before, was still the cheerful New York bray it had always been, the voice that had made people call him the Happy Warrior. Maybe he didn't want anyone else to know his job was killing him. Maybe he didn't know himself. "What have you got for me, Flora? Malcolm said you said it was important."

"It is, sir. A colored man escaped from Virginia gave me these. . . ." She set the manila envelope on the desk between them. "I hope you have a strong stomach. This is proof the Confederates aren't just mistreating their Negroes, the way they always have. They're slaughtering them."

"Let's see." He set reading glasses on his nose, which only made him look like a learned skeleton. He went through the photos one by one, nodding every now and then. When he was through, he eyed Flora over the tops of the glasses. "All right. Here they are. What do you want me to do about it?"

"Shout it from the housetops!" she exclaimed. "When the world knows they're doing this, they'll have to stop."

"Will they?" Smith said. "Remember when the Ottomans started killing Armenians?" He waited. When Flora didn't answer, he prodded her: "Remember?"

"I remember," she said, a sudden sinking feeling at the pit of her stomach.

"We protested to the Sultan," the President said. "You'd know about that—Hosea was Vice President then, wasn't he? We protested. Even the Kaiser said something, I think. And the USA and Germany had fought on the same side as Turkey during the Great War. How much attention did anybody in Constantinople pay?"

Again, he stopped. Again, she had to answer. Miserably, she did: "Not much."

"Not any, you mean," Al Smith said. "They went on killing Armenians till there weren't a whole lot of Armenians left to kill. We're not the Confederates' allies. We're enemies. They'll say we're making it up. Britain and France will believe them, or pretend to. Japan won't care. And people here won't much care, either. Come on, Flora—who gives a damn about *shvartzers*?" Of course a New York Irish politician knew the Yiddish word for Negroes.

"They're *slaughtering* them, Mr. President," Flora said stubbornly. "People can't ignore that."

"Who says they can't?" Smith retorted. "Most people in the USA don't care what happens to Negroes in the CSA. They're just glad they don't have to worry about very many Negroes here at home. You can like that or not like it, but you can't tell me it isn't true." He waited once more. This time, Flora had nothing to say. But even saying nothing admitted Smith was right. Nodding as if she *had* admitted it, the President continued, "And besides, Sandusky's fallen."

"Oh . . . dear," Flora said, in lieu of something stronger. It wasn't that she hadn't expected the news. But it was like a blow in the belly even so.

"Yeah," Smith said, trying to seem as upbeat as he could. He put Caesar's photographs back in the envelope. "So if we start going on about this stuff right now, what will people think? They'll think we're trying to make 'em forget about what we couldn't do on the battlefield. And will they be wrong?"

"But this—this is the worst wickedness the world has ever seen!" The word was old-fashioned, but Flora couldn't find another one that fit.

"We're already in a war full of bombed cities and poison gas," Smith said. "When we're doing that to each other, who's going to get all hot and bothered about what the Confederates are doing to their own people?"

"Mr. President, this isn't war. This is murder. There's a difference," Flora insisted.

"Maybe there is. I suppose there is. If you can make people see it, more power to you," Al Smith said. "I'm very sorry—I'm more sorry than I know how to tell you—but I don't think you can."

Flora wanted to hit him, not least because she feared he was right. Instead, keeping her voice under tight control, she said, "Would you say the same thing if they were Jews and not Negroes?"

"I don't know. Maybe not. People in the USA are more likely to get hot and bothered about Jews than they are about Negroes, don't you think?" Smith sounded horribly reasonable. "If you can make it go, I'll get behind you. But I won't take the lead here. I can't."

"I'm going to try," Flora said.

The worst had happened. That was what everybody said. The Confederates had sliced up through Ohio and cut the United States in half. If the worst had already happened, shouldn't that have meant that men from the USA and CSA weren't killing one another quite so often now? It didn't, not so far as Dr. Leonard O'Doull could tell.

U.S. forces were trying to strike back toward the west and cut through the Confederate corridor. The Confederates, for their part, were doing their best to push eastward, toward Pennsylvania. So far, nobody seemed to be making much progress. That didn't mean an awful lot of young men on both sides weren't getting maimed, though.

O'Doull's aid station lay a few miles west of Elyria, Ohio—about halfway between lost Sandusky and Cleveland. Elyria had been the town with the largest elm in Ohio: a tree with a spread of branches of over a hundred thirty feet and a trunk almost sixty-five feet thick. It had been, but no more: Confederate artillery and bombs had reduced the tree to kindling—along with much of what had been a pleasant little place.

"Burns are the worst," O'Doull said to Granville McDougald. "Some of the poor bastards with burns, you just want to cut their throats and do them a favor."

"This tannic acid treatment we're using now helps a lot," the corpsman answered. McDougald was resolutely optimistic.

"We're saving people we wouldn't have in the last war—no

doubt of that," O'Doull said. "Some of them, though . . . Are we doing them any favors when we keep them alive?"

"We've got to do what we can," McDougald said. "Once they get the pain under control, they thank us."

"Yeah. Once," O'Doull said tightly. He was seeing a lot more burn cases this time around than he had in the last war. Men who bailed out of barrels usually had to run a gauntlet of flame to escape. During the Great War, barrels had been latecomers and oddities. They were an ordinary part of the fighting here. With so many more of them in action, so many more horrible things could happen to their crews.

In the last war, O'Doull didn't remember anyone asking to be killed so he could escape his torment. It might well have happened, but he hadn't seen it. He did now. More than once, he'd been tempted to ignore the Hippocratic oath he'd sworn and give the victims what they wanted.

"That's why God made morphine, sir," McDougald said.

"God made morphine—and we make addicts," O'Doull replied.

"If you're in pain, that's the least of your worries," the corpsman said. "All you want to do is stop hurting. You can get over morphine addiction once you're not hurting any more. As long as the burns are giving you hell, you might as well be dead."

O'Doull thought of addiction as a personal failing, even if pain relief caused it. He eyed McDougald thoughtfully. The corpsman had a different slant on things. "You look at it from the patient's point of view, don't you? Not the doctor's, I mean."

"I'm not a doctor," McDougald said, which was formally true. He went on, "And we're here for the patients, aren't we?"

A lot of people at aid stations thought they were there to advance their own careers, or to stay out of the front-line fighting. And there were some men from churches that did not approve of members who carried guns, but that had nothing against helping the wounded. "Everybody ought to think the way you do," O'Doull said. "We'd all be better off."

The corpsman only shrugged. "Maybe yes, maybe no. My guess is, we'd just be screwed up a different way."

"Doc! Hey, Doc!" O'Doull had come to dread that call. It meant another wounded man coming in. Sure enough, the corpsman outside went on, "Got a belly wound for you, Doc!"

"Oh, hell," O'Doull said. Even with sulfa drugs, belly wounds were always bad news. The chance for peritonitis was very high, and a bullet or shell fragment could destroy a lot of organs a person simply couldn't live without. O'Doull raised his voice: "Bring him in."

The corpsmen were already doing it. They lifted their stretcher up onto the makeshift operating table that had been someone's kitchen table till the Medical Corps commandeered it. The soldier on the stretcher wasn't groaning or screaming, as men with belly wounds often did. He'd passed out—a mercy for a man with an injury like that. He was ghost pale, and getting paler as O'Doull eyed him.

"I don't think you'd better wait around real long, Doc," said the corpsman who'd shouted for O'Doull.

"I don't intend to, Eddie," O'Doull answered. He turned to McDougald. "Pass gas for me, Granny?" McDougald wasn't an anesthetist, either, but he'd do a tolerable job.

He nodded now. "I'll take a shot at it." He grabbed the ether cone and put it over the unconscious man's face. "Have to be careful not to give him too much, or he's liable to quit breathing for good."

He was liable to do that anyway. He looked like the devil. But he was still alive, and O'Doull knew he had to give it his best shot. He said, "Eddie, get a plasma line into his arm. We're going to have to stretch his blood as far as it'll go, and then maybe another ten feet after that."

"Right, Doc." Eddie grabbed for a needle. O'Doull hoped it wasn't one he'd just used on some other patient, but he wasn't going to get himself in an uproar about it one way or the other. This wounded man had more important things to worry about. Surviving the next half hour topped the list.

When O'Doull opened him up, he grimaced at the damage. The bullet had gone in one side and out the other, and had tumbled on the way through. There were more bleeders than you could shake a stick at, and they were all leaking like hell.

Granville McDougald said, "You don't want to waste a lot of time, Doc. He's just barely here."

"What's his blood pressure, Eddie?" O'Doull asked. His hands automatically started repairing the worst of the damage.

"Let me get a cuff on him," the corpsman said. "It's . . . ninety over sixty, sir, and falling. We're losing him. Down to eighty over fifty . . . Shit! He's got no pulse."

"Not breathing," McDougald said a moment later, and then, "I'm afraid he's gone."

Eddie nodded. "No pulse. No BP. No nothin'." He loosened the cuff and pulled the needle from the plasma line out of the soldier's— the dead soldier's—arm. "Not your fault, Doc. You did what you could. He got hit too bad, that's all. I saw what you were trying to fix up. His guts were all chewed to hell."

"That they were." Leonard O'Doull straightened wearily. "Get his identity disk. Then call the burial detail and Graves Registration. Somebody's going to have to notify his next of kin."

"That's a bastard of a job," McDougald said. "In the last war, no one wanted to see a Western Union messenger coming to the door. Everybody was afraid he had a 'deeply regret' telegram. It's gonna be the same story this time around, too."

O'Doull hadn't thought spending the last war in a military hospital had shielded him from anything. Now he discovered he was wrong. People in Quebec hadn't had to worry about telegrams with bad news—not in the part of Quebec where he'd been stationed, anyhow. Farther west, Quebec City and Montreal had held out for a long time before falling. Francophones had defended them along with English-speaking Canadians.

Lucien doesn't have to worry about the war. He can get on with his life. That was a relief, anyhow. Quebec's conscription law wasn't universal, and Lucien had never had to be a soldier. And with the Republic formally neutral—even if it did lean toward the USA and help occupy English-speaking Canada—it wasn't likely the younger O'Doull would ever have to aim a rifle in anger.

That bothered the elder O'Doull not at all. He'd seen too much of what rifles aimed in anger could do in the last war. The refresher course he was getting now—including the poor son of a bitch who'd just died on the table—had done nothing to change his opinion.

He discovered he was still holding the scalpel. He chucked it into a wide-mouthed jug of rubbing alcohol. The jug had a big red skull and crossbones on it, plus a warning label in red capital letters: POISON! DO NOT DRINK! He hoped that would keep thirsty soldiers from experimenting. You never could tell. He'd heard that sailors were draining the alcohol fuel from torpedo motors and drinking it.

But that really was ethyl alcohol, and wouldn't hurt them unless they were pigs. Rubbing alcohol was a different critter. It was poison even in small doses.

He scrubbed his hands with strong soap. He could get the dead soldier's blood off of them easily enough. Getting it off his mind . . . ? He shook his head. That was another story. If anybody could sympathize with Lady Macbeth, a battlefield surgeon was the one to do it. *Here's the smell of the blood still. All the perfumes of Arabia will not sweeten this little hand.* And Macbeth himself:

> *Will all great Neptune's ocean wash this blood*
> *Clean from my hand? No, this hand will rather*
> *The multitudinous seas incarnadine,*
> *Making the green one red.*

Macbeth, unlike his lady, had borne up under what he'd done. O'Doull had to do the same.

"Can't save them all, Doc," Eddie said.

It was meant to be sympathy. O'Doull knew as much. He wanted to punch the corpsman even so. Instead, he hurried out of the tent. He gaped and blinked in the sunshine like some nocturnal creature unexpectedly caught out by day. That wasn't so far wrong. He spent most of his time under canvas trying to patch up what the fierce young men on either side were so eager to ruin.

For the time being, the front was pretty quiet. The Confederates had got what they wanted most. The United States hadn't yet decided how their real counterattack would go in. Only an occasional shot or brief burst of gunfire marred the day.

O'Doull pulled out a pack of Raleighs. They were spoil of war: taken from a dead Confederate soldier and passed on to him in appreciation of services rendered. The C.S. tobacco was a hell of a lot smoother than what the USA grew. Even since he'd got to the front, O'Doull had noticed a steep dive in the quality of U.S. cigarettes as stocks of imported tobacco got used up. These days, brands like Rose Bowl and Big Sky tasted as if they were made of dried, chopped horse manure.

He still smoked them when he couldn't get anything better. They relaxed him and calmed his nerves even if they did taste lousy. Most of the time, his hands steadied down when he got to work. Still, a dose of nicotine didn't hurt.

Raleighs, now, Raleighs had it all. They gave your nerves what you craved, and they tasted good, too. How could you go wrong? O'Doull stopped with the half-smoked cigarette halfway to his mouth. How could you go wrong? He wouldn't have been enjoying this savory smoke if some kid from North Carolina or Mississippi or Texas hadn't stopped a bullet or a shell fragment. Things had gone wrong for the Confederate soldier, and they'd never go right for him again. O'Doull started to throw down the cigarette, then checked himself. What was the point of that? It wouldn't do the dead man any good. But the smoke didn't taste as good now when he raised it to his lips.

He finished the Raleigh, then stomped it out. Behind the line, U.S. guns began to roar. Shells flew through the air with freight-train noises. Gas rounds gurgled as if they were tank cars full of oil or molasses. O'Doull's mouth twisted. The Confederates would respond in kind, of course. Each side always did when the other used gas.

"Different kinds of casualties," he muttered. "Happy goddamn day." He ducked back into the tent to get ready for them.

They put Armstrong Grimes' company into two boxcars. It wasn't quite the 8 HORSES OR 40 MEN arrangement the French had used during the Great War—Armstrong didn't think the cars had housed horses or cattle or anything similarly appetizing. But he did come to feel a strong and comradely relation with a sardine. The only difference was, they hadn't poured olive oil in after his buddies and him. Maybe they should have. The grease might have kept the men from rubbing together so much. Just getting back to the honey buckets was trial enough.

"How come we're so lucky?" he grumbled.

"Can't you figure it out for yourself?" Corporal Stowe asked. "I thought you were a smart fellow. You graduated high school and you stayed alive, right? That's why you made PFC."

Armstrong was convinced simply staying alive had more to do with the stripe on his sleeve than the high-school diploma did. He had that more because his old man would have walloped the snot out of him if he'd quit beforehand than for any other reason. Yeah, only about one guy in three in the USA did, but so what? It didn't mean anything to him.

He said, "Maybe I'm a moron especially for today, but I don't see what you're driving at."

"No, huh?" The grin the corporal sent his way wasn't especially friendly or amused. "All right—I'll spell it out for you. We're going where we're going on account of we ended up west of fucking Sandusky when the Confederates cut the country in half. If we'd been east of the goddamn place, they'd've done something different to us—I mean, with us."

"Oh." Armstrong Grimes thought it over. It made more sense than he wished it did. Getting from, say, Cleveland to Utah would have been hard, long, and dangerous. Getting from western Ohio to Mormon country was a straight shot—except, with luck, nobody would be shooting at them till they got there. He nodded. "Yeah, I guess maybe you're right."

"Bet your ass I am." Stowe's laugh was the laugh of a man waiting for the gallows the next morning. "I'll tell you something else, too: I'd sooner fight Featherston's fuckers than the damned Mormons. The Confederates play by the rules, pretty much. The Mormons, it's you or them, and they don't quit till they're dead."

"How do you know that?" Grimes asked.

"That's how it was in the last war, anyway," Stowe answered. "Men, women, kids—they threw everything at us but the kitchen sink. And they probably loaded that full of TNT and left it for a booby trap."

"Oh, boy," Armstrong said in a hollow voice. His father hadn't fought in Utah, and so he'd never had much to say about the Mormons. History books in school made them out to be bad guys, but didn't talk about them a whole lot. The books seemed to take the attitude that if you didn't look at them, they'd go away. All he knew about them was that they wanted to have lots of wives and they hated the U.S. government. The wives didn't seem to matter. Hating the U.S. government did.

The train rattled west. Every so often, it would stop at a siding. They'd open the doors to the boxcars and let the soldiers out to stretch. The country gradually got flatter and drier. They clattered over the Mississippi between Quincy, Illinois, and Hannibal, Missouri. The bridge had a nest of antiaircraft guns around it. Armstrong doubted they would have done much good had Confederate bombers come calling.

Missouri gave way to Kansas. Armstrong discovered why they called them the Great Plains. Nothing but miles and miles of miles and miles. Western Colorado was the same way. But then, in the distance, the Rockies poked their way up over the horizon. Those were *mountains*. Nothing Armstrong had ever seen in the eastern part of the USA prepared him for country like that.

The next day, the train went over them. Even the passes were high enough to make his breath come short. He was glad he didn't have to do anything serious there. The train went down the other side, but not so far down.

It stopped again in Grand Junction, Colorado, where the Gunnison and Colorado Rivers came together. Again, Armstrong was glad to get out and stretch. A sign on the train station said, BIGGEST TOWN IN COLORADO WEST OF THE ROCKIES. That might have been true, but it didn't strike him as worth bragging about. If Grand Junction had ten thousand people, that was pushing things. It was full of frame houses, most of them painted white. Not far from the railroad yards, several factories and packing plants dominated the business district.

Railroad workers hooked up a car full of coal and scrap iron in front of the locomotive. Pointing, Armstrong asked, "What the hell's going on there?"

Corporal Stowe laughed. Again, the sound didn't hold a whole lot of mirth. "Goddamn Mormons are mining the train tracks. Better if they blow up a car full of junk than an engine with people in it."

"Oh." Armstrong thought that over. "Yeah, I guess so." He eyed the forward car. "Bastards really are playing for keeps, aren't they?"

"I said so before. You better believe it," Stowe answered. Behind them, somebody blew a whistle. The noncom grimaced. "Time to get back in."

"Mooo!" Armstrong said mournfully. Stowe laughed once more, this time as if he really meant it.

Armstrong couldn't have said for sure when they crossed from Colorado into Utah. The train went at a crawl all the way. If that warning car did touch off a mine, the engineer wanted the damage to be as limited as possible. He was probably thinking more of his own neck than of his passengers'. Armstrong didn't mind. He was in no great hurry to meet the Mormons.

Nothing blew up in the trip across the rebellious state, for which he was duly grateful. The train stopped at a place called Woodside. Soldiers threw the doors to the cars open. "Out!" they yelled. "Out! Out! Out! This here's the end of the line."

"Jesus!" Armstrong said when he got a look around. "It sure as hell looks like the end of the line."

Grand Junction had been a small city. Woodside, Utah, was barely a wide place in the road. Along with a railroad depot, it boasted two gas stations and, between them, a trickle of water that had a sign above it: WOODSIDE GEYSER. DO NOT DRINK.

Armstrong jerked a thumb toward the sign. "What the hell's that?"

"Bad water, that's what," answered one of the men who looked to have been there for a while. "Railroad dug for water back around the turn of the century and got a gusher they couldn't cap. Only trouble was, it was *bad* water. People couldn't drink it. Cows kept trying—and kept dying. Ain't much of a geyser now, but from what the old-timers say it really used to be something."

"Oh, boy." Armstrong tried to imagine what being an old-timer in Woodside, Utah, would be like. If you had a chance between living here for fifty or sixty years and blowing out your brains, wouldn't you think hard about picking up a rifle?

But even the old-timers had probably never seen Woodside the way it was now. Green-gray tents spread out in all directions. For reasons known only to itself and possibly to God, the Army had decided to make this miserable place its chief staging area for moves against the Mormon rebels farther west. The rebels were holding the parts of Utah worth hanging on to. They seemed perfectly willing to let the Army have the rest.

Off in the distance, artillery muttered and growled. Armstrong was more familiar with that noise than he wished he were. He wasn't sorry to hear it at a distance, though. He'd heard artillery at much closer ranges than this. He'd heard soldiers after shells landed among them, too. He shoved that thought out of his mind. He didn't want to remember what happened when things went wrong.

For the rest of that day, things went right. He and his buddies lined up for showers—presumably not in water from the Woodside Geyser. They lined up again for chow. They got steaks and french fries, the first meal that didn't come out of cans they'd had since leaving Ohio. It wasn't a great steak, but the only thing really wrong with it in Armstrong's eyes was that it was too damn small.

He slept on a real steel-framed cot with a real mattress that night. When first conscripted, he'd hated Army cots. They weren't a patch on his bed back home. Compared to the floor of a jouncing freight car, though, or to sleeping in a muddy foxhole, this one was a good approximation of heaven. He got rid of at least a few of the kinks of travel before reveille the next morning.

Breakfast was even better than supper had been. Bacon and real scrambled eggs, biscuits with gravy, fresh-brewed coffee . . . He ate till he was groaningly full. He wasn't the only one, either. The cooks had a devil of a time keeping ahead of the ravening hordes of hungry men.

Content with the world, Armstrong was slowly walking back to his tent when a metallic buzzing in the air made him look west. "What the hell's that?" he said.

"Looks like a crop-duster," another soldier said. The fabric-covered biplane certainly wasn't very impressive. Armstrong felt as if he could run as fast as it flew. He knew that wasn't so, but the impression remained.

A few men pointed at the biplane. More paid no attention to it at all as it sputtered along over the Army encampment at Woodside. Armstrong might have been the only one who saw a crate tumble out of it. He had time for no more than a startled, "What the—?" before the crate hit the ground.

Boom! The next thing Armstrong knew, he was on the ground. That wasn't the blast—it was reflex painfully acquired on the battlefield. When something blew up, you hit the dirt. You did if you wanted to keep breathing, anyhow.

A soldier off to his right didn't hit the dirt fast enough—and let out a startled squawk of pain. He pulled a tenpenny nail out of his arm. The nail was red and wet with his blood from point to head.

"Find an aid station," Armstrong said. "There's a Purple Heart for you."

The soldier just gaped at him. Ignoring the man, Armstrong jumped to his feet and ran toward the place where the makeshift bomb had gone off. The biplane, meanwhile, buzzed off in the direction from which it had come. Nobody took a shot at it. Very likely, only a handful of people had any idea it had dropped the improvised bomb.

Makeshift, improvised, or not, the bomb did everything its equivalent from a fancy ordnance factory might have done. It knocked things down. It blew things—and soldiers—up. It sprayed fragments of sharp metal (nails, here) all over the place. What more could you ask for from something that fell out of an airplane?

Armstrong tripped over a leg and almost fell. He gulped. Breakfast nearly came up. The rest of the man wasn't attached to the leg. A little closer to where the Mormons' explosive had hit, he found a soldier as neatly disemboweled as if he'd be cut up for butcher's meat in the next few minutes. Then he came upon someone he could actually help: a sergeant with a mangled hand trying without much luck to bandage himself with the other. Kneeling beside him, Armstrong said, "Here, let me do that."

"Thanks, kid," the noncom got out through clenched teeth. "What the hell happened?" Armstrong told him in a few words. The sergeant swore. "Ain't that a son of a bitch? Goddamn Mormons got bombers?"

"Looks that way." Armstrong stared west, then shook his head. "Who knows what else they've got, too?"

Brigadier General Abner Dowling rode a train east toward Philadelphia. The journey was one he would much rather not have made. He'd known it was coming, though. He hadn't been recalled by the War Department. That would have been bad enough. But instead, he'd been summoned by the Joint Committee on the Conduct of the War. That was at least ten times worse.

Congress had formed such a committee once before, during the War of Secession. It hadn't proved a good idea then. The committee had crucified officers it didn't like, and terrorized more than it crucified. It hadn't done a damn thing to keep the war from being lost. And now, just to prove how clever the elected rulers of the country were, they'd decided to reprise what hadn't worked before.

And, of course, Abner Dowling was the first, to say nothing of the most obvious, target the committee had chosen. People from

Bangor to San Diego were going to be yelling, "Who lost Ohio?" They were going to be pointing fingers and shouting for heads. And there was Dowling, right square in the crosshairs. They didn't even need to look very hard.

If a Congressman can spot me, I must be obvious, Dowling thought savagely. He could make a good guess about what would happen when he got to the de facto capital. They were going to pin everything on him. They would say that, if the U.S. forces in Ohio had had a general who knew his ass from a hole in the ground, everything would have gone fine, and soldiers in green-gray would have chased those butternut bastards all the way down through Kentucky and into Tennessee, if not into Alabama and Mississippi.

They'd expect him to fall on his sword, too. What else could he do? He'd issued the orders—the orders that hadn't worked. If he'd issued some different orders, wouldn't things have turned out differently? Wouldn't they have turned out better?

Of course they would. That was how Congress, with its infinite wisdom and twenty-twenty hindsight, was bound to see things, anyhow.

"Oh, yes. Of course," Dowling muttered. The woman across the aisle from him gave him an odd look. He ignored her.

An hour out of Pittsburgh, the train slowed and then stopped. They hadn't come to a town, not even a whistlestop. They were out in the middle of nowhere, or as close to the middle of nowhere as you could get in a crowded state like Pennsylvania. A telegraph line ran next to the tracks. A big crow—a raven?—sat on the wire staring in through the window at Dowling. *I'm not dead yet,* he thought. Then he wished that last word hadn't occurred to him.

An important-looking man in an expensive suit and a dark homburg reached up and grabbed the cord that rang for the conductor. In due course, that blue-uniformed worthy appeared. "See here," the important-looking man said. "I demand to know what has happened to this train. I have an urgent engagement in the capital."

Dowling had an urgent engagement in the capital, too. He wasn't eager enough to make a fuss about it, though. As far as he was concerned, the train could sit there as long as it pleased. He glanced out at the big black bird on the wire. *If we do wait a long time, you'll starve before I do.*

The conductor was a tall, pale, skinny man who looked as if

he'd been working on trains forever. "Well, I'll tell you," he said in a broad Down East accent. "Th' engineer calls it sabotage." He stretched out the final *a* till it seemed to last about a minute and a half.

"Sabotage!" Half a dozen people in the car echoed the word; all of them pronounced it much faster than the conductor had.

"Ayuh," he said. Dowling needed a moment to understand that meant yes. "Hole in the track up ahead. Hole in the *ground* up ahead. Damn *big* hole." He spoke with a certain dismal satisfaction.

"How long are we going to be stuck here?" the important-looking man asked. "My missing that meeting would be a disaster— a disaster, I tell you."

"Well, if you care to, you can walk." The conductor stretched that last *a* as far as he had the one in *sabotage*. The important-looking man glared furiously. Several other people snickered. That only made Mr. Urgent Meeting more unhappy. The conductor continued, "They got a crew workin' on it. Be another hour, hour and a half, I reckon."

Some passengers sighed. Some groaned. The important-looking man fumed. Dowling wondered just how much sabotage the Confederates were bringing off in the USA. *Not as much as we are in the CSA, I hope.* He also wondered how Lucullus Wood and the other stubborn blacks in Kentucky were doing. Maybe the Confederates would have hit Ohio even harder than they had if not for Negro sabotage. But they'd hit plenty hard enough as things were, dammit.

The promised hour to an hour and a half stretched out to closer to three. Dowling hadn't expected anything different. The crow or raven flew away. The important-looking man almost had a fit of apoplexy. Dowling almost hoped he would.

By the time the general got into Philadelphia, night had fallen. The train crawled in with blackout curtains over the windows and with no light on the engine. No one knew if Confederate bombers would come over; no one wanted to give them targets if they did. The station had black cloth awnings stretched over the platforms. Dim lights gathered arriving passengers through double curtains of black cloth into the more brightly lit interior.

"General Dowling?" The officer who waited inside was tall and lean and fair—pale, really—almost to the point of ghostliness. He wore eagles on his shoulder straps. His arm-of-service colors were the gold and black of the General Staff.

"Hello, Colonel Abell," Dowling said stiffly. *Et tu, Brute?* was what went through his mind. He had not got on well with General Staff officers since the days of the Great War. Part of that was guilt by association; he'd served with George Custer and Irving Morrell, both men who had little use for the stay-at-homes in Philadelphia and weren't shy about letting those stay-at-homes know it. And part of it was that Abner Dowling felt the same way. If John Abell and his fellow high foreheads were to help the Joint Committee on the Conduct of the War ease Dowling out . . .

"We have a car waiting for you, sir," Abell said. "If you'll just come with me . . ."

"I have a suitcase," Dowling said.

"It will be taken care of," the bloodless General Staff officer promised. "That sort of thing, after all, is why God made enlisted men."

He led Dowling out to a Chevrolet with headlights reduced to slits. A dent in one fender said the little bit of light they threw hadn't always been enough. "Nice of you to meet me," Dowling said as they got in. The driver—an enlisted man—started up the engine and put the auto in gear.

Colonel Abell lit a cigarette and offered Dowling the pack. He leaned close to give Dowling a light. Then he smiled—a surprisingly charming smile from someone usually so cold. "Don't worry, General," he said, amusement—amusement? yes, definitely amusement—lurking in his voice. "Our interests here run in the same direction."

"Do they?" Dowling said. Had the General Staff officer told him the sun was shining, he would have gone to a window and checked.

Abell laughed. The noise was slightly rusty, as if from disuse, but unmistakable. "As a matter of fact, they do. You don't want the Joint Committee crucifying you for losing Ohio, and the War Department doesn't want the Joint Committee crucifying it for allowing Ohio to be lost."

"Ah," Dowling said. That *did* make sense. In the War of Secession, the Joint Committee on the Conduct of the War had run rampant over the Army. No wonder Colonel Abell and his superiors were anxious to avoid a repeat performance.

"Are you a quick study, General?" Abell asked.

"Tolerably," Dowling answered. Anyone who'd served under Custer had to be a quick study, to find ways to get his superior out of the trouble he insisted on getting himself into. "Why?"

"Listen to me for about twenty minutes. With things the way they are, getting you to BOQ will take that long anyhow." Colonel Abell proceeded to fill Dowling's head with the inadequacies of U.S. military budgets, starting in the early 1920s and continuing to the present day. Dowling found himself nodding again and again. Abell finished, "You know perfectly well we could have put up a much stronger defense in Ohio if we'd had more and better matériel. I want you to let the Joint Committee know, too."

"They won't want to hear it," Dowling said. "Congress never wants to hear that anything is its fault. But I will tell them. I'll be delighted to—and I thank you for the chapter and verse."

"My pleasure, sir," Abell said as the Chevrolet pulled up in front of Bachelor Officer Quarters.

"Not altogether, Colonel," Dowling said. "Not altogether."

His suitcase had beaten him there. He wondered how that had happened. He slept better than he'd thought he would, and it wasn't just because the Confederates didn't come over that night.

The next morning, as another noncom drove him to the hall where the Joint Committee met, he got a look at what the bombers had done to Philadelphia when they did come over. It wasn't pretty. On the other hand, he'd seen worse in Ohio. Oddly, that thought steadied him. When he got to the hall and was sworn in, his first interrogator was a white-maned Socialist Senator from Idaho, a state that might never have seen a real, live Confederate and surely had never seen a hostile one. "Well, General, to what besides your own incompetence do you ascribe our failures in Ohio?" the Senator brayed.

"Sir, I think one of our worst problems is the fact that Congress put so little money into the military after the end of the Great War," Dowling answered. "And when the Confederates did start loading up, we didn't try to match them as hard as we might have. As I recall, sir"—as Colonel Abell had briefed him—"you last voted for an increased military appropriation in 1928—or was it '27?"

He'd heard about men standing with their mouths hanging open while nothing came out. He wasn't sure he'd ever seen it, not till that moment. The sight was sweeter than the sugar he'd spooned into his morning coffee. After close to half a minute, the Senator recovered enough to say, "How dare you blame this august body for your own dismal failings?"

"Sir, war's been staring us in the face ever since Jake Featherston got elected. That's almost eight years ago now," Dowling said. "Anyone could see it. Plenty of people did see it. Why was Congress so slow about giving us the money to build and develop the tools we need to lick the son of a bitch?"

More bellows and barks followed, but the Senator from Idaho seemed more than a little disconcerted by answers he hadn't expected. He acted relieved to turn the grilling over to a Congresswoman from New York City. Flora Blackford said, "Instead of snarling at each other, what can Congress and the Army do to work together and gain the victory we have to have?"

A sensible question! Dowling had wondered if he'd hear any. "Get all our factories humming," he answered. "Make sure the raw materials reach them. Make sure the weapons reach the front. Keep the Confederates as busy as we can—never let 'em relax. Uh, knock Utah flat. And while we're at it, get the niggers in the CSA plenty of guns, as many as we can. That'll make sure Featherston's boys stay hopping."

It went on and on. There was more hostility from the committee members, but also, increasingly, a wary respect. Dowling had no idea whether they were really listening to him or just posturing for the hometown papers. He also had no idea whether he was saving his career or sinking it forever. The strange thing was, he didn't care. And it was amazing how liberating that could be.

Jake Featherston looked at the engineer in his cramped, glassed-in booth. Saul Goldman was in there with the engineer. The little Jew didn't usually look over people's shoulders like that—he wasn't pushy, the way sheenies were supposed to be. But this was a big speech. Featherston was glad to see Goldman there. When something needed doing, the director of communications made sure he was on the spot.

The engineer pointed through the glass. Jake nodded. The light on the wall above the booth glowed red. He was on.

"I'm Jake Featherston," he said, "and I'm here to tell you the truth." How many times had he said that on the wireless? More than he could count, by now. While he was saying it, he believed it every single time, too. That was what let him make other people believe it right along with him.

"Truth is, we never wanted this here war with the United States. Truth is, they forced it on us when they wouldn't listen to our reasonable demands. Well, now they've paid the price for being stupid. They've got their country cut in half, and they've seen they can't hope to stand against us. Our cause is just and right, and that only makes us stronger.

"But I'm a reasonable man. I've always been a reasonable man. I want to show I don't hold a grudge. And so I'm going to offer terms to the USA, and I do believe they're terms so kind and generous that nobody could possibly say no to 'em.

"First off, as soon as the United States agree to 'em, we'll pull out of U.S. territory fast as we can. We didn't want Yankees on our soil in 1917, and we don't want to be on theirs now." He'd won, or come as close to winning as didn't matter to him. Now was the time to sound magnanimous. "All we want is what's rightfully ours. I'll tell you what I mean.

"At the end of the last war the USA took Sequoyah and chunks of Virginia and Sonora away from us. We want our country back. We've got a right to have our country back. And it's only fitting and proper for the United States to give back everything they took."

In the engineer's booth, Saul Goldman nodded vigorously. Saul was a good guy, as solid as they came. If he worried a little more than most Freedom Party men, well, what could you expect from a Jew? Plenty of Party men had all the balls in the world. Featherston knew he needed some with brains, too. Goldman fit the bill there.

"And it's only fitting and proper that the United States should pay back the reparations they squeezed out of us when we were down," Featherston went on. "Paying them killed our currency and damn near ruined us. There was a time when, instead of carrying your money to the store in your pocket and your groceries home in your basket, you needed the basket for your money and you could take home what you bought in your pocket. We don't ever want that to happen again."

He didn't mention that the United States had stopped demanding reparations after a Freedom Party man gunned down the Confederate President in Alabama. If Grady Calkins hadn't died in that park, Jake would have killed him. He would have stretched it out over days, maybe even weeks, to make sure Calkins suffered the way he should have. The assassin had come closer to murdering the Party than any of its enemies.

And if the United States came down with their own case of galloping inflation . . . If they did, wouldn't that just be *too* bad. Jake grinned wolfishly. Seeing the USA in trouble would break his heart, all right.

"We don't want to have to worry about Yankee aggression any more, either," he went on. "We don't mind if the United States keep their forts around Washington. That's all right. George Washington was the father of their country, too, even if he was a good Virginian. But except for those, we want a disarmed border. No more forts within a hundred miles of the frontier. No barrels within a hundred miles, either, or war airplanes. We will have the right to send inspectors into the USA to make sure the Yankees hold up their end of the bargain."

He didn't say anything about letting U.S. inspectors travel on the Confederate side of the border. There were good reasons why he didn't, chief among them that the only way he intended to let U.S. inspectors into the CSA was over his dead body. After the Great War, U.S. snoops had worn out their welcome in a hurry. He didn't intend to dismantle his fortifications, either, or to move back his fighters and bombers and armor. The United States had let down their guard after the Great War. He wasn't about to make the same mistake.

Saul Goldman had stopped nodding. He wore a frown. He wanted to make *really* easy terms with the USA. Featherston couldn't see that. He was on top, by God. What point to being on top if you didn't take advantage of it? And he needed to squeeze the United States while he *was* on top. They were bigger and richer and more populous than the Confederate States. He never forgot that. No Confederate leader could afford to forget it. However badly the Whigs had botched the Great War, it had proved the Yankees could be dangerous foes, not just a bunch of bumbling fools.

Featherston continued, "And both we and the United States have internal troubles we need to deal with. Unlike some countries I could name, *we* don't interfere in other nations' private business." He didn't care about selling the Mormons of Deseret down the river. The USA didn't need to know he'd supplied the Mormons with weapons and advice. The damnyankees could probably figure it out for themselves, but figuring it out and proving it were two different critters.

And the damnyankees might think he would wait till this war was over to settle accounts with blacks in the CSA. He wanted to laugh. He was going to take care of that business anyway, come hell or high water.

"It's a shame we had to fight again," he said. "Now that things are decided, let's get back to business as usual. It's time for peace. We only want what's ours. Too bad we had to go to war to get it, but that's how things work out sometimes. I'm just waiting on Al Smith to set things to rights. Thank you, and good night."

The red light went out. He wasn't on the air any more. He gathered up his speech and left the soundproofed studio. Saul Goldman came out into the hallway to meet him and be the first to shake his hand. "I think that went very well, Mr. President," Goldman said.

"Thank you kindly, Saul," Featherston said. "Me, too, matter of fact."

"I hope President Smith takes you up on it," the director of communications said. He was good, amazingly good, at what he did, but no, he didn't have the fire in his belly that a lot of Freedom Party men did.

"So do I. I expect he will," Jake said. "Why wouldn't he? It's been two months, hardly even that, and we've knocked the snot out of the USA. We've done a damn sight better than the French and the British and the Russians have against Germany and Austria-Hungary, and you can take that to the bank."

Goldman nodded at that last. As they had in the last war, the Russians had tried to drown the Central Powers in oceans of blood. Against the barrels and artillery the new Kaiser's army could hurl at them, they'd made small gains for high cost—though Jake did think the Central Powers were going to lose most of the Ukraine, which had always been more nearly subject than ally.

France had reached the Rhine, driving through the rugged country to the west of the river. But she hadn't been able to cross the river, and the Germans claimed they were rallying. *Action Française* denied that with particular venom, which made Jake all the more inclined to believe it true. And the British end run through Norway had accomplished nothing but infuriating the Norwegians and pushing them over to the German side. Churchill had got himself a black eye with that one.

Only the Anglo-French thrust through the Low Countries was still going well. The Belgians had welcomed the French and British as liberators, the way the Ukrainians welcomed the Russians. The Dutch were more pro-German, but the Germans had had a lot of other things on their plate. Holland was lost to them, and some of the North German plain. If Hamburg fell . . . But it hadn't fallen yet.

Jake's smile showed sharp teeth. His allies might be having trouble, but he'd done what he'd set out to do. "Yeah, I reckon Smith'll come around," he said. *Come across* came closer to what he really meant.

"I do hope he does," Saul Goldman said earnestly. "I wish you hadn't put in that part about demilitarizing the border. He won't like that."

"He may not like it, but he'll swallow it," Featherston said. "I know my man."

He thought he did. He'd slickered Smith into agreeing to the plebiscite that brought Kentucky and the abortion called Houston back into the CSA. And Smith had believed him when he said he wouldn't put troops into the redeemed states for years. Finding an excuse to do what you needed to do anyway was never hard.

If Smith could be suckered on a deal like that, couldn't he also be suckered into leaving himself open for the next punch Jake Featherston planned to throw? Jake didn't see why not. The Yankees needed one more licking after this one, maybe even two, before they'd roll over and play dead for a good long time, the way they had after the War of Secession and the Second Mexican War. And Smith was dumb enough and weak enough—ballsless enough—to cave in one more time. Jake was so sure . . . "Bet you a stonewall," he said.

"Sir?" Goldman said.

"Five dollars in gold says Al Smith caves."

The communications director shook his head. "I wouldn't bet

against you, Mr. President. You've shown you know what you're doing. I hope you're right again."

He wasn't saying that for the sake of flattery. More than most people around Jake, he spoke his mind. And Featherston didn't think he declined the bet because he was a cheap Jew, either. That was a measure of the respect Jake had for Goldman. The other man had turned it down because he'd thought he would lose, which was a hell of a good reason to turn down a bet.

"I reckon I am." Jake generally thought he was right, and he generally *was* right. He'd proved it again and again, in the Freedom Party's rise and in the way things had gone since he took the oath of office.

He was on his way back to the Gray House through the blacked-out streets of Richmond when air-raid sirens began to scream. The racket penetrated even the bulletproof glass of his armored limousine. So did the harsh, flat *crump*s of exploding Yankee bombs a few minutes later.

"You want me to find a shelter for you, Mr. President?" the driver asked.

The man was a Freedom Party guard. He was as tough as they came. He wasn't worried about his own neck, only about Featherston's safety. Jake knew that. All the same, he wished Willy Knight's hired guns hadn't done in Virgil Joyner. His old driver hadn't just taken care of him. He'd *known* him, as much as any man could.

Jake had to answer this fellow. "Hell, no, Mike," he said. "Keep going—that's all. We'll be back pretty damn quick, and this here auto can take anything but a direct hit."

"All right, sir." The driver's broad shoulders moved up and down in a shrug. "Reckoned I better ask. You suppose this raid is the damnyankees' answer to you?"

That was a different question, and a different kind of question. After a moment's thought, Featherston shook his head and said, "No, I don't believe so. They'll need a while to think about it. This here is nothing but business as usual."

He did go to the shelter when he got to the Presidential residence. He didn't want to; he would rather have stayed out and watched the show. But he knew he had to keep himself safe. Nobody else was up to the job of leading the CSA against the USA—nobody came close. The Yankees stayed over Richmond for close to two hours. Not all their bombs hit targets worth hitting, but the Confederates had the same problem when they bombed U.S. cities. Featherston still hoped Al Smith would say yes to him. The USA hadn't gone away yet, though.

Clarence Potter listened to U.S. wireless broadcasts. Had he been just anybody in the CSA, he might have got in trouble for that. But rank had its privileges. So did belonging to Intelligence. He needed to know what the enemy was saying.

Finding out wasn't always easy. The CSA and the USA jammed each other's stations. Very often, in places as close to the border as Richmond, you got nothing but howls of static as you spun the dial.

As usual, though, patience paid off. So did a wireless set a good deal more sensitive than the ones ordinary Confederates could buy. Potter brought in a Philadelphia station that broadcast President Smith's response to President Featherston's call for an end to the fighting.

Smith wasn't half—wasn't a quarter—the speaker Featherston was. All the same, he left no doubt about where he stood. Through buzzes and hisses and pops, he said, "The United States have lost a battle. We have not lost the war. As John Paul Jones said when the British called on him to surrender, 'I have not yet begun to fight!' By treacherously attacking after loudly pledging peace, the Confederate States have gained an early advantage. I cannot deny that. I cannot conceal it. I do not intend to try. But we are still in the fight. We will stay in the fight. And wars are not decided by who starts ahead, but by who wins in the end. In the Great War, the CSA occupied Washington and threatened Philadelphia. We won even so. We can win again. We will win again. Jake Featherston has shown he is a man who cannot be trusted even when he sounds most reasonable. He has shown he cannot be trusted *especially* when he sounds most reasonable. We will not disarm. We will not open our borders to future aggression. This war is not over. The Confederate States started it. We will finish it. Good day."

"Shit," Clarence Potter said, and turned off the wireless. Al Smith had been slow figuring out his Confederate opponent, but he had Jake Featherston down cold now. And if the United States wouldn't curl up and die just because they'd taken a hard right to the chops, the Confederate States would have to knock them flat. Could they?

We're going to find out, Potter thought unhappily. Standing toe to toe with a bigger foe and trading punches till one side couldn't stand up any more hadn't worked during the Great War. Would it this time?

Potter shrugged. The Confederate States were better at knocking things flat than they had been a generation earlier. Unfortunately, so were the United States. The attack on Richmond the night before had been one of the worst of the war. Confederate antiaircraft gunners had fired away like madmen. Searchlights had swung through the sky. Fighters had searched the blackness for the U.S. bombers tormenting their city. But only a handful of Yankee airplanes had gone down.

The North American air war struck Potter as a duel with machine guns at a pace and a half. The CSA and USA faced each other across a long, long border. When they started smashing up each other's cities, they could hardly miss. The Confederates had got off to a better start. They'd begun gearing up for the war before their enemies had, and they'd begun with the advantage of surprise.

But the damnyankees hadn't thrown up their hands or thrown in the sponge. That they would try to ride out the CSA's first blows, stay in the war, and use their greater numbers and strength had always been Potter's worst fear. Placed where he was, he thought he understood the USA better than most of his countrymen (including Jake Featherston) did. He looked like he was right, too. That worried him.

The United States were still cut in half. Potter nodded to himself—that would help a lot. Even the biggest body still needed food. If the factories in the Northeast couldn't get the raw materials they had to have, they couldn't make guns and shells for all the millions of U.S. soldiers to shoot at their Confederate counterparts. And if the USA's soldiers couldn't shoot, what difference did it make how many of them there were? They'd lose any which way.

If I were a Yankee logistics officer, what would I be doing now? Potter wondered. He had a pretty good idea. He'd be seeing what he could get aboard freighters on the Great Lakes, and he'd be seeing how much the Canadian railroad lines north of Lake Superior could carry and how fast he could bump up their capacity.

And would all that add up to anything that could replace the rail lines and highways the Confederacy had cut? Not a chance in church. Potter didn't need to be a logistics officer to know that much. Would it add up to enough to keep the United States breathing? That was a harder question, and one for which he didn't have the answer. Neither did anybody else in the Confederate States. In one sense, that was why people fought wars: to find out such things.

Lost in calculations—and even more lost because he didn't have all the information he needed to make them—Potter jumped a little when the telephone rang. "Intelligence—Potter speaking," he said into the mouthpiece; no one on the other end of the line would know he'd been startled.

"Hello, Potter, you sly son of a bitch." That was Jake Featherston's perpetually angry rasp.

"Good morning, Mr. President. To what do I owe the honor of this call?" Potter, on the other hand, was perpetually ironic, or near enough to make no difference: an asset for an Intelligence officer.

Featherston went on, "You're laughing your ass off, aren't you, on account of you figured the United States'd keep fighting and most folks here didn't? I didn't myself, and that's a fact. I reckoned Al Smith'd see reason." He sounded angry that Smith hadn't, too.

Of course, what he called reason meant *what Jake Featherston wants.* Featherston didn't, couldn't, see that. And Al Smith finally saw it clearly. Potter said, "Sir, I'm not laughing. There's nothing funny about it. I wish the United States had rolled over and played dead, believe you me I do."

"Well, if they won't roll over, we goddamn well have to *roll* 'em over," Featherston said. He didn't quit when things failed to go the way he wanted them to. That was one of the things that made him so dangerous—and so successful.

"Yes, sir." Potter had a good deal of stubbornness in his system, too. He didn't like admitting, even to himself, that the President of the CSA had more. But he knew it was true, however little he liked it. "What can I do for you now? Besides not gloating, I mean?"

After a couple of seconds of surprised silence, Featherston offered him an anatomically unlikely suggestion. Then the President of the CSA laughed. "You've got your nerve, don't you?" He sounded more admiring than otherwise. "We've got to keep the damnyankees hopping, is what we've got to do. What sort of ways can you pump up those Mormon maniacs in Utah?"

"It would be easier if you hadn't offered them to the USA on a platter," Potter said dryly.

"Potter, it doesn't matter for hell—not for hell, you hear me?" Featherston said. "If the Devil could get those sorry sons of bitches guns, they'd take 'em and they wouldn't say boo. You gonna tell me I'm wrong about that?"

"Not me," Clarence Potter said, and he meant it. "The Mormons love the USA about as much as our niggers love the Freedom Party."

"Yeah." For once, Featherston sounded not only unhappy but also unsure of himself. He rarely hesitated, but he did now. At last, he went on, "Goddamn Yankees know about that, too. They use it to give our nuts a twist whenever they can. That one's a bitch to get a handle on."

One way to reduce the problem would have been to give Negroes in the CSA privileges to match those of whites. The Whigs had taken tentative steps in that direction during the Great War—they'd granted Confederate citizenship, as opposed to mere residence, to colored men who honorably completed a term of service in the C.S. Army. Potter had never thought that was a smart idea. What had it done but given a large cadre of Negroes training in how to shoot white men and the certain knowledge that they could?

He said, "The harder we press the United States on their home grounds, the harder the time they'll have poking us down here."

"That's how I figure it, too," Featherston said. "The best defense is giving the other bastard a good kick in the teeth before he gets his dukes up." If that wasn't Jake Featherston to the core, Potter had never heard anything that would be. Like a lot of things Featherston said, it held its share of truth. Also like a lot of things the President said, it wasn't so simple as he made it out to be.

"Even if Smith did say no, we're off to a pretty good start on that," Potter said.

"You bet we are," Featherston said, though he still sounded furious that the President of the USA hadn't done as he'd hoped. "Reason I called you, though—along with the Mormon business, I should say—is that I want your people to step up sabotage east of what we're holding in Ohio. The United States are building up to try and cut off the base of our salient, and I want 'em to have all the trouble they can handle doing it—all they can handle and then some."

"I'll take care of it, Mr. President," Potter said. That was his bailiwick, all right. "Do you have anything in particular in mind, or just general mischief?"

"Always general mischief," Featherston answered, "but not just general mischief. If nasty things happen to bridges strong enough to take barrels, the Yankees'll have a harder time coming at us, and that's what I've got in mind."

"Yes, sir," Potter said crisply, even though he couldn't help adding, "Bombing will help, too."

Jake Featherston had a nasty laugh most of the time. He sure did now. "Don't teach your granny to suck eggs. Trouble is, the high-level bombers are good for tearing hell out of a city, but the only way they can hit a bridge is fool luck. Our airplane and bombsight makers kind of sold us a bill of goods on that one."

"Looks like the USA's people sold them the same bill of goods," Potter remarked.

"Yeah, you got that right. Those high-forehead types are the same wherever you find 'em." With one casual sentence, Featherston dismissed scientists and intellectuals. He went on without even noticing what he'd done: "Mules, now, Mules can hit bridges they aim at. But the damnyankees have got antiaircraft guns coming out of their assholes, and Asskickers turn out to be sitting ducks when the other guy's waiting for them. We've lost more airplanes and more pilots than we can afford. So . . . sabotage where we can."

Again, that made sense. Featherston, after all, had spent three years in combat in the Great War. He'd been in at the start, and he'd still been shooting at the Yankees when the Confederacy finally threw in the sponge. When he talked about the battlefield, he knew what he was talking about.

"Sabotage where we can," Potter agreed. "I'll see who's in place in that area—and then we'll find out who talks a good game and who's serious about this business."

"Fair-weather friends," Featherston fleered.

"It happens, sir," Potter said. "Happens all the time, in fact. Some people just talk about helping us. Some will pass information, but that's all. Some, though, some *will* put their necks on the line."

"I reckon you'll know which ones are which," Featherston said.

"I have my notions, but I could be wrong," Potter said. "It's not like giving orders to soldiers, sir. These men are volunteers, and we mostly can't coerce them if they don't do what we say. They're behind the enemy's lines, after all. If we push them too hard, they can just go . . . selectively deaf, you might say."

"They better not, by God." Rage clotted the President's voice. "Might be worth exposing one or two who don't go along to the damnyankees. That'd make the rest shape up."

Pour encourager les autres, Potter thought, but Jake Featherston wouldn't have heard of Voltaire, not in a million years. Potter remembered having a similar notion himself. Thinking like the President worried him. He spoke carefully: "We need to make sure we don't scare people away from working with us."

"Handle that. I reckon you know how," Featherston said.

"I hope so, Mr. President." *And I hope you go on remembering it.* But Clarence Potter knew saying that would do more harm than good. He could come closer than many to being frank with the man he'd once known as a sergeant. Coming closer, though, wasn't the same as going all the way. Potter also knew that, only too well.

Colonel Irving Morrell rode along with his head and shoulders out of the cupola on his barrel's turret. He'd been doing that since the Great War, when he'd had a machine gun mounted in front of the barrel commander's hatch. Most good barrel commanders rode that way whenever they could. You could see so much more when you were actually out there looking. Riding buttoned up and peering through periscopes wasn't the same.

Of course, the better you could see, the better the enemy could see you. Barrel commanders who exposed themselves too much turned into casualties in short order. Morrell didn't want to be a casualty. He had Agnes and Mildred at home, and he hoped to come back to them. He couldn't let that get in the way of doing his job, though. Unless things improved in a hurry, the United States were in trouble.

Here, at least, he didn't have to worry so much about getting picked off. He wasn't trying to keep the Confederates from reaching the Great Lakes any more. They'd already done it. His guessing they would try that crippling stroke consoled him only a little. *I should have been more ready to stop them, dammit.*

Given what he'd had to work with, he supposed he'd done

about as well as he could. The CSA had got serious about fighting before the USA had, and the United States were paying the price.

A green-gray barrel had pulled off the road under the shade of a spreading elm. Two men were attacking the engine with wrench and pliers. One of them aimed an obscene gesture into the air as Morrell's barrel clattered by. The rest of the crew sprawled on the grass in the shade, smoking cigarettes and probably thanking God they were out of the war—if only for a little while.

Barrels broke down more often than Morrell wished they did. They were large, heavy, complicated machines often forced to go as hard as they possibly could. In the Great War, breakdowns had put far more of them out of action than enemy fire had. Things weren't quite so bad so far in this fight, but they weren't good. From what Morrell had seen, C.S. barrels needed repair about as often as their U.S. counterparts. That was something, anyhow.

The highway leading from Martins Ferry, Ohio, down toward Round Bottom would need repair, too, after the column of barrels finished going by. Pavement plenty good enough for motorcars crumbled when caterpillar treads supporting fifteen or twenty times the weight of a motorcar dug into it. Morrell's barrel took newly gouged potholes and chunks of asphalt gouged out of the surface in stride.

Several barrels ahead of Morrell's had halted at a stream called—he checked the map—Sunfish Creek. "What the hell?" Morrell said, or perhaps something a little more pungent than that. He ducked down into his barrel to get on the wireless to the leading machine. "Why aren't you moving forward?" he demanded.

"Sir, the bridge is out," answered the lieutenant commanding that barrel.

"What the hell?" Morrell said again—or, again, words to that effect. "How did that happen? I hadn't heard anything about it."

"It looks blown, sir," the lieutenant said.

This time, Morrell's profanity drew a glance of wonder and admiration from Sergeant Michael Pound. Morrell tore the earphones off his head, climbed out of his halted barrel, and trotted south toward Sunfish Creek. He'd been wounded in the leg not long after the Great War started. Even after all these years, the thigh muscle twinged painfully when he exerted himself. That pain was as much a part of him as the thud of his heartbeat. He paid it no more mind.

Sun dapples sparkled across the surface of the stream. Oaks and willows grew down close to the bank. Thrushes hopped beneath them, careless of man's killing tools close by. Midges droned. Morrell smelled engine exhaust, hot iron, his own sweat, and, under them, the cool green odors of vegetation and running water.

Sunfish Creek flowed swiftly. That meant it was probably more than three feet deep: the depth a barrel could ford without special preparation. And someone had dropped the bridge across the creek right into it. The concrete span had a good fifteen-foot gap blown from the center. If it wasn't a professional job, the amateur who'd done it sure had promise.

"You see, sir," said the lieutenant in the lead barrel.

"I see, all right," Morrell agreed grimly. "I see sabotage, that's what I see. Somebody ought to dance at the end of a rope for this."

"Er—yes, sir." That didn't seem to have occurred to the young officer. "But who?"

"We'll set the constables or county sheriffs or whatever they've got at Round Bottom trying to figure that out," Morrell answered. "Have you sent men into the creek to find a ford?"

"Not yet, sir," the lieutenant said.

"Then do that, by God," Morrell told him. "I'll be damned if I'm going to sit around here with my thumb up my ass waiting for Army engineers to repair this span."

Two crews' worth of barrel men emerged from their machines. They seemed glad to strip off their coveralls and plunge, naked, into Sunfish Creek. The day was hot and sticky, and they'd been cooped up inside iron bake ovens since sunrise. In fact, the men seemed more inclined to swim and splash one another than to do what needed doing. "Quit skylarking, you sorry bastards!" the lieutenant shouted. "Do you want to keep Colonel Morrell waiting?"

Morrell was gratified to find that the question *did* get the men moving. If it hadn't, he would have jumped into the creek himself. The water looked mighty inviting. "Here you go!" a man shouted from downstream, his voice thin across perhaps a hundred yards of distance. "I can keep my balls dry all the way across—there's a little sandbar or something right here."

How badly would a column of barrels tear up that sandbar? Enough to flood the machines that came at the end? Some officers would have hesitated. Morrell didn't, not for an instant. "Well done!" he yelled to the soldier. "Go on over to the far side and mark the ford. We'll cross to you."

"Can't I get my clothes back first?" the man asked.

"No. One of your buddies will bring them. You can dress on the other side," Morrell told him. He turned to the lieutenant and added two words: "Get moving."

"Uh, yes, sir," the youngster said. He didn't get moving quite so fast as Morrell would have liked; one of the crews looking for a ford was his. They reluctantly emerged, all dripping and cool-looking, and even more reluctantly dressed again. Still, less than five minutes went by before the barrel's engine came to flatulent life. As soon as it did, Morrell jogged back to his own machine.

"A ford, sir?" Sergeant Pound asked when he got in again. Unlike that lieutenant, Pound seemed capable of independent thought. Morrell didn't have to provide the brains for him.

"That's right," the officer answered. "A ford—but a sabotaged bridge."

"We ought to take hostages," Pound said. "If there's any more trouble, we ought to execute them." Everything seemed simple to him.

"Unfortunately, this is our own country," Morrell pointed out.

"Well, sir, in that case the people around here ought to act like it," Pound said. "If they don't, they don't deserve our protection, do they?" He was calm, reasonable, and altogether bloodthirsty.

Here, Morrell was inclined to agree with him. Wasn't helping armed enemies of the United States treason? Weren't they shooting and hanging Mormons out in Utah for doing things like blowing bridges? Why shouldn't the same rules apply here in Ohio? Morrell had no answers, only questions. Setting policy wasn't his job. Carrying it out was.

He found no help in Round Bottom, Ohio, which turned out to be nothing but a wide spot in the road—and not a very wide spot, at that. It had neither policemen nor sheriff. It had a general store, a saloon, and eight or ten houses. A sign in front of the general store said WELCOME TO ROUND BOTTOM. POPULATION 29. The census-takers had been there before the war. If half that many people lived in the hamlet now, Morrell would have been astonished.

He had to check the map to find the closest real town: Woodsfield, the seat—such as it was—of Monroe County. He sent a barrel west to inform the local sheriff of the sabotage. It didn't get there as fast as he would have liked. A wireless message came crackling: "Sir, the road goes over something called Sandingstone Run."

Morrell had to look at the map again to find out where Sandingstone Run was. He discovered it was, of all things, a tributary to Sunfish Creek. "Well?" he said ominously.

"Sir, the bridge is blown," the barrel commander said.

That disgusted Morrell without surprising him. "Find a ford," he growled. "Don't waste time doing it, either. By the look of that run on the map, if you piss in it you'll send it over its banks."

He got a burst of startled laughter. "It's a little bigger than that, sir, but not a hell of a lot," the barrel commander said. "All right. We'll take care of it."

Fifteen minutes later, the barrel commander reported he was over the stream. *Another delay*, Morrell thought unhappily. And how many more bridges in eastern Ohio had gone splashing into the streams they crossed? More than a few, unless he missed his guess.

Maybe I should have gone to Woodsfield myself, he thought. A sheriff would pay more attention to a bird colonel than he would to Joe Blow in a barrel. Then Morrell laughed at himself. Anybody in a barrel could command attention. All he had to do was aim his cannon at the sheriff's station and threaten to start blowing things up unless he got what he wanted. Civilians couldn't do much about that except knuckle under.

And then Morrell remembered Featherston Fizzes. Somebody in what had been the state of Houston had figured out that a bottle of gasoline with a lit wick would set a barrel on fire easy as you please. Barrels were inflammable things any which way, what with paint and grease all over them. Spill burning gasoline down through the engine-decking louvers onto the motor and you really had yourself a problem.

"Sir?" The barrel commander's voice sounded in his earphones.

"I'm here," Morrell said.

"Yes, sir. Well, truth is, this town got bombed to hell and gone back I don't know when—not too long ago. Sheriff's dead. Nobody's sent out a replacement yet."

"Oh, for Christ's sake," Morrell said. But it wasn't that surprising. A replacement for a county sheriff would have been chosen in Columbus. Columbus had had other things to worry about than sending somebody with a badge out to a place where nothing ever happened anyway. These days, the Stars and Bars, damn them, flew over the capital of Ohio. Nobody there would care about Monroe County now.

"What do you want me to do, sir?" the barrel commander asked.

"Hold your position. We'll move up and join you. Describe where the ford is relative to the bridge," Morrell said. He got the column moving again. They rumbled through forest country. A sniper could have had a field day picking off barrel commanders. But there were no snipers. *The things I'm grateful for these days,* Morrell thought sourly. How much delay would the blown bridges between here and the start of the counteroffensive impose? And what would that do to the attack when it did get going? Nothing good. He shook his head. No, nothing good at all.

XI

Mary Pomeroy didn't like going to the post office in Rosenfeld any more. Wilf Rokeby knew too much. He never said anything, not after the first time, but he knew. Sooner or later, she was going to have to do something about that. She hadn't figured out what yet. Whatever it was, it had to be something that didn't draw suspicion down on her.

She wished she didn't see the need. But he had a hold on her. He could use it to blackmail her, or he could go to the occupying authorities. He'd got along with them ever since 1914. He'd had to get along with them if he wanted to stay postmaster—and, as far as Mary could tell, being postmaster had been his whole life, even if he was finally retiring at the end of the year. He'd never married. He lived by himself. Maybe because he was so fussy and precise, some people wondered if he was a pansy, but nobody had anything even resembling proof of that. It was just something to gossip about when folks were in a more scandalous mood than usual.

A bomb? Bombs were always Mary's first thought. She was, after all, her father's daughter. Arthur McGregor had hit back hard at the Yanks for years till his luck ran out. But Wilf would surely be alert to anything that came in the post. As far as Mary could see, the only thing worse than not trying to get rid of him was trying and failing. That would surely send him off to the authorities.

Poison? Similar objection. She could bake an apple pie, lace it with rat poison, and smile sweetly while she gave it to him. No matter how sweetly she smiled, though, would he eat any of the pie? Would he eat more than one bite if it tasted even the least bit funny? Not likely.

Pretending the brakes on the auto failed and running him down in the street? She could do it, but she didn't see how she could keep from going to jail once she did. That wasn't what she had in mind.

Frustration gnawed at her. What she really wanted was to plant bombs on the railroad tracks outside of town. Canadian railroads were suddenly a lot more important to the USA than they had been before the war. The Yanks couldn't ship through their own country, because the Confederates had split it in two (and the Mormons were also sitting astride one of their transcontinental routes). If they wanted to move things from west to east or from east to west, they had to go through Canada. Damaging the railroads could really hurt them now.

But damaging the railroads would also make Wilf Rokeby sit up and take notice. And what would he do if he did take notice? Mary couldn't tell. She couldn't very well ask him, either. He wouldn't give her a straight answer, and the question would only put his wind up.

That left . . . waiting and seeing what happened next. Mary didn't like that. It meant the ball was in Wilf's hands. What happened next might be U.S. soldiers—or, worse, Quebecois soldiers—banging on her door in the middle of the night. If they searched the apartment building, they would find her bomb-making tools. Everything would be all over then. She wondered if she could die as bravely as her brother, Alexander, had during the Great War. She had her doubts. Alexander hadn't been old enough to believe death could really happen to him. Mary knew better.

The irony was, Canada had started seething like a pot coming to the boil since the war broke out. Fresh signs had gone up in the post office, warning not just of Japanese spies (a ridiculous notion in Rosenfeld) but also of British agents (perhaps not so ridiculous after all). The *Rosenfeld Register* trumpeted out the same warnings.

Pointing to one of those stories in the weekly, Mary said, "Seems some of us remember the mother country after all."

"Does look that way." Mort Pomeroy eyed her from across the dining-room table. "You don't want to say that kind of thing outside the apartment, though, or to anybody but me."

Such were the lessons of occupation. Mary had learned them,

too. She nodded. "I know, Mort. You didn't marry a fool." *You married a bomber's daughter. You knew that. You still don't know you married a bomber, too.*

He smiled. "I wouldn't have married a fool. That's not what I was looking for."

And Mary found what *she* was looking for a few days later, in Karamanlides' general store. She didn't realize what she'd found, not at first. It was a folded piece of cheap pulp paper stuck between cans of tomatoes. She pulled it out, wondering why anyone would have wasted time sticking an advertising circular there.

When she unfolded it, she found it wasn't an advertising circular—not one of the usual sort, anyway. A cartoon at the top showed a Satanic-looking Uncle Sam with a scantily clad maiden labeled CANADA slung over his shoulder. He was heading up a stairway, plainly intending to visit a fate worse than death upon her when he got to the room at the top. A nasty little dog with a Frenchman's face—labeled QUEBEC—bounded along behind him. God only knew what the dog would do up there. Whatever it was, it wouldn't be pretty.

FIGHT FOR YOUR COUNTRY! FIGHT FOR THE MOTHER COUNTRY! shouted the headline below the cartoon. The text under that was as vicious a denunciation of the USA as Mary had seen since the Yanks came into Rosenfeld in the first place.

Automatically, she tucked the flyer into her handbag. She had no idea what she'd do with it, not right then. But it encouraged her even so. Somebody in town besides her couldn't stand the Yanks. That was plenty to make her feel good all by itself. British agents, indeed!

She got what she needed and brought it up to the counter. Karamanlides added it up. "Eight dollars and eighteen cents," he said, his accent part Yank and part Greek. She gave him a ten and waited for her change. The storekeeper had come up from the USA and brought out Henry Gibbon, who'd run this place for years and years. No wonder the person with the flyer had stuck it here—this was one place where what had happened to Canada was obvious. It was the same reason Mary had planted a bomb here.

Karamanlides wasn't a bad fellow, not as an individual. He was honest enough. He carried a wide variety of goods, probably even more than Henry Gibbon had. He didn't give anybody any trouble.

But he was a Yank. If Canada were a free country, he never would have come up here. That made all the difference in the world.

Mary carried the groceries and sundries back to her apartment building and up the stairs. Alec was still busy with the fortress of blocks and toy soldiers he'd been playing with when she went to the general store. He was getting bigger; she didn't need to keep an eye on him every minute of every day.

After she'd put things away, she pulled the delicious flyer out of her purse and reread it. It was just as wonderful the second time through. The Yanks and the Frenchies would have kittens if they saw it. She suspected it did come from Britain. A couple of turns of phrase weren't quite Canadian. It was good to see that the British hadn't forgotten their colony, even if it lay in enemy hands.

And then, all at once, Mary started to laugh. "What's so funny, Mommy?" Alec called from the front room. "Tell me the joke."

"It's for grownups, sweetheart," Mary answered. Alec made a disappointed noise. A minute later, though, he was blowing things up again. He had quite a war going on here. Mary decided to take advantage of that. She said, "I'm going over to the post office. Do you want to come along?"

Had he said yes, she would have had to bring him. But he shook his head. She'd hoped he would, and thought so, too. He didn't like it there; he always fidgeted. And he really was engrossed in the lead-soldier war.

"I won't be too long," she said. He hardly heard her. She closed the door behind her and went out again.

The post office was only a five-minute walk. Nothing in Rosenfeld was more than a five-minute walk from anything else. Mary nodded to several people on the street as she strolled along. No point to acting as if she were in a hurry.

As usual, Wilf Rokeby had a fire going in the potbellied stove in one corner of the post office. It made the room too warm on a mild summer day. It also seemed to bring out the spicy smell of his hair oil.

"Good morning, Mrs. Pomeroy," he said, polite as usual. "Please excuse me for just one moment, if you'd be so kind." He ducked into a back room, closing the door behind him. No one else was in the building.

Better and better! Mary hurried behind the counter. She took the subversive flyer out of her purse and stuffed it into a drawer with the words POSTAGE FOR FOREIGN COUNTRIES neatly stenciled on the front. She was back on her side before the toilet flushed.

Rokeby came out and nodded briskly. "Sorry to keep you waiting there. What can I do for you today?"

"I need twenty stamps, please," Mary said.

"Coming right up." Rokeby counted them off a roll. "That'll be one dollar."

"A dollar!" Mary said. "Aren't they still three cents apiece?"

"New surcharge—I just got these in." The postmaster tapped one of the stamps with a fingernail. Sure enough, it had +2 printed in black over President Mahan's face. Rokeby went on, "It's to help pay for the war, I expect."

Mary expected he was right. Now that she thought back on it, she remembered her father grumbling about such things during the Great War. She sighed as she reached into her purse. "They get you every which way, don't they?"

"Seems like it sometimes, that's for sure." Wilf Rokeby put the dollar bill in the cash box. "I thank you very much."

Waiting six days after that was one of the harder things Mary had done. If Rokeby happened to reach into that drawer in the meantime . . . But how many people in sleepy little Rosenfeld needed postage for foreign countries—especially these days, when a censor was bound to take a long, hard look at any letters bound for distant lands?

At the end of the wait, Mary went to Rosenfeld's only telephone booth, which stood beside one of the town's three gas stations (all run by Americans). She folded the glass door shut behind her and put a nickel in the coin slot. When the operator came on the line, she said, "Occupation headquarters, please." She made her voice squeakier than usual so Maggie McHenry, who ate at the diner about three times a week, wouldn't recognize it.

"Yes, ma'am," was all the woman at the switchboard said.

"*Allo?* Who is this?" a Frenchy said in accented English when he picked up the call.

Again, Mary did her best not to sound like herself. She also did her best to sound as if she was very excited. And so she was, but not in the way she was pretending. "Horrible treason!" she gasped. "Wilf Rokeby! At the post office! Filthy pictures! Hid it when I came in, but— Oh, my God! Horrible!"

"Who is this?" the Quebecois demanded. "What do you say?"

"Treason!" Mary repeated, and then, "I've got to go. They're looking." She was proud of that. It could have meant anything at all. She hung up and left the phone booth in a hurry.

She strolled home as calmly as if she had nothing in the world on her mind. The Frenchies probably wouldn't have the brains to question Maggie. Even if they did, she hadn't sounded as if she knew Mary's voice. And now whatever happened with Wilf Rokeby would happen. Mary nodded and kept walking.

"Hear the news?" Mort asked at supper that night.

Mary shook her head. "I've been here almost all day. Just stepped out once for a second. Didn't talk to anybody." That should forestall Alec, who might have given her the lie if she said she hadn't been out at all. She looked interested, which wasn't hard—not a bit. "What's up?"

"Frenchies hauled Wilf Rokeby off to jail," Mort said solemnly. "Story is, they found subversive literature at the post office, if you can believe it. Wilf Rokeby! My God! Who would've figured him for that kind of thing? What was he going to do when he retired—start shooting at Frenchies and Yanks for the fun of it?"

"That's terrible. Terrible!" Mary knew she had to sound dismayed. Once she'd done it, she took another bite of meat loaf.

Hipolito Rodriguez was as happy as a man with a son in the Army could be during time of war. Everything else in his life was going well, and nothing had happened to Pedro. This war, from what the wireless said and from the way the front moved, was a different sort from the one he'd known. You weren't stuck in trenches all the time, waiting for enemy machine-gun bursts to knock over anyone careless enough to show even a bit of himself. A war of movement, people called it.

Did it mean it was a war in which ordinary soldiers were less likely to get killed? So far, it seemed to. Rodriguez sometimes lit candles in the hope that would go on. At Freedom Party meetings,

Robert Quinn kept telling everybody how well things were going. The wireless said the same thing, over and over again. Every day, it seemed, the men who read the news announced some new triumph. Most people who heard the news believed every word of it. Why not? Nothing else in the Confederate States challenged the reporting. One evening after a Freedom Party meeting, though, Rodriguez went to *La Culebra Verde* for a few drinks. If Magdalena yelled at him when he got home, then she yelled at him, that was all. He didn't feel like standing at the bar; he spent too much time on his feet in the fields. He and Carlos Ruiz took a table against the wall. When the barmaid came up and asked what they wanted, they both ordered beers.

Away she went, hips swinging in her flounced skirt. Rodriguez's eyes followed her—in a purely theoretical way, he told himself. Magdalena, no doubt, would have had another word for it. He shrugged. He was a dutiful enough husband. He hadn't done more than look at another woman since coming home from the war. If he'd gone upstairs with a few *putas* while he wore butternut . . . well, he'd usually been drunk first, and he'd been a lot younger, and he'd been a long way from home, with no assurance he'd ever see his wife again. What she didn't know and couldn't find out about wouldn't hurt her.

He noticed Ruiz wasn't watching the barmaid. "Are you all right?" he asked his old friend. "She's pretty."

Ruiz started. His laugh sounded embarrassed. "I wasn't even thinking about her. I was thinking about the war." He had two sons in the Army.

"Oh." Rodriguez couldn't tease him about that. He said, "*Gracias a Dios,* everything goes well."

His friend made the sign of the cross. "I hope so. By all the saints, I hope so. They tell us about victory after victory—heaven knows that's true."

"That proves the war is going well, *sí*?" Rodriguez said. The barmaid came back and set two foam-topped mugs on the table. He smiled at her. "Thank you, sweetheart."

Her answering smile was a professional grimace that showed white teeth. "You're welcome." She hurried away, her backfield in motion.

Rodriguez raised his mug. "*Salud.*" He and Carlos Ruiz both drank. Rodriguez sucked foam off his upper lip. "Why aren't you happy about the war, then?"

Ruiz eyed his beer. "If it's going as well as they say it is, why haven't *los Estados Unidos* given up?"

"They're the enemy," Rodriguez said reasonably.

"Well, yes." Ruiz finished his beer and waved to the barmaid for a refill. Rodriguez hadn't intended to pour his down, but he didn't want to fall behind, either. He gulped till the mug was empty. Ruiz, meanwhile, went on, "But in 1917 they beat us over and over. They beat us like a drum." He'd fought in Kentucky and Tennessee, where the worst beatings had happened. "And when they'd beaten us hard enough and long enough, we had to give in. Now everyone says we're beating them like that. So why aren't they quitting, the way we had to?"

Rodriguez shrugged. "We'd been fighting for three years then. We couldn't fight any more. This war is hardly even three months old yet."

"And if it goes on for three years, we will probably lose again," Carlos Ruiz said gloomily. "If a little man fights a big man, sometimes he can hit him with a chair right at the start and win like that. But if the big man gets up off the floor and keeps fighting, the little man is in trouble."

"Countries aren't men," Rodriguez said.

Ruiz shrugged again. "I hope not. Because we've knocked the United States down, but we haven't knocked them out."

The barmaid set fresh beers on the table and took away the empty mugs. Her smile might have been a little warmer—or maybe Rodriguez's imagination was a little warmer. He was pretty sure she did put more into her walk this time. *She's just trying to get a bigger tip out of you,* he told himself. He enjoyed watching her even so. Thinking about the war took a real effort. "We've cut the United States in half," he said.

"*Sí, es verdad,*" Ruiz said. "But even if it is true, so what? *Why* did we cut *los Estados Unidos* in half? To make them quit fighting, yes? If they don't quit fighting, what good does it do us?" He started emptying his second mug of beer as methodically as he'd finished the first.

"Well . . ." Rodriguez thought for a little while. "If they're cut in half, they can't send men and supplies from one part to the other.

That's what *Señor* Quinn says, and the wireless, too. How can they fight a war if they can't do that? They'll run out of men and food and guns."

"They still have men on both sides. They still have food on both sides, and factories, too." Carlos Ruiz seemed determined to be glum. "We've made it harder for them, *sí, sin duda*. But also without a doubt, we haven't beaten them unless they decide they're beaten. It isn't like it was with us at the end of the last war, when we couldn't stand up any more. They can go on for a long time if they decide they want to, and it looks like they do." He tilted back his mug. His throat worked. He set the mug down empty and waved to the barmaid again.

Rodriguez had to gulp to get his mug dry, too, by the time she walked over. He said, "At the rate we're going, *you're* not going to be able to stand up any more, and neither am I." But he nodded when his friend ordered refills for both of them.

Ruiz said, "I'll be able to get home. I'm not worried about that. But if I get drunk tonight—so what? I don't do it very often any more. If I have a headache tomorrow, I'll have a headache, that's all. That's tomorrow. Tonight, I'll be drunk."

Magdalena would have something besides *so what?* to say to getting drunk. Rodriguez suspected Carlos' wife would, too. That didn't make the idea any less tempting. Rodriguez didn't get drunk very often any more, either. Did that mean he couldn't do it every once in a while if he felt like it? He didn't think so. The two beers he'd already drunk argued loudly that they ought to have some company.

Here came the barmaid. She had company for those beers in her hands. "Here you are, *señores*," she said, bending low to set the fresh mugs on the table. Rodriguez tried to look down her ruffled white blouse. By the way Carlos Ruiz craned his neck now, so did he. By the way the barmaid giggled, she knew exactly what they were doing, and knew they wouldn't—quite—have any luck.

They drank. The barmaid brought over a plate of *jalapeños*. Those were free, but they made the two men thirstier. They drank some more to put out the fire. They weren't the only ones doing some serious drinking tonight, either. Somebody at the bar started to sing. It was a song Rodriguez knew. Joining in seemed the only right thing, the only possible thing, to do. He'd never sounded better, at least in his own ears. And the rest of the audience wasn't inclined to be critical, either. It was two in the morning when he and Carlos staggered out of *La Culebra Verde.* "Home," Rodriguez said, and started to laugh. Everything was funny now. It might not be when Magdalena saw the state he was in, but he wasn't going to worry about that. He wasn't going to worry about anything, not right this minute. He embraced his friend one last time. They went their separate ways.

The long line of power poles pointed the way home. They went straight across the countryside. Hipolito Rodriguez didn't, but he did go generally in the same direction. And he found the power poles convenient in another way, too. He paused in front of one of them, undid his trousers, and got rid of a good deal of the beer he'd drunk. A couple of miles farther out of Baroyeca, he did the same thing again.

The night was cool and dry. Days here in late summer kept their bake-oven heat, but the nights—growing longer now—were much more tolerable. Crickets chirped. Moths fluttered here and there, ghostly in the moonlight. Bigger flying shapes were bats and night-jars hunting them.

A coyote trotted past, mouth open in an arrogant, almost-doggy grin. *Have to look out for my lambs,* Rodriguez thought, wondering if he'd remember when he got home. Farmers around here shot coyotes on sight, but the beasts kept coming down out of the mountains and stealing stock.

There was the house, a light on in the front window. He approached with drunken caution; if the light was on, Magdalena might be waiting up for him. And if Magdalena was waiting up, she wouldn't be very happy.

He tiptoed up the steps. Somehow, he wasn't so quiet as he wished he would have been. He managed to slam the front door behind him. Even that didn't bring out his wife. Maybe she'd stayed up till an hour or so ago, and was deep asleep now. That would save him for the time being, but she'd be twice as angry in the morning, and he'd be hung over then. He didn't look forward to that.

He didn't want to be *very* hung over in the morning. He knew it was too late to block all the aftereffects of what he'd drunk tonight.

Maybe he could ease the pain to come, though, at least a little. He went into the kitchen and flipped on the light in there. He didn't have to fumble around lighting a lamp. A flick of the switch was all it took. A good thing, too; he might have burned down the house fooling around with kerosene and matches.

In the refrigerator were several bottles of beer. Rodriguez let out a silent sigh of relief; Magdalena might have thrown them all away. He reached for one. It might take the edge off the headache he'd have in the morning. He was *still* drunk, and proved it by knocking over a pitcher of ice water next to the beer on the top shelf.

A desperate, drunken, miraculous grab kept the pitcher from crashing to the floor and bringing Magdalena out with every reason to be furious. It didn't keep the whole pitcher's worth of water from splashing down onto the floor and all over everywhere. He jumped and cursed. The cold water froze his toes. He'd hardly felt them for quite a while, but they announced their presence now.

Still swearing under his breath, he fumbled for rags. He did a halfhearted—a very halfhearted—job of cleaning up the mess, or at least that part of it right in front of the refrigerator. Puddles still glittered on the floor in the light of the electric lamp. He started to go after some of them, then shook his head. It was only water. It would dry up. And getting down on his hands and knees was making his head hurt. He didn't just want that beer. He needed it.

He opened it. He drank it. It wasn't just delicious, though it was that. It was medicinal. His headache retreated. He started to smile. Maybe he would get away with this after all. He set the bottle on the counter. Then he smiled a sly smile and put it in the trash instead. Magdalena wouldn't have to know. He wasn't as sly as he thought, though, and he was drunker than he thought.

As he reached for the light switch, his sandal splashed in one of the puddles he hadn't bothered sopping up. The instant he touched the switch, he realized he'd made a dreadful mistake. Current coursed through him, stinging like a million hornets. He tried to let go, and discovered he couldn't. *Just a stupid mistake,* he thought over and over. *Just a stupid . . .*

Honolulu. The Sandwich Islands. Paradise on earth. Warm blue water. Tropic breezes. Palm trees. Polynesian and Oriental and even white women not overencumbered with inhibitions or clothes. Bright sunshine the whole year round.

Every paradise had its serpent. The bright sunshine was Sam Carsten's.

He'd had duty in Honolulu before. It had left him about medium rare, the way bright sunshine always did. He was too fair to stand it, and he wouldn't tan. He just burned, and then burned some more. He wished the *Remembrance* were charged with protecting Seattle or Portland, Maine, or, for that matter, Tierra del Fuego. At least then he could stick his nose out on deck without having it turn the color of raw beef.

Staying below in warm weather was no fun, either. The ship's ventilators ran all the time, but heat from the sun and from the engine room combined to defeat them. Sometimes that drove him topside. He stayed in the shade of the carrier's island when he could, which helped only so much. Even the reflection of the sun off the Pacific was plenty to scorch him.

The exec noticed his suffering. "Are you sure you want to stay aboard?" Commander Cressy asked. "If you want to transfer to a ship in the North Atlantic—one that's out to keep the British from sneaking men and arms to Canada, say—I'll do all I can to put your transfer through."

"Sir, I've been tempted to do that a few times," Sam answered. "I've been tempted, but I'd rather stay here. This is where the action is."

"Plenty of action everywhere, I'd say," Cressy observed. "But I do take your point. And if you don't want to leave us, well, you'd better believe we're glad to have you. You're a solid man. You've proved that plenty of times—and you may get the chance to do it some more."

"Thank you very much, sir," Sam said. The exec's good opinion mattered to him, probably more than that of any other officer on the ship. Cressy was a man who would soon have a ship of his own, if not a fleet of his own. Hoping to take advantage of his friendly mood, Sam asked, "When do we go into action against the Japs?"

"Damn good question," Cressy told him. "What I haven't got for you is a damn good answer. Right now, I'd say it's more up to Tokyo than to us. We're playing defense here, trying to make sure they don't take the Sandwich Islands away from us. We've got the

Remembrance for mobility, and we've got as many land-based air-planes as we could ferry over here. We've got submersibles—oh, and battleships and cruisers, too. The enemy won't have an easy time if he comes."

"Yes, sir," Sam said. Back during the Great War, the battlewag-ons and cruisers would have taken pride of place. He knew that full well; he'd served aboard the *Dakota* back then. In this fight, Com-mander Cressy tossed them in as an afterthought, and that was only fitting and proper. They could still hit hard—if they ever got close enough to do it. But airplanes, either land-based or flying off carri-ers, were likely to sink them before they got the chance. Even in the Pacific War, airplane carriers had attacked one another without coming over the horizon.

"The other thing we've got is Y-ranging," Cressy said. "That gives us early warning. We don't think the Japs do. Most of their en-gineering is pretty good; their ships and airplanes measure up to anybody's."

"Oh, yes, sir," Carsten agreed. "We've found that out the hard way."

"So we have," the exec said. "But they're just a little bit slow in electrical engineering. Most of their gear is like what we were using, oh, five years ago. They get the most out of it—never underestimate their skill. It's one place where we know a few tricks they don't, though."

"That could be a big edge," Sam said.

"It could be, yes. Whether it will be . . ." Commander Cressy shrugged. "It's like anything else: it's not only what you've got, it's how well you use it." He nodded. "I always enjoy passing the time of day with you, Lieutenant. But now, if you'll excuse me . . ." He hurried away. He always hurried. That added to the impression that nothing ever got by him.

When Sam got leave, he took the trolley from Pearl Harbor east to Honolulu. Hotel Street was where the ratings congregated: an avenue full of bars and dance halls and brothels, all designed to make sure a sailor out on a spree didn't leave any money in his wal-let and had a good time with what he spent. Shore patrolmen tramped along in groups of three or four; traveling in pairs wasn't enough. Men called them names behind their backs, and sometimes to their faces.

Sam sighed. Being an officer meant he was slumming here. He didn't really belong, the way he had during the Great War. There were some quieter, more discreet establishments an officer could visit without losing face. Carsten liked rowdiness as much as the next sailor on leave. But he was conscious that, as a mustang, he couldn't get away with certain things other officers might have. His superiors had warned him against acting as if he were still a CPO. Mustangs had the deck stacked against them anyhow. They made things harder for themselves if they remembered what they had been and forgot what they were.

He was walking toward one of those discreet establishments when a plump blond woman not far from his own age came up the street toward him. He started to go past her, then stopped and did a double take. "I'll be a son of a gun," he said. "You're Maggie Stevenson, aren't you?"

"Hello, Lieutenant," she said, pronouncing it *Leftenant* in the British way. A wide, amused smile spread across her face. "I take it we've met before?"

"Just once," he replied with genuine regret. "That was the only time I could scrape so much cash together back in the last war. But you see I never forgot."

Her smile got wider yet. "I always wanted satisfied customers," she said. "Every so often, a man who was here back then recognizes me. It's flattering, in a way." During the Great War, she'd been the undisputed queen of Honolulu's women of easy virtue. She'd charged thirty bucks a throw, ten times the going rate for an average girl, and she'd made sailors think they got their money's worth, too. She eyed Carsten's shoulder boards. "You've come up in the world a bit since then."

He shrugged. "Maybe a bit. How about you?" She couldn't be in the business any more, but she didn't look as if she'd missed any meals. She'd made money hand over fist back then. Had she managed to hold on to any of it?

She laughed. "Lieutenant, I own about half of Hotel Street. Every time some horny able seaman gets a piece, I get a piece of his piece. I get a piece of what he drinks, too, and of what he eats, whatever that is." She laughed again. "I haven't done too badly for myself."

"Good," he said. Broken-down, penniless whores who'd got too old to turn tricks any more were a dime a dozen. Whores who'd made a killing in real estate, on the other hand . . . Well, now he'd met one. "Good for you, by God!"

"You really mean it," Maggie Stevenson said wonderingly.

"Why wouldn't I?"

"Plenty of reasons, starting with that boring text about the wages of sin. For me, the wages of sin turned out to be pretty good, I had a lot of fun earning them, and I don't regret a goddamn thing. What do you think of that?"

"You sure gave a lot of fun," Sam said. "I'm glad you had some, too. I've known quite a few working girls who didn't—don't."

"So have I." She nodded. "I'm lucky. I *have* been lucky, most ways. So where are you headed, Lieutenant?"

"I was going to the Excelsior Hotel."

She made a face at him. "That's not one of mine. Would you rather visit the Oceanview?"

From what he'd heard, the Oceanview was the best officers' place in Honolulu. It was also the most expensive. "Sure," he said, "or I would if I could afford it."

"Don't worry about that." She took a business card and a pen from her purse. She wrote on the card, then handed it to Sam. "Show them this at the door. On the house. For old times' sake, you might say."

"Thanks very much." He eyed the card. She'd written, *Anything—Maggie* in a bright purple ink. The printed card described her as a caterer. She catered to all kinds of appetites. "Thanks *very* much."

"You'll pay me back. Just keep the Japs away. They'd be hell on business. Good luck, Lieutenant." Off she went, the same determination in her stride as when she'd gone on to the next eagerly waiting sailor after leaving Sam. He looked down at the card again, smiled, and shook his head in wonder.

The bouncers at the door to the Oceanview could have played professional football. They were used to seeing commanders and captains and even admirals, not an overage lieutenant, junior grade. "Help you, sir?" one of them rumbled. *Help you get lost?* he no doubt meant. Sam displayed Maggie Stevenson's card, wondering what would happen next.

"Oh," the bouncer said. He actually came to attention, and nudged his even beefier pal so he did the same. "Didn't know you knew the owner." He handed back the card, nothing but respect on his blunt-featured face. "Have a good time, sir."

"I do believe I will," Sam said, bemused. He walked in. The place wasn't whorehouse gaudy. Everything had an air of quiet elegance. You could see the money, but it didn't shout. And the purple ink on that card was a potent Open, Sesame.

With that card in hand, his own money was no good in there. No one would take it, not even for tips. The food was good. The booze was better. After a while, he picked himself a girl. Just making the choice wasn't easy; the Oceanview had girls to match anyone's taste, as long as that taste was good.

Sam finally settled on a blue-eyed brunette named Louise. She did whatever he wanted, and smiled while she was doing it. He didn't ask for anything fancy or jaded; his own habits didn't run that way. He didn't think he warmed her, but she was pleasant all the way through.

She didn't throw him out of bed so she could go on to her next customer right away, either, the way girls in houses usually did. Instead, she lay beside him for a lazy cigarette and a brandy. "How did you get to know the Boss?" she asked; he could hear the capital letter.

"Same way I just got to know you," he answered, patting her round behind. He wondered if he could manage a second round. He'd been at sea a long time.

Louise's eyes widened. "She gave you that card for a roll in the hay years ago?" She didn't say, *You must have been better with her than you were with me.* Even if she didn't, Sam could tell what she was thinking.

He shrugged. "Maybe she was feeling sentimental." That sent Louise into gales of laughter. Well, Maggie Stevenson didn't strike Sam as the sentimental type, either. But what other explanation made sense?

And, in the end, what difference did it make? With Louise on top the second time, Sam did succeed again. He went back to the *Remembrance* thinking there were worse places to fight a war than Honolulu in spite of the tropical sun.

*   *   *

Jefferson Pinkard always dreaded telephone calls from Richmond. When people in Richmond phoned Camp Dependable, it was usually to tell him to do things he didn't want to do. Some things they didn't want to put in writing, even in something as ephemeral as a telegram.

"Hello, Pinkard." Ferdinand Koenig sounded almost offensively cheerful this morning. Why not? The Attorney General gave orders. He didn't have to take them. "How are you today?"

"Fine, sir," Jeff answered. Hopefully, he added, "Connection isn't real good."

"No? I hear you just fine," Koenig said—so much for that. "There's something you need to take care of for me."

"What's that?" Jeff asked, trying to hide the resignation he felt.

"You still have Willy Knight there, right? Nothing's happened to him or anything?"

"No, sir. Nothing's happened to him. We've still got him right here," Pinkard said. He'd never included the former Vice President of the CSA in a population reduction. What you once did, you couldn't undo. "How come? You need him again?" If they were crazy enough to want to use Knight to rally the country, or some small part of it, they could. Pinkard didn't think it would work, but nobody'd asked his opinion, and nobody was going to, either.

"Need him? Jesus Christ, no!" Ferd Koenig hadn't lost all of his mind, then. "He's never going to have any use for anybody again. Time to dispose of him."

"Dispose of him?" Pinkard wanted to make sure he had that right before he did anything. "Shall I expect something in writing that tells me the same thing? You people change your mind about that, whose ass is in a sling? Mine."

"Nobody's going to put anything in writing about this," Koenig said. "I'll call you back tomorrow, that's all." He hung up.

"Shit." Jefferson Pinkard hung up, too. The Attorney General hadn't said what would happen if he called back and found Willy Knight still breathing. Pinkard didn't need anybody to draw him a picture, though. He could figure it out for himself. Somebody else would do Knight in—and he'd trade his uniform for prison coveralls, if the powers that be didn't decide to dispose of him instead.

It had to be done, then. And he had to *see* it done. You never could tell which guard was a secret Knight sympathizer. If the man got loose, especially now with a war on . . . Pinkard supposed that was why Richmond had decided it didn't want to keep him around any more. If he ever escaped, the damnyankees could use him against the CSA. Or he could rally the black rebels, maybe even join them to white troublemakers. No wonder the Freedom Party didn't want to take the chance of letting him keep breathing, even in a place like Camp Dependable.

When Jeff walked out of the office compound and into the very different world of the camp itself, he wasn't surprised to have Mercer Scott come over to him within a couple of minutes. "What's up?" the guard chief asked.

He knew Pinkard had got a call from Richmond. He didn't even bother hiding that. But he didn't know, or didn't let on that he knew, what the call was about. Maybe he was sandbagging. Jeff didn't think so. He hoped not, anyway. He said, "Have Atkins and Moultrie and McDevitt bring Willy Knight here right away. Those three, nobody else. Anybody fucks this up, Mercer, it may cost me my ass, but I promise you you'll go down with me."

Again, Scott didn't bother pretending he didn't know what Jeff was talking about. He said, "You want to come along with me, see I don't talk to nobody else?"

"Yeah," Jeff said after a moment's thought. "I guess maybe I do. No offense, Mercer, but this here's important."

"Soon as you said it was about Willy, I reckoned it was," Mercer Scott answered. "His clock finally run out?"

Pinkard didn't answer that, not in so many words. "Let's just go get him, separate him off from the rest of the prisoners." He laughed. "One thing—he won't be hard to find." Except for the guards, Knight was still the only white man in the camp.

Braxton Atkins, Clem Moultrie, and Shank McDevitt were guards personally loyal to Pinkard. Mercer Scott had his own favorites, too. A guard chief would have been a damn fool not to. But Jeff was going to stand and fall with *his* people on this. Things still might go wrong, but they wouldn't go wrong because he hadn't done everything he could to make them go right.

All five white men carried submachine guns with big, heavy snail-drum magazines when they went after Willy Knight. If anybody tried to give them trouble, they could spray a lot of lead around before they went down. The Negroes in the camp had been taken in arms against the Confederate States. They knew what sort of weapons the guards had, and no doubt why. They also knew the men in uniform wouldn't hesitate to start shooting, not even a little bit. They gave them a wide berth.

Pinkard and his followers found Knight coming back from the latrine trenches. When the former Vice President realized they were heading his way, he straightened into a mocking parody of attention. "Well, gents, what can I do for you?"

"Got a message for you from Richmond," Pinkard answered stolidly. "It's waiting back at the compound."

"A message? What kind of message?" Hope warred with fear on Knight's scrawny, care-worn face. Did any part of him really imagine Jake Featherston would ever let him off the hook? Maybe so, or the hope wouldn't have been there.

"I don't know. A message. They wouldn't let me look at it." Pinkard lied without compunction. This *had* to go smoothly. The way to make sure that happened was to keep Knight soothed, keep him eager, till the very last instant.

And it worked. He believed because he wanted to believe, because he had to believe, because not believing meant giving up. "Well, lead me to it, by God," he said, more life in his voice than Jeff had heard there for years.

"No, Mr. Knight. You go first. You know the way," Pinkard said. That *Mister* sealed the deal. Knight hurried on ahead of the guards. Behind his back, Mercer Scott gave Jeff a look filled with reluctant respect. He brought his free hand up to touch the brim of his juice-squeezer hat, as if to say, *You know what you're doing, all right.*

Once Pinkard had Willy Knight away from the rest of the prisoners, he knew things would go the way he wanted them to. He nodded to his three loyalists. They all raised their weapons and shot Knight several times each. He died hopeful, and he died fast. There were worse ways to go out—plenty of them. The camp gave examples every day.

"Good job," Jeff told the guards. His ears still rang from the gunfire. "Take what's left here and get rid of it." They dragged Willy

Knight's body away by the feet. That way, they didn't get their uniforms so dirty. The corpse left a trail of red behind it. Flies started settling on the blood and buzzed round the body.

"Well, there's one loose end taken care of," Scott said.

"I was thinking the same thing," Jeff answered. He was also thinking that another one had just shown up. Now the guard chief knew for sure who three of his chief backers were. He didn't see what he could have done about that, but he knew he would have to get some less obvious followers, too.

"Just complicated our lives, having him around," Mercer Scott added.

"You think I'm gonna tell you you're wrong, you're nuts," Jeff said. "Now I'm gonna go call the Attorney General back, tell him it's been taken care of." He didn't aim to wait for Ferdinand Koenig to telephone him again. He would have liked to call Koenig something worse than his formal title. He would have liked to, but he didn't, not where Scott could hear. The guard chief had his own channels back to Richmond. Giving him dirt to report was just plain stupid.

"I liked the way you handled that. Slick as hell," Scott said.

"Thanks," Pinkard said. Maybe good reports could go back to the capital, too. Maybe. He wouldn't have bet anything much above a dime on it.

He placed the call to Koenig's office. Hisses and pops and clicks on the telephone line said it was going through. Every once in a while, Jeff could hear operators talking to each other. They sounded like faraway ghosts. And then, also from some considerable distance but not quite from the Other Side, the Attorney General said, "Koenig here."

"Hello, sir. This is Pinkard. Wanted to let you know it's all done."

"Good. That's good," Koenig said. "You didn't waste any time, did you?"

"Didn't reckon I ought to," Jeff answered. "Never can tell what'll happen if you dick around on something like this."

"Well, you're right about that." The Attorney General paused. "You're sure about it?"

Jeff had expected that. He found himself nodding, even though Ferd Koenig was a thousand miles away. "Sir, I saw it with my own eyes. I made sure I did. Can't take chances on something so important."

"All right. I reckon you know why I have to make certain," Koenig said. Pinkard nodded again. That meant the Attorney General would also check with Mercer Scott, and maybe with some other people at Camp Dependable, too, people about whom neither Pinkard nor Scott knew anything. Jeff didn't know Koenig had people like that here, but he would have in the other man's shoes. The Attorney General went on, "I'll let the President know what a good job you did."

"I thank you kindly." Jeff meant that. "How do you want me to put it in the books, sir? 'Shot while attempting to escape' or 'natural causes'?"

" 'Natural causes,' " Koenig answered after a bare moment's hesitation. "His heart stopped, didn't it?"

"Sure as hell did."

"All right, then. Leave it at that. The less we stir up those waters, the better off everybody'll be," Ferdinand Koenig said.

Jeff found himself nodding one more time. "That's how it'll be, then." There were still more than a few people who liked Willy Knight. They mostly kept their mouths shut if they wanted to stay healthy, but they were out there. No point getting them all hot and bothered, not if you could help it. *Natural causes* could mean anything.

"All right." Koenig paused once more. "Sounds like it went off smooth as can be. I'll let the President know about that, too."

"Thanks. Thanks very much." Pinkard beamed. Most of the time, nobody ever gave a jailer the respect he deserved.

After a few more polite noises—ones that didn't matter nearly so much—Koenig hung up. Jeff let out a long sigh. If it wasn't one thing, it was another. But he'd handled it.

He nodded to himself. If it wasn't one thing, it was another, all right. And he had a pretty good notion of what the next thing would be: a new population reduction. How many more of those could the guards take and still keep their marbles? He didn't want them blowing out their own brains or finding other ingenious ways to kill themselves, the way Chick Blades had.

What could he do about it, though? He didn't have the room or the food to keep all the blacks who flooded into Camp Dependable. If he tried, he'd touch off an explosion here. He couldn't do that, not when the Confederate States were fighting for their lives. He had to make things here run as well as he could. He wasn't supposed to cause trouble. He was supposed to stop it.

At least he didn't have Willy Knight to worry about any more. No more bad dreams about Knight escaping, either. That was something, anyhow.

When Cincinnatus Driver went to a drugstore to buy himself a bottle of aspirins, he had to wait till the druggist took care of every white customer in the place before he could give the man his money. Back before the Great War, he'd taken such humiliations for granted. After a quarter of a century of living as a citizen rather than a resident, though, they galled him. He couldn't do anything about that, not unless he wanted to get his population reduced, but he was muttering to himself as he made his slow, halting way out the door.

He'd been lucky, after a fashion. Another white man came in just as he was going out: a tall, jowly fellow, still vigorous despite his white hair, with a mournful face and the light brown eyes of a hunting dog. He held the door open for Cincinnatus, saying, "Here you go, uncle."

"Thank you kindly, suh," Cincinnatus said. That *uncle* still grated, too. But it wasn't the reason he leaned against the sooty brickwork of the drugstore's front wall. Nobody bothered him there. Why would anyone? He was just a decrepit, broken-down nigger soaking up some sunshine. He could have been sprawled on the sidewalk with a bottle in his hand. Nobody would have bothered him then, either, unless a cop decided to beat on him or run him in for being drunk.

A pigeon strutted by, head bobbing. It could walk about as fast as Cincinnatus could. He opened the bottle of aspirins and dry-swallowed a couple of them. They wouldn't get rid of all his aches and pains, but they would help some. And the sun did feel good on his battered bones.

After five or ten minutes, the man with the white hair and the hunting-hound eyes came out of the drugstore. He was carrying a small paper sack. He would have walked past Cincinnatus without a second glance, but the Negro spoke in a low voice: "Mornin', Mistuh Bliss."

The man stopped dead. Just for a moment, his eyes widened. Surprise? Fear? Cincinnatus would have bet on surprise. Luther Bliss was a first-class son of a bitch, but nobody'd ever said he scared easy. Cincinnatus wondered if he'd deny being who he was. He didn't; he just said, "Who the hell are you? How do you know who I am? Speak up, or you'll be sorry."

Sorry probably meant *dead*. His voice still held the snap of command. When Kentucky belonged to the USA, he'd headed up the Kentucky State Police—the Kentucky Secret Police, for all intents and purposes. He'd battled Negro Reds and Confederate diehards with fine impartiality, and he'd got out of the state one jump ahead of the incoming Confederates. If he was back now . . .

Cincinnatus said, "I holler for a cop, we see who's the sorriest." That brought Luther Bliss up short. Cincinnatus went on, "I spent time in your jail. Your boys worked me over pretty good."

"You probably deserved it." No, nobody'd ever said Bliss lacked nerve.

"Fuck you," Cincinnatus said evenly.

That made Bliss jump; no Negro in his right mind would say such a thing to a white man here. But the former—or not so former—secret policeman was made of stern stuff, and shrewd as the devil, too. "You want to holler for a cop, go ahead. You'll help the CSA and hurt the USA, but go ahead."

"Fuck you," Cincinnatus said again, nothing but bitterness in his voice this time. Luther Bliss had found the switch to shut him off, all right.

Seeing as much, Bliss managed a smile that did not reach his eyes. "This time, I reckon we're on the same side. Any . . . colored fellow who isn't on the USA's side, he's got to have something wrong with him." He didn't say *nigger*, but his hesitation showed he didn't miss by much.

He wasn't wrong, either. Cincinnatus wished he were. And sure as hell he wasn't a coward. If the Confederates caught him here, they'd take him apart an inch at a time. "What the devil you doin' in Kentucky again?" Cincinnatus asked him.

Bliss gave back that unamused smile once more. "Raising Cain," he answered matter-of-factly. Those light brown eyes—an odd, odd color, one that almost glowed in the sunlight—measured Cincinnatus like a pair of calipers. "I remember you. That Darrow bastard sprung you. Old fool should have kept his nose out of what was none of his business."

"I hoped to God I'd never see you again," Cincinnatus said.

"Well, you're about to get your wish," Bliss replied. "Like I say, you want to yell for a cop, go right ahead." He didn't bother with a farewell nod or anything of the sort. He just walked away, turned the corner, and was gone, as if he were a bad dream and Cincinnatus suddenly awake.

Shaking his head, Cincinnatus walked to the corner himself. When he looked down the street, he didn't see Luther Bliss. The ground might have swallowed up the secret policeman. Cincinnatus shook his head again. That was too much to hope for. "Do Jesus!" he muttered, shaken to the core. Ghosts kept coming back to life now that he was here in Kentucky again.

He made his slow return to the colored part of town. No drugstores operated there. A couple had been open while Kentucky belonged to the USA, run by young, ambitious Negroes who'd managed to get enough education to take on the work. The Confederates had made them shut down, though. The Freedom Party didn't want capable colored people. As far as Cincinnatus could tell, the Freedom Party didn't want colored people at all.

A policeman in a gray uniform strode up to Cincinnatus on an almost visible cloud of self-importance. "What're you doing out of the quarter, boy?" he demanded. *Boy* was even worse than *uncle*.

"Got me some aspirin, suh." Cincinnatus displayed the bottle. "I'm crippled up pretty bad, an' they help—some."

"Let me see your passbook."

"Yes, suh." Cincinnatus handed him the all-important document. The cop studied it, nodded, and handed it back with a grudging nod. Like Luther Bliss, he walked away without a backward glance.

Cincinnatus stared after him, then slowly put the passbook in his pocket once more. He despised and feared Luther Bliss, but he was damned if he would tell a Confederate cop about him. One thing he'd learned and learned well was the vital difference between bad and worse. Bliss was bad, no doubt about it. Anything that had to do with the Freedom Party was bound to be worse.

Now that he was back in his own part of town, Cincinnatus had to be extra careful where he set his cane and where he put his feet. Sidewalks here were bumpy and irregular and full of holes. In the white part of Covington, they got repaired. Here? Not likely. This part of town was lucky to have sidewalks at all. The USA hadn't spent much more money here than the Confederate States had while they ran Kentucky.

One slow, painful step at a time, Cincinnatus trudged over to Lucullus Wood's barbecue place. As usual, the smell made him drool blocks before he got there. Also as usual, Lucullus had customers both black and white. Freedom Party stalwarts might hate Negroes on general principles. That didn't mean they didn't know good barbecue when they sank their teeth into it.

The heat inside was terrific. Pig carcasses and great slabs of beef turned on spits over glowing hickory coals. Cincinnatus recognized one of the men turning the spits. "Can I see Lucullus?" he asked.

"Sure. Go on back," the turner answered. "He ain't got nobody with him now."

"Come in," Lucullus called when Cincinnatus knocked on the door. The barbecue cook had a hand in the top drawer of his desk. If Cincinnatus had been an unwelcome visitor, Lucullus probably could have given him a .45-caliber reception. But he smiled and relaxed and showed both hands. "Sit yourself down. What you got on your mind?"

Sitting down felt good—felt wonderful, in fact. Cincinnatus didn't like being on his feet. Baldly, he said, "Luther Bliss is back in town."

"My ass!" Lucullus exclaimed. "If he was, I reckon I'd known about it. How come you got the word ahead o' anybody else? I don't mean no disrespect, but you ain't nobody special."

"Never said I was," Cincinnatus answered. "But he was goin' into Goldblatt's drugstore when I was comin' out. I ain't nobody special, but I ain't nobody's fool, neither. I seen him, I recognized him—you better believe I recognized him—an' I talked to him. He got white hair now, but he ain't changed much otherwise. Luther Bliss, all right."

Lucullus drummed his plump fingers on the desktop. "Confederates catch him, he take a looong time to die."

"I know. I thought o' that." Cincinnatus nodded. "Man's a bastard, but he's a brave bastard. I always figured that."

"What the hell he doin' here?" Lucullus asked. Cincinnatus could only shrug. Lucullus waved away this motion. "I wasn't askin' you. Ain't no reason for you to know. But *I* ought to have. I got me connections up in the USA. They shoulda told me he was comin' back."

"Back in the days when Kentucky belonged to the United States, Bliss cared more about chasin' your daddy than about workin' with him," Cincinnatus said.

"Well, that's so, but times is different now. You gonna tell me times ain't different now?" Lucullus sent Cincinnatus a challenging stare.

Cincinnatus shook his head. "Not me. I oughta know. Still and all, though, Bliss, he works with white folks. He likely come down here for some special nasty trick or another, an' he got his people all lined up an' ready to go. I don't reckon he wants nobody else to know he's here."

"You got to be right about that." Lucullus eyed Cincinnatus again, this time speculatively. "You got to be lucky he don't decide to dispose o' you for knowin' who he is."

"He thought about it," Cincinnatus said. The sun hadn't been the only thing glowing in Luther Bliss' eyes. "He thought hard about it, I reckon. He probably figured no nigger's gonna give him away."

"He a damn fool if he think like that. Plenty o' niggers sell their mama for a dime." Lucullus held up a hand, pale palm out. "I don't mean you. I know better. You is what you is. But a lot o' niggers is just plain scared to death—an' the way things is goin', *to death* is just about the size of it."

"I ain't gonna do nothin' to help the Confederates an' the Freedom Party," Cincinnatus said. "Nothin', you hear me?"

"I done said I don't mean you. I said it, an' I meant it. You got to listen when you ain't talkin'," Lucullus said. "Bliss was at Goldblatt's, was he? He likely ain't stayin' real far from there, then."

"Mebbe," Cincinnatus said. "Never can tell with him, though. That there man taught the Mississippi to be twisty."

"You ain't wrong," Lucullus said. "And I is much obliged to you fo' passin' on what you seen. I should know that sort o' thing. Luther Bliss!" He whistled mournfully. "Who woulda thunk it?"

The cook heaved himself to his feet and led Cincinnatus out of the office. At his shouted order, one of the youngsters behind the counter gave Cincinnatus a barbecued-beef sandwich so thick, he could barely get his mouth around it. He walked back to his father's house engulfing it like a snake engulfing a frog. But all the barbecue in the world couldn't have taken the taste of Luther Bliss from his mouth.

Just swinging a hammer felt good to Chester Martin. Watching a house go up, making a house go up, seemed a lot more satisfying than tramping along the sidewalk with a picket sign on his shoulder. He'd never been thrilled about taking on a general's role in the war against capitalist oppression.

So he told himself, anyhow—and told himself, again and again. With patriotic zeal, one big builder after another had made his peace with the construction workers' union. Nobody could afford strikes any more. Everyone from the President on down was saying the same thing. People were actually acting as if they believed it, too. Love of country trumped love of class. That was one of the lessons of 1914, when international solidarity of the workers hadn't done a damn thing to stop the Great War. A generation of peace had let memories grow hazy. Now the truth came to light again.

Martin found himself quietly swearing at Harry T. Casson as he rode the trolley home from work one hot afternoon. The building magnate had known him better than he knew himself. Try as he would to get back to normal, to return to being an ordinary working man, he *missed* the class struggle, *missed* heading the proletariat's forces in that struggle. Was ordinary work enough after such a long, bruising fight?

When he got off the trolley a few blocks from his place, a newsboy on the corner was hawking the *Daily Mirror*—Los Angeles' leading afternoon paper—with shouts of, "Sabotage! Treason! Read all about it!"

That was a headline Chester would have expected from the *Times*. In fact, half a block away another newsboy was selling the afternoon edition of the *Times* with almost identical cries. In the *Times*, they were usually aimed at union organizers and other such subversives. Chester bought a copy of the *Daily Mirror*. That way, he didn't have to give the *Times* any of his money.

He discovered that the *Daily Mirror*—and, presumably, even the *Times* for once—meant their headlines literally. A U.S. offensive against the Confederates in Ohio had been blunted because Confederate sympathizers blew bridges, took down important road signs, and otherwise fouled things up. One of them had been caught in the act. He'd killed himself before U.S. forces could seize him and, perhaps, squeeze answers out of him.

"Fighting the enemy is hard enough. Fighting the enemy and our own people at the same time is ten times worse," an officer was quoted as saying. Right next to his bitter comment was a story about the secondary campaign in Utah. The Mormons were using lots of land mines against U.S. soldiers and U.S. barrels, making the advance toward Provo hideously expensive.

Chester almost walked past his own building. He folded the newspaper under one arm and thumped his forehead with the heel of his other hand. Then he went inside and went upstairs. He sniffed when he let himself into the apartment. "What smells good?" he called.

"It's a tongue," Rita answered from the kitchen. Chester smiled. When times were good, back in the 1920s, he would have turned up his nose at tongue. He and Rita had started eating it when times went sour. They'd kept on eating it afterwards because they both found they liked it. So did their son. Rita went on, "How did it go today?"

"All right, I guess." Chester did his best not to think about his discontent. To keep from flabbling about what he was doing, he flabbled about external things instead: "War news isn't very good."

"I know. I've been listening to the wireless," his wife said. "Not much we can do about it, though."

He walked into the kitchen, opened the refrigerator, and took out a bottle of Lucky Lager. "Want one?" he asked. When Rita nodded, he opened the beer, put it on the counter by her, and got another one for himself. They clinked the brown glass bottles together before drinking.

Not much we can do about it. Rita knew he sometimes thought about putting on the uniform again. He wasn't afraid of getting shot at. Her knowing he might get shot at? That made him shiver.

"Ahhh! That hits the spot!" Chester said after a third of the bottle ran cold down his throat. Rita, who'd taken a smaller sip, nodded. Chester drank again, then went on, "At least it doesn't look like the Confederates are going to take Toledo away from us."

"Thank God for small favors." Rita's second swig was a hefty one. Chester understood that. They'd come to Los Angeles from Toledo after he lost his job at a steel mill there. Both of them still had family in the town. If the Confederates had decided to drive west after reaching Lake Erie at Sandusky . . .

But they hadn't. Chester added, "Last letter we got from my old man, he says even the bombers aren't coming over as often as they did."

"They don't need to so much, not any more," Rita said.

One more truth, Chester thought. Till the Confederates cut the USA in half, all sorts of cargoes rolled through Toledo, bound for points farther east. Now those cargoes couldn't go much farther east—not on land, anyhow. "I'll bet the docks are booming," Chester said.

His wife gave him a look. "Of course they are. That's why the bombers still come over at all: to make them go boom."

Chester groaned. "I didn't mean it like that." Whether he'd meant it or not, it was still so. He usually made the jokes in the family, but he'd walked right into this one. He said, "You can get rich sailing on a freighter in the Great Lakes today."

"You can get blown to kingdom come sailing in one of those freighters, too," Rita pointed out. Pay was high because the chances of running the Confederate gauntlet were low. Chester finished his beer with a last gulp and opened another one. Rita didn't say anything. He wasn't somebody who made a habit of getting smashed after he came home from work. He certainly wasn't somebody who made a habit of pouring down a few boilermakers before he came home from work. He'd known a few—maybe more than a few— steelworkers like that. Builders drank, too, but mostly not with the same reckless abandon.

"I'm home!" Carl shouted. The front door slammed. Feet thundered in the hall.

"Oh, good," Chester told his son. "I thought we were in the middle of an elephant stampede."

Carl thought that was funny. He also thought his father hadn't been joking. Rita said, "Go wash your hands and face. With soap, if you please. Supper's just about ready."

Despite the warning, Carl's cleanup was extremely sketchy. Like any boy his age, he was not only a dirt magnet but proud of it. When he came out of the bathroom with the dirt still there and not even visibly rearranged, Chester sent him back. "Do a better job or you won't have to worry about supper," he said. "And it's tongue tonight."

That got Carl moving—yes, he loved tongue. Nobody'd told him it was poor people's food. He just thought it tasted good. When he emerged this time, there was no doubt water had touched his face. Chester wasn't so sure about soap. But when he went into the bathroom himself to unload some of that beer, he found the bar of Ivory had gone from white to muddy brown.

"For Pete's sake, wash the soap after you use it," he told his son when he came out.

Carl giggled. "That's a joke, Daddy! You wash *with* the soap."

"If anybody washes with the soap after you've been anywhere near it, he'll get dirtier, not cleaner," Chester said. Carl thought that was funny, too. Chester wondered if anything this side of a clout in the ear would make him change his mind.

Along with the tongue, supper included potatoes and carrots and onions. Sometimes Rita made tongue with cloves, the way most of her cookbooks recommended. Chester liked it better with lots of salt and horseradish. Carl couldn't stand horseradish—it was too strong for him. Chester hadn't liked it when he was a kid, either. Too big a mouthful was like a dagger up into your head.

After supper, Rita washed dishes and Carl unenthusiastically dried. Chester turned on the wireless. He spun the dial, going from quiz show to comedy to melodrama to music. Not a football game anywhere. He muttered to himself, even though he'd known there wouldn't be. The war had put paid to football leagues strong and weak all across the country. Travel for nothing more important than sport seemed unpatriotic—and a lot of football players were wearing uniforms of green-gray, not some gaudier colors.

Chester missed the broadcasts even so. He'd played a lot of football when he was younger—not for money, but he knew the game. And listening to announcers describing far-off action was one of the best ways he knew to wind down after a long, hard day.

Without any games, he settled on an adventure story set in Canada. The hero was trying to forestall Japanese agents from touching off an uprising. The Japs sounded like characters from a bad imitation of Gilbert and Sullivan. The Canadians who stayed loyal to the USA were almost as good as real Americans; the ones who didn't were truly despicable. All in all, the show was pretty dumb, but it made half an hour go by and it sold shaving cream—to say nothing of selling the Stars and Stripes.

At the top of the hour came five minutes of news. Stations had to have some if they wanted the government to renew their broadcast licenses. This was a pretty bare-bones setup—the reader droned away, presenting copy plainly taken straight from the wire services: "U.S. pilots have pounded strategic targets in Richmond, Louisville, and Nashville for the third night in a row. Damage is reported heavy. Only a few Confederate raiders appeared over Philadelphia last night. Several of them were shot down, while those that escaped did little harm."

Chester wondered how much of that he could believe. All of it? Any of it? What were the people who could actually see what was happening hearing on the news? Was it so relentlessly upbeat? He wouldn't have bet anything on it.

"Confederate authorities have denied reports that former Vice President Willy Knight was killed while attempting to escape," the newsman said. "Knight has been imprisoned since failing in his attempt to overthrow President Featherston. When asked about his current whereabouts and condition, Confederate spokesman Saul Goldman declined comment."

Again, more questions than answers. Was Willy Knight still alive? Had he died not attempting escape? Chester Martin shrugged. He wished Knight had managed to get rid of Featherston. The CSA wouldn't have been so dangerous without that maniac in charge.

"President Smith has announced that the United States are preparing strong counterblows against the Confederate States. 'We are one people. We are strong and determined, and we will prevail,' the President said to war workers in a factory outside Philadelphia. Long and tumultuous applause greeted his remarks."

Well, Chester knew what that meant: nothing at all. It was only wind and air. Of course the United States were preparing counterblows. Whether any would work was a different question. So far, the Confederates had been ready for everything the United States threw at them.

After a couple of local stories, the announcer said, "Coming up next is the popular *Marjorie's Hope*. Stay tuned." *Marjorie's Hope* wasn't popular with Chester. He turned off the wireless.

XII

When George Enos, Jr., joined the Navy, he thought he would go aboard a warship right away. Why not? He'd been a seaman for years. What more did he need to know? In his mind, the answer to that was *nothing*. The Navy had other ideas.

The Navy's ideas won. When the Navy's ideas bumped up against his, they always won. That was annoying, but it was how things worked.

It was also one of the things he had to learn before he could go from fisherman to Navy man. As the saying went, there was a right way, a wrong way, and a Navy way. If you did things the Navy way, you couldn't get in too much trouble. The training camp outside Providence drove that home.

George had been hundreds of miles out to sea. Except for his honeymoon at Niagara Falls, the train ride to Providence was the longest one he'd ever made. He was jammed up against a window. He liked that fine, except when he had to fight his way to the aisle to go to the toilet. Otherwise, he pressed his nose to the dirty, smeary glass and gaped at the countryside rolling by.

Training camp wasn't what he'd expected, either. The Navy seemed determined to make soldiers, not sailors, out of its recruits. George didn't mind the calisthenics, though the fellows ten years younger than he was had an easier time with them. He didn't mind making his cot up just so; he understood the need to keep things tidy in cramped places. He *did* mind the endless marching in formation. He saw no point to it. "Are we going to do close-order drill on a battleship deck, for crying out loud?" he grumbled one hot, sticky evening before lights-out.

"You know what it is? I'll tell you what it is," a skinny New York kid named Morris Fishbein said. His accent and George's were much further apart from each other than the miles separating their home towns; sometimes they hardly seemed to be speaking the same language. "They want to pound the individualism out of us, that's what they want to do."

"What do you mean?" George asked.

Before answering, Fishbein lit a cigarette. He smoked in quick, nervous puffs. Everything he did seemed fast and herky-jerky. His thoughts went the same way, leaping over the mental landscape where George had to plod one mental step at a time. Blowing out smoke, Fishbein said, "Only stands to reason. We all gotta act the same way on a ship. We all gotta do what they tell us, no matter what the hell it is, without even thinking about it. We don't do that, we get in trouble and maybe we put the ship in trouble. We gotta do it automatic-like, you know what I mean? So that's what close-order drill is for."

Maybe he was right. Maybe he was wrong. Right or wrong, he was sure as hell plausible. When George was marching and counter-marching and turning to the left flank and the right, he didn't feel like an individual. He barely felt like a human being. He was just one gear in an enormous machine where all the pieces worked smoothly together. Maybe that was what Fishbein was talking about.

Every once in a while, something would go wrong in the machinery. Somebody would turn right when he should have turned left, or else keep going straight when he should have counter-marched. What happened to such luckless people didn't bear thinking about. CPOs descended on them like a swarm of cats on a mouse. The abuse they screamed startled George, who'd been working at T Wharf and going to sea since before he started shaving, and who thought he'd heard it all.

"They should treat us better," he complained.

"Yeah, and then you wake up," Morrie Fishbein said scornfully.

"All we're there for is to get work out of us. Military proletariat is what we are. They don't have to treat us good. We fuck up, they replace us."

"You talk too much like that, they'll come down on you," George said.

"I'm a Socialist. So what? So's the President. It's still a free country—more or less. I'm not talking about the revolt of the proletariat. I don't want that. I want to blow the reactionaries in the goddamn CSA to hell and gone. We need an Army and a Navy for the job. But I know a class structure when I see one."

A big, slow-talking Midwesterner named Oswald Schmidt said, "I know something you don't know." His flat accent sounded nothing like George's or Fishbein's.

"Oh, yeah? What's that?" Fishbein bristled at the very idea.

"I know you talk too goddamn much."

It could have been the start of a fight. But everybody who heard it laughed too hard for anything to get started. And everybody except possibly Morris Fishbein knew he *did* talk too much.

Reveille at half past five made a lot of people groan every morning. George took it in stride. He put in longer hours at sea than the Navy made him put up with. Navy cooks weren't anything special— they couldn't very well be, not cooking for so many men. But quantity counted, too. Bacon and eggs and fried potatoes and plenty of coffee made the day worth facing.

George also learned to shoot a Springfield as if he were in the Army. He supposed that gave him a certain mental discipline, too. From rifles, he graduated to machine guns, and then to one-pounder antiaircraft guns. He felt a certain thrill firing one of those—his father had helped tend the same kind of weapon in the Great War.

Some of the recruits had no idea how to take care of weapons, or how to fix them when part of their mechanism went out of whack. George had no problems there. Any fisherman had to be a pretty good jackleg mechanic. If something broke down while you were out on the Grand Bank, you couldn't take it to the nearest repairman. You damn well had to fix it yourself, with whatever you had on your boat.

A couple of petty officers noticed that George's hands knew what they were doing. "Keep that up and you'll be a machinist's mate in jig time," one of them said.

"I don't much want to be a machinist's mate," George answered.

"Why not? People who can put things back together like you don't grow on trees. The Navy needs as many of 'em as it can get," the chief said, scowling at George for daring to have a mind of his own.

George shrugged. "If I have my druthers, I'll be a gunner. That's what my father was. Besides, I'd sooner blow up the other guys if I'm going to be in the scrap at all."

The chief stuck out his chin farther than should have been humanly possible. "Listen, Enos, you're in the Navy now. You don't get your druthers, and you ain't gonna have 'em, neither. You'll do what we tell you, or else you'll be the sorriest son of a bitch ever born—and then you'll do what we tell you. You got that?"

"Yes, Chief Isbell. Sure do." George knew better than to come right out and argue. That would have asked to get his square peg self rammed into a round hole. But he didn't volunteer for special machinist's training, either. He wondered if anybody would volunteer him. No one did. He let out a discreet sigh of relief, making sure none of the fearsome chiefs could hear him when he did it.

Before long, the raw seamen started training cruises in a destroyer that hadn't been new in the Great War and was downright ancient now. The *Lamson*'s decrepitude made her a better ship to learn in than a newer vessel would have been. Things were always going wrong with her. Her hull wasn't much more than rust covered by paint. That gave the aspiring sailors endless practice at chipping paint and polishing metal, two skills any seaman needed.

She was so old, she burned coal. George did a stretch in the black gang, shoveling it into her furnace. He came off those shifts exhausted and looking like the end man in a minstrel show. He coughed up black-streaked phlegm for days afterwards.

Once upon a time, the *Lamson* had been able to make twenty-eight knots. The only way she could do that these days was by falling off a cliff. Her boilers had more wheezes than a sanatorium full of consumptives. George knew diesels, but he'd never worked with steam before. He found himself interested in spite of his vow to steer himself toward gunnery.

He had a hammock and a duffel bag to call his own: even less in the way of space and belongings than he'd had on the *Sweet Sue*. For him, though, the adjustment was small. Some of the landsmen groused all the time. A couple of them just couldn't take it. They'd managed the barracks outside of Providence, but couldn't stand the even tighter quarters at sea. Or maybe it was the heads that did them in. They had no partitions. You did your business sitting next to somebody else who was doing his business, and if what you saw and heard and smelled put you off your stride, you got more and more constipated. The pharmacist's mates did a booming—so to speak—business in castor oil.

The *Lamson* had five three-inch guns. They hadn't been much back when she was built, and they were only popguns by today's standards. But they were big enough to give the crew practice at loading, firing, and shooting real artillery pieces.

An ensign with peach fuzz on his cheeks asked, "What would you do, men, if we were attacked by a British cruiser?"

Get blown to hell and gone, George thought, but that probably wasn't what the baby-faced officer wanted to hear. Morrie Fishbein said, "Launch torpedoes, sir. They'd be our best chance against anything that outgunned us by so much."

The ensign frowned. That was a good answer, but not the one he'd been looking for. He said, "But how would you fight back with our guns?"

"Shoot like hell and hope for the best, sir," Fishbein answered. "One hit from a six-inch gun and we're scrap iron anyway." He was right there, too. Destroyers weren't armored against shellfire. They couldn't be; they depended on speed instead. Armor added weight and would have slowed them down.

After that, the ensign asked fewer questions.

George did everything at the *Lamson*'s guns: he jerked shells, loaded, handled the altitude and azimuth screws, and finally commanded the piece. If he served a gun once he was assigned to his own ship, he knew he would start as a shell jerker. That was low man on the totem pole. He didn't care. As long as that gun was shooting at the Confederates—or the British, or the French, or the Japanese—he didn't care at all.

Some of the men on the *Lamson* got dreadfully seasick. The waves did pick her up and toss her around a good deal. That fresh-faced ensign turned almost as green as the Atlantic. George took the destroyer's motion in stride. Whatever the ocean did to her, it wasn't a patch on a fishing boat riding out a storm. Once you'd been through that, nothing else on the ocean would faze you . . . unless you were the luckless sort who never did find his sea legs. In that case, the Navy—or at least a warship—was a ghastly mistake.

There were men who kissed the dirty, splintery planks of the wharf when the *Lamson* got back to port in Providence. Nobody laughed at them. Everyone had been through enough to feel *There but for the grace of God go I.* If the grace of God didn't decide who made a good sailor and who didn't, George couldn't imagine what would.

As usual, the land seemed to reel when he came ashore. He was used to a constantly shifting surface under his feet; one that stayed in place felt wrong. So did a horizon that failed to roll and pitch. He knew the abnormalities would subside in a little while, which made them no less strange while they were going on.

Routine returned, including close-order drill. George endured it, waiting for his next cruise. The Navy had more nonsense in it than he'd expected when he put on the uniform. Once he was at sea, though, most of it went away. And that was what really mattered.

These days, cops with submachine guns patrolled the bus stop where blacks in the Terry went off to Augusta's war plants. They made sure nobody could repeat the atrocity that had scarred the colored part of town. Scipio didn't care. He went a couple of blocks out of his way every day so he didn't have to walk past that bus stop.

He knew avoiding it might not save him. There weren't enough cops in Augusta to examine every automobile in the Terry, let alone every one in the whole town. And a bomb didn't have to hide inside an auto. A creative terrorist had plenty of other choices.

Fewer whites joked about his penguin suit as he walked to the Huntsman's Lodge. Fewer joked at all. Hard suspicion filled most of the glances he got. His passbook got checked two or three times in the trip up to the restaurant.

Bathsheba said the same thing happened to her when she went to clean houses. More and more, whites in Augusta didn't want Negroes coming out of the Terry at all unless they rode on those buses.

Scipio wondered what the whites thought they would do if they started excluding waiters and cleaners and barbers and others who served them and made their lives easier and more comfortable. Would they start waiting on one another? He couldn't believe it. In the Confederate States, that was nigger work. The whole point of being a white in the CSA was that you didn't have to do nigger work. All whites were equal, above all blacks. Why else had the Confederate States seceded, if not to preserve that principle?

He slipped into the Huntsman's Lodge with a sigh of relief. As long as his shift lasted, everything would probably be all right. He knew his role here. He knew what to expect from his boss and the cooks and the other waiters and the customers. They wouldn't be wondering if he aimed to blow the place to hell and gone. The most they'd worry about was whether the steak they'd ordered rare would come back medium-rare. They'd look down their noses at him, but in a familiar way.

"Hello, Xerxes," Jerry Dover said when he came in. "You know a colored fella about your age named Aurelius? He said you did."

"Yes, suh, I knows Aurelius," Scipio answered. "How come *you* knows he?"

"He's looking for work here. Place he was at's closing down."

"Do Jesus! John Oglethorpe's place closin' down?" Scipio said in altogether unfeigned dismay. "He give me my first job waitin' tables in dis town—alongside Aurelius—when I come here durin' de las' war. What fo' he closin' down?"

"Got somethin' wrong with his ticker—he's not strong enough to keep the place open any more," Dover answered. "Too damn bad—I know he's been here a long time. This Aurelius knows his stuff, then?"

"Oh, yes, suh," Scipio said at once. "I reckon you knows about Oglethorpe's. Ain't no fancy place—just a diner. But Aurelius, he always put out de right forks an' spoons, an' he put dey where dey goes. I walk in dere lookin' for work, he check me on dat first thing."

He wondered if he'd just talked too much. Jerry Dover might ask him where he'd learned such things, if not at Oglethorpe's. On the other hand, Dover already knew Anne Colleton claimed he'd worked for her. If the restaurant manager had an ounce of sense, he knew that claim was true, too. He'd protected Scipio, but for the restaurant's sake more than the Negro's. And now Anne was dead. Scipio still found that hard to believe.

All Dover did ask was, "You reckon he can do the job?" That didn't just mean keeping the customers happy and knowing which fork went where. It meant showing up on time every day no matter what. It meant not making yourself intolerable to the cooks. It meant a good many other things, too, but those were the big ones.

Scipio nodded without hesitation. "Yes, suh. He do it. Dat man don't give you no trouble, not fo' nothin'."

"All right, then. I expect I'll take him on. We both know that Marius fella isn't working out."

This time, Scipio's nod was reluctant. Marius meant well. Scipio was convinced of that. But he also knew which road good intentions paved. The young waiter *would* come in late, and without letting Dover know ahead of time he'd be late. He was clumsy, and the cooks ragged him because of it. Like any cooks, the ones here were merciless when they scented weakness. And Marius couldn't take ribbing, and he was no damn good at giving it back.

Jerry Dover clapped Scipio on the back. "Don't worry about it. You're not the one who's going to can his ass. I am." He laughed. "And he'll probably end up in a war plant two days after I do it. Getting fired might be the best thing that ever happens to him."

"Yes, suh," said Scipio, who didn't believe it for a minute. Working in a war plant was better than getting shipped off to a camp, but it wasn't a whole lot better. The hours were long, the work was hard, and the pay was lousy. Very few blacks complained where whites could hear them. By all appearances, nobody did that more than once.

Out to the dining room Scipio went. It hadn't started filling up yet. A couple of businessmen sat smoking Habanas and going on in low voices about the killings they were making. Blacks might not gain much from the war plants. More than a few whites did.

Off at a corner table, a Confederate captain was spending a week's pay to impress a pretty blond girl. Scipio wondered if he'd get as much return for his investment as the businessmen did for theirs. He must have thought so, or he wouldn't have brought her here.

Scipio smiled at the eagerness blazing from the young officer. Confederate soldiers bothered him much less than Freedom Party stalwarts or guards. Soldiers mostly looked outward, not inward. The Party oppressed Negroes. Soldiers aimed at the USA.

And yet . . . Scipio wished he hadn't thought about *and yet*. He'd killed a Confederate officer in 1916, as the Congaree Socialist Republic fell to pieces. Plenty of other officers and soldiers had helped to break it. He wished he could forget those days, but he didn't think he'd ever be free of them.

Before long, more people started coming into the Huntsman's Lodge. Scipio was glad enough to serve them, and wished there were more still. As long as he stayed busy, he didn't have to think. Not thinking, these days, counted for a blessing.

Bathsheba would have wagged a finger at him if he'd said something like that where she could hear it. Her faith sustained her. Part of Scipio wished he too believed in God and in good times to come. He wished he could. But what kind of God would let people go through what the Negroes in the CSA were enduring? No kind that Scipio wanted anything to do with.

When his shift ended, he made his way home. That was plenty to put the fear of God in him. Since the two auto bombs went off, black predators weren't all he had to worry about in the Terry. Whites with pistols or rifles or submachine guns often came in after night fell and shot up the place almost at random. They'd hit his building only once, and never the floor where he and his family lived. Who could say how long that would last, though?

Sometimes people in the Terry would shoot back. But that carried its own risks. The only thing that would guarantee a Negro a more horrible death than killing a white man was raping a white woman. No matter how desperate for self-defense the blacks of Augusta were, any serious resistance would bring more firepower than they could hope to withstand down on their heads.

Damned if we do, damned if we don't, Scipio thought miserably. Somebody not too far away chose that exact moment to fire off a whole magazine from a submachine gun. It punctuated his bitter thoughts. So did the laughter—without a doubt from a white throat—that followed.

"Praise the Lord you're here," Bathsheba said when Scipio finally walked into their apartment.

"Praise de Lawd," Scipio echoed, tasting his own hypocrisy. He added, "You should oughta be sleepin'."

"Guns woke me." By the calm way his wife said it, it might have been an everyday occurrence. Increasingly, it was. As Scipio got out of his tuxedo, Bathsheba asked, "What's the news?"

He had some this evening: "Look like Aurelius be comin' to work at de Huntsman's Lodge."

"How come?" Bathsheba asked. "Don't you tell me Mr. Oglethorpe threw him out. I don't believe it." John Oglethorpe was the most decent white man either of them knew. He would have clouted anybody who told him so in the side of the head with a frying pan. In an odd way, that too was a measure of his decency.

Scipio shook his head. "Mistuh Oglethorpe closin' down on account of he ain't well no more. Aurelius got to find what he kin."

"I pray for Mr. Oglethorpe," Bathsheba said. Scipio nodded. Prayer couldn't hurt. On the other hand, he didn't think it would do much good. Oglethorpe had to be pushing eighty, or maybe past it. When you got to that age, you didn't sit down and start *War and Peace.*

Sliding his nightshirt on over his head, Scipio brushed his teeth at the sink and then lay down beside Bathsheba. Had he been in a mood to thank God for anything, it would have been for good teeth. He still had all but two of the ones he'd been born with, and they didn't give him much trouble. He knew how lucky he was by the misery so many people went through.

Then again, he still had the skin he was born with, too. That caused him lots of misery all by itself. That kind of skin caused millions of people in the CSA misery. And who cared about them? Nobody in this country. Nobody in the United States, or they would have protested louder when the Confederates started abusing Negroes over and above the ways they'd always abused them. Nobody in the Empire of Mexico. Nobody in Britain or France, not when they were on the same side as Jake Featherston.

Nobody at all.

"Ain't easy, bein' a nigger," he muttered.

"What you say?" Bathsheba asked sleepily. He repeated himself, a little louder this time. She nodded; he could feel the bed move. "Never was, never is, never gonna be. You ain't used to that by now?"

Her words paralleled his thoughts all too well. But, for once, however bad it had been, however bad it might be, didn't measure up to how bad it was now. Scipio started to say so. But his wife's breathing had gone soft and regular; she'd fallen back to sleep.

Scipio wished he could do the same. No matter what he wished, he couldn't. He had too much on his mind. What if a white man sent a burst of submachine-gun fire through this flat in the next five minutes? What if a black man set off an auto bomb in front of the building? What if . . . ?

What if you relax and get some rest? Scipio shook his head. Those other things might happen. They were only too likely to happen. Rest and sleep were unlikely to come any time soon. He didn't know what he could do about that. He didn't think he could do anything. And that by itself made a perfectly good reason not to be able to sleep.

Armstrong Grimes loped in the direction of Provo, Utah. Barrels rumbled along with the advancing U.S. infantry. Most of them couldn't go any faster than he could. The Army had hauled Great War machines out of storage and put them to work against the Mormons. Philadelphia needed its modern barrels for the fight against the CSA, and must have figured these antiques would do well enough here.

In a way, Armstrong could see the War Department's point of view. Against an enemy with no barrels of his own, any old barrels would do. But these beasts had enormous crews, broke down if you looked at them sideways, and couldn't get out of their own way. It did make him wonder how seriously the folks back East took this fighting.

A machine gun in a farmhouse up ahead started chattering. Armstrong dove behind a boulder and shot back. He didn't know how much good that would do. A lot of the houses here were built like fortresses. The Mormons defended them as if they were fortresses, too. Armstrong had already discovered that.

One of those slow, awkward barrels turned toward the farmhouse. Since it had a prow-mounted cannon instead of a rotating turret, it had to turn to make the gun bear on the target. It waddled forward. Bullets from the machine gun spanged off its armor. It could ignore those, though any cannon shell would have ripped into it like a can opener.

Confident in its immunity, the barrel moved in for the perfect shot—and ran over a buried mine. *Whump!* Armstrong didn't know how many tons the barrel weighed, but the mine made it jump in the air. Smoke and flames poured out of the cannon port and all the machine-gun ports. They poured from the escape hatches, too, when those flew open. Only a handful of crewmen managed to get out, and the Mormon machine gunners remorselessly shot most of them down.

Ammunition started cooking off inside the carcass of the machine. The *pop-pop-pop* sounded absurdly cheerful, like firecrackers on the Fourth of July. By then, whoever was still inside the barrel had to be dead.

"Son of a bitch," Armstrong muttered. A moment later, another barrel hit a mine and started to burn. "*Son* of a bitch!" he said. The Mormons had known what they'd be up against, all right, and they were ready to fight it. *Did anybody know what* we'd *be up against?* he wondered.

Whistling screams in the air made Armstrong dig in for dear life. The shells that came down on the U.S. soldiers weren't of the ordinary sort. The Mormons had some conventional artillery, but not a whole lot. As they had with their biplane bomber, they'd improvised. Large-caliber mortars didn't shoot very far, but you didn't want to be on the receiving end when the bombs landed.

The earth shook under Armstrong. He jammed his thumbs into his ears and yelled as loud as he could. That eased the blast, a little. Dirt and small stones—and a couple not so small—thrown up by near misses pattered down on his back.

Corporal Stowe jumped in the foxhole with him. The squad leader shouted something. Armstrong took his thumbs out of his ears. Stowe shouted it again: "Gas!"

"Shit," Armstrong said, and grabbed for his mask. If it was mustard gas or nerve gas, even the mask might not help. Those could get you through the skin—you didn't have to inhale them.

More mortar bombs thudded home. They were obviously homemade. What about the poison gas in them? Did the Mormons have labs cranking it out in the desert somewhere? That wasn't impossible; who paid attention to anything in Utah but the stretch from Provo up to Ogden? But it was also possible that the rebels here had had some help from others who called themselves Rebels. The Confederates would have to be crazy *not* to do all they could for the Mormons. As long as this uprising tied down large numbers of U.S. soldiers, those soldiers wouldn't go into action against the CSA.

Armstrong breathed in air that tasted of rubber. He peered out through little portholes that needed cleaning.

A U.S. barrel was shelling the house that held the machine gun. Part of the roof had fallen in, but the machine-gun crew was still in business. Muzzle flashes and the streaks of tracers made that very clear. Sooner or later, U.S. forces would drive the Mormons out of that house, but at what price? The USA had already lost two barrels and most of the big crews the lumbering Great War machines carried. And another old-fashioned barrel wasn't moving and wasn't shooting. Had gas got the men inside? Armstrong wouldn't have been surprised.

We aren't buying anything cheap today, he thought. Whatever the price, in the end the United States could afford to pay it and the Mormons couldn't. Just because the United States could, though, didn't necessarily mean they should. That seemed obvious to PFC Armstrong Grimes. He wondered if it had occurred to anybody in the War Department. On the evidence, it seemed unlikely.

U.S. artillery started pounding the machine-gun position. More U.S. shells fell farther back: counterbattery fire against the Mormon mortars. Of course, the mortar crews might not have hung around to get pounded. Mortars were much lighter and more portable than regular artillery. Again, did anybody on the U.S. side think in those terms?

Any which way, Armstrong knew what his job was. He jumped out of his foxhole, ran forward twenty or thirty feet, and threw himself into a crater one of the mortar bombs had made—they hadn't all been loaded with poison gas. The machine gun's stream of bullets came searching for him, but too late. He'd reached new cover.

Have to stay here a while, till they forget about me. He panted. Running hard in a gas mask wasn't easy. It was, in fact, damn near impossible. The filter cartridge wouldn't let you suck in enough air.

He could have all the air he wanted if he took off the mask. Of course, he would also keel over in short order if he got unlucky. Some men didn't care. They took big chances with poison gas, just because they couldn't stand their gas masks. Armstrong took his share of chances, too, but not like that.

When artillery failed to silence the Mormon machine gun, dive bombers paid it a call. They didn't scream like Confederate Asskickers, but they flattened the house. The machine gun fell silent at last. U.S. soldiers, Armstrong among them, cautiously moved forward.

No one shot at them from the shattered house any more. But as they drew near, somebody stepped on a cunningly buried land mine. The man in green-gray screamed, but not for long—he'd been blown to red rags below the waist. And another machine gun a couple of hundred yards father back, whose crew seemed to have waited for just that, opened up on the Americans.

Armstrong didn't know whether to shit or go blind. He threw himself to the ground, wondering if explosives hidden beneath it would blast him sky-high an instant later. Bullets stitched malevolently through the dirt all around him, kicking dust off the portholes of his gas mask. He crawled for the shelter of a rock. It wasn't much shelter, because it wasn't much of a rock. He gratefully took anything he could get.

Behind him, an American machine gun opened up. Bullets zipped over his head—not far enough over it, as far as he was concerned. They'd probably nail some of his buddies, not that the gunners would give a damn. He didn't shed a tear when machine gunners got shot. They were almost as bad as snipers.

And they couldn't knock out the Mormon machine gunners, which made them all the more worthless. He had no idea where or if the Mormons had done their basic training. Wherever it was, they all fought like ten-year veterans. They never showed much of themselves, they always had gun positions supporting other gun positions, and they didn't seem to have heard of retreat. The only way U.S. soldiers moved forward was over their dead bodies.

Armstrong spotted Corporal Stowe sprawled behind another rock. He pointed toward the Mormons ahead—making sure he exposed no part of himself to their fire—and shouted, "Why can't we turn these fuckers loose against the Confederates? They'd kick Featherston's ass." Through the mask, he sounded disembodied, unearthly.

"Tell me about it," Stowe yelled back. "Only trouble is, they'd rather shoot us."

"Yeah. I know." Armstrong started digging in behind his rock. The corporal was only too right.

As usual, U.S. artillery went into action to try to neutralize the latest Mormon machine-gun nest. *Neutralize* was a nice, meaningless word. If you neutralized somebody, you just took him off the board like a captured checker. You didn't blow his arm off halfway between the elbow and shoulder or drive red-hot metal shards through his balls or take off the top of his skull like the shell from a hard-boiled egg. Of course, he was trying to do all those charming things to you, too. You couldn't afford to waste a lot of grief on him. Not wasting grief on him was what brought words like neutralize front and center.

The machine gun stopped shooting. Armstrong stayed right where he was. He'd seen soldiers play possum before. If you thought they were really down for the count, you'd pay for it. Armstrong's goal in life was to make the other guy pay for it. So far, he'd managed.

He glanced over to Corporal Stowe. The two-striper wasn't going anywhere, either. Armstrong just hoped some whistle-ass lieutenant wouldn't order everybody forward. That would show whether the Mormons were fooling, all right—probably show it the hard way.

Before a junior officer could do anything stupid, some dumb kid did it for him, standing up so he could move toward the objective. Somewhere up the road was a town romantically called Thistle. That was about as good as naming a place Dandelion or Poison Ivy.

As the kid walked forward and a couple of other soldiers stood up to go with him, Armstrong hoped the artillery had got lucky. It could happen; a direct hit from a 105 would make even a sandbagged machine-gun nest say uncle.

Armstrong still sat tight. He wanted to see what was happening before he put his neck on the line. He didn't always get the chance, but he wanted to. Then more trusting soldiers trotted forward. They carried their Springfields at the ready. *Fat lot of good it'll do them,* Armstrong thought.

Fat lot of good it did them. The machine gun, very much unsubdued, opened up again. Several advancing soldiers fell. Others dove for cover. *Fools. Suckers,* went through Armstrong's mind. He was no great brain, but he could figure out when somebody was lying in wait for him. Maybe some of the men who'd managed to take cover would learn that lesson now. The sorry bastards who'd stopped bullets wouldn't get the chance.

Eventually, a barrel shelled the machine gun into silence. Armstrong scurried forward. Would Thistle be worth having once the Army finally took it? Not likely. And what would happen after that? They'd push on to Provo, where the Mormons would fight from house to house, and which was big enough to have a lot of houses. How many men would go through the grinder there? How many would come out the other side? And the most important question of all: *will I be one of them?*

Alec Pomeroy wrinkled his nose when he walked into the barn on his grandmother's farm. "It smells like animal poop in here!" he said.

"Well . . . yes." His mother fought not to laugh. To Mary Pomeroy, the smell of a barn was one of the most normal, natural things in the world. She'd grown up with it. Even now, she took it altogether for granted. But Alec was town-raised. Farm life and farm smells didn't come natural to him. Mary said, "Don't you like it?"

"No! Eww! It's nasty! It's disgustering!" Alec hadn't quite learned how to say that, but he knew what he meant.

"Well, why don't you go back to Grandma at the farmhouse, then?" Mary said. "If you ask her nicely, maybe—just maybe—she'll let you have another piece of rhubarb pie."

"Do you think so?" Alec's eyes got big.

"You'll never know till you try, will you?" Mary said. Alec was off like a shot.

Mary breathed a sigh of relief. She'd hoped the odor of the barn would be enough to get her son out of her hair for a little while. She didn't need long. The old wagon wheel still lay in the same old place. Moving it took an effort, but not an enormous one. She scraped away the dirt under it, and then lifted up the flat board the dirt concealed.

Under the board was a hole her father had dug. Mary nodded to herself. She'd taken years to find that hole. No one else ever had. It had kept Arthur McGregor's bomb-making tools safe, even though the Yanks had searched the farm at least a dozen times.

And now it would keep them safe again. Mary was carrying the biggest handbag she owned, one the size of a young suitcase. It was plenty big enough to hold the dynamite and blasting caps and fuse and crimpers and other specialized tools of the bomber's trade.

She took them out of the purse and put them back in the hole from which she'd exhumed them years before. *You're not going in there forever,* she thought, *only for a while.* Who could say whether Wilf Rokeby would tell the occupiers what he knew about her? If he decided she was the one who'd planted that flyer in the post office, he would. She wanted the evidence out of the way, just in case.

With the explosives and tools stowed once more, she replaced the board and pushed dirt and straw over it till it looked like the rest of the barn's floor. Then the old wagon wheel went back where it belonged. She scuffed around the dirt where it had lain after she'd moved it, so that place looked ordinary, too.

Then she had to clean her hands as best she could on her skirt. Fortunately, it was beige, so the dust hardly showed. She looked around one more time. Satisfied she'd set everything to rights, she went back to the farmhouse herself.

As she always did, she felt as if she were falling back into her childhood when she went inside. But how had her mother got old? Maude McGregor's hair was supposed to be as red as her own, not this dull, lifeless gray. And when had her back begun to bend?

Alec was devastating an enormous chunk of rhubarb pie. Mary's mother looked up with a smile on her face. It slipped a little when her eyes met Mary's. "Did you take care of whatever needed taking care of?" she asked.

Maude McGregor had never said much of anything about what Arthur McGregor had done. She'd known. Mary was sure of that. Her mother couldn't have failed to know. But she'd got into the habit of keeping quiet, and she'd stuck with it. She'd never said much of anything about what Mary was up to, either. Plainly, though, she also knew about that—or knew enough, anyhow.

Mary nodded now. "Everything's fine, Ma. Everything's just fine."

"Good," her mother said. "Always nice to have you visit, dear. Don't want to see any trouble. Don't want to see any trouble at all. We've had enough, haven't we? Come back whenever you need to."

"Can I have some more pie?" Alec asked.

"If you eat any more pie, you'll turn into a rhubarb," Mary said. That was the wrong approach; Alec liked the idea. He would have liked it even better if he'd had any idea what a rhubarb looked like.

He'd eaten enough rhubarb pie and other things to fall asleep on the trip home. He hardly ever did that any more, however much Mary wished he would. He'd be grumpy when he woke up, grumpy and then bouncy. Mary knew he wouldn't want to go to bed tonight. She'd worry about that later. *You sure will,* she told herself.

On the way back into town, the Oldsmobile bumped over the railroad tracks. Alec stirred and muttered, but didn't rouse. Mary smiled to herself. *One of these days before too long . . . but not quite yet.*

"I hope you told your mother hello for me," Mort said when he got home that night.

"Of course I did," Mary said.

"That's good." His smile was wide and genial, as usual. "I'm glad. You haven't been out there for a while. Is she still all right by herself?"

With a parent getting older, that was always a worry, and Mary had noticed how the years were starting to lie heavy on her mother's shoulders. Even so, she nodded. "For a while longer, I think. She hangs on. That farm is her life—that and her grandchildren." For some reason, Alec wasn't much interested in supper. Mary didn't scold him, not after what she knew he'd put away.

Three days later, someone knocked on the door in the middle of the afternoon. When Mary opened it, she found herself facing a tall, skinny, swarthy officer in a blue-gray uniform. "Mrs. Pomeroy?" he asked in accented English. "I am Captain Brassens of the Army of the Republic of Quebec." He touched one corner of the skinny black mustache that made him look like a cinema villain. Behind him stood four or five soldiers, Frenchies all.

"Yes?" Mary said. "And so? What do you want with me? I haven't done anything."

"It could be," Captain Brassens said. "Or it could be otherwise. We shall see. Do you know a certain Mrs. Laura Moss, formerly Laura Secord, of Berlin, Ontario?"

"Never heard of her," Mary said at once. Wilf Rokeby was throwing mud, then. She might have known. She *had* known.

Brassens's raised eyebrow was Gallic almost to the point of self-parody. "You deny, then, that you posted to the said Mrs. Moss a package shortly before a bomb burst in her flat, killing her and her young daughter?"

"Of course I deny it," Mary said. "I've never heard anything so ridiculous in all my born days."

"This may be true. Or, on the other hand, this may be something other than true." Captain Brassens turned to the men at his back and spoke to them in French. Mary knew next to nothing of what had been Canada's other language. The soldiers showed her what their commander had said, though. They turned her apartment upside down.

"I don't suppose you have a warrant," she said as they got to work.

The Quebecois officer shook his head. "I have none. I need none. Military occupation takes precedence. You should know this." He looked at her reproachfully, as if to say he might have to give her a low mark because of her ignorance. But she knew. She'd just wanted to get her protest on the record.

And she had one more protest to add: "I think it's a crying shame you can do this to an innocent person who's never done anybody any harm."

"So you say," Captain Brassens answered coldly. "But is it not true that your brother was shot for sabotage? Is it not true that your father was a notorious bomber who killed many? It could be that you are an innocent person. It could be, yes. But it also could be that you are not. We shall see."

Wilf Rokeby must have been singing like a meadowlark in spring. *He has a yellow belly like a meadowlark, too,* Mary thought. "You can't blame me for what my family did—and my brother never did anything," she told Brassens. "Go ahead and look as much as you please. I've got nothing to hide." *That's the truth. I already hid it.*

The soldiers were gentle with Alec. They didn't let him interfere, but they didn't smack him or even shout at him. He seemed to decide they were making a mess for the fun of it. To a little boy, that was a perfectly reasonable conclusion. He started throwing things around, too. The Frenchies thought that was funny.

After they'd done their worst, they reported back to Captain Brassens. They spoke French, so Mary didn't know what they said. He asked them several sharp questions in the same language. After they'd answered, he turned to her and said, "*Eh bien,* it appears—it

appears, mind you—that you have been telling the truth and someone else is the liar. We shall remember that."

"I hope you do," Mary said—raw relief helped her sound angry,
the way she was supposed to. She drew herself up and glared at Captain Brassens. "And I hope you'll have the common decency to
apologize for being wrong."

He stared steadily back at her. "I am sorry . . ." he began, and
she could tell he meant, *I am sorry we did not catch you.* But then,
after a pause, he finished, ". . . we have disturbed your tranquility.
Good day." He started to turn away.

"Wait," Mary said. The Quebecois officer stopped in surprise.
"There's some of our stuff stored in the basement, too," she told
him. "If you're going to do this to me, you might as well do everything at once."

"Oh. I see. You need not worry yourself about that, Mrs.
Pomeroy," the Frenchy said. "We searched those things before paying a call upon you. Had we found anything of interest there, we
would have paid a different sort of call. On that, you may rely." He
spoke to his men in their own language. They tramped away.

"Look what they did, Mommy!" Alec said. "Are they going to
come back and do it some more?"

"I hope not," Mary answered. "Will you help me try to put
things back together?"

He did try. She gave him credit for that. But he was much more
interested in making messes than in repairing them. He got bored in
a hurry. Mary hadn't realized how much she and Mort had till she
saw it all spilled on the floor. The soldiers in blue-gray had enjoyed
mess-making as much as Alec did. They'd even pawed through her
underwear, though explosives were unlikely to be lurking there.

She'd got things about half repaired by the time Mort came
home from across the street. "What happened here?" he asked.
"Our own private earthquake?"

"You're close," Mary answered. "The Frenchies searched the
place."

Her husband blinked. "Why would they do that?"

"Because my father . . . did what he did. Because my brother . . .
was who he was," she said. *Because Wilf Rokeby is trying to save
his own skin,* she added, but only to herself. She wasn't supposed to

know anything more than the usual gossip about how and why the longtime postmaster had ended up in trouble with the occupying authorities.

Mort gave her a hug. "Those dirty bastards," he said, which was about as rough as he ever talked around her. "They've got no business doing that. None, you hear me?"

"They've got the guns," Mary said bleakly. "They can do whatever they want."

She hated that kind of argument when Mort used it on her. By his sour expression, he didn't like it coming back at him, either. He said, "It's not right. They can't tear your place to shreds for no reason at all." It wasn't for no reason at all, but he didn't know that. Mary didn't intend to let him find out, either.

Big, snorting trucks brought the latest shipment of Negroes to Camp Dependable. The trucks were painted butternut and had butternut canvas covers over the back. From the outside, they looked just like the vehicles that hauled Confederate soldiers here and there. And, in fact, the differences were minor. The biggest one was that these trucks were fitted with manacles and leg irons to make sure their passengers didn't depart before they got where they were going.

Jefferson Pinkard came out to watch the unloading, the way he always did. His men had it down to a science. He watched anyway. The Negroes coming into his camp had nothing to lose, and they probably knew it. If some of them could beat the restraints before they got here, they might grab a guard who was releasing them and turn his gun on the others. Even science could go wrong, especially if you got careless.

Nobody here got careless. That was another reason Jeff came to the unloadings. When men worked under the boss's eye, they worked by the book. They didn't get smart. They didn't get cute. They just did what they were supposed to do. Nothing went wrong, which was exactly what Jeff wanted.

"Good job," he told Mercer Scott when the last Negro had been processed through into the camp.

"Yeah." The guard chief nodded. He paused to light a cigarette, then held out the pack. Jeff took one, too. Scott went on, "All the same, though, I wonder why the hell we bother."

"How do you mean?" Jeff asked.

Scott's gesture left a small trail of smoke in its wake. "Well, shit, we could get rid of these niggers as soon as they come in the gates, blow their goddamn brains out while they're still in the trucks, and save ourselves the bother of leadin' 'em out to the swamp later on."

"Population reductions," Pinkard said distastefully. They still offended his sense of order. He was a *jailer,* dammit, not a . . . a. . . . He didn't have the word for what his superiors were turning him into, didn't have it and didn't want to go looking for it very hard. After a moment, he shook his head. "Wouldn't work so good. They'd have to shoot 'em, and then they'd have to get rid of their bodies, 'stead o' just letting 'em fall into the trenches like they do now. We'd have more people eating their guns and going out like Chick Blades."

"Shit," Scott said again, but he didn't try to tell Jeff he was wrong. Instead, he suggested, "We could let the niggers who're still alive dispose of the others."

That sounded halfhearted. There were good reasons why it should, too. Pinkard pointed that out: "This place is antsy enough as is. We start doin' our population reductions right here and let the niggers know for sure we're doin' 'em, it's gonna blow up right in our faces. You want to tell me any different?"

"No." Mercer Scott scowled, but he could see the obvious when you rubbed his nose in it. "No, goddammit."

"All right, then," Jeff said. "We'll keep on doin' it the same old way till we come up with somethin' better. *Better,* you hear me?"

"I hear you." Scott threw his butt on the ground and crushed it out under his boot heel. He probably would have sooner crushed Jeff under it, but even a guard chief didn't always get his druthers.

For that matter, a camp commandant didn't, either. Jeff went back to his office muttering to himself. He hated the way Camp Dependable worked now, but he hadn't been able to come up with anything better, either. Trucks came in. Shackled prisoners shambled into the swamp. They didn't come out. And, every so often, a Chick Blades would run a hose from his auto's exhaust pipe into the passenger compartment, turn on the motor, and. . . .

The obvious. And maybe, maybe, the not so obvious. Instead of sitting down at his desk, Pinkard started pacing around it. After half a dozen revolutions, he paused, an unaccustomed look of wonder spreading across his fleshy face. "Well, fuck me!" he exclaimed. "Maybe I *am* a genius."

If he was, he needed something to prove his genius on. He hurried out of the office again. To his relief, not all the trucks had left. He kept one of them and sent the driver back with a pal. When the man squawked, Pinkard said, "You tell your boss to give me a call. I'll square it with him—you bet I will." The driver grumbled some more, but Jeff had the bulge to get away with it.

"What's going on?" Mercer Scott asked, attracted by the argument.

"Need me a truck," Jeff answered.

Scott scratched his head. "How come?"

"You'll see," was all Pinkard said. If this worked, it was his baby. If it didn't work, he'd have to fix it up with the fellow from whose bailiwick he'd lifted the truck. He figured he could. One truck and one miffed driver were small change in the bureaucratic skirmishes that ate so much of his life these days. He clapped Scott on the back. "I'm going into town for a little while. Try not to let the niggers steal this place or burn it down while I'm gone, all right?"

Scott staring after him, he drove the truck into Alexandria. He was glad traffic was light. He'd never tried handling anything so big, and he wasn't used to a gearshift with five forward speeds instead of the usual three. But he didn't hit anything, and he wasn't grinding the gears when he shifted nearly so much by the time he got where he was going: a garage named Halliday's, on the outskirts of town.

Stuart Halliday was a compact man with battered, clever hands. "What can I do for you, buddy?" he asked when Jeff descended from the truck.

Jeff told him what he wanted, finishing, "Can you handle it?"

The mechanic rubbed his chin. "Sheet metal all the way around there . . . Gasketing on the doors . . ."

"Gotta be sturdy sheet metal," Pinkard said.

"Yeah, I heard you." Halliday thought for a little while, then nodded. "Yeah, I can do it. Set you back two hundred and fifty bucks."

"I'll give you one seventy-five," Jeff said. They haggled good-naturedly for a little while before settling on two and a quarter. Jeff asked, "How soon can you let me have it?"

"Be about a week." Halliday sent Pinkard a curious look. "What the hell you want it like that for?"

"Camp business," Jeff answered. If the snoopy garage man couldn't work it out for himself, that was all to the good. Then Pinkard coughed. In all of this, he hadn't figured in one thing. "Uh— you give me a lift back to camp?"

Halliday carefully didn't smile. "Why, sure."

When Jeff came back without the truck, Mercer Scott sent him a stare full of hard suspicion. He didn't care. He knew what he was doing, or thought he did. Over the week, while Halliday was over-hauling the truck, he made a few preparations of his own. Till he saw how this would go, he intended to play his cards close to his chest.

He paid Halliday when the mechanic delivered the revised and edited machine. He used camp money. If the thing didn't work, he'd pay it back out of his own pocket. Halliday stuffed brown bank-notes into his coveralls. "I left that one hole, like you said," he told Jeff. "I don't understand it, not when the rest is pretty much airtight, but I did it."

"You got paid for doin' the work," Jeff answered. "You didn't get paid for understanding."

One of Halliday's kids drove him away from Camp Dependable. Unlike Jeff, he'd thought ahead. After he was gone, Jeff did some of his own work on the truck. He drew a small crowd of guards. Most of them hung around for a while, then went off shrugging and shaking their heads.

Mercer Scott watched like a hawk. Suddenly, he exclaimed, "You son of a bitch! You *son* of a bitch! You reckon it'll work?"

Pinkard looked up from fitting a length of pipe to the hole that had puzzled Stuart Halliday. "I don't know," he said, "but I aim to find out."

"Chick Blades ought to get a promotion for giving you the idea," Scott said. "Goddamn shame he's too dead to appreciate it."

"Yeah." Jeff examined his handiwork. Slowly, he nodded to himself. "That ought to do it. Now I'll just announce a transfer to another camp. . . ."

Getting Negroes to volunteer to hop into the truck was so easy, it almost embarrassed him. The hardest part was picking and choosing among them. They knew that when they got shackled together and marched out into the swamp, they weren't coming back. But a transfer to another camp had to be an improvement. Maybe there wouldn't be population reductions somewhere else.

Pinkard drove the truck himself that first time. It was his baby. He wanted to see how it went. He closed the gasketed doors behind the Negroes who'd got in. The lock and bar to keep those doors closed were good and solid. Halliday hadn't skimped. Jeff would have skinned the mechanic alive if he had.

He started up the engine and drove out of camp. It wasn't long before the Negroes realized exhaust fumes were filling their compartment. They started shouting—screaming—and pounding on the metal walls. Jeff drove and drove. After a while, the screams subsided and the pounding stopped. He drove a little longer after that, just to be on the safe side.

When he was satisfied things had worked out the way he'd hoped, he took a road that the prisoners had built into the swamp. Mercer Scott and half a dozen guards waited at the end of it. Jeff got out of the cab and walked around to the back of the truck. "Well, let's see what we've got," he said, and opened the rear doors.

"By God, you did it," Scott said.

The Negroes inside were dead, asphyxiated. All the guards had to do was take them out and throw them in a hole in the ground. Well, almost all. One of the men held his nose and said, "Have to hose it down in there before you use it again."

"Reckon you're right," Jeff said. But he was just about happy enough to dance a jig. No fuss, no muss—well, not too much—no bother. Guards wouldn't have to pull the trigger again and again and again. They wouldn't have to see what they were doing at all. They'd just have to . . . drive.

And, best of all, the Negroes inside Camp Dependable wouldn't know what was happening. Their pals who got in the truck were going to another camp, weren't they? Sure they were. Nobody expected them to come back.

Mercer Scott came up and set a hand on Pinkard's shoulder. "You know how jealous I am of you? You got any idea? Christ, I'd've given my left nut to come up with something so fine."

"It really did work, didn't it?" Jeff said. "You know what? I reckon maybe I will try and bump poor Chick up a grade or two. It'd make his missus' pension a little bigger."

Scott gave him a sly look. "She'd be right grateful for that. Not a bad-lookin' woman, not a bit. Maybe I oughta be jealous of you twice."

Jeff hadn't thought of it like that. Now that he did, he found himself nodding. She'd been haggard and in shock at the funeral, but still. . . . Business first, though. "Other thing I'm gonna do," he said, "is I'm gonna call Richmond, let 'em know about this. They been tellin' me stuff all along. By God, it's my turn now."

Ferdinand Koenig strode into Jake Featherston's office in the Gray House. The Attorney General was a big, bald, burly man with a surprisingly light, high voice. "Good to see you, Ferd. Always good to see you," Jake said, and stuck out his hand. Koenig squeezed it. They went back to the very beginnings of the Freedom Party. Koenig had backed Jake at the crucial meeting that turned it into *his* party. He came as close to being a friend as any man breathing; Jake had meant every word of his greeting. Now he asked, "What's on your mind?"

"Head of one of the camps out in Louisiana, fellow named Pinkard, had himself a hell of a good idea," Koenig said.

"I know about Pinkard—reliable man," Jake said. "Joined the Party early, stayed in when we were in trouble. Wife ran around on him, poor bastard. Went down to fight in Mexico, and not many who weren't in the hard core did that."

Koenig chuckled. "I could've named a lot of people in slots like that—slots lower down, too—and you'd know about them the same way."

"Damn right I would. I make it my business to know stuff like that," Featherston said. The more you knew about somebody, the better you could guess what he'd do next—and the easier you could get your hooks into him, if you ever had to do that. "So what's Pinkard's idea?"

"He's . . . got a whole new way of looking at the population-reduction problem," Koenig said.

Jake almost laughed out loud at that. Even a tough customer

like Ferd Koenig had trouble calling a spade a spade. Jake knew what he aimed to do. Koenig wanted to do the same thing. The only difference was, Ferd didn't like talking about it. He—and a bunch of other people—were like a hen party full of maiden ladies tiptoeing around the facts of life.

The laugh came out as an indulgent smile. "Tell me about it," Jake urged. Koenig did. Featherston listened intently. The longer the Attorney General talked, the harder Jake listened. He leaned forward till his chair creaked, as if to grab Koenig's words as fast as they came out. When the other man finished, Jake whistled softly. "This could be big, Ferd. This could be really, really big."

"I was thinking the same thing," Koenig said.

"A fleet of trucks like that, they'd be easy to build—cheap, too," Featherston said. "How much you tell me it cost Pinkard to fix that one up?"

Koenig had to check some notes he pulled from a breast pocket. "He paid . . . let me see . . . $225 for the sheet-metal paneling, plus another ten bucks for the pipe. He did the work with that himself— didn't want the mechanic figuring out what was going on."

"He *is* a smart fellow," Featherston said approvingly. "We get a fleet of those bastards made, we're out of the retail business and we go into wholesale." Now he did laugh—he was wondering what Saul Goldman would say to that. But he got back to business in a hurry. "Shooting people in the head all day—that's hard work. A lot of men can't take it."

"That's what Pinkard said. He said this guard named"—Koenig glanced at the notes again—"named Blades killed himself with car exhaust, and that's what gave him the idea. He asked if Blades' widow could get a bigger pension on account of this turned out to be so important."

"Give it to her," Jake said at once. "Pinkard's right. Like I say, shooting people's hard work. It wears on you. It'd be harder still if you were shootin' gals and pickaninnies. But, hell, you load 'em in a truck, drive around for a while, and the job's taken care of— *anybody* can do that, anybody at all. Get a 'dozer to dig a trench, dump the bodies in, and get on back for the next load."

"You've got it all figured out." Koenig laughed, but more than a little nervously.

"Bet your ass I do," Featherston said. "This is part of what we've been looking for. We've always known what we were going to do, but we haven't found the right way to go about it. This here may not be the final solution, but we're sure as hell gettin' closer. You get to work on it right away. Top priority, you hear me?"

"How many trucks you reckon we'll need?" Koenig asked.

"Beats me," Jake said. "Find some bright young fella with one o' them slide rules to cipher it out for you. However many it is, you get 'em. I don't give a damn what you got to do—you get 'em."

"If it's too many, the Army may grumble," Koenig warned.

"Listen, Ferd, you leave the Army to me," Featherston said, his voice suddenly hard. "I said top priority, and I meant it. *You get those trucks.*"

He hardly ever spoke to Ferd Koenig as superior to inferior. When he did, it hit hard. "Right, boss," the Attorney General mumbled. Jake nodded to himself. When he gave an order, that was what people were supposed to say.

After some hasty good-byes, Koenig all but fled his office. Featherston wondered if he'd hit *too* hard. He didn't want to turn the last of his old comrades into an enemy. *Have to pat him on the fanny, make sure his feelings aren't hurt too bad,* he thought. He cared about only a handful of people enough for their feelings to matter to him. Ferd Koenig probably topped the list.

Lulu stepped in. "The Vice President is here to see you, sir."

"Thank you, dear," Featherston said. His secretary smiled and ducked back out. She was also one of the people whose feelings he cared about.

Don Partridge, on the other hand . . . The Vice President of the CSA was an amiable nonentity from Tennessee. He had a big, wide smile, boyishly handsome good looks, and not a hell of a lot upstairs. That suited Jake just fine. Willy Knight had been altogether too much like him, and he'd barely survived the assassination attempt Knight put together. Well, the son of a bitch was dead now, and he'd had a few years in hell before he died, too. *I pay everybody back,* Jake thought. The United States were finding out about that. So were the Negroes in the Confederate States, and they'd find out more soon. *Have to do something nice for that Pinkard fellow . . .*

Jake worried about no coups from Don Partridge. Not having to worry about him was why he was Vice President. "Well, Don, what's on your mind?" he asked. *Not a hell of a lot,* he guessed. "Got a joke for you," Partridge said. He went ahead and told it. Like a lot of his jokes, it revolved around a dumb farm girl. This time, she wanted to make a little record to send to her boyfriend at the front, but she didn't have the money to pay the man at the studio in town. ". . . and he said, 'Get down on your knees and take it out of my pants.' So she did. 'Take hold of it,' he said, and she did. And then he said, 'Well, go ahead.' And she said, 'Hello, Freddie . . .' "

Partridge threw back his head and guffawed. Jake laughed, too. Unlike a lot of the jokes Don Partridge told, that one was actually funny. "Pretty good," Jake said. "What else is going on?"

"That's what I wanted to ask you, Mr. President," Partridge said. He knew better than to get too familiar with Jake. "You've got me out making speeches about how well everything's going, and sometimes folks ask when the war's going to be over. I'd like to know what to tell 'em."

He was earnest. He didn't want to do the wrong thing. He also had to know Featherston would come down on him like a thousand-pound bomb if he did. Jake didn't mind being feared, not even a little bit. He said, "You tell 'em it's Al Smith's fault we're still fighting. I offered a reasonable peace. I offered a just peace. He wouldn't have it. So we'll just have to keep knocking him over the head till he sees sense."

"Yes, sir. I understand that." Don Partridge nodded eagerly. "Knocking the damnyankees over the head is important. I know it is." He stuck out his chin and tried to look resolute. With his big, cowlike eyes, it didn't come off too well. "But the trouble is, sometimes the Yankees hit back, and people don't much like that."

"I don't like it, either," Jake said, which was a good-sized understatement even for him. "We're doing everything we can. As long as we hang in there, we'll lick 'em in the end. That's what you've got to let the people know."

The Vice President nodded. "I'll do it, sir! You can count on me."

"I do, Don." *I count on you to stay out of my hair and not cause me any trouble. There are plenty of things you're not too good at, but you can manage that.*

"I'm so glad, sir." Partridge gave Jake one of his famous smiles. From what some of the Freedom Party guards said, those smiles got him lady friends—or more than friends—from one end of the CSA to the other. This one, aimed at a man older than he was, had a smaller impact.

"Anything else I can do for you?" Featherston didn't quite tell Partridge to get the hell out of there, but he didn't miss by much. The Vice President took the hint and left, which he wouldn't have if Jake had made it more subtle.

He's a damn fool, Featherston thought, *but even damn fools have their uses. That's something I didn't understand when I was younger.* One thing he understood now was that he couldn't afford to let the damnyankees kill him before he'd won the war. He tried to imagine Don Partridge as President of the Confederate States. When he did, he imagined victory flying out the window. Damn fools had their uses, but running things wasn't one of them.

Featherston looked at a clock on the wall, then at a map across from it. He'd got Partridge out early; his next appointment wasn't for another twenty minutes. It was with Nathan Bedford Forrest III. The general was no fool. Railing against the Whigs, Jake had cussed them for being the party of Juniors and IIIs and IVs, people who thought they ought to have a place on account of what their last name was. Say what you would about Forrest, but he wasn't like that.

He came bounding into the President's office. He didn't waste time with hellos. Instead, he pointed to the map. "Sir, we're going to have a problem, and we're going to have it pretty damn quick."

"The one we've seen coming for a while now?" Jake asked.

Nathan Bedford Forrest III nodded. "Yes, sir." His face was wider and fleshier than that of his famous ancestor, but you could spot the resemblance in his eyes and eyebrows . . . and the first Nathan Bedford Forrest had had some of the deadliest eyes anybody'd ever seen. His great-grandson (the name had skipped a generation) continued, "The damnyankees have seen what we did in Ohio. Looks like they're getting ready to try the same thing here. After all, it's not nearly as far from the border to Richmond as it is from the Ohio River up to Lake Erie."

"Like you say, we've been looking for it," Featherston replied. "We've been getting ready for it, too. How much blood do they want to spend to get where they aim to go? We'll give 'em a Great War fight, only more so. And by God, even if they do take Richmond, they haven't hurt us half as bad as what we did to them farther west."

"I aim to try to keep that from happening," Forrest said. "I think I can. I hope I can. And you're right about the other. What we've done to them will make it harder for them to do things to us. But we're going to have a hell of a fight on our hands, Mr. President. You need to know that. Life doesn't come with a guarantee."

"I haven't backed down from a fight yet," Jake said. "I don't aim to start now."

XIII

On the shelf. Abner Dowling hated it. Oh, they hadn't thrown him out of the Army altogether, as he'd feared they might. But he was back in the War Department in Philadelphia, doing what should have been about a lieutenant colonel's job. That was what he got for letting Ohio fall.

He'd been George Armstrong Custer's adjutant for what seemed like forever (of course, any time with Custer seemed like forever). He'd been a reasonably successful military governor in Utah and Kentucky. These days, Utah was in revolt and Kentucky belonged to the CSA, but none of that was his fault.

Then they'd finally given him a combat command—but not enough barrels or airplanes to go with it. He hadn't done a bang-up job with what he had. Looking back, he could see he'd made mistakes. But he was damned if he could see how anyone but an all-knowing superman could have avoided some of those mistakes. They'd seemed like good ideas at the time. Hindsight said they hadn't been, but who got hindsight ahead of time?

Dowling swore under his breath and tried to unsnarl a logistics problem. Right this minute, the war effort was nothing but logistics problems. That was the Confederacy's fault. Getting from east to west—or, more urgently at the moment, from west to east—was fouled up beyond all recognition. Everybody thought he deserved to go first, and nobody figured he ought to wait in line.

"I ought to give 'em a swat and make 'em go stand in the corner," Dowling muttered. If Army officers were going to act like a bunch of six-year-olds, they deserved to be treated the same way. Too bad his authority didn't reach so far.

Someone knocked on the frame to the open door of his office. A measure of how he'd fallen was that he didn't have a young lieutenant out there running interference for him. "General Dowling? May I have a few minutes of your time?"

"General MacArthur!" Dowling jumped to his feet and saluted. "Yes, sir, of course. Come right in. Have a seat."

"I thank you very much," Major General Daniel MacArthur said grandly. But then, Daniel MacArthur was made for the grand gesture. He was tall and lean and craggy. He wore a severely, almost monastically, plain uniform, and smoked cigarettes from a long, fancy holder. He was in his mid-fifties now. During the Great War, he'd been a boy wonder, the youngest man to command a division. He'd commanded it in Custer's First Army, too, which had made for some interesting times. Custer had never wanted anybody but himself to get publicity, while MacArthur was also an avid self-promoter.

"What can I do for you, sir?" Dowling asked.

"You may have heard I'm to head up the attack into Virginia." MacArthur thrust out his long, granitic chin. Like Custer, he was always ready—always eager—to strike a pose.

"No, sir, I hadn't heard," Dowling admitted. He wasn't hooked into the grapevine here. Quite simply, not many people wanted to talk to an officer down on his luck. He put the best face on it he could: "I imagine security is pretty tight."

"I suppose so." But Daniel MacArthur couldn't help looking and sounding disappointed. He was a man who lived to be observed. If people weren't watching him, if he wasn't at the center of the stage, he began to wonder if he existed.

"What can I do for you?" Dowling asked again.

MacArthur brightened, no doubt thinking of all the attention he would get once he became the hero of the hour. "You have more recent experience in fighting the Confederates than anyone else," he said.

"I guess I do—much of it painful," Dowling said.

"I hope to avoid *that*." By his tone, MacArthur was confident he would. Custer had had that arrogance, too. A good commander needed some of it. Too much, though, and you started thinking you were always right. Your soldiers commonly paid for that—in blood. MacArthur went on, "In any case, I was wondering if you would be kind enough to tell me some of the things I might do well to look out for."

Abner Dowling blinked. That was actually a reasonable request. He wondered if something was wrong with MacArthur. After some thought, he answered, "Well, sir, one thing they do very well is coordinate their infantry, armor, artillery, and aircraft, especially the damned barrels. They'd studied Colonel Morrell's tactics from the last war and improved them for the extra speed barrels have these days."

"Ah, yes. Colonel Morrell." MacArthur looked as if Dowling had broken wind in public. He didn't much like Morrell. The barrel officer had gained breakthroughs last time around where he hadn't. Morrell was *not* a publicity hound, which only made him more suspicious to MacArthur.

"Sir, he's still the best barrel commander we've got, far and away," Dowling said. "If you can get him for whatever you're going to do in Virginia, you should."

"Colonel Morrell is occupied with affairs farther west. I am perfectly satisfied with the officers I have serving under me."

"Is it true that the Confederates have recalled General Patton to Virginia?" Dowling asked.

"I have heard that that may be so." Daniel MacArthur shrugged. "I'm not afraid of him."

Dowling believed him. MacArthur had never lacked for courage. Neither had Custer, for that matter. He was as brave a man as Dowling had ever seen. When it came to common sense, on the other hand . . . When it came to common sense, both MacArthur and Custer had been standing in line for an extra helping of courage.

"Flank attack!" Dowling said. "The Confederates kept nipping at our flanks with their armor. You'll have to guard against that on defense and use it when you have the initiative."

"I intend to have the initiative at all times," MacArthur declared. The cigarette holder he clenched between his teeth jumped to accent the words.

"Um, sir . . ." Dowling cast about for a diplomatic way to say what damn well needed saying. "Sir, no matter what you intend, you've got to remember the Confederates have intentions, too. I hope you'll mostly be able to go by yours. Sometimes, though, they'll have the ball."

"And when they do, I'll stuff it down their throat," MacArthur said. "They cannot hope to stand against the blow I will strike them."

He sounded very sure of himself. So had Custer, just before the start of one of his big offensives. More often than not, the ocean of blood he spent outweighed the gains he made. Dowling feared the same thing would happen with Daniel MacArthur.

But what can I do? Dowling wondered helplessly. Nobody would pay attention to a fat failed fighting man who'd been put out to pasture. Lord knew MacArthur wouldn't. Everything already seemed perfect in his mind. To him, everything *was* perfect. What the real world did to his plans would come as a complete and rude shock, as it always had to Custer.

"If you already have all the answers, sir, why did you bother to ask me questions?" Dowling inquired.

Some officers would have got angry at that. Invincibly armored in self-approval, MacArthur didn't. "Just checking on things," he replied, and got to his feet. Dowling also rose. It didn't help much, for MacArthur towered over him. Smiling a confident and superior smile, MacArthur said, "Expect to read my dispatches from Richmond, General."

"I look forward to it," Dowling said tonelessly. Major General MacArthur's smile never wavered. He believed Dowling, or at least took him literally. With a wave, he left Dowling's office and, a procession of one, hurried down the corridor.

With a sigh, Abner Dowling sat back down and returned to the work MacArthur had interrupted. It wasn't a grand assault on Richmond—assuming the grand assault got that far—but it wasn't meaningless, either. He could tell himself it wasn't, anyhow.

He jumped when the telephone on his desk rang. He wondered if it was a wrong number; not many people had wanted to talk to him lately. He picked it up. "Dowling here."

"Yes, sir. This is John Abell. How are you today?"

"Oh, I'm fair, Colonel, I guess. And yourself?" Dowling couldn't imagine what the General Staff officer might want.

"I'll do, sir," Abell answered with what sounded like frosty amusement—the only kind with which he seemed familiar. "Did you just have a visit from the Great Stone Face?"

"The Great—?" Dowling snorted. He couldn't help himself. "Yes, Colonel, as a matter of fact I did."

"And?" Colonel Abell prompted.

"He's . . . very sure of himself," Dowling said carefully. "I hope he had reason to be. I haven't seen his plans, so I can't tell you about that. You'd know more about it than I would, I'm sure."

"Plans go only so far," John Abell said. "During the last war, we saw any number of splendid-sounding plans blown to hell and gone. Meaning no offense to you, our plans in the West at the start of this war didn't work as well as we wish they would have."

"It does help if the plans take into account all the enemy can throw at us," Dowling replied, acid in his voice.

"Yes, it does," Abell said, which startled him. "I told you I meant no offense."

"People tell me all kinds of things," Dowling said. "Some of them are true. Some of them help make flowers grow. I'm sure no one ever tells you anything but the truth, eh, Colonel?"

Unlike Daniel MacArthur, Colonel Abell had a working sarcasm detector. "You mean there are other things besides truth, sir?" he said in well-simulated amazement.

"Heh," Dowling said, which was about as much as he'd laughed at anything the past couple of months. Then he asked, "Is the General Staff concerned about Major General MacArthur's likely performance?"

Perhaps fifteen seconds of silence followed. Then Colonel Abell said, "I have no idea what you're talking about, General."

He said no more. Dowling realized that was all the answer he'd get. He also realized it was more responsive than it seemed at first. He said, "If you're that thrilled with him, why isn't somebody else in command there?"

After another thoughtful silence, Abell answered, "Military factors aren't the only ones that go into a war, sir. General MacArthur came . . . highly recommended by the Joint Committee on the Conduct of the War."

"Did he?" Dowling kept his tone as neutral as he could make it.

"As a matter of fact, he did. His service in Houston before the plebiscite particularly drew the committee's notice, I believe." Abell sounded scrupulously dispassionate, too. "It was decided that, by giving a little here, we might gain advantages elsewhere."

It was decided. Dowling liked that. No one had actually had to decide anything, it said. The decision just sort of fell out of the sky. No one would be to blame for it, not the General Staff and certainly not the Joint Committee. If MacArthur got the command, the committee would leave the War Department alone about some other things. Dowling didn't know what those would be, but he could guess. You scratch my back and I'll scratch yours. "I hope it turns out all right," he said.

"Yes. So do I," Colonel Abell answered, and hung up.

The knock on Seneca Driver's door came in the middle of the night, long after evening curfew in the colored district in Covington. Cincinnatus' father and mother went on snoring. Neither of them heard very well these days, and a knock wouldn't have meant much to her anyhow. Nothing much meant anything to her any more.

But a knock like that meant something to Cincinnatus. It meant trouble. It didn't sound like the big, booming open-right-now-or-we'll-kick-it-in knock the police would have used. That didn't mean it wasn't trouble, though. Oh, no. Trouble came in all shapes and sizes and flavors. Cincinnatus knew that only too well.

When the knocking didn't stop, he got out of bed, found his cane, and went to the door. He had to step carefully. Darkness was absolute. Police enforced the blackout in this part of town by shooting into lighted windows. If they saw people, they shot to kill. They were very persuasive.

Of course, Luther Bliss didn't run the Kentucky State Police any more. He might come sneaking around to shut Cincinnatus up. That occurred to Cincinnatus just as he put his hand on the knob. He shrugged. He couldn't move fast enough to run away, so what difference did it make?

He opened the door. That wasn't Luther Bliss out there. It was another Negro. Cincinnatus could see that much—that much and no more. "What you want?" he asked softly. "You crazy, comin' round here this time o' night?"

"Lucullus got to see you right away," the stranger answered.

"During curfew? He nuts? You nuts? You reckon I'm nuts?"

"He reckon you come," the other man said calmly. "You want I should go back there, tell him he wrong?"

Cincinnatus considered. That was exactly what he wanted. Saying so, though, could have all sorts of unpleasant consequences. He muttered something vile under his breath before replying, "You wait there. Let me get out of my nightshirt."

"I ain't goin' nowhere," the other man said.

I wish I could tell you the same. Cincinnatus put on shoes and dungarees and the shirt he'd worn the day before. When he went to the door, he asked, "What do we do if the police see us?"

"Run," his escort said. Since Cincinnatus couldn't, that did him no good whatever.

They picked their way along the colored quarter's crumbling sidewalks. Cincinnatus used his cane to feel ahead of him like a blind man. In the blackout, he almost was a blind man. Starlight might have been beautiful, but it was no damn good for getting around.

His nose proved a better guide. Even in the darkness of the wee small hours, he had no trouble telling when he was getting close to Lucullus Wood's barbecue place. The man with him laughed softly. "Damn, but that there barbecue smell good," he said. "Make me hungry jus' to git a whiff." Cincinnatus couldn't argue, not when his own stomach was growling like an angry hound.

The other man opened the door. Cincinnatus pushed through the blackout curtains behind it. He blinked at the explosion of light inside. He wasn't much surprised to find the place busy regardless of the hour. Several white policemen in gray uniforms were drinking coffee and devouring enormous sandwiches. Cincinnatus would have bet they hadn't paid for them. When did cops ever pay for anything?

All the customers were out after curfew. The policemen didn't get excited about it. They didn't jump up and arrest Cincinnatus and his companion, either. They just went on feeding their faces. The sandwiches and coffee and whatever else Lucullus gave them looked like a good insurance policy.

The other black man took Cincinnatus to a cramped booth closer to the police than he wanted to be. The other man ordered pork ribs and a cup of coffee. Cincinnatus chose a barbecued beef sandwich. He passed on the coffee: he still nourished a hope of getting back to sleep that night. He knew the odds were against him, but he'd always been an optimist.

To his amazement, Lucullus Wood lumbered out and took a place in the booth. It had been cramped before; now it seemed full to overflowing. "What you want that won't keep till mornin'?" Cincinnatus asked, doing his best to keep his voice down.

Lucullus didn't bother. "What you know about trucks?" he asked in turn.

"Trucks?" Whatever Cincinnatus had expected, that wasn't it. "Well, I only drove 'em for thirty years, so I don't reckon I know much."

"Funny man." Lucullus scowled at him. "I ain't jokin', funny man."

"All right, you ain't jokin'." Cincinnatus paused, for the food arrived just then. After a big bite from his sandwich—as good as always—he went on, "Tell me what you want to know, and I'll give you the answer if I got it."

"Here it is," Lucullus said heavily. "You got a Pegasus truck—you know the kind I mean?"

"I've seen 'em," Cincinnatus answered. The Pegasus was the CSA's heavy hauler. You could fill the back with supplies or with a squad of soldiers—more than a squad, if you didn't mind cramming them in like sardines. A Pegasus would never win a beauty contest, but the big growling machines got the job done.

"Good enough," Lucullus said, and then, loudly, to a waitress, "You fetch me a cup of coffee, Lucinda sweetie?" Lucinda laughed and waved and went to get it. Lucullus turned back to Cincinnatus. "You know how it's got the canvas top you can put up to keep rain off the sojers or whatever other shit you got in there?"

"I reckon I do," Cincinnatus answered. "White truck had the same kind o' thing in the last war. What about it?"

"Here's what," Lucullus said. "How come you'd take a bunch o' them trucks and take off that whole canvas arrangement and close up the back compartment in a big old iron box?"

"Who's doin' that?" Cincinnatus asked.

Now Lucullus did drop his rumbling bass voice. "Confederate gummint, that's who," he said solemnly. Lucinda set the coffee in front of him. He swatted her on the behind. She just laughed again and sashayed off.

"Confederate government?" Cincinnatus echoed. Lucullus nodded. Cincinnatus did a little thinking. "This here ironwork armor plate?"

"Don't reckon so," Lucullus answered. "Ain't heard nothin' 'bout no armor. That'd be special, right?—it ain't no ordinary iron."

"Armor's special, all right. It's extra thick an' extra hard," Cincinnatus said. Lucullus started to cough. After a moment, Cincinnatus realized he was trying not to laugh. After another moment, he realized why. "I didn't mean it like that, goddammit!"

"I know you didn't. Only makes it funnier," Lucullus said. "Figure this here is regular ironwork, anyways."

"Well, my own truck back in Iowa's got an iron cargo box. Keeps the water out better'n canvas when it rains. Keeps thieves out a hell of a lot better, too."

"These here is Army trucks—or trucks the gummint took from the Army," Lucullus said. "Reckon they gonna be where there's sojers around. Ain't got to worry 'bout thievin' a whole hell of a lot."

This time, Cincinnatus laughed. "Only shows what you know. You ain't never seen the kind o' thievin' that goes on around Army trucks. I *know* what I'm talkin' about there—you'd best believe I do. You start loadin' stuff in Army trucks, and some of it's gonna walk with Jesus. I don't care how many soldiers you got. I don't care how many guns you got, neither. Folks steal."

Maybe his conviction carried authority. Lucullus pursed his lips in what was almost a parody of deep thought. "Mebbe," he said at last. "But it don't quite *feel* right, you know what I mean? Like I told you, these here ain't exactly no Army trucks no more. They was took from the Army. I reckon they be doin' somethin' else from here on out."

"Like what?" Cincinnatus asked.

"Don't rightly know." Lucullus Wood didn't sound happy about admitting it. "I was hopin' you could give me a clue."

"Gotta be somethin' the government figures is important." Cincinnatus was talking more to himself than to Lucullus. "Gotta be somethin' the government figures is *real* important, on account of what's more important than the Army in the middle of a war?"

He couldn't think of anything. Lucullus did, and right away:

"The Freedom Party. Freedom Party *is* the goddamn gummint, near enough." He was right. As soon as he said it, Cincinnatus nodded, acknowledging as much. Lucullus went on, "But what the hell the Freedom Party want with a bunch o' gussied-up trucks?"

"Beats me." Cincinnatus finished his sandwich. "That was mighty good. I wish you didn't haul me outa bed in the middle o' the night to eat it."

"Didn't get you over here for that." Lucullus' face could have illustrated *discontented* in the dictionary. "I was hopin' you had some answers for me."

"Sorry." Cincinnatus spread his hands, pale palms up. "I got to tell you, it don't make no sense to me."

"I got to tell you, it don't make no sense to me, neither," Lucullus said, "but I reckon it makes sense to somebody, or them Party peckerheads over in Virginia wouldn't be doin' it. They got somethin' on their evil little minds. I don't know what it is. I can't cipher it out. When I can't cipher out what the ofays is gonna do next, I commence to worryin', an' that is a fac'."

"Sorry I'm not more help for you," Cincinnatus said again. "I know trucks—you're right about that. But you know a hell of a lot more about the Freedom Party than I do. I ain't sorry about that, not even a little bit. I wish to God I didn't know nothin' about 'em."

"Don't we all!" Lucullus said. "All right, git on home, then." He turned to the man who'd brought Cincinnatus to the barbecue place and sat silently while he and Lucullus talked. "Git him back there, Tiberius."

"I take care of it," the other man promised. "Don't want no trouble." He caught Cincinnatus' eye. "You ready?"

Slowly, painfully, Cincinnatus rose. "Ready as I ever be." That wasn't saying a hell of a lot. He knew it, whether Tiberius did or not.

They went out into the eerie, blackout-deepened darkness. Everything was quiet as the tomb: no bombers overhead tonight. A police car rattled down a street just after Cincinnatus and Tiberius turned off it, but the cops didn't know they were around. Lights were for emergencies only. Tiberius laughed softly. "Curfew ain't so hard to beat, you see?" he said.

"Yeah," Cincinnatus answered. Tiberius stayed with him till he went up the walk to his folks' house, then disappeared into the night.

Cincinnatus' father was up waiting for him. "You *did* come home. Praise the Lord!" Seneca Driver said.

"Wasn't the *po*lice at the door, Pa," Cincinnatus answered. "Sorry you woke up while I was tendin' to it."

"Don't worry about that none," his father said. "Got us plenty o' more important things to worry about." Cincinnatus wished he could have told him he was wrong. And he could have, too—but only if he were willing to lie.

T om Colleton felt proud of himself. He'd managed to wangle four days of leave. That wasn't long enough to go home to South Carolina, but it did let him get away from the front and down to Columbus. Not worrying about getting shelled or gassed for a little while seemed a good start on the road to the earthly paradise.

It also proved too good to be true. As he got on the train that would take him from Sandusky to Columbus, a military policeman said, "Oh, good, sir—you've got your sidearm."

"What about it?" Tom's hand fell to the pistol on his hip.

"Only that it's a good idea, sir," the MP answered, his white-painted helmet and white gloves making him stand out from the ordinary run of noncoms. "The damnyankees down there aren't real happy about the way things have gone."

"Unhappy enough so that a Confederate officer needs to pack a pistol?" Tom asked. The MP gave back a somber nod. Tom only shrugged. "Well, if U.S. soldiers couldn't kill me, I'm not going to lose too much sleep over U.S. civilians." That got a grin from the military policeman.

The train was an hour and a half late getting into Columbus. It had to wait on a siding while workmen repaired damage— sabotage—to the railway. Tom Colleton fumed. "Don't get yourself in an uproar, sir," advised a captain who'd evidently made the trip several times. "Could be a hell of a lot worse. Leastways we haven't had any fighters shooting us up this time around."

"Gurk," Tom said. No, he hadn't come far enough to escape the war—not even close.

And he was reminded of it when he got into Columbus. The city had been at the center of a Yankee pocket. The U.S. soldiers who'd held it had fought hard to keep the Confederates from taking it.

They'd quit only when they ran too low on fuel and ammunition to go on fighting. That meant Columbus looked as if rats the size of automobiles had been taking big bites out of most of the buildings.

The porter who fetched suitcases from the baggage car for those who had them was a white man. He spoke with some kind of Eastern European accent. Tom stared at him. He'd rarely seen a white man doing nigger work, and in the CSA few jobs more perfectly defined nigger work than a porter's.

This fellow stared right back at him. That wasn't curiosity in his eyes. It was raw hatred. *Measuring me for a coffin*, Tom thought. He'd wondered if the MP had exaggerated. Now he saw the man hadn't. The weight of the .45 on his hip was suddenly very comforting.

Union Station was a few blocks north of the state Capitol, whose dome had taken a hit from a bomb. Fort Mahan, which had been the chief U.S. military depot in Ohio, was now where visiting Confederates stayed. It lay a few blocks east of the station, on Buckingham Street. Sentries checked Tom's papers with scrupulous care before admitting him. "You think I'm a Yankee spy?" he asked, amused.

"Sir, we've had us some trouble with that," one of the sentries answered, which brought him up short.

"Have you?" he said. All three sentries nodded. Two of them had examined his bona fides while the third covered them and Tom with his automatic rifle. Tom asked, "You have a lot of problems with people shooting at you, stuff like that?"

"Some," answered the corporal who'd spoken before. "We gave an order for the damnyankees to turn in their guns when we took this here place, same as we always do." He made a sour face. "Reckon you can guess how much good that done us."

"I expect I can," Tom said. If the United States had occupied Dallas and tried to enforce the same order, it wouldn't have done them any good, either. People in both the USA and the CSA had too many guns and too many hiding places—and the Yankees hated the Confederates just as much as the Confederates hated the Yankees, so nobody on either side wanted to do what anyone on the other side said.

The sentry added, "It's not shooting so much. We've hanged

some of the bastards who tried that, and we've got hostages to try and make sure more of 'em don't. But there's sabotage all the time: slashed tires, busted windows, sugar in the gas tank, shit like that. We shot a baker for mixing ground glass in with the bread he gave us. They even say whores with the clap don't get it treated so as they can give it to more of us."

"Do they?" Tom murmured. He hadn't been with a woman since the war started. But Bertha was a long way away. What she didn't know wouldn't hurt her. He'd thought he might . . . Then again, if what this fellow said was true, he might not, too.

"I don't know that that's so, sir," the corporal said. "But they do say it." He gave Tom his papers again. "Pass on, and have yourself a good old time."

Don't eat the bread, Tom thought. *Don't lay the women. Sounds like a hell of a way to have a good old time to me. At least he didn't say the bartenders were pissing in the whiskey.*

He found the Bachelor Officers' Quarters without any trouble. Fort Mahan bristled with signs, some left over from when the USA ran the place, others put up by the Confederates. He got a room of his own, one of about the same quality as he would have had in the CSA. Two stars on each collar tab helped. Had he been a lieutenant or a captain, he probably would have ended up with a roommate or two.

Since the sentry hadn't warned that they were pissing in the booze, he headed for the officers' club once he'd dumped his valise in the room. He got another jolt when he walked in: the barkeep was as white as the railroad porter. Tom walked up to him and ordered a highball. The man in the boiled shirt and black bow tie didn't bat an eye. He made the drink and set it on the bar. "Here you go, sir," he said quietly. His accent declared him a Yankee.

Tom sipped the highball. It was fine. Even so . . . "How long have you been tending bar?" he asked.

"About . . . fifteen years, sir," the fellow said after a moment's pause for thought. "Why, if you don't mind my asking?"

"Just wondering. What do you think of the work?"

"It's all right. Money's not bad. I never did care for getting cooped up in a factory. I like talking with people and I listen pretty well, so it suits me."

"Doesn't it, oh, get you down, having to do what other folks tell you all the time? Serving them, you might say?"

He and the bartender both spoke English, but they didn't speak the same language. The man shrugged. "It's a job, that's all. Tell me about a job where you don't have to do what other people tell you. I'll be on that one like a shot."

Tom decided to get more direct: "Down in the Confederate States, we'd call a job like this nigger work."

"Oh." The barkeep suddenly found himself on familiar ground. "Now I see what you're driving at. Some other people have asked me about that. All I got to tell you, pal, is that you're not in the Confederate States any more."

"I noticed that." Shaking his head, Tom found an empty table and sat down. The man behind the bar plainly didn't feel degraded by his work. A white Confederate would have. *You're not in the CSA any more is right,* Tom thought. That was true.

A couple of other officers came in and ordered drinks. One of them nodded to Tom. "Haven't seen you before," he remarked. "Just get in?"

"That's right," Tom answered. "Nice, friendly little town, isn't it? I always did enjoy a place where I could relax and not have to look over my shoulder all the time."

The officer who'd spoken to him—a major—and his friend—a lieutenant-colonel like Tom—both laughed. After they'd got their whiskeys, the major said, "Mind if we join you?"

"Not a bit. I'd be glad of the company," Tom said, and gave his name. He got theirs in return. The major, a skinny redhead, was Ted Griffith; the other light colonel, who was chunky and dark and balding, was Mel Lempriere. He had a pronounced New Orleans accent, half lazy and half tough. Griffith sounded as if he came from Alabama or Mississippi.

They started talking shop. Aside from women, the great common denominator, it was what they shared. Ted Griffith was in barrels, Lempriere in artillery. "We caught the damnyankees flat-footed," Lempriere said. "It would've been a lot tougher if we hadn't." Actually, he said *woulda,* as if he came from Brooklyn instead of the Crescent City.

"Reckon that's a fact," Griffith agreed. "Their barrels are as good as ours, and they use 'em pretty well. But they didn't have enough, and so we got the whip hand and ripped into 'em."

"Patton helped, too, I expect," Tom said. He got to the bottom of his highball and waved for a refill. The bartender nodded. He brought over a fresh one a minute later.

"Patton drives like a son of a bitch," Lempriere said. "Sometimes our guys had a devil of a time keeping up with the barrels." He and Major Griffith both finished their drinks at the same time. They also waved to the barkeep. He got to work on new ones for them, too.

Once Griffith had taken a pull at his second drink, he said, "Patton's a world-beater in the field. No arguments about that. If the Yankees hadn't had their number-one fellow here, too, we'd've licked 'em worse'n we did. Yeah, he's a damn good barrel commander."

He didn't sound as delighted as he might have. "But . . . ?" Tom asked. A *but* had to be hiding in there somewhere. He wondered if Griffith would let it out.

The major made his refill disappear and called for another. *Dutch courage?* Tom thought. "Patton's a world-beater in the field," Griffith repeated. "He does have his little ways, though."

Mel Lempriere chuckled. "Name me a general officer worth his rank badges who doesn't."

"Well, yeah," Griffith said. "But there's ways, and then there's ways, if you know what I mean. Patton fines any barrel man he catches out of uniform, right down to the tie on the shirt underneath the coveralls. He fines you if your coveralls are dirty, too. How are you supposed to run a barrel without getting grease and shit on your uniform? I tell you for a fact, my friends, it can't be done."

"Why's he bother?" Tom asked.

"Well, he likes everything just so," Griffith answered, which sounded like an understatement. "And he likes to say that a clean soldier, a neat soldier, is a soldier with his pecker up. I suppose he's got himself a point." Again, he didn't say *but*. Again, he might as well have.

Lieutenant-Colonel Lempriere laughed again. "You know any soldier in the field longer'n a week who *hasn't* got his pecker up?"

That brought them around to women. Tom had figured they'd

get there sooner or later. He asked about the local officers' brothels, and whether the girls really did steer clear of cures for the clap. Lempriere denied it. He turned out to be a mine of information. As Tom had, he'd been in the last war. Ted Griffith was too young. He listened to the two lieutenant-colonels swap stories of sporting houses gone by. After a while, he said, "Sounds like bullshit to me, gentlemen."

"Likely some of it is," Tom said. "But it's *fun* bullshit, you know?" They all laughed some more. They ended up yarning and drinking deep into the night.

When the USS *Remembrance* sortied from Honolulu, Sam Carsten had no trouble holding in his enthusiasm. The airplane carrier wasn't going any place where the weather suited him: up to Alaska, say. She could have been. The Tsars still owned Alaska, and Russia and the United States were formally at war. But they hadn't done much in the way of fighting, and weren't likely to. The long border between the U.S.-occupied Yukon and northern British Columbia on the one hand and Alaska on the other was anything but the ideal place to wage war.

The western end of the chain of Sandwich Islands, now . . .

Midway, a thousand miles north and west of Honolulu, had a U.S. base on it. The low-lying island wasn't anything much. Aside from great swarms of goony birds, it boasted nothing even remotely interesting. But it was where it was. Japan had seized Guam along with the Philippines in the Hispano-Japanese War right after the turn of the century, and turned the island into her easternmost base. If she took Midway from the USA, that could let her walk down the little islands in the chain toward the ones that really mattered.

Japan didn't have anyone to fight but the USA. The United States, by contrast, had a major land war against the Confederate States on their hands. They were trying to hold down a restive Canada. And the British, French, and Confederates made the Atlantic an unpleasant place—to say nothing of the Confederate submersibles that sneaked out of Guaymas to prowl the West Coast.

Sam wished he hadn't thought about all that. It made him realize how alone out here in the Pacific the *Remembrance* was. If something went wrong, the USA would have to send a carrier around the

Horn—which wouldn't be so easy now that the British and Confederates had retaken Bermuda and the Bahamas. The only other thing the United States could do was start building carriers in Seattle or San Francisco or San Pedro or San Diego. That wouldn't be easy or quick, either, not with the country cut in two.

Most of the crew enjoyed the weather. It was mild and balmy. The sun shone out of a blue sky down on an even bluer sea. Carsten could have done without the sunshine, but he had special problems. Zinc oxide helped cut the burn a little. Unfortunately, a little was exactly how much the ointment helped.

He glanced up to the carrier's island every so often. The antenna on the Y-range gear spun round and round, searching for Japanese airplanes. Midway also had a Y-range station. Between the two of them, they should have made a surprise attack impossible. But Captain Stein was a suspenders-and-belt man. He kept a combat air patrol overhead all through the day, too. Sam approved. You didn't want to get caught with your pants down, not here.

Fighters weren't the only things flying above the *Remembrance* and the cruisers and destroyers that accompanied her. As she got farther out into the chain of Sandwich Islands, albatrosses and their smaller seagoing cousins grew more and more common. Watching them always fascinated Sam. They soared along with effortless ease, hardly ever flapping. The smaller birds sometimes dove into the ocean after fish. Not the albatrosses. They swooped low to snatch their suppers from the surface of the sea, then climbed up into the sky again.

They were as graceful in the air as they were ungainly on the ground. Considering that every landing was a crash and every take-off a desperate sprint into the wind, that said a great deal.

The other impressive thing about them was their wingspan, which seemed not that much smaller than an airplane's. Sam had grown up watching hawks and turkey buzzards soar over the upper Midwest. He was used to big birds on the wing. The goony birds dwarfed anything he'd seen then, though.

"I hear the deck officer waved one of them off the other day," he said in the officers' wardroom. "Fool bird wasn't coming in straight enough to suit him."

"He didn't want it to catch fire when it smashed into the deck," Hiram Pottinger said. "You know goonies can't land clean."

"Well, sure," Sam said. "But it shit on his hat when it swung around for another pass."

He got his laugh. Commander Cressy said, "Plenty of our fly-boys have wanted to do the same thing, I'll bet. If that albatross ever comes back, they'll pin a medal on it."

Sam got up and poured himself a fresh cup of coffee. He was junior officer there, so he held up the pot, silently asking the other men if they wanted any. Pottinger pointed to his cup. Sam filled it up. The head of damage control added cream and sugar. Before long, the cream would go bad and it would be condensed milk out of a can instead. Everybody enjoyed the real stuff as long as it stayed fresh.

Pottinger asked Commander Cressy, "You think the Japs are out there, sir?"

"Oh, I know they're out there. We all know that," the exec answered. "Whether they're within operational range of Midway—and of us—well, that's what we're here to find out. I'm as sure that they want to boot us off the Sandwich Islands as I am of my own name."

"Makes sense," Sam said. "If they kick us back to the West Coast, they don't need to worry about us again for a long time."

Dan Cressy nodded. "That's about right. They'd have themselves a perfect Pacific empire—the Philippines and what were the Dutch East Indies for resources, and the Sandwich Islands for a forward base. Nobody could bother them after that."

"The British—" Lieutenant Commander Pottinger began.

Sam shook his head at the same time as Commander Cressy did. Cressy noticed; Sam wondered if the exec would make him do the explaining. To his relief, Cressy didn't. Telling a superior why he was wrong was always awkward. Cressy outranked Pottinger, so he could do it without hemming and hawing. And he did: "If the British give Japan a hard time, they'll get bounced out of Malaya before you can say Jack Robinson. They're too busy closer to home to defend it properly. The Japs might take away Hong Kong or invade Australia, too. I don't think they want to do that. We're still on their plate, and they've got designs on China. But they could switch gears. Anybody with a General Staff worth its uniforms has more strategic plans than he knows what to do with. All he has to do is grab one and dust it off."

Pottinger was Navy to his toes. He took the correction without blinking. "I wonder how the limeys like playing second fiddle out in the Far East," he remarked.

"It's Churchill's worry, not mine," Cressy said. "But they're being good little allies to the Japs out here. They don't want to give Japan any excuses to start nibbling on their colonies. They make a mint from Hong Kong, and it wouldn't last twenty minutes if Japan decided she didn't want them running it any more."

"Makes sense," Hiram Pottinger said. "I hadn't thought it through."

"Only one thing." Sam spoke hesitantly. Commander Cressy waved for him to go on. If the exec hadn't, he wouldn't have. As it was, he said, "The Japs may not need any excuse if they decide they want Hong Kong or Malaya. They're liable just to reach out and grab with both hands."

He waited to see if he'd made Cressy angry. Before the exec could say anything, general quarters sounded. Cressy jumped to his feet. "We'll have to finish hashing this out another time, gentlemen," he said.

Neither Sam Carsten nor Hiram Pottinger answered him. They were both on their way out of the wardroom, on their way down to their battle stations below the *Remembrance*'s waterline. Panting, Sam asked, "Is this the real thing, or just another drill?"

"We'll find out," Pottinger answered. "Mind your head."

"Aye aye, sir," Sam said. A tall man had to do that, or he could knock himself cold hurrying from one compartment to another. He could also trip over his own feet; the hatchway doors had raised sills.

Some of the sailors in the damage-control party beat them to their station. They'd been nearby, not in the wardroom in officers' country. "Is this the McCoy?" Szczerbiakowicz asked. "Or is it just another goddamn drill?"

He shouldn't have talked about drill that way. It went against regulations. Sam didn't say anything to him about it, though. Neither did Lieutenant Commander Pottinger. All he did say was, "We'll both find out at the same time, Eyechart."

"I don't hear a bunch of airplanes taking off over our heads," Sam said hopefully. "Doesn't feel like we're taking evasive action, either. So I hope it's only a drill."

The klaxons cut off. The all-clear didn't sound right away,

though. That left things up in the air for about fifteen minutes. Then the all-clear did blare out. Commander Cressy came on the intercom: "Well, that was a little more interesting than we really wanted. We had to persuade a flight patrolling out from Midway that we weren't Japs, and we had to do it without breaking wireless silence. Not easy, but we managed."

"That could have been fun," Sam said.

Some of the other opinions expressed there in the corridor under the bare lightbulbs in their wire cages were a good deal more sulfurous than that. "What's the matter with the damn flyboys?" somebody said. "We don't look like a Jap ship."

That was true, and then again it wasn't. The *Remembrance* had a tall island, while most Japanese carriers sported small ones or none at all. But the Japs had also converted battleship and battle-cruiser hulls into carriers. Her lines might have touched off alarm bells in the fliers' heads.

"Nice to know what was going on," a junior petty officer said. "The exec may be an iron-assed son of a bitch, but at least he fills you in."

All the sailors nodded. Sam and Hiram Pottinger exchanged amused glances. They didn't contradict the petty officer. Commander Cressy was supposed to look like an iron-assed son of a bitch to everybody who didn't know him. A big part of his job was saying no for the skipper. The skipper was the good guy. When, as occasionally happened, the answer to something was yes, he usually said it himself. That was how things worked on every ship in the Navy. The *Remembrance* was no exception. Some executive officers reveled in saying no. Cressy wasn't like that. He was tough, but he was fair.

Chattering, the sailors went back to their regular duties. Sam went up onto the flight deck, braving the sun for a chance to look around. Nothing special was going on. He liked that better than rushing up to jury-rig repairs after a bomb hit while enemy fighters shot up his ship. All he saw were vast sky and vaster sea, the *Remembrance*'s supporting flotilla off in the near and middle distance. A couple of fighters buzzed overhead, one close enough to let him see the USA's eagle's head in front of crossed swords.

And a pair of albatrosses glided along behind the *Remembrance*.

They really did look almost big enough to land. He wondered what they thought of the great ship. Or were they too birdbrained to think at all? But this was their home. Men came here only to fight. That being so, who really were the birdbrains here?

Flora Blackford's countrymen had often frustrated her. They elected too many Democrats when she was convinced sending more Socialists to Powel House and to Congress and to statehouses around the United States would have served the country better. But she'd never imagined they could ignore large-scale murder, especially large-scale murder by the enemy in time of war.

Whether she'd imagined it or not, it was turning out to be true. She'd done just what she told Al Smith she would do: she'd trumpeted the Confederacy's massacres of Negroes as loudly and as widely as she could. She'd shown the photographs Caesar had risked his life to bring into the USA.

And she'd accomplished . . . not bloody much. She'd got a little ink in the papers, a little more in the weekly newsmagazines. And the public? The public had yawned. The most common response had been, *Who cares what the Confederates are doing at home? We've got enough problems on account of what they're doing to us right here.*

She shook her head. No, actually that wasn't the most common response. She would have known how to counter it. And even a response like that would have meant people in the USA were talking about and thinking about what was going on in the CSA. Against silence, against indifference, what could she do?

Confederate wireless hadn't called her a liar. The Freedom Party's mouthpieces hadn't bothered. Instead, they'd started yelling and screaming and jumping up and down about what they called the USA's "massacre of innocents" in Utah. They didn't bother mentioning that the Mormons had risen in rebellion.

Flora's mouth twisted as she sat in her office. She supposed the Confederates might claim Negroes had risen in rebellion against Richmond. As far as she was concerned, that served Richmond right. The Confederate States oppressed and repressed their blacks.

The United States had given the Mormons full equality—and they'd risen anyhow.

Besides, the Mormons who died died in combat. The Confederates seemed to have set up special camps to dispose of their Negroes. Gather them in one place, get rid of them, and then bring in a fresh batch and do it again. It all struck her as being as efficient as a factory. If Henry Ford had decided to produce murders instead of motorcars, that was how he would have gone about it.

Bertha knocked on the office door, which took her out of her unhappy reverie. "Yes?" she said, a little relieved—or maybe more than a little—to return to the here and now.

Her secretary looked in. "The Assistant Secretary of War is here, Congresswoman."

"Oh, yes. Of course." Flora shook her head again. It was eleven o' clock. She'd had this appointment for days. This whole business with those photos really was making her forget everything else. "Please tell him to come in."

"All right." Bertha turned away. "Go on in, Mr. Roosevelt, sir." She held the door open so he could.

"Thank you very much," Franklin Roosevelt said as he propelled his wheelchair past her and into Flora's office. He was only distantly related to Theodore Roosevelt, and a solid Socialist rather than a Democrat like his more famous cousin. He did seem to have some of his namesake's capacity for getting people to pay attention to him when he said things.

"Good to see you, Mr. Roosevelt." Flora stood up, came around the desk, and held out her hand.

When Franklin Roosevelt took it, his engulfed hers. He had big hands, wide shoulders, and a barrel chest that went well with the impetuous, jut-jawed patrician good looks of his face. But his legs were shriveled and useless in his trousers. More than twenty years earlier, he'd come down with poliomyelitis. He hadn't let it stop him, but it had slowed him down. Some people said he might have been President if not for that mishap.

"Can I have Bertha bring you some coffee?" Flora asked.

"That would be very pleasant, thanks," Roosevelt replied in a resonant baritone.

"I'd like a cup, too, Bertha, if you don't mind," Flora said. She and Roosevelt made small talk over the steaming cups for a little while. Then she decided she might as well get to the point, and asked, "What can I do for you today?"

"Well, I thought I would come by to thank you for your excellent work on publicizing the outrages the Confederate States are committing against their Negroes," Roosevelt answered.

"You did?" Flora could hardly believe her ears. "To tell you the truth, I'd begun to wonder if anyone noticed."

"Well, I did," Roosevelt said. "And you can rest assured that the Negroes who are fighting for justice in the CSA have noticed, too. The War Department has made a point of being careful to let them know the government of the United States sympathizes with them in their ordeal."

"I . . . see," Flora said slowly. "I didn't say what I said for propaganda purposes."

"I know that." Roosevelt beamed at her from behind small, metal-framed spectacles. "It only makes things better. It shows we understand what they're suffering and want to do something about it."

"Does it?" Flora had held in her bitterness since discovering she couldn't even raise a tempest in a teapot. Now it came flooding out: "Is that what it shows, Mr. Roosevelt? Forgive me, but I have my doubts. Doesn't it really show that a few of us may be upset, but most of us couldn't care less? What the Confederate States are doing is a judgment on them. And how little it matters here is a judgment on us."

Franklin Roosevelt pursed his lips. "You may be right. That may be what it really shows," he said at last. "But what the Negroes in the CSA think it shows also counts. If they think the United States are on their side, they'll struggle harder against the CSA and the Freedom Party. That could be important to the war. When you play these games, what people believe is often as important as what's really so. I'm sure you've seen the same thing in your brand of politics."

Flora studied him. That was either the most brilliant analysis she'd ever heard—or the most breathtakingly cynical one. For the life of her, she couldn't decide which. Maybe it was both at once. Was that better or worse? She couldn't make up her mind there, either.

Roosevelt smiled. When he did, she wanted to believe him.

When Jake Featherston talked, people wanted to believe *him*. Roosevelt had some of the same gift. How much had poliomyelitis taken away from the country?

Or, considering to whom she'd just compared him, how much had it spared the country? Either way, no one would ever know.

"You see?" he said.

With his eyes twinkling at her, she wanted to see things his way. "Maybe," she said, though she hadn't expected to admit even that much. "It hardly seems fair, though, to use them for our purposes when they're so downtrodden. They'll grab at anything they see floating by." She realized she'd just mixed a metaphor. Too late to worry about it now.

"This is a war," Roosevelt said. "You use the weapons that come to hand. The Confederates have used the Mormons. The British and the Japanese have both worked hard to rouse the Canadians against us. Should we waste a chance to make the Confederates have to fight to keep order in their own country? Isn't that a choice that would live in infamy?" He thrust out his chin.

He had a point, or part of one. Flora said, "In that case, we shouldn't let the Negroes in the CSA live on hope and promises. If they're going to fight Confederate soldiers and Freedom Party goons, they ought to have the guns to make it a real fight. Otherwise, we just set them up to be massacred."

"We *are* sending them guns, as we can," Roosevelt replied. "They do live in another country, you know. Smuggling in weapons isn't always easy. We did some in the Great War. We can do more now, because we can drop more from bombers. It's less than I would like, but it's better than nothing. If we give them the tools, they can finish the job."

Finish the job? It was a fine phrase, but Flora didn't believe it. Blacks in the Confederate States would always be outnumbered and outgunned. They could rebel. They could cause endless trouble to the whites in the CSA. They couldn't hope to beat them.

Could they hope to live alongside them? That would take changes from both whites and blacks. Flora wished she thought such changes were likely. When she asked Franklin Roosevelt whether he did, he shook his head. "I wish I could tell you yes," he said. "But if people are going to change, there has to be a willingness on both sides to do it. I don't see that there. What Negroes want is very far removed from what whites will give."

Flora sighed. "I'm afraid it seems that way to me, too. I was hoping you might tell me something different."

"I'd be happy to, if you want me to lie," Roosevelt said. "I thought you would rather have a straight answer."

"And I would," Flora said. "I tell you frankly, I would also like to have the executive branch say some of the things I'm saying. If it did, the Negroes in the Confederate States might have some real reason to hope."

"I have two things to say about that," Roosevelt replied. "The first is that if you want to persuade the executive branch to say anything in particular, you need to persuade the President, not the Assistant Secretary of War."

"President Smith has a view of this matter somewhat different from mine," Flora said unhappily.

Roosevelt shrugged those broad shoulders. "That's between you and him, then, not between you and me. The other thing I would tell you, though, is that you should watch what the administration does, not just what it says. I am sure the President has his reasons for not wanting to make the sort of statement you wish he would. You may not agree with them, but he has them. No matter what he *says*, we are *doing* what we can to arm Negroes in the Confederate States. If they can fight back, they're less likely to be slaughtered, don't you think?"

Carefully, Flora said, "I wish we were doing it for reasons of justice and not just for political and military considerations."

When Teddy Roosevelt's cousin shook his head, he showed a lot of his more famous namesake's bulldog determination. "There, meaning no offense, I have to say I disagree with you. Whenever someone talks about doing something for reasons of justice, you should put your hand in your pocket, because you're about to get it picked. That's not always true—your own career proves as much— but it's the way to bet."

"Thank you for making the exception," Flora murmured, wondering if he really meant it.

"Any time," he said cheerfully. He was too smart to make any protestations that he had. She wouldn't have believed those. Instead, he went on, "Political and military reasons are the ones you should rely on, if you care to know what I think. They have self-interest behind them, and that makes them likely to last. Principles are pretty, but they go stale a lot faster."

Again, Flora wondered whether that was wisdom or some of the most appalling cynicism she'd ever heard. Again, she had a devil of a time coming up with an answer.

The more Clarence Potter learned about the intelligence assets the Confederates had in place in the USA, the more he respected his predecessors. Some of the people who contrived to send word south of the border had been quietly working in the U.S. War Department and Navy Department and Department of State since before the Great War broke out. Most of the time, they were what they pretended to be all the time: clerks and bookkeepers who did their jobs and didn't worry about anything else. They did their jobs, all right, but every now and then they did worry about something else.

Seeing what they did also made Potter worry about something else. He dared not assume U.S. spymasters were any less clever than those on his own side. That made him wonder who in the C.S. War Department had ways to get word of this, that, or the other thing to the damnyankees. Who was in the C.S. State Department but not fully of it?

Trying to find out wasn't his province. He had plenty to keep his own plate full—not least those reports that came out of Philadelphia and Washington. They helped confirm what he'd suspected for some time: that the United States were getting ready to try an offensive of their own, and that Virginia, the obvious target, was the one they had in mind.

But he did do what anyone who'd spent a while in government service would have done: he wrote a memorandum. He sent it to his opposite number in Counterintelligence, and sent a copy to Nathan Bedford Forrest III as chief of the Confederate General Staff. He thought about sending a copy to Jake Featherston, too, but decided against it—that would be going over too many people's heads.

Instead of having the President descend on him like a ton of bricks, then, he had the head of the General Staff pay him the same kind of call. Potter jumped to his feet and saluted when Forrest barged into his office unannounced. Nathan Bedford Forrest III was not a man to cross, any more than his great-grandfather was said to have been.

"At ease," Forrest said, and then, "By God, General, once I started looking at your note, I started doubting whether anybody here would ever be at ease again."

"One of the things we've found out over and over again, sir, is that anything we can do to the Yankees, they can damn well do to us," Potter said. "We didn't believe it in the Great War, and look at the price we paid for that." Part of the price the Confederate States had paid was Jake Featherston. Potter still thought so, but not even he was bold enough to say so out loud.

"I don't think I much care for the sound of that," Forrest observed. "Do you think they could pull off an armored attack like the one that took us up to Lake Erie?"

"Give that Colonel Morrell of theirs enough barrels, for instance, and I expect he could," Potter answered. "One of the things that goes some little way towards easing my mind about what's building up to the north of us here is that Morrell's nowhere near it."

Forrest chewed on the inside of his lower lip as he thought that over. At last, he nodded. "A point. But that's not what I came here to talk to you about. Do you truly believe we've got us some damnyankee gophers digging out what we're up to here in the War Department?"

"Gophers." Potter tasted the word. He nodded, too—he liked it. He could all but see spies gnawing underground, chomping away at the tender roots of Confederate plans. "Unfortunately, sir, I do. Why *wouldn't* the United States want to do something like that? No reason I can see. And they'll have people who can sound as if they belong here, same as we have people who can put on their accent."

"You're one of those," Forrest said. "Every now and then, I get calls about you from nervous lieutenants. They think you're a spy."

"And so I am—but not for the United States." Potter allowed himself a dry chuckle. "Besides, I only sound like a Yankee to somebody who's never really heard one. I do sound a little like one, but only a little. Comes of going to college up there. That turned out to be educational in all kinds of ways."

"I'll bet it did," Forrest said.

"Sir, you have no idea how much in earnest those people were," Potter said. "This was before the Great War, you understand. We'd licked them twice, humiliated them twice. They were bound and determined to get their own back. That holiday of theirs, Remembrance Day . . . They wanted the last war more than we did, and they got it."

"Well, now that shoe is on the other foot," Forrest said. He was right. The Confederates had been whipped up into a frenzy of vengeance, while U.S. citizens hadn't cared to think about a new fight. The chief of the General Staff brought things back to what he wanted to know: "If we've got gophers, how do we find 'em? How do we go about getting 'em out of their holes?"

"I can tell you the ideal solution," Potter said. Forrest raised an eyebrow. His eyes and eyebrows were much like his famous ancestor's, more so than the lower part of his face. Clarence Potter went on, "The ideal solution would be for our gophers in Washington and Philadelphia to dig up a list of U.S. gophers here. That could solve our problem."

"Could, hell!" Forrest said. "That *would* do it."

"Well, sir, not necessarily," Potter said. "If the Yankees knew we were looking for that kind of list, they could arrange for us to find it—and to shoot ourselves in the foot with it."

Nathan Bedford Forrest III raised both eyebrows this time. "You have a damn twisty mind, General."

"Thank you, sir," Potter answered. "Considering the business I'm in, I take that for a compliment."

"Good. That's how I meant it." Forrest pulled a pack of Raleighs out of his pocket. He stuck one in his mouth and held out the pack. Potter took one, too. Forrest had a cigarette lighter that could have done duty for a flamethrower. He almost singed Potter's nose giving him a light. After they'd both smoked for a little while, the head of the General Staff said, "Something I want you to do for me."

"Of course, sir." Potter gave the only kind of answer you were supposed to give to a superior officer.

"If you get word that that Morrell is moving from Ohio to the East, I want you to let me know the instant you do. The instant, you hear me? I don't care if I'm on the crapper with my pants down around my ankles. You barge in there yelling, 'Holy Jesus, General, the damnyankees have transferred Morrell!' "

Potter laughed. Nathan Bedford Forrest III wagged a finger at him. He wasn't kidding. "If I have to do that, I'll do it," Potter promised.

"You'd better." Forrest got to his feet. "And if you have any good ideas about how to make a gopher trap, I wouldn't mind hearing those."

"That's really more Counterintelligence's cup of tea, sir. I just wanted to alert you to the possibility," Potter said. "I don't want to step on General Cummins' toes any more than I have already."

"Oh, I'll put him on it, too. Don't you worry about that," Forrest said. "You've already done some thinking about this, though. Kindly do some more." Trailing smoke, he hurried out the door.

"Gopher traps," Potter muttered. He did some more muttering, too, while he finished the cigarette and stubbed it out. It wasn't as if he weren't already riding herd on 127 other things, all of which *were* in his bailiwick. And it wasn't as if General Cummins weren't a perfectly competent officer. Potter wanted to put the whole business on the back burner.

He wanted to, but he found he couldn't. He kept worrying at it in odd moments. It might have been a bit of gristle stuck between his teeth. It kept drawing his attention no matter how much he wished it wouldn't.

"Gopher traps." He kept saying it, too. If only Forrest hadn't come up with such a good phrase. It commanded attention whether Potter felt like giving it or not.

For the next few days, as he watched the growing U.S. storm in the north, he tried hard not to think about catching any possible spies in the War Department. He was, in fact, clacking away at a report summarizing news from spies in Kansas and Nebraska when he suddenly stopped and stared out the window, his eyes far away behind his spectacles.

His gaze returned to the report. It was as dull as it deserved to be. Not a hell of a lot was going on in Kansas and Nebraska. Not a hell of a lot had ever gone on in that part of the USA. In spite of that, he started to smile. In fact, he started to laugh, and the report had not a single funny word in it.

He walked over to Lieutenant General Forrest's office. The chief of the General Staff wasn't in the men's room. That being so, Potter had no trouble getting in to see him. *The power of these wreathed stars,* he thought. He'd never expected to become a general officer. He'd ten times never expected to become a general officer with Jake Featherston as President of the CSA. But here he was.

Nathan Bedford Forrest III looked up from whatever paperwork jungle he'd been hacking his way through. "Morrell?" he asked. "If he's up there, the other shoe'll drop on us any day now."

"No, sir. Haven't heard a thing about him." Potter shook his head. "I may have found a gopher trap, though."

"Well, that's interesting, too." Forrest waved him to a chair. "Why don't you sit down and tell me all about it?"

"Let me show you this first." Potter set the report on Kansas and Nebraska on Forrest's desk. "Glance over it, sir, if you'd be so kind." After Forrest did, he nodded. Potter explained. He finished, "You see how I could do that, don't you, sir?"

"I believe I do." Forrest looked the report over one more time. "It would mean a good deal of extra typing for you—because if you take this on, you're not going to trust it to a secretary."

"Oh, good heavens, no, sir. Of course not." Potter was shocked. "The thought never once crossed my mind."

"Good. I believe you—you sound like a schoolteacher talking about the bawdyhouse next door to her apartment building." The chief of the General Staff chuckled. Potter was less amused, but let it pass. Chuckling still, Forrest went on, "I should have remembered you run spies. You think about these things more than an ordinary officer is liable to."

"Well, I should hope so!" Clarence Potter exclaimed. "Ordinary officers . . ." He shook his head. "I read a memoir once, by one of Robert E. Lee's couriers. In the Pennsylvania campaign, he almost lost a set of Lee's special orders—the damned fool had wrapped them around three cigars. If McClellan had found out how badly Lee had divided the Army of Northern Virginia, who knows how much mischief he could have done? An enlisted man saw the orders fall and gave them back. If he hadn't, that courier's name would be mud all over the CSA."

"You do have to pay attention to little things," Forrest agreed. He tapped the report with his fingernail. "Go ahead with what you've got in mind. I'll be interested to see what you turn up."

"Yes, sir." Potter's smile was all sharp teeth. "What—and who."

XIV

Colonel Irving Morrell hadn't read the *Iliad* since he got out of the Military Academy, almost thirty years ago now. Chunks of it still stuck in his mind, though. He didn't remember the anger of Achilles so much as the Greek hero sulking in his tent after he'd quarreled with Agamemnon.

All things considered, Morrell would rather have sulked in Achilles' tent than in Caldwell, Ohio, where he found himself ensconced for the moment. Caldwell was a town of fifteen hundred or two thousand people, a few miles west of Woodsfield. It was the county seat for Noble County, as a sign in front of the county courthouse declared. That made him feel sorry for the rest of the county.

Caldwell was a coal town. People had been mining coal there for more than sixty years, and it showed. The air was hazy with coal dust. When Morrell needed to hawk and spit, he spat black. There were no red brick buildings in Caldwell. There were no white frame houses, either. The brick buildings were murky brown, the frame houses gray. The people seemed as subdued as their landscape. A lot of them seemed covered in a thin film of coal dust, too.

All things considered, Caldwell would have made Irving Morrell gloomy even if he'd gone into the place cheery as a lark. Since he'd gone in sullen, he would have been satisfied to come away without hanging himself. Even that much sometimes seemed optimistic. Caldwell was where what would have been his grand attack against the base of the Confederate salient in Ohio had ingloriously petered out. Sabotage and Confederate Asskickers had brought his armor to a standstill.

That wasn't the worst of it, either. He'd thought it would be, but he'd been wrong. As he watched some of his precious barrels chained onto flatcars bound for the East Coast, his fury and frustration grew too large to hold in. He turned to Sergeant Michael Pound, who was always good for sympathy over imbecilities emanating from the War Department. "I'm being robbed, Sergeant," he said. "Robbed, I tell you, as sure as if they'd held a gun to my head and lifted my wallet."

"Yes, sir," Pound said. "If they're going to take your barrels, the least they could do would be to take you, too. Seems only fair."

"They don't want me anywhere near Philadelphia," Morrell said. "They want me to keep fighting here in Ohio. They've said so."

"They just don't want to give you anything to fight with," Sergeant Pound said. "They'll probably set you to making bricks without straw next."

"You mean they haven't?" Morrell said. "By God, I was doing that for years at Fort Leavenworth. We had the prototype for a modern barrel twenty years ago—had it and stuck it in a back room and forgot about it. Christ, Sergeant, you went back to the artillery when they closed down the Barrel Works."

"I'm glad you don't hold it against me, sir," Pound said.

"A man has to eat. There's nothing in the Bible or the Constitution against that," Morrell said. "If there were no barrels to work on—and there damn well weren't—you needed to be doing something."

"That was how I looked at it, too." Pound suddenly snapped his fingers. "I'll bet I know one of the reasons why they're taking your barrels away from you."

"More than I do," Morrell said sourly. "Tell me."

"They're the biggest bunch we can get our hands on this side of the Confederate salient," Pound said. "Everything west of here has to go the long way around, up through Canada—either that or on Great Lakes freighters that the enemy can bomb."

Morrell eyed him. "Normally, Sergeant, when I say somebody thinks like a General Staff officer, I don't mean it as a compliment. This time, I do. That makes much more sense than anything I've been able to think of." He paused. "How would you like me to recommend you for a commission? You have the brains to do well by it. You have more in the way of brains than four out of five officers I know, maybe more."

"Thank you very much, sir." Michael Pound smiled a crooked smile. "If it's all the same to you, though, I'll pass. I've seen what officers do. There's a lot more nonsense in it than there is when you've just got stripes on your sleeve. Gunner suits me fine. It's simple. It's clean. I know exactly what I have to do and how to do it—and I'm pretty damn good at it, too. My notion is, the Army needs a good gunner more than it needs an ordinary lieutenant, which is what I'd be."

"Oh, I wouldn't say that." Morrell's smile lifted only one corner of his mouth. "Whatever else you were, you'd be an *extraordinary* lieutenant. You talk back to me as a sergeant. If you got a gold bar on your shoulder, you'd probably talk back to the chief of the General Staff."

"Seeing how the war is going, wouldn't you say somebody ought to?" Pound sketched a salute and ambled off. He was blocky as a barrel himself—and solid as a barrel, too. And, when he went up against something he didn't like, he could also be as deadly as a barrel.

Morrell looked east. Then he looked west. Then he muttered something uncomplimentary about Jake Featherston's personal habits, something about which he was in no position to have firsthand knowledge. Sergeant Pound was altogether too likely to be right. The thrust up to Lake Erie was starting to hurt the USA. Morrell wondered what the exact problem was. Could they ship enough fuel or enough barrels on the rail lines north of the Great Lakes, but not both at once? Something like that, he supposed. Logistics had never been his favorite subject. No good officer could afford to ignore it, but he preferred fighting to brooding about rolling stock.

Of course, if not for rolling stock he'd still have had his barrels with him. They would have broken down one after another if they'd had to get to eastern West Virginia under their own power. Breakdowns kept almost as many of them out of action as enemy fire did. Morrell wished it were otherwise, but it wasn't. The weight of armor they carried stressed engines and suspensions to the point of no return, or sometimes past it.

Half a dozen barrels still in Caldwell had their engine decking off. Soldiers were attacking them with wrenches and pliers. Some, maybe even most, of them hadn't broken down. A barrel whose crew kept it in good running trim didn't fail as often as one whose crew neglected it.

Far off in the distance, artillery rumbled. Morrell cursed under his breath. He should have been up there punching, not stalled in this jerkwater town. And how could he ever hope to land any punches if they kept siphoning away his strength? He couldn't, but they'd blame him because he didn't.

The Constitution said U.S. soldiers weren't supposed to quarter themselves on civilians. Like most rules, that one sometimes got ignored when bullets started flying. Morrell didn't ignore it, though. He was perfectly happy in a tent or a sleeping bag or just rolled in a blanket—he *liked* the outdoors. That was a concept General Staff officers back in Philadelphia had trouble grasping.

He was glad he had a tent when it started to pour about eight that night. Rain bucketed down out of the sky. It wasn't a warm summer rain, either: not the kind you could go out in and enjoy. The nasty weather said the seasons were changing. It would turn everything but paved roads into soup, too. Morrell muttered to himself. Enough mud could bog down barrels. That would slow things here.

He did some more muttering a moment later. If it also rained like this in Virginia, it wouldn't do the building U.S. offensive any good. That wasn't his campaign, but he worried about it. He worried about it all the more *because* it wasn't his campaign. But all he could do was worry. The weather did as it pleased, not as he pleased.

He'd just stretched out on his cot when Confederate bombers came over Caldwell. The drumming rain drowned out the drone of their motors. The first he knew that they were around was a series of rending crashes off in the woods east of the little town. Frightened shouts came from nearby houses. Morrell almost laughed. Civilians got a lot more excited about bombing than soldiers did.

With those clouds overhead, the Confederates were bombing blind. Morrell didn't worry that they would actually hit Caldwell . . . until the bomb impacts started walking west from those first blasts. The lead bombers had missed their targets by a lot. But the ones behind them, trying to bomb from the same point as they had, released their bombs too soon, an error that grew as it went through the formation.

That sort of thing happened all the time. Here, though, it was bringing the bombs back toward where they should have fallen in the first place. Morrell had taken off his boots to get comfortable. He put them on again in a tearing hurry, not bothering to tie them. Then he bolted from his tent and ran for the closest shelter trench.

He splashed and squelched getting down into it. It filled rapidly with cursing crewmen from his remaining barrels. However much they cursed, they kept their heads down. A chunk of bomb could do as neat a job as a headsman's axe—but a messy one would leave you just as dead.

"Here they come," somebody said as bombs started falling inside Caldwell. The ground shook. Fragments hissed and screeched not nearly far enough overhead. As Morrell bent to tie those boots, he hoped the civilians had had the brains to go down into their basements.

One crash was especially loud, and followed by a flash of light. "Fuckin' lucky bastards," a soldier said. "If they didn't just blow a barrel to hell and gone, I'm a monkey's uncle." Ammunition cooking off inside the stricken machine proved him right.

Another, different-sounding, crash probably meant a bomb had come down on a house. Going to the basement wasn't likely to save the poor bastards who'd lived there. Morrell sighed a wet sigh. Nothing to be done about it—and it wasn't as if U.S. bombers weren't visiting the same kind of hell on Confederate civilians.

"Pay those stinking sons of bitches back for getting me all wet and muddy," a barrel man said. Civilian casualties worried him even less than Morrell. His own discomfort was another story.

The bombs stopped falling. Morrell stood up straight and looked out of the trench. The barrel that had taken a direct hit was still burning in spite of the rain. By that yellow, flickering light, Morrell saw that two or three houses had fallen in on themselves. They were trying to burn, too, but weren't having an easy time of it in the downpour.

"Come on," he said. "Let's see what we can do for the locals."

A civilian lay in the middle of one of the streets, suddenly and gruesomely dead. What had he been doing out there? Watching the bombs come down? Did he think it was sport? No one would ever know now.

Other people came staggering out of houses. Some of them were wounded. Some were simply in shock, and crying out their terror to whoever would listen, or maybe to the world at large. "My baby! My baby!" a woman shrieked. She was holding the baby, which was also shrieking.

A corpsman took the baby from her. After looking it over—carefully, because fragments could produce tiny but deadly wounds—he spoke in tones of purest New York City: "Lady, ain't nuttin' wrong wid dis kid but a wet diaper."

"But the poor thing is frightened half to death!" the woman said.

What the corpsman said after that was memorable, but had very little to do with medicine. The woman squawked indignantly. Irving Morrell filed away some of the choicer—the corpsman would have said *chercer*—phrases. When he found a moment, he'd aim them at Philadelphia.

When Scipio looked in his pay envelope, he thought the bookkeeper at the Huntsman's Lodge had made a mistake. That had happened before, two or three times. As far as he could tell, the bookkeeper always erred in the restaurant's favor. He took the envelope to Jerry Dover. "I hates to bother you, suh, but I's ten dollars light."

Dover shook his head. "Sorry, Xerxes, but you're not."

"What you mean?" For a second, Scipio thought the restaurant manager thought he'd pocketed the missing banknote before complaining. Then he realized something else was going on. "You mean it's one o' them—?"

"Contributions. That's right. Thought you might have seen the story in the *Constitutionalist* yesterday, or maybe heard about it on the wireless. It's on account of the bombing in the Terry."

"Lawd!" Scipio burst out. "One o' dem bombs almost kill me, an' now I gots to *pay fo' it*? Don't hardly seem fair." It seemed a lot worse than unfair, but saying even that much to a white man carried a certain risk.

Jerry Dover didn't get angry. He just shrugged. "If I don't short you and the rest of the colored help, my ass is in a sling," he said. If it came to a choice between saving his ass and the black men's, he'd choose his own. That wasn't a headline that would make the *Augusta Constitutionalist*.

Scipio sighed. Only too plainly, he wasn't going to get his ten dollars. He said, "Wish I seen de newspaper. Wish I heard de wireless. Wouldn't be such a surprise in dat case."

"How come you missed 'em?" Dover asked. "You're usually pretty well up on stuff." He didn't even add, *for a nigger.* Scipio had worked for him a long time now. He knew the colored man had a working brain.

"One o' them things," Scipio said with a shrug of his own. He'd missed buying a paper the day before. He hadn't listened to the wireless very much. He did wonder how he'd managed not to hear the newsboys shouting the headline and the waiters and cooks and dishwashers grousing about it. "Been livin' in my own little world, I reckon."

"Yeah, well, shit like that happens." Dover was willing to sound sympathetic as long as he didn't have to do anything about it.

Before Scipio could answer, a dishwasher came up to their boss. "Hey, Mr. Dover!" he said. "I got ten clams missin' outa my envelope here!"

"No, you don't, Ozymandias," the manager said, and went through the explanation again. Scipio knew a certain amount of relief that he hadn't been the only one not to get the word.

Ozymandias, a young man, didn't take it as well as Scipio had. He cussed and fumed till Scipio wondered whether Jerry Dover would fire him on the spot. Dover didn't. He just let the Negro run down and sent him out the door. Quite a few white men boasted about being good with niggers. Most of them were full of crap. Jerry Dover really was good with the help at the Huntsman's Lodge, though he didn't go around bragging about it.

Of course, Dover was good with people generally, whites as well as Negroes. *We are people, dammit,* Scipio thought. The Freedom Party had a different opinion.

Dover said, "You be careful on the way home, you hear? Don't want your missus and your young ones grieving on account of some bastard who's out prowling after curfew."

"I's always careful," Scipio said, and meant it. "But I thanks you fo' de thought."

He went out into the black, black night. Augusta had never been bombed, but remained blacked out. Scipio supposed that made sense. Better safe than sorry was a pretty good rule.

The weather was cooler and less muggy than it had been. As fall came on, the dreadful sticky heat of summer became only a memory. It wasn't cold enough to put all the mosquitoes to sleep for the winter, though. Scipio suspected he'd get home to his apartment with a new bite or two. He couldn't hear the mosquitoes buzzing any more unless they flew right past his ears. Those nasty whines had driven him crazy when he was younger. He didn't miss hearing them now—except that they would have warned him the flying pests were around.

An auto slid past, going hardly faster than Scipio was. Masking tape reduced its headlights to slits. They cast a pallid glow that reached about as far as a man could spit. At least the driver here didn't have the delusion he could do more than he really could. Accidents were up even though fewer motorcars were on the road. That meant one thing and one thing only: people were driving like a bunch of damn fools.

As usual, Scipio had no trouble telling when he got to the Terry, even though he could hardly see a hand in front of his face. As soon as the sidewalk started crumbling under his feet, he knew he'd come to the colored part of town.

He skirted the shortest way home, which took him past what had been the bus stop for war workers. It remained a sea of rubble. Repairs got done slowly in the Terry—when they got done at all. Some of the buildings white mobs had burned in the pogroms after the Freedom Party took over remained ruins after seven years.

He'd almost died then. Two different auto bombs had almost killed him. He'd lived through the bloody rise and even bloodier fall of the Congaree Socialist Republic. He'd outlived Anne Colleton, and he never would have bet anything on that. *After what I've been through, maybe I'll go on forever,* he thought.

A bat flittered past, not a foot in front of him. It was out of sight almost before he realized it had been there. He wondered if the war had brought hardship to bats. Without street lights to lure insects, wouldn't they have to work harder to get enough to eat? Strange to imagine that one man's decision in Richmond might affect little furry animals hundreds of miles away.

"Hold it right there!" The harsh, rasping voice came out of an alley not ten feet away. "Don't even breathe funny, or it'll be the last thing you ever do."

Scipio froze. Even as he did it, he wondered if it was the worst thing he could do, not the best. If he ran, he might lose himself in the darkness. Of course, if he ran, he might also give the owner of that voice the excuse to blast him to hamburger with a charge of buckshot. He'd made his choice. Now he had to see what came of it.

"All right, nigger. Suppose you tell me what the fuck you're doin' out after curfew."

He'd *thought* that was a white policeman there, not a black robber. He would have been more likely to run from a man of his own color. "Suh, I works at de Huntsman's Lodge," he answered. "Dey don't let me off till midnight. I goes home at all, I gots to go after curfew."

"Likely tell," the white man said. "Who's your boss, damn you? Make it snappy!"

"Jerry Dover, suh," Scipio said quickly. "Mebbe he still dere. I ain't left but fifteen minutes ago. He tell you who I is."

Footsteps crunching on gravel, thumping on cement. A dark, shadowy shape looming up in front of Scipio. The silhouette of the juice-squeezer hat the other man wore said he really was a policeman. He leaned forward to peer closely at Scipio. "Holy Jesus, you're in a goddamn penguin suit!"

"I gots to wear it," Scipio said wearily. "It's my uniform, like."

"Get the fuck outa here," the cop said. "Nobody's gonna be dumb enough to go plantin' bombs or nothin' in a lousy penguin suit."

"I thanks you kindly, suh," Scipio said. If the policeman had been in a nasty mood, he could have run him in for being out after curfew. Scipio thought Jerry Dover or the higher-ups at the restaurant would have made sure he didn't spend much time in jail, but any time in jail was too much.

"A penguin suit," the cop said one more time—another dime Scipio didn't have. "Shit, the boys at the station'll bust a gut when I tell 'em about this one."

With a resigned chuckle and a dip of his head to show he was a properly respectful—a properly servile—Negro, Scipio made his way deeper into the Terry. He peered carefully up and down every street and alley he came to before crossing it. How much good that would do, with so many inky shadows for robbers to hide in, he didn't know. But it was all he could do.

When he came to a couple of the places where he was most likely to find trouble—or it was most likely to find him—he wished he had that foul-mouthed policeman at his side. He shook his head, ashamed and embarrassed at wanting a white man's protection against his own people. Ashamed and embarrassed or not, though, he did. The Terry was a more dangerous place these days than it had been a few years before. Sharecroppers and farm workers forced from fields when tractors and harvesters took their jobs away had poured into Confederate cities, looking for whatever they could find. When they could find nothing else—which was all too often— they preyed on their fellow Negroes. And Reds sheltered here, too. They weren't above robbery (from the highest motives, of course) to keep their cause alive.

He got through the worst parts safely. His last bad moment was opening the fortified door to his building. If somebody came up while he was doing that . . . But nobody did. He quickly shut the door behind him, locked the lock, and used the dead bolt. Then he breathed a sigh of relief. *Made it through another night,* he thought.

As the fear dropped away, he realized how tired he was. The climb up the stairs to his flat felt as if he were going up a mountain. He'd had that happen before, too. He didn't know what he could do about it. If he didn't work at the Huntsman's Lodge, he'd be waiting tables somewhere else. And if he couldn't do it anywhere, what would he be doing then? Prowling the alleys, looking for someone unwary to knock over the head?

Scipio laughed, not that it was funny. He might make the *Constitutionalist* if he tried it. What would the headline be? Augusta's oldest strongarm man? Augusta's dumbest strongarm man? Oldest *and* dumbest? That would probably do the job.

He trudged down the hall and opened his front door. A light was burning inside. Blackout curtains made sure it didn't leak out. Here as in other colored districts throughout the CSA, blackout wardens and cops were likelier to shoot through lighted windows than to bother with a warning and a fine.

As usual, he got out of his tuxedo with nothing but relief. Putting on his nightshirt felt good, where even that much in the way of clothes had been a sore trial in the hot weather not long before. Bathsheba murmured sleepily when he lay down beside her. "How'd it go?" she asked.

"Not too bad," he answered automatically. But then he remembered that wasn't quite true. "Got my pay docked ten dollars, though." He couldn't hide that from his wife—better to let her know right away, then.

The news got her attention, no matter how sleepy she was. "Ten dollars!" she said. "What you do?"

"Didn't do nothin'. Everybody git docked," Scipio said. "De gummint fine de niggers here fo' de auto bombs."

"Ain't fair. Ain't right," Bathsheba said. "Gummint don't fine no ofays when *they* do somethin' bad."

"I ain't sayin' you wrong," Scipio replied. "But what kin we do 'bout it?" The answer to that for Negroes in the CSA had always been *not much.*

Jonathan Moss led his squadron of Wright fighters out over Lake Erie. They were looking for trouble. They would probably find it, too. Just in case they couldn't on their own, they had help. The wireless set sounded in Moss' earphones: "Red-27 leader, this is Mud Hen Base. Do you copy?"

"Go ahead, Mud Hen Base," Moss said. "I read you five by five." Mud Hen Base was the Y-ranging station back in Toledo. For reasons known only to God, the Toledo football team was called the Mud Hens. They didn't play in one of the top leagues, so maybe Confederate wireless men monitoring the conversation—and there were bound to be some—wouldn't figure out where the fellow on the other end of the circuit was for a while.

And maybe the stork brings babies and tucks them under cabbage leaves, too, Moss thought.

"We have bogies on the lake. Range about seventy, bearing oh-seven-five. I say again, range about seventy, bearing oh-seven-five."

"Roger that," Moss said, and repeated it back. "We'll have a look. Out." He checked a small map, then got on the circuit with the rest of the airplanes he led. After passing on what he'd got from the Y-ranging station, he added, "Sounds like they're somewhere out east of Point Pelee Island. Let's see if we can't catch 'em."

Point Pelee Island lay north of Sandusky. Before the Great War, it had belonged to the province of Ontario. It had been fortified to hell and gone, too; reducing it had cost most of a division. Technically, Moss supposed it still belonged to Ontario. That didn't matter now, though—it was under U.S. management.

When the island came into sight, he led the squadron north around it. Some of the U.S. antiaircraft down there opened up on the fighters anyway. "Knock it off, you stupid sons of bitches!" Moss shouted in the cockpit. The gunners, of course, paid no attention to him. They probably wouldn't have even if he'd been on the wireless with them—how could they be sure he wasn't a Confederate who could put on a Yankee accent?

U.S. guns had already shot at Moss quite often enough to last him several lifetimes. They hadn't hit him yet. He knew of pilots who weren't so lucky. He also knew of pilots who hadn't come home because their own side shot them down.

Nobody got hit here. Someone—Moss couldn't tell who—spoke in his earphones: "I'd like to go down there and strafe those assholes." That had occurred to him, too.

Once past the danger, he peered east. He also looked down to the surface of the lake every now and again. The Confederates would be out hunting freighters. With the rail lines and railroads through Ohio cut, the United States had to do what they could to move things back and forth between East and West. And the Confederates had to do what they could to try to stop the USA.

He hoped he'd find Mules buzzing along in search of ships to dive on. The CSA's Asskickers were formidable if you were underneath them. To a fighter pilot, they might have had SHOOT ME DOWN! painted on their gull wings. They couldn't run fast enough to get away, and they couldn't shoot back well enough to defend themselves.

"There they are—eleven o' clock!" The shout crackled with excitement.

Moss peered a little farther north than he'd been looking. He spotted the sun flashing off cockpit glass, too. "Well, let's go see what we've got," he said. "Stick with your wingmen, keep an eye on your buddies, and good hunting."

His own wingman these days was a stolid squarehead named Martin Rolvaag. He came on the circuit to say, "They don't look like Mules, sir."

"I was thinking the same thing," Moss answered. "Razorbacks, unless I miss my guess." The medium bombers couldn't outrun Wrights, either, but they carried more machine guns than Mules did, and had to be approached with caution. And . . . "They've got Hound Dogs escorting them."

"They've seen us," Rolvaag said.

Sure enough, the Confederate fighters peeled away from the Razorbacks and sped toward the U.S. airplanes. Their numbers more or less matched those he had. So did their performance. They were a little more nimble, while the Wrights climbed and dove a little better.

Moss didn't want to fight the Hound Dogs. He wanted to punish the Razorbacks. Knocking them out of the sky was the point of the exercise. They could sink the ships the United States had to have. Confederate fighters could shoot up ships, but couldn't send them to the bottom.

But if Moss wanted the Razorbacks, he had to go through the Hound Dogs. The C.S. fighter pilots understood what was what as well as their U.S. counterparts. They were there to make sure the bombers got through.

Elements—lead pilots and their wingmen—were supposed to hold together. So were flights—pairs of elements. And so were squadrons—four flights. In practice, damn near everything went to hell in combat. Lead pilots and wingmen did stick together when they could; you didn't want to be naked and alone out there. Past that, you did what you could and what you had to and worried about it later.

Head-on passes made you pucker. You and the other guy were zooming at each other at seven hundred miles an hour. That didn't leave much time to shoot. And if you both chose to climb or dive at the same instant . . . The sky was a big place, but not big enough to let two airplanes occupy the same small part of it at the same time.

The Hound Dog coming at Moss started shooting too soon. You couldn't hit the broad side of a barn from half a mile out. That told Moss he was flying against somebody without a whole lot of experience. Anybody who'd done this for a while knew you had to get in close to do damage. Moss waited till the Hound Dog—painted in blobs of brown and green not much different from those on his Wright 27—all but filled the windshield before thumbing the firing button.

He missed anyway. The Hound Dog roared past him and was gone. He swore, but his heart wasn't in it. "Watch my back, Marty," he called to his wingman. "Let's go after the bombers."

"Will do." Nothing fazed Rolvaag. That went a long way toward making him a good pilot all by itself. If he didn't quite have a duelist's reflexes and a duelist's arrogance . . . That went a long way toward making him a good pilot but not a great one.

His calm answer had to fight its way through the shouts—some wordless, others filled with extravagant obscenity—from the other pilots in the squadron. A flaming fighter tumbled toward the lake far below. Moss couldn't tell if it bore the eagle and crossed swords or the Confederate battle flag. Like the USA and the CSA, their fighter aircraft bore an alarming resemblance to each other.

Bombs rained down from the Razorbacks. The bombers had no target—all they'd kill were fish. But they were faster and less likely to go up in a fireball if they got rid of their ordnance. As soon as they'd done it, they streaked for the deck. In a dive, they were damn near as fast as a fighter.

Damn near, but not quite. Moss picked his target. Once he heeled over into a dive, he stopped worrying about the Hound Dogs. They couldn't catch him from behind. The dorsal and portside machine gunners on the Razorback opened up on him. He respected their tracers, but didn't particularly fear them. They had to aim those single guns by hand. Hits weren't easy.

He, on the other hand, needed only to point his Wright's nose at the Razorback's wing root. The bombers carried fuel in their wings. Confederate self-sealing gas tanks were as good as the ones the USA used, but they weren't perfect. No tanks were. Put enough armor-piercing and incendiary bullets through them and they'd burn, all right.

This one did. Fire licked back from the wing. The portside engine started burning, too. "You nailed his ass!" Rolvaag shouted as the Razorback's pilot lost control and the bomber spiraled down toward the water.

"Yeah," Moss said. As long as he was in his dive, he didn't have to worry about Hound Dogs. Once he came out . . . Once he came out, he was down here, and they could dive on him.

You traded speed for altitude. To gain speed, you had to give up altitude. That was why fights that started three miles up in the sky often finished just above the ground. To get the altitude back, you had to give up speed. You were vulnerable to the fighters that hadn't dropped so low.

Another bomber plunged down toward Lake Erie. A moment later, so did the U.S. fighter that had shot it down. Moss eyed it, hoping the pilot could get out before it went into the water. No such luck. The squadron leader swore. Another one of the bright, eager youngsters he commanded wouldn't be coming home.

The Hound Dogs were a little slower down to the deck than the U.S. Wrights. Once they got there, though, they got between the U.S. fighters and the fleeing Razorbacks. By then, the Razorbacks were streaking towards occupied Ohio. The Confederates had brought up what seemed like all the antiaircraft in the world. Going after the bombers, especially down low like this, was liable to prove expensive.

Moss got on the all-squadron circuit: "Let's head for home, boys. We did what we were supposed to do. Those Razorbacks won't bother our shipping for a while."

"Some of those bastards won't ever bother it again," somebody said. Moss thought that was Red Geoffreys, who had every ounce of the killer instinct Marty Rolvaag was a hair short on. He couldn't be sure, though. There was a lot of other wireless traffic, and the earphones didn't reproduce anybody's voice real well.

A few pilots grumbled, but no one complained very much when he swung back toward the west. The Hound Dogs followed the Razorbacks down to the south. They were content to let the Wrights go. Moss nodded to himself. That was always a sign the guys on the other side had had enough of you.

He'd seen two Razorbacks go down. He knew his own squadron had lost at least one fighter. As the Wrights went back to their airstrip, the men made their claims about enemy aircraft shot down. To listen to them, the Confederates had lost half their Razorbacks and at least half a dozen Hound Dogs. Moss had heard—and made—enough excited claims to take all of them with a grain of salt. If you didn't see an airplane crash, you couldn't be sure it was really downed. Even if you did, two or three guys were liable to think they were the one who'd shot it out of the sky.

Rolvaag came on the element-only circuit: "Looks like we're down two, Major."

"Shit," Moss said. His wingman had done the count before he'd had the chance to. He wondered how many U.S. fighters the Hound Dogs would claim once they got back to *their* airstrip. If it were only two, he would have been amazed.

How much punishment could the Confederates take over Lake Erie before they decided their attacks cost more than they were worth? How much damage were they doing to U.S. shipping? How much to the U.S. airplanes that opposed them? Moss had no idea. He wondered whether anybody on either side did.

After too much experience with too many wars, he wouldn't have bet on it. They'd just go on till one side or the other couldn't stand it any more. Which one that would be, how long the whole bloody business would take . . . There alone in the cockpit, he shrugged. No way to tell, not ahead of time.

He wondered if he'd be around to see the end of it. He shrugged again. He'd got through the Great War in one piece. He hadn't even been scratched. But what did that prove? Nothing, and he knew it too well.

George Enos didn't mind getting bounced out of bed at half past five every morning. He didn't mind the calisthenics that followed, either. He would have got up earlier and worked harder had he been bringing in cod out on the Grand Bank.

Some people grumbled about the chow. He'd figured out nobody could do anything about that, not when the cooks here turned out meals for hundreds at a time. It wasn't terrible food, and you could make a pig of yourself, which he did. He poured down coffee with every meal, too. Sometimes he thought he'd have trouble going to sleep without it.

After breakfast came gunnery practice. He'd graduated from a one-pounder like those his father had served to a twin 40mm cannon. That gun probably would have amazed his old man. It sure amazed him. It was a Swedish design, built under license in the USA, and it could put a hell of a lot of shells in the air.

Chief Isbell, the gunnery instructor, was another one of those broad-beamed, gray-stubbled CPOs. The Navy seemed to have a factory that turned them out as needed. They were, if not the brains of the outfit, at least its memory. Behind Isbell's back—but only behind his back—the raw seamen he taught called him the Bald Eagle: when he took off his cap, which he did as little as he could, he showed the world a wide expanse of shining scalp.

He knew his business, though. "They come after you, you start shooting like a bunch of mad bastards, you hear?" he said one morning. "Start shooting before you really start aiming. Just point it sorta at the fuckers comin' your way and let fly."

"What the hell good will that do, Chief?" somebody asked.

Isbell spelled it out like a third-grade teacher working on the multiplication table with a class full of dumbbells: "I'll tell you what, by God." He laid an affectionate hand on the barrel of the gun, the way a husband might on his wife's behind. A stab of longing for Connie pierced George to the root, but only for a moment, for Isbell went on, "For one thing, you're liable to scare him away. These babies put out muzzle flashes as long as your arm. He sees 'em, he knows you're going after him. Not everybody's a hero. Sucker in that airplane may decide he'd rather go home to his girlfriend than press home and maybe get shot down. Even if he does press home, he won't do it as well as he would have if you weren't banging away at him. You see what I mean?"

A few would-be sailors nodded.

"*You see what I mean?*" Isbell growled.

"Yes, Chief!" the men chorused.

Isbell nodded. "That's more like it. I spend my breath talking to you puppies, I want to know you're paying attention. I don't like wasting my time, you know what I mean?" He paused and lit a cigarette. After his first drag, he made a face. "Damn thing tastes like horseshit." That didn't stop him from smoking it down to a tiny butt as he continued, "Other thing you gotta remember is, ammo's cheap. Ships are a lot more expensive." He looked the trainees up and down. "You guys might be worth a little somethin', too, but I wouldn't count on it a whole hell of a lot."

So there, George thought. An old-fashioned two-decker flew back and forth, towing a cloth target at the end of a long line. No matter how long the line was, one eager-beaver group almost shot down the target tug instead of the target. The Bald Eagle waxed eloquent on the shortcomings of the material the Navy had to use these days. That, in its way, was also rather like walking into an unexpected volley of 40mm ammunition.

George's group did better. He wasn't sure they hit the target, but they did scare it. "I've seen worse," Isbell declared. From him, that was high praise.

After the session, George went up to the chief and said, "My father used to serve a one-pounder on a destroyer in the last war."

"Those goddamn things." Isbell spoke with a mixture of affection and exasperation that George understood from training on such a gun. "You had to be lucky to hit an airplane with 'em, but you sure could make a sub say uncle if you caught it on the surface. What ship, kid?"

George was past thirty. Nobody'd called him *kid* for quite a while. If anyone had the right, though, it was somebody like the Bald Eagle. "He was on the *Ericsson*," he answered.

Isbell's face changed. Every Navy veteran knew about the *Ericsson*. "At the end?" he asked. George nodded. To his amazement, the Bald Eagle set a hand on his shoulder. "That's rough, kid. I'm sorry as hell." All at once, the chief's gaze sharpened. "Wait a minute. You're Enos. Are you related to the Enos gal who . . . ?"

"Who shot the Confederate submersible skipper? That was my mother," George said proudly.

"Fuck me." Isbell made the obscenity sound like a much more sincere compliment than the one he'd given the gun crew. "You want antiaircraft duty, kid? You been making noises like you do. I bet you can have it. Personnel ain't gonna say no, not to somebody with your last name."

"I've . . . thought about that," George said. "I don't want to get anything just on account of who my mother and father were."

"You've got an angle. You've got an in. You'd have to be nuts not to use 'em," Isbell said. "Life gives you lemons, make lemonade."

George had heard plenty of advice he liked less. He said, "Is there any way I can get to sea faster than usual?"

But Isbell just laughed at that, laughed and shook his head. "Nope. Sorry, Enos, but that ain't gonna happen. You gotta know what you gotta know, and the Navy's gotta know you know what you gotta know. Nothing personal—don't get me wrong—but if they put you on a ship before that, you're liable to be more of a menace than a help, if you know what I mean."

With a tight, sour smile, George changed the subject. He did know what the Bald Eagle meant, and wished he didn't. A couple of times, he'd gone on a fishing run with men who didn't know what the hell they were doing, men who were trying the fisherman's life for the first time. Even when they were eager to work, they might as well have been so many kittens. They got in everybody's way and caused more trouble than they were worth.

And then he realized that, once upon a time, he'd been one of those kittens himself. How had the old-timers put up with him when he first started going out to fish? He'd been sixteen, seventeen, something like that: somebody the phrase *green as paint* was made for. The other guys had probably remembered what they were like when they first put to sea. That was the only explanation that made any sense to him. If he saw any of them again, he'd have to buy them a beer and thank them for their patience.

He worked hard on antiaircraft gunnery. He got practice firing bigger guns, too, as he had on the *Lamson*. The men in training didn't get to handle full-sized big-gun ammunition. The guns had subcaliber practice rounds, which couldn't do as much harm if something went wrong and which, as the CPO in charge of those guns (a near twin to Bald Eagle Isbell, except that he had a full head of graying hair) pointed out, were a hell of a lot cheaper than the real thing.

And he tried to learn the other things the Navy threw at him. Like anybody who'd made more than a few fishing runs, he was a pretty fair amateur mechanic. He'd fiddled with the *Sweet Sue*'s diesel several times, and made things better more often than he'd made them worse. He'd learned on the *Lamson*, though, that, just as sailing on a fishing boat wasn't enough to let him go to sea right away on a warship, so fiddling with a diesel didn't teach him what he needed to know about the care and feeding of a steam turbine.

Some guys bitched about the classwork. Morris Fishbein asked the overage lieutenant who was teaching them, "Why do we need to know this, sir? Most of us aren't going into the black gang."

"I know that, Fishbein," the officer answered. "But if your ship takes a bomb or a shell or a torpedo and they have casualties down there, the men left alive will be screaming for help as loud as they can. And when they get it, they won't want a bunch of thumb-fingered idiots who don't know their ass from the end zone. They'll want people who can actually do them some good. Not all of you will be gunners, either, but you're learning to handle guns. Well, a ship's engine is just as much a weapon as her guns are."

The answer made more than enough sense to keep George happy. And the Navy knew how to ram home what people needed to learn. He wished his high-school teachers had been half as good. He might have stayed in long enough to graduate.

By the time he had both the training and the hands-on work on the *Lamson,* he thought he could have built an engine from scratch. He was wrong, of course, but a little extra confidence never hurt anybody.

Men applied for specialist schools: those who really would go into the black gang, men who'd handle the wireless and Y-ranging gear, cooks. There was a gunnery school, too. George put in for it. He let Bald Eagle Isbell know he had.

"Way to go, kid," the CPO said. "Tell you what I'll do. I'll bend a few people's ears. I know the right ones to talk to. I'd goddamn well better by now, eh? I've been at this business long enough."

"Thanks very much, Chief," George said.

"You're welcome," Isbell answered matter-of-factly. "I wouldn't do it if I didn't think you had the makings. That wouldn't be fair to whoever you shipped with. But you can do the job, so why the hell not?"

Lists of those assigned to this, that, or the other school appeared on the door outside the camp's administrative offices. George scanned them eagerly. His name wasn't on the one for the gunnery school, but it wasn't on any of the other lists, either. He wondered if the Navy really wanted him for anything at all.

And then, after a week of what felt like the worst anticlimax in the world, he found his name. Actually, Morrie Fishbein, who was standing beside him to check the lists, found it for him. Fishbein gave him a nudge with an elbow and said, "Hey, George, here you are."

"What? Where? Lemme see," George said. Fishbein pointed. George looked. "Gunnery school! Yeah!" He pumped his fist in the air. Then he remembered the other man. "What about you, Morrie? You anywhere?"

"Doesn't look like it." Fishbein sounded mournful. "I don't think anybody gives a damn about me." George hadn't been the only one with such worries, then.

A yeoman came out of the office and stuck another list to the door with a piece of masking tape. Morrie turned away in dejection. George took a look at it. " 'Fishbein, Morris D.,' " he read. "It's the antisubmersible-warfare list. They're going to teach you to throw ashcans at subs—either that or put earphones on you and show you how to really use that sound-ranging gear they've got."

"Oh, yeah?" The other man turned back. George aimed an index finger to show him his name. Fishbein thought it over. "Antisub . . . That's not too bad. They could've sent me plenty of worse places. Minesweeping, for instance." He shuddered at the mere idea.

"If I didn't get gunnery, I would've wanted antisub," George said. "You sink one of those bastards for me, you hear?"

"Sure as hell try," Fishbein said. "If you don't get them, they get you."

"You'd best believe it," George said. "Like the chaplain tells us every Sunday—it is better to give than to receive."

He realized too late that Fishbein listened to *his* chaplain on Saturday, if he listened at all. But the New Yorker laughed. "That's pretty goddamn funny, George."

George checked the lists again. "They're going to ship us out this afternoon. Better throw your stuff in your duffel."

"Uh-huh." Fishbein stopped laughing. "Ain't that a pisser? Everything you got in the world, and you can sling it over your shoulder."

"Just one of those things," George answered with a shrug. He'd been used to living with not much more than a duffel's worth of stuff for weeks at a time when he went on a fishing run. To someone new to the sea, though, it couldn't be easy.

He stared at the list again. Gunnery school. He nodded to himself. He thought the father he didn't remember well enough would approve.

Hipolito Rodriguez turned off the lights in the farmhouse kitchen. As always these days, he did it with enormous respect, after first making sure the floor under his feet was dry. He'd been careless once, and it had almost killed him. If Magdalena hadn't come out of the bedroom and knocked him away from the switch he couldn't let go of on his own, it would have finished the job in short order.

From what he'd heard since, she was lucky she hadn't stepped in the water herself, or the treacherous electricity would have seized her, too. Electricity was a strong servant, yes. Like anything strong, though, it could use its strength for good or ill. He'd found that out. He hoped one lesson would last him a lifetime.

When he went into the front room, Magdalena asked, "How are you?"

"I'm all right. I'm not made of glass, you know," he answered. His wife gave him a look that said she didn't believe a word of it. He still hadn't got back all his strength and coordination. Sometimes he wondered if he ever would, or if he'd remain a lesser man than he once had been.

He frowned. He wished he hadn't thought of it like that. He was a lesser man than he had been in some other ways, too. He wasn't quite no man at all, but the electricity hadn't done that any good, either.

Magdalena hadn't complained. She'd done everything she could to help him. He was discovering that women got less upset about such things than did the men to whom they happened. That was a small relief, even if one he would rather not have had.

To keep from worrying about his shortcomings, he said, "I'm going to turn on the wireless. It's just about time for the news."

"All right." Magdalena didn't tell him to be careful when he turned on the set. She never told him anything like that. She knew he had his pride. Whether she said it or not, though, he knew what she was thinking. And he *was* careful when he turned it on. He thought he always would be.

Click! The set was on. He stepped away from it. Nothing had happened to him. Absurd to feel relief at that, but he did. Then he stepped back and turned the tuning knob to the station he wanted.

As usual when the wireless hadn't been on for a while, the sound needed a bit of time to show up. When it did, the announcer was in the middle of a sentence: "—the news in a moment, after these brief messages." An improbably cheerful chorus started singing the praises of a brand of kitchen cleanser. By Magdalena's sniff, it wasn't a brand she thought much of.

Another chorus, this one full of deep, masculine voices, urged people to buy Confederate war bonds. Rodriguez had already done that: as many as he could afford. "Bonds and bullets, bonds and bombs!" they chanted, drums thudding martially in the background. Just hearing them made you want to give money to the cause. Their music faded. The familiar fanfare that led off the news followed. "Now it is time to tell you the truth," the announcer said. "Yankee air pirates were severely punished in raids over Virginia and Kentucky last night. Confederate bombers struck hard at Yankee shipping in the Great Lakes yesterday. U.S. industry cannot keep making munitions if it cannot get supplies."

"Es verdad. Tiene razón," Rodriguez said. His wife nodded—she thought it was true and the newsman was right, too.

"In Utah, poison-gas attacks did not make the Mormon freedom fighters rebelling against Yankee tyranny pull back from Provo," the newsman went on. "And in New Mexico, a daring raid by the Confederate Camel Corps caused the destruction of a U.S. ammunition dump outside of Alamogordo. The shells and bombs would have been used against Confederate women and children in Texas."

Rodriguez found himself nodding. That was how the damnyankees did things, all right.

"There were minor raids by Red *mallate* bandits in Mississippi, Georgia, and South Carolina over the past few days," the newsreader said. "None of them did much damage, and the Negroes were driven off with heavy losses." Rodriguez nodded again. If blacks in the CSA took up arms against the government, they deserved whatever happened to them. Even if they didn't . . .

"And in Richmond, President Jake Featherston announced the formation of the Confederate Veterans' Brigades," the newsman said. "These men, while no longer fit for the demands of modern war, will free younger men now serving behind the lines to go up to the front."

More singing commercials followed. Rodriguez listened to them with half an ear. When they went away, the newsman gave football scores from across the CSA. Rodriguez waited for the score of the Hermosillo-Chihuahua match. It had ended up 17–17. He sighed. He'd hoped for a win, but Chihuahua had been favored, so he didn't suppose he could be too disappointed that the team from the Sonoran capital had managed to earn a tie.

After the sports came the weather forecast. Rodriguez did about as well by going outside and watching the clouds and feeling the breeze as the weathermen did with all their fancy gadgets. He listened anyway, not least so he could laugh at them when they turned out to be wrong.

Music came back after more commercials. He listened for a while, then got up and yawned and stretched. "*Estoy cansado.* I'm going to bed," he said.

"I'm tired, too," his wife agreed. She turned off the wireless. Rodriguez didn't say anything. If he had, she would have told him she was closer to the set than he was. It would have been the truth, too, but not all of the truth.

When they lay down together, he wondered if he would know the sweetness of desire. It had been a while. But nothing happened. He sighed once more, yawned, rolled over, and fell asleep.

He was chivvying a chicken into the henhouse the next morning when an auto pulled off the road and stopped not far from the barn. He blinked. That didn't happen every day—or every month, either. The motorcar wasn't new, and hadn't been anything special when it was: a boxy, battered Birmingham with bulbous headlights that stuck out like a frog's eyes. Out of it stepped Robert Quinn.

The Freedom Party organizer hadn't come to Baroyeca to get rich—or if he had, he'd been out of his mind. He hadn't got rich, either. That was one of the reasons he commanded so much respect in town. He was doing what he believed in, not what would serve his own selfish interests.

Rodriguez waved to him. "*Hola, Señor* Quinn. What can I do for you today?"

"Well, I thought I'd come by and see how you were doing, *Señor* Rodriguez," Quinn replied. "How do you feel?"

"From what the doctor said, I am doing about the way I should be," Rodriguez said. "I wish I were better, but I could be worse. I am not shockingly bad, anyhow."

Quinn made a face at him. "I see the electricity did not fry your brains—or maybe I see that it did."

"Would you like to come in the house?" Rodriguez asked. "If you have the time, we could drink a bottle of *cerveza.*"

"*Muchas gracias.* I would like that," Quinn said. "I have a question I would like to ask you, if you don't mind." *I want something from you,* was what he meant. But he was too smooth, too polite, to say so straight out. Maybe he would have when he first came to Baroyeca from the more bustling northeast of the Confederate States. But he'd learned to fit into the Sonoran town's slower rhythms.

"I would be very pleased to hear it," Rodriguez said. "Just let me attend to this miserable hen first. . . ." He waved his hat. The hen, which had paused to peck in the gravel, squawked irately and retreated. He got it back where it belonged and slammed the door on it. Then he raised his voice: "Magdalena, we have company. *Señor* Quinn has come to ask me something."

His wife came out onto the front porch. She nodded to Robert Quinn. "Very good to see you, *señor.*"

"And you as well." Quinn's answering nod was almost a bow.

"Come in, come in," Rodriguez said. "Magdalena, would you get us some beer, *por favor?*"

"Of course," she answered. If they'd been down to their last bottle of beer and had nothing else on the farm, Quinn would have got it. Not only that—he would have got it in a way that said they had plenty more, even if they didn't.

Rodriguez settled his guest in the most comfortable chair. That was the one he usually sat in himself, but the next best would do. Magdalena brought in two bottles of beer. She served Quinn first. "Thank you very much," he said, and raised his bottle to Rodriguez. "*¡Salud!*"

The simple toast—*health*—meant more than it would have before Rodriguez almost electrocuted himself. "*¡Salud!*" he echoed feelingly. He sipped at the beer. "Ask me your question, *Señor* Quinn."

"I will, never fear." Quinn nodded to the wireless set. "Did you hear any news last night?"

"Some," Rodriguez said, surprise in his voice: that wasn't the sort of question he'd expected.

Robert Quinn went on, "Did you hear the news about what President Featherston is calling the Confederate Veterans' Brigades?"

"Yes, I did hear that," Rodriguez answered. "It struck me as being a good idea."

"It struck me the same way," Quinn said. "It is something this country needs when we fight an enemy larger than we are. I was wondering if you had thought about joining the Veterans' Brigades yourself."

"I see," Rodriguez said. "Before my . . . my accident, I was wondering whether *los Estados Confederados* would call me back to the colors to fight at the front, not behind it."

"*Así es la vida,*" Quinn said. "The way things are now, you would probably not do well with a Tredegar automatic rifle in your hands." He was being polite, and Rodriguez knew it. If he put on the butternut uniform again, he would be almost as big a danger to his own *compadres* as he would to the damnyankees. Robert Quinn added, "But you also serve your country if you free up a fitter man to fight. That is what the Confederate Veterans' Brigades are for."

"I understand. But one thing I am not so sure I understand is who would take care of the farm if I went away. My one son is already in the Army. The other two are bound to be conscripted soon. Magdalena cannot possibly do everything by herself."

"People can do all sorts of things when they find they have to," Quinn remarked. "But the Freedom Party looks out for the people. You would have your salary, of course. And the Party would pay your wife an allowance that would go a long way toward making up for your being gone."

"Well, that is not so bad," Rodriguez said. "It gives me something to think about, anyhow."

"You might do better not to think too long. So far, the Confederate Veterans' Brigades are voluntary." Quinn paused to let that sink in before continuing, "I do not know when, or if, men our age will be conscripted into them. But I know it could happen. This is war, after all. If you volunteer, you will have the best chance to get the assignment you might want. You could patrol the dams in the Tennessee Valley to guard against sabotage, or you could guard the *mallates* taken in arms against the Confederate States, or—"

He knew what levers to pull. He even knew not to name guarding the Negroes first, lest it seem too obvious. "I *will* think about that," Rodriguez said. Robert Quinn didn't even smile.

The fighting off to the west, in the direction of Sandusky, had picked up again. If the racket of the small-arms and artillery fire hadn't told Dr. Leonard O'Doull as much, the casualties coming into the aid station near Elyria, Ohio, would have. There seemed to be no easy times, just hard ones and harder.

O'Doull stepped out of the tent for a cigarette. He made sure everyone did that, and set his own example. Smoking around ether wasn't the smartest thing you could do. All he'd had before was green-gray canvas with a big Red Cross on it between him and the noise of battle. Somehow, things sounded much louder out here. Back in the tent, of course, he'd been concentrating on his job. That helped make the world go away. A cigarette couldn't equal it.

He smoked anyway, enjoying the ten-minute respite he'd given himself. His boots squelched in mud as he walked about. It wasn't raining now, but it had been, and the gray clouds rolling in off the lake said it would again before too long. He would have thought both sides would have to slow down in the rain. Things had worked like that in the Great War, anyhow. Here, they didn't seem to.

And then the shout of, "Hey, Doc! Doc!" made him stamp out the cigarette and mutter a curse under his breath. So much for the respite. War didn't know the meaning of the word.

"I'm here," he yelled, and ducked back into the tent.

Stretcher-bearers brought in the casualty half a minute later. At first, O'Doull just saw another wounded man. Then he noticed the fellow wore butternut, not green-gray. He made a small, surprised noise. Eddie—one of the corpsmen—said, "We found him, so we brought him in. Their guys do the same for our wounded. Some-times we bump into each other when we're making pickups—swap ration cans for good tobacco, shit like that."

Such things were against regulations. They happened all the time anyhow. O'Doull wasn't about to get up on his high horse about them. They wouldn't change who won and who lost, not even a little bit. And he had the wounded Confederate here. "What's going on with him?" he asked.

What was going on was pretty obvious: a shredded, bloodied trouser leg with a tourniquet on it. "Shell blew up too damn close," Eddie answered. "You think you can save the leg?"

"Don't know yet," O'Doull said. "Let's get his pants off him and have a look." As the corpsman started cutting away the cloth, O'Doull added, "You gave him morphine, right? That's why he's not talking and yelling and raising a fuss? He's not shocky? He doesn't look it."

Eddie nodded. "Right the first time, Doc. Gave him a big old dose. He was screamin' his head off when we found him, but the dope's taken hold pretty good."

The wounded Confederate opened his eyes. They were startlingly blue. O'Doull wasn't sure the man was seeing him or anything else this side of God. In a faraway voice, the soldier said, "Don't hardly hurt at all no more."

"Good. That's good, son." O'Doull tried to sound as reassuring as he could. One look told him that leg was going to have to come off. It was a miracle the Confederate hadn't bled out before Eddie got to him. Or maybe not a miracle—his hands were all bloody. Maybe he'd held on literally for dear life and slowed things down enough to give himself a chance to survive. O'Doull turned to Granville McDougald. "As soon as he's on the table, get him under. We've got work to do." With the soldier conscious, he didn't want to say any more than that.

McDougald nodded. "Right, Doc." He didn't say anything else, either. But he could see what was what at least as well as O'Doull could.

Grunting, Eddie and the other corpsman got the Confederate off the stretcher and onto the operating table. Granville McDougald stuck an ether cone over the soldier's nose. The fellow feebly tried to fight; ether was nasty stuff. Then he went limp. Eddie said, "You are gonna have to amputate, aren't you?" He could see what was what, too.

"You bet," O'Doull answered. "Got to be above the knee, too. That makes learning to walk with an artificial leg harder, but look at his thigh. I'll be damned if I see how the burst missed cutting the femoral artery. That would've been curtains right there. But it sure as hell tore everything else to cat's meat."

"If it's above the knee anyhow, do it pretty high," McDougald advised. "You can pack more tissue below the end of the bone for a good stump."

"Right," O'Doull said. "You want to do it yourself, Granny? He'd have just as good a result with you cutting as he would with me." He meant it; the other man was a thoroughly competent medical jack of all trades.

But McDougald shook his head. "Nah. You go ahead. You got me up here passing gas. I'll go on with that." He didn't say he made a better anesthetist than O'Doull would. Whether he said it or not, they both knew it was true.

"All right, then." The more O'Doull considered the wound, the less happy he got. "It will have to be high. Some of this flesh is just too damn tattered to save. *Tabernac!*" Every once in a while, he still swore in Quebecois French. Constant use had brought his English out of dormancy in a hurry, though.

He got to work, repairing what he could, removing what he had to, picking out shell fragments and bits of cloth driven into the Confederate's wounds, and dusting sulfa powder over them. That could have gone on a lot longer than it did, but he didn't need to worry about the damage below mid-thigh.

"Give me the bone saw, Eddie," he said when he was ready for it. The corpsman handed it to him. He used it. Cutting through even the longest, strongest bone in the body didn't take long. The leg fell away from its former owner.

"Very neat, Doc," McDougald said. He'd watched the whole procedure with his usual intelligent interest. "You fixed that up better than I thought you could."

It wasn't over yet. O'Doull still had to make the fleshy pad below the femur and suture the flaps of skin he'd left attached for that purpose. But McDougald was right: that was just follow-up. He'd finished the challenging part.

"How's he look?" he asked.

"He's pretty pink. Pulse is strong. These young ones are tough. He's got a decent chance of coming through," McDougald answered.

"Keep him doped up," O'Doull said. "I don't want him feeling all of this till it's had the chance to settle down a little bit. Be a shame to lose him to shock when we've got what looks like such a good result."

"Too bad he's not one of ours," Eddie said, though he'd brought in the Confederate.

"Nothing we can do about that," O'Doull said. "Geneva Convention says we take care of wounded from both sides the same way. Only common sense that we do, too. If we don't, the Confederates won't for our guys."

"I suppose." But Eddie still didn't sound happy about it.

"We can question him while he's all doped up," Granville Mc-Dougald said. "If he knows anything, he'll spill his guts."

That bent the rules if it didn't actually break them. O'Doull thought about saying so. Then he looked at the Confederate soldier's tunic: two stripes on his sleeve. The man was only a corporal. Whatever he knew, it wouldn't matter much. Besides, O'Doull had no doubt the Confederates did the same thing. Who wouldn't? He kept his mouth shut.

Eddie took the canteen off his belt and sloshed it suggestively. "Want to celebrate pulling him through?"

Where had he come up with booze? O'Doull laughed at himself for even wondering. It wasn't hard. The corpsman would just claim it was medicinal if anyone came down on him for it. He didn't let whatever he scrounged interfere with the job he did. As far as O'Doull was concerned, nothing else mattered.

As for the offer . . . The doctor shook his head. "Ask me when I'm not on duty and I'll say yes. Till then, I'll pass. I don't want to do anything that might make me screw up a case. That wouldn't be fair to the poor sorry bastards who depend on me to patch 'em up the best way I know how."

"I know plenty of docs who'd say yes so fast, it'd make your head swim," Eddie said.

O'Doull only shrugged. "That's their business. I've got to mind mine."

"All right. All right." By his shrug, Eddie thought O'Doull was nuts, but most likely in a harmless way. The corpsman went on, "I'm going to clean up and go see who else got lucky out there." He spoke with a casual lack of concern that sounded more cold-blooded than it was. When he went out there, he could "get lucky" as easily as anyone else—more easily than most, for he exposed himself to more fire than any normal soldier in his right mind would have. Yes, he wore Red Cross armbands and smock and had Red Crosses on the front and back of his helmet, but not everybody paid attention to that kind of thing. And machine-gun bullets and shell fragments flew more or less at random. What did they care about the Red Cross? Not a thing, not a single thing.

After Eddie headed off toward the front, McDougald said, "You've got pretty good sense, Doc."

"Oh, yeah? Then why did I put the uniform back on? What the hell am I doing here?" O'Doull said. "It isn't for the pay and it isn't for the scenery, that's for goddamn sure."

The other man chuckled. "Why? On account of you're good at what you do, that's why. Sometimes, if you're good at what you do, you've got to go do it where it's hardest or where you can do the most good with it. That's how it looks to me, anyway. But what the deuce do I know? If I had any brains, I'd be out in California laying on the beach and soaking up something with a lot of rum in it."

O'Doull scrubbed at his hands with water and disinfectant. He used soap and a toothpick to get blood out from under his nails. He always kept them trimmed short, which helped, but not enough. Lying on a beach soaking up something with a lot of rum in it sounded pretty good to him, too. But he knew what sounded better: "I wish I were home."

"Yeah, there is that, too." McDougald nodded. "For you there is, anyway. Me, I'm a lifer at this—and if that doesn't prove I haven't got any brains, screw me if I know what would."

"You said it yourself, Granny," O'Doull answered. "You're good at what you do, and you're doing it where it counts most. Next question?"

He got another small laugh from McDougald. "Well, maybe I have picked up a trick or two over the years. I'd better. I've been at this game long enough, you know." He wasn't one to parade his knowledge, which was at least as extensive as O'Doull's even if less formally gained. He wasn't one to make a big fuss about anything— something a lot of men who'd spent a lot of time in the Army had in common.

"I'm glad to have you here, I'll tell you that," O'Doull said, "especially when the chips are down."

"Well, thanks very much. I expect you're making more out of it than there is to make, but thanks all the same," McDougald said. "I'm just a gas-passer who can do a little sewing and cutting when I have to, that's all."

"Bullshit." O'Doull didn't always cuss in French. Sometimes only English had the word he needed. "Maybe you couldn't teach this stuff at a medical school, but you can sure as hell do it better than most of the docs who do teach it. When the war's done, you ought to go back to school and pick up your M.D."

Granville McDougald shrugged. "Have to pick up a bachelor's first. Hell, I'm lucky I got out of high school."

Before O'Doull could answer, a salvo of Confederate shells roared by overhead. Somebody'd be sorry when they came down. "You call this luck?" O'Doull asked. McDougald only shrugged.

XV

From Los Angeles, the war back East seemed a quarrel in another room. Chester Martin followed it as closely as anyone, but that wasn't so closely as he would have liked. The wireless and the newspapers gave him the broad outlines of the stories, but only the broad outlines. He always wanted to learn more. Not being able to ate at him.

Even the Mormon uprising in Utah was hundreds of miles away. Martin kept trying to figure out how many U.S. divisions it was tying down. Try as he would, he couldn't. The papers and the wireless were coy as could be about stuff like that. He muttered and fumed. Those were divisions that should have been in action against the CSA. They should have, but they weren't.

When he muttered and fumed once too often in front of Rita, she said, "Why don't you stop flabbling about it? They aren't going to come out and tell you. If you can't figure it out from what you hear and what you read, maybe the Confederates won't be able to, either."

"Oh." Chester felt foolish. He wanted to say several things. They were things he wasn't supposed to say in front of his wife, so he didn't. What he did say was, "Well, sweetheart, when you're right, you're right." Anyone who'd been married for a while learned to use that phrase pretty often.

Rita just nodded, as if she knew she'd got her due. "The only way they'd pay as much attention to the war as you want would be if it came here."

Chester snorted. "Fat chance."

"You're right. Fat chance," Rita agreed. "And you know what else? I'm not sorry, not even a little bit. We've paid everything we owe anybody." She'd lost her first husband in the Great War. Chester had scars on his arm that would never go away and a Purple Heart stashed in a nightstand drawer. Rita repeated, "*Everything.*" She knew he still thought about putting on the uniform again. She did everything she could to keep him from going out and signing up.

Four days later, on a cool, gray morning as close to autumnal as L.A. got (not very close, not as far as Chester was concerned, not when the leaves were mostly still on the trees and mostly still green), the *Times* and the wireless went nuts. A submersible—Confederate? Mexican? Japanese? nobody knew for sure—had surfaced off the coast near Santa Barbara, northwest of Los Angeles. Its deck gun fired maybe a dozen rounds at a seaside oil field. Then it slipped below the surface and disappeared. It was long gone before flying boats and destroyers got to the neighborhood.

At a construction site on the west side of town, Chester observed the hysteria with more than a little amusement. "You've almost got to hand it to the Confederates or whoever the hell it was," he said. "Sneaking up the coast took balls."

"We got ours draped over a doorknob, that's for damn sure," another builder said.

"You wait. You watch. Now we're going to have air-raid alerts and blackouts and all the other crap we've done without since just after the war started," Chester predicted. "Talk about a pain in the ass . . ."

But the other man said, "Maybe we need 'em. If the Confederates put bombers in Sonora, they could get here. Look at a map if you don't believe me."

Martin thought about it. Slowly, he nodded. "Maybe you're right, Frank. I guess they could. Whether it'd be worth their while is a different story, but they *could.*"

Perhaps the powers that be were looking at the same map. By that afternoon, fighters started buzzing above Los Angeles, something else that hadn't happened since the war was new. They would dash across the sky like bad-tempered little dogs looking for rats to tear to pieces. No rats seemed to be in evidence. That relieved Chester, but only so much. Bombers on both sides that came overhead in daylight got shot down in large numbers. Night was the time when they could fly in something resembling safety.

He rode the trolley home with more than a little apprehension. What would the night be like? When he got off in Boyle Heights, newsboys on all the corners were still shouting about the submarine and what it had done. As a matter of fact, it hadn't done much. What it had done wouldn't change the way the war turned out by even the thickness of a hair.

But Rita greeted Chester at the door with, "Wasn't that horrible? Right off our coast, bold as brass! What's the world coming to?"

"I don't know, babe," he answered. "Somebody was asleep at the switch, is what it looks like to me."

That sort of thing was not what the authorities wanted people to be thinking. The wireless crackled with bulletins and commands all through the evening. Coast-watching battalions would be set up all the way from the border with Baja California to San Francisco. Airship patrols would be doubled and redoubled. And, as Chester had gloomily foretold, the blackout returned.

"We want to make sure the cunning enemy has no opportunity to strike us unawares," brayed the man who made that announcement.

Chester laughed out loud. "What do they think just happened?" he asked.

"Oh, hush," Rita said. "This is important."

"Yeah, it is," he agreed. "It's so important, they want us to forget they just got caught with their pants down. But they darn well did."

"We'll manage," Rita said. "I never threw out the blackout curtains I made. I'll put 'em up again tomorrow. It won't be so bad in the fall and winter. They made the place beastly hot in the summertime. You couldn't open a window and get a breath of fresh air unless you turned out all the lights. . . ."

She didn't want to think about what had gone wrong. She just wanted to go on from day to day. And if she thought that way, how many hundreds of thousands of others in Los Angeles did, too? Magnified, that attitude probably showed how people back East on both sides of the border got on with their lives even though bombers appeared overhead almost every night.

Another announcer said, "Mayor Poulsen and Brigadier General van der Grift, commandant of the Southern California Military District, have jointly declared that the area is in no danger and there is no cause for alarm. Steps are being taken to ensure that what Mayor Poulsen termed 'the recent unfortunate incident' cannot possibly recur. General van der Grift was quoted as saying, 'Our state of readiness is high. Anyone who troubles us is asking for a bloody nose, and we will give him one.' "

"Where were they before this sub started shooting at us?" Chester asked. But Rita hushed him again.

She was already busy putting up the blackout curtains when he left for work the next morning. He didn't say anything. It needed doing. And she seemed convinced it would go some little way toward winning the war. Maybe she was even right. *But if she is, God help us all,* Chester thought. That was one more thing he didn't say.

He bought a *Times* on the way to the trolley stop. The front page showed a shell hole in the oil field, as if no one had ever seen such a thing before. That made Martin want to laugh out loud. He'd seen shell holes so close together, you couldn't tell where one stopped and the next one started. Seen them? He'd huddled in them, hoping the next shell wouldn't come down on top of him. How many men his age hadn't?

But a lot of people these days were younger than he was. And women hadn't had to go to war. Talk at the trolley stop was about nothing but the shelling. Having the trolley pull up was something of a relief, but not for long. As soon as everybody got settled, the talk started up again. And the people already aboard the car must have been talking about the shelling, too, for they chimed right in.

Chester tried to concentrate on the newspaper, but had little luck. Across the aisle from him, another man who was starting to go gray also kept out of the conversation. They caught each other's eyes. The fellow across the aisle tapped his chest with a forefinger and said, "Kentucky and Tennessee. How about you?"

"Roanoke front and then northern Virginia," Chester answered. "I thought you had the look."

"I thought the same thing about you," the other middle-aged man said.

"Yeah, well . . ." Martin shrugged. "Everybody's running around like a chicken after the hatchet comes down. We've seen the real thing, for Christ's sake. Next to that, this isn't so much of a much."

"Yup." The other man nodded. "Try and tell anybody, though. Whoever did it stuck a pin in us so we'd jump up and down and yell, 'Ouch!' Sure got what they wanted, too, didn't they?"

"You'd better believe it," Chester said.

Hardly anything is more pleasant than talking about why other people are a pack of damn fools. Chester and the veteran across from him enjoyed themselves till the other man climbed to his feet and said, "I get off here. Take care of yourself, Roanoke."

"You, too, Kentucky," Martin said. They nodded to each other.

A lot of the builders at the construction site were veterans, too—more than would have been true before the war started. Some of the younger men had gone into the Army or the Navy. Others were working in armament factories, hoping that would keep the government from conscripting them. Chester suspected that was a forlorn hope, but it wasn't his worry.

Most of the men who'd seen the elephant reacted the same way as Chester and the vet on the trolley had: they couldn't believe everyone else was making such a fuss over a nuisance raid. "It's here, that's why," somebody said. "The *Times* just had to send photographers up the coast a little ways and they got the pictures they needed for the goddamn front page. Hell, I could piss in one of those lousy little holes and fill it up."

That got a laugh. "You'd need three or four beers first, Hank," somebody else said, and got a bigger one.

Another builder spat a couple of nails into the palm of his hand. He said, "And the mayor's against people shooting at us. He's got a lot of guts to take a stand like that, doesn't he?"

"He's like the rest," another man said. "If it's got a vote in it, he's all for it. Otherwise, he thinks it's a crappy idea."

"Not a hell of a lot of votes in getting shelled," Chester observed.

"And did you notice the general came out and said we'll clean their clocks the next time they try something like this? He didn't say a word about how come the sub got away *this* time."

"Oh, hell, no," Hank said. "That'd show everybody what an egg-sucking dog he really is."

"I think trying to cover it up is worse," Chester said. "How dumb does he think we are, anyway? We're not going to notice nobody sank the damn thing? Come on!"

"Tell you what I wish," another man said. "I wish Teddy Roosevelt was President. He'd give that Featherston bastard what-for. Smith tries hard, and I think he means well, but Jesus! The way Featherston picked his pocket last year, they ought to throw him in jail. I voted for Smith, on account of we didn't have to fight right then, but it looks like I got my pocket picked, too."

Several men nodded at that. Chester said, "I voted for Taft because I was afraid Featherston would cheat. I wish I was wrong. I've voted Socialist almost every time since the Great War. I don't like it when I don't think I can. Hell, I wish we had TR back again, too."

Were Roosevelt alive, he would have been in his eighties. *So what?* Chester thought. George Custer had been a hero one last time at that age. Would TR have let the general with whom his name was always linked upstage him? Martin shook his head. Not a chance. Not a chance in church.

When the door to Brigadier General Abner Dowling's office opened, he swung his swivel chair around in surprise. Not many people came to see him, and he didn't have a hell of a lot to do. He'd been staring out at the rain splashing off his window. There'd been a lot of rain lately. Watching it helped pass the time. His visitor could have caught him playing solitaire. That would have been more embarrassing.

"Hello, sir." Colonel John Abell gave him a crisp salute and a smile that, like most of the General Staff officer's, looked pasted on. "I hope I'm not interrupting anything important."

Dowling snorted. They both knew better. "Oh, yes, Colonel. I was just finishing up my latest assignment from the President—the plan that will win the war in the next three days. Remember, you heard it here first." Dowling hardly cared what he said any more. How could he get an assignment worse than this one? Abell smiled again. This time, he actually bared his teeth. That was as much reaction as Dowling had ever got from him. He said, "Are you prepared to take command of General MacArthur's First Corps in Virginia?"

Dowling's jaw dropped. His teeth clicked together when he closed it. "If this is a joke, Colonel, it's in poor taste." *Kicking a man when he's down,* was what went through his head. Did Abell think he was too far down to take revenge? If Abell did . . . he was probably right, dammit.

But the slim, pale officer shook his head and raised his right hand as if taking an oath. "No joke, sir. General Stanbery's command car had the misfortune to drive over a mine. They think he'll live, but he'll be out of action for months. That leaves an open slot, and your name was proposed for it."

"My God. I'm sorry to hear about Sandy Stanbery's bad luck. He's a fine soldier." Dowling paused, then decided to go on: "I think I'd better ask—*who* proposed me? As much as I'd like to get back into action, I don't want to go down there and find out that General MacArthur wishes somebody else were in that position."

"Your sentiments do you credit," Abell said. "You don't need to worry about that, though. MacArthur asked for you by name. He said you were very helpful in his recent meeting with you, and he said bringing you in would cause fewer jealousies than promoting one of General Stanbery's subordinates to take his place."

That made some sense, anyhow. Dowling didn't know that he'd been so helpful to MacArthur, but he wasn't about to argue. He did ask, "How will this sit with the Joint Committee on the Conduct of the War?"

"Well, sir, I would say that's largely up to you." Abell's pale eyes—Dowling never could decide if they were gray or light, light blue—measured him. "If the attack succeeds, how can the Joint Committee complain? If it fails, on the other hand . . ." He let that hang in the air.

"Yes. On the other hand." Dowling left it there, too. He hadn't thought much of what he'd heard of MacArthur's plans. He didn't think Colonel Abell had, either. *Do I really want this assignment?*

Am I sure I do? But he did, and he was. Anything was better than sitting here counting raindrops. "I'll do my best. Can you get me a copy of the plan? I'll want to be as familiar as I can with what I'm supposed to do by the time I get down to the border. The attack should begin soon." The attack should have begun a while ago, but he didn't mention that. All the rain that had fallen lately wouldn't make things any easier.

"I'm sorry. I should have brought one with me, but I wanted to make sure you would say yes first," Abell said. "I'll have a runner get you one right away. How soon do you plan on going down to the border?"

"As soon as I can throw a change of clothes into a duffel bag—sooner, if they need me there right away," Dowling answered.

"I'll put a motorcar at your disposal," Abell said. "It will have a civilian paint job—nothing to draw special notice from the air."

"Thanks," Dowling said, and then, in a different tone of voice, "Thanks. I'll do everything I can." Colonel Abell nodded, saluted, and left.

Two hours later, Dowling was rolling south in a middle-aged Ford that was indeed thoroughly ordinary. He paid little attention to the landscape. He did notice bomb damage dropped off sharply once the motorcar got out of Philadelphia. It didn't pick up again till the Ford went through Wilmington, Delaware.

For the most part, though, he found the three-ring binder spread out on his ample lap much more interesting than the countryside. Daniel MacArthur—or rather, the clever young officers on his staff—had planned everything down to the last paper clip. MacArthur knew exactly what he wanted the First Corps to do. If everything went according to Hoyle, it could handle the job, too.

If. As usual, the word was the joker in the deck. One of the few things Dowling found inadequate in the enormous plan was its appreciation of Confederate strength. MacArthur's attitude seemed to be that the men he commanded would brush aside whatever enemy soldiers they happened to run into, march into Richmond, and hold a victory parade past the Confederate White House and Confederate Capitol.

Maybe things would work out that way. Every once in a while, they did. If the Confederate thrust through Ohio hadn't gone according to plan, Dowling would have been amazed. He shifted in the back seat. He'd been on the receiving end of that plan. Getting his own back would be sweet . . . if he could.

"You all right, sir?" the driver asked. He must have seen Dowling fidget in the rearview mirror.

"Yes." Dowling hoped he meant it.

The sun started to sink below the horizon as they passed from Delaware to Maryland. Dowling held the plan ever closer to his nose so he could go on studying it. One other thing that seemed to be missing from it was any notion of how bad weather would affect it. Listening to rain drum on the roof of the Ford, Dowling found the omission unfortunate. The driver turned on the slit headlights that were all anyone could use these days. They were inadequate in good weather, and almost completely useless in this storm. The motorcar slowed to a crawl. Dowling hoped other drivers would have the sense to slow to a crawl, too. Every so often, he got glimpses of wreckage hauled off to the side of the road. He could have thought of lots of things that would have done more for his confidence in the good habits of other drivers.

Outside of Baltimore, the Ford stopped crawling. That didn't mean it sped up: it stopped moving at all. "What the hell?" Dowling said irritably, wondering if Abell shouldn't have laid an airplane on for him instead.

"Some kind of mess up ahead. We'll find out when we get there." The driver sounded philosophical.

That did little to ease Dowling's irritation. "If we get there, you mean," he growled. There was barely enough light to let him see the driver's shoulders go up and down in a shrug.

They took twenty minutes to go half a mile to the trouble. A bomb crater rendered the road impassable south- and northbound. Engineers had just finished spreading steel matting of the sort that made instant airstrips out to either side of the damage. Without it, motorcars would have bogged down in the mud when they went off the road and onto the shoulder. With it, Dowling felt as if he were being shaken to pieces. He breathed a sigh of relief when the Ford got on the road again.

The relief didn't last. No sooner had they got into Baltimore than the Confederates started bombing it. With that cloud cover overhead, the enemy bombers couldn't hope to be accurate. But they didn't seem to care. The bombs would come down somewhere on U.S. soil. If they didn't blow up ships in the harbor or factories or warehouses, they'd flatten shops or apartments or houses. And if they hit a school or a hospital or a church—well, that was just one of those things. U.S. pilots didn't lose sleep over it, either.

Cops and civil-defense wardens were shouting for everybody to get off the streets. "Keep going," Dowling told the driver. The man shrugged again and obeyed.

Somewhere near the middle of town, a warden stepped in front of the Ford. He almost got himself run over for his trouble. "Are you out of your frigging mind?" he yelled as a bomb crashed down a few hundred yards away. "Get into a cellar, or the undertaker will bury you in a jam tin."

"What do we do, sir?" the driver asked Dowling. "Your call."

Before Dowling could answer, a bomb went off much closer than the one a minute before. A fragment of casing clanged into the Ford's trunk. Another pierced the left front tire, which made the auto list. And another got the civil-defense warden, who howled and went down in the middle of the wet street.

"I think we just had our minds made up for us," Dowling said as he opened the door. "Let's give this poor bastard a hand, shall we?"

The warden was lucky, if you wanted to call getting wounded lucky. The gouge was on the back of his calf, and fairly clean as such things went. He was already struggling back to his feet again by the time Dowling and the driver came over to him. "Let me get bandaged up and I'll go back on duty," he insisted.

Dowling doubted that; the wound was larger and deeper than the warden seemed to think it was. But it hadn't hamstrung him, as it would have were it a little lower. "Where's the closest cellar?" Dowling asked. "We'll get you patched up, and then we'll worry about what happens next."

"Just you follow me," the civil-defense warden said. Dowling and the driver ended up hauling him along with his arms draped over their shoulders. Trying to put weight on the leg showed him he was hurt worse than he'd thought. He guided them to a hotel down the block. Dowling was soaked by the time he got there. Manhandling the warden down the stairs to the cellar was another adventure, but he and the driver managed.

People in the cellar exclaimed at the spectacle of a bedraggled brigadier general. All Dowling said was, "Is there a doctor in the house?" For a wonder, there was. He went to work on the wounded warden. Dowling turned to his driver. "Do you think you can fix that flat once the bombs stop falling?"

"I'll give it my best shot, sir," the driver said resignedly.

It took more work than he'd expected, for the fragment that got the trunk had torn into the spare tire and inner tube. The driver had to wait till a cop came by, explain his predicament to him, and wait again till the policeman came back with a fresh tire and tube. They didn't get moving again till well after midnight.

As Dowling fitfully dozed in the back seat, he hoped the driver wasn't dozing behind the wheel. The Ford didn't crash into another auto or go off the road, so the driver evidently managed to keep his eyes open.

More problems with the road stalled them outside of Washington. The driver did start snoring then. Dowling let him do it till things started moving again. They didn't get through the de jure capital of the USA until after dawn. That let Dowling see that Confederate bombers had hit it even harder than Philadelphia. Still, it wasn't the almost lunar landscape it had been after the USA took it back from the CSA in the Great War.

The Confederates had knocked out the regular bridges over the Potomac. Engineers had run up pontoon bridges to take up the slack. The Ford bumped into what had been Virginia and was now an eastern extension of West Virginia.

Daniel MacArthur made his headquarters near the little town of Manassas, scene of the first U.S. defeat—but far from the last—in the War of Secession. As Dowling, wet and weary, got out of the motorcar, he hoped that wasn't an omen.

Waiting for the first big U.S. attack to go in wasn't easy for Flora Blackford. If it succeeded, it would bring the war back to something approaching an even keel. If it failed . . . She shook her head. She refused to think about what might happen if it failed. It would succeed. It *would*.

Ordinary business had to go on while she waited along with the rest of the United States. Studying the budget was part of ordinary business. If you looked long enough, you learned to spot all sorts of interesting things.

Some of the most interesting were the ones that were most puzzling. Why was there a large Interior Department appropriation for construction work in western Washington? And why didn't the item explain what the work was for?

She called an undersecretary and tried to find out. He said, "Hold on, Congresswoman. Let me see what you're talking about. Give me the page number, if you'd be so kind." She did, and listened to him flipping paper. "All right. I see the item," he told her. Close to half a minute of silence followed, and then a sheepish laugh. "To tell you the truth, Congresswoman, I have no idea *what* that's about. It does seem a little unusual, doesn't it?"

"It seems more than a little unusual to me," Flora answered. "Who would know something about it?"

"Why don't you try Assistant Secretary Goodwin?" the undersecretary said. "Hydroelectric is his specialty."

"I'll do that," Flora said. "Let me have his number, please." She wrote it down. "Thanks very much." She hung up and dialed again.

Assistant Secretary Goodwin had a big, deep voice. He *sounded* more important than the junior functionary with whom she'd spoken a moment before. But when she pointed out the item that puzzled her, what he said was, "Well, I'll be . . . darned. What's that doing there?"

"I was hoping you could tell me," Flora said pointedly.

"Congresswoman, this is news to me," Goodwin said. She believed him. He seemed angry in a special bureaucratic way: the righteous indignation of a man who'd had his territory encroached upon. She didn't think anyone could fake that particular tone of voice.

Tapping a pencil on her desk, she asked, "If you don't know, who's likely to?"

"It would have to be the secretary himself," Goodwin answered. "Let's see which one of us can call him first. I aim to get to the bottom of this, too."

The Secretary of the Interior was a Midwesterner named Wallace. The first time Flora tried to reach him, his secretary said he was on another line. Goodwin must have dialed faster. "I'll have him call you back, if you like," the secretary added.

"Yes. Thank you. Please do that." Flora gave her the number and returned the handset to its cradle. She did some more pencil tapping. Were they just passing the buck? Her mouth tightened. If they were, they'd be sorry.

She jumped a little when the telephone rang a few minutes later. Bertha said, "It's Assistant Secretary Roosevelt, Congresswoman."

"Oh!" Flora said. She'd been expecting the Secretary of the Interior. She wondered what Roosevelt wanted. More propaganda? She shrugged. Only one way to find out. "Put him through, please."

"Hello, Congresswoman." As usual, Franklin Roosevelt sounded jaunty. No one who didn't know would ever imagine he couldn't get out of his wheelchair. "How are you this lovely morning?"

It wasn't lovely; it was still raining. Even so, Flora couldn't help smiling. "I'm well, thanks," she answered. "And you?"

"In the pink," Roosevelt said. "I just had a call from Hank. He thought I might be able to tell you what was going on."

"Hank?" Flora echoed with a frown. "Hank who? You're a step or two ahead of me."

"Wallace," Roosevelt told her. "You've been talking to people about that Washington State item in the Interior Department budget. It's no wonder nobody over there knows anything much about it. It really has more to do with my shop, if you must know."

"With the War Department?" Flora said. "Why isn't it listed under War Department appropriations, in that case?" *Curiouser and curiouser,* she thought.

Roosevelt coughed a couple of times. He sounded faintly embarrassed as he answered, "Well, Congresswoman, one reason is that we didn't want to draw the Confederates' notice and make them wonder what we were doing way out there." He laughed. "So we drew your notice and made you wonder instead. Seems we can't win."

"So you did," Flora said. "What *are* you doing way out there? Something large, by the size of the appropriation you're asking for."

"I'm sorry, but I can't tell you what it is," Roosevelt said.

"What?" Now Flora really did start to get angry. "What do you mean, you can't? If you don't want to talk to me here, Mr. Roosevelt, you can answer questions under oath in front of the Joint

Committee on the Conduct of the War. Now—what sort of boondoggle has the War Department got going on in Washington State?"

"We don't believe it's a boondoggle. We wouldn't be working on
it if we did," Roosevelt answered. "And you can summon me to the
Joint Committee, no doubt about it. But if you do, I will lie like Ana-
nias. That will be the best possible way for me to serve my country.
I will be convincing, too. Your colleagues, or enough of them, will
believe me. And, of course, I will deny we ever had this conversation."

He meant every word of it. Flora had dealt with a lot of recalci-
trant bureaucrats. Once in a great while, one of them would dig in
his heels and refuse to move. Plainly, that was what was happening
here. Flora didn't understand why, though. "What could possibly be
so important?" she asked.

"I can't tell you that, either," Roosevelt said. "I will tell you that
it is more important than my job. If you want to send me to the cala-
boose for contempt of Congress, I will cheerfully go. It is *that* important. It is so important, I am going to ask you to let me sell you
a pig in a poke and trust me without asking any more questions. If
you do, I will thank you. If you don't, Jake Featherston will. Up to
you."

He meant every word of that, too. Whether he was right or
wrong was a different question—and he didn't want to give Flora
any clues that would let her decide. She said, "You don't make this
easy, do you?"

"Few things in wartime are easy. Figuring out whether to keep
this secret is one of them," he answered.

"If you turn out to be wrong, Mr. Roosevelt, there is no place in
the world you can hide from me," Flora said.

"That's fair," Roosevelt said at once. "If you have a price, I will
pay it. The administration will pay it. You were unhappy President
Smith hasn't said more about the way the CSA treats its Negroes. He
could. He would. He will, if you like."

"The last time we talked about this, you said it was between the
President and me," Flora reminded him. "You told me you couldn't
do anything about it. I believed you." Of course she'd believed him.
What he'd told her was the way things always worked in the U.S.
government—or any other. "Why have you changed your mind?
Why do you think he'll change his?"

"Because he agrees with me about how important this is—and how important keeping it secret is," Franklin Roosevelt answered. Flora didn't ask him if he could deliver. She had no doubt he could. But what was so very important out there by the Pacific that Al Smith would change a political position he'd taken after the coldest of calculations? She started to ask the Assistant Secretary of War. Only one thing held her back: the certainty that he wouldn't tell her.

Slowly, she said, "I think I will take you up on that. This war has a moral element. We aren't just fighting it to protect ourselves, though we certainly are doing that. But the Confederates are committing crimes against humanity. They need to be stopped."

"Crimes against humanity," Roosevelt echoed. Flora could hear the faint scrape of pen on paper. "It's a good phrase, a telling phrase. You'll hear it again. Is there anything else?"

There was one thing more—the secret Roosevelt was willing to pay any price to preserve. Again, though, Flora knew he wouldn't tell her. "No, I don't think so," she answered, and wondered what sort of deal she'd just made. Franklin Roosevelt wasn't her idea of the Devil—but how could she be sure?

She couldn't. That bothered her more than anything. She'd done it anyhow. Done what, exactly? Agreed to keep quiet about something he wished she'd never found in the first place. It was almost as if she'd discovered him being unfaithful to his wife.

Would she have kept quiet about something like that? She didn't suppose she would have gone out of her way to talk about it, but. . . . She didn't suppose Roosevelt could have offered such a tempting bargain about that, either.

What on earth *was* going on out there to make them willing to go so far to cover it up? Flora laughed. She almost wanted to be difficult just so she could find out.

She wondered if they were developing some fancy new poison gas. Western Washington was full of empty square miles. If you wanted to experiment with something toxic, you wouldn't do it in New York City. You'd go someplace where a mishap wouldn't turn into a disaster.

Slowly, Flora nodded to herself. If she had to bet, she would have put her money on something like that. The longer the Confederates didn't know what was going on, the shorter the time they'd have to start working on an antidote or new protective clothing or whatever they'd need to neutralize the weapon once the United States trotted it out.

She nodded again. That left her more or less satisfied, but it also left her more than a little miffed. No matter how she'd threatened Roosevelt, she wasn't about to start screaming about a new poison gas from the housetops. She wanted this war won, too. Didn't Roosevelt see that? Evidently not. He'd promised her the sun, moon, and little stars to keep her mouth shut instead.

The telephone in the outer office rang. Bertha answered it. She called, "Congresswoman, it's the President."

Flora picked up the phone on her desk. "Hello, Mr. President," she said.

"Hello, sweetheart," Al Smith answered. "So you want me to squawk about the *shvartzers*, do you? So all right, I'll do it." Like a lot of New York Irish politicians, he could sound very Jewish when he wanted to.

"That's . . . kind of you, sir," Flora said. "I still don't quite understand why you're raising such a fuss."

"I know," Smith said. "Franklin made the deal with you so you wouldn't ask questions, remember, not so you would."

"Oh, yes. I remember. I'm not likely to forget," Flora answered. "If you meet your end, I'll meet mine." She said that with a curious reluctance. "I won't ask any questions. I won't poke my nose where it doesn't belong. But if you think I won't be ready to blow up from curiosity, you'd better think again."

Al Smith laughed. Even then, he sounded tired. "Well, I've been worrying about some bigger bangs than that lately."

"Not likely," Flora said. The President laughed again. He made a kissing noise over the telephone and hung up. Flora smiled as she did, too. She was still curious, but she didn't feel quite so bad about the bargain now.

Major Jonathan Moss bounced to a stop at an airstrip outside a Maryland town with the odd name of Texas. One after another, the rest of his fighter squadron landed behind him—all except one pilot, who'd had engine trouble and had to come down somewhere in western Pennsylvania. Moss hoped the missing man would get repairs and rejoin the squadron soon. By the looks of things here in the East, they were going to need all the help they could get.

Led by a groundcrew man with wigwag flags, Moss taxied into a revetment. As soon as his prop had stopped spinning, more groundcrew men spread camouflage netting over his Wright. He slid back the canopy and climbed out.

"Looks like the balloon's going to go up here pretty soon," he remarked.

"Beats me," the groundcrew man answered. "Far as I'm concerned, we've already been sitting around too long with our thumbs up our asses."

A man of strong convictions, Moss thought, amused. But then again, why not? Everybody in the USA seemed to wonder why the attack here in the East hadn't started yet. Moss' flying boots dug into mud as he walked out of the revetment. The rain had messed things up. He knew that. And the high command here was pulling together whatever it could to add to the fight. But didn't the powers that be think the Confederates were doing the same damn thing?

Martin Rolvaag came out of another revetment. Moss' wingman waved to him. "At least we didn't have to fight our way across Ohio," Rolvaag said.

"That occurred to me, too," Moss admitted. "Can't say I'm sorry we didn't."

"Way it looks to me, we can't do more than one big thing at a time, and neither can the Confederates," Rolvaag said. "As soon as one side or the other manages to run two full-scale attacks at once, it'll have the edge."

"Makes sense," Moss said. Rolvaag usually did. Along with the rest of the pilots from the squadron, they walked toward the biggest camouflaged tent nearby. Either that would hold local headquarters, in which case they could get billeted, or it would be the local officers' club, in which case they could get lit.

It turned out to be local headquarters. Several fliers looked disappointed. Moss was a little disappointed himself, but only a little. They'd be going into action soon, and he didn't want to fly hung over. Some of the younger guys didn't give a damn. Back in the Great War, he hadn't given a damn, either.

The captain who let them know where they'd be eating and sleeping (and who told them where the officers' club was, so they could drink, too) only shrugged when Moss asked him when the U.S. push toward Richmond would start. "Sir, when the orders come in, they'll get to you, I promise. We won't leave you on the ground," he said. "Past that, you know as much as I do."

"I don't know a damn thing," Moss complained. The captain just nodded, as if to say they were still even.

After supper, Moss did find his way to the officers' club. Blackout curtains inside the tent flap made sure no light leaked out. The fog of cigarette smoke inside would have done a pretty good job of dimming the light even without the curtains. Along with tobacco, the air smelled of beer and whiskey and sweat.

Moss made his way up to the bar and ordered a beer. He reminded himself that drink wasn't spelled with a *u*. As he sipped, he listened to the chatter around him. When he discovered that the three men immediately to his left were reconnaissance pilots, he started picking their brains. If anybody could tell him what the Confederates were up to, they were the men.

But they couldn't tell him much. One said, "Bastards know how to palm their cards as well as we do. If they haven't got more than they're showing, we'll waltz into Richmond. 'Course, I hope to hell they're saying, 'Sure don't look like them damnyankees got much up there a-tall.' " His impression of a Confederate accent was less than successful.

"Here's hoping," Moss agreed. A second beer followed the first. He had a few more over the evening. He didn't get drunk—he was sure of that—but he did get happy. He heard about as many opinions of Daniel MacArthur as there were people offering them.

Not long after he hit the sack, Confederate bombers came overhead. They were doing their best to disrupt what they had to know was coming. Moss ran for a damp trench. He didn't think any of their load hit the airstrip, but it wasn't coming down very far away. He hoped U.S. bombers were paying similar calls on the defenders. Soldiers who went without sleep didn't fight as well as those who got their rest.

Orders for his squadron came in the next morning. He'd wondered if they'd been sent east to escort bombers. They hadn't had any training or practice in that role. But instead the command was ground attack. Moss nodded to himself. They could handle that just fine. And he had a date—three days hence. He talked with men who'd been in Maryland longer about local landmarks and Confederate antiaircraft.

The day of the attack dawned cold and gloomy. Moss yawned as he went to his fighter. He didn't like the low clouds overhead. They would make it harder for him to find his targets. He managed a shrug. His squadron wouldn't be the only one hitting the Confederates. He could probably tag along with someone else.

He ran through his flight checks with impatience, but was no less thorough because he was impatient. Like a modern automobile, the Wright had a self-starter. No groundcrew man needed to spin the prop for him. He poked the button. The engine roared to life; the propeller blurred into a disk.

He raced down the runway and flung himself into the air. One by one, the airplanes in his squadron followed. They rocketed south toward Virginia and the enemy. Moss got the feeling of being part of something much bigger than himself. He'd known it in the Great War, too, but seldom in this fight.

As they got farther south, the clouds began to break up. That was a relief. Maybe the people who'd ordered the attack weren't complete idiots after all. Then again, you never could tell. Moss got a quick glimpse of Washington, D.C., before he zoomed over the Potomac. Plumes of smoke rose here and there from the formal capital—for all practical purposes, the former capital. Confederate bombers must have visited there the night before. Not even Y-ranging had helped fighters do much to track bombers by night.

After the Potomac, the next good-sized river was the Rappahannock. If U.S. soldiers could get over the Rappahannock and the Rapidan, the next stop was Richmond, which lay on the north bank of the James.

Crossing the Rappahannock wouldn't be a whole lot of fun, though. Confederate artillery was zeroed in on the river, and pounded the pontoon bridges U.S. military engineers were running up under the not quite adequate cover of their own artillery. Asskickers were out dive-bombing those bridges, too. Moss watched one crash into the Rappahannock in flames. Somebody had thought to bring plenty of antiaircraft guns forward, then. Good.

And there were plenty of Confederate antiaircraft guns right up at the front, too. Shells began bursting around Moss and his squadron even while they were on the U.S. side of the Rappahannock. He hoped those came from Confederate guns. He didn't like the idea of getting shot down by his own side. Come to that, he didn't like the idea of getting shot down by the enemy, either.

He dove on a battery of Confederate artillery pieces. He could damn well shoot back at the bastards on the other side. He thumbed the firing button. His Wright seemed to stagger a little in the air from the recoil of the guns. Soldiers in butternut scattered as he roared past overhead. Muzzle flashes showed that some of them were taking potshots at him with whatever small arms they carried. He wasn't going to lose any sleep over that—he was gone before they could hope to aim.

He had more targets than he could shake a stick at. The Confederates had known this attack was coming, and they'd spent a lot of time getting ready for it. That worried Moss. When the Confederates struck for Lake Erie, they'd caught the USA by surprise. Maybe they shouldn't have, but so what? Surprise had helped them go as far and as fast as they had.

Surprise wouldn't do the USA a nickel's worth of good here. Could a major armored thrust succeed without it? Moss didn't know. One way or the other, he'd find out. And so would everybody else.

He shot up another artillery position, and a battalion's worth of infantrymen he caught in the open. He'd pitied the poor foot soldiers in the last war. Their lot was, if anything, worse now. The fighters he and the Confederates were flying now were ever so much more deadly as ground-attack machines than their Great War ancestors had been. Barrels were correspondingly more dangerous, too. Even the poison gas was more poisonous than it had been a generation earlier.

When Moss tried to strafe some more infantrymen, his guns emptied in the middle of the burst. *Time to head for home,* he thought, and hoped no Hound Dog would jump him on the way back to Maryland. All he could do was run away.

From the squadron's wireless traffic, a lot of the other pilots were in the same boat. "Let's go back," Moss said. "They can reload us, and then we'll hit 'em again." Savage sounds of approval dinned in his earphones.

Finding Texas, Maryland, wasn't easy, even though the clouds had thinned out up there, too. He knew how things had looked going from north to south. They didn't look the same coming back from south to north. They never did. Anyone who drove a motorcar knew that. The problem was ten times worse in an airplane.

He finally spotted the town by the nearby ponds that had once been mine shafts. If they were there, then the airstrip was . . . there. He bumped to a landing. It wasn't pretty, but he'd take it.

Groundcrew men swarmed over the fighters. He got refueled. Armorers took out the empty ammunition belts and loaded in full ones. An officer came out of the headquarters tent with a map. He pointed a few miles west of where Moss and his squadron had been strafing. Moss called his pilots to gather around so they got a look at the map, too. After a little while, everybody nodded. Moss thought he knew how to get there.

As it happened, the squadron never did. They'd come into U.S.-held West Virginia and were heading for Confederate Virginia when they ran into a squadron of Hound Dogs flying north to shoot up the men in green-gray who wanted to invade their country. Fliers from each side spotted the other at about the same time. Both sides started shooting at about the same time, too.

Nobody'd planned the fight. Nobody'd expected it. Nobody backed away from it, either. It was a wild mêlée. Both Wrights and Hound Dogs were already on the deck; they had no altitude to give up. They just darted and swooped and fired. Gunners down below— Moss was damned if he knew *whose* gunners—seemed to blaze away impartially at both sides.

Moss thought he hit a Hound Dog, but the Confederate fighter kept flying. A Wright smashed into the ground. A fireball blossomed where it went down. He swore. That was one of his men surely dead; nobody could hope to bail out this low. A Hound Dog limped off toward the south trailing smoke. Moss hoped it crashed, too.

After several more airplanes went down or had to pull out of the fight, both sides broke off, as if licking their wounds. Moss and his squadron didn't shoot up the Confederates in northern Virginia. The Hound Dogs didn't shoot up U.S. soldiers in eastern West Virginia (they would have called it occupied northern Virginia). They'd battled one another to a standstill. At the moment, as far as he was concerned, that would have to do.

Armstrong Grimes sat cross-legged in front of a campfire on the outskirts of Provo, Utah. He leaned close to the flames. The night was chilly, and he had his tunic off. He was sewing a second stripe onto his left sleeve, and not having an easy time of it. "My aunt ought to be doing this, goddammit," he grumbled.

Across the fire from him, Rex Stowe was sewing a third stripe onto his sleeve. He raised an eyebrow. "Your aunt?"

"Yeah." Armstrong nodded. "She's only two years older than me. My granny got married again right when the Great War ended, and she had a kid just a little before my ma did. Clara would be good at this—and it would piss her off, too. We fight like cats and dogs."

"All right." Stowe laughed and shrugged. "Whatever makes you happy."

"What'd make me happy is getting the hell out of here," Armstrong said. "You fix that up for me, Corp—uh, Sarge?"

Stowe laughed again. "In your dreams. And now all the fresh young dumb ones can call *you* Corporal. Looks to me like we've got two ways to leave Utah any time soon. We can get wounded—or we can get killed."

It looked like that to Armstrong, too. He'd hoped Stowe would tell him something different. Not too far away, a machine gun started hammering. Armstrong and Stowe both paused in their sewing. Tunics or no tunics, they were ready to grab their rifles and do whatever they had to do to keep breathing. Then the gunfire stopped. The two noncoms looked at each other. "Is that good or bad?" Armstrong asked.

"Dunno," Stowe answered. "If they just overran one of our machine-gun nests, it's pretty bad, though." He pointed to a couple of privates. "Ustinov! Trotter! Go see what the hell's going on with that gun. Try not to get killed while you're doing it, in case the Mormons have got the position."

"Right, Sarge." The two men slipped away. Grimes didn't *think* a machine gun could fall with so little fuss, but the Mormons had already come up with too many surprises to leave him sure of anything.

He waited. If Ustinov and Trotter didn't come back pretty soon, the Army was going to need a lot more than two guys to set things right. Stowe must have thought the same thing. He put his tunic back on even though his new stripes were only half attached. So did Armstrong.

No gun suddenly turned the wrong way started spitting bullets. A sentry not far from the fire called a challenge. Armstrong heard a low-voiced answer. He couldn't make out what it was. That was good, because one of the Mormons' little games was to steal countersigns and use them to sneak infiltrators in among the U.S. soldiers. If Armstrong couldn't hear the countersign, odds were the enemy couldn't, either.

He shook his head at that. Up till a few weeks before, the Mormons hadn't been the enemy. They'd been his fellow citizens. But they didn't want to stay in the USA, any more than the Confederates had. The Confederates had made secession stick. They were genuine, sure-as-hell foreigners these days. The Mormons wanted to be, but the United States weren't about to let them go.

Ustinov and Trotter came back in. Trotter said, "Gun's still ours, Sergeant. He squeezed off a burst on account of he thought he saw something moving out in front of him."

"Thanks," Stowe said. "You guys did good. Sit your butts down and take it easy for a couple minutes."

Ustinov laughed. He was a big bear of a man; the noise reminded Armstrong of a rockslide rumbling down the side of a valley. "You take it easy around here, you start talking out of a new mouth," he said, and ran a finger across his throat in case anybody had trouble figuring out what he meant.

He wasn't wrong, either. The Mormons were playing for keeps. They'd tried rising up once before. The USA had pushed their faces into the dirt and sat on them for twenty years afterwards. They had to know that whatever happened to them if they lost again would be even worse. And they had to know the odds were all against their winning. They'd risen again anyhow. That spoke of either amazing stupidity or undying hatred—maybe both.

Hardly any Mormons surrendered. Not many U.S. soldiers were

in much of a mood to take prisoners even when they got the chance. Every now and again, the Mormons took some. Oddly, Armstrong had never heard that they mistreated them. On the contrary—they stuck to the Geneva Convention straight down the line.

When he mentioned that, Sergeant Stowe spat into the campfire. "So what? Bunch of holier-than-thou sons of bitches," he said. Heads bobbed up and down. Armstrong didn't argue. How could he? If the Mormons hadn't been a pack of fanatics, would they have rebelled against all the might the United States could throw at them?

Later that night, U.S. bombers paid a call on Provo. They weren't the most modern models. Those went up against the Confederates—Armstrong hoped the attack in Virginia was going well. But the Mormons didn't have any night fighters, and they didn't have much in the way of antiaircraft guns. Second-line airplanes were plenty good enough for knocking their towns flat.

After the explosions to the north and west had stopped, a couple of Mormon two-deckers buzzed over the U.S. lines and dropped small—probably homemade—bombs on them. "Goddamn flying sewing machines," Armstrong grumbled, jolted out of a sound sleep by the racket.

Antiaircraft guns and machine guns turned the sky into a fireworks display with tracers. As far as Armstrong could tell, they didn't hit anything. If they fired off a lot of ammo, people would think they were doing their job. The racket killed whatever chance he'd had of going back to sleep.

When morning came, the Mormons started firing the mortars they used in place of conventional artillery. Like what passed for their air force, the mortars weren't as good as the real thing. Also like the makeshift bombers, the ersatz artillery was a lot better than nothing. And cries of, "Gas!" made Armstrong snarl curses as he put on his mask.

He wasn't the only one. "How are we supposed to fight in these goddamn things?" Trotter demanded.

Sergeant Stowe took care of that: "Can't very well fight if you suck in a gulp of mustard gas, either." He already had his mask on. From behind it, his voice sounded as if it came from the other side of the grave, but he wore the mask to make sure it didn't.

U.S. artillery wasted little time in answering. Some of the shells the U.S. guns flung gurgled as they flew: they were gas rounds, too.

In a way, that pleased Armstrong; he wanted the Mormons to catch hell. In another way, though, it mattered very little, because the U.S. bombardment didn't do much to stop the hell he was catching. Somebody not nearly far enough away started screaming like a damned soul. That was a man badly wounded, not somebody who'd been gassed. The ordinary Mormon mortar rounds produced a hail of nasty fragments and splinters when they burst. Some poor bastard had stopped at least one.

Mortar bombs were still falling, too. Some of them made the ground shake when they hit. Armstrong didn't know much about earthquakes, not when he'd grown up in Washington, D.C. He did know he wanted *terra* to stay *firma* under him.

The wounded man kept screaming. Armstrong swore under his breath. Someone had to go get the sorry son of a bitch and bring him in. Someone, at the moment, looked remarkably like him. He was no hero. All he wanted to do was get out of this war with a whole skin. But if that were him screaming, he would also have wanted his buddies to bring him in if they could.

Scrambling out of his hole was one of the hardest things he'd ever made himself do, and he'd been in combat since the Confederates bombed Camp Custer. Once in the open, he flattened out like a toad after a steamroller ran over it. His belly never left the ground as he crawled ahead and sideways. Sharp rocks poked him in the stomach. With bullets and sharper fragments snarling by much too close overhead, the pebbles were the least of his worries.

He found the wounded man. It was Ustinov. His left arm ended just above the wrist. He was holding on to the stump with his right hand, slowing the bleeding. "Oh, shit," Armstrong said softly. He bent and pulled the lace out of one of Ustinov's shoes. "Hang on, pal. I'll fix you a tourniquet." Ustinov nodded. He didn't stop screaming.

Armstrong tied the tourniquet as tight as he could. Maybe that cost Ustinov some extra agony. Maybe he was already feeling as much as one man could. The noise he made never changed. Armstrong fumbled at his belt till he found the morphine syringe every soldier carried. Awkwardly, he stuck the wounded man and pushed the plunger home.

He hoped for some immediate change, but didn't see one.

Shrugging, he said, "We've got to get you out of here. I'll help you out of the hole. Then you climb on my back, and I'll do the best I can." He was a good-sized man himself, but Ustinov was bigger.

Getting Ustinov out of the foxhole was a bitch. Again, Armstrong wasn't sure whether he hurt the other man worse by shoving him up. He was afraid he did. But it had to be done. When Ustinov got on top of him, he felt as if he'd been tackled. He crawled on anyhow. He was about halfway back to his own foxhole when Ustinov sighed and stopped screaming. The morphine must have taken hold at last.

Trotter and Yossel Reisen were on their way out after him when he brought Ustinov in. When Trotter saw what had happened to Ustinov, he said some of the same things as Armstrong had.

"Where the hell are the corpsmen?" Armstrong growled.

"They were coming up," Reisen answered. "A mortar burst caught them. They're both down."

"Oh." With news like that, Armstrong had nothing else to say.

"Neither one of them is as bad off as he is." Reisen pointed to Ustinov.

"One second I was fine. The next . . . I looked down, and my hand was gone." Ustinov sounded quiet and calm. That was the morphine talking.

"Take him back, you two," Armstrong told Trotter and Reisen.

"Right, Corporal," the privates said together. They couldn't complain. Armstrong had already done his share and then some.

He got back into his foxhole with nothing but relief. "You ought to pick up a Bronze Star for that," Sergeant Stowe said. "Maybe a Silver Star."

"Fuck it," Armstrong said. "Not a guy here who wouldn't do the same for his pals. I don't give a damn about the medal. He was making a racket, and I wanted him to shut up."

"There you go." Stowe laughed, or at least bared his teeth and made noises that sounded amused. "You were a brand new conscript when this shit started, weren't you?" Armstrong nodded. The sergeant said, "Well, you're sure as hell not a raw conscript any more, are you?"

"Doesn't look that way," Armstrong allowed.

Dive bombers roared down on the Mormon positions at the

southern edge of Provo. Armstrong hoped they were blowing up the mortars that had caused so much torment. He wouldn't have bet too much on it, though. Unlike ordinary artillery pieces, mortars broke down easily into man-portable loads. They were made to shoot and scoot.

Three barrels of Great War vintage waddled up to the front. Their crews must have been wearing masks, for the gas didn't faze them. A Mormon with a bottle of burning gasoline—a Featherston Fizz—incinerated one at the cost of his own life. The other two led U.S. foot soldiers, Armstrong among them, deeper into Provo.

Like most of Richmond, Clarence Potter lived suspended between hope and fear. The damnyankees were coming—everybody knew that. Whether they'd get there was a different question. Brigadier General Potter hoped it was, anyhow.

Unlike most of the people in the Confederate States, he knew U.S. forces were over the Rappahannock and pushing down toward the Rapidan. The wireless just talked about heavy defensive fighting. Broadcasts also had a lot to say about the losses Confederate forces were inflicting on the enemy. As far as Potter could tell, those losses were genuine. But the wireless didn't mention whatever the Yankees were doing to the Confederate defenders.

Even before the latest U.S. push, people in Richmond had been able to hear the artillery duels to the north. Now there was no escaping that low rumble. It went on day and night. If it was louder than it had been a few days earlier, if the guns were closer than they had been . . . Potter tried not to dwell on that. By the way other people talked, they were doing the same thing.

His work at the War Department kept him too busy to pay too much heed to the battle to the north. He knew what he would do and where he would go if he got an evacuation order. Plans had long since been laid for that. Until the hour, if it came, he would go on as he always had.

As he always had, he worked long into the night. Now, though, U.S. bombers visited Richmond every night after the sun went down. Wave after wave of them pounded the Confederate capital. Potter spent more time than he would have wanted in the shelter in the bowels of the building instead of at his desk. Even if everything above ground fell in, a tunnel would take people in the shelter to safety. Potter wished he could take his work with him. He even longed for the days when he'd been subterranean all the time. His prewar promotion to an office with a window had its drawbacks. In the general shelter, too many unauthorized eyes could see pieces of what he was up to. Security trumped productivity.

Considering one of his projects, that was very true indeed. He still waited for results from it. He had no idea how long he would have to go on waiting, or if it would ever come to fruition. Logically, it should, but whether evidence that it had would ever appear to someone who could get word back to him was another open question.

Before the U.S. onslaught, Jake Featherston had called him about it two or three times. Featherston didn't have the patience to make a good intelligence man. He wanted things to happen right now, regardless of whether they were ripe. That driving, almost demoniac, energy had taken the Confederate States a long way in the direction he wanted them to go, but not all problems yielded to a hearty kick in the behind. The President of the CSA sometimes had trouble seeing that.

People who came to the office every day spoke of the pounding Richmond was taking. Potter hardly ever got out of the War Department, and so saw less of that destruction than most people.

The U.S. attack disrupted his news gathering—his spying—on the other side of the border more than he'd thought it would. Some of his sources were too busy doing their nominal jobs to have the chance to send information south. That frustrated him to the point where he reminded himself of Featherston.

He ate when he got the chance. As often as not, he had someone go to what passed for the War Department canteen and bring him back something allegedly edible. Half the time, he didn't notice what it was. Considering what the canteen turned out, that might have been a blessing.

Every once in a while, he emerged from his lair. He felt like a bear coming out of its den after a long winter when he did. By the way the inside of his mouth tasted after too much coffee and too many cigarettes, the comparison was more apt than he would have liked.

Once, he walked into the canteen at the same time as Nathan Bedford Forrest III. The head of the Confederate General Staff looked even more weary, rumpled, and disheveled than he did. Forrest was also in a perfectly foul temper. Fixing Potter with as baleful a stare as the spymaster had ever got, the younger officer growled, "God damn those nigger sons of bitches to hell, so the Devil can fry 'em even blacker than they are already."

"What now?" Potter asked with a sinking feeling.

"We had two big trainloads of barrels that were supposed to get up here from Birmingham, so we could gas 'em up, put crews in 'em, and throw 'em into the fight against the damnyankees. Two!" Forrest said. "Fucking niggers planted mines under both sets of train tracks. Blew two locomotives to hell and gone, derailed God only knows how many freight cars, and now those stinking barrels won't get here for another three days at the earliest. At the earliest!" He was extravagantly dismayed and even more extravagantly furious.

"Ouch!" Potter said. He didn't ask what the delay would do to the defense of northern Virginia. The answer to that was only too obvious: nothing good. Instead, he chose the question that touched him professionally: "How did the coons find out those trains were on the way?"

Lieutenant General Forrest looked even grimmer than he had before. "I've asked General Cummins the very same thing. So far, he hasn't come up with answers that do me any good." His expression said that the head of Counterintelligence had better come up with such answers in a tearing hurry if he wanted to keep his own head from rolling.

The canteen line snaked forward. Potter picked up a tray and a paper napkin and some silverware. So did Forrest. Potter got a dispirited salad and a ham sandwich. Forrest chose a bowl of soup and some of the greasiest fried chicken Potter had ever seen. He wondered what the cooks had fried it in. Crankcase oil? He wouldn't have been surprised.

Forrest followed him to a table. They sat down together. The head of the General Staff went right on cursing and fuming. Potter had the rank and the security clearance to listen to his rant. After a while, when Forrest ran down a little, Potter asked, "Do you think the damnyankees knew about those trains and tipped off the raiders?"

"That's the way I'd bet now." Nathan Bedford Forrest III demolished a drumstick, plainly not caring what he ate as long as it filled his belly. "General Cummins says it isn't possible. I wish I thought he was right, but I just can't believe it. The timing was too goddamn good. For them to nail both those trains within an hour of each other . . . They knew they were coming, all right."

"I agree," Potter said crisply—which was not a word he could use to describe the lettuce in his salad. "You can only bend the long arm of coincidence so far before you break it."

"Yeah." Forrest slurped up soup with the same methodical indifference he'd shown the chicken. "General Cummins thinks otherwise . . . but he's got his prestige on the line. If the niggers figured it out all by themselves, then his shop doesn't look bad."

Potter didn't say anything to that. Instead, he took a big bite of his ham sandwich—and regretted it. Virginia made some of the finest ham in the world, none of which had gone between those two slices of bread. But Forrest was liable to see any comment he made about Cummins as self-serving.

Forrest scowled across the table at him. "What can you tell me about this business? Anything?"

"Right this minute, sir, no," Potter answered. "If the Yankees are getting messages to our niggers, I don't know how they're doing it. I don't know how they're getting word of our shipments, either. That's probably not too hard for them or the niggers, though. They could do it here, or in any one of half a dozen—likely more—railroad dispatch offices, or at the factories in Birmingham."

"I'd like to put you in charge of finding out," Forrest said. "You seem to have more ideas about it than General Cummins does."

Part of Potter craved the extra responsibility. The rest of him had more sense. He said, "Sir, there aren't enough hours in the day for me to give it the attention it ought to have. General Cummins is a good officer. If he can't track down what's going on, odds are nobody can."

"He hasn't done it yet, and he's had his chances," the chief of the General Staff said. "You're right, Potter: he's sound. I know that. But he hasn't got the imagination he needs to be really top-notch."

"If that means you think I do, then I thank you for the compliment," Potter said. "But I'm sure General Cummins has some bright young officers in his shop. Give one of them his head, or more than one. They'll have all the imagination you could want—probably more than you can use."

"With Cummins in charge, they won't get the chance to use it. He'll stifle them," Forrest predicted.

"Sir, there are ways to finesse that." The word made Potter wonder when he'd last played bridge. He loved the game. Like so much of his life, the chance to sit at a table for a few hands had been swallowed up by duty.

"I know there are," Forrest said. "I'd still rather the imagination came from the top. That idea you had for finding spies here—"

"Has come to exactly nothing so far," Potter pointed out.

"It will, though." Forrest sounded more confident than Potter felt. "I don't know when, but it will. Soon, I hope. What I do know is, Cummins wouldn't have had the idea in a million years."

"Somebody over there would have," Potter said.

Nathan Bedford Forrest let out a deeply skeptical grunt. "I don't think so. The President doesn't think so, either."

"Really?" Potter pricked up his ears. "I would have thought I'd have heard that from the President himself if it were so."

"Not lately. He's been at the front a lot." Forrest made a face and dropped his voice. "You didn't hear that from me, dammit."

"Yes, sir." Clarence Potter smiled. Forrest still didn't. He'd let his mouth run freer than it should have, and it worried him. Considering Featherston's temper, it should have worried him, too. Smiling still, Potter went on, "What's he doing up there, playing artilleryman again?"

Now the chief of the General Staff gaped at him. "How the devil did you know that?"

"Well, I didn't know for sure, but I thought it was a pretty good bet," Potter answered. "Remember, the two of us go back to 1915. We go back longer than he does with any of his Freedom Party buddies. We haven't always got along"—now there was an understatement; Potter remembered the weight of the pistol in his pocket when he came up to Richmond for the 1936 Olympics—"but I do have some notion of the way he thinks." *And he has a notion of how I think, too, dammit. Otherwise, I wouldn't be in uniform right now.*

"All right, then." Forrest didn't sound sure it was all right, but he nodded. "Yeah, he's done some shooting. But you didn't hear that from me, either."

"Hear what?" Potter said blandly. Forrest made a face at him. Potter decided to see if he could squeeze some extra information out of the younger man now that he'd caught him embarrassed: "Sir, are we going to hold Richmond?"

"We'll find out, won't we, General?" Forrest answered. Nodding, Potter dropped it. He could tell he'd got as much as he would get.

XVI

Tom Colleton had a rain slicker on over his uniform. The hood was made to cover his head even when he wore a helmet. In spite of slicker and hood, cold water dripped down the back of his neck. And he had it better than the damnyankees looking his way from a small forest between Sandusky and Cleveland: the rain was at his back, while it blew into their faces. He'd never liked rain in the face. Some of the Yankee soldiers, like some of his own, wore glasses. For them, rain in the face wasn't just an annoyance. It could be deadly if it blurred an approaching enemy.

A barrel rumbled up the road toward him. He wouldn't have wanted to try sending barrels anywhere except along roads right now. The rain had turned an awful lot of dirt into mud. He'd seen a couple of bogged-down barrels. They needed specialized recovery vehicles to get them out of their wallows.

The man commanding the barrel rode with his head and shoulders out of the cupola. Tom approved of that, especially in this weather. A lot of people would have stayed buttoned up and dry and comfortable inside the turret—and if they couldn't see quite as much that way, well, so what? If you took care of your job first and yourself second, you were more likely to live to keep on doing your job.

As the barrel drew near, the commander ducked down into the turret. He must have given an order, for the machine stopped, engine still noisy even while idling. The commander popped up out of the cupola again like a jack-in-the-box. He waved to Tom. "What's going on up here?" he called, pitching his voice to carry over the engine and through the rain.

Probably a lieutenant or a sergeant himself, he had no idea he was talking to a lieutenant-colonel. Tom gave the same answer any foot soldier who'd seen some action would have: "Not a hell of a lot, thank God."

"Sounds good to me," the barrel commander said. By his accent, he came from Texas, or possibly Arkansas—somewhere west of the Mississippi, anyhow. He wiped the back of his hand across his face. "I don't mind the rain one goddamn bit, let me tell you."

"Because of the lull, you mean?" Tom asked. As if to belie the word, an automatic rifle not too far away stuttered out a short burst. Several shots from Springfields answered. Tom waited to see if anything big would flare up.

So did the barrel commander. When the firing died away instead, his smile showed nothing but relief. "Partly the lull, yeah," he said. "But there's one thing more: weather like this here, all the poison gas in the world ain't worth shit."

"You've got a point," Tom said. He didn't want to think about wearing a gas mask in a driving rain like this. All his thoughts about eyeglasses came back, doubled and redoubled. With a gas mask's portholes, you couldn't even peer over the tops if the lenses got spattered. You were stuck trying to see through drip-filled glass.

"Damnyankees throw that stuff around like it's going out of style." The barrel commander patted the cast steel of the cupola. "Sometimes inside here, we don't know they've done it till too late."

"Hadn't thought of that," Tom admitted. He imagined rattling along inside the noisy barrel, maybe firing its cannon and machine guns to add to the din. If gas shells started bursting near you, how would you know? Likely by getting a lungful of the stuff, which wasn't the best way. Colleton asked, "Haven't you got any filters to keep it out?"

"Yeah, but we have to seal everything up for 'em to work at all, and you don't want to do that most of the time, on account of you can't see out so good," the man standing in the cupola replied, illustrating his own point. "Besides, it's cooled down now, but in the summertime you purely can't stand getting all cooped up in here. They throw some potatoes in with us, they could serve us up for roast pork."

Tom's stomach did a slow lurch. In the last war and this one, he'd smelled burnt human flesh. It did bear a horrid resemblance to pork left too long on the fire. Would it taste the same way? He didn't want to know.

The barrel commander disappeared down into the turret again. As he emerged, the engine noise picked up. The barrel started forward. "Don't go too far into the woods, or you'll run into the Yankees," Tom shouted. The commander cupped a hand behind his ear. Tom said it again, louder this time. The barrel commander waved. Tom hoped that meant he understood, not that he was just being friendly.

A few minutes later, two more Confederate barrels rattled down the road after the first one. Tom Colleton frowned. Had some kind of push been ordered, one nobody'd bothered to tell him about? He wouldn't have been surprised; that kind of thing happened too often. On the other hand, maybe the barrels' crews thought something was going on when it really wasn't. In that case, they were likely to get a nasty surprise.

Frowning, Tom shouted for a wireless man. The soldier with the heavy pack on his back seemed to materialize out of thin air. One second, he was nowhere around. The next, he stood in front of Colleton, asking, "What do you need, sir?"

"Put me through to division HQ in Sandusky," Tom answered. "I want to find out what the hell's going on up here."

When the wireless man wanted to, he had a wicked laugh. "What makes you think they'll know?"

That held more truth than Tom wished it did. "Somebody has to," he said. "They're as good a bet as any, and better than most. Come on, get on the horn with them."

"Right." The wireless man got busy. Before he could raise Sandusky, though, an antibarrel cannon went off in the direction the Confederate barrels had taken. It fired several rounds. Those weren't big guns; a crew could serve them lickety-split. A machine gun started to answer, undoubtedly trying to shoot down the gunners, but fell silent all at once. A moment later, Tom heard ammunition start to cook off. At least one of those barrels was history.

He muttered a curse and set a hand on the wireless man's shoulder. "Never mind. I just got my answer." Pulling his pistol from its holster, he ran forward to see what he could do for the luckless barrel men.

Some of them came running or staggering back toward him. Most were wounded. A couple of the soldiers in butternut coveralls turned around and went with him. The others kept going. Tom didn't suppose he could blame them, not after what had just happened.

And it turned out not to matter any which way. All three barrels were burning. Tom couldn't get close to any of them. Several men, including the commander of that first barrel, lay dead near the dead machines. Tom swore again. They'd walked into a buzzsaw. He hoped the end had come quickly for them. Sometimes, in war, that was as much as you could hope for.

A burst of machine-gun fire chewed up the fallen leaves not far from his feet. He dove for cover and swore one more time, now at himself. He hadn't come up here to be a target. Of course, the poor bastards in the barrels hadn't, either, and what had happened to them?

The damnyankee behind the machine gun squeezed off another burst. *Hunting me, the son of a bitch,* Tom thought as he rolled and scrambled toward and then behind the thickest tree he could find. The U.S gunner's fire went a little wide. Tom lay there panting for a couple of minutes. In the last war, he might have laughed at himself for getting into and out of a scrape like that. He didn't feel like laughing any more.

Careful not to draw the machine gunner's notice again, he crawled off to the west, putting as many trees between himself and the enemy as he could. Only when he was sure he could do it without getting shot did he climb to his feet. By then, he was so wet, he might as well not have bothered with the rain slicker. He felt like a cat that had fallen into a pond.

To add insult to injury—or, here, almost to add injury to insult—some Confederate soldiers hurrying into the woods came close to shooting him for a Yankee. *No good deed goes unpunished,* he thought as he finally made it back out into open country.

His wireless man looked him over. "Sir, you're a mess."

"Thanks. Thanks a hell of a lot, Rick," Tom said. "I never would have figured that out without you."

Rick took his canteen off his belt. "Here you go, sir. Have a knock of this." *This* turned out to be a good deal more potent than water. Tom swigged gratefully.

"Ahhh," he said when the fire in his gullet had faded a little. "That hit the spot. *Now* get on the horn to divisional headquarters. They need to know the damnyankees have got antibarrel guns and all sorts of other little delights lurking in those woods."

"I'll do it, sir," the wireless man said, and he did. Tom spoke with heat perhaps partly inspired by the liquid flames he'd just drunk.

"Well, we'll see what we can do about it." The staff officer back in Sandusky didn't sound very worried. Why should he be? He was far enough behind the lines that nobody was shooting at him. He went on, "Can't really send out the Mules in weather like this, you know."

He was bound to be dry and under a roof, too. More cold water trickled down the back of Tom Colleton's neck. He was amazed his anger didn't turn it to steam. "Have you ever heard of artillery?" he growled.

"Oh, yes, sir," the staff officer said brightly. "I told you, sir— we'll see what we can do. Things are spread a little thin right now."

"What's left of three crews' worth of barrels is spread pretty thin right now, too," Tom said. "They didn't know what they were walking into. Now they've found out the hard way. The Yankees need to pay for that."

"Yes, sir," the staff officer said. That wasn't agreement; Tom had listened to too many polite but unyielding staff officers to mistake it for any such thing. The man was just saying that he heard Tom. He went on, "I'm afraid I can't make you any promises, but I'll do what I can."

"Right. Thanks. Out." Tom's *thanks* wasn't gratitude, either. It was rage. He turned away from the wireless set before he said something worse.

Rick understood that perfectly. "Don't worry, sir," he said. "I broke the link as soon as you said, 'Out.' "

"Thanks." This time, Tom did mean it. "I won't say you saved me a court-martial, but I won't say you didn't, either. Those goddamn behind-the-lines types are all the same. No skin off their nose what happens up here, because it isn't happening to them."

The wireless man looked at him with real surprise. "You sound like a noncom grousing about officers, sir. Uh, no offense."

Tom laughed. "You think we don't know what noncoms say about us? It's the same as privates say about noncoms."

Rick looked surprised again, this time in a different way. "You know what? I reckon you're right. I know what I called sergeants before I got stripes on my sleeve."

Artillery did start falling on the forest. The bombardment wasn't as hard as Tom would have liked to see it, but it was heavy enough to let division HQ think they'd taken care of the problem—and to say so if the people who gave them orders ever asked about it. Tom could have called Sandusky again and complained, but he didn't see the point. He was getting what Division had to give. If the Confederates had planned a big push through those woods, that would have been a different story. He would have squawked then no matter what. Now? No.

Before long, U.S. artillery started shooting back at the C.S. guns. The counterbattery fire also seemed halfhearted. How much had the United States moved from Ohio to Virginia? Would the Confederate defenders there be able to hold on? From where Tom was, he could only hope so.

As he always did when he went to the front, Jake Featherston was having the time of his life. He often wished he could chuck the presidency, put on his old sergeant's uniform, and go back to blowing up the damnyankees. Of course, that would leave Don Partridge in charge of the country, which was a truly scary thought.

But what could be better than yanking the lanyard, hearing the gun roar, and watching another shell fly off to come down on some U.S. soldiers' heads? This was what Jake had been made for. Everything that came after he took off the uniform . . . There were times when it might have happened to somebody else.

And he loved the automatic rifles Confederate soldiers carried. He had a hell of a time filling the air with lead when Yankee fighters shot up the gun pits. He hadn't hit anything yet, but he kept trying. It drove his bodyguards nuts.

He wished the Confederates had thrown back the U.S. attack without letting it get across the Rappahannock. In a perfect world, things would have worked out like that. *If wishes were horses, then beggars would ride,* Featherston thought. The damnyankees *were* over the Rappahannock, and driving for the Rapidan. They weren't slicing through the C.S. defenders the way the Confederates had sliced through the Yankees in Ohio, but they were still going forward. And they didn't have to go all that far before they got to Richmond.

"Sir? Mr. President?" somebody shouted right next to Jake.

He jumped. What with the bellowing guns of the battery and his own thoughts, he hadn't even realized this crisp-looking young captain of barrels had come up. "Sorry, sonny," he said. "Afraid I've got a case of artilleryman's ear. What's up?" Too much time by the guns *had* left him a little hard of hearing, especially in the range of sounds in which people spoke. But he was also selectively deaf. When he didn't feel like listening to somebody, he damn well didn't, regardless of whether he heard him.

"Sir, General Patton's come up to talk with you," the captain answered.

"Has he, by God?" Featherston said. The young officer nodded. Jake slapped him on the back, hard enough to stagger him. "Well, lead the way, then. I'm always interested in what General Patton has to say."

Again, he wasn't lying. He'd picked George Patton as a winner before the barrel commander helped put the Confederates in Sandusky. Patton's driving aggressiveness reminded him of his own. The general always had his eye on the main chance. You wouldn't go anywhere in this world if you didn't.

A butternut Birmingham with Red Crosses prominent on the roof and sides waited for Featherston. He felt not the least bit guilty about the ruse. If anything happened to him, the whole Confederacy would suffer. He knew that. Remembering it while he was blazing away with an automatic rifle was a different story.

Patton's camouflage-netted tent stood with several others in among some trees not far south of Culpeper, Virginia. The deception would have been better in the summertime. With leaves gone from trees, the tents were noticeable in spite of the netting. With luck, though, the Red Crosses on the auto would make Yankee pilots think they made up a field hospital.

"Mr. President!" Patton jumped out of a folding chair, sprang to stiff attention, and saluted. "Freedom!" he added.

"Freedom!" Jake echoed automatically. "At ease, General. Are we ready to twist the damnyankees' tail?"

"Just about, sir," Patton answered. He had some of the palest, coldest eyes Featherston had ever seen. They lit up now with a glow like the northern lights shining on Greenland ice. "Then we don't just twist it. We land on it with both feet."

"And won't they yowl when we do!" Featherston said.

"That's the idea." Patton pointed north toward the din of battle. "These head-on attacks—all they prove is that General MacArthur hasn't figured out what to do with all the tools his War Department gave him."

"Well, General, if you think I mind, you can damn well think again," Jake said. "When you're ready, I want you to do just what you said. We'll bundle these bastards out of your country with their jumped-on tails between their legs."

"We'll do it, Mr. President. We're better men than they are. We always have been," Patton said. "And while wars may be fought with weapons, they are won by men. It is the spirit of the men who follow and of the man who leads that gains the victory."

When he spoke of the man who led, he thought of himself. When Jake Featherston heard it, he thought of *himself.* He nodded. "You've got that right, General. The triumph of the will is going to take us where we want to go, and the United States won't be able to do a thing about it."

"In war nothing is impossible, provided you use audacity," Patton said. "We have it. The Yankees don't. To win battles you do not beat weapons—you beat the soul of man of the enemy first."

"Damn right!" Jake said enthusiastically. "When the Freedom Party was down in the '20s, we could have folded up our tents and packed it in. But I hung tough, and that made people stick with me. I knew our time would come around."

"That is the way it works, Mr. President," Patton said. "And I hope the way things work in our counterattack will be to your satisfaction. My only concern is that the U.S. forces have General Dowling commanding their right wing."

"Why worry about him?" Featherston said. "You beat him in Ohio. You can do it again."

"Well, sir, I hope so. But he was sensitive to his flanks there," Patton replied. "He didn't fight a bad campaign, given what he had to work with. Of course, Colonel Morrell commanded his armor then, and Morrell is still in the West, for which I am glad."

"You're not the first officer I've heard who talks about Morrell like that," Jake observed. "Maybe something ought to happen to him."

"Maybe something should," Patton agreed. "It's not what you would call sporting, but war is not a sporting business. I don't give a damn about good losers. I want the tough bastards who go out there and win, no matter how."

"That sure as hell sounds right to me. When I get back to Richmond, I'll see what we can do about it." Jake made a sour face. He didn't want to go back to the Confederate capital. In a lot of ways, he really would rather have been an artilleryman than President. But he talked about duty to other people. He couldn't go on pretending it didn't matter for him.

He motored back to Richmond in the Birmingham with the prominent Red Crosses. No Yankee airplanes attacked it, though a couple of flights of fighters roared by at not much above tree-top height, looking for things to shoot up. He got out of the auto at the foot of Shockoe Hill, and rode to the Presidential mansion near the top in his armored limousine. He didn't want the auto with the Red Crosses seen near the Gray House. That might give the damn-yankees ideas they would be better off not having.

"Good to have you back, Mr. President," Lulu said.

He smiled at his secretary. "Thank you kindly, sweetheart. It's good to be back." He was lying through his teeth, but he didn't want Lulu to know it. He didn't care to hurt her feelings by making her think he would sooner have been away from her.

His desk was piled high with papers. He swore under his breath, even though he'd known it would be. He wished he could aim a 105 at it and blow it to hell and gone. If he'd known how much paperwork being President of the CSA entailed, he wouldn't have wanted the job so much. Despite hating it, he had to keep up with it. If he gave it all to flunkies, he wouldn't be able to watch what went on. Nobody was going to get away with any private empire-building, not if he could help it.

He sifted through things as fast as he could, writing *Yes—J.F.* on some and *No—J.F.* on others and setting still others aside for consultation before he decided what to do about them. You had to use experts—you couldn't know everything yourself. But you had to watch them, too; otherwise they'd spend you out of house and home. Jake chuckled wryly, remembering the professor who'd wanted a fortune to play around with uranium. There were plenty more like him, too.

Every once in a while, something interested Featherston enough to make him slow down and read carefully instead of skimming. England was doing something new with airplane engines, something that didn't use a propeller but that promised a better turn of speed than anyone had managed with props. *We need to find out everything we can about this,* Jake wrote.

That might not be easy. In the last war, both sides had had a rough time crossing the Atlantic. Even submersibles had had trouble. The Yankees had been ready to copy a German fighting scout, but the sub carrying an example of the airplane got sunk. That set the USA back for months. The same thing could happen to any ship leaving the UK for the CSA. It could—but it had better not.

A note from Ferdinand Koenig also drew Jake's full attention. Things at Camp Dependable and some of the others were going the way everybody'd hoped they would. Featherston nodded to himself. That was good news.

Fewer bombers than usual came over Richmond that night; the ones that did seemed to strike mainly at the railroad yards. Most of the U.S. bombers dropped their loads farther north, at the Confederates defending against the Yankee onslaught. Jake hoped antiaircraft guns and night fighters knocked down a lot of them. No matter what he hoped, he knew better than to be too optimistic. U.S. gunfire hadn't badly hurt the Confederate airplanes that struck at Washington, Philadelphia, Pittsburgh, and other cities north of the border.

At dawn the next morning, the distant crashing of guns announced General Patton's counterattack out of the foothills of the Blue Ridge Mountains. Telephones in the Gray House started ringing right away. Aides brought Featherston notes on how things were going. As soon as he finished breakfast, the notes stopped satisfying. He had the calls routed to his own line, and started tracing progress on a map of Virginia that had gone up on his office wall next to the map of Ohio.

Before long, he was muttering to himself. Things weren't going as well as he'd hoped they would. Things never went as well as he hoped they would. In his mind, every campaign was a walkover till it turned out not to be. But reports of heavy enemy resistance all along the U.S. right flank did nothing to improve his temper. He barked at everyone who came in to see him except Lulu, and he never barked at her.

He tried to talk directly to Patton. He found out he couldn't; the general commanding the barrels was in one himself. There was another way in which the two men were very much alike: they both wanted to get out there and fight. Most people didn't have the stomach—or the balls—for it. Even a lot of officers were happier well back of the line. But Jake and Patton both enjoyed mixing it up with the enemy—and if he shot back, well, so what?

As the day wore along, the news gradually got better. The Yankees began falling back from positions they'd tenaciously defended all morning. But Jake's vision of cutting off their salient looked more like a pipe dream with each passing hour.

On the other hand, it didn't look as if U.S. forces were driving so hard for the Rapidan. Some units that had been spearheading the U.S. attack turned back to help deal with Patton's counterblow. Featherston nodded to himself. In war, you rarely got everything you wanted. He hadn't smashed the Yankees, or he didn't think he had, but he'd slowed them down, maybe even stopped them. That would do. It would definitely do.

Jefferson Pinkard felt awkward in a civilian suit. He could hardly remember the last time he'd worn one. Lately, he'd just about lived in his uniform. The gray flannel suit smelled of mothballs. It didn't fit too well, either. His shirt collar was tight around his neck. He'd added a few pounds since the last time he got into ordinary civvies.

But he didn't think he ought to call on Edith Blades in his camp commandant's uniform. It would only remind her that her husband had worn one like it, if less fancy. That didn't seem to be the right thing to do, not after Chick Blades had killed himself.

Before going on to Edith's house, Jeff stopped at a florist's in Alexandria and picked up a bouquet of daisies and chrysanthemums. He felt callow as he carried it up the walk and knocked at her front door. That made him want to laugh. There was a feeling he hadn't had in a hell of a long time—not since before the Great War. He had it again, though.

He knocked on the door. She opened it. She was wearing dark gray, too: not quite widow's weeds, but not far from them. "Hello, Mr. Pinkard, uh, Jeff," she said.

"Hello." Awkwardly, Jeff thrust the flowers at her. "I brought you these."

"Thank you. They're very pretty." She stepped aside. "Why don't you come in for a minute while I put 'em in something?"

"I'll do that." The house was small and cramped. Another woman with Edith's dark blond hair and strong cheekbones sat on the sofa keeping an eye on the two small boys wrestling on the floor not far away. Jeff nodded to her. "Ma'am."

"I'm Judy Smallwood," she said. "I'm Edith's sister"—as if Jeff couldn't figure that out for himself—"and I'll be riding herd on these two terrors tonight." The terrors kept on trying to assassinate each other.

Edith brought the flowers out in a green pressed-glass vase not quite big enough for the job. She started to put the vase on the coffee table in front of the sofa, then thought better of it. The top of the wireless cabinet made a safer choice. Once she'd set the vase there, she nodded to Jeff. "Well, I'm ready," she said, and she might have been challenging the world or herself to tell her she wasn't.

"Let's go, then," he said.

"Have a good time," Edith's sister called after them. Jeff held the door open for Edith and closed it again after she went through. He opened the Birmingham's passenger-side door, too, then went around and got in behind the wheel himself.

As he started the auto, Edith said, "I want to thank you again for everything you did about Chick's pension. That was kinder'n anybody had any need of bein'."

"Least I could do." He put the motorcar in gear and pulled away from the curb. "He gave his life for his country, just like he got shot at the front." That was more true than the prison guard's widow knew.

Edith Blades looked down at her hands. She wasn't wearing a wedding ring any more, but Jeff could still see the mark on her finger. "Thank you," she repeated, not much above a whisper.

He parked right across the street from the Bijou. The theater wasn't going to be crowded tonight. People came up by ones and twos. No line stretched along the sidewalk out from the ticket counter, the way it did when a hit came to town. If a hit had been in town, he would have taken her to it. As things were, he had to make do. He set two quarters on the counter, got two poorly printed tickets, and gave them to the attendant at the door, who tore them in half.

At the refreshment counter, he bought popcorn and candy and waxed cardboard cups of fizzy Dr. Hopper. Edith called up a faint smile. "Been a while since I went to a picture show," she said. "Even before Chick . . . died . . . It's been a while."

"Well, we're here," Jeff said. "Let's have the best time we can." She nodded.

The plush seats creaked when they sat down in them. The seats needed reupholstering; too many backs and bottoms had rubbed against them since they were new. Everything about the Bijou was overdue for a fix-up. The carpet had seen better years. The gold paint on the lamps was dusty and peeling. The curtain in front of the screen had frayed, threadbare spots.

And all of that stopped mattering the minute the lights went down and the threadbare curtain pulled back. All that mattered were the pictures on the screen. The newsreel came first, of course. There was President Featherston, firing a cannon at the Yankees. There were General Patton's barrels rumbling forward. There were burnt-out Yankee barrels and throngs of dirty, disheveled U.S. prisoners trudging into captivity with their hands above their heads. There were Confederate bombers blasting U.S. cities. Patriotic music blared. The announcer gabbled. By what he said, the war was as good as won. Jeff hoped he was right.

The serial was installment number nine—or was it number ten?—about a blond heroine kidnapped by Red Negro guerrillas and constantly threatened with a fate worse than death, a fate she somehow kept evading episode after episode. The Negroes mugged and rolled their eyes and showed their teeth. They seemed to know they'd get what was coming to them in the last reel. Jeff knew they'd get worse than that if they didn't shut up and do as they were told. They might end up in Camp Dependable, for instance.

In the feature, a loose-living woman from New York City (was there any other kind?—in the CSA, the place was a synonym for depravity) tried to seduce military secrets from a Confederate aeronautical engineer. His love for the girl he'd left behind him kept him from yielding to temptation, and everything turned out for the best. In films, it always did.

When the lights came up again, Jeff sighed. He didn't want to face the real world. But here it was, whether he wanted it or not. "I'll take you home," he told Edith Blades.

"All right," she answered. "Thank you again for asking me out."

"You're welcome. I'd like to do it again, if you care to," he said. She nodded. He smiled. He felt like a kid having a pretty good time on a first date. If that wasn't silly at his age, he didn't know what would be. Silly or not, it was real.

He walked her up to her front door when they got back to her house. "Good night," she said, and squeezed his hand. He wondered if he ought to try to kiss her. Something told him it wouldn't be a good idea, so he held off. She opened the door, went inside, and softly closed it behind her.

Even without a kiss, a broad grin stretched over Jeff's face as he drove back to Camp Dependable. In the morning, Mercer Scott would grill him about what he'd done. He was as sure of that as he was of the coming sunrise. He didn't know if the guard chief would care for the story he spun. He didn't much care, either. If Mercer Scott wanted to play Peeping Tom, he could watch prisoners, not his boss.

Sure as hell, the first thing Scott said the next morning was, "How'd it go?"

"Fine," Jeff answered. "She's a nice gal." After that, he went back to his ham and eggs and grits and toast and coffee.

"Well?" Scott went on. "Where'd you go? What did you do?"

"Went to the Bijou. Spy picture there's not bad." Jeff pointed. "Pass me that strawberry jam, would you?" Fuming, Scott did. He asked a few more questions. Pinkard sidestepped most of them, which only annoyed the guard chief more. The harder the time Scott had hiding it, the more Jeff wanted to laugh out loud.

Instead of laughing, he prowled through the camp after breakfast, the way he did almost every morning. Things felt quieter than they had when bands of Negroes were led out into the swamps every so often and didn't come back. Some of the desperation, the certainty they had nothing left to lose, was gone from the prisoners. That eased Jeff's mind. A man with nothing left to lose would lash out against the people holding him. Why not? If he figured he'd last a while, though, he'd think twice.

Nobody made a fuss when a fleet of trucks pulled up in front of the camp. "Come on!" the guards shouted. "Get your raggedy asses lined up, niggers. Some of y'all are goin' to Texas! Be good to see the last of you, you miserable bastards. Free up space in the camp, and about time, too."

The black men who boarded the trucks didn't fuss at talk like that. White men had talked to them like that since they were babies. Had the guards spoken softly and politely, it would have made them suspicious. Ordinary, bantering abuse they were used to.

They didn't give anyone any trouble as they filled one truck after another. Why should they? Texas was a big place. Camps there were bound to be big, too, with more room than this one had. Guards slammed the rear doors of the trucks. None of the Negroes flabbled at those metallic clangs, or at the thud of the bar coming down across the doors. Naturally, the white men wouldn't want them getting away. At least they weren't shackled into place in the cargo box. It might get a little crowded in there, but it wouldn't be too bad . . . would it?

One after another, the loaded trucks rolled away. A couple of the guards waved good-bye. Jefferson Pinkard saw that. As soon as the trucks were gone, he summoned those guards to his office. "You *ever* do that again, I will fire your sorry asses so fast, it'll make your heads swim," he snarled. "Ever! You don't like those niggers well enough to wave if they're going to Texas. Only thing that'd make you wave is if something else is goin' on."

"But, sir, somethin' else is—" one of the guards began.

"Shut up," Jeff told him. "Every time you open your mouth, your brains try and fall out. You may know somethin'. I doubt it, but you may. I may know somethin'. Matter of fact, I damn well do. But do we want the niggers here gettin' a whiff of it? *Do* we, you stupid son of a bitch?"

The guard stood mute, which was the smartest thing he could have done. Pinkard jerked his thumb toward the door. The guards almost tripped over each other in their eagerness to escape. They left the door open. Jeff shouted after them. One came back and closed it. Jeff listened to his footsteps recede.

That afternoon, Mercer Scott said, "Don't you reckon you came down on my boys a little hard?"

"Sorry, Mercer, but I don't," Jeff answered. "I want things to go smooth around here. That means I *don't* want some damn fools tryin' to be funny spookin' the spooks. They get the wrong idea"— by which he meant the right idea—"and we're right back where we were at before." He didn't go into detail. They were out in the open. It wasn't likely anybody could overhear them if they talked quietly, but it wasn't impossible, either.

Scott understood what he was saying—and what he wasn't. The guard chief didn't want Camp Dependable simmering at the edge of revolt the way it had been when Negroes were marched off into the swamps any more than Jeff did. "I don't reckon they'll make that mistake again," he said.

"They'd better not, or they're gone," Jeff said. "That's how come I came down on 'em like I did. They've got to know I won't put up with that shit. And if you want to talk to your friends in Richmond about it, you go right ahead. I don't aim to back down on this one."

He watched Scott weighing his chances. By the downward curve of the guard chief's mouth, he didn't think they were good. Jeff didn't, either. He was sure right lay on his side. And he was in favor in Richmond because of the transport trucks that did more than transport. Put right and favor together and you were pretty hard to beat.

From the way the papers and the wireless news in Covington, Kentucky, were crowing, Cincinnatus Driver feared that the U.S. offensive in Virginia had come to grief. He didn't completely trust the papers or the wireless; he'd seen they told more lies than a husband coming home with lipstick on his collar and whiskey on his breath. But Lucullus Wood was gloomy, and he had more ways of knowing than what the papers and the wireless said.

Cincinnatus made a habit of visiting Lucullus' barbecue joint every so often. If the police ever asked him what he was doing there, he could truthfully say he was a regular and have witnesses to back him up. How much good that would do him he didn't know, but it couldn't hurt.

Lucullus often came out from the back of the place and sat with him when he did show up. Cincinnatus got the feeling the cook who was more than a cook was looking for somebody to talk to, somebody who he could be sure wouldn't go to the police with whatever he said.

"Yeah, the USA screwed up," Lucullus said mournfully. "Got over the Rappahannock, but they ain't over the Rapidan yet, an' I dunno if they ever git that far. All depends on how much bleedin' they wanna do."

"Great War was like that," Cincinnatus said after swallowing a bite from his barbecued-pork sandwich. "This here one wasn't supposed to be. Goddamn Confederates done it right."

"Yeah, well . . ." Lucullus' broad shoulders went up and down in a shrug. "Where they went, they caught the Yankees by surprise. Daniel MacArthur sure didn't surprise them none." He took a swig of coffee, as if to wipe a bad taste from his mouth.

"Too bad," Cincinnatus said: a two-word epitaph for the Lord only knew how many men and how many hopes.

"Uh-huh. You said it. Too bad is right." By the way Lucullus agreed, his hopes were among those that lay bleeding between the two Virginia rivers.

Trying to change the subject, Cincinnatus asked, "You ever run across Luther Bliss?"

Lucullus had been raising the coffee cup again. It jerked in his hand—only a little, but Cincinnatus saw. "Funny you should ask me that," the barbecue cook said. "He come in here the other day."

"Is that a fact?" Cincinnatus said. Lucullus nodded. Cincinnatus wagged a finger at him. "And you called me a liar when I said he was back in town."

Lucullus shifted uncomfortably. "Yeah, well, looks like I was wrong."

"Looks like," Cincinnatus agreed. "What did he want?"

The other man hesitated. Cincinnatus understood that: the less Lucullus said, the less anybody could tear from *him*. At last, the barbecue cook answered, "He's interested in makin' trouble for folks he don't like an' we don't like."

For the Confederates, Cincinnatus thought. "Do Jesus!" he said, as if astonished such an idea could have crossed Luther Bliss' mind.

Hearing the sarcasm, Lucullus made a sour face. "He want you to know more, I reckon he tell you more his ownself."

That put Cincinnatus in his place, all right. The last thing he wanted was Luther Bliss telling him anything at all. He'd hoped he would never see the secret policeman again. Like so many of his hopes, that one had been disappointed. He changed the subject once more: "You ever find out anything more about them trucks?"

"They usin' 'em in the camps," Lucullus replied. "They usin' 'em to ship niggers between the camps. Now you knows as much as I does." He didn't sound happy confessing his ignorance.

"Well, that explains it, then," Cincinnatus said. It did for him, anyhow. "They use 'em in the camps, they reckon that's important—maybe even important enough to take 'em away from the Army."

"Maybe." But Lucullus sounded deeply dubious. "But what they use 'em *for?*"

"You done said it yourself: to ship niggers from one place to the next."

"Yeah, I done said it. But it don't add up, or it don't add up all the way. They already had trucks for that kind o' work. Ordinary Army trucks with shackles on the floor . . . You put a nigger in one o' them, he ain't goin' nowhere till you let him loose. How come they change, then?" Lucullus was as suspicious of change as the most reactionary Freedom Party man.

Cincinnatus could only shrug. "They don't always do stuff on account of it makes sense. Sometimes they just do it for the sake of doin' it, you hear what I'm sayin'?"

"I hears you. I just don't think you is right," the barbecue cook answered. "What the Freedom Party does don't always make sense to us. But it always make sense to *them.* They gots reasons fo' what they does."

That made sense to Cincinnatus. He wished it didn't, but it did. He said, "But you don't know what those reasons are?"

"No. I don't know. I ain't been able to find out." By the way Lucullus said it, he took not knowing as a personal affront.

Cincinnatus said something he didn't want to say: "You reckon Luther Bliss knows?"

Lucullus started to answer, then checked himself. He eyed Cincinnatus with pursed lips and a slow nod. "Your mama didn't raise no fools, did she?"

"My mama—" Cincinnatus broke off. What his mother had been bore no resemblance to the husk she was these days.

"I'm sorry 'bout your mama now. That's a tough row to hoe. I didn't mean it like that," Lucullus said. Cincinnatus made himself nod, made himself not show most of what he was thinking. Lucullus went on, "I ain't talked to Bliss about none o' this business. Didn't cross my mind to. Didn't, but it damn well should have. Reckon I will next time I sees him."

"All right. Meanwhile—" Cincinnatus got to his feet. He was smoother at it than he had been even a few weeks earlier, and it didn't hurt so much. Little by little, he *was* mending, but he didn't expect to try out for a football team anytime soon. "Meanwhile, I'll be on my way."

"You take care o' yourself, you hear?" Lucullus said.

"Do my best," Cincinnatus said, which promised exactly nothing. "You be careful, too, all right?"

The barbecue cook waved that aside. "Ain't the time for nobody to be careful. Time to do what a man gotta do. If you ain't a man at a time like this, I don't reckon you is a man at all."

That gave Cincinnatus something to chew on all the way home. It was tougher and less digestible than the sandwich he'd eaten, but it too stuck to the ribs. Three airplanes buzzed high overhead: C.S. fighters on guard against U.S. bombers sneaking over the border by daylight. Bombers mostly came by night, when the danger facing them was smaller. Back East, where defenses were concentrated, day bombing was suicidal. Here, though, the country was wider and airplanes and antiaircraft guns fewer and farther between. Raiders from both sides could sometimes cross the border, drop their bombs, and scoot before the enemy hunted them down.

Cincinnatus always looked both ways before crossing the street. The cane in his right hand and the pain that never went away were reminders of what happened when he didn't. So was the brute fact that he and his father and mother remained stuck in Covington instead of being safe in Des Moines, far away from the war and from the Freedom Party.

"Hello, son," Seneca Driver said when Cincinnatus came in. The older man looked as gloomy as Cincinnatus felt.

"Hello. How's Ma?" Cincinnatus asked.

"Well, she sleepin' right now." His father sounded relieved. Cincinnatus understood that. When his mother was asleep, she wasn't getting into mischief or wandering off. She didn't do anything out of malice, or even realize what she was doing, but that was exactly the problem. Seneca went on, "How is things down to Lucullus'?"

"They're all right." Cincinnatus stopped and did a double take. "How you know I was there?"

"I ain't no hoodoo man. I ain't no Sherlock Holmes, neither," his father said. "You got barbecue sauce on your chin."

"Oh." Cincinnatus felt foolish. He pulled a rumpled handkerchief out of his pocket and dabbed at himself. Sure enough, the hankie came away orange.

His father said, "Lucullus, he's a pretty smart nigger, same as his old man was. He got one trouble, though—he reckon he so smart, nobody can touch him. Ain't nobody that smart. He gonna pay the price one day. Anybody too close to him gonna pay the price, too."

That sounded much more likely than Cincinnatus wished it did. He said, "I'm bein' as careful as I can."

"Good. That's good." To his relief, his father didn't push it. He just sighed and said, "If Livia hadn't chose that one day to wander off . . ."

"Uh-huh." Cincinnatus nodded. That came close to paralleling the thought he'd had walking home. He managed a shrug. "Ain't nothin' nobody can do about it now."

"Ain't it the truth?" Seneca smiled a sweet, sad smile. "I's sorry you down here. Shouldn't oughta happen on account of our troubles."

"Do Jesus, Pa!" Cincinnatus exclaimed. "If your troubles ain't my troubles, too, whose is they? Everything shoulda gone fine when I came down. It just . . . didn't, that's all."

"Leastways you ain't got that Luther Bliss bastard breathin' down your neck no more. That's somethin', anyhow," his father said.

"Yeah, somethin'." Cincinnatus hoped his voice didn't sound

too hollow. Bliss wasn't exactly breathing down his neck, true. But the former head of the Kentucky State Police hadn't been happy to have Cincinnatus recognize him. Bliss might yet decide dead men couldn't go blabbing to the Confederates. Cincinnatus didn't know what to do about that. He couldn't hide and he couldn't run.

"Still and all, I reckon you do better goin' to Lucullus' place'n down to the saloon," his father said.

"I'm all grown up, Pa." Now Cincinnatus knew he sounded patient. "And I never knew you was a temperance man."

"Temperance man?" Seneca Driver shook his head. "I ain't. I never was. Don't reckon I ever will be. But I tell you, too many people does too much listenin' at the saloons. Too many people does too much talkin', too, an' a lot of 'em ends up sorry afterwards."

Cincinnatus had had that thought himself. He said, "I never been one to run my mouth, not even when I get liquored up. I don't get liquored up all that often, neither, not even after . . . all this happen." He gestured with his cane to show what he meant.

"All right, son. All right. I's glad you don't." His father raised a placating hand. "But I ain't wrong. Lucullus watch what goes on in his place for his sake. Some o' the niggers in them saloons, they watch what goes on for the gummint's sake." Cincinnatus was damned if he could tell him he was wrong.

No matter how many strings Colonel Irving Morrell pulled, he couldn't get sent to the Virginia front. From southern Ohio, he listened with growing dismay to the reports of a bogged-down U.S. offensive. He also listened to them with considerable sympathy. Why not, when he presided over a bogged-down offensive himself? If the War Department had given him enough barrels, he might have accomplished something with them. They hadn't; they'd taken. And he'd accomplished nothing.

"It's enough to drive a man to drink, Sergeant," he told Michael Pound. They hadn't moved from Caldwell. The front a few miles to the west hadn't moved, either. The only thing that had moved was the calendar, and it was not in the USA's favor. The longer the Confederates held their corridor through Ohio, the worse they squeezed the United States.

"Nobody would blame you if it did, sir," Pound answered.

"The War Department would," Morrell said dryly.

"Well, if those idiots in Philadelphia aren't a pack of nobodies, who is?" As usual, Pound sounded reasonable. If you already despised the powers that be, he could give you more reasons for doing so than you'd thought of yourself.

Morrell laughed. If he didn't laugh, he'd start swearing. He'd already done that a time or six. He didn't think doing it again would help. "You're thoroughly insubordinate, aren't you, Sergeant?"

"Who, me?" Pound might have been the picture of innocence. "I don't know what you're talking about, sir. Have I ever been insubordinate to you?"

"Well, no," Morrell admitted.

"There you are, sir. As long as somebody shows he knows what he's doing, I don't have any trouble with him at all. Some numskull who thinks he's a little tin Jesus because he's got oak leaves on his shoulder straps, now . . ."

"You've taken that thought about as far as it ought to go," Morrell said. Pound had known that for himself, or he wouldn't have stopped where he did. Sometimes a reminder didn't hurt, though. Morrell's principal concern was with numskulls who thought they were big tin Jesuses because they had stars on their shoulder straps. They could do more damage than the ones Pound had named.

Shrugging, the gunner said, "What *are* we going to do to get this war rolling the way it should?"

By the way he asked the question, he thought he and Morrell could take care of it personally. Morrell wished he thought the same thing. He said, "I'm going to do whatever my superiors tell me to. And you, Sergeant, you're going to do whatever your superiors tell you to. If you'd let me promote you, you wouldn't have so many superiors. Wouldn't you like that?"

"There'd still be too many," Pound said. The only way he would be happy, Morrell realized, was to have no superiors at all. In the military, that wasn't practical. *Why not?* Morrell wondered. *Would he do so much worse than the people we have in charge now?* The answer was bound to be yes, but the fact that Morrell could frame the question didn't speak well for what was going on back at the War Department.

Pound took out a pack of cigarettes, stuck one in his mouth, and offered them to Morrell. "Thanks," Morrell said. Pound flicked a cigarette lighter. Both men inhaled. Both made sour faces when they did. Morrell took the cigarette out of his mouth and looked at it. He neighed, suggesting where what passed for the tobacco had come from. Sergeant Pound got a case of the giggles. "Can you tell me I'm wrong?" Morrell asked him.

"Not me, sir," Pound said. "But we keep smoking them just the same."

"We do, don't we? Bad tobacco's better than no tobacco." Morrell studied the cigarette before he put it back in his mouth. "I wonder what that says about us. Nothing good, probably."

Still puffing on it, he walked towards a barrel whose crew was working on the engine. One of the men in dark coveralls looked up and waved. "I think we've finally got the gunk out of the goddamn carburetor," he called.

"Good. That's good." Morrell kept his distance. The barrel crew had the sense not to smoke while they messed around with the engine. That deserved encouragement. He looked out toward the woods that ringed Caldwell. With the leaves off the trees, they seemed much grimmer than they would have in summertime.

Because he was looking out toward them, he saw the muzzle flash. The rifle report came a split second later—right on the heels of the bullet that slammed into his shoulder.

"Oh, shit!" he exclaimed, and clapped his other hand to the wound. Blood dripped out through his fingers. For a couple of seconds, he felt only the impact—as if somebody'd belted him with a crowbar. Then the pain followed. He howled like a wolf. The next thing he knew, he was sitting on the muddy ground, with no memory of how he'd got there.

"Holy shit! The colonel's down!" Three people said the same thing at the same time. Another shot rang out. This one cracked past Morrell's ear.

Sergeant Pound ran over to him. The gunner grabbed Morrell and heaved him across his broad back. Morrell howled again, louder this time—getting manhandled like that hurt worse than getting shot had. Michael Pound paid no attention to him. He ran for cover, shouting, "Doc! Hey, Doc! Some son of a bitch shot the colonel!"

One more bullet snarled by, much too close for comfort. *That's not just somebody picking off whoever he can get,* Morrell thought dazedly. *He wants* my ass. *Christ, I wish that's where he'd shot me.*

Morrell hadn't thought about the aid station in a while. The medics and the doctor there hadn't had to worry about anything worse than cuts and burns for a bit, not since the planned U.S. offensive stalled. They'd probably been playing poker in their tent before Pound burst in, still carrying Morrell. "For God's sake, Doc, patch him up," the gunner panted.

The doctor attached to the force was a New Yorker named Sheldon Silverstein. "Get him on the table," he said. The corpsmen obeyed, taking Morrell from Sergeant Pound. Morrell tried to bite down on a shriek as they shoved him around. He succeeded less well than he wished he would have.

Silverstein looked down at him. The doctor settled a gauze mask over his nose and mouth. His eyes were dark and clever. "Morphine," he said, and one of the corpsmen stuck a needle in Morrell. Silverstein went on, "I'm going to have to poke around in there, Colonel. I'm sorry, but I've got to figure out what's going on."

When he did, pieces of broken bone grated. Morrell tried to rise up off the table like Lazarus. The corpsmen and Michael Pound held him down. He called them and Silverstein every name in the book— and a couple he invented specially for the occasion.

"Smashed up your clavicle, sure as hell," Silverstein said, as if he and Morrell were discussing the weather. "Doesn't look *too* bad after that—bounced off a rib and exited under your arm."

"Hot damn," Morrell said, or perhaps something rather warmer.

Dr. Silverstein smiled a thin smile. "I'll see how we do," he said. An ether cone came down over Morrell's face. He feebly tried to pull it off—it reminded him too much of poison gas. Somebody grabbed his good hand. Then the ether took him away from himself.

When he came back to the real world, things hurt less than they had before he went under. He croaked something even he couldn't understand. A corpsman called, "Hey, Doc! He's awake!" The man gave Morrell a small swig of water.

Silverstein looked down at him from what seemed a great height. "How do you feel?" he asked.

"I was born to hang," Morrell said feebly.

"Wouldn't be a bit surprised." Nothing fazed Silverstein—he worked at it. "Can you move the fingers on your right hand?"

"Don't know." As more cobwebs came off his brain, Morrell realized a good many were still there. He tried to move those fingers.

The effort made him grunt. "I—think so." He wasn't sure whether he'd succeeded.

But Dr. Silverstein nodded. "Yeah. That means the bullet didn't tear up the nerve plexus in there. You should do pretty well now, as long as you don't get a wound infection."

Even dopey and doped-up as he was, Morrell winced. "Had one of those in the last war. Damn near lost my leg."

"Well, we can do some things this time around they didn't know about then," the doctor told him. "I think you've got a pretty good chance."

"That's nice." Morrell yawned. Yes, he still felt disconnected from the physical part of himself. Considering what had happened to his physical part, that was just as well. "How long will I be on the shelf?"

"Depends on how you do," Silverstein said, which was no answer at all. He seemed to realize that. "My best guess is a couple of months, maybe a little longer than that. You aren't as young as you used to be."

When Morrell was young, he'd lain in the dust in Sonora wondering if he'd bleed to death. Was this an improvement? "Should be sooner," he said, and yawned again. Whatever Dr. Silverstein told him, he didn't hear it.

He woke later with something closer to his full complement of wits. He also woke in more pain, because the morphine they'd given him was starting to wear off. He was in a different place—a real building with walls and a ceiling, not a tent. A corpsman he'd never seen before asked him, "How do you feel?"

"Hurts," he answered—one word that covered a lot of ground.

"I believe it, buddy. Stopping a bullet's no fun at all." The corpsman gave him a shot. "Here you go. This'll make things better pretty soon."

"Thanks," Morrell said. What was pretty soon to the medic seemed like forever to him. He tried to think, hoping that would distract him from the fire in his shoulder. The fire made thinking hard work, and all he could think about was how he'd got wounded. He was behind the line when he got hit. How had the Confederates sneaked a sniper that far into U.S.-held territory?

After a little while, he realized *how* might not be the right question. *Why* had the Confederates sneaked a sniper that deep into

U.S.-held territory? The only answer that came to mind was to knock off a certain Irving Morrell. The bastard had been shooting at him—at him and nobody else—even while Sergeant Pound was hauling him to Dr. Silverstein's tent.

It was an honor, of sorts. It was one he would gladly have done without. He tried to move the fingers on his right hand again. When he did, it was as if he'd put a bellows to the fire in his shoulder. The Confederates thought he was dangerous to them, did they? He wondered if the United States were trying to assassinate Confederate officers who'd hurt them. Neither side had fought that way in the Great War. This time, it looked to be no holds barred.

Little by little, the new shot of morphine sneaked up on him. It built a wall between his wound and the part of him that mattered. It also slowed his thinking to a crawl . . . and that wasn't such a bad thing, either.

Part of Mary Pomeroy was glad to see Alec in kindergarten. It meant she didn't have to keep an eye on him every hour of every day. She'd almost forgotten what having time to herself felt like. Finding some again was even better than she'd thought it would be.

But, however convenient it was for her, it came at a price. What didn't? In kindergarten and all the years of school that followed, Alec's teachers would do their best to turn him into a Yank, or at least into somebody who thought like a Yank. Some of what they taught him would be small and probably harmless. Would it really matter if he spelled in the U.S. style, writing *color* for *colour* and *check* for *cheque*? Maybe not. As far as Mary was concerned, though, it would matter a lot if he decided the United States had had right on their side in the War of 1812—or, for that matter, in the Great War.

Her own father had pulled her out of school when he saw what the Yanks were up to. She couldn't do that with Alec. The rules were tighter now than they had been a generation before—and she was in town, not on a farm. If she held him out, she'd draw questions. They'd investigate her. They might look harder at what Wilf Rokeby had claimed about her. She couldn't take the chance. And so Alec went off to school every day, and never knew about his mother's misgivings.

He had none of his own. He loved school. He said over and over that he was the biggest boy in his class, and the toughest. He had fights on the schoolyard, and he won them. Every once in a while, his teacher paddled him. He seemed to take that in stride—part of the price of being exuberant. Mary still sometimes had to whack him to get his attention, too.

"He's a little hell-raiser, isn't he?" Mort said, more proudly than not, one day after Alec came home with a torn shirt and a fat lip.

"Does he take after you?" Mary asked.

"Oh, I expect so," Mort answered. "I got into trouble every now and again. Not a whole lot of kids who don't, are there? Boys, anyway, I mean. Girls are mostly pretty good."

"Mostly," Mary said, and Mort laughed. He didn't know about the bomb she'd put in Karamanlides' general store, or about the one she'd sent to Laura Moss. She had no intention that he find out, either.

The laugh drew Alec into the kitchen. "What's so funny?" he asked.

"You are, kiddo," Mort said.

"I'm not funny. I'm tough," Alec said.

"You sure are, kiddo," Mort said. "Here—put up your dukes." He and Alec made as if to turn the kitchen into Madison Square Garden.

"You'd better be careful, champ, or he'll knock you out when you aren't looking," Mary said. Alec threw haymakers with wild enthusiasm. Mort caught them with his hands. He didn't let his chin get in the way of one. When Alec stepped on Mary's toes twice in the space of half a minute, she chased him and her husband out of the kitchen. Had she married a different man, she might have threatened him with having to do his own cooking. That didn't work with Mort, though.

"Good chicken," he said once she finally got it on the table. Threats might not work with him, but his compliments counted for more than they would have from a man who didn't know anything about food.

Alec gnawed all the meat off his drumstick, then thumped it against his plate. That was taking the word too literally for Mary. "Cut it out," she said, and then, louder, "Cut it out!" Next stop was a spanking. Alec knew as much, and did cut it out. His mother sighed. "He *is* a little . . . what you said earlier."

"A what?" Alec asked. "What am I? I'm a what?"

"You're a what, all right," Mort Pomeroy said. "Try to be a good what, and do what your mother tells you to."

"I'm a what! I'm a what! What! What!" Alec shouted. He liked that so well, he wasn't about to pay attention to anything else.

When supper was done, Mary got up from the table, saying, "I'm going to wash dishes. How would you like to dry them, what?"

The what didn't like that idea at all. He retreated into the living room, where he loudly told the cat what he was. If Mouser was impressed, he hid it very well. Mort said, "I'll dry. I'm less likely to drop things than Alec is, anyway."

"I'm not Alec! I'm a what!" The what, like a lot of little pitchers, had big ears.

Most husbands who volunteered to dry would have got nothing but gratitude from their wives. Mort made Mary feel guilty. She said, "You mess around with dishes all day long."

"A few more won't hurt me," he said gallantly, and then, lowering his voice, "Besides, maybe we can talk a little without the hell-raiser listening in." Since Alec didn't know he was a hell-raiser, he didn't rise to that.

Mary started running water in the sink. The splashing helped blur their voices. "What's up?" she asked, also quietly.

"They gave Wilf Rokeby ten years," Mort answered as he grabbed a dish towel. "Five for having subversive literature, and five for lying about you and that bomb. He swore up and down that he wasn't lying, but he would, wouldn't he?"

"He knew my father. He remembered what happened to my brother. He thought the Yanks—well, the Frenchies—would believe any old lie about me on account of that." Mary had no trouble sounding bitter. She *was* bitter about everything the USA had done to her family and made it do to itself. That the postmaster was telling the truth was something only he and she knew—an odd sort of intimacy, but no less real for that. In an abstract way, she pitied him. He had to be out of his mind with rage and frustration because he couldn't make anybody believe him.

"He's got a lot of . . . darn nerve, trying to get you in trouble on account of what happened a long time ago." Mort slung a couple of forks into the silverware drawer. He was furious, even if he didn't raise his voice.

"Ten years is a long time. He'll be an old man when he gets out, if he doesn't die in there," Mary said.

Mort slipped an arm around her waist and kissed the back of her neck. "You're a peach, you know that? I want to murder Wilf Rokeby, and here you are sticking up for him after he did his best to ruin you."

He had his reasons, too. The only difference is, I managed to ruin him instead. Mary shrugged. "He didn't. He couldn't. Not even the Frenchies would believe him without evidence, and he didn't have any." *I made sure of that.*

"I should hope not!" Mort let his hand rest on the swell of her hip.

She looked back over her shoulder at him. "Sooner or later, you-know-who's got to go to bed." She didn't name Alec, and so he didn't notice that.

"Well, I guess he does." Mort gave her a quick kiss. "I can hardly wait."

To Mary's surprise, Alec didn't stay up too late, or fuss too much about going to sleep. Maybe he'd worn himself out running around at school, or maybe the chasing game he played with the cat—who was chasing whom wasn't always obvious—did the trick. Mort read him a story from England about a talking teddy bear and his animal friends. Even the Yanks enjoyed Pooh; Alec adored him. As usual, he listened, entranced, till the end of the tale. Then he kissed Mort and Mary and went off to his room. Five minutes later, he was snoring.

Those snores brought a particular kind of smile to Mort's face. "Well, well," he said. "What did you have in mind?"

"Oh, I don't know," Mary answered demurely. "I suppose we could think of something, though."

And they did. Mort locked the bedroom door and left one of the bedside lamps on, which made everything seem much more risqué than it did in the usual darkness. Mary wasn't sure whether it would excite her or embarrass her. It ended up doing a little of both. Her nails dug into his back.

Then it was over, and he suddenly seemed very heavy on her. "You're squashing me," she said, sounding . . . squashed.

"Sorry." He rolled off and reached for a pack of cigarettes on the nightstand. "Want one?"

"No, thanks." Mary had tried to smoke, but didn't care for the burning feeling in her chest. She put on a housecoat, belted it around her, and went into the bathroom to freshen up. When she came back, Mort was blowing smoke rings. She liked that as much as Alec did. It was the one reason she'd ever found that made smoking seem worthwhile.

He went out to the bathroom in a ratty old bathrobe. By the time he got back, Mary had got into a flannel nightgown and bundled under the covers. He put on pajamas and got in beside her. "Time for long johns soon," he said.

Mary sighed and nodded. "I hate them, though," she said. "They itch."

"Wool," Mort said, and Mary nodded again. He went on, "You need 'em, whether you like 'em or not."

"I know." Mary thought about going out without long underwear when it got down to fifteen below. Even the thought was plenty to make her shiver.

Mort leaned over and gave her a kiss. "Good night. I love you."

"I love you, too," she said, and she did. She yawned, rolled over, twisted once or twice like a dog getting the grass just right, and fell asleep. Next thing she knew, the alarm clock started having hysterics. Mort killed it. Yawning, Mary went out to the kitchen to make coffee. She would rather have had tea, but it was impossible to come by with the USA at war with Britain and Japan. Coffee was harsher, but it did help pry her eyes open.

After a hasty morning smooch, Mort hurried across the street to the diner. It was still dark outside; the sun came up later every day. Mary poured herself a second cup of coffee and turned on the wireless. Pretty soon she'd haul Alec out of bed and start getting him ready for school, but not quite yet. She had a few minutes to herself.

"And now the news," the announcer said. "Confederate claims of victory in Virginia continue to be greatly exaggerated. U.S. forces continue to advance, and have nearly reached the Rapidan in several places. Further gains are expected."

Mary had been listening to U.S. broadcasters for as long as she'd had a wireless set. By now, she knew what kinds of lies they told and how they went about it. When they said the other side's claims were exaggerated, that meant those claims were basically true. Mary hoped they were. She had no great love for the Confederate States, but they'd never bothered Canada.

"U.S. bombers punished targets in Virginia, Kentucky, Arkansas, and Texas in reprisal for the terrorist outrages the Confederates have inflicted on the United States," the newsman continued. "Damage to the enemy was reported to be heavy, while C.S. antiaircraft fire had little effect."

Again, no details, but it sounded good to anyone who already liked the USA. Since Mary didn't, she hoped the Yanks were lying again. She expected they were. What else did Yanks do but lie? They'd lied about Alexander, lied so they could line him up against a wall and shoot him.

What goes around comes around, Mary thought. *And it hasn't finished coming around yet.* One of these days, she would get back to the farm where she'd grown up. Not yet—the time wasn't ripe quite yet. But it would be.

XVII

Robert Quinn looked up from the papers on his desk when Hipolito Rodriguez walked into Freedom Party headquarters in Baroyeca. "*Hola, Señor* Rodriguez," Quinn said. "I don't often see you except on meeting nights."

"Usually, I am working on the farm during the day," Rodriguez said. "But I've been thinking about what you said about the Confederate Veterans' Brigades."

"Ah. Have you?" Quinn smiled broadly. "I'm glad to hear it, *señor*. And what have you decided about them?"

"I would like to join," Rodriguez said simply.

"*¡Bueno!*" Quinn jumped up from his chair and stuck out his hand. He pumped Rodriguez's. "Congratulations! I think you are doing the right thing for yourself and the right thing for your country."

"For myself, I'm sure I am," Rodriguez replied. "I've studied what the law gives, and it's generous. It gives more than I could make if I stayed on my farm." He knew why that was so, too, though he didn't mention it. The law that set up the Veterans' Brigades was bound to be geared to the richer Confederate northeast. What would have been barely enough to get by on there seemed like a lot more in Sonora and Chihuahua. He went on, "Do you have the papers I will need to sign?"

Quinn shook his head. "No. They are not here. You will find

them at the *alcalde*'s office. This is a government matter, not a Freedom Party matter."

"What is the difference?" Rodriguez asked, honestly confused.

"Many times, it is not so much," Quinn admitted. "But military affairs—except for the Freedom Party guards—belong to the government, and even the guards end up getting their gear through the Attorney General's office. So yes, you do this there."

"Then I will. *Muchas gracias, señor.* Freedom!"

Back before the Freedom Party rose to power, the *alcalde*'s office had been a sleepy place. It had been a center of power, yes, but a small one. The dons, the big landowners, were the ones who'd given the orders. But the Party had broken them; Rodriguez had been in a couple of the gunfights that turned the trick. These days, the *alcalde* and the *guardia civil* took orders from Hermosillo and from Richmond, which meant from the Party. If those orders sometimes came through Robert Quinn, they did so unofficially.

All the same, the clerk to whom Hipolito Rodriguez spoke seemed unsurprised to see him. The man had the paperwork ready for him to fill out. He even had a voucher for a railroad ticket, though not the exact date. A telephone call to the train station took care of that. "You leave for Texas day after tomorrow. The train goes out at twenty past ten in the morning. You must be here by then."

"I will." Rodriguez knew the train often ran late. But it didn't always, and he didn't think he could get away with taking a chance here. In the last war, the Army had been very unhappy with people who ran late.

"One other thing," the clerk said. "How is your English? You will have to use it when you go to the northeast."

They'd both been speaking the English-laced Spanish that remained the dominant language in Sonora and Chihuahua. Rodriguez shrugged and switched to what he had of real English: "I do all right. Learn some when I fight before, learn some from *niños*, learn some from wireless. No is *muy* good, but is all right."

"*Bueno*," the clerk said, and then, "That is good." His English was smoother than Rodriguez's—almost as good as, say, Robert Quinn's Spanish. He went on in the CSA's leading language: "Be on the train, then, the day after tomorrow."

Rodriguez was. His whole family—except for Pedro, who was

in Ohio—came with him to the station to say good-bye. He kissed everybody. The train pulled in two minutes early. He'd hoped for more time, but what you hoped for and what you got too often had little to do with each other. He climbed on board, showed the conductor the voucher, and took a seat by the window. He waved to his wife and children till the train chugged off and left them behind.

He hadn't gone this way since he headed off for basic training more than half a lifetime before. He'd been jammed into the middle of a crowded car then, and hadn't had much chance to look out. Now he watched in fascination as the train climbed up through the Sierra Madre Occidental and then down into the flatter country in Chihuahua.

Some Chihuahuans got on the train as it stopped at this town or that one. They and the Sonorans jeered at one another in the same mixture of Spanish and English. To English-speaking Confederates, Sonorans and Chihuahuans alike were just a bunch of damn Mexicans. They knew how they differed, though. Rodriguez made as if he were playing an accordion. *Norteño* music, with its thumping, German-based rhythms and wailing accordions, was much more popular in Chihuahua than in Sonora, though some musicians from the northern part of his state played it, too.

More things than the music changed when the train got into northern Chihuahua. Rodriguez started seeing bomb damage. Once, the train sat on a siding for most of a day. Nobody gave any explanations. The men going into the Veterans' Brigades hadn't expected any—they'd been in the service before, after all. Rodriguez's guess was that the damnyankees had managed to land a bomb, or maybe more than one, on the tracks.

Eventually, the train did start rolling again. When it went over a bridge spanning the Rio Grande between El Paso del Norte and El Paso, it crossed from Chihuahua into Texas. Rodriguez braced himself. So did a lot of the other middle-aged men in the car with him. They weren't entering a different country, but they were coming into a different world.

Some of the men who got on near the Rio Grande were short and dark and swarthy like most of them, and spoke the same English-flavored Spanish. But some—and more and more as the train rolled north and east—were big, fair, light-eyed English-speakers. They eyed the men already aboard with no great liking. They thought of

Rodriguez and his kind as greasers and dagos—not quite niggers, but not white men, either. Rodriguez remembered his soldier days, and threatening to kill a white man who'd called him names once too often. He wondered if he'd have to do it again.

Then one of the Texans peered through bifocals at one of the men who'd got on the train in Chihuahua. "Luis, you stinking son of a bitch, is that you?"

The other fellow—Luis—stared back. "Jimmy? *Sí, pendejo,* is me." He got up. The two men embraced and showered each other with more affectionate curses in English and Spanish.

"This little bastard drug me back to our lines after I got hit on a trench raid over in Virginia—drug me on his back, y'all hear?" Jimmy said. "I coulda bled to death or been a prisoner for a coupla years, but he done drug me instead. Doc patched me up, an' I was back in the line in three weeks."

"Then he save me," Luis said in English no better than Rodriguez's. "He—*¿como se dice?*—he kick grenade away before it go off."

"Hell, I was savin' my own ass along with yours," Jimmy said. "It wasn't nothin' special."

After that, none of the other white men in the car acted rude toward the brown men they rode with. Rodriguez didn't know what they were thinking. He doubted that had changed much. But so what? A man's thoughts were his own business. What he did, he did in public.

When the train stopped in Fort Worth, the conductor shouted, "All out for guard training here!"

Rodriguez had to push past his seatmate on the aisle. "Excuse, please. Is me." He grabbed his denim duffel bag from the rack above the seats, slung it over his shoulder, and went up the aisle to the door. A good many others, some brown like him, others ordinary Texans, got out, too.

Stretching his legs on the platform felt good. A man in a uniform of military cut but made from gray rather than butternut spoke in a loud voice: "I am Assault Troop Leader Billy Joe Hamilton. I have the honor and privilege to be a Freedom Party guard. Freedom!" The last word was a fierce roar.

"Freedom!" Rodriguez and his comrades echoed.

Assault Troop Leader Billy Joe Hamilton sneered at all of them impartially, caring no more for white than for brown. "Y'all have a lot to learn, and you won't learn some of it till you get to a *real* camp," he said. "Come on, now, let's get you off to where you're supposed to be at, get your paperwork all done, and then we'll see what the hell we got in you. Follow me." He did a smart about-face and marched off the platform.

"Ain't it nice they're so glad to see us?" Jimmy didn't bother to keep his voice down. Assault Troop Leader Billy Joe Hamilton's back got even stiffer than it was already; Rodriguez hadn't thought it could. The Freedom Party guard didn't stop or turn around, though.

Buses waited outside the station. The recruits for the Veterans' Brigades filled two of them. Rodriguez got into the second one. The cloud of black, stinking smoke that belched from the tailpipe of the first almost asphyxiated him. If the Confederate States weren't using it for poison gas, they should have been. His own bus coughed out the same sort of fumes, but he didn't have to breathe those. Gears grinding, the bus groaned into motion.

Decatur, Texas, was about forty miles northwest of Fort Worth. Getting there took an hour and a half—not bad, not as far as Rodriguez was concerned. The town was bigger than Baroyeca, but not very big. It stood on what the locals called a hill. To Rodriguez, who knew what mountains were supposed to be, it seemed like nothing more than a swell of ground, but he saw no point in arguing.

On the flat land below Decatur stood a compound surrounded by barbed wire. There was a ramshackle barracks hall inside; a guard tower with a machine gun stood at each corner. The guard towers were manned. Negroes wandered inside the barbed-wire perimeter. Outside the compound were neat rows of butternut tents.

Assault Troop Leader Billy Joe Hamilton said, "This here is Training Camp Number Three. Y'all are gonna learn to take care of nigger prisoners by taking care of the stinkin' sons of bitches. Ain't no better way to learn than by doin' what you got to do. Am I right or am I wrong?" When the men didn't answer fast enough to suit him, he donned an ugly scowl. "I said, *Am I right or am I wrong?*"

He may have a funny rank because he is a Party guard and not a soldier, but he is nothing but a top sergeant, thought Rodriguez, who remembered the breed well. "You are right, Assault Troop Leader!" he shouted along with the rest of the veterans. By the way some of them smiled, they were remembering their younger days, too.

The paperwork was about what Rodriguez expected: fitting pegs into slots. He had to ask for help two or three times; he spoke more English than he read. He didn't feel bad or embarrassed about it. Others from Sonora and Chihuahua were doing the same thing, some more often than he.

He got a gray uniform like Hamilton's but plainer. He got a pair of shiny black marching boots. He got a submachine gun, but no ammunition for it yet. And he got assigned to a cot in one of those tents. His tentmate turned out to be a Texan named Ollie Parker. "You ain't no nigger-lover, are you?" Parker demanded. Rodriguez shook his head. Parker, who'd looked worried, relaxed. "In that case, I reckon we'll get on just fine."

Rain poured from the night sky. Scipio put on his galoshes and his raincoat and took his umbrella out of a wastebasket at the Huntsman's Lodge. He'd get wet walking home anyway. He knew that ahead of time, and knew how inconvenient it was. He also knew he couldn't do anything more than he'd already done.

"See you tomorrow, Xerxes," Jerry Dover said.

"Reckon so," Scipio answered, although, since it was half past one, his boss would really see him again later today.

He slid out the door and started for the Terry. The thick, black clouds overhead only made it darker than it would have been otherwise—which is to say, very dark indeed. He tried to stride carefully, feeling with each foot as well as stepping. He didn't want to walk off the curb and fall in the gutter or land in a pothole and sprain his ankle.

He'd got almost to the Terry when a flashlight beam stabbed into his face from up ahead. He gasped in surprise and fear. With the raindrops drumming down on his umbrella, he hadn't heard anyone up there. And, coming out of the gloom, the beam felt bright as a welder's torch.

"What the hell you doin' out after curfew, nigger?" The voice that snapped the question belonged to a white man.

Scipio realized the raincoat hid the tuxedo that told without words what he did. "Suh, I waits table up at de Huntsman's Lodge," he answered. "I jus' git off work a few minutes gone by."

By now, just about every cop in Augusta had stopped him at one time or another. From behind the flashlight, this one said, "Show me you got on your fancy duds under that there raincoat."

"Yes, suh. I do dat." Scipio shifted the umbrella from his right hand to his left and used his right to undo the top couple of buttons on the coat and tug it wide so the policeman could see the wing collar and bow tie beneath it.

"It's him, all right," another policeman said. "I almost blew the bastard's head off a few weeks ago." Scipio still couldn't see anything but the dazzling beam of light and the raindrops falling through it. He heard more cops muttering agreement. How many were out there? He got the idea there were quite a few.

"Whereabouts exactly you live, uncle?" asked the policeman behind the flashlight.

After giving his address, Scipio buttoned the raincoat to keep out the November chill. "How come you wants to know dat, suh?" he asked. "I ain't done nothin' wrong."

"You're out after curfew. We wanted to jug you, we sure as hell could," the cop said, and the cold of a winter from much farther north took root in Scipio's vitals. But the white man went on, "You just get your sorry black ass home, then. This here ain't got nothin' to do with you."

"This here what?" Scipio inquired.

"Cleaning out transients and terrorists." Abruptly, the flashlight beam winked out. Green and purple afterimages danced in front of Scipio's eyes. Aside from them, he couldn't see a thing. He'd hardly been able to before, but this was even worse. "Come on through," the policeman told him. "Come on. You'll be fine."

Had he ever heard a white man say something like that before? Maybe, but not for a long time. Since the Freedom Party took over? He wouldn't have been surprised if he hadn't.

And the cop didn't lie. Nothing happened to him when he went by however many white men stood out there in the rain. No colored night runners tried to redistribute the wealth, either. The Negroes had enough sense to stay in where it was dry. Scipio had already unlocked the front door to his apartment building before he started wondering why the police didn't. He shrugged. They'd let him alone. If they got rid of some of the predators who preyed more on their own kind than on whites, he wouldn't shed many tears.

He slipped into bed without waking Bathsheba. He was awakened an hour or so later himself, though, by harsh barks that effortlessly pierced the patter of the rain on the windows. Bathsheba woke, too. "Do Jesus!" she said. "What's that?"

"Guns," Scipio answered, and told her of the policemen in the Terry. He finished, "Reckon some o' dem terrorists an' transients don't fancy gettin' cleaned out."

"How fussy the *po*lice gonna be, figurin' out who is one o' them bad folks and who ain't?" his wife asked.

Scipio hadn't thought about that. How often *were* cops fussy when they dealt with blacks? Not very. But he said, "Dey didn't run me in."

Bathsheba laughed. "Oh, you is real dangerous, you is."

That infuriated Scipio. He brought up the educated white man's voice he hardly ever used: "Once upon a time, more than a few people believed I was."

"Oh." Bathsheba laughed again, this time nervously. "I done forgot about that."

He returned to the dialect of the Congaree to say, "Somewhere in South Carolina is folks who don't never forget." Anne Colleton hadn't forgotten. She might have kept after him if the Yankees' bombers hadn't put an end to her career. She couldn't be the only one in that part of the state who refused to give up the hunt, either.

More gunfire split the night. In spite of it, Scipio yawned. By now, he knew more about gunfire than he'd ever wanted to learn. This wasn't getting any closer. As long as it stayed away, he wouldn't get too excited about it. Gunfire or no gunfire, he fell asleep.

When he woke, watery sunshine was trying to get through the blackout curtains. Bathsheba had gone off to clean white men's houses. Scipio put on dungarees and an undershirt and went out to fix breakfast for himself.

His son was in there washing everyone else's breakfast dishes. Cassius liked that no better than any other thirteen-year-old boy would have, but he did it when his turn came up. He looked back over his shoulder at Scipio. "Noisy in the nighttime," he said.

"Sure enough was," Scipio agreed.

"You know what was goin' on?" By the eager bounce in Cassius' voice, he wished he'd been a part of it, whatever it was. Scipio had named him for the Red rebel who'd led the Congaree Socialist Republic to its brief rise and bloody fall. This Cassius didn't know to whom he owed the name, but he seemed to want to live up to it. He also seemed surprised when Scipio nodded and said, "Cops goin' after riffraff in de Terry. You don' want to mess wid no *police*. Buckra gots mo' guns'n we. You always gots to 'member dat. You ain't right if you is shot." Maybe, just maybe, he could make his son believe it. So many didn't or wouldn't, though, and had to find out for themselves. Whites never tired of teaching the lesson, either.

"What do the ofays call riffraff?" Cassius asked.

"Dunno," Scipio admitted. "Dey reckon I weren't las' night, though. Dey lets me go on pas' 'em to git here. I finds out when I goes to work."

Cassius' expression said being passed like that was cause for shame, not pride. But he didn't push it, which proved he had some sense, anyhow. Then, as if to show he didn't have much, he said, "I could go out now an' take a look."

"You could stay here, too, and you gwine stay here," Scipio said. "Mebbe still trouble out dere. We already gots enough troubles. Don't need to go lookin' for mo'."

"Nothin' happen to me." Cassius was sure as could be.

"I say you stay here. You hear me?" Scipio sounded as firm and fatherly as he could. Cassius was getting to the age where they butted heads. Scipio knew that sort of thing happened. But he didn't want his son disobeying him here. The way things were in the CSA these days, this was a matter of life and death. Scipio hated clichés. He hated them all the more when they were literally true.

Some of his urgency must have got through to his son, for Cassius nodded. "I hear you, Pa."

"Good. Dat's good. You is a good boy." As soon as the words were out of his mouth, Scipio hoped they wouldn't make things worse. They might have with him when he was Cassius' age.

When it was time to head for the Huntsman's Lodge, Scipio put on his boiled shirt and black bow tie, his tuxedo jacket and satin-striped trousers. Not trusting the weather, he carried his raincoat and umbrella. But it was clear and sunny outside. The rain had washed the mugginess out of the air. It was the kind of crisp, cool fall day Augusta didn't get very often. Scipio savored the breeze against his cheek. The only thing he missed was the sharp smell of burning leaves, but after last night's downpour a man would have to drench them in gasoline to get them to burn.

As he usually did, he skirted the bus stop where the auto bombs had gone off. He hadn't gone much farther toward the white part of town when he stopped in astonishment. By the way things looked, the Augusta police hadn't just been after transients and terrorists in their raid the night before. Doors hung open in house after house, tenement after tenement. Not a shop near there was doing business. A stray dog whined and ran up to Scipio, looking for reassurance on the empty, quiet street.

Scipio had none, not for the dog, not for himself. The breeze swung one of those open doors on squeaky hinges. The small, shrill noise made the black man start violently. "Do Jesus!" he said, and wished he had even a fraction of his wife's faith. "The buckra done clean out dis whole part o' de Terry."

He hurried up into white Augusta as if fleeing ghosts. And so he might have been, for there were no living souls to flee in that part of the colored district. No one in the white part of town seemed to notice anything out of the ordinary. The newsboys hawking the *Augusta Constitutionalist* shouted about the fighting in Virginia, not what had happened here. Scipio bought a copy anyhow. The story had to go in the paper somewhere . . . didn't it?

He found what he was looking for buried near the bottom of page four. It didn't say much: just that the Augusta police had cleaned out some criminals in the Terry. *In the course of the investigation, more than a few Negroes were discovered not to possess papers authorizing them to dwell in our fair city,* the reporter wrote. *They have been removed for resettlement. Some minor resistance was encountered, but soon overcome.*

Anyone who'd listened to the gunplay the night before would have known the resistance was more than minor. And anyone who'd walked through that part of the Terry could see the cops had cleared out everybody, not just people without the right stamps in their passbooks. But how many white men were likely to do that? And how many were likely to give a damn if they did?

When Scipio got to the Huntsman's Lodge, he wasn't surprised to find Jerry Dover in a state. "We're missing a waiter, a cook, and a busboy!" Dover exclaimed. "No word, no nothing. They just aren't here. Three at once! That's crazy."

"Reckon this here gots somethin' to do wid it." Scipio showed him the *Constitutionalist*.

"Well, shit!" Dover said. "How the hell am I supposed to run a restaurant? Got to get on the phone, get those boys back where they belong." Off he went, to use what pull he and the Huntsman's Lodge had. Because he was doing that, Scipio hardly even minded the *boys*. But Dover returned with a fearsome scowl on his face. Pull or no pull, he'd plainly had no luck.

Aurelius nodded to Scipio when they bumped into each other in the kitchen. "I was afraid I wasn't gonna see you no more, Xerxes," the other waiter said.

"I been afeared o' the same thing 'bout you," Scipio answered. They clasped hands. *Still here*, Scipio thought. *We're both still here. But for how much longer, if they start cleaning out whole chunks of the Terry at a time?*

"The Star-Spangled Banner" blared from the wireless set in Chester Martin's living room. The announcer said, "Ladies and gentlemen, the President of the United States!"

"Good evening, ladies and gentlemen," Al Smith said. It was nine o'clock back East, but only six here in Los Angeles—evening in the autumn, yes, but just barely, especially since summer time stayed in force all year around now that the war was on. The President continued, "Some of the things I have to tell you are less pleasant than I wish they were, but this has never been a country that lived in fear of bad news. Unlike our enemies, we don't need to lie every time we open our mouths to keep our people in the fight."

At the kitchen table, Carl wrestled with arithmetic homework. To him, that was more important than anything the President had to say. Who was to say he didn't have the right attitude, either? Chester lit a cigarette and held out the pack to Rita. She shook her head. He set the pack on the little table by the sofa.

"Things in Virginia haven't gone as well as we wish they would have," Smith said. "If they had, we'd be in Richmond by now. But we have moved down from the Rappahannock to the Rapidan, and we haven't given up. We still hold the initiative."

Chester blew out a plume of smoke. He'd heard officers talk that way on the Roanoke front in the last war. Add *things haven't gone as well as we wish* and *we haven't given up* together, and what did you get? The answer was easier to figure out than Carl's arithmetic problems. What you got was simple—a hell of a lot of dead soldiers.

"I'm not claiming any great victories down there," the President continued. "But we've hurt the Confederate States, and we aim to go right on hurting them. I said when we declared war that they might have started this fight, but we were going to finish it. I said it, and I meant it, and I still mean it." The jaunty New York rasp in his voice made him sound all the more determined.

He paused and coughed. "There's something else you need to know about, something I wish I didn't have to tell you. It says a lot about the people we're at war with, and what it says isn't very pretty. You may have heard this before, but it's the truth, and not the garbage Jake Featherston puts out with that label on it. Those Freedom Party maniacs and butchers really are massacring Negroes. There's no doubt about it, and they're doing more of it, and worse, than even the Confederates have ever before.

"We know this is true because we have photographs that prove it. Some were taken by Negroes who escaped or who came upon piles of bodies before they were buried. Others were taken by Confederate murderers who were proud of what they did. I know that seems incredible, but it's the truth, too."

Chester looked over at Rita. She was also looking his way. Almost at the same time, they both shrugged. Not many Negroes lived in Los Angeles. Come to that, not many Negroes lived anywhere in the USA. Dealing with the ones who'd fled Kentucky when it returned to the CSA had stirred enough hard feelings. He might have been listening to a report about a flood in China. It was too bad, certainly, but it didn't affect him much.

The President tried hard to persuade him that it did: "We can't let people who do these terrible things beat us. Who knows where they would stop? Who knows if they would stop anywhere? We must show them that no one in the world will tolerate even for a moment the crimes against humanity they are committing. We have to stop them. We have to, and with your help and God's we will. Thank you, and good night."

"That was the President of the United States, Al Smith," the announcer said, as if anyone could have imagined it was, say, the mayor of St. Paul. "We now return you to your regularly scheduled programming." Music came out of the speaker.

"He's done better," Rita said.

"He sure has," Chester agreed. "It was like he was saying things weren't going so well in Virginia, so he'd give us something else to get all hot and bothered about. Except I don't think very many people will start flabbling about this."

"Why should we?" his wife said. "It's going on in another country—and when was the last time you saw a Negro around here, anyway?"

"I don't know. I was trying to think of that myself while he was talking," Chester said. "I couldn't—not right away, anyhow."

"I think there was a colored woman at the grocery store a few weeks ago," Rita said. "But she wasn't buying much. She looked like she was just passing through, not like she really lived around here."

"Once during the last war, I passed a Negro through our lines," Chester said. "I expect he was one of the blacks who rose up against the Confederates a little later on. Served 'em right, the way they treated Negroes even back then."

His wife nodded. "I suppose so. But when the colored people down there keep on fighting against the government, why would anybody think the government would want to give 'em a kiss?"

"Beats me," Chester said. "The Confederates treat their Negroes like dirt, so the Negroes raise Cain, and that makes the Confederates treat 'em worse. Of course, the Freedom Party would treat 'em bad no matter how they behave—I know that. It's a mess, yeah. But is it really our mess? I don't think so."

Rita nodded again. "That's a better way to put it. It's terrible, like you say, but it isn't really anybody's fault. It's . . . one of those things that happen."

Carl looked up from his homework. "Can I have a snack?" The President might have been talking about the cost of cauliflower for all the attention he'd paid to the speech.

"How much have you done?" Rita asked—Carl had been known not to pay too much attention to the homework, too.

He held up the sheet of cheap pulp paper—so cheap it was closer to tan than white, with little bits of wood that hadn't quite been pulped embedded here and there—he'd folded to make individual squares for all twelve problems. "More than half. See?"

"Have you done them *right*?" Chester asked. Carl nodded vigorously. "We'll check," Chester warned. "Arithmetic comes in handy all sorts of places. A builder like me needs it every day. Go on and have your snack—but then finish your work."

"I will, Dad." And, after Chester had inhaled half a dozen chocolate cookies and a glass of milk, he did buckle down. *Fortified,* Chester thought. His son waved the paper in triumph to show he'd finished.

Rita went over to check it. "This one's wrong . . . and so is this one."

"They can't be! I did 'em right." Carl stared at the paper as if his answers had mysteriously changed while he wasn't looking.

"Well, you can darn well do 'em over," Rita told him. "And you'd better not get the same answers this time, or you'll be in real trouble."

"I'll try." Carl might have been sentenced to ten years at San Quentin. He erased what he'd done and tried again. When he was done, he pushed the paper across the table to his mother. "There."

She inspected the revised problems. "That's more like it," she said. Carl brightened. But she wasn't going to let him off the hook so soon. "If these answers are right, that means the ones you got before were wrong, doesn't it?"

"Uh-huh," Carl said unwillingly.

"How come you didn't get 'em right the first time?"

"I don't know. I thought I did."

" 'Cause you were goofing around, that's why. Are you going to goof around when your teacher gives you a test?" Rita asked. He shook his head. He knew that question had only one safe answer. His mother continued, "You'd better not. I'm going to be looking for that test paper when you come home with it. If you only get a C, I'll make you sorry. And don't think you can hide it from me if you do bad, either, 'cause that won't work. I'll call up Mrs. Reilly and find out what you got. Do you hear me?"

"Yes, Mommy," Carl said in a very small voice. Telephoning the teacher was a parent's ultimate weapon. Kids had no defense against it this side of running away from home.

"All right, then." Rita seemed satisfied that she'd bombed him into submission. "Do you have any more homework?" He shook his head again. She ruffled his hair. "Then go take a bath and get into your pajamas, why don't you?"

A spark of resistance flared. "Do I hafta?"

She ruthlessly squashed it. "Yes, you have to. Go on. Scoot." Routed, Carl retreated to his bedroom. He came out in pajamas: the garments of surrender.

"Honestly," Rita said after she and Chester had played with him and read to him and finally kissed him good night. "Getting him to do anything is like pulling teeth." She scowled at Chester. "Why are men always like that?"

"Because women would walk all over us if we weren't," he answered, and tickled her. There was probably something in the Geneva Convention about that, especially since he wasn't ticklish himself, which meant she couldn't retaliate in kind.

They did have a more enjoyable way of unknotting such problems than the earnest diplomats at Geneva had imagined. Afterwards, they both smoked cigarettes. Then Chester turned out the lamp on his nightstand. Rita stayed up a while with a mystery. As he rolled himself into a cocoon of blankets—one more Geneva violation—she said, "You do remember Sue and Otis and Pete are coming over for dinner tomorrow night?"

"I do now," he said, and fell asleep.

He was glad to see his sister and brother-in-law and nephew. Sue had a beaky face much like his. Where he was going gray, her hair remained a time-defying sandy brown. He suspected a bottle helped her defy time, but he'd never asked. Otis Blake had a wide, perfect part along the top of his head—the scar from a bullet crease. An inch lower and Sue never would have had the chance to meet him. Their son was several years older than Carl.

"I'm working with glass again," Otis said. "When they found out I had plate-glass experience, they put me on cockpits." Till the war boom started, he'd been in and out of work since coming to California. He'd spent years in a plate-glass plant in Toledo before the business collapse got him along with so many others.

"Good for you, Otis." Chester meant it. He'd helped out when he could. Otis had done the same for him back in Ohio when Chester lost his steel-mill job there while his brother-in-law still had work.

"You ought to get a war-plant job," Otis said. "I'm making more money than I ever did before."

"I'm doing all right where I am," Chester said. "I like building better than steel, too."

"You're losing money," his brother-in-law declared.

"Not much," Chester answered. "We're getting raises. The contractors know they've got to give 'em to us, or else we darn well will quit and start making airplanes or shells or whatever else the war needs."

"Before too long, I'll be able to start paying back some of what I owe you," Otis said. "Haven't wanted to show my face around here till I could tell you that."

Chester shrugged. "Hey, I never worried about it. It's not like you didn't carry me for a while. If you can do it without hurting yourself, great. If you can't—then you can't, that's all."

"You're all right, Chester," Sue said softly.

Framed on the wall of the front room was a note from Teddy Roosevelt hoping Chester would recover from his war wound. They'd met on one of TR's tours of the Great War trenches. From that day to this, Chester had never found any words that mattered so much to him. Now maybe he had.

The USS *Remembrance* lay at anchor off the town of Lahaina on the island of Maui. The airplane carrier hadn't come back to Pearl Harbor after her cruise up to Midway. Somebody with a lot of braid on his sleeves had decided that putting an extra ninety miles or so between the *Remembrance* and a Japanese attack from the west would help keep her safe. Sam Carsten wasn't completely convinced, but nobody except the sailors in the damage-control party cared about his opinion.

His boss wasn't thrilled, either. "If they bomb us in Pearl Harbor, we sink in shallow water and we're easy to refloat," Lieutenant Commander Hiram Pottinger grumbled at a general-quarters drill. "If they bomb us here, down we go, and they never see us again. There's a hell of a lot of water underneath us."

"If we can figure that out, how come the brass can't?" Szczerbiakowicz asked.

"Beats me, Eyechart," Sam said. "You want stuff to make sense all the time, why the hell'd you join the Navy?"

"You got me there, Lieutenant," the Pole said. "Why the hell did *you* join the Navy?"

"Me?" Sam hadn't thought about it for a while. "Mostly because I didn't want to walk behind a horse's ass the rest of my life, I guess. My folks had a farm, and I knew that was hard work. I figured this would be better. And it is—most of the time."

"Yeah, most of the time," Szczerbiakowicz agreed dryly. Everybody laughed, not that it was really funny. You weren't likely to run into dive bombers and battleships and submarines on a farm.

When the all-clear sounded, Sam went up to the flight deck. Destroyers and cruisers flanked the *Remembrance* to the west; their antiaircraft guns would help defend the vital ship if the Japs figured out she wasn't at Pearl Harbor. To the east lay Maui. Lahaina had been the capital of the Kingdom of Hawaii till 1845. It had been a boomtown in whaling days. Now it seemed to have forgotten its lively past, and slumbered the days away—until Navy ships anchored offshore, when it perked up amazingly. Sam had seen the enormous banyan tree in the town square, which had to shade an area a couple of hundred feet across. Any town whose main attraction was a tree wasn't the most exciting place God ever made.

Fighters buzzed high overhead. The *Remembrance*'s Y-ranging antenna swung round and round, round and round. *Nobody's going to catch us with our pants down,* Sam thought approvingly. But how many carriers did the Japanese have? It was possible—hell, it was easy—to be ready for battle in a tactical sense but to get overwhelmed strategically.

That thought came back to haunt him at supper. He was halfway through a good steak—he couldn't remember the last time he'd had a better one—when the intercom suddenly announced, "Midway reports itself under attack by Japanese aircraft. The island has launched aircraft along the vector given by the enemy machines. We are proceeding to lend our assistance."

No sooner had the metallic words died away than the engines rumbled to life under Sam's feet. Somebody down the table from him said, "Godalmighty—we're not wasting any time, are we?"

Commander Dan Cressy had been swearing under his breath.

The officer's remark made him revert to straightforward English: "We've wasted more than three hours just by being here instead of in Honolulu. Now we get to find out how much that costs us."

"We have all the supplies we need, sir?" Sam asked.

"We have enough fuel to get us to Midway, and we have enough aviation gas to fly our airplanes," Cressy answered. "What more do we need past that?"

Carsten said the only thing he could: "Nothing, sir." If they had enough fuel to come home from Midway, the exec hadn't said a word about it. He hadn't said anything about food, either. They could get there, and they could fight once they did. Past that . . . well, they could worry about everything else afterwards.

Captain Stein came on the intercom a little later, urging men who weren't on duty to go out on the flight deck and keep an eye peeled for periscopes. "We have fancy new sound gear since the last war," the captain said, "but nothing is perfect. One of you may see something everybody else misses. It's worth a try."

Sam would have gone out anyway. If the Japs were attacking Midway, they might well have sent subs out ahead of their fleet to pick off American reinforcements rushing up from the main Sandwich Islands. The *Remembrance*'s anchorage off Lahaina might actually have done the ship and its escorts some good. Submarines would be most likely to prowl the line between Pearl Harbor and Midway. The carrier and her flanking ships would take a different course.

Several sailors called out alarms. None of them came to anything—all they'd seen was an odd wave or a bird diving into the sea or, once, a spouting whale that had three or four men shouting at the same time.

Some sailors stayed on the flight deck even after the sun went down. That wasn't the worst gamble in the world; a periscope might leave a phosphorescent trail against dark water or might be spotted by moonlight. Sam went over to the wireless shack to see if he could find out what the *Remembrance* was liable to be walking into. But the yeomen didn't have a lot to say: Midway was under attack from the air, and had launched aircraft against the enemy. That much Sam already knew, and so did everyone else. The men with the earphones wouldn't tell him on which vector the U.S. airplanes had gone out from Midway. They did allow that no Japanese troops had landed on the low, flat island. That was good news, anyhow.

He decided to hit the sack early. Even at top speed, the *Remembrance* was a day and a half from Midway. When she got there, she'd be busy. Grabbing what rest he could seemed like a good idea. He had no idea how much that would be. An alert or a real attack might bounce him out of his bunk any old time.

Except for shoes and hat, he slept in his uniform. If he looked rumpled when he got up—well, so what? To his surprise, he got most of a full night. He woke at 0400, feeling refreshed and ready for whatever lay ahead. He went to the galley for food and coffee. As with sleep, no telling how soon he'd have a chance for more.

Commander Cressy sat there with a steaming mug in front of him. Sam's guess was that he'd had no sleep since the *Remembrance* set out. The exec nodded to him. "Midway thinks there are three Jap carriers out there," he said, as calmly as if he were talking about shoelaces.

"Three?" Sam made a face. "That's not so good, sir." He filled his plate with bacon and eggs—real ones, not the powdered kind— and hash browns. "Airplanes from the island do them any harm?"

"They say they did." By Cressy's sour smile, he didn't believe it. After a sip from the thick white mug, he explained why: "The incoming waves haven't stopped, and they aren't getting smaller, either. What does that tell you?"

Sam's smile was sour, too. "No damage to the Jap carriers, sir, or not much, anyway. Uh—where are they?"

"North of Midway, and a little west—about where you'd expect," the exec answered. "Maybe we can give them a surprise. Here's hoping." He raised the mug.

Sam grabbed a nap in the afternoon, and sacked out early in the evening. That proved wise—they went to general quarters about midnight. He ran to his post in his stocking feet and put on his shoes only when he got there. Then it was a long wait for anything to happen. The mess gang brought sandwiches and coffee down to the damage-control party. The men wolfed down the chow.

"Sunday morning," Lieutenant Commander Pottinger said. "I'd rather being going into Lahaina for liberty. I'd really rather be going into Honolulu for liberty."

"Three weeks till Christmas, too," Sam said. "Well, two and a half weeks, if you want to get fancy."

At just past six, airplanes started taking off from the *Remembrance*'s flight deck. "Must be getting light," Pottinger said. Down where they were, day and night had no meaning. He added, "Here's hoping they've got good targets."

An hour and a half went by. The intercom came to life. "Y-ranging gear reports aircraft bound this way, about half an hour out. They are not believed to be friendly. All hands stand by for action."

Not believed to be friendly . . . They were Japs, for Christ's sake! Japan didn't have Y-ranging gear, or the USA didn't think she did. They'd probably spotted U.S. airplanes coming from the *Remembrance* or her escorting cruisers and flown along the reciprocal of their courses. That was how the U.S. aircraft from Midway had attacked the Japanese carriers. However they'd done it, they meant trouble.

Even in the bowels of the carrier, Sam heard the ships around the *Remembrance* start shooting. Then her guns started banging away, too. Her engines revved up to emergency full. She started twisting and dodging for all she was worth. How much *was* she worth, though? Compared to an airplane, she might have been nailed to the surface of the Pacific.

A bomb burst in the water nearby, and then another. Szczerbiakowicz worked a set of rosary beads. Sam wondered if he knew he was doing it. And then a bomb hit near the bow, and he stopped worrying about things that didn't matter. "Let's go!" He and Pottinger shouted it in the same breath.

Another bomb hit, also well forward, as the damage-control crew rushed to do what they could. The engines kept running, which meant they had power for hoses and pumps. "Gotta get the flight deck fixed," Pottinger panted while he ran. "If our aircraft can't land and take off, we're screwed."

Then a bomb hit near the stern, and all the fire alarms started going off. That was where they stored the aviation fuel. Ice ran through Carsten. They were liable to be screwed any which way.

When he got up on deck, he saw they were. The two hits at the bow were bad enough. The *Remembrance* didn't have enough steel plates to cover those gaping gaps. But the fierce flames leaping up through the hole in the stern were ten times worse. If they didn't get a handle on that fire right now, it would roar through the whole ship.

Sam grabbed a hose, careless of Japanese fighters whizzing by low overhead and spraying the flight deck with machine-gun bullets. "Come on!" he shouted to a couple of his men, and ran back toward the flames.

But even high-pressure seawater at a range close enough to blister his face wasn't enough to douse that inferno, or to slow its spread very much. "Back!" somebody shouted. Sam ignored him. Then a hand grabbed his arm. He shook it off. "Back, Lieutenant Carsten! That's an order!" He turned his head. There was Commander Cressy. Even as Sam started to yell a protest, the pressure in the hose went from high to zero. "You see?" the exec said grimly. "We aren't going to save her. The abandon-ship order went out five minutes ago."

"It did?" Sam stared in amazement. He'd never heard it.

"Yes, it did. Now come on, God damn your stubborn, two-striped squarehead soul, before you cook."

Only when Sam was bobbing in the Pacific did he realize he'd also been promoted. A j.g. was addressed as a lieutenant, yes, but wore only one and a half stripes. Carsten grabbed a line flung from a surviving destroyer. Five minutes after he'd clambered up onto her deck, the *Remembrance* went to the bottom. He burst into tears.

"**M**ail call!"

That was always a welcome sound. Dr. Leonard O'Doull looked up from the little chessboard over which he and Granville Mc-Dougald sat hunched. "I resign, Granny," he said. "You'd get me anyway."

"Quitter," McDougald said. "You're only down two pawns."

"Against you, that's plenty." O'Doull won some of the time against the other man. If he hadn't, he wouldn't have kept playing him. But if McDougald got an edge, he wasn't the sort to give it up. "Besides, mail's more interesting."

"For you, maybe." McDougald had been in the Army a long time. He didn't have anybody on the outside who wrote him very often. This was his life. To O'Doull's way of thinking, it wasn't much of a life, but Granny didn't lose sleep over what he thought.

Eddie carried a fat wad of envelopes into the tent. "Got three for you, Doc," the corpsman said. "One for you, too, Granny." He passed the rest out to the other medics.

"Holy Jesus," McDougald said. "Somebody must have decided I owe him money." He opened the envelope, unfolded the letter inside, and sadly shook his head. "See? I knew it."

"What is it really?" O'Doull asked. His letters stood out from the rest. They bore bright red stamps from the Republic of Quebec. These all showed General Montcalm fighting bravely against the British during the French and Indian War. His bravery hadn't done him a damn bit of good. He'd lost and got killed, and Quebec had spent the next century and a half as a sometimes imperfectly willing part of British-created Canada.

"Letter from an old-maid cousin of mine in Pittsburgh," Granville McDougald answered. "She complains about everything to everybody, and my number happened to be up. Prices are too high, and there isn't enough of anything, and bombers are annoying when they come over, and why don't I fix all of it? Trudy's kind of stupid, but she makes up for it by being noisy."

"Er—right." O'Doull recognized Nicole's handwriting on his envelopes. He made sure he opened the one with the earliest postmark first. By now, he was so used to English that he had to shift gears to read his wife's French.

Unlike McDougald's cousin, Nicole had better sense than to complain about how things were back in Rivière-du-Loup. Since Pittsburgh *was* getting bombed, Cousin Trudy had some right to complain—but not to a man who saw at first hand what war did every day and who had to try to repair some of the damage.

Keeping track of her two brothers and three sisters and their families let Nicole ramble for a page and a half before she even got around to town gossip. O'Doull soaked it all in; it had been his life, too, ever since the Great War. Who was putting on airs because she'd got a telephone and who'd knocked over a mailbox because he'd taken his Buick out for a spin while he was drunk was big news in Rivière-du-Loup.

And Lucien sends his love, Nicole wrote. *He is home for the holidays from the university, and says he did well on his examinations.*

O'Doull read that with relief. His son wasn't always an enthusiastic student, and had dawdled a good deal on his way to a bachelor's degree. That he was going to college at all made him an object of wonder to his throng of cousins.

The other two letters had much the same theme. Only the details changed, and not all of them: Jean Diderot had assassinated another mailbox by the time Nicole finished her last letter. *Someone should take away his keys before he hurts a person instead,* she wrote indignantly. O'Doull was nodding as he read. He'd patched up plenty of drunks and the people they hit—that wasn't quite so bad as battle damage, but it came close.

"I wish I were back there," he said.

"It's your own damn fault that you're not, Doc," Granville McDougald said. "See what you bought for volunteering?"

"You should talk," O'Doull retorted. "How long have you been doing this?"

"A while," McDougald allowed. "I hope your news is better than what's coming out of the Pacific."

"It is, yeah," O'Doull said. "We hurt the damn Japs, anyhow. We sank one of their carriers and damaged another one."

"But they got the only one we had out there, and they got their people ashore on Midway, and that's what counts," McDougald said. "Now they're the ones who can build it up, and we'll have to worry about getting things through to Oahu. We can't send a carrier with our ships for protection till we build more or pull one out of the Atlantic and send it around the Horn."

"If we pull one, that makes things tougher against England and France and the CSA," O'Doull pointed out.

"I didn't say it didn't," McDougald answered. "But we can fly airplanes out of Honolulu and we can fly them out of San Francisco, and there's still that space in between that neither bunch can really cover. And if I can figure that out from the map, you bet your ass some smart Jap admiral can do the same thing and stick a carrier up there somewhere to make our lives difficult."

"Makes sense," O'Doull said. "That doesn't mean it's true, mind you, but it makes sense." He hesitated, then went on, "Hey, I've got one for you, Granny."

"Shoot," the medic told him.

"What do you think about what Smith said on the wireless a little while ago—about the Confederates slaughtering their Negroes, I mean?"

Granville McDougald frowned. "Well, I don't know. In the last war, the limeys told stories about how the Germans marched along with Belgian babies on their bayonets, called 'em Huns, and that was a crock of shit. I figure it's about even money that he's trying to whip things up on the home front because the offensive in Virginia isn't going the way he hoped it would. The Confederates are bastards, yeah, but are they crazy bastards?"

"Featherston is," O'Doull said, to which McDougald only grunted. O'Doull added, "Smith said he had photos. The limeys never said that about the Germans."

"I haven't seen any photos." McDougald shrugged. "Come to think of it, that Congresswoman—you know, the one who was poor damned Blackford's wife—said *she* had photos. I didn't see those, either. I wonder if they're the same ones. Till I see the evidence with my own eyes, I'm going to keep this one in the 'not proven' column."

"All right." O'Doull had trouble quarreling with that, even though he wanted to. As far as he was concerned, Jake Featherston should have been locked up in a loony bin instead of running a country. He struck O'Doull as nuttier than a three-dollar fruitcake, and he'd driven the Confederate States nuts along with him.

Up at the front, several machine guns started stuttering. Everybody in the tent with the Red Crosses on it swore with varying degrees of imagination. It had been quiet up there for a while. The weather'd been nasty, and both sides were throwing most of their energy into the fighting back East. But now one side or the other had put on a raid—or maybe somebody'd just imagined he'd seen something and opened up on it, which made everybody else open up, too.

"Come on," Eddie told the other corpsmen. "We better shag ass up there. Sure as hell, somebody's gonna be bleeding." Off they went.

"You and me," Granville McDougald said to O'Doull.

"Let's hope it stays that way," O'Doull answered. "My best kind of day here is one where I don't do a goddamn thing."

But the first casualty came back about ten minutes later. He got there under his own power, clutching a wounded hand. Trying to encourage him, McDougald said, "It could have been worse—it could have been the other one."

"Screw you," the soldier said. "I'm a lefty."

"Let's get him under, Granny," O'Doull said. Looking as nonplused as O'Doull had ever seen him, McDougald nodded. Because it was the man's skilled hand, O'Doull took special pains to do the best job of patching it up he could. With so many bones and tendons in the palm smashed up, though, he didn't know how much use the soldier would have when he recovered. *Hope for the best,* he thought.

"That's very neat work, Doc," McDougald said when O'Doull finished at last. "I'm not sure I could handle anything that delicate myself."

"Nice of you to say so," O'Doull answered. "I don't know what kind of result he'll get out of it, though. He'll just have to wait and see how he heals." O'Doull himself would probably never find out; the wounded man would be sent farther back of the line as soon as possible.

He and McDougald dealt with three more wounded soldiers in the course of the afternoon, none of them, luckily, with life-threatening injuries. Knowing someone would come back to something approaching full health once he recovered was a good feeling. For a day, at least, O'Doull could pretend he'd won a round against death.

Darkness fell early—not so early as it would have up in Rivière-du-Loup at this season of the year, but early enough. The gunfire died away to occasional spatters. It had never been a full-strength exchange; neither side brought barrels and artillery into it. That strengthened O'Doull's impression that the firefight had started more by accident than for any real reason.

He was spreading a can of deviled ham over a couple of crackers when a runner stuck his head into the tent. He wasn't a man O'Doull remembered seeing before. "Get ready to shut this place down," he announced. "Whole division's pulling out of the line here and heading for Virginia."

"Jesus!" O'Doull exclaimed. "Nice to give people a little warning, isn't it?"

"You've got a little warning, sir," the runner answered. "This is it." He wasn't even sarcastic. He meant it. As far as O'Doull was concerned, that made things worse, not better.

"Who's taking our place?" Granville McDougald asked.

"Two regiments from a new division—the 271st," the runner said. Two regiments from a full-strength division would match the number of effectives facing the Confederates, all right. Even casual firefights like the one earlier in the day caused casualties, and they happened all the time.

"Why didn't they ship the 271st to Virginia?" O'Doull asked bitterly. The runner didn't answer that. O'Doull had no trouble finding his own answers. The obvious one was that they wanted to send veteran troops up against the Confederate defenders. That was a compliment of sorts, but one O'Doull could have done without. If they kept feeding veteran units into the sausage machine, they wouldn't have any veteran units left before too long.

Nobody cared about a Medical Corps major's opinion. He looked at McDougald. The Army medic shrugged and said, "Looks like we've got to take care of it. I hear Virginia is really shitty this time of year."

"Wouldn't be surprised," O'Doull agreed. But the other man was right—they had to take care of it.

And they did. It wasn't as if they had no practice moving the aid station; they'd done it whenever the front went forward or back. They weren't doing it under fire this time, and, though it was chilly, it wasn't raining. Things could have been worse. The medics bitched, but O'Doull would have thought something was wrong with them if they hadn't. He bitched, too; he didn't like climbing into a truck at two in the morning any better than anybody else. Like it or not, he did it. The truck jounced off down a road full of potholes. He was leaving the war behind—and heading straight towards it.

George Enos, Jr., slung his duffel bag over his right shoulder. Leaning to the left to balance the weight, he strode up the Boston Navy Yard gangplank to the USS *Townsend*. He felt good about coming home to Boston to get a ship, and felt even better to have a ship at last.

When he stepped from the gangplank to the destroyer, he saluted the colors and the officer of the deck and said, "Permission to come aboard, sir?"

"Granted," the OOD said, returning the salute. "And you are . . . ?"

"Seaman George Enos, Junior," George said, and rattled off his pay number.

"Enos." The OOD looked down at his clipboard and made a checkmark. "Yeah, you're on the list. Specialty?"

"Antiaircraft gunnery, sir."

The young j.g. wrote something beside his name. "All right. Gather with the other new fish there, and one of our petty officers will take you to your bunk."

"Thank you, sir." About a dozen men stood by the rail. Some were raw kids. Others, like George, had been around the block a few times. Two or three of them had good-conduct hashmarks on their sleeves that spoke of years in the Navy. Part of George felt raw when he saw those. Telling himself he'd been going to sea for years helped some, but only some.

Five or six more men came aboard after him. The OOD stared down at his clipboard and muttered to himself. George didn't need a college degree to figure out what that meant: a few sailors hadn't shown up. They were probably out drunk somewhere. George didn't know just what the Navy did to you for missing your ship. He didn't want to find out, either.

Finally, still muttering, the officer of the deck called, "Fogerty! Let's get this show on the road. If they show up, they show up. If they don't . . ."—he muttered some more, grimly—"it's their funeral."

"Aye aye, sir." Fogerty was a CPO with a big belly and an impressive array of long-service hashmarks. He glowered at the new men as if they were weevils in the hardtack. "Come on, youse guys. Shake a leg."

The *Townsend* was larger and bound to be faster than the *Lamson*, the Great War relic on which George had trained. She was every bit as crowded as the training ship, though: with her bigger displacement, she carried more weapons and more men. They ate up the space.

George's bunk turned out to be a hammock. He did some muttering of his own. What fun—he could sleep on his back or fall on his face. And he lay on his belly when he had a choice. No help for it, though. If he got tired enough, he'd sleep if he had to hang himself by his toes like a bat.

"Youse guys know your way around?" Fogerty asked, and then answered his own question: "Naw, of course youse don't. Come on, if you want to after you all get your bunks, and I'll give youse the tour."

When George accompanied him, he got more than he'd bargained for. Fogerty prowled from bow to stern and from the Y-ranging antenna down to the bilges. George hoped he would remember everything he'd seen.

One thing he made sure he'd remember was the OOD reaming out a hung-over sailor who'd shown up later than ordered. He didn't want that happening to him. And at least one man was still missing, because the officer had spoken of *they* to Chief Fogerty.

With or without the missing man or men, the *Townsend* sailed that afternoon. The *Lamson*'s engines had wheezed. These fairly thrummed with power. Asking one of the men who'd been aboard her for a while, George discovered that she was rated at thirty-five knots, and that she could live up to the rating. The training ship had been a tired old mutt. This was a greyhound.

He got assigned to an antiaircraft gun near the *Townsend*'s forward triple five-inch turret. They made him an ammunition passer, of course; men with more experience held the other positions, all of which took more skill. A shell heaver just needed a strong back—and the guts not to run away under attack.

They steamed south. Men not on duty stood at the rail. Some were watching for submersibles. Others were just puking; the Atlantic in December was no place for the faint of stomach. George took the heaving sea in stride. He'd known plenty worse, and in a smaller vessel.

"Not sick, Enos?" asked the twin 40mm's loader, a hulking kraut named Fritz Gustafson.

"Nah." George shook his head. "I was a Boston fisherman since before I had to shave. My stomach takes orders."

"Ah." Gustafson grunted. "So you're a sailor even if you're not a Navy man." He let out another grunt. "Well, it's something."

"Sure as hell is." The gun chief was a petty officer called Fremont Blaine Dalby—he described himself as a Republican out of a Republican family. With most of the USA either Socialist or Democrat, that made him a strange bird, but he knew what he was doing at the gun mount. Now he went on, "There's guys who've been in since the Great War who still lose their breakfast when it gets like this. North Atlantic this time of year ain't no joke."

"That's the truth. I've been on a few Nantucket sleigh rides myself." George had been on more than a few, riding out swells as high as a three-story building. He didn't want to brag in front of men senior to him, though. They were liable to make him pay for it later. That turned out to be smart, as he found out when he asked, "You know where we're headed?"

Dalby and Gustafson both stared at him. "They didn't tell you?" Dalby asked.

"Nope. Just to report aboard."

Fritz Gustafson grunted again. "Sounds like the Navy, all right. We're heading for the Sandwich Islands. We get to go around the Horn. You think the waves up here are bad? The ones down there make this look like a dead calm."

Now it was George's turn to grunt. He'd heard stories about going around the Horn—who hadn't? "Have to see what that's like," he said. "I've been east a ways, but I haven't been south."

"So you're a polliwog, are you?" Gustafson asked with a cynical laugh. Enough fishermen came out of the Navy and had crossed the Equator to let George know what that meant. He nodded. Gustafson laughed again. "Well, you'll get yours."

"Rounding the Horn shouldn't be *too* bad," Dalby said. "It'll be summer down there, or what passes for it. Going through in winter is worse. Then it's just mountains of water kicking you in the teeth, one after another after another."

"People have been talking about a canal through Central America damn near forever," Gustafson said. "I wish they'd finally get around to building the fucker."

"Yeah, but who'd run it?" George said.

Gustafson and Dalby looked at each other. "He's no dope," Dalby said. No doubt it was possible to build a canal through Colombia's upper neck or through Nicaragua. The USA and the CSA had both examined the project. Each had threatened war if the other went ahead with it. It might have happened after the Great War, when the Confederate States were weak, but the United States had been putting themselves back together then, too. And after the bottom fell out of the economy, nobody'd had the money or the energy for a project like that.

The *Townsend* joined three more destroyers and a heavy cruiser that came out of New York harbor. The flotilla also picked up a pair of oilers from Philadelphia. The ships would have to refuel before they swung around the southern tip of South America. The Empire of Brazil was technically neutral, but wasn't friendly, not when it was getting rich off fees from Argentine, British, French, Spanish, and Portuguese freighters hauling beef and wheat through its territorial waters for the dash across the Atlantic to Dakar in French West Africa. There were no guarantees that U.S. ships would be able to top off there.

My father went this way, George thought. *He didn't go around the Horn—I don't think he did, anyhow—but he was here before me.* He nodded to himself. *I'll pay 'em back for you, Pa.*

"Gonna be a little interesting, sliding past Bermuda and the Bahamas," Dalby said. "Yeah, just a little. How many ships and patrol airplanes do the limeys and the Confederates have?"

George's father hadn't had to worry about airplanes, or not very much. Warships were terribly vulnerable from the air. The loss of the *Remembrance* drove that home, in case anyone had forgotten. "What do we do if they spot us?" George asked.

Fremont Blaine Dalby let his hand rest on the right barrel of the twin 40mm. "Why, then, we give 'em a big, friendly hello and we hope for the best," he said. "That's why we're here, Enos—to make sure they get that big hello."

"Right," George said, as nonchalantly as he could. The rest of the men in the gun crew laughed at him. He kept his mouth shut. He knew they'd go right on laughing till he showed what he was worth. He'd had the same thing happen the first time he went out on a fishing run—and, in the days since, he'd jeered at other first-timers till they showed they were worth something.

As the flotilla went down past Maryland and Delaware toward Virginia and the CSA, it swung ever farther from shore, both to avoid Confederate patrol aircraft and to take a course halfway between the Bahamas and Bermuda. The men on the hydrophones worked around the clock. Sailors stayed on deck whenever they could, too, watching for death lurking in the ocean.

They ran between the enemy's Atlantic outposts on a dark,

cloudy midnight. No bombs or bullets came out of the sky. No torpedoes slid through the sea. The farther south they went, the calmer
that sea got, too. That mattered less to George than to some afflicted
with seasickness, but he didn't enjoy swinging in his hammock like
a pendulum weight when the rolling got bad.

Not that he was in his hammock when the *Townsend* ran the
gauntlet. He stayed at his battle station through the long night.
When the east began to lighten, Fritz Gustafson let out a long sigh
and said, "Well, the worst is over."

"May be over," Fremont Dalby amended.

"Yeah. May be over." Gustafson pointed up to the gray sky.
"Long as the ceiling stays low like this, nothing upstairs can find us."

Having been shot up aboard the *Sweet Sue,* George wouldn't
have been sorry never to see another airplane carrying guns. He said,
"Which means all we've got to worry about is submarines. Oh,
boy."

"We can shoot subs, or drop ashcans on 'em, or even run away
from 'em if we have to," Dalby said. "Can't run from a goddamn
airplane—looks like that's the number one lesson in this war so far."

Gustafson shook his head. "Number one lesson in this war so
far is, we should've been ready for it five years before it started. And
we weren't. And we're paying for it. We ever make that mistake
again . . ." He spat over the rail.

"But Featherston's a nut," George said. It wasn't quite a protest.
He answered himself before the others could: "Yeah, I know. It's not
like he didn't advertise." Dalby and Gustafson both nodded. George
sighed. The *Townsend* steamed south.

#

The wind that roared down on Provo, Utah, felt as if it had started somewhere in Siberia. Snow blew almost sideways. Armstrong Grimes huddled behind a wall that blocked the worst of it. Most of the house of which the wall had been a part had fallen in on itself. Armstrong turned to Sergeant Stowe and said, "Merry Christmas."

Rex Stowe needed a shave. So did Armstrong, but he couldn't see himself. Snowflakes in the other man's whiskers gave him a grizzled look, old beyond his years. Armstrong sure as hell felt old beyond his. Stowe said, "The fuck of it is, it *is* a merry Christmas. Goddamn Mormons aren't shooting at us. Far as I'm concerned, that makes it the best day since we got to this shitass place."

"Yeah." Armstrong cupped his hands and lit a cigarette. Arctic wind or not, he got it going first try. He hardly even noticed the blasphemy and obscenity with which Stowe had decked the day of Jesus' birth. He would have done it himself had the other noncom given him a Merry Christmas before he spoke. He said, "Nice to have a smoke without worrying some sniper'll spot the coal and blow my head off."

"Uh-huh." Stowe nodded. "Truce looks to be holding pretty good. If the Mormons want to make like they're holier'n we are 'cause they proposed it, I don't care."

"Me, neither," Armstrong said. "Amen, in fact."

He could even stick his head up over the wall without worrying about anything more than wind and snow. He could, but he didn't.

He knew what the rest of Provo looked like: the same sort of lunar landscape as the part the U.S. Army had already clawed away from the rebellious Mormons.

His old man had talked about how the truce in 1914 almost knocked the war into a cocked hat. At Christmas the next year, both sides had fired endless artillery salvos to make sure it didn't happen again. The truce here wasn't anything like that. As soon as the clock hit 12:01 A.M., both sides were going to start banging away at each other again. The only thing either felt for the other was hatred—that and, possibly, a wary respect.

And then that howling wind brought something strange with it: the sound of men singing carols. When Army chaplains talked about the Mormons at all, they insisted the folk who liked to call this place Deseret weren't really Christians. They tried to make the fight sound like a crusade.

Armstrong had never paid much attention to that. He didn't feel like a knight in shining armor. He was filthy and fleabitten and probably lousy again. If they would have put him on a train and shipped him home, he wouldn't even have turned around to wave good-bye. He was here because the Army told him to be here and would shoot him if he bailed out, not because he thought God willed it. God was bound to have better things to do with His time.

But hearing "Silent Night" and then "O Little Town of Bethlehem" gave him pause. "Reminds me of the days when I was a kid and I'd go caroling in the streets," he said.

"You did that?" Stowe said. "I did, too. I guess there aren't a hell of a lot of people who didn't—except for sheenies, I mean."

"Well, yeah, sure," Armstrong said, thinking of Yossel Reisen. "But I didn't think these Mormon bastards had the same songs ordinary people do."

As if to prove him wrong, the men who'd been trying to kill him sang "The Twelve Days of Christmas" and "Deck the Halls" and "Hark, the Herald Angels Sing." They were pretty good. Armstrong wondered if any of them belonged to the Mormon Tabernacle Choir. It had come back to life the minute Mormonism turned legal again, even before the Mormon Tabernacle was rebuilt. By now, Armstrong was willing to bet U.S. bombers had knocked the Tabernacle flat again.

How long would it be before the Army fought its way into Salt

Lake City for a firsthand look? Armstrong wished he hadn't had that thought. It led to too many others. Chief among them were, *How many men will get shot between Provo and Salt Lake?* and *Will I be one of them?* He'd stayed lucky so far. How long could it go on?

Somebody behind Armstrong—a U.S. soldier like him—started singing "Oh, Come, All Ye Faithful." He and Stowe both joined in at the same time. He hadn't sung carols in years, and he'd never had what anybody would call a great voice. He sang out anyhow, for all he was worth. It felt good.

He wondered if the Mormons would try to outshout their enemies. They could do it; they had that howling wind at their backs. Instead, they joined in. Tears stung his eyes and started to freeze his eyelashes together. He rubbed at his eyes with his knuckles. He would have been more embarrassed if the hard-bitten Stowe weren't doing the same thing.

Both sides caroled for half an hour or so. When the singing ended, they gave each other a hand. Armstrong didn't mind clapping for the Mormons. It was Christmas, after all. And he knew it didn't truly mean anything. The war might hold its breath, but it wouldn't go away.

Somebody from the other side of the line called, "You guys sing like you're nice people. Why don't you ever just leave us alone to do what we want?" He didn't even drawl, the way Confederate soldiers did. He sounded like anybody else: he had a vaguely Midwestern accent like half the guys in Armstrong's platoon. That made Mormons deadly dangerous infiltrators. It also made their uprising harder for Armstrong to fathom. They seemed like people no different from anybody else. They seemed like that—but they weren't.

"Why don't you stay here in the USA where you belong?" someone on the U.S. side yelled back.

That brought angry shouts from the Mormons—so angry that Armstrong looked to make sure he could grab his Springfield in a hurry. The truce felt on the edge of falling apart. He also found out a few things he hadn't known before. Nobody'd ever told him the Mormons had come to Utah before the First Mexican War exactly because they'd wanted to escape the USA even back then, only to find themselves under the Stars and Stripes again whether they wanted to be or not.

"Jesus," Stowe said: an appropriate comment on the day. Less appropriately, he went on, "These assholes have wanted to secede even longer than the goddamn Confederates."

"Yeah, well, how can they?" Armstrong asked. "They're right here in the middle of us. You can't make a country like that. Besides, they're a bunch of perverts. They ought to straighten out and fly right."

"Tell me about it," Stowe replied with a filthy leer. But then, as the shouting went back and forth between the lines, he added, "I wish to God they weren't shooting at us. Then we could make a couple of Mormon divisions and throw 'em at Featherston's fuckers. That would use 'em up in a hurry." He chuckled cynically.

"Maybe not. They might just mutiny and go over to the CSA," Armstrong said.

Stowe grunted. "You're right, dammit. They might. Plain as the nose on your face the Confederates are giving 'em as much help as they can."

In the end, nobody on either side started shooting in spite of the curses that flew back and forth. It stayed Christmas to that extent, anyhow. And Armstrong went back to the field kitchen without worrying about Mormon snipers. The cooks served ham and sweet potatoes and something that was alleged to be fruitcake but looked as if it came from a latrine. It did taste all right, and it gave the soldiers the chance to razz the cooks. They always liked that.

Once they returned to their positions at the front line, Stowe pulled a flask from his jacket pocket. He brought it to his mouth, then passed it to Armstrong. "Here. Have a knock of this."

"Thanks." Armstrong swigged, trying not to be too greedy. Brandy ran down his throat, smooth as a pretty girl's kiss. "Where'd you come up with this shit? Damn Mormons aren't supposed to have any."

"Musta been a gentile's house," Stowe said.

"Hope the Mormons didn't poison it and leave it for us," Armstrong remarked.

Stowe gave him the finger. "There's a hell of a thing to go and say. I've had hooch poison me a time or three, but I haven't got enough in here for that."

Armstrong did his best to look worldly-wise. He'd done some drinking in the Army, but hardly any before. His folks would take a drink every now and then, but they didn't make a big thing out of it.

His father would have walloped the tar out of him if he ever came home smashed. As for the swig of brandy the sergeant had given him, it sent a little warmth out from his stomach, but otherwise left him unpoisoned.

He rolled himself in a down-filled quilt. That was a bit of his own war booty, and a hell of a lot warmer than an Army-issue wool blanket. He used the folded-up blanket for a pillow. As he fell asleep, he wondered when he'd last lain in a real bed. It had been a while.

Some time in the middle of the night, he woke up. There were occasional flurries of gunfire, nothing to get excited about. If he'd let stuff like this bother him, he wouldn't have been able to sleep at all near the front. Only after he'd wiggled around for a little while did he think, *Oh. It must be after midnight.* Then he went back to sleep. If the shooting picked up, he knew he'd wake again.

What happened instead was that Sergeant Stowe shook him awake. The sun still hadn't come up, but the sky behind the mountains to the east was beginning to go gray. "Welcome back to the war," Stowe said.

"Screw the war." Armstrong yawned. "Screw you, too."

"I don't want you. I want a blonde with big tits," Stowe said. "Only trouble is, the gals like that carry rifles around here. They'd sooner blow my brains out than blow me."

As it got lighter, bombers came overhead and started pounding the parts of Provo the Mormons still held. The bombers were not only outmoded but flying above the clouds. Thanks to both those things, they weren't the most accurate bombing platforms God or U.S. factories had ever made. Some of the bombs came down on the U.S. side of the line.

The handful of Mormon antiaircraft guns banged away at the bombers overhead. Firing blind, they didn't have much hope of hitting them. All the same, Armstrong—who'd got dirt down the back of his neck from a near miss by his own side—snarled, "I hope they shoot those fuckers down."

"Bet your ass," Stowe said. "Goddamn bombers can't hit the broad side of a barn."

"Oh, I don't know about that," Armstrong said. "If they're aiming at us, they're pretty good shots."

"Ha! That'd be funny if only it was funny, you know what I mean?"

"Hell, yes," Armstrong said. "If I ever run into one of those fly-boys, I hope I come as close to killing him as he just came to killing me."

"Yeah! That's good!" Stowe said. "If I run into one of 'em, I think I would kill him. It's what he was trying to do to me. Only difference is, I'm good at what I do, and those bastards aren't."

Mortar bombs came whispering down on U.S. trenches and fox-holes. The Mormons often tried to repay whatever the USA did to them. After the ordnance the bombers had expended on their own men, the mortar rounds hardly seemed worth getting excited about. Again, Armstrong wondered how long he would take to get out of Utah and if he could somehow do it alive and in one piece.

As a lieutenant, junior grade, Sam Carsten had worn a thick gold stripe and a thin one on his jacket cuffs for a long time. A lieutenant wore two full stripes. Carsten didn't give a damn about the promotion. Some things were too dearly bought. He would rather have been a j.g. aboard the *Remembrance* than a lieutenant waiting for new orders at Pearl Harbor and contemplating a gloomy New Year.

Too many men were gone. He didn't know what had happened to Lieutenant Commander Pottinger. All he knew was that nobody'd fished the chief of the damage-control party out of the Pacific. Eye-chart Szczerbiakowicz hadn't made it back to Oahu, either. Some-body had said the sailor was wounded going into the drink and hadn't been able to stay afloat. And Captain Stein, an officer of the old school, had gone down with the *Remembrance*. Word was that he'd got a Medal of Honor for it. Much good the decoration did him.

Gloomily, Sam trudged over to the officers' club. He intended to see 1942 in smashed. He'd feel like grim death when he sobered up tomorrow morning, but he didn't care. He was too sorrowful to face the world sober.

Despite the loss of Midway—and of the only U.S. airplane carrier in the Pacific—a lot of officers were living it up. Some of them had wives along, others girlfriends. The band played a bouncy tune that mimicked Confederate rhythms without being too blatant about it.

Here and there, though, sat other gloomy men with slumped

shoulders, intent on the serious business of getting drunk. At the bar, one of them waved to Sam. Dan Cressy had four stripes on his sleeves these days. They'd promoted him to captain. By all the signs, that delighted him no more than Sam liked *his* promotion.

"Happy New Year, Carsten." Yes, if Cressy was happy, Sam wouldn't have wanted to see him sad.

Carsten sat down by the *Remembrance*'s exec and ordered a shot over ice. Even before the drink got there, he said, "It's a bastard, sir."

They made an odd pair: the aging lieutenant and the young, promising captain. They'd been through a lot together, though. Cressy said, "It's a bastard and a half, is what it is." He emptied his glass and signaled for a refill. "I'm ahead of you."

"Oh, that's all right," Sam answered. "I expect I can catch up." He got the shot, poured it down, and waved for another.

Both new drinks arrived at the same time. Cressy stared moodily into his. "This isn't how I wanted to get promoted, God damn it." He bit the words off one by one.

"No, sir. Me, neither," Sam said.

"I tried to get him to come away." Cressy was talking more to himself than to Sam. "I tried. I said the Navy needed him. I said the country needed him. I said . . . Well, it doesn't matter what I said. He looked at me and he told me, 'This is my ship, and she's sinking. Get off her, Commander. Good-bye and good luck.' So I got off her. What else could I do?"

"Nothing I can see. You got me off her the same way," Sam said.

"You." Commander—no, Captain—Cressy seemed to come back to himself, at least a little. He managed a smile of sorts for Sam. "I'd've kicked myself for the rest of my days if anything had happened to you."

That made Sam blink even as he knocked back his shot and waved for another reload. "Me?" His voice squeaked in surprise. He wondered when he'd last squeaked like that. Probably not since he'd joined the Navy, which was a hell of a long time ago now. "Nothing special about me, sir. Just a mustang who's long in the tooth."

With whiskey-fueled precision, Cressy started ticking off points on his fingers. "Item: there aren't that many mustangs to begin with. Coming up through the hawse hole's never been easy. Item: most of the mustangs I've known don't make very good officers. That doesn't mean they're not good men. They are, just about every one of them. And they have fine records as ratings, or they wouldn't have made officer's grade in the first place. But most of 'em don't have the imagination, the, the *breadth,* to make good officers. You're different."

"Thank you kindly. I don't know that it's true, but thank you. I try to do the best work I can, that's all."

The vehemence with which Captain Cressy shook his head spoke of how much he'd put away. "No. Any mustang, near enough, will do his particular job pretty well. Most of them won't care about anything outside their assignment, though. You aren't like that. How many times did you get chased out of the wireless shack?"

"Oh, maybe a few, sir," Sam allowed. "I like to know what's going on."

"That's what I'm saying," Cressy told him. "And you would always come up with something interesting in the officers' wardroom— always. You don't just want to know what's going on. You think about it, too, and you think straight."

Sam only shrugged. Praise made him uncomfortable. "Sir, you know ten times as much as I do."

"More, yes, but not ten times. How much schooling did you have before you enlisted?"

"Eighth grade, sir. About what you'd expect."

"Yes, about what I'd expect. On the other hand, I've got one of these." Cressy tapped his Annapolis class ring with the forefinger of his other hand. "If you had one of these, you'd hold flag rank now. You've . . . picked up your learning other ways, and that's a slower, harder business. I was talking about breadth a little while ago. You can make officer's rank with an eighth-grade education, but if you haven't got something more than that on the ball you won't go anywhere even if you do. That's what sets you apart from most mustangs. You've got that extra something."

"Fat lot of good it did me," Sam said bitterly. "I could know everything there was to know and I wouldn't've been able to douse that fire aft on the *Remembrance.*"

"Some things are bigger than you are, that's all," Cressy said. "You weren't the only one trying, you know."

"But I was in charge, dammit," Carsten said. "Well, Lieutenant Commander Pottinger was, God rest his soul, but I was the fellow with a hose in my hand."

"Some things are bigger than you are," Cressy repeated. "That fire was bigger than a man with a hose."

Sam wanted to argue with him. However much he wanted to, he knew he couldn't. The *Remembrance* had taken too many hits for any damage control to help. He changed the subject: "You'll have your own command now, sir. A cruiser at least—maybe a battleship."

"Not the way I wanted to get it," Cressy said once more. "And if I do go into business for myself, I'd sooner do it in another flattop. Trouble is, we haven't got any that are short a skipper, and we won't till they launch the ones that are building. And the carriers have the same trouble everything else has—getting stuff and people from A to B when A is west of Ohio and B is east or the other way round."

"What the hell can we do about that, sir?" Sam asked.

"Fight. Keep fighting. Not give up no matter what," Cressy answered. "The Japs can't hope to lick us. Oh, if we screw up bad enough, they may drive us out of the Sandwich Islands"—he grimaced at the thought—"but even if they do, they won't land three divisions south of Los Angeles. Britain and France can't lick us— same argument on the East Coast. And I don't see how the Confederates can lick us, either. They can hurt us. But I think we're too big and too strong for them to knock us flat and hold us down. We're the only people who can lick us. If we give up, if we lay down, we're in trouble. As long as we don't, we'll stay on our feet longer than anybody who's in there slugging with us."

Sam waved to the barkeep for another shot. Noticing Cressy's glass was also empty, he pointed to it and held up two fingers. The bartender nodded. As the man poured the drinks, Sam said, "I hope you're right, sir."

Cressy gave him a sad, sweet smile he never would have shown sober. "Hell, Carsten, so do I." He waited till the bartender brought the fresh drinks, then lifted his glass in salute. "And here's to you. Since they fished you out of the Pacific, where do you want to go from here?"

"I haven't really worried about it all that much, sir," Sam answered. "I'll go wherever they send me. If they want to leave me in damage control, well, I'll do that. I don't like it a whole lot, but I'm good at it by now. If they put me back in gunnery, that'd be better. Or if they finally give me something to do with airplanes, I'd like that the most. It's why I transferred over to the *Remembrance* in the first place, back when I was still a petty officer."

"If I were running the Bureau of Personnel, that's not what I'd do with you," Captain Cressy said.

"Sir?" A polite question was always safe.

"If it were up to me, I'd give you a ship," Cressy said, which made Sam want to jam a finger in his ear to make sure he'd heard right. The other officer went on, "I would. I'd give you a destroyer or a minelayer or a minesweeper. You could handle it, and I think you'd do a first-rate job."

"Th-Thank you, sir," Sam stammered. "I'm gladder than hell you think so." He wasn't nearly so sure he thought so himself, or that he wanted so much responsibility. But if he didn't, why had he tried to become an officer in the first place?

This time, Captain Cressy's smile was knowing. "Don't pop a gasket worrying about it, because the odds are long. BuPers doesn't know you the way I do. But they may stick you in a destroyer as exec under a two-and-a-half striper. Or they may give you something little—a sub chaser, say—and let you show what you can do with that."

"Well," Sam said wonderingly, and then again: "Well." Command hadn't occurred to him. Neither had serving as exec. He raised his glass in a salute of his own. "If they do give me the number-two slot somewhere, sir, the man I'll try to imitate is you."

"That's a real compliment," Cressy said. "I know who my models are. I suppose a few people in the Navy have picked up a pointer or two from me." He was sandbagging, and doubtless knew it. He pointed at Sam. "You'll have to do it your own way in the end, though, because you're you, not me. You've got years on me, and you've got all that experience as a rating. Use it. It'll do you good."

"Me? Command?" Sam didn't squeak this time, but he still did sound wondering, even to himself. He wondered if he could swing it. He'd understudied poor dead Pottinger in the damage-control party for years. The men had obeyed him about as well as they had the lieutenant commander. He'd always figured he could run the party if something ever happened to Pottinger. Now something damn well had, but it had happened to the *Remembrance,* too.

"You can do the job, Carsten. You can get the men to do what they're supposed to do, too," Cressy said. "You think I would say that if I didn't mean it?" He eyed Sam with owlish, booze-fueled intensity.

"Command," Sam said once more. He was feeling the whiskey, too. "Well, it's up to BuPers, not me." But now he couldn't help wondering what sort of orders the clerks back in Philadelphia would cut for him.

Sometimes January south of the Potomac was almost as bad as January up in Ontario. Sometimes, though, January here could feel like April up there. A high up close to fifty? A low above freezing? That hardly seemed like winter at all to Jonathan Moss.

He remembered flying in the Canadian winter during the Great War. More to the point, he remembered *not* flying most of the time. Bad weather—either snow or just low clouds—had kept fighters on the ground more often than not. Things weren't so bad here.

And the U.S. soldiers on the ground needed all the help they could get. They were trying to gain footholds on the south bank of the Rapidan, and not having a whole lot of luck. The only place where they'd gained any lodgement at all was in some truly miserable second-growth country that was marked on the map as the Wilderness. Having flown over it, Jonathan could see how it had got the name. The only reason the Confederates hadn't thrown the Army back into the river there was that they had as much trouble bringing men up to defend as the U.S. forces did in expanding their little bridgehead.

Moss' squadron listened in a tent as he briefed them. He whacked a large-scale map with a wooden pointer. "This is a ground-attack mission, gentlemen," he said. "We're going to shoot up the Confederates. Then we'll come home, gas up, get reloaded, and go back and do it again. We'll keep on doing it till they break. Have you got that? Any questions?"

Nobody said anything. Moss had a question of his own: *what happens if we keep hammering and they don't break?* He'd seen that more times than he could count in the last war. What happened was that a lot of men ended up dead and maimed. But he was the only Great War veteran here. The pilots he led were young and eager. He envied them. He was neither.

Eager or not, he was good at what he did. He wouldn't have lived through one war and the first six months of another if he hadn't been. And, eager or not, he was reasonably confident he'd come back to this airstrip once he and his men had worked over the Confederate positions. He'd made a lot of flights. What was one more?

The groundcrew men said his Wright was in fine fettle. He ran down the checklist himself just the same. They weren't going up there. He damn well was. Everything did seem all right. It almost always did. The day he didn't double-check, though, was bound to be the day when something went wrong.

Engine roaring, the fighter jounced along the runway and sprang into the air. Moss climbed quickly. He circled above the field, waiting for the men he led to join him. "Ready?" he called on the wireless.

"Ready!" The word dinned in his earphones.

"Then let's go." He flew south. A few puffs of smoke from bursting antiaircraft shells sprouted around the squadron. What dinned in Jonathan's earphones then were curses. He added a few of his own, or more than a few. They were still in U.S.-held territory, which meant their own side was doing its best to shoot them down. That its best wasn't quite good enough failed to reassure him.

Before long, they left the overenthusiastic gunners behind. From the air, the battlefield looked much more like those from the Great War than the Ohio ones had. Because the front had moved slowly here, things on both sides of it had been pounded and cratered in a way they hadn't farther west. The bombed-out landscape took Jonathan back half a lifetime across the years.

There was the Rappahannock. Hardly the blink of an eye later, there was the Rapidan, and the U.S. toehold on the far bank. The Wilderness had surely looked like what it was even before war came to it. Bombs and artillery and entrenchments did nothing to improve it.

Moss didn't want to shoot up his own side, even if his own side hadn't been shy about shooting at him. Green flares went up from the ground to mark U.S. positions. Anything beyond them was fair game. He swooped low over the battlefield, shooting up trenches and trucks and anything that caught his eye. A column of men in butternut tramping up a road dissolved like maple sugar in water under machine-gun fire.

Whoops of glee filled Moss' earphones. He let out shouts when he was shooting things up, too. It was fine sport—none finer—if you didn't think about the havoc you were wreaking on the ground. Watching trucks go up in flames, watching ant-sized men scatter in all directions, was like being inside an adventure film.

This had a drawback adventure films didn't: people shot back at you here. Confederate antiaircraft gunners and machine gunners and riflemen filled the air with lead. Strafing runs were more dangerous than bomber escort because of all the small-arms fire that couldn't touch you at altitude. Moss never worried about it very much. It was just something that came with the mission.

He was clawing his way up off the deck to go around for another pass when his engine suddenly quit. Smoke and steam gushed from it. Oil streamed back and smeared his windshield. A chunk of metal from the cowling slammed off the bulletproof glass, too.

"Shit," he said, and then something stronger. He gave the altimeter a quick glance—two thousand feet. If he didn't get out now, he never would. He cranked back the canopy, stood up in his seat, and bailed out.

He got away from the stricken fighter without smashing against the tail—always an escaping pilot's first worry. As soon as he was free, he yanked the ripcord. He didn't have a lot of time to waste, not down that low. The parachute opened with a loud *whump!* Moss' vision went red for a few seconds, then slowly cleared.

Another, smaller, *whump!* was a bullet going through the silk canopy above his head. He was a target hanging up here in the sky. If the Confederates on the ground wanted to shoot him, they could. They could shoot him by accident, too. Till he got down, he couldn't do anything about anything.

A tall column of black, greasy smoke rising from the ground not too far away had to be the Wright's funeral pyre. He shuddered. If the canopy had jammed, it would have been his funeral pyre, too.

Here came the ground. He steered away from a stand of trees

and towards a clearing. Then he wondered if he'd made a mistake, because soldiers in butternut came out of the woods. No help for it now. He bent his knees, bracing for the landing. He twisted an ankle, but that was all.

As he struggled to get out of the parachute harness, the soldiers ran up to him. He looked down the barrels of several automatic rifles and submachine guns. "Surrender!" three men yelled at the same time.

"Well, what the hell else am I going to do?" Moss asked irritably. "There!" He shed the harness. He knew of a man who'd had to cut his way free, and had cut off the tip of his thumb without even noticing till later.

One of the Confederates had a single bar on either side of his collar: a second lieutenant. "Can you walk, Yankee?" he asked.

"Let's see." Gingerly, Moss got to his feet and put weight on that ankle. "Kind of."

"Pull his teeth, somebody," the lieutenant said. A corporal plucked the .45 automatic from Moss' belt. The downed fighter pilot looked at it as if it belonged to somebody else—which it did, now. He'd been about as likely to yank it out and start shooting as to sprout wings and fly away without his airplane. Of course, the Confederates didn't know that. To them, if not to himself, he was still a dangerous character.

They also relieved him of his wristwatch. That was a different story. He let out a squawk: "My wife gave me that watch." It was one of the last things he had by which to remember Laura.

The lieutenant stuck it in his pocket. "And so?" he asked coolly. Moss wondered whether a sob story would do him any good. He didn't wonder for more than about three seconds, though. They didn't *have* to take prisoners, no matter what the Geneva Convention said. Not every fighting man who fell into enemy hands ended up in a POW camp. If they shot him now, who'd know? Who'd care? Nobody and nobody, respectively. When Moss kept his mouth shut, the lieutenant nodded and said, "I reckoned you were a smart fellow. Now get moving."

He got moving. He couldn't go very fast, but they didn't push him. As long as they were herding him along, they were doing something clearly line-of-duty and just as clearly not very hard. That came close to a soldier's ideal. One of them even cut a branch off a pine and trimmed it with his bayonet to make Moss a walking stick. He took it gratefully. It helped.

They'd spread camouflage netting and branches over their tents. That must have worked; they didn't seem to have been shot up. The lieutenant took Moss into a tent where a man in his thirties with three bars on each side of his collar—a captain—sat behind a folding table doing paperwork. "Captured the damnyankee flier we heard going down," the lieutenant said proudly.

"Good work." By the casual way the captain said it, this sort of thing happened every day, which was bullshit of the purest ray serene. The captain looked at Moss and said, "For you, the war is over."

How many bad films about the Great War had he seen, to come out with a line like that? Moss almost laughed in his face. But it wasn't really a laughing matter, not when he could still suffer an unfortunate accident—and when the captain was right. "Looks that way to me, too," Moss said.

The captain got down to business. "Give me your particulars."

"Jonathan Moss. Major, U.S. Army." He rattled off his pay number. He knew it as well as he knew his name.

"What was your mission?" the Confederate officer asked.

"I've told you everything the laws of war say I have to," Moss answered, and waited to see what happened next. If the captain felt like giving him the third degree . . . he couldn't do a whole hell of a lot about it.

But the man just said, "Well, we can't keep you here. We don't have the setup to hold prisoners. Jenkins!"

"Yes, sir!" the lieutenant said.

"Take him into Spotsylvania. They'll have a jail there. He won't get out till they can take him down to the Carolinas or Georgia or one of those places where they've got themselves POW camps."

"Yes, sir," the lieutenant repeated. Into Spotsylvania Moss went. *Hell of a name for a town,* he thought, but that was one more thing he kept quiet about. The auto was of Confederate make, but looked and performed like one built in the USA. Two soldiers with submachine guns sitting behind Moss discouraged any thoughts of adventure.

The jail was a squat red-brick building. The sheriff considerately gave Moss a cell as far away from the drunk tank as he could. It had a cot and a chamber pot and a pitcher and cup and basin. The water was cool, not cold. Moss drank it anyway. The bars all looked very solid. He rattled them. They were. He sighed and lay down on the cot. *For you, the war is over.* And so it was.

Brigadier General Abner Dowling was not a happy man. For Dowling, that made anything but a man-bites-dog headline. What with long service under George Armstrong Custer, even longer service in hate-filled Utah, and brief service trying to hold back the Confederate thrust into Ohio, he hadn't had a lot to be happy about. When some of your fonder memories were of a Salt Lake City sporting house, you hadn't lived life for the fun of it.

He wasn't enjoying himself much here in Virginia, either. His corps had borne the brunt of the Confederate flank attack. They'd contained it, but they'd been badly battered in the process. The counterattack against the right and the coming of winter had slowed the U.S. advance—intended to be as quick and ferocious as the Confederate drive that had opened the fighting—to a crawl right out of 1915.

And now Daniel MacArthur had a new brainstorm. As Dowling's driver took him over the icy roads to MacArthur's headquarters in Warrenton, he wondered what the army commander had come up with this time. MacArthur's last inspiration had led to this bloody stalemate. Dowling was more than a little surprised to see the flamboyant officer get a second chance. He wondered what MacArthur would do with it.

When fighters roared by overhead, he wondered if he would live to find out. The Confederates still came over and harried road traffic in U.S.-held territory, just as U.S. airplanes shot up motorcars farther south. But either these were U.S. fighters or the Confederates didn't think the middle-aged Buick worth wasting ammunition on, for he came through unscathed.

Warrenton was nothing special. It had gone from Virginia to West Virginia, from the CSA to the USA, after the Great War, and had never got over it. YANKEES GO HOME! graffiti, others saying

FREEDOM!, and whitewashed patches covering up more such love notes scarred the walls. Dowling saw no U.S. soldiers by themselves. Everybody always had at least one buddy along, which spoke volumes about how much the locals thought of themselves as U.S. citizens.

Daniel MacArthur had appropriated the fanciest house in town for his headquarters. That struck Dowling as utterly in character. If MacArthur had made one more Warrentonian turn scarlet about the United States and everything they stood for . . . Dowling, frankly, wasn't going to give a damn.

The neoclassical columned portico made him feel as if he were walking into a government building in Philadelphia or Washington. The only difference was, the architect here had shown better taste and more restraint than builders in the USA's capitals were in the habit of doing.

"Good afternoon, General." MacArthur greeted him in the foyer.

It was getting on toward evening, but Dowling didn't argue. "Good afternoon, sir." He saluted. Grandly, MacArthur returned the courtesy. His long, lean toothpick of a body was made for the grand, arrogant gesture. Built more along the lines of a refrigerator, Dowling had to make do with competence. He asked, "What have you got in mind, sir? Some way to punch through the Wilderness?" He didn't think any such way existed. His superior was all too likely to own a different opinion. Which of them turned out to be right might prove a different question, but MacArthur had more stars on his shoulder straps than Dowling.

The cigarette in MacArthur's long, fancy holder quivered. Excitement? Disdain? Who could tell? "Come with me to the map room," the U.S. general commanding said. You couldn't fight a war without maps. Only MacArthur would make it sound as if he never looked at them outside of this one room.

He led Dowling to a chamber that was indeed full of maps. To Dowling's surprise, he pointed to a large-scale one that showed all over Virginia and the surrounding states, both U.S. and C.S. "I'm sorry, sir, but I can't make it out from this alone," Dowling said.

"No?" By MacArthur's tone, he'd just proved himself a moron. "What I aim to do, General, is force the Confederates to divide their forces by making a surprise landing at the mouth of the James and advancing on Richmond along the river." He struck a pose, plainly waiting for Dowling to acclaim his genius.

Whatever else you could say about him, he didn't think small. But there *were* other things to say. Dowling didn't scream, *Are you out of your goddamn mind, sir?* He was proud of himself because he didn't. It showed commendable restraint on his part—that was how he saw it, anyway.

"Didn't General McClellan try that same move during the War of Secession?" he inquired, hoping to lead MacArthur back to reality by easy stages.

"He did indeed," MacArthur said. "But he didn't move fast enough. The only thing about McClellan that might have moved fast enough was his bowels."

Dowling fought back a startled giggle. From everything he'd read about McClellan, that was gospel truth. Even so, he said, "But you have to worry about things he didn't—the Confederates' Navy and their bombers, for instance. If you do land a force, can you supply it?"

"By God, I can. By God, I will." MacArthur stuck out his granite chin, as if to say he needed nothing but determination.

It wasn't that simple, as Dowling knew too well. "Sir, they'll have artillery that can reach our rear, too," he said. "General McClellan didn't have to worry about that kind of thing, either."

Outside the map room, light drained from the sky. MacArthur looked at him as if he'd just crawled out, all pallid and moist, from under a flat rock. "I had hoped you would show confidence in the fighting ability of the American soldier, General," he said stiffly.

"Sir, I do. I'm more confident of that than of just about anything else in the world," Dowling answered. "But I also think we shouldn't have to depend on his fighting ability by itself. I think he ought to go into battle with a plan that gives him the best chance to win without getting slaughtered."

Now Daniel MacArthur looked as if he wanted to step on what had crawled out from under the flat rock. "Are you saying my plan does not meet that criterion? I must tell you, I beg to differ." He didn't beg to differ; he demanded.

Instead of answering directly, Dowling asked, "What does the General Staff think of your scheme?"

MacArthur snapped his fingers with contempt a Shakespearean

actor might have envied. "That for the General Staff!" he said. "If they fart, they'll blow their brains out."

Custer would have agreed with that, and would have laughed himself into a coughing fit when he heard it. Dowling persisted: "Have you submitted this plan to them?"

"I don't need to," MacArthur said. "I command in the Virginia theater."

"Well, yes, sir. Of course, sir." Dowling might have been trying to soothe a dangerous lunatic. As far as he was concerned, that was exactly what he was doing. He went on, "But if you're going to land troops at the mouth of the James, you'll need some help from the Navy, you know."

"Oh, I have that." MacArthur waved away such trivial concerns. "Rear Admiral Halsey, the commander of the Southern Shore Naval District, is confident he can give me everything I need along those lines."

"Is he?" Dowling said tonelessly. He hadn't known the Navy also had a wild man running around loose. He supposed it was fate—probably a malign fate—that let this other officer link up with MacArthur. "Does the Navy Department have any idea what he's up to?"

"General Dowling, your continual carping questions grow tiresome in the extreme," MacArthur said. "I thought you would be eager to come to grips with the enemy in some new place. I see I was unduly optimistic."

"I would have been more eager to come to grips with him here in northern Virginia if the attack hadn't been delayed so long," Dowling said.

Daniel MacArthur's face went a dusky, blotchy red. "Good evening," he choked out.

"Good evening, sir." Dowling saluted again and left MacArthur's sanctum sanctorum. If the other man wanted to relieve him, Dowling wouldn't lose any sleep over it. Even going back to Philadelphia might be a relief after serving under such a prima donna. *I've done this before. I don't need to do it again,* Dowling thought.

His driver was smoking a cigarette when he got out to the motorcar. When the man said, "Where to now, sir?" he had whiskey as well as smoke on his breath. Either he carried a flask or he'd made a friend while waiting for Dowling to emerge.

"Back to my headquarters," Dowling said, and then, "Do you want me to do the driving?"

"Oh, no, sir. I'm fine," the driver assured him, unabashed. "I just had a nip. I didn't get smashed or anything."

"All right." Dowling waited to see if it was. It seemed to be. The driver shifted gears smoothly, didn't speed, and didn't wander all over the road. Considering that the taped-over headlamps didn't reach much farther than a man could spit, not speeding was an especially good idea.

Dowling kept a hand on his sidearm all the way back. Confederate bushwhackers sometimes took potshots at passing autos. He didn't intend to go down without shooting back. What he intended to do and what he got a chance to do might prove two different things. He understood that, even if he didn't want to think about it.

He wondered whether Daniel MacArthur had ever grasped the difference between intention and reality. All the signs said he hadn't, any more than George Custer had before him. Once, Custer had proved spectacularly right. By substituting his own view of what barrels could do for War Department doctrine, he'd gone a long way toward winning the Great War for the USA. Before that, though, how many soldiers in green-gray had he slaughtered in his headlong attacks on entrenched Confederate positions? Tens of thousands, surely.

Maybe MacArthur's plan for a landing at the mouth of the James and a drive on Richmond from the southeast was a brilliant move that would win the war. Then again, maybe it wasn't. It hadn't been for McClellan, eighty years ago now. MacArthur was without a doubt a better general than McClellan had been. Of course, saying that was like saying something smelled better than a skunk. It might be true, but how much did it tell you?

Once Dowling had got back, he went to his code book for the five-letter groups that let him ask Colonel John Abell, WHAT IS GENERAL STAFF'S VIEW OF PROPOSED LANDING? He handled that personally; he didn't want even his signals officer knowing anything about it. MacArthur would probably guess where the leak came from. *Too bad,* Dowling thought.

The answer, also coded, came back inside half an hour. That didn't surprise Dowling. Colonel Abell damn near lived at his desk.

Dowling also did his own decoding. WHAT PROPOSED LANDING? Abell asked.

"Ha!" Dowling said, and found the groups for a new message: SUGGEST YOU INQUIRE COMMANDING GENERAL THIS THEATER. If the General Staff decided the plan was brilliant, they'd let MacArthur go ahead. So Dowling told himself, anyhow. But he also told himself somebody other than the scheme's originator ought to look at it before it went forward.

He didn't hear from Colonel Abell again. He also didn't receive a detonation from Daniel MacArthur. Abell knew when to be subtle, then. MacArthur pulled no troops from Dowling's command to go into a landing force. That didn't leave Dowling downhearted, not at all. Sometimes what didn't happen was as important as what did.

In spite of everything, reports from Philadelphia did get back to Richmond. They took a while, but they got here. Clarence Potter, unlike a lot of people in the Confederate government and military these days, was a patient man. Sooner or later, he expected he would find out what he needed to know.

One of the things he'd grown interested in was how reports got from Richmond to Philadelphia, to whatever opposite numbers he had there. A clerk in the U.S. War Department had sent by a round-about route a U.S. report that . . . quoted Potter, as a matter of fact.

I believe the situation with regard to the Negroes in Mississippi is hectic, and our response to it must be dynamic. Seeing his own words come back was interesting—and exciting, too. He'd written several versions of that report. In another, he called the situation *distressing* and the needed response *ferocious;* in yet another, the key-words were *alarming* and *merciless;* and so on. He had a list of where the report with each set of keywords had been distributed. He kept that list in his wallet. No one but him could possibly get at it.

When he took out the list, he checked to see where the relevant words were *hectic* and *dynamic.* Then, whistling to himself, he went to Lieutenant General Forrest's office. He had to cool his heels in an anteroom for half an hour before he could see the chief of the Confederate General Staff. By the glum expressions on the faces of the two major generals who emerged from Forrest's inner office, they would have been glad to let him go before them.

"Good morning, General," Nathan Bedford Forrest III said when Potter came in at last. "Sometimes you have to take people out to the woodshed. It's not a hell of a lot of fun, but it's part of the job."

"Yes, sir. You're right on both counts." Potter closed the door behind him and lowered his voice: "You're right on both counts, and you've got a Yankee spy somewhere in the Operations and Training Section."

"Son of a bitch," Forrest said. "*Son* of a bitch! So your cute little scheme there paid off, did it?"

"Yes, sir." Clarence Potter nodded in somber satisfaction. "When I drafted that report on the guerrilla situation in Mississippi, I varied the words in some of the most important sentences. Each version went to a different section here in the War Department and in the State Department. If a spy sent it north and one of our people in the USA got it back to me, I'd know where it came from. I've had to wait longer than I wanted to, but that's part of the game."

"Operations and Training, eh?" A savage gleam came into Forrest's eyes. His great-grandfather had probably worn that same expression just before he drew his saber and charged some luckless damnyankee cavalryman. "You have any idea who the snake in the grass is?"

"No, sir," Potter answered. "I can't even prove he's the only spy in the War Department. But I know he's there, and I can think of a couple of different ways to get after him."

"I'm all ears," Forrest said.

"One would be to do the same thing I did this time: make several versions of a report, one for each subsection of O and T. The problem with that is, getting results back from the USA is slow and uncertain," Potter said. "The other one is the usual—seeing who has a grudge, seeing who's spending more money than his salary accounts for, seeing who all had access to the report, and on and on. You'll have plenty of people who can do that for you; you don't need me to give them lessons."

"Let's try both approaches," Nathan Bedford Forrest III said after only the barest pause for thought. "You fix up another report— hell, make it on the organization and training of spies. They'll sit up and take notice of that. We'll use it to winnow out suspects, or we'll try to, anyway. And we'll do the usual things, too. We don't want to miss a trick here."

Potter nodded. "All right, sir. I'll take care of it. I wonder how much this bastard has given the USA without our ever noticing it."

"When we catch him, we'll squeeze him like an orange," the chief of the General Staff promised. "Oh, yes. I have plenty of people who can take care of that for me, too."

"No doubt, sir." Now Potter did his best to hide his distaste. Intelligence work wasn't always about friendly persuasion. Potter didn't shrink from straightforward brutality, but he didn't relish it, either. Some people did. They usually made better Freedom Party stalwarts and other sorts of strongarm men than they did spies— usually, but not always.

"You did a terrific job here, Potter," Forrest said. "Your country won't forget."

"This is just a start. When we catch this son of a bitch, then I've done something," Potter said.

"Well, at least we're looking in the right place now—or one of the right places." Forrest looked harried. "Jesus Christ! We're liable to be ass-deep in these stinking Yankees."

"Every one we ferret out is one we don't have to worry about later." Potter didn't say that one captured spy would lead to others. It was possible, but not likely. If the Yankees had the brains God gave a blue crab, they'd have each spy sending what he found to someone he never saw, didn't know, and would have a hard time betraying. Jack Smith wouldn't know that Joe Doakes three desks over was also selling out his country. They could eat lunch together every day for twenty years without finding out about each other. He'd organized things in Philadelphia and Washington that way. His counterparts in green-gray would do the same thing.

"You fix up some fresh bait." Nathan Bedford Forrest III might have been on a fishing trip. And so he was—but he hoped to fry up a nastier catch than crappie or bluegill. "We'll take it from there."

Potter recognized dismissal when he heard it. He got to his feet and saluted. "Yes, sir." Out he went, coldly pleased with himself. He wished he could have talked with Anne Colleton about what he'd done. She would have appreciated it. She might have thought of it herself—she'd been nobody's fool. If she hadn't gone down to Charleston the day the Yankee carrier raided . . .

He shrugged. Bad luck came to everybody. You had to look at it that way, or else the voices that came to you in the wee small hours of bad nights started showing up at all hours every day. You weren't good for anything then, to yourself or to anybody else. Bury your dead, drink a toast to them now and again, and move on. As long as you kept moving, you made a hard target.

They'd get you anyway, of course. Odds were, though, they'd take longer.

He sat down at his desk. It wasn't as if he had nothing to do. He'd pile those bait reports on top of everything else. *No rest for the weary,* he thought. Or was it *for the wicked?* He never could remember. And what difference did it make? It fit either way.

He swore when the telephone rang. There went a perfectly good train of thought. He wondered if he'd be able to find it again. The telephone went on ringing. He picked it up. "Clarence Potter here." Anybody who didn't know he was in Intelligence had no business calling on this line.

"Hello, Potter, you sly son of a bitch. General Forrest tells me you really are as smart as you think you are."

"Thank you, Mr. President—I suppose." Potter wasn't inclined to let anyone praise more faintly than he did.

Neither was Jake Featherston. Laughing, he said, "You're welcome—I reckon." His good humor never lasted long. He went on, "That was a good piece of work. We've got to make sure the damnyankees aren't looking over our shoulder and reading our cards before we ever set 'em down."

"Yes, sir." Potter hoped his resignation didn't show. In spite of everything the Confederate States could do, the United States *were* going to find out some of what they were up to. The countries were too similar and shared too long a border to keep that from happening. He went on, "As long as we find out more about what they're up to, we're ahead of the game."

"I don't just aim to be ahead of the game. I aim to win it and then kick over the goddamn table." Featherston sounded perfectly serious. He also sounded as angry as usual—*not at me,* Potter judged, *but at the USA.*

Really whipping the United States, whipping them to a point where they couldn't hope to fight back, had always been the Confederate dream. Featherston still believed it. Maybe that made him crazy. Potter had long thought so. He wasn't so sure any more.

"Gotta knock 'em flat," Featherston went on. "Gotta knock 'em flat and never let 'em build up again. They tried it with us at the end of the Great War, but they couldn't make it stick. When we do it, we'll fuckin' do it right."

Potter remembered U.S. inspectors in Charleston harbor making sure the Confederate States adhered to the armistice they'd signed. But Jake Featherston was right; the USA hadn't kept that up for long. The United States had wanted to forget about the war, to enjoy what they'd won. They were able to afford it—they *had* won. For the Confederates, everything since then had been about getting even. With Featherston, everything still was.

If he made the damnyankees say uncle, he wouldn't forget about holding them down. He wanted nothing more than to stand on them with a boot on their neck. For as long as he lived, the United States would go through hell on earth. And if anything could make Jake Featherston a happy man—which was by no means obvious—that would be it.

What would happen after Jake finally went? Potter wondered if the President of the CSA had ever wondered about that. The Intelligence officer doubted it. Everything was personal with Jake Featherston. If it didn't have him in it, he didn't give a damn. Whatever happened after he was gone would just have to take care of itself.

"How would you like to run the operation that makes sure the damnyankees keep on being good little boys and girls?" Featherston asked.

Not only was everything personal with him, he knew who had an axe to grind, and which axe it was. He assumed everybody took things as personally as he did. *He knows just what to offer me, by God,* Potter thought. He said, "If we get there, I'll do that job for you, Mr. President."

"Oh, we'll get there. Don't you worry about that. Don't worry about it even for a minute." As usual, Jake sounded messianically certain. By being so sure himself, he made other people sure, too. And when they were sure, they could do things they never would have imagined possible before.

The Confederate States had done some things Clarence Potter wouldn't have imagined possible. Could they do more? Could they flatten the United States? A smaller country flatten a bigger one and hold it down? Before this war started, Potter never would have believed it. Now—and especially after he listened to Jake Featherston for a while—he really thought he did.

Hipolito Rodriguez hadn't needed long to decide that Assault Troop Leader Billy Joe Hamilton put him in mind of his Great War drill sergeant. "I want y'all to listen up. Listen up real good, you hear?" he'd say several times a day, sticking out his chin to seem even meaner than he did already. "Y'all better listen up good, on account of I ain't got the time to say this shit over and over."

He gave his warning over and over. He didn't seem to realize that. Rodriguez didn't challenge him on it. Neither did any of the other men in his training group. Challenge an instructor and you lost even if you won.

"Anybody here ever hear people talk about a population reduction?" Hamilton asked one day.

A few men from the Confederate Veterans' Brigade raised their hands. The ones Rodriguez knew came from big cities—Richmond, Atlanta, New Orleans.

"Means 'I'll fix you,' somethin' like that, right?" Hamilton said. "Folks say, 'I'll reduce your population, you son of a bitch,' right? Doesn't make a whole hell of a lot of sense, but who said the way people talk's gotta make sense, right? *Right?*"

"Right!" the men chorused. If loud agreement was what the Freedom Party guard wanted, they'd give it to him.

"That's a bunch of bullshit," he said now. "When *we* talk about reducing population, we goddamn well mean it. Too many niggers in this country, right? Gotta do somethin' about that, right? *Right?*"

"Right!" The chorus sounded odd this time. Some of the men bayed out the word in voices full of savage enthusiasm, while others sounded oddly doubtful. Rodriguez's tones were somewhere in the middle. He had no use for *mallates,* but he'd never been filled with blood lust, either.

The Party guard studied his students. "Some of you sorry sons of bitches are gonna puke like you wouldn't believe when we get rolling on this here job. Some of y'all won't be able to cut it. We'll have to ship your asses home—either that or put you in an easier line of work."

"How come?" somebody in back of Rodriguez called.

"How come?" Billy Joe Hamilton echoed. "You'll find out how come. Bet your balls you will. I got one other thing to tell you, too— no matter how tough y'all reckon you got it, you don't know squat about what tough is. Fellas who were doin' this before we got the system down, they're the ones who can talk about tough. What they saw is tougher'n any battlefield."

"Bullshit." This time, it was a man off to Rodriguez's left. Rodriguez was thinking the same thing himself. Nothing was worse than a battlefield. Nothing could be. He was convinced of that. The Devil hadn't known how to run hell before he took a long look at a Great War battlefield.

"I heard that," Hamilton said. "You go ahead. You think that way. Y'all'll find out what it's like now. But that ain't a patch on what camp guards *were* doin'. No, sir, not even a patch."

Rodriguez remained dubious. Everybody who was an old-timer at this, that, or the other thing always went on and on about how tough things had been before all these new fellows came in. Talk was cheap. Talk was also commonly nonsense.

Camp guards learned by doing. They ran their own camp, out there past Decatur, Texas. They were Great War veterans, every man jack of them. They knew all they needed to know about barbed wire and machine guns. Most of them had taken prisoners, too. Some of them had *been* prisoners, which also taught a lot about what they needed to know.

Submachine guns were new to Rodriguez, but easy to learn. For guard duty, they were better than the bolt-action Tredegar he'd carried during the last war. No one bullet had the stopping power of a Tredegar round, but you could do a lot of shooting mighty fast with a submachine gun. If you got in trouble in the camp, that mattered more.

"Never trust the niggers here. Never believe the niggers here," Assault Troop Leader Hamilton told his pupils. "You do, you'll end up with your throat cut. They didn't get in here on account of they was nice people. They got here on account of they was trouble."

That Rodriguez believed. The blacks in the camp looked like men who would raise hell if they ever got the chance. They looked like captured enemy soldiers, as a matter of fact. In essence, they were. Rodriguez figured he would have been safer guarding Yankee prisoners. They would have been less desperate than the Negroes here.

A truck with an iron box of a cargo compartment pulled up to the camp. At the morning roll call, the experienced guards picked twenty Negroes from the lineup. "You men are going to be transferred to another camp," one of them told the blacks.

There were the usual grumbles. "I jus' got here two weeks ago," a prisoner complained. "How come you shippin' me somewheres else?"

"To confuse you. Working pretty good, isn't it?" the guard answered. The prisoner scratched his head. He didn't know how to take that, and so he warily accepted it.

Rodriguez was one of the guards outside the barbed-wire perimeter who made sure the Negroes didn't try to run off on their way to the truck. The black men gave no trouble. Most of them seemed glad to get away from where they were. One of the experienced guards closed the doors behind the prisoners and dogged them shut. The bar that did the trick seemed exceptionally sturdy.

"We'll need a driver," Hamilton said. Rodriguez didn't volunteer; he couldn't drive.

They packed him and the other trainee prison guards into a couple of ordinary trucks with butternut canvas canopies over their beds. Those trucks followed the one with the Negro prisoners. Rodriguez wondered where they were going. He didn't know of any other camps close by. Of course, Texas had more empty space than it knew what to do with. Maybe there were others, somewhere not too far over the horizon.

His truck ride lasted about an hour. Looking out at where he'd been—he couldn't see where he was going—he found he'd passed through a gate in a perimeter marked off by barbed wire. *Maybe it's another camp after all*, he thought.

The truck stopped. "Everybody out!" Billy Joe Hamilton yelled. "Y'all got work to do!"

Out Rodriguez came. Like a lot of the other middle-aged men who'd ridden with him, he grunted and stretched. His back ached. The truck had been anything but comfortable.

The other truck, the one with the Negroes in it, had stopped, too, at the edge of a long, deep trench a bulldozer had scraped in the ground. Rodriguez looked around. All he saw was prairie. They were a long way from anything that mattered. He nodded to himself. He remembered this kind of landscape from when he'd fought in the Great War, though he'd been farther west then.

"You!" Hamilton pointed to him. "Open the rear doors on that there truck."

"Yes, Assault Troop Leader!" Rodriguez answered. His pure English would never be great, but he followed what other people said to him, and he could speak enough to get by. Nobody'd complained about the way he talked.

He went over to the truck with the iron box for a passenger compartment. He needed a moment, but no more than a moment, to figure out how the heavy bar that kept the doors closed was secured. He got it loose before the Freedom Party guard either showed him or brushed him aside as a goddamn dumb greaser. That done, he grabbed the handles and pulled the doors open.

"¡Madre de Dios!" he exclaimed as the fecal stink poured out of the compartment and into the chilly air. He crossed himself, not once but two or three times in quick succession. None of the blacks in the truck remained alive. They sprawled atop one another in unlovely, ungainly death.

"Isn't this smooth?" Hamilton said. "We take 'em out, we drive 'em off, and they're dead by the time they get where they're goin'. Matter of fact, the only place they're goin' is straight to hell." He shook his head, correcting himself. "Nope—other place they're goin' is right into this here ditch. Y'all drag 'em out of the truck and fling 'em in. Then the 'dozer'll scrape the dirt back over 'em, and that'll be the end of that. Good riddance to bad rubbish." He made hand-washing motions.

Nobody said no. The trainees did the job willingly enough. It didn't bother Rodriguez all that much once he got over his first horrified astonishment. The Freedom Party hadn't been kidding when it said it wanted to put Negroes in their place. After all the trouble they'd caused the Confederate States, he wasn't going to lose much sleep over what happened to them.

Into the ditch thudded the corpses, one after another. They were still limp; they hadn't started to stiffen. *Good riddance to bad rubbish,* the Freedom Party guard had said. To him, and to Hipolito Rodriguez as well, that was all they were. Rubbish.

Somebody asked what struck him as a practical question: "Can we kill 'em off faster'n they breed?"

"Oh, you bet your ass we can." Assault Troop Leader Hamilton sounded as if he hadn't the slightest doubt. "If we want to bad enough, we can do any goddamn thing we please. And Jake Featherston wants to do this really bad. Whatever we have to do to take care of it, well, that's what we do. Pretty soon, we don't got to worry about niggers no more."

The guards murmured among themselves. Most of the murmurs sounded approving to Rodriguez. Nobody who didn't see this as at least a possibility would have volunteered for camp-guard duty.

Wiping his hands on his trousers, a trainee asked Hamilton, "How come this used to be a tougher duty than it is now?"

"On account of these trucks are new," the Freedom Party guard answered. "Up until not so long ago, guards had to shoot the niggers they needed to get rid of." His voice was altogether matter-of-fact. "That was hard on everybody. Some guards just couldn't stand the strain, poor bastards. And the niggers knew what was comin' when they got marched outa camp, too. Made 'em twice as dangerous as they would've been otherwise. Some fella named Pinkard, runs a camp over in Mississippi or Louisiana—one o' them places—came up with this here instead."

"*¡Madre de Dios!*" Rodriguez said again, this time in an altogether different tone of voice.

"What's eatin' you?" the Party guard asked.

"I know this Pinkard—or a Pinkard, anyhow," Rodriguez answered. "We fight together here in Texas in the Great War. Not many with this name, I think."

"Reckon maybe you're right," the Freedom Party man agreed. "Ain't that a kick in the nuts? This here Pinkard, he's come up a long ways since then. Runnin' a camp, that's like commanding a regiment."

Rodriguez tried to imagine Jefferson Pinkard as a high-ranking officer. It wasn't easy. It was, in fact, damn hard. The Pinkard he'd known had been an ordinary soldier—till he started having woman trouble. After that, all he'd cared about was killing damnyankees. Up until then, he'd been like any sensible fighting man, more interested in staying alive himself than in getting rid of the enemy. But afterwards . . . Afterwards, he hadn't cared whether he lived or died.

Evidently he'd lived. And now a lot of *mallates* were efficiently dead because he had. Rodriguez shrugged and pulled one of them out of the truck. Who'd miss them, after all?

XIX

They'd sent Irving Morrell to a military hospital outside of Syracuse, New York. The sprawling wooden building had enormous Red Crosses painted on the roof, in case Confederate bombers came that far north. Up till now, none had. Syracuse had to seem like the end of the world to the Confederates. It sure as hell seemed like the end of the world to Morrell.

Dr. Silverstein had told him his shoulder would heal well. And it was healing—but not nearly fast enough to suit him. He looked at the snow blowing by outside and asked, "How long before I get out of here?"

The sawbones currently in charge of him was named Conrad Rohde. "I don't know, exactly," he answered. "A few weeks, I expect."

"That's what everybody's been telling me for—a few weeks now," Morrell said irritably.

Dr. Rohde shrugged. He was a big, blond, slow-moving man. Nothing seemed to faze him. A bad-tempered colonel sure didn't. "Do you *want* a wound infection?" he inquired. "You told me you had one of those the last time you got shot. You're older than you were then, you know."

"Oh, yeah? Since when?" Even Morrell's sarcasm drew nothing more than a chuckle from Rohde. Morrell did know he was older than he had been in 1914. Even with the wound infection that didn't want to go away, he'd got his strength back then a hell of a lot faster than he was now.

"Do your exercises," Rohde told him, and went off to inflict his resolute good cheer on some other injured soldier.

"Exercises." Morrell said it as if it were a four-letter word. He started opening and closing and flexing his right hand. It didn't hurt as much as it had when he'd begun doing it. Then it had felt as if his whole right arm were being dipped in boiling oil. Now he just imagined he had a wolverine gnawing at his shoulder joint. This was progress, of a sort.

Dr. Rohde insisted that the more he did the exercises, the easier they would become. To Morrell, that only proved that Dr. Rohde, no matter how smart and well trained he was, had never got shot. Morrell wished he could say the same thing.

Instead, he got an oak-leaf cluster for his Purple Heart, an honor he would gladly have done without. The decoration looked absurd on the green-gray government-issue pajamas he wore.

Even though the exercises hurt, he did keep up with them. He'd done that with his wounded leg, too, once it finally healed enough to let him. His thigh still twinged every once in a while, but he could use it as well as the other. Dr. Rohde beamed at him a few days later. "You are a conscientious man, Colonel."

"Doc, what I am is one stubborn son of a bitch." The two phrases meant the same thing, but Morrell preferred his version. He went on, "Long as you're here, Doc, I've got a question for you."

"If I know the answer, you will have it." Rohde still looked and sounded mighty cheerful for a medical man. Morrell wondered if he'd been getting into the prescription brandy.

Well, if he had, that would only make his tongue flap more freely. Morrell asked, "Am I the only officer you know of who's been specifically targeted, or are the Confederates really trying to knock off people who know what they're doing?"

"I did not know you had been, let alone any others," Rohde said.

So much for that, Morrell thought. Aloud, he said, "I damn well was. That sniper bastard took two more shots at me after I got hit, when they were carrying me off to cover." *And thank God for Sergeant Pound's strong, broad back.* "He missed me by a gnat's whisker both times, and he didn't even try for anybody else. So am I just lucky, or is Jake Featherston trying to kill officers who've shown that they're competent?"

"Let me try to find out." Dr. Rohde pulled a notepad from the breast pocket of his long white jacket. He scribbled something on the pad, then stuck it back in the pocket.

"You going to be able to read that?" Morrell gibed.

Rohde took the pad out again, wrote something else in it, tore out that sheet of paper, set it on Morrell's bed, and left his room. Morrell picked up the paper with his good hand. *Mind your own goddamn beeswax,* he read. The script was an elegant copperplate; a schoolteacher would have envied it. Morrell laughed out loud. There went one cliché, shot down like a dive bomber with a fighter on its tail.

For the next few days, Conrad Rohde was all business. Morrell wondered if he'd really offended the doctor. He didn't think he should have, but how could anybody know for sure? Maybe he'd been the fourth guy to rag on Rohde's writing in the space of an hour and a half. That would frost anybody's pumpkin.

At the end of the examination, though, the doctor said, "I haven't forgotten about what you asked. I'm trying to find out."

"All right," Morrell said mildly. "Uh—thanks."

"You're welcome," Rohde answered. "For whatever you may think it's worth, some of the people to whom I've put your question seem to think it's very interesting."

"I'd rather they thought I was full of hops," Morrell said. "The war would be easier if they did."

Rohde didn't say anything about that. He just finished writing up Morrell's vital signs and left the room. When he came back that afternoon, he set another sheet of paper from his notepad on the bed. Again, he left without saying a word.

Morrell read the sheet. In that same precise script—*rub it in, Doc, why don't you?* he thought—Rohde had listed seven names. Beside four of them, he'd written KIA. Beside the other three was the word *wounded.* Morrell recognized five of the names. He knew two of the men personally, and knew of the other three. They were all officers who were good at whatever they happened to do: infantry, artillery, one a genius at logistics. That lieutenant-colonel had KIA by his name; someone else, someone surely less capable, was filling his slot now.

The doctor didn't return till the following morning. By then, Morrell had all he could do not to explode. "They are!" he exclaimed. "The sons of bitches damn well are!"

"So it would seem," Rohde answered. "You've certainly found a pattern. Whether the pattern means something is now under investigation."

"If it's there, it has to mean something," Morrell said.

But the doctor shook his head. "If you're in a crap game and somebody rolls four sevens in a row, that just means he's hot. If he rolls fourteen sevens in a row, or twenty—"

"That means he's playing with loaded dice," Morrell broke in.

"Exactly," Rohde said. "So—which is this? Four sevens in a row, or fourteen? All these officers have served at or near the front. Plenty of people who'd never make your list have got shot, too. So maybe this is a coincidence. But maybe it isn't, too. And if it isn't, you're the one who spotted it."

"Thanks a lot," Morrell said. "There's one more prize I'd just as soon not win."

"Why?" Rohde said. "We can do a better job of protecting our people if we know this than we could before we knew. That may come to matter, and not a little, either."

Morrell's grimace, for once, had nothing to do with his shattered shoulder. "And what else will we do? Go after the Confederates the same way?"

"I wouldn't be a bit surprised," Dr. Rohde said.

"Neither would I." Morrell pulled another horrible face. "Makes the war even more wonderful than the bombing raids and the poison gas and the machine guns, doesn't it?"

Rohde shrugged. "No doubt. You're the one who makes his living fighting it, though, you and the fellows like you on the other side. I just make mine patching up the ones you don't quite kill."

"Thanks a lot, Doc. I love you, too."

"I'm not saying we don't need soldiers. I've never said that. There's no way to get rid of such people, not without everybody doing it at the same time. If you think twenty sevens in a row are unlikely . . . But don't expect a doctor to get all misty-eyed and romantic about war, either. I've seen too much for that."

"So have I," Morrell said soberly. "Plenty of people have ugly jobs. That doesn't mean they don't need doing."

"Well, all right—we're not so far from the same page, anyhow," Rohde said. "I'll tell you, though, I've heard plenty who won't admit even that much."

Somebody down the hall shouted his name. He muttered something vile under his breath, then hurried off. *Patching up another one my Confederate counterparts didn't quite kill,* Morrell thought. *They'll get reprimanded if they don't quit screwing up like that.* He chuckled, though it wasn't really funny. Up till now, he'd never thought about war from a doctor's point of view.

Here he was, flat on his back again. For the first time since he'd got shot in 1914, he had plenty of time to lie there and think about things. He couldn't do much else, as a matter of fact. After he asked for a wireless set, he had it to help him pass the time. Sometimes the saccharine music and the sports shows and the inane quizzes made him want to scream. Sometimes what passed for news in the civilian world made him want to scream, too.

He solved that problem by turning off the wireless. Then he stared at the set sitting there on the little table by the bed. What good was it to him if he didn't listen to it? On the other hand, what good was it to him if it drove him out of his mind?

He was still trying to work that out three days later when he had a visitor. "Good God in the foothills!" he exclaimed. "I didn't know they let you out of Philadelphia except when you needed to make a mess on the floor."

Colonel John Abell gave him a thin, cool smile—the only kind the cerebral General Staff office seemed to own. "Hello," Abell said. "You do pose interesting questions, don't you? Well, I've got a question for you—can you open this?" He handed Morrell a small box covered in felt.

"Damn straight I can. I can do almost anything one-handed these days." Morrell proceeded to prove himself right—and then stared at the pair of small silver stars inside the box.

"Congratulations, General Morrell," Abell said.

"Oh, my," Morrell whispered. "Oh, my." He went on staring. After some little while, he realized he ought to say a bit more. Softly, he went on, "The last time I felt something like this, I was holding my new daughter in my arms."

"Congratulations," Abell repeated. "If the Confederates think you're important enough to be worth killing, I daresay you're important enough to deserve stars."

Morrell gave him a sharp look. The General Staff officer looked back blandly. He probably wasn't kidding. He almost surely wasn't, in fact. What Morrell had done in the field looked unimpressive to Philadelphia. What the enemy thought of him was something else again. That mattered to the powers that be. In the end, though, how Morrell had got the stars hardly mattered. That he'd got them made all the difference in the world.

Jefferson Pinkard swore when the telephone in his office jangled. Telephone calls were not apt to be good news. He always feared they'd be from Richmond. As far as he could remember, calls from Richmond had never been good news. When his curses failed to make the telephone stop ringing, he reluctantly picked it up. "Pinkard here."

"Hello, Pinkard. This is Ferd Koenig. Freedom! How are you this morning?"

"Freedom! I'm fine, sir. How are you?" *What the hell do you want with me?* But that wasn't a question Jeff could ask the Attorney General.

"Couldn't be better," Koenig said expansively, which only made Jeff more suspicious. The Attorney General continued, "Got a question for you."

"Shoot." What else could Pinkard say? Nothing, and he knew it.

"You reckon Mercer Scott's ready to take over Camp Dependable?"

Ice ran through Pinkard's veins. "I reckon that depends, sir," he said cautiously.

"Depends on what?"

Caution flew out the window. "On what you intend to do with me, sir. I've run this here camp since we took it over from that goddamn Huey Long. Don't think I've done too bad a job, either. Just in case you forgot, I was the fellow came up with those trucks. Nobody else—me."

"Easy, there. Easy. I do remember. So does the President. Nobody's putting you on the shelf," Ferdinand Koenig said. "It's not like that at all. Matter of fact, I've got a new job for you, if you want it."

"Depends on what it is," Pinkard said, dubious still.

"Well, how long have you been complaining that Camp Dependable isn't big enough for everything it's supposed to do?"

"Only forever."

Koenig laughed, which did nothing to make Jeff feel any easier. "All right, then," the Attorney General said. "How would you like to run a camp that's big enough for everything? Not just run it, but set it up from scratch. You've got practice at that kind of thing, don't you?"

"You know damn well I do, sir," Jeff answered. "Wasn't for me startin' up a camp in Mexico, I never would've got into this here line of work at all." *And there's plenty of times I wish I never did.* "Whereabouts'll this new camp be at?"

"Texas," Koenig said. "We'll put you out on the goddamn prairie, so you'll have plenty of room to grow. There'll be a railroad spur out to the place so you can ship in supplies easy. Won't be any trouble shippin' in plenty of niggers, either."

"*That* kind of camp again?" Pinkard said heavily. "I was hopin' you'd let me handle real prisoners of war."

"Any damn fool can do that," Ferd Koenig said. "We've got plenty o' damn fools doing it, too. But this other business takes somebody with brains and somebody with balls. That's you, unless. . . ."

Unless you haven't got the balls to do it. That hurt. Angrily, Pinkard said, "I've never backed away from anything you threw at me, Koenig, and you know it goddamn well. I'll do this, and I'll do it right. I just wish I had my druthers once in a while, is all."

He waited. If the Attorney General felt like canning him because he had the nerve to answer back . . . If he did, then he would, that was all. Jeff refused to worry about it. He'd paid his dues, and he'd given the Freedom Party everything it could possibly have asked from him. He could always find other things to do now. He was too old to make a likely soldier, but he still had his health. Factories lined up to hire people like him these days.

Instead of getting angry, Koenig said, "Keep your shirt on, Jeff. I know what you've done. Like I told you, the President knows, too.

Why do you think I called you first? This is going to be the top camp job in the whole country. We want the best man for it—and that's you."

Koenig had never been the sort to flatter for the sake of flattery. As Jake Featherston's right-hand man, he'd never needed to. He meant it, then. Since he meant it, Pinkard didn't see how he could say no. He drummed his fingers on the desktop. But he also had reasons he hadn't mentioned for being unenthusiastic about saying yes. He asked, "How long would it be before I have to go out to this place in Texas?"

"Part-time, pretty damn quick. Like I said, you'll be doing a lot of the setup," Koenig answered. "Full-time? A few months, I expect. You can ease Scott into your slot there while you're away, finish showing him whatever he needs when you come back to Louisiana. How's that sound?"

"Fair, I reckon," Jeff said, still with something less than delight. "A little longer might be better."

To his surprise, Ferd Koenig laughed out loud. "I know what part of your trouble is. You're courting that guard's pretty widow."

Pinkard growled something he hoped the Attorney General couldn't make out. Of course the government and the Freedom Party—assuming you could tell one from the other—were keeping an eye on him. He'd risen high enough that they needed to. He didn't like it—how could anybody like it?—but he understood it.

"Well, what if I am, goddammit?" he said. He almost said, *God damn you,* but managed not to. "I don't sit in this office or prowl around the camp *every* minute of the day and night."

"Didn't say you did," Koenig told him. "All right—how's this? When you go to Texas full-time, bring her along. Call her a secretary or whatever the hell you please. If she really does some work, that's fine. If she doesn't, nobody's gonna lose any sleep over it. We'll pay her a salary on top of the pension either way. We want you there, and if that means forking over a little extra on the side, then it does, and we'll live with it. That's why we've got bookkeepers."

"Thank you kindly, Mr. Koenig." Now Jeff was glad he hadn't aimed his curses straight at the Attorney General. "That's mighty handsome of you. I'll do it, and I'll see if she wants to come along."

"Good," Koenig said. "I'll tell you one more thing, long as I'm on the line: if she doesn't want to go to Texas with you, chances are it wouldn't have worked out even if you stayed in Louisiana."

Pinkard grunted. That was probably gospel, too. He said, "She's got young 'uns, you know. There a place close by this here new camp for them to go to school?"

"Beats me," the Attorney General said. "But if there isn't, there will be by the time you move there for good. You've got my word on it. You're an expensive proposition, you know that?"

"You said you wanted the good stuff. I don't come cheap," Pinkard answered.

Ferdinand Koenig laughed again. "We'll take it from there, then," he said, and hung up.

"Yeah. I guess maybe we will," Pinkard said to the dead line. He set the telephone back in the cradle.

When he went out into the yard, he wasn't surprised to find Mercer Scott coming up to him inside a minute and a half. The guard chief knew when he got a telephone call. Jeff had never found out how, but Scott knew. "What's the latest?" the hard-faced man asked casually.

"Congratulations," Jeff said, his own features as tightly shuttered as if he were in a high-stakes poker game. "Looks like you're gonna be takin' over this here camp in a few months' time."

"Oh, yeah?" Mercer Scott had a pretty good poker face, too, but it failed him now, shattering into astonishment. "What the hell's goin' on? You ain't in trouble far as I know, so help me God." He had to be wondering what sort of revenge Jeff had planned for him.

"Nah, I ain't in trouble," Jeff allowed after letting the other man stew for a little while. "They're startin' up a new camp in Texas, and they want me to go over there, get it up and running, and then take it over."

"Ah." Scott's narrow eyes were shrewd. "Good break for you, then. It'll be a big son of a bitch, I bet. They wouldn't waste you on anything pissant-like. So you'll be able to set it up the way you want to, will you?"

"That's what Koenig says, anyways," Jeff answered. "I'll find out how much he means it when I get there. Some—I'm pretty sure o' that. All the way? Well, Jesus walked on water, but there ain't been a hell of a lot of miracles since."

"Heh," Scott said. "Yeah. That'd be funny, if only it was funny. Well, you earned it—screw me if you didn't." He stuck out his hand. Jeff solemnly shook it. The clasp seemed less a trial of strength than their handshakes usually did. Still shrewd, Scott went on, "What's Edith Blades gonna think about it?"

Pinkard shrugged. "Dunno yet. I only just found out myself. I got to see what she thinks, see if she feels like packin' up and headin' west."

"You're serious," Scott said in some surprise.

"Expect I am," Jeff agreed. "She's a nice gal. She's a *sweet* gal. She wouldn't play around on you, not like—not like some." He didn't need to tell Mercer Scott the unhappy story of his first marriage.

Scott didn't push him. Maybe the guard chief already knew. He just said, "Good luck to you." His voice was far away. His eyes weren't quite on Jeff, either. He was looking around Camp Dependable. Jeff had no trouble figuring out what he was thinking about: things he'd do different when he took over.

That would be his worry. Jeff had plenty of things to think about, too. Paying a call on Edith once he got off duty topped the list, but only barely. Part of his mind was already way the hell out in Texas. Just like Mercer Scott, he was thinking about what he'd do when he started his new post. But Edith did come first.

He couldn't telephone her. She didn't have a telephone. He drove on over that evening after sundown. Her boys said, "It's Mr. Pinkard!" when she opened the door. They sounded glad to see him. That made him feel good. He'd never had much to do with kids since he stopped being one himself, not till now.

"Well, so it is," she said. "Come on in, Jeff. What brings you here?"

He told his story all over again. This time, he finished, "An' I was wondering, if I was to go to Texas, whether you'd like to come along—you and the kids, of course." He didn't want her thinking he didn't give a damn about the boys. He wasn't even trying to fool her, because he did like them.

She said, "That depends. I could go out there and we'd keep on seeing each other like we been, or I could go out there married to you. I'm not saying you've got to propose to me now, Jeff, but I tell you straight out I *won't* go out there in between the one of those and the other, if you know what I mean."

He nodded. He knew exactly what she meant. He liked her better for meaning it, not less. He would gladly have slept with her if she'd let him, but he never would have thought about marrying her if she had. He said, "I'd be right pleased to marry you, if that's what you want to do." His heart pounded. *Would* he be pleased? One way or the other, he'd find out.

"That's what I'd like to do," she said. "I'd be proud to go to Texas as your fiancée. I'd like to wait till Chick's dead a year before I marry again, if you don't mind too much."

"I don't mind," Jeff said. *Too much,* he thought.

Tom Colleton had hoped to land another leave down in Columbus. Then the USA threw a fresh attack at Sandusky. It was more an annoyance than a serious effort to drive the Confederates out. The blizzard that blew into the U.S. soldiers' faces as they advanced from the east didn't make their lives any easier, either. After a couple of days of probing and skirmishing, they sullenly drew back to their own lines—those who could still withdraw, of course.

Whatever else the attack accomplished, it made the Confederate high command nervous. An order canceling all leaves came down from on high. Privates and sergeants hoping for some time away from the front were disappointed. So was Tom Colleton. *One more reason to hate the damnyankees,* he thought as the arctic wind off Lake Erie threatened to turn him into an icicle.

For a wonder, the Confederate powers that be actually suspected they might have disappointed their men. From officers of such exalted grade, that was almost unprecedented. Colleton put it down to Jake Featherston's influence on the Army. Say what you would about the President of the CSA, but he'd been a noncom up close to the front all through the Great War. He knew how ordinary soldiers thought and what they needed. Some of that knowledge got through to the people directly in charge of the Army these days.

They tried to make up for banning leaves by sending entertainers up to Sandusky. It wasn't the same—they didn't send a brothel's worth of women up there, for instance—but it was better than nothing.

There were some women in the troupe: singers and dancers. The soldiers who packed a high-school auditorium whooped and cheered and hollered. Officers were no less raucous than enlisted men. They might have charged the stage if a solid phalanx of military policemen with nightsticks hadn't stood between them and the objects of their desire.

Most of the acts that didn't have girls in them met a reception as frigid as the weather outside. A comic who told jokes about the war but was plainly making his closest approach to anything that had to do with combat by being here almost got booed off the stage.

"You cocksucker, you'd shit your drawers if you saw a real Yankee with a real gun in his hands!" somebody yelled. A fierce roar of approval rose from the crowd. It was all downhill from there for the luckless comic.

One exception to the rule was a Negro musical combo called Satchmo and the Rhythm Aces. Negro musicians had been part of life in the Confederate States since long before the War of Secession— and Satchmo was a trumpeter the likes of whom Tom Colleton had never seen or heard. The rest of the Rhythm Aces were good without being especially memorable. Backing the brilliant Satchmo, they shone brighter in the light of his reflected glory.

With a harsh spotlight on him, he looked like nothing so much as a big black frog. His eyes and his cheeks bulged in a way that would have been comical except for the sounds that came out of his horn. A man who made music like that? No matter what he looked like, you couldn't help taking him seriously.

A man sitting in the row behind Tom said, "I'll be goddamned if that nigger don't look scared to death."

He was right. Colleton realized as much almost at once. He'd taken Satchmo's grimaces and contortions as some ill-advised comedy thrown into the act. Colored performers often did things like that when they played in front of whites. But these weren't the usual nigger's smirks and simpers. They didn't come close to fitting the music, either, and Satchmo wasn't the sort of man who would have sullied that.

What was he so afraid of? Nobody here was going to do anything to him. On the contrary: the soldiers were listening in the enchanted silence only the finest performers could earn. When Satchmo finished a number, the cheering nearly tore the roof off the auditorium.

What, then? Tom shrugged. You couldn't expect Negroes to love the CSA. As far as Tom was concerned, they deserved a lot of what they were getting. He remembered the way the Marshlands plantation had been, and the ruin it was now. If the colored Reds hadn't risen up, that wouldn't have happened. But blacks didn't like it so much now that the shoe pinched the other foot.

Tom didn't know everything the Freedom Party was doing down in the CSA. He did know he wasn't sorry for it, whatever it was. He'd never asked himself where the phrase *population reduction* came from. Few whites had, though they used it. Had the question occurred to him, he might have understood why terror lay under Satchmo's music.

When the trumpeter and the Rhythm Aces finished their set, they got another thunderous hand. Tom wasn't the only man who leaped to his feet to show how much he'd liked them. They played an encore and got even more applause, enough to prompt a second encore. They could have played all night, as far as the soldiers went. At last, though, Satchmo mimed exhaustion.

"I thanks you right kindly, gentlemen," he said in a deep, gravelly voice, "but we gots us another gig in the mornin'. When the gummint done sent us up here to Yankeeland, they made sure they kep' us busy."

How many shows did they have to play? How much rest did they get between them? The answers were bound to be *lots* and *not much,* respectively. Reluctantly, the Confederate soldiers let them go—and then jeered the white song-and-dance man who had the misfortune to come on after them.

Quite a few men got up and left after Satchmo and the Rhythm Aces quit the stage. They might have been saying they were sure they wouldn't see anything else worth watching. Tom sat through the rest of the evening. He saw a few more pretty girls than the soldiers who'd walked out early, but that was about it.

He tramped back through the snow to the house where he'd been staying since his regiment reached Sandusky. The Yankees who'd lived there before him had either got out or been killed. The house itself had taken some damage, but not a lot. With wood in the fireplace and coal in the stove, it was cozy enough, even in wintertime.

A commotion—men running every which way and shouting—woke Tom before sunup the next morning. He put on his boots and the greatcoat he'd piled on top of his blanket and went out to see what the hell was going on. The only thing he was sure of was that it wasn't the damnyankees: nobody was shooting and nobody was screaming in the way only wounded men did.

He got his answer when a soldier burst out, "Them goddamn niggers've run off!" By the fury in his voice, he might have been an overseer back in the days before the Confederate States manumitted their slaves.

"Satchmo and the Rhythm Aces?" Tom asked. He couldn't imagine men making such a fuss over either of the other colored acts in the show.

"That's right. Goddamn stinking ungrateful coons," the soldier said. "We catch their black asses, we'll make 'em sorry they was ever born."

"They're probably already sorry," Tom said. "And if they aren't now, they will be pretty damn quick. Even if they do make it through our lines, they'll find out the damnyankees don't like niggers a hell of a lot more than we do."

The soldier—a sergeant who needed a shave—nodded. "That's a fact, sir. But I want to make 'em as sorry as they can be. They got themselves a nerve, playin' like that last night and then runnin' away. Like I said, ungrateful bastards."

"Which way did they go?" Tom asked. "In this snow, they should have left a trail a mile wide."

"What it looks like they done is, it looks like they stole themselves a command car," the noncom said. "Once they got on the eastbound road, their goddamn tire tracks look like everybody else's."

He was right about that. Command cars often mounted machine guns, too. Whoever tried to stop the blacks might get a nasty surprise. "Did you send a wireless message on ahead, warning people the niggers are liable to be on the way?" Tom asked.

"Sure did, sir," the unshaven sergeant answered, "but Christ only knows how much good it'll do. We only just found out they was gone—reckon the ruction's what rousted you out of the sack—and they have hours of start. They could've gone a hell of a long ways before we knew they took off."

He was right about that, too. Tom said, "God help their sorry necks if we do catch 'em. They'll get their population reduced faster than you can whistle 'Dixie.' "

"Just goes to show you can't trust a nigger no matter what," the noncom said. "Somebody down in the CSA figured those spooks wouldn't make a break for it if he let 'em get close to the damnyankees. That's what he figured, but it sure looks like he was full of shit."

Another soldier came running out of regimental headquarters. "Son of a bitch!" he shouted. "Just got word back from the east. They found a picket post, looks like it was all shot to hell. Shot to hell from *this* side, mind you, not like the Yankees done it. Hell with me if those coons didn't get away."

Tom and the sergeant both swore. Evidently the stolen command car had carried a machine gun. Had one of the Rhythm Aces, or maybe even Satchmo himself, served a weapon like that in the uprisings of 1915 and 1916? Or—worse thought yet—had one of them served in the C.S. Army during the Great War and learned to use a machine gun there? So much for gratitude: if he had, he'd just bitten the hand that fed him.

And the Confederate pickets would have been paying attention to the U.S. troops in front of them, not to a command car coming up from behind. They would have figured an officer was coming up to look things over. It would have been the last mistake they ever made.

"How far from there to the Yankees' positions?" Tom asked.

"Not very far, sir," answered the soldier who'd heard the report.

"Any sign of dead niggers between the outpost and the U.S. lines?"

"No, sir."

"They got away, then, sure as hell." Tom cussed some more. So did the sergeant. After a moment, so did the man who'd brought the news. Tom went on, "The real pisser is, odds are they won't let any more niggers come up and perform after this. I bet they ship the other colored acts in this troupe back home, too. It's a damn shame for soldiers, is what it is. We aren't using niggers to fight. If we can't use 'em to entertain, what are they good for?"

"Who says niggers are good for anything?" the sergeant growled. "It'd be a better country if we didn't have to worry about 'em no more."

The other soldier standing there in the snow nodded. Tom didn't argue. He wouldn't have been sorry to see all the blacks in the CSA disappear, either. He didn't have the stomach for killing them all himself, but he wouldn't shed a tear if the Freedom Party found men who did. As for Satchmo and the Rhythm Aces . . . "I can think of some we don't have to worry about any more—unless the Yankees use 'em to mock us." That could be a nuisance. But, as long as he stood here by Lake Erie, it couldn't be much more than a nuisance.

Flora Blackford picked up the telephone in her office. "Yes? What is it?" she said.

"Mr. Roosevelt wants to speak to you, Congresswoman," her secretary answered.

"Thank you, Bertha. Of course I'll talk to him," Flora said. When the Assistant Secretary of War came on the line, she continued, "Good morning, Mr. Roosevelt. What can I do for you today?"

"Hello, Congresswoman." As always, Franklin Roosevelt sounded jaunty in spite of his paralysis. "I've just run into something that I thought might interest you."

"What is it?" Flora asked.

"Seems some colored musical ensemble that was up in Ohio to entertain Confederate soldiers decided the grass was greener on our side of the fence. They got away. I gather they shot up some Confederates doing it, too."

"Good for them!" Flora exclaimed. "They didn't get shot when they walked into our lines?"

"They drove in, as a matter of fact—they stole a command car. That's what gave them their firepower," Roosevelt answered. "No, they didn't get shot. I'm not sure they know how lucky they are."

"What are we going to do with them? We can't very well send them back—that would be murder," Flora said.

"No, we'll keep them. We can use their testimony about Confederate atrocities. And they're supposed to be pretty good musicians, if you like that kind of thing." Roosevelt's laugh was a little self-conscious. "Not really to my taste, I'm afraid: too wild. But some people are excited that they've made it over the border. Satchmo and the Rhythm Aces, they're called."

"Satchmo?" Flora wasn't sure she'd heard straight.

"That's right." Franklin Roosevelt laughed again. "I gather he was named, er, Sennacherib, but nobody who knew him could pronounce it. I believe that—I can't pronounce it myself."

"Sennacherib is a fancy handle even for a Negro from the Confederate States," Flora agreed. "Will we be bringing, uh, Satchmo and the—the Rhythm Aces, did you say?—to Philadelphia? This is where the wireless networks have their headquarters."

"Yes, I think we'll do that. I don't know how much broadcasting we'll have them do, though. What we call English and what they call English are almost two different languages, I'm afraid."

"I'd like to see them when they get here," Flora said.

"Actually, I was hoping you'd say that." The Assistant Secretary of War sounded pleased. "You've taken the lead in telling the world about what the Confederates are doing to their colored population."

"It's worse than what the Ottomans did to the Armenians during and after the Great War," Flora said. "If the Russians started killing off their Jews, that might come close, but even it wouldn't be the same."

"The Russians or the Germans," Roosevelt said. "With the Kingdom of Poland a German puppet, the Kaiser rules over as many Jews as the Tsar does."

"Yes, but the Russians have pogroms for the fun of it, and to distract people from what a mess the Tsar's government is," Flora answered. "The Germans are too civilized for that kind of thing, thank God."

"Half their brain trust are Jews, too. They can't afford to do without them," Roosevelt said. "But that's beside the point. Satchmo and the Rhythm Aces have heard about you, too. So I'm doubly glad you want to meet them, because they've already said they want to meet you."

"How have they heard about me? Do you know?" Flora asked.

"From the wireless, mostly, I think," Roosevelt told her. "That's good to hear; it shows some of our propaganda is getting through. Would you like to be there on the platform when they come in?"

"That might be nice." Flora sighed reminiscently. "When I was first elected to Congress and came down here to start my term, Hosea met me on the platform and took me to my flat. That was the first time we met. I had no idea it would go the way it did."

"He was a good man. A *good* man," Franklin Roosevelt said. "I've always thought it was horribly unfair to blame the business collapse on him. If it weren't for that, he would have made a fine President. No, that's not right—he *did* make a fine President. It's just that the times were against him."

"Thank you. I've always thought the same thing," Flora said.

"And we elected Coolidge—and got Hoover. Coolidge wouldn't have made things better, and Hoover didn't. And the Confederates chose Jake Featherston, and the French got *Action Française* and a king, and the English got Mosley and Churchill. That's a lot to pin on an Austro-Hungarian bank failure, but it's the truth."

"If you toss a pebble into a snowbank, you can start an avalanche that will wipe out everything down below," Roosevelt said. "The first failure was a pebble, and the avalanche rolled downhill from there."

"Didn't it just!" Flora said mournfully.

When Roosevelt spoke again, it was after a paper-shuffling pause: "Satchmo and the Rhythm Aces get into town at the Broad Street station, Platform 27, at . . . let me see . . . at half past nine tomorrow night. That's when they're scheduled, I should say. Confederate bombers and Confederate saboteurs may change everyone's plans."

"Oh, yes, I know," Flora replied. "Well, I'll get there on time—unless an air raid changes *my* plans."

"Thank you very much." Franklin Roosevelt hung up.

To Flora's relief, the sirens didn't howl that night. The Confederates weren't coming over Philadelphia quite so much these days. More of their airplanes were staying home to attack the U.S. forces slogging forward through an ocean of blood in Virginia. She had no trouble getting a cab and going over to the Broad Street station.

Platform 27 wasn't the one where she'd got off the train from New York City all those years ago. *Too bad,* she thought. She'd wondered if Franklin Roosevelt would also be there to greet the escaped musicians. He wasn't, but several lesser War Department dignitaries were.

The train ran late. Some years before, there'd been an Italian politician who'd promised to make the trains run on time if he were elected. He hadn't been; nobody had believed he could do it. Flora tried to remember his name, but couldn't, which only went to show how unimportant he'd been. U.S. trains weren't so bad as their Italian counterparts were said to be, but they weren't all that good, either. And the war had done nothing to help.

At ten, Flora was resigned. At half past, she was annoyed. At eleven, she didn't know whether to be furious or worried. The train finally pulled into the station at ten minutes to twelve. That irked her all over again. She'd decided to give the laggard locomotive till midnight. After that, she could have gone home and gone to bed in good conscience. She wouldn't see bed at even a halfway reasonable hour now.

People who got off before Satchmo and the Rhythm Aces shook their heads and grumbled, often profanely, about delays and detours. A few of them muttered apologies to Flora as they walked by. One of the foulest-mouthed passengers, though, was a woman, and she was in no mood to apologize to anybody for anything.

Flora had no trouble recognizing the men she was looking for. In the bright light under the platform, the Negroes seemed all eyeballs and teeth. They wore green-gray uniform tunics and trousers with the highly polished shoes that must have accompanied more formal wear. They stared every which way, plainly with no idea what to do next.

She stepped up to them, gave her name, and said, "Welcome to Philadelphia. I'd say welcome to freedom, but there's a party down in the CSA that's given the word a bad name."

All five of the black men grinned and nodded. "Ain't it the truth!" said the one who stood out a little from the rest. If he wasn't Satchmo, she would have been very surprised. He had a deep, raspy voice and an engagingly ugly face. "We're right pleased to make your acquaintance, Mrs. Blackford. Ain't that right, boys?" The other Negroes nodded again, in unison.

The men from the War Department were a few paces behind Flora. Since they were the ones who were going to take charge of the newcomers, she stepped aside and let them introduce themselves. Then she asked, "What is it *like* for a Negro in the Confederate States these days?"

"Ma'am, I reckon you got a notion already that it's pretty bad," Satchmo said. Flora didn't need to nod to show she did. The musician went on, "All right. Well, for true, it's a hundred times that bad." The other Rhythm Aces murmured agreement, as if he were a lead singer and they his backup vocalists.

"Do most of the Negroes in the CSA know what the Freedom Party is doing to them—to you?" Flora asked.

One of the Aces spoke on his own for the first time: "If we didn't, ma'am, you reckon we take the chance o' doin' what we done?"

"But musicians like you travel all over the place. You hear things most people wouldn't," Flora persisted. "What about ordinary Negroes who stay in one spot? Do they know what's happening in those Freedom Party camps?"

A major asked, "Do they hear our wireless broadcasts? We try to let them know what's going on." He had to be in Intelligence or Propaganda. Nobody who wasn't could have made that sound so smooth.

"They hear some, I reckon, but the Freedom Party jams you pretty good, suh," Satchmo replied. "Don't want nobody, white or colored, listenin' to the damnyankee wireless."

Flora had heard white Confederates say *damnyankee* as if it were one word. She hadn't expected a black man to do the same. "How do they know, then?—the black people in the CSA, I mean."

The musicians looked at her. One of them said, "Everybody know somebody done got sucked into a camp. Ain't nobody know nobody who ever come out again. We ain't educated. White folks in the CSA always been afraid o' what'd happen if we git educated. But we ain't stupid, neither. Don't gotta be no sly, sneaky Jew to figure out what folks goin' in an' not comin' out means."

He knew as little of Jews as Flora did of Negroes, probably less. She had to remind herself of that. And he'd made his point. She said, "Well, you're safe here—as long as a bomb doesn't fall on your head. We all take that chance."

"Thank you, ma'am. God bless you, ma'am," Satchmo and the Rhythm Aces chorused together.

"You're welcome," Flora said. "And I'll do whatever I can to stop those Freedom Party goons from massacring your people. I don't know how much that will be, but I'll do my damnedest." She hardly ever swore, but it seemed fitting now.

"God bless you," Satchmo repeated. "Nice to know somebody

here cares a little, anyways. Ain't nobody south of the border cares at all."

How many people north of the border cared at all? Too few, too few. Flora didn't care to tell Satchmo that. He and his friends had just escaped from worse. Let them find out a little at a time that they hadn't come to paradise. That way—maybe—their hearts wouldn't break.

Cincinnatus Driver couldn't believe he'd been stuck in Covington more than a year. He knew he was lucky his father hadn't had to bury him here, but he wasn't always sure his luck in surviving had been good.

Just the same, he *had* made progress. He still used a cane, and feared he would for the rest of his life. He was fairly spry with it now, where he had been an arthritic tortoise. He didn't get headaches as often as he had not long after the accident, either, and the ones that did come weren't so blinding. Progress. He laughed. It was either that or cry. He'd gone from worse to bad. Huzzah!

His mother, now, his mother went from bad to worse. She still knew who Seneca was, and sometimes Cincinnatus, but that was almost her only hold on the real world. She made messes like a toddler. The first time Cincinnatus cleaned her, he burst into tears as soon as he got out of the room. He had to harden himself to do it over and over again. He never cried after that once, but it tore at his heart every time. It wasn't right. It wasn't natural. She'd done this for him when he was little. That he should have to do it for her . . .

He found himself looking at his father. Would he have to do the same for him one day? The horror of that thought drove Cincinnatus out of the house. He could have gone to the Brass Monkey; getting drunk would—well, might—have kept him from dwelling on it. Instead, he headed for Lucullus'. He couldn't buy a drink there, not officially, but that didn't mean he couldn't get something to wet his whistle if he wanted to. Knowing the proprietor had its advantages.

The place wasn't crowded when he limped in. He hadn't thought it would be, not on a drizzly Tuesday afternoon. But it wasn't empty, either. As far as he knew, Lucullus' place was never empty. The barbecue was too good for that. Negroes and whites both came here. As usual, whites sat at some tables, blacks at others, and. . . . There, a white man and a Negro sat across from each other at the same table. That was out of the ordinary not only at Lucullus' but anywhere in the CSA.

Then Cincinnatus saw the Negro at the table was Lucullus himself. The bulky barbecue chef broke the rules whenever he pleased. The white man glanced up as Cincinnatus came in. The fellow didn't look to be far from a skid row bum. His gray hair came down in odd tufts from under a disreputable hat. He'd needed a shave for three or four days. His scruffy sweater had had spots on it before barbecue sauce added a more colorful one.

None of that had anything to do with the icy lizards that walked up Cincinnatus' back. Going around like somebody who'd been hitting the bottle too hard for too long might fool most people, but not Cincinnatus. He would have recognized Luther Bliss in pancake makeup and a little black dress, let alone this outfit.

His face must have given him away. Bliss said something to Lucullus, who looked up. He waved to Cincinnatus and beckoned him over. Cincinnatus would sooner have jumped into a nest of rattlesnakes. He didn't see what choice he had, though. Moving even more slowly than he had to, he approached.

"Well, well. Damned if it ain't little Mary Sunshine." Bliss sounded like a crack-brained derelict, too, which was harder than looking like one. His eyes, though, his eyes he couldn't disguise. They were too alert, too clever, to match the rest of his pretended persona.

"What you doin' here?" Cincinnatus asked as he sat down—by Lucullus. Nothing in the world would have made him sit down by Luther Bliss.

"Me? Goin' to and fro in the earth, and walking up and down in it," Bliss answered.

For a moment, that made no sense to Cincinnatus. Then it did. It was from the Book of Job. "You don't gotta do much talkin' to make me believe you're the Devil," Cincinnatus said.

Bliss brayed out a loud, stupid laugh. "Love you, too," he said, and blew Cincinnatus a kiss.

Cincinnatus turned to Lucullus. "What you doin' with this man? Whatever it is, he ain't doin' it for you. He's doin' it for his ownself, nobody else." Bliss laughed again, even more raucously.

Cincinnatus glared at him once more. All that did was prove looks couldn't kill.

Before saying anything of consequence, Lucullus waved for a waitress and told her to fetch Cincinnatus a plate of pork ribs and a bottle of Dr. Hopper. Only after she went away did he remark, "Ain't always who you're for what matters. Sometimes who you're against counts fo' mo'."

"Yeah, sometimes." Cincinnatus pointed at Luther Bliss. "He's against you, for instance, on account of you're a Red." Keeping his voice down so the whole place wouldn't hear what he was saying took almost more willpower than he had in him.

"I got bigger worries right now, bigger fish to fry." Bliss talked normally. He just made sure nobody in his right mind would want to listen. That was a considerable talent. He had a lot of them. Getting Cincinnatus to trust him would never be one.

The waitress brought the food and the soda pop. Nobody said anything till she left. Cincinnatus wondered whether that was wasted caution. People who worked for Lucullus were probably involved in his schemes up to their eyebrows. Then the delicious aroma of the ribs distracted him. He dug in, and promptly got a stain on his shirt to match the one on Luther Bliss' sweater.

"How'd you like to help us give the Confederate States of America one right in the nuts?" Lucullus asked.

He might have asked, *How'd you like to buy a pig in a poke?* Or he might have asked, *How'd you like to get killed?* Cincinnatus suspected all three questions boiled down to the same thing. "Depends," he said. "What do I gotta do?"

"I knew he didn't have the balls for it," Luther Bliss said scornfully.

Cincinnatus didn't raise his voice as he said, "Fuck your mother, Luther."

Bliss' mahogany eyes opened very wide, perhaps at the obscenity, perhaps because a black man had presumed to call him by his first name. Before he could say anything, Lucullus beat him to it: "That'll be enough outa both o' you." He glowered at white man and black in turn, as if to say they'd have to quarrel with him before they could go at each other.

If Luther Bliss wanted a fight, Cincinnatus was ready. He didn't even worry about being a cripple. He intended to use his cane to knock the white man ass over elbow. He didn't figure Bliss would fight fair, so why should he?

"You reckon you can drive a truck?" Lucullus asked him.

"Can I? Hell, yes," Cincinnatus answered. "Why do I want anything to do with this ofay bastard, though?" He pointed across the table at Bliss.

"Because it'll heap coals of fire on Jake Featherston's head." Lucullus could quote Scripture for his purpose, too. "Next to that, what else matters?"

That was a potent argument with any Negro, but not necessarily potent enough with Cincinnatus. "Jake Featherston never lured me down here so he could throw me in jail," he snarled. "This here asshole did."

Bliss didn't deny it. How could he, when it was true? He said, "Featherston's killing spades by the tens of thousands—hell, maybe by the hundreds of thousands now. You gonna piss and moan about a jail cell next to that?"

He had an odd way of arguing, which didn't mean it wasn't effective. He didn't care what Cincinnatus thought of him. He just worried about what the black man did. Cincinnatus didn't look at him or speak to him. Instead, he turned to Lucullus. "Where's this truck at? Where do I got to drive it to?"

"It's by the train station," Lucullus answered. "You got to bring it over to the river."

"The Ohio?" Cincinnatus asked. You could almost spit from the station to the Ohio.

Lucullus shook his head. The soft flesh under his chin wobbled. That made Cincinnatus think of the barbecue chef's father. Apicius Wood's flesh had been the only soft thing about him. Lucullus said, "No, not the Ohio. The Licking, here in the colored part o' town."

That made sense. Cincinnatus wasn't sure a colored truck driver could get near the Ohio without challenge. The tributary was bound to be a different story. "What's the truck got in it?" Cincinnatus asked.

"Something I arranged," Luther Bliss said. "You don't need to know what."

Cincinnatus started to get to his feet. "Obliged for the ribs," he told Lucullus. "Reckon you don't need me for no driver."

"Git down off your high horse. You are the *proudest* damn nigger," Lucullus said querulously. Cincinnatus didn't deny it. He didn't leave, either. He waited. If he got an answer, that was one thing. If he didn't . . . He could always leave then. Lucullus muttered under his breath. Then he stopped muttering and spoke in that same low, breathy voice: "Got us some mines to dump in the river."

"Do Jesus!" Cincinnatus said. Luther Bliss doubtless had connections with the U.S. War Department. Even so, smuggling infernal devices like that across the border couldn't have been easy. Since Bliss had managed to do it, or somebody had managed to do it for him . . . "When you want me there?" Cincinnatus asked.

Two days later, wearing a pair of overalls and a cloth cap furnished by Lucullus, he made his way toward the truck. A gray-uniformed cop checked his passbook and let him go on without asking exactly where he was going and why. The Confederates thought everything in Covington was under control. Cincinnatus' carnivorous smile said otherwise.

He found the truck right where Lucullus said it would be. One of the keys in his pocket opened the door. Another fit the ignition. The motor roared to life when he turned that key and stamped the starter.

Releasing the hand brake and putting the truck in gear felt good. He'd been driving for more than thirty years. He'd taken his surname because of what he did. Driving was a big part of his life, and he hadn't been able to do it since coming down to Covington. Now he could.

He shook his head and clucked sadly as he went through the colored quarter. A lot of houses stood empty; their owners had been sensible enough to get across the Ohio to the USA when the CSA won the plebiscite. Cincinnatus sighed. He'd been sensible himself. Fat lot of good it had done him.

The derelict garage where Lucullus had told him to pull in was hard by the river. The building faced away from the Licking, but had a back door that opened on it. Even before Cincinnatus killed the engine, half a dozen black men stepped out from the gloom and darkness inside the garage.

"You brung 'em?" one of them asked.

"Yeah," Cincinnatus answered. The men took half a dozen

crates out of the back of the truck. They pried up the tops and carefully removed the mines, one after another. Two men on each mine, they carried them down to the river. Cincinnatus didn't see how they placed them: whether they dropped them in, had a rowboat waiting, or what. As soon as the last mine was gone, he fired up the truck again and drove off. Lucullus' crew of men with strong backs also broke up in a hurry.

The truck went back where he'd found it. He returned the keys to Lucullus. The barbecue chef gave him a conspiratorial wink. He returned it, then limped out of the barbecue shack and headed home.

Jake Featherston scowled as he read the report from Kentucky. A Confederate gunboat on the Licking River had blown sky-high when it hit a mine. Two dozen men dead, another eight or ten badly hurt, an expensive piece of machinery gone to hell . . . He cursed under his breath, and then out loud.

After he'd thought for a few seconds, his curses got nastier. The Licking ran *into* the Ohio. You couldn't drop a mine into the Ohio and expect it to go up the Licking. Sure as hell, the damnyankees had sneaked people and at least one mine from the USA into the CSA. Either that or they'd sneaked in the explosives and then used white traitors or niggers to do their dirty work for them.

After a few *more* seconds, Jake swore even louder. That *at least one mine* stuck in his head. How much time and money and manpower would the authorities in Covington have to spend before they made sure there weren't any others—or before they got rid of the ones they found? Too much, too much, and too much, respectively.

Back before Kentucky and the abortion called Houston came home to the CSA, pro-Confederate demonstrators had been as nasty and as noisy as they could. Yankee backers in the redeemed states were quieter. If they showed what they thought, the police and Freedom Party stalwarts and guards would land on them with both feet. The Yankees had been soft-headed and let their enemies shelter under the protection of the Constitution. In the CSA, the Whigs had made the same mistake—and they'd paid for it, too.

Unfortunately, the damnyankees had wised up. They'd figured

out how to play nasty, and they'd turned out to be pretty good at it. Featherston swore once more, this time at himself. He'd misread Al Smith. The man—and the country Smith led—turned out to have more backbone than he'd expected. He'd been so sure the Yankees would go for his peace offer after the CSA's smashing victories in Ohio. He'd been sure, and he'd been wrong.

"Well, if the bastards won't lay down on their own, we'll just have to knock 'em flat, that's all," he muttered. "And we goddamn well will." The telephone rang. He picked it up. "Yeah? What is it, Lulu?"

"General Potter is here to see you, sir," his secretary answered.

"Send him in," Jake said, and hung up. When Clarence Potter walked into the President's office, Featherston fixed him with a glare. "You know about the goddamn mess in Covington?"

"Yes, sir, I do," Potter answered. Jake's glare, which reduced a lot of men to quivering jelly, had disappointingly little effect on the Intelligence officer. Potter went on, "That's one of the things I was coming to talk to you about. We've got reports Luther Bliss has been seen in Covington. Does that name mean anything to you?"

"I hope to shit it does!" Featherston burst out. "That cold-blooded bastard was nothing but trouble for us while the USA held on to Kentucky."

Potter's face never showed a whole lot. Even so, the slight twitch of an eyebrow gave Jake some idea of what was going through his devious mind. If it wasn't something like, *Takes one to know one,* the President of the CSA would have been mightily surprised.

"I can't prove he had anything to do with the mines in the Licking," Potter said. "I can't prove it—but that's the way to bet."

"You'd better believe it," Jake said. "I want that son of a bitch taken out. He can cause us more trouble than a regiment of regular Yankee soldiers."

"We're working on it," Potter said. "Trouble is, he's a professional, too. I'd guess he's been in place there a good long while, getting set up and so on, but I first got word of him just a few days ago. He's not going to be there by himself. He'll have friends lending a hand."

"Niggers lending a hand," Featherston said savagely. "You see why we're on our way to taking care of them."

"Oh, yes, Mr. President. I've never had any trouble with that," Potter said.

Jake eyed him. He hadn't quite come out and said he did have trouble with other things the Freedom Party had done, but he might as well have. "How the hell did I get me a goddamn stiff-necked Whig running my spies?" Jake asked Potter—or possibly God.

God, as usual, kept quiet. Potter, as usual, didn't. Giving Jake a crooked smile, he answered, "Well, sir, looks to me like it's because you aren't a wasteful man."

Among his other annoying traits was being right most of the time. He'd sure put a hole right in the middle of this bull's-eye. Featherston remained sure Potter had come up to Richmond in 1936 to put a hole right in the middle of *his* bull's-eye. He'd accidentally become a hero instead, and made the most of things since.

The really crazy part was that, if he'd just stayed down in Charleston as an ordinary loud-mouthed Whig, he would have got arrested and gone into a camp for politicals, the way so many others had. Or maybe, since he was tougher than most, he would have been shot while resisting arrest. He would have been out of the picture, though, for sure.

But here he was—not only alive but useful. He'd done better for himself as a would-be assassin than he ever could have as an ordinary loud-mouthed Whig.

"That was part of what you wanted to tell me," Featherston said. "What else have you got?"

Clarence Potter smiled again. This time, a leopard wouldn't have been ashamed to show its teeth like that. "We've found one of the spies in the War Department, anyhow—sniffed him out with another round of multiversion reports."

"There you go!" Jake slammed a fist down on the desk. Papers and even the gooseneck lamp jumped. "Who was it?"

"A mousy little file clerk in Operations and Training named Samuel Beauchamp Smith," Potter answered. "He's been shuffling and filing papers since 1912, God help us, and he's probably been passing things along all that time, too."

"Peel him," Featherston said. "Peel him like an onion, and make him hurt every time you strip off a new layer. He's been hurting us all that time—he should hurt for a long time himself. Just be sure you keep him alive so he can go on answering questions, that's all."

"It's being taken care of, sir." Clarence Potter didn't bat an eye. He didn't lose any sleep over playing a dirty game. He understood you sometimes had to get answers any way you could. If that was hard on the bastard who didn't want to give them . . . well, too bad for him.

"All right," Featherston said. "And a good job on that sniper who shot Morrell."

"Not good enough." Potter said. "He's on the shelf, but I wanted him dead."

Potter was a perfectionist. Unless things went exactly the way he wanted them to, he wasn't happy. That was not the least of the things that made him so useful to the CSA in spite of his godawful politics. Featherston said, "By your report, the Yankees scooped him up and got him out of harm's way pretty damn quick."

"First shot should have finished him off." Yes, Potter was discontented. "One of our snipers would have. But this was so far in back of their lines, I had to rely on local talent—and the local talent wasn't talented enough."

"You'll have other chances at other officers," Featherston said. "If we can knock the brains out of the U.S. Army, it'll be that much easier to lick."

"Yes, sir. But the Yankees have figured out that that was an assassination try," Potter said. "I'd suggest you beef up security for our own best men."

"I've already done it," Featherston said. "And, to tell you the truth, there's a few generals I wouldn't mind seeing 'em knock off. I won't name names, but I reckon you can figure some of 'em out for yourself."

"Could be." Potter's voice and chuckle were dry. But he quickly grew serious again. "The other thing is, you ought to beef up *your* security, too. The war effort goes down the drain if we lose you."

"Don't you worry about *my* security. That's not your department, and it's tight as an old maid's. . . ." Featherston didn't finish, but he came close enough to make Potter chuckle again. And the truth was, he didn't worry all that much about his security, at least not in the way Potter meant. If it was good enough to keep blacks and disgruntled Freedom Party men from knocking him off, it was bound to be good enough to hold the damnyankees at bay, too.

And if it wasn't . . . If it wasn't, Don Partridge became President of the CSA. Jake didn't think Partridge could run things, even if he did have the title. Who would? Ferd Koenig, from behind the scenes? Nathan Bedford Forrest III, from even further behind them?

Featherston only shrugged. If he wasn't there to see the unlucky day, what difference did it make to him? "Anything else?" he asked.

"Only the thought that, since the damnyankees didn't quit after we got up to Lake Erie, we might do better finding a peace both sides can live with than butting heads for God knows how long," Potter answered. "That kind of fight favors them, not us."

"I want your opinion on how to run my business, you can bet I'll ask for it," Featherston growled. "Till I do, you can damn well keep your mouth shut about it. So long, General Potter."

"So long, Mr. President." Potter wasn't the least bit put out as he left the office. He'd probably said what he'd said for no better reason than to rattle Jake's cage.

I don't care why he said it. He can goddamn well shut up about it, Featherston thought. Defiantly, he looked north. He'd taken Confederate arms where they'd never gone before, where none of his predecessors had ever dreamt they could go. He still intended to lick the United States, to lick them so they stayed licked. It might take longer than he'd thought when he set out, but that didn't mean he couldn't do it.

"I can, and I will," he said, as if someone had denied it. All he had to do to make something real was to want it, to keep going after it, and not to quit no matter what. Sooner or later, it would fall into his hands. *I'm sitting here in the Gray House, aren't I?*

He nodded. Even if the Whigs didn't like it, he *was* here. He belonged here. And he intended to take the Confederate States with him where he wanted to go. By the time they were someone else's worry, they would look the way he'd wanted them to all along. No one else would be able to change them back to the way they were now.

As for the United States . . . Featherston's swivel chair squeaked as he swung it around toward the north, too. All right, they hadn't given up the way he'd thought they would. That didn't mean they couldn't be beaten down. He intended to do just that. By the time he got finished, the Confederate States would be the number-one power on this continent.

They'd stay number one, too. He intended to fix things so even a dunderhead like Partridge couldn't mess them up. And everyone would always remember the name of the man who'd put them on top. His name. Him. Jake Featherston.

The Sandwich Islands. Home of perfect weather, sugar cane, pineapple, and women of several races wearing no more than the perfect weather required. Home of the ukulele, the instrument the Devil had invented when he was trying for the guitar. Home of romance. That was what the tourist brochures said, anyhow.

George Enos, Jr., didn't have the chance to pay attention to the tourist brochures. He didn't have time to pay attention to the pineapple or the sugar cane or even the women and what they were or weren't wearing. He'd been away from Connie for quite a while. His interest might have been more than theoretical. He didn't get the chance to find out.

As soon as the *Townsend* pulled into Pearl Harbor, she refueled and steamed northwest toward Midway. Even though the island was lost to the Japanese, the USA seemed determined to defend Oahu as far forward as possible. That would have been farther forward still if the *Remembrance* hadn't lain at the bottom of the Pacific. As things were, the Americans didn't poke much beyond the distance air cover from the main islands could reach.

Out beyond that distance lay . . . the Japs. *They* had carriers in the neighborhood, and they'd proved airplanes could do more to ships than other ships could. The *Townsend* did have Y-ranging gear, which struck George as something not far from black magic. Black magic or not, though, how much would it help? Airplanes were so much faster than ships—you couldn't run away even if you saw the other guy long before he saw you.

Hydrophone gear listened for Japanese submersibles. Old-timers—the *Townsend* had a handful—said the gear was greatly improved over what the Navy had used in the last war. It could hear a sub while the destroyer's engines were going. If they hadn't been able to do that in the Great War, George wondered how any surface ships had survived. His mouth tightened. Too many hadn't, including the one with his father aboard.

When he wasn't chipping paint or swabbing the deck or doing one of the nine million other jobs the Navy had to keep all hands from knowing any idle moments, he stuck close to the 40mm mount. If anything came within range of the destroyer, he wanted the best chance to blast it he could get. When the klaxons sounded general quarters, he ran like a man possessed. So did his crewmates. In these waters, it was too likely no drill.

"We're trying to find their subs, and they're trying to find us," Fremont Blaine Dalby said one morning. The gun chief peered out over the blue, blue water, as if expecting to see periscopes lined up like city workers waiting for the trolley. He might not have been so far wrong, either. He went on, "Whoever plays the game better gets to play it again. Whoever screws up . . ." A shrug. "It's a hell of a long way down in this part of the Pacific."

"Happy day," George said.

"Ain't it?" That was Fritz Gustafson. The loader seldom had a whole lot to say, but he never left any doubt where he stood. He jerked a thumb at Dalby. "Just our luck to have a damn Jonah bossing this gun."

"A Jonah?" Dalby swelled up like a puffer fish. "What do you mean, a Jonah?"

"What I said," Gustafson answered. "Named for Republicans. Phooey! Bunch of goddamn losers."

"Could be worse," George said helpfully. "His mama could have called him Lincoln."

Dalby gave him a more venomous look than the one he'd sent Gustafson. He and the loader had been together for a long time. They'd probably been needling each other just as long, too. George was still a new kid on the block. He was showing some nerve by joining in.

Before Dalby could call him on it, if he was going to, the klaxons began to hoot. Feet clanged on metal decks. George started to laugh. He was already at his battle station. The only thing he did was button up his shirt and roll down his sleeves. Orders were to cover as much of yourself as you could when combat was close. That could be uncomfortable in warm weather, but it could also be a lifesaver. Flash burns from exploding ordnance often killed even when shrapnel didn't turn a man to butcher's work.

The *Townsend*'s engines took on a deeper note. The destroyer sped up and started zigzagging. The men on the gun crew looked at one another. They all said the same thing at the same time: "Uh-oh."

When the klaxons stopped, it wasn't to sound the all-clear. An officer's voice came over the speakers: "Now hear this. We've picked up airplanes heading this way from the northwest. They are unlikely to be friendly. That is all."

"Unlikely to be fucking friendly." Fremont Dalby spat. "Yeah."

With Midway gone, the USA had no bases northwest of where the *Townsend* steamed. However many Japanese carriers were up there, they had the best of both worlds. They could launch their airplanes at American ships while staying out of range of retaliation from Oahu or Kauai. They might lose fighters or bombers. They wouldn't expose themselves to danger.

Y-ranging gear had a range far beyond that of the Mark One eyeball. It gave the gun crews fifteen or twenty minutes to get as ready for the onslaught as they could. Everyone started toward the northwest. Somebody opened up on a particularly majestic goony bird. The shells screamed past it. The goony bird altered course not a bit.

But then shouts rang out up and down the *Townsend*. Those dark specks weren't birds, goony or otherwise. They were enemy airplanes.

The *Townsend*'s five-inch guns could fight both ships and airplanes. They opened up first. The blast from them was like the end of the world. George felt it as much as he heard it. Black puffs of smoke appeared among the incoming Japs. None of them tumbled out of the sky, not yet. They didn't even break formation. The Pacific War had proved Japanese pilots knew their stuff. Nothing that had happened in this one made anybody want to change his mind.

"Let's get 'em!" Dalby shouted. The twin 40mm guns started

hammering away. George fed shells as fast as he could. Fritz Gustafson might have been a mechanism designed for nothing but loading. The rest of the crew swung the guns toward their targets. Flame spurted from the gun barrels. Shell casings leaped from the breeches. George passed more ammo. The noise of the twin antiaircraft guns was terrific, but not so overwhelming as the roar of the dual-purpose five-inchers not far away. They kept shooting, too, adding bass notes to the cacophony.

Bombs burst in the sea, much too close to the *Townsend*'s flank. George remembered destroyers were built for speed, and sacrificed all armor plate to get it. He could have done without the thought. Great plumes of white water flew up. Some of it splashed him. He wondered what flying fragments from the casing were doing to the hull. Nothing good.

A fighter streaked for the *Townsend*, machine guns blazing. Tracers from several guns converged on it. It blew up in midair; the remains splashed into the Pacific. "Scratch one Jap!" George yelled in delight, even if he was far from sure his gun had put the fatal round into the enemy fighter.

But plenty of Japanese airplanes were left unscratched. A dive bomber screamed down on the *Townsend*. Fritz Gustafson swiveled the antiaircraft gun with desperate haste to bring it to bear on the bomber. Tracers swung toward the hurtling plane, swung into it, and left it a smoking, flaming ruin that crashed into the sea—but not before it loosed the bomb.

George watched it fall. He felt the *Townsend* heel sharply—but not sharply enough. The bomb struck home at the destroyer's stern. It struck home . . . but it didn't burst.

"Thank you, Jesus!" George said. He'd nominally turned Catholic to marry Connie, but he didn't feel it. That was too bad. Crossing himself and really meaning it would have felt good just then.

"Fuck me." Fremont Dalby sounded as reverent as George did, even if he'd chosen different words. "A dud!" Those were beautiful words, too.

Gustafson shook his head. "I bet it isn't. I bet they put an armor-piercing fuse on it, and it didn't hit anything tough enough to make it go off. It would have raised all kinds of hell on a cruiser or a battle-wagon."

"Fuck me," Dalby said again, this time much less happily. "I bet you're right. That means we've got a real son of a bitch in there somewhere."

"It'll go off if somebody sneezes on it, too, most likely." Gustafson spoke with a certain somber satisfaction.

Another dive bomber stooped on the destroyer. One of the *Townsend*'s five-inch guns got this one. When that kind of shell struck home, the enemy airplane turned into a fireball. The dive bomber behind it flew past the edge of the fireball, so close that George hoped it would go up in flames, too. It didn't. It released its bomb and zoomed away only a few feet above the waves.

Maybe evading the fireball had spoiled the pilot's aim, because the bomb went into the Pacific, not into the *Townsend*. It also failed to explode, which suggested all the dive bombers bore badly fused bombs. George expended some more hope on that.

Even if it was so, the *Townsend* wasn't out of the woods yet. More bombs rained down from the level bombers high overhead. None had hit yet, but they kept kicking up great spouts of water when they splashed into the sea. Nothing was wrong with *their* fuses. And fighters buzzed around the destroyer like so many malevolent wasps. They strafed the deck again and again. Someone on the *Townsend* shot down another one, but cries for medics said the fighters' machine guns were doing damage, too.

After what seemed forever but was by the clock eighteen minutes, the Japanese airplanes flew back in the direction from which they'd come. Fritz Gustafson nodded to George. "Well, rookie, you're a veteran now," he said.

George looked around. There were bullet holes and dents much too close for comfort. Blood streaked the deck at the next 40mm mount. *That could have been me,* he thought, and started to shake.

Gustafson slapped him on the back. "All right to get the jimjams now," the loader said. "You did good when it counted."

"We all did good when it counted," Dalby said. "Damn Japs didn't buy anything cheap today."

"Unless that bomb goes off," Gustafson said. Dalby gave him the finger.

Men from the damage-control party brought the bomb up on deck in a canvas sling. Ever so gently, they lowered it over the side.

All the sailors watching cheered as it disappeared into the depths of the Pacific.

"Still here," George breathed. He hardly dared believe it. If that carrier decided to send more airplanes after the *Townsend*, it might not last. Nothing seemed better, though, than taking the enemy's best shot—and coming through.

Scipio didn't like going through the Terry any more. He especially didn't like going through the northern part, the part that had been emptied out by police and Freedom Party stalwarts and guards. Scavengers prowled it, pawing through what the inhabitants had had to leave behind when they were sent elsewhere. A lot of the houses and apartments there weren't uninhabited any more. They had no electricity, water, or gas, but the people in them didn't seem to care. For some, they turned into homes. For others, they were no more than robbers' dens.

Every time Scipio got into the white part of Augusta, he breathed a sigh of relief. That felt cruelly ironic. Whites were doing horrible things to blacks all over the CSA. No one could deny it. But a white man wouldn't murder him on the street for the fun of it or for whatever he had in his pockets. A black man might. He hated that knowledge, which didn't mean he didn't have it.

He grumbled about it during the waiters' hasty supper at the Huntsman's Lodge. Now that Aurelius was also working there, he had someone to talk to, someone who'd been through a lot of the things he had. *Two gray heads*, he thought.

"Ain't nothin' to be done about it," Aurelius said. "Things is what they is. Ain't for the likes of us to change 'em. We just got to git through 'em."

"I knows it," Scipio said. "Don't mean I likes it."

"Tell you what the difference is 'tween niggers and ofays," Aurelius said.

"Go on," Scipio urged him. "Say your say, so's I kin tell you what a damn fool you is." He smiled to show he didn't intend to be taken seriously.

Aurelius ignored the gibe altogether, which showed how seriously he took it. Before he went on, though, he looked around to make sure neither Jerry Dover nor any other white was in earshot. That *was* serious business. Satisfied, he said, "Difference is, when niggers kill whites, they does it one at a time. When the ofays decide they gonna kill niggers, they does it by city blocks an' by carloads. If I was forty years younger . . ." He didn't finish that.

What would you do? But Scipio didn't wonder for long. What could the other man have meant but that he would pick up a gun and use it against the whites? Scipio said, "We tries dat, we loses. They gots more guns, an' they gots bigger guns, too. Done seen dat in de las' war."

"Yeah." Aurelius didn't deny it. He couldn't very well; it was self-evident truth. But he did say, "We don't try it, we loses, too. Can't very well turn the other cheek when the ofay jus' hit you there soon as you do."

Scipio grunted. That also held more truth than he wished it did. Before he could say anything, Jerry Dover stuck his head into the room and said, "Eat up, people. We've got customers coming in, and the floor has to be covered." He disappeared again.

The floor has to be covered whether you're done eating or not, he meant. Waiters and busboys could eat, as long as they did it in a way that didn't interfere with their work. If it came to a choice between work and food, work always won.

Gulping down a last bite of chicken breast cooked with brandy, Scipio went out onto the floor. He stood straighter. He walked with dignity. He put on some of the airs he'd shown as Anne Colleton's butler at Marshlands. Assuming all of them would have been laying it on too thick, but customers here expected a certain amount of well-trained servility. Giving them what they wanted put a little extra money in his pocket.

As he took orders and recommended specials, he thought about Marshlands, now a ruined ghost of its former self. Anne Colleton dead . . . That still amazed him. One of her brothers had died—bravely—at the very start of the black revolt in 1915. The other one, as far as Scipio knew, was still alive.

After the war, Tom Colleton had turned out to be more dangerous and more capable than he'd expected. The white man had crushed what was left of the Congaree Socialist Republic. Till then, Scipio hadn't thought of him as anything but a lightweight. It only went to show, you never could tell.

That was probably true for almost all white men. Scipio laughed, not that it was funny. Whites in the CSA probably said the same thing about blacks. No, they certainly said the same thing about blacks. Hadn't he overheard them often enough, at Marshlands and here at the Huntsman's Lodge and plenty of places between the one and the other whenever they didn't think blacks could listen?

Of course, when whites talked among themselves, they often didn't pay enough attention to whether blacks were in earshot. Why should they, when blacks were hewers of wood and drawers of water? Blacks talking about whites? That was a different story. Blacks had known for hundreds of years that a white man overhearing them could spell disaster or death.

A white man at one of Scipio's tables waved to him. "Hey, uncle, come on over here!" the man called.

"What you need, suh?" Scipio asked, obsequious as usual.

"How long do they need to do up a steak in the kitchen? Have they all died in there? Of old age, maybe?" He was playing to the rest of the whites at the table. His friends or business associates or whatever they were laughed at what passed for his wit.

"It come soon, suh. Dey needs a little extra time, git it well-done de way you wants it."

"Oh. All right. Thanks, uncle. Make sure you bring it out the minute they get it finished." The white man, mollified, forgot about Scipio, even though he was still standing right there.

"Yes, suh. I do dat." Scipio could have laughed in the man's face. He could have, but he didn't. It wouldn't have been polite. But he knew the kitchen was glad to get well-done orders. They let it dispose of meat too nasty to serve before searing it thoroughly enough to destroy all the flavor. They also let it get rid of meat too tough to be worth eating; once cooked well-done, almost all meat was too tough to be worth eating. If the customer couldn't tell the difference—and the customer never could—the kitchen only smiled.

After Scipio brought that dinner and the rest of the food to that table, he got a better tip than he'd expected. He thought that was pretty funny, too. No matter what he thought, his face never showed a thing.

It had looked like rain when he came to work, but the clouds had blown through by the time he left the restaurant. A big yellow moon hung in the sky; its mellow light went a long way toward making up for the street lamps that shone no more. Farther north, they would have called it a bombers' moon, but no bombers had come to Augusta.

Scipio and Aurelius walked along side by side. Scipio was glad to have company on the way back to the Terry. Neither of them said much. They just walked in companionable silence, both of them puffing on cigarettes. Then, about a block and a half from the edge of the colored part of town, Aurelius stopped. So did Scipio, half a step later. Aurelius pointed ahead. "Somethin' goin' on up there, Xerxes."

"I sees it." Scipio squinted. The moonlight wasn't enough to let him make out what it was. It seemed as if it ought to be that bright, but it wasn't. Moonlight had a way of letting you down when you needed it most. Suddenly, absurdly, Scipio remembered a girl from more than fifty years before, not long after he was manumitted. She'd seemed pretty enough by moonlight. Come the day . . . Come the day, he wondered what he'd been thinking the night before. He *hadn't* been thinking the night before, which was exactly the point.

Aurelius had similar doubts. "Reckon we ought to find out what it is?" he asked.

"Can't stay here," Scipio said. "The buckra find we here in de mornin', we gwine wish we was dead."

"Uh-huh." Aurelius took a couple of steps forward, then stopped again. "We go on, maybe we *be* dead."

"We gots to go on," Scipio said. "They catches we in de white folks' part o' town, we be dead then, too. Either that or they puts we in jail, and only one place a nigger go from jail dese days—to one o' dem camps."

Aurelius plainly wanted to argue. No matter what he wanted to do, he couldn't. With dragging feet, he and Scipio approached. "Halt! Who goes there?" a white man barked at them, and then, "Advance and be recognized."

Even more hesitantly, the two Negroes obeyed. As Scipio drew near, he saw that uniformed white men were surrounding the Terry with barbed wire. There were gateways; he and Aurelius were coming up to one. Trying to keep his voice from shaking, he asked, "What you do?"

"Too many troublemakers getting in and out," the white man answered briskly. "High time we kept a closer eye on things, by God. And what the hell are you coons doing out after curfew anyways?"

"We works at the Huntsman's Lodge, suh. Dey closes late," Scipio answered.

"Yeah? If that's so, you'll have fancy dress on under those topcoats. Let's have a look," the white—a Freedom Party stalwart—said. Scipio and Aurelius hastily unbuttoned their coats to display the tuxedos beneath.

"I know them two niggers, Jerry," an Augusta cop told the stalwart. "They are what they say they are. They don't give anybody trouble." He pointed at Scipio and Aurelius with his nightstick. "Ain't that right, boys?"

"Yes, suh!" the waiters chorused.

"Any nigger'll give trouble if he gets the chance." Jerry spoke with great conviction. But then he shrugged. "All right—have it your way, Rusty. Pass on, you two."

"Yes, suh!" Scipio and Aurelius said again. The gates were barbed wire, too, strung on wooden frames instead of fastened to metal posts. Scipio doubted the barrier would stop all unsupervised traffic between the Terry and the outside, but it was bound to slow that traffic to a trickle.

Once they got on their own side of the barbed wire, he and Aurelius let out identical exhalations: half sigh, half groan. "Do Jesus!" Scipio said. "We is caged in."

"Sure enough," Aurelius agreed. "They kin feed us through the bars—if they want to. An' if they want to, they kin poke us through the bars, too."

"Or they kin take we out an' git rid o' we if they wants to." Scipio paused. "But why dey bodder? Dey done made de whole Terry a camp."

Aurelius' jaw worked, as if he were literally chewing on that. "We're in trouble," he said in a low voice. "All the niggers in Augusta is in trouble."

"In Augusta?" Scipio's fears reached wider than that. "You reckon dis here the onliest place in the country where dey runs up de barbed wire?"

Now Aurelius was the one who whispered, "Do Jesus!" That bright, cheerful moon showed how wide his eyes went. "You suppose they doin' this everywhere?"

"You got a wireless?" Scipio asked. The other Negro nodded. Scipio went on, "Reckon the news say one way or de other. If they do it all over everywhere, they won't hide it. They brag an' be proud."

Slowly, Aurelius nodded. Scipio shivered, there in the night. He'd finally found something he feared more than the regime's hatred of blacks. Its grim certainty that it was doing right frightened him far worse.

The move from Ohio to Virginia had changed life very little for Dr. Leonard O'Doull. He still worked in an aid station not far behind the line. The wounds he and his crew faced changed not at all. The weather was a little milder, but he had scant leisure to notice it. Going outside the aid tent for a quick cigarette every now and then hardly counted.

Repair, stabilize, send the successes back out of harm's way, send the failures back for burial . . . Sometimes he thought the wounded were war's mistakes—if everything had gone just the way the enemy planned, they would be dead. Or would they? In his more cynical moments, he reminded himself that a wounded soldier made the USA spend more resources on him than an easily replaceable dead one did.

When he mentioned that to Granville McDougald, the medic only nodded. "Same thing's occurred to me, Doc—you bet it has," he said. "Take a look at mustard gas, for instance. That shit hardly ever kills outright. It just makes casualties."

O'Doull hadn't even thought about mustard gas. "Tabernac!" he said.

McDougald laughed at him. "When you get excited, you start talking like a Frenchy."

"I know. I spoke French every day for almost twenty-five years, remember. I wasn't sure my English would come back as well as it has." O'Doull paused, then said, "Son of a bitch! There. You feel better now, Granny?"

He got another laugh out of McDougald. "Sure. Much better. I'll take two aspirins and you can see me in the morning."

"What I'd like to see in the morning is home," O'Doull said. His longing for Rivière-du-Loup suddenly pierced like an arrow. "I feel like nothing but a goddamn butcher down here."

"That's not right," McDougald said. "The butchers are the ones with the stars on their shoulder straps—and that maniac down in Richmond. If it weren't for Featherston, you'd be in Quebec and I wouldn't be worrying about anything more urgent than shortarm inspections."

"With the new drugs, we can even do something about a dose of the clap." O'Doull preferred thinking of gonorrhea to mustard gas. "Who would have figured that ten years ago?"

"Oh, irrigation with permanganate would cure some of the time," McDougald said. "Of course, most of the guys who went through it would sooner have had the disease."

"It wasn't pleasant," O'Doull agreed. He'd had to administer that treatment a good many times himself. Quebecois civilians were no fonder of it than U.S. soldiers. "A few pills or shots are a lot easier—and they work a lot better, too."

"And what's that going to do, Doc?" McDougald asked. "If we can screw as much as we want without worrying about coming down with VD, don't a lot of the old rules fly right out the window?"

"You come up with the most . . . interesting questions," O'Doull said admiringly. "I don't think the rules go till women don't have to worry about getting knocked up whenever they sleep with a guy. Rubbers aren't reliable enough for that, and a lot of men don't want to use 'em."

"Makes sense." Granville McDougald started to nod, then caught himself. He pointed a finger at O'Doull. "You're a Catholic, Doc. Won't you get in trouble with the Church for saying stuff like that?"

"In trouble? I doubt it. The Church isn't the Freedom Party, and the Pope isn't Jake Featherston. Nobody's going to come and burn me at the stake for having a mind of my own. The Spanish Inquisition went out of style a long time ago, even in Spain."

"Well, all right." McDougald seemed happy enough to return to the point: "You think we can do that? Make really good contraceptives, I mean?"

"Sure we can," O'Doull said. "It's just a matter of putting our minds to it and doing the research. It'll happen. I don't know when, but it will. And the world will be a different place."

Far above the tent with the Red Cross on each side, shells flew back and forth. O'Doull gauged how the fighting was going by the quality of those sounds. If more came in from the Confederate side of the line than went out at the C.S. forces, he might have to pull back in a hurry. If U.S. gunfire was outdoing the enemy's, he might have to move up quickly, which could be almost as big a nuisance. Right now, things seemed pretty even.

McDougald was listening, too, but in a different way. "Goddamn gurglers," he said. "I hate those goddamn gurglers. They're throwing gas around again. You'd think we had more sense than that. Hell, you'd think the Confederates had more sense than that."

"No such luck," O'Doull said sadly.

"I don't know what the hell good gas is." McDougald sounded bitter. "It kills people and it ruins people, and that's about it. You can't win a battle with it, not when both sides use it. It's only one more torment for the poor damned fools with guns in their hands."

"Every word you say is true," O'Doull answered. "Every single word. But saying it, no matter how true it is, doesn't make anybody on either side change his mind."

"Don't I know it? Haven't we seen it? Christ!" The way McDougald took the name of the Lord in vain wasn't so far removed from the Quebecois habit of swearing by the host and the chalice. He went on, "At least we have an antidote that does some good against nerve gas, as long as the casualties get here before it's too late. But mustard gas? Once you've got mustard gas on you or in your lungs, it will do what it does, and that's that."

A shell landed a couple of hundred yards away: not close enough to be dangerous—though O'Doull wouldn't have believed that when he first put on a uniform again—but plenty close enough to be alarming. "Was that a short round of theirs or a short round of ours?" O'Doull wondered.

"What difference does it make?" McDougald asked. "Whoever it comes down on is screwed either way."

O'Doull sighed. "Well, I'm not going to tell you you're wrong, because you're right. How many have we treated where our own guns did the damage?"

"I don't have the slightest idea, and neither do you," McDougald said. "The only thing I can tell you is, it's too goddamn many."

He was right again. Accidents of all sorts were only too common in war. Some of them made O'Doull think God had a nasty sense of humor. Two U.S. companies would attack the same bit of high ground from different directions. Maybe neither would know the other was in the neighborhood. Maybe somebody in one or the other—or both—would see soldiers moving toward him and open up regardless of what uniform they wore. In a split second, dozens of soldiers would be blazing away at one another, trained reflex overriding thought . . . and adding to the casualty lists.

Artillery wasn't always the infantryman's friend, either. Very often, U.S. and C.S. lines would lie close together. Rounds didn't have to fall short by much to come down on soldiers in green-gray rather than those in butternut. Some of the fault, no doubt, lay in mismanufactured shells and in powder that didn't do everything it was supposed to. And some, just as surely, lay in the calculations artillerymen botched when they were in a hurry—and sometimes when they weren't. All those blunders bloated the butcher's bill.

"One thing," O'Doull said.

"What's that?" Granville McDougald inquired.

"Over on the other side of the line, there are bound to be a couple of Confederate medics bitching about the same thing."

"Oh, yeah." McDougald nodded. "But does that make it better or worse?"

That was another of those . . . interesting questions. How you answered it depended on how you looked at war. It was better for the USA if the Confederates also killed and maimed their own. It was better for the USA, yes, but much worse for a good-sized group of men who would either die too young or go through life with puckered scars and perhaps without fingers or a foot or their eyesight or testicles.

O'Doull answered with a question of his own: "Are you asking me as an American or as a doctor?"

"That's for you to figure out, wouldn't you say?" McDougald was enormously helpful when dealing with the wounded, much less so when he and O'Doull were making the time pass by.

Another round burst closer than it should have. O'Doull swore in English and in Quebecois French. Somebody on one side of the line or the other didn't know his ass from the end zone. No one set out to shell an aid station, but that was also one of the accidents that happened.

"I think we'd better—" O'Doull began.

Granville McDougald was already doing it. O'Doull followed him out of the tent. Both men jumped into a zigzagging trench not far away. O'Doull was glad they had no wounded lying in the tent right that minute. Getting them out would have been a nightmare. The doctor thought he would sooner have stayed in the tent himself and taken his chances.

"Cigarette?" McDougald held out a pack.

"Thanks." O'Doull took one. They were Niagaras, a U.S. brand, and tasted as if they were made of hay and horseshit. Even bad tobacco, though, was better than no tobacco at all. O'Doull sucked in smoke. "Yeah, thanks, Granny. I needed one there."

Another shell screamed in. A man who listened closely could tell which rounds were long, which short, and which right on the money. O'Doull ducked and threw his hands up over his head. So did McDougald, who'd judged the incoming round the same way he had.

The shell burst between the trench and the aid tent. Shrapnel whined through the air not far enough over their heads; dirt pattered down on them. Some slid down the back of O'Doull's neck. He knew that would drive him crazy later. Nothing he could do about it now.

Cautiously, he stuck his head up above the rim of the trench. The explosion had shredded the green-gray canvas of the aid tent; the Red Cross on the side was ventilated with several rips and tears. And what the fragments would have done to them had they stayed in the tent . . . "You know something? I'm not what you'd call sorry we vacated the premises."

"Now that you mention it, neither am I." McDougald looked up to survey the damage, too. He whistled mournfully. "No, that wouldn't have been a hell of a lot of fun, would it?"

"No. Looks to me like we could have practiced sewing each other up," O'Doull said.

"Suture self, Doc," McDougald said. O'Doull sent him a reproachful stare. The other man didn't seem to notice he'd been reproached. Anyone who'd say something like that probably wouldn't notice such a thing.

Then O'Doull threw himself flat in the trench again. Two more shells came down, one on the tent, the other close by it. He and McDougald would have been in no position to do any sewing after that. *Light a candle for me, Nicole,* he thought, and wondered if he'd ever see Rivière-du-Loup again.

Mary Pomeroy hugged her mother. "So good to see you, Ma," she said.

"You, too, dear," Maude McGregor answered. "It was a nice visit, wasn't it?"

"I sure thought so," Mary answered. "Easier to get out of town now that Alec's in kindergarten." She made a sour face. "Even so, I wish I didn't have to send him. The Yanks make teachers fill up the children's heads with the most fantastic lies you ever heard."

"You don't want to get in trouble for leaving him out, though," her mother said. "You don't want to get in trouble at all, especially after all the lies Wilf Rokeby told about you."

"I know, Ma," Mary said, and said no more. She knew Wilf Rokeby hadn't told lies. She knew her mother knew, too. Maude McGregor never would have said so, though, even if you put her on the rack. There were things she carefully didn't see. She hadn't seen them when her husband was alive, and she didn't see them when she looked in her daughter's direction, either.

She'd never asked, for instance, why Mary spent half an hour or an hour or an hour and a half of each recent visit to the farm out in the barn by herself. She never came out to see what her daughter was doing there. She didn't want to know—or rather, to know officially.

All she said now was, "Whatever you're doing, be careful about it."

Gently, Mary answered, "I'm always careful, Ma," and her mother nodded. Mary knew she hadn't been careful enough with Wilf. She'd dodged the immediate danger, but the postmaster had brought her to the occupiers' notice.

The Yanks suspected Pa, but he kept on going, Mary thought fiercely. *I can, too.* As long as they only suspected, what could they do? They'd never found any evidence against her. They'd never found any evidence against her father, either, till things went wrong when he threw the bomb at General Custer. And if Custer hadn't been more alert than an old man had any business being, Pa might have got away with that, too.

"I'll see you before too long," Mary said. Her mother nodded. The two women embraced. Mary went out to the Oldsmobile. She started the auto and drove away from the farm where she'd grown up.

What went through her mind was, *I have to be extra careful now.* If the Frenchies caught her with a bomb in the Olds, everything was over. They had no particular reason to search it, but. . . .

Even when she used the bomb, she had to be extra careful. If it went off somewhere too close to Rosenfeld, that would make the occupiers wonder. She muttered to herself as she drove across the vast, wintry Manitoba prairie. The Olds was almost the only motorcar on the road. What she didn't know was how active the overall resistance against the Yanks was. How many things happened that never got into the newspapers or on the wireless? If the Americans were smart—and they were, damn them; they were—they would keep most of those things quiet.

If she wasn't the only one fighting the Yanks in this part of the province, though, then one more bomb wouldn't mean so much. It wouldn't necessarily make the occupiers look toward *her*. If nobody else was giving them trouble, that was a different story.

She sighed. She hadn't heard anyone else's bombs blow up in Rosenfeld. A lot of the farmers in these parts were Mennonites who went along with the central authority, whatever it happened to be. But there had been that pamphlet, the one she'd turned against Rokeby. *Somebody* had put it out.

About ten miles west of Rosenfeld lay Coulee, an even smaller town. Like Rosenfeld, Coulee would have had no reason to exist if not for the railroad. It was a place where people loaded grain; Mary had trouble imagining anyone getting off the train in Coulee without the immediate, intense desire to get right back on again. People in Rosenfeld hardly ever thought about Coulee; when they did, it was usually with a condescending smile. Even in Rosenfeld, people needed someone to feel superior to.

The paved road to Coulee paralleled the train tracks. It went on right through the town. Mary got off the paved road before Coulee, went around the place on lesser tracks like the one that led to her family's farm, and then got back on to drive for another couple of miles.

She stopped the auto there and pulled off to the side of the road. When she got out of the Olds, she looked both east and west. Nobody coming in either direction—that was what she'd wanted to see. She remembered the Quebecois soldiers who'd appeared out of nowhere while her family was picnicking. Having a patrol show up now wouldn't do at all.

No patrol. There were too many miles of railroad, not enough soldiers to keep an eye on all of them all the time. Mary opened the trunk. She carried the box in it over to the railroad tracks, then came back. As she returned, she scuffed and kicked the footprints she'd made in the snow till they were unidentifiable. She drove the auto back onto the road and did the same thing to the tire tracks. The occupiers would be able to figure out where she'd planted the bomb. The explosion itself would tell them that. Who she was, or even that she was a she? No. Not if she could help it.

Mary drove back to Rosenfeld the same way as she'd come west, skirting Coulee. Nobody in the town would see the Oldsmobile. She tried to use different little country roads heading east. She didn't want a farmer remembering he'd seen the same auto coming and going in a short stretch of time.

She got back to her apartment less than an hour later than she would have if she'd come straight from the farm. Who was to say when she'd broken off her visit with her mother? Mort might notice that the gas gauge on the motorcar was down a little farther than it should have been. But so what? Even if he did, would he turn her in to the occupiers? Not likely!

All the way back to Rosenfeld, she'd listened for an explosion. She hadn't heard one. Maybe no train had gone through during her drive. Maybe she'd got too far away for the sound to carry. Or maybe the bomb had failed. That was an unwelcome possibility, but one she couldn't ignore.

As soon as she got into the apartment, she used a nail file to get rid of the dirt from the barn and washed her hands. Drying them, she felt a little like Lady Macbeth—another stubborn Scotswoman advancing her cause no matter what.

Music blared from the wireless when she turned it on. It was twenty minutes to the hour, so she had a while to wait before she could hear the news. She used the time to good advantage, making herself a cup of coffee and sitting down with a mystery story set in Toronto before the Great War. She knew what she was doing— pretending things hadn't changed since. Again, so what?

When the news came on, it talked about an American submersible torpedoing a Japanese cruiser somewhere in the Sandwich Islands. It talked about U.S. bombing raids on Confederate cities, and about Confederate terror attacks on U.S. cities. Mary sneered. She knew propaganda when she heard it. The wireless talked about U.S. progress in Utah. It talked about an Austro-German counterattack against the Tsar's armies in the Ukraine, and about a German counterattack against the British near Hamburg.

It talked about cuts in the coal ration for Canada, and about reductions in civilian seat allocations on the railroads here. Bombs on the tracks? Not a word.

Mary said a word—a rude one. Maybe it was too soon to get the news on the air. Maybe no train had gone along that stretch of track, which didn't strike her as very likely. Or maybe something had gone wrong. Could a patrol have found the bomb before a train went over it? Worry settled over her like the clouds that presaged a snowstorm.

After Alec got back from kindergarten, even worry had to stand in line. He rampaged through the apartment. Mouser had been asleep under a chair. Alec blew a horn right by him, which horrified him and Mary both. He fled, squalling. "Leave the cat alone!" Mary shouted at Alec, who wanted to do no such thing.

She kept the wireless on, wondering whether she would get news from it or a knock on the door. At last, three hours after that first newscast, the announcer started inveighing against saboteurs who tried to put a spike in the American war effort. "These evildoers hurt their Canadian brethren by further decreasing the number of seats available in the railway system as a whole. Southern Manitoba is particularly afflicted, but authorities have every confidence they will

soon hunt down the murderers and depraved individuals responsible
for these dastardly acts of terrorism." The man sounded ready to
flop down on the floor and start chewing up the carpet.

Hearing that report took the nervous edge off Mary's temper.
Alec kept after the cat. Before long, Mouser had had enough and
scratched him. He ran to Mary, crying. She managed to be sympathetic, and painted the wounds with Mercurochrome, which didn't
sting, and not with Merthiolate, which did.

"He's a bad kitty," Alec declared, glowering at the orange-red
blotches on his arm.

"He is not. If you tease him, he's going to scratch." Mouser
rarely bit, thank heaven. Mary and Mort had trained him out of that
when he was a kitten. "How would you like somebody blowing a
horn in your ear when you were asleep and chasing you all over
everywhere?"

Alec looked as if he thought that might be fun. Mary might have
realized he would. And then, all at once, an amazingly knowing expression passed over his face—he saw he shouldn't have let her notice that. *He's growing up,* she thought, and couldn't decide whether
to laugh or to cry.

When Mort came home from the diner that evening, he was
oddly subdued. She wondered if he'd had a row with his father. She
didn't want to ask him about it till after Alec went to bed. Then her
husband beat her to the punch: "They say a train got bombed, other
side of Coulee."

Uh-oh, Mary thought. Voice somewhere between casual and
savage, she answered, "I heard something about it on the wireless.
They didn't say much, though. I hope it gave the Yanks a good kick
in the slats."

Mort made a small production out of lighting a cigarette. He
said, "When the Frenchies turned this place upside down, they didn't
find anything."

"Of course they didn't. There wasn't anything to find." *I made
damn sure of that,* Mary added, but only to herself.

"They never found any of the stuff your father used, either," he
said.

That rocked her again; she didn't think he'd ever come right out
and talked about Arthur McGregor and what he'd done before. She
made herself nod. "No, they never did."

"Mary . . ." Mort paused, maybe not quite sure how to go on. He drew on the cigarette till the coal glowed tomato red. "For God's sake watch yourself, Mary. This isn't a game. They'll kill you if they catch you. I don't think I could stand that. I know Alec couldn't."

How long had he known and kept quiet? If he could add two and two, how many other people in Rosenfeld could do the same thing? "I always watch myself, Mort," Mary said, but she knew she would have to be more watchful yet.

A corner drugstore not far from Chester Martin's house in East L.A. had gone belly-up a few months before the war started. Times were still hard; the building had stood vacant ever since, the door padlocked, the GOING OUT OF BUSINESS! sign painted on the window slowly fading in the harsh California sun.

And then, quite suddenly, the place wasn't vacant any more. Off came GOING OUT OF BUSINESS! A new sign went up on the window: a fierce-looking bald eagle in left profile in front of crossed swords, and below it, in red, white, and blue, the legend U.S. ARMY RECRUITING STATION.

Chester eyed that with thoughtful interest. He smiled a little when he thought about the men who'd be working there. They had a tough job, didn't they? Talking other people into carrying rifles and going off to shoot Confederates was a hell of a lot safer than carrying a rifle and going off to shoot Confederates yourself.

His wife couldn't have been more horrified if a bordello had opened up in that building. By the hard, set expression on Rita's face, she would rather have seen a bordello there. Chester knew why, too—she was afraid the recruiting station would take him away from her.

He knew what she was waiting for: for him to laugh and joke and tell her she was worrying over nothing. Then she would have relaxed. For the sake of family peace, he wished he could have. But the eagle's hard golden stare reproached him every time he saw it. He knew what he could do for the country; he'd been through the mill. He just hadn't decided whether the country truly needed him to do it.

"You haven't been in there, have you?" she anxiously asked him one Sunday afternoon, as if it *were* a house of ill repute.

All he wanted to do was drink a bottle of beer, eat a corned-beef sandwich, and listen to the football game on the wireless. President Smith had decreed that football was essential to U.S. morale, so some leagues had resumed play. Some of their stars had joined the armed forces, and some of the players they were using wouldn't have had a chance of making their squads before the shooting started. But the Dons were still the Dons, no matter who wore their black and gold. Today they were in Portland, squaring off against the Columbias.

"Well?" Rita said when he didn't answer right away. "Have you?"

He washed down a bite of the sandwich with a swig of Lucky Lager. "No, I haven't been in there," he said. "I am curious—"

"Why?" Rita broke in, her voice sharp with fear. "Don't you already know everything you ever wanted to about getting shot?"

"You bet I do." Chester wore a long-sleeved shirt, so the scars on his arm didn't show. That didn't mean he'd forgotten them. You couldn't forget something like that, not ever. After another pull at the Lucky, he went on, "No, what I'm curious about is who's doing things in there. Have they got real soldiers, or are they cripples or Great War retreads? You'd think they'd want every able-bodied man up at the front."

"What difference does it make?" Rita wouldn't see reason on this. She'd made that very plain. "You don't need an oak-leaf cluster on your Purple Heart. I don't need a Western Union boy knocking on my door. I've already done that once."

Most of the time, the kids who delivered telegrams were welcome visitors. Not when the USA and CSA grappled with each other. Then they were all too likely to bring bad news, a dreaded Deeply Regret message from the War Department. Their uniforms were a little darker than U.S. green-gray. People watched them go by on their bikes and prayed they wouldn't stop. One of those kids had rung Rita's doorbell in 1916.

Chester said, "I haven't been in there. I—" He stopped. The Portland crowd was yelling its head off. The Dons had just fumbled. Having Rita in the same room with him inhibited his choice of language.

"You what?" she asked suspiciously.

"I wish we could find a halfback who can hold on to the darn ball, that's what."

"That isn't what you were going to say, and we both know it." Rita spoke *ex cathedra*, as the Pope or an upset wife had the right to do.

He sighed. "Like I said before, the only thing I'm curious about is who they've got in there."

Rita rolled her eyes. "Like *I* said before, what the devil difference does it make? Whoever they are, what are they selling? The chance to get killed. They already gave you that once. Are you dumb enough to want it again?"

"No," he said, but even he heard the doubt in his own voice.

"Don't you want to live to see Carl grow up? Don't you want to live to see your grandchildren?" His wife had no more compunction about fighting dirty than did the officers on both sides of this war who fired poison gas at their foes.

"That's not fair," Chester protested, a complaint that did him no more good with Rita than it did an ordinary soldier on the battle-field.

She got the last word, as wives have a way of doing: "All you care about is how sharp you'll look in the uniform, even if they have to use it to lay you in a coffin. What the hell makes you think there'll be enough of you left to bury?" She stormed out of the living room in tears.

Chester swore mournfully. How the deuce was he supposed to enjoy a football game—or even a corned-beef sandwich and a bottle of beer—after that?

Rita eased up on him during the week, but turned up the heat on the weekends. To her, that no doubt seemed perfectly logical. During the week, he was busy working, so he wasn't likely to have the time to do anything she disapproved of. On the weekend, he could run loose. He could—but she didn't aim to let him.

He didn't always vote the straight Socialist ticket the way she did, but he understood the way the dialectic worked. A thesis created an antithesis that reacted against it. The more Rita told him to stay away from the recruiting station, the more he wanted to go in-side. He almost wished it were a whorehouse. He could have had more fun if he did.

The clash of thesis and antithesis generated a synthesis. Chester never wondered what that might be. A more thoroughgoing Social-ist might have.

He hoped Rita believed him when he said he was going out to get a haircut two Sundays after their big argument. It wasn't that he was lying; he did visit the barbershop. He got a shave, too—an unusual luxury for him, because he took care of that himself most mornings. But it was also camouflage of a sort. If he came back to the house smelling of bay rum, Rita couldn't doubt where he'd been.

No bell chimed when he walked into the recruiting station. He'd half expected a carillon to play "The Star-Spangled Banner." Inside, a first sergeant with row after row of fruit salad on the chest of his dress uniform was talking earnestly with a man in his mid-thirties. Chester had expected to see kids here. He needed only a moment to figure out why he didn't, though. Kids would get conscripted anyhow. The Army didn't need to recruit them. This place was geared to persuading people like him to put on the uniform again.

Another noncom in a fancy uniform nodded to him. "Hello, sir," the man said in friendly tones. "What can I do for you today?"

"I don't know that you can do anything for me," Chester answered. "I just came in for a look around."

"Well, you can do that," the recruiter said easily. "Want a cup of coffee while you're doing it?"

"Thanks. I wouldn't mind one a bit," Chester said, even though he was thinking, *Step into my parlor, said the spider to the fly. . . .*

"We've got a hot plate back here. You take cream and sugar?" the noncom asked. He walked over to the pot on the hot plate with a peculiar rolling gait. Chester had seen that before; it meant the man had an above-the-knee amputation. He wouldn't be any good in combat. He had to be a smooth talker, though, or they wouldn't have let him keep wearing the uniform.

Once he'd doctored the coffee to Chester's taste, he brought it back. "Thanks," Chester said again.

The recruiter eyed him. "You saw the elephant the last time around, I'd say," he remarked.

"Oh, yeah." Chester sipped the coffee. It tasted about the way coffee that had sat on a hot plate since early morning usually tastes: like battery acid diluted with cream and sugar.

"What did you top out at, you don't mind my asking?"

Chester didn't answer. The guy in his thirties got up and left. The sergeant to whom he'd been talking pushed back his chair—and Chester saw it was a wheelchair. He had legs, but they evidently weren't any good to him. "Are you sure you guys are recruiting?" Chester blurted.

He wondered if the noncom who'd brought him coffee would deliberately misunderstand. The man didn't. He didn't even blink. "Yes, we are," he said. "If you went through it, you already know what can happen. We don't need to be able to run and jump to do this job. In the field, we would. Here, we can still help the country. So . . . You were in the last one, you said."

"Yeah, from start to finish. I ended up a sergeant. I was in charge of a company for a while, till they scraped up an officer for it."

"Wounded?"

"Once—in the arm. It healed up pretty good. I was lucky."

"You sure as hell were," the recruiter agreed soberly. "What have you done since?"

"Steel. Construction. Union organizing." Chester wondered if that would faze the Army man.

It didn't. The fellow just nodded. "If you can command a company, you can run civilians, too. As long as you're not a Freedom Party stalwart or a Mormon, I don't care about your politics. And if you're a loyal Mormon—there are some—and you take the oath, we'll find some kind of place for you. The other stuff? Socialist? Democrat? Republican? Nobody gives a damn. You can argue about it in the field. It helps the time go by."

"Interesting," Chester said, as noncommittally as he could.

The recruiter looked him in the eye. "What have you got to say for yourself? Did you just come here to window shop, or are you serious about helping the country?"

There it was, right out in the open. Chester licked his lips. "If I go back in, can I hold off induction for a month? I'm not a kid any more. I'm going to need to straighten out some things."

"It's a seller's market," the noncom said. "However you want us, we want you." He stuck out his hand. Chester shook it. *Rita's gonna kill me,* he thought.

Air-raid sirens screamed. Flora Blackford and her son hurried downstairs to the basement of their block of flats. Joshua said, "They haven't come over Philadelphia for a while." He sounded excited, not afraid.

"I'd just as soon they didn't," Flora answered. A very fat man—he was a lobbyist for the meat-packing business—was taking the stairs at a snail's pace, which was as fast as he could go. He filled the stairwell from side to side, so nobody could get around him. Flora felt like giving him a push and going over his back. Bombs were already bursting in the city.

"I'd just as soon they didn't, too," Joshua said. "It means we aren't putting enough pressure on them in Virginia—they think they can use their bombers up here instead of against the troops."

Flora almost asked if she should send him over to the General Staff. The only thing checking her was the certainty that he'd say yes. He'd take it for an invitation, not sarcasm. He studied war with a passionate intensity altogether alien to her—and, she was convinced, understood its permutations in ways she didn't. Maybe he would do some good on the General Staff. You never could tell.

At last, the fat lobbyist came to the bottom of the stairs. People surged around him to either side in the hall. He placidly rolled on at his own pace. If that pace had happened to kill him and a lot of people behind him . . . But, yet again, it hadn't, so why flabble?

People in the shelter mostly wore flannel pajamas. Some of them had thrown robes over the PJs. Men's-style nightwear was now de rigueur for women in cities likely to be bombed. Filmy peignoirs lost most of their allure when you were liable to be showing off for everyone in your apartment building.

Thump! Thump! Thump! The ground shook under Flora's feet. Several people in the basement groaned. The lights flickered. The sound on the old wireless set faded out for a moment, but then came back to life.

"There is an enemy bomber going down in flames!" the announcer said excitedly. "I don't know whether our antiaircraft guns or a night fighter got him, but he's a goner."

Three or four people clapped their hands. A few more applauded when the Confederate bomber hit the ground. The blast when it did was different from ordinary bomb impacts: larger, more diffuse. Most of the men and women down there just waited to see what would happen next. The CSA lost some bombers whenever it sent them over Philadelphia. The Confederates never lost enough to keep them from sending more.

On and on the pounding went. It always seemed to last an eternity, though the bombers rarely loitered more than an hour. The building, so far, had lived a charmed life. Its windows had lost glass, but not many buildings in Philadelphia kept unshattered glass these days. No bomb had landed on it. That counted most.

The wireless announcer went on giving a blow-by-blow account of the fight against the airplanes from the CSA. Not all of that blow-by-blow account would be the truth, though. The Confederates— both in the air and down in Virginia—would be monitoring the stations broadcasting from cities they bombed. Keeping them guessing about what they actually accomplished struck the U.S. powers that be as a good idea. Flora normally extolled the truth. Here, she could see that telling all of it might not be a good idea.

Twenty minutes after bombs stopped dropping, the warbling all-clear sounded. A man in front of her and a woman in back of her both said the same thing at the same time: "Well, we got through another one." The same thought had been in her mind, too.

Along with everybody else, she wearily trudged up the stairs. She wondered whether she would be able to sleep when she got back to her flat. Joshua seldom had trouble dropping off again, but he lived in the moment much more than she did. She couldn't help brooding on what might have been and what might be.

Brooding or not, she was drifting toward sleep when someone knocked on the door. She looked at the clock on the nightstand. The glowing hands told her it was a quarter to three. Like anyone else with an ounce of sense, she was convinced nothing good ever happened at a quarter to three. But the knocking went on and on.

She got out of bed and went to the door. "Who is it?" she called without opening up. Robbers prowled blacked-out Philadelphia.

"It's Sydney Nesmith, Congresswoman—assistant to the House Sergeant at Arms." And it was; she recognized his voice. He went on, "Please come with me to Congress right away. Someone would have telephoned, but the lines to this building are down, so I came in person."

Flora did open the door then, saying, "Good heavens! What's happened?"

"Everything will be explained once you get there, ma'am," Nesmith answered, which told her nothing—but if it weren't important, he wouldn't have been here.

"Let me change," she said, and started to turn away.

"People aren't bothering," he said.

"What is it, Mom?" Joshua asked from behind her.

"I don't know," she answered, thinking, *Nothing good, all right*. She nodded to Nesmith. "I'll come."

"Thank you, ma'am. An auto is waiting down below." Nesmith started to turn away, then checked himself. "Beg your pardon, but I've got a couple of more to get up in this building."

"Do what you have to do." Flora closed the door. If he was going to wake others, she had a minute, no matter what he said. She threw on a dress and a topcoat.

"Something terrible has happened, hasn't it?" Joshua said as she did start out into the hallway.

"I'm afraid it has. I'll let you know what it is as soon as I can. Try to go back to sleep in the meantime." That sounded foolish as soon as Flora said it, but what else was her son supposed to do? She hurried downstairs.

The waiting motorcar was an enormous Packard. It had room for the driver, for Sydney Nesmith, and for all the members of Congress from her building. Some of the others had put on clothes, as she had, but a couple were still in pajamas. "Step on it, Fred," Nesmith said as the auto pulled away from the curb.

Stepping on it in a blacked-out city just after an air raid struck Flora as a recipe for suicide. Fortunately, Fred paid no attention to the Sergeant at Arms' assistant. The only lights in Philadelphia were the ones from fires the bombing had started. Their red, flickering glow seemed brighter and carried farther than it would have without pitch darkness for a backdrop.

Flora and the other members of Congress tried to pump Nesmith about why he'd summoned them. He refused to be pumped, saying, "You'll find out everything you need to know when you get there, I promise." By the time the Packard pulled up in front of the big, slightly bomb-battered building that took the place of the Capitol here, he'd said that a great many times.

They all hurried inside. Flora blinked several times at the bright electric lights. They too seemed all the more brilliant because of the darkness from which she'd just emerged.

Sydney Nesmith shepherded his charges toward the House chamber. Flora would have gone there anyway; it was her natural habitat. She saw Senators as well as Representatives in the large hall.

That was nothing too far out of the ordinary. When Congress met in joint session, it met here: the hall had room for everybody.

Vice President La Follette and the Speaker of the House, Joe Guffey of Pennsylvania, sat side by side on the rostrum. Again, that didn't surprise Flora; it was where the two presiding officers belonged. But Charlie La Follette, normally a cheerful man, looked as if a bomb had gone off in front of his face, while the Speaker seemed hardly less stunned. When Flora spotted Chief Justice Cicero Pittman's rotund form in the first row of seats in front of the rostrum, ice ran through her. All at once, she feared she knew why all the Senators and Representatives had been summoned.

"*Alevai omayn,* let me be wrong," she murmured. At the same time, an Irish Congressman from another New York City district crossed himself. That amounted to about the same thing.

Members of Congress kept crowding in. By the look of things, not everyone had figured out what might be going on. Some people couldn't see the nose in front of their face. Some, perhaps, didn't want to.

At 5:22—Flora would never forget the time—the Speaker nodded to the Sergeant at Arms. He in turn waved to his assistants, who closed the doors to the chamber. The Sergeant at Arms banged his gavel to call Congress to order, then yielded his place to the Speaker.

Guffey approached the microphone like a man approaching the gallows. "Ladies and gentlemen, I would give anything I own not to be where I am right now and not to have to make this announcement," he said heavily. He needed a moment to gather himself, then went on, "The President of the United States—Al Smith—is dead."

Gasps and cries of horror rang through the hall. Yes, some had been caught unawares. Flora gasped, too, but only in dismay to find her fears confirmed. Swallowing a sob, Guffey continued, "He took shelter from the raid as he should have, but three bombs hit the same place in Powel House—a million-to-one shot, the War Department assures me. The first two cleared obstructions from the path of the third, which . . . which destroyed the shelter under the Presidential residence. There were no survivors."

More cries rose. Men wept as unashamedly as the handful of women in Congress. Speaker Guffey paused to take off his reading glasses and dab at his streaming eyes. "But, while the loss to our nation is incalculable, we must go on—and we shall go on. Here to administer the oath of office to the new President is Chief Justice Pittman."

Flora saw what looked like the collar of bright red pajamas peep out from under the Chief Justice's judicial robes for a moment. She swallowed a tear-filled giggle. Charles La Follette—he wouldn't be Charlie any more, she supposed—towered over Pittman. He set his left hand on a Bible, raised his right hand, and took the oath: "I do solemnly swear that I will faithfully execute the Office of President of the United States, and will to the best of my Ability preserve, protect and defend the Constitution of the United States."

Very solemnly, he shook hands with the Chief Justice, and then with the Speaker of the House. That done, he looked out to the Senators and Representatives staring in at him. "As Speaker Guffey said, all I have I would have given gladly not to be standing here today. When they told me what had happened, I felt like the moon, the stars and all the planets had fallen on me. Al Smith was the leader this country chose, and he did well to the very last instant of his life. Even when days looked darkest, he never gave up hope. While we are not where we would wish to be in this war, neither are we where the enemy would have us. The road to victory may be long, but we will walk it. With God's help, we will walk it to the end."

Applause thundered through the sobs. Flora clapped till her palms burned. The United States were bigger than any one man. Were the Confederate States? She had her doubts.

About the Type

This book was set in Sabon, a typeface designed by the well-known German typographer Jan Tschichold (1902–74). Sabon's design is based on the original letterforms of Claude Garamond and was created specifically to be used for three sources: foundry type for hand composition, Linotype, and Monotype. Tschichold named his typeface for the famous Frankfurt typefounder Jacques Sabon, who died in 1580.